THE WARRIOR-PROPHET

Also by R. Scott Bakker

The Darkness That Comes Before:
The Prince of Nothing, Book One

THE WARRIOR~PROPHET

THE PRINCE OF NOTHING
BOOK TWO

R. SCOTT BAKKER

THE OVERLOOK PRESS
Woodstock & New York

First published in paperback in the United States in 2005 by
The Overlook Press, Peter Mayer Publishers, Inc.
Woodstock & New York

WOODSTOCK:
One Overlook Drive
Woodstock, NY 12498
www.overlookpress.com
[for individual orders, bulk and special sales, contact our Woodstock office]

NEW YORK:
141 Wooster Street
New York, NY 10012

Cataloging-in-Publication Data is available from the Library of Congress

Manufactured in the United States of America
ISBN 1-58567-728-0
2 4 6 8 10 9 7 5 3 1

To Bryan

—— ⊗⊗⊗ ——

my brother,
both of heart and vision

Acknowledgments

Since I had over fifteen years to write *The Darkness That Comes Before*, I really had no idea what I was getting into when I committed to finishing *The Warrior-Prophet* within one year. I had thought a year was a long time, but now, after watching the seasons flicker past my window quicker than commercials, I know better. As a consequence of my miscalculation, I inadvertently complicated the lives of all those around me, both professionally and personally. Never have I been so indebted to so many. I would like to thank:

First and foremost, my fiancée, Sharron O'Brien, for her love, support, and brilliant critiques.

My brother, Bryan Bakker, for giving me more great ideas than I care to admit!

My agent, Chris Lotts, and the wonderful crew at Ralph M. Vicinanza Ltd.

My family and all my friends, for forgiving me my frequent absences—and for recognizing my voice those few times I called.

My students at Fanshawe College for cutting me slack when my deadlines loomed large.

Michael Schellenberg for his instincts, Barbara Berson for her positively biblical patience, and Meg Masters for her editorial genius. I would also like to thank Tracy Bordian, Martin Gould, Karen Alliston, Lesley Horlick, and the whole Penguin Canada family.

Wil Horsley and Jack Brown at for their tremendous and talented support.

Ur-Lord, Mithfânion, and Loosecannon for putting the virus in viral marketing!

And, of course, Steven Erikson, for kicking open the ballroom door.

For those interested in exploring Eärwa beyond the boundaries of these covers, you can visit www.princeofnothing.com or Wil and Jack's message board at www.three-seas.com.

Here we see philosophy brought to what is, in fact, a precarious position, which should be made fast even though it is supported by nothing in either heaven or earth. Here philosophy must show its purity as the absolute sustainer of its laws, and not as a herald of laws which implanted sense or who knows what tutelary nature whispers to it.

—IMMANUEL KANT, FOUNDATIONS OF THE METAPHYSICS OF MORALS

Contents

PART III: The Third March

Appendices

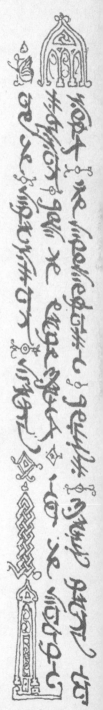

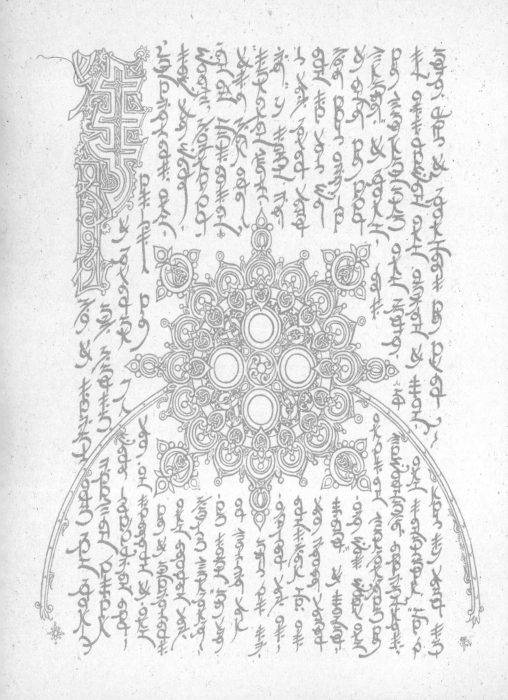

What Has Come Before ...

The First Apocalypse destroyed the great Norsirai nations of the North. Only the South, the Ketyai nations of the Three Seas, survived the onslaught of the No-God, Mog-Pharau, and his Consult of generals and magi. The years passed, and the Men of the Three Seas forgot, as Men inevitably do, the horrors endured by their fathers.

Empires rose and empires fell: Kyraneas, Shir, Cenei. The Latter Prophet, Inri Sejenus, reinterpreted the Tusk, the holiest of artifacts, and within a few centuries the faith of Inrithism, organized and administered by the Thousand Temples and its spiritual leader, the Shriah, came to dominate the entire Three Seas. The great sorcerous Schools, such as the Scarlet Spires, the Imperial Saik, and the Mysunsai, arose in response to the Inrithi persecution of the Few, those possessing the ability to see and work sorcery. Using Chorae, ancient artifacts that render their bearers immune to sorcery, the Inrithi warred against the Schools, attempting, unsuccessfully, to purify the Three Seas. Then Fane, the Prophet of the Solitary God, united the Kianene, the desert peoples of the southwestern Three Seas, and declared war against the Tusk and the Thousand Temples. After centuries and several jihads, the Fanim and their eyeless sorcerer-priests, the Cishaurim, conquered nearly all the western Three Seas, including the holy city of Shimeh, the birthplace of Inri Sejenus. Only the moribund remnants of the Nansur Empire continued to resist them.

Now war and strife rule the South. The two great faiths of Inrithism and Fanimry continually skirmish, though trade and pilgrimage are tolerated when commercially convenient. The great families and nations vie for military and mercantile dominance. The minor and major Schools squabble and plot, particularly against the upstart Cishaurim, whose sorcery, the Psûkhe, the Schoolmen cannot distinguish from the God's own world. And the Thousand Temples pursue earthly ambitions under the leadership of corrupt and ineffectual Shriahs.

The First Apocalypse has become little more than legend. The Consult, which had survived the death of Mog-Pharau, has dwindled into myth, something old wives tell small children. After two thousand years, only the Schoolmen of the Mandate, who relive the Apocalypse each night through the eyes of their ancient founder, Seswatha, recall the horror and the prophecies of the No-God's return. Though the mighty and the learned consider them fools, their possession of the Gnosis, the sorcery of the Ancient North, commands respect and mortal envy. Driven by nightmares, they wander the labyrinths of power, scouring the Three Seas for signs of their ancient and implacable foe—the Consult.

And as always, they find nothing.

Book One: The Darkness That Comes Before

The **Holy War** is the name of the great host called by Maithanet, the leader of the Thousand Temples, to liberate Shimeh from the heathen Fanim of Kian. Word of Maithanet's call spreads across the Three Seas, and faithful from all the great Inrithi nations—Galeoth, Thunyerus, Ce Tydonn, Conriya, High Ainon and their tributaries—travel to the city of Momemn, the capital of the Nansur Empire, to become Men of the Tusk.

Almost from the outset, the gathering host is mired in politics and controversy. First, Maithanet somehow convinces the Scarlet Spires, the most powerful of the sorcerous Schools, to join his Holy War. Despite the outrage this provokes—sorcery is anathema to the Inrithi—the Men of the Tusk realize they need the Scarlet Spires to counter the heathen Cishaurim, the sorcerer-priests of the Fanim. The Holy War would be doomed without one of the Major Schools. The question is why the Scarlet Schoolmen would agree to such a perilous arrangement. Unknown to most, Eleäzaras, the Grandmaster of the Scarlet Spires, has waged a long and secret war against the Cishaurim, who for no apparent reason assassinated his predecessor, Sasheoka, ten years previous.

Second, Ikurei Xerius III, the Emperor of Nansur, hatches an intricate plot to usurp the Holy War for his own ends. Much of what is now heathen Kian once belonged to the Nansur, and recovering the Empire's lost provinces is Xerius's most fervent desire. Since the Holy War gathers in the Nansur Empire, it can march only if provisioned by the Emperor, something he refuses to do until every leader of the Holy War signs his Indenture, a written oath to cede all lands conquered to him.

Of course, the first caste-nobles to arrive repudiate the Indenture, and a stalemate ensues. As the Holy War's numbers swell into the hundreds of thousands, however, the titular leaders of the host begin to grow restless. Since they war in the God's name, they think themselves invincible, and as a result see little reason to share the glory with those yet to arrive. A Conriyan noble named Nersei Calmemunis comes to an accommodation with the Emperor, and convinces his fellows to sign the Imperial Indenture. Once provisioned, most of those gathered march, even though their lords and a greater part of the Holy War have yet to arrive. Because the host consists primarily of lordless rabble, it comes to be called the Vulgar Holy War.

Despite Maithanet's attempts to bring the makeshift host to heel, it continues marching southward, and passes into heathen lands, where— precisely as the Emperor had planned—the Fanim destroy it utterly.

Xerius knows that in military terms the loss of the Vulgar Holy War is insignificant, since the rabble that largely constituted it would have proven more a liability than an advantage in battle. In political terms, however, the Vulgar Holy War's destruction is invaluable, because it has shown Maithanet and the Men of the Tusk the true mettle of their adversary. The Fanim, as the Nansur well know, are not to be trifled with, even with the God's favour. Only an outstanding general, Xerius claims, can assure the Holy War's victory—a man like his nephew, Ikurei Conphas, who after his recent victory over the dread Scylvendi at the Battle of Kiyuth has been hailed as the greatest tactician of his age. The leaders of the Holy War need only sign the Imperial Indenture and Conphas's preternatural skill and insight will be theirs.

Maithanet, it seems, now finds himself in a dilemma. As Shriah, he can compel the Emperor to provision the Holy War, but he cannot compel him to send Ikurei Conphas, his only living heir. In the midst of this controversy arrive the first truly great Inrithi potentates of the Holy War: Prince Nersei Proyas of Conriya, Prince Coithus Saubon of Galeoth, Earl Hoga Gothyelk of Ce Tydonn, and King-Regent Chepheramunni of High Ainon. The Holy War amasses new strength, though it remains in effect a hostage, bound by the scarcity of food to the walls of Momemn and the Emperor's granaries. To a man, the caste-nobles repudiate Xerius's Indenture and demand that he provision them. The Men of the Tusk begin raiding the surrounding countryside. In retaliation, the Emperor calls in elements of the Imperial Army. Pitched battles are fought.

In an effort to forestall disaster Maithanet calls a Council of Great and Lesser Names, and all the leaders of the Holy War gather in the Emperor's palace, the Andiamine Heights, to make their arguments. Here Nersei Proyas shocks the assembly by offering a many-scarred Scylvendi Chieftain, a veteran of past wars against the Fanim, as a surrogate for the famed Ikurei Conphas. The Scylvendi, Cnaiür urs Skiötha, shares hard words with both the Emperor and his nephew, and the leaders of the Holy War are impressed. The Shriah's Envoy, however, remains undecided: the Scylvendi are as apostate as the Fanim, after all. Only the wise words of Prince Anasûrimbor Kellhus of Atrithau settle the matter. The Envoy reads the decree demanding that the Emperor, under pain of Shrial Censure, provision the Men of the Tusk.

The Holy War will march.

Drusas Achamian is a sorcerer sent by the School of Mandate to investigate Maithanet and his Holy War. Though he no longer believes in his School's ancient mission, he travels to Sumna, where the Thousand Temples is based, in the hopes of learning more about the mysterious Shriah, whom the Mandate fears could be an agent of the Consult. In the course of his probe, he resumes an old love affair with a harlot named Esmenet, and despite his misgivings, he recruits a former student of his, a Shrial Priest named Inrau, to report on Maithanet's activities. During this time, his nightmares of the Apocalypse intensify, particularly those involving the so-called "Celmomian Prophecy," which foretells the return of a descendant of Anasûrimbor Celmomas before the Second Apocalypse.

Then Inrau dies under mysterious circumstances. Overcome by guilt and heartbroken by Esmenet's refusal to cease taking custom, Achamian flees Sumna and travels to Momemn, where the Holy War gathers under the Emperor's covetous and uneasy eyes. A powerful rival of the Mandate, a School called the Scarlet Spires, has joined the Holy War to prosecute their long contest with the sorcerer-priests of the Cishaurim, who reside in Shimeh. Nautzera, Achamian's Mandate handler, has ordered him to observe them and the Holy War. When he reaches the encampment, Achamian joins the fire of Xinemus, an old friend of his from Conriya.

Pursuing his investigation of Inrau's death, Achamian convinces Xinemus to take him to see another old student of his, Prince Nersei Proyas of Conriya, who's become a confidant of the enigmatic Shriah. When Proyas scoffs at his suspicions and repudiates him as a blasphemer, Achamian implores him to write Maithanet regarding the circumstances of Inrau's death. Embittered, Achamian leaves his old student's pavilion certain his meagre request will go unfulfilled.

Then a man hailing from the distant north arrives—a man calling himself *Anasûrimbor* Kellhus. Battered by his recurrent dreams of the Apocalypse, Achamian finds himself fearing the worst: the Second Apocalypse. Is Kellhus's arrival a mere coincidence, or is he the Harbinger foretold in the Celmomian Prophecy? Achamian questions the man, only to find himself utterly disarmed by his humour, honesty, and intellect. They talk history and philosophy long into the night, and before retiring, Kellhus asks Achamian to be his teacher. Inexplicably awed and affected by the stranger, Achamian agrees.

But he finds himself in a dilemma. The reappearance of an Anasûrimbor is something the School of Mandate simply has to know: few discoveries could be more significant. But he fears what his brother Schoolmen will do: a lifetime of dreaming horrors, he knows, has made them cruel and pitiless. And he blames them, moreover, for the death of Inrau.

Before he can resolve this dilemma, Achamian is summoned by the Emperor's nephew, Ikurei Conphas, to the Imperial Palace in Momemn, where the Emperor wants him to assess a highly placed adviser of his—an old man called Skeaös—for the Mark of sorcery. The Emperor himself, Ikurei Xerius III, brings Achamian to Skeaös, demanding to know whether the old man bears the blasphemous taint of sorcery. Achamian sees nothing amiss.

Skeaös, however, sees something in Achamian. He begins writhing against his chains, speaking a tongue from Achamian's ancient dreams. Impossibly, the old man breaks free, killing several before being burned by the Emperor's sorcerers. Dumbfounded, Achamian confronts the howling

Skeaös, only to watch horrified as his face peels apart and opens into scorched *limbs* ...

The abomination before him, he realizes, *is a Consult spy*, one that can mimic and replace others without bearing sorcery's telltale Mark. A skin-spy. Achamian flees the palace without warning the Emperor and his court, knowing they would think his conviction nonsense. For them, Skeaös can only be an artifact of the heathen Cishaurim, whose art also bears no Mark. Senseless to his surroundings, Achamian wanders back to Xinemus's camp, so absorbed by his horror that he fails to see or hear Esmenet, who has come to rejoin him at long last.

The mysteries surrounding Maithanet. The coming of Anasûrimbor Kellhus. The discovery of the first Consult spy in generations ... How can he doubt it any longer? The Second Apocalypse is about to begin.

Alone in his humble tent, he weeps, overcome by loneliness, dread, and remorse.

Esmenet is a Sumni prostitute who mourns both her life and her daughter. When Achamian arrives on his mission to learn more about Maithanet, she readily takes him in. During this time, she continues to take and service her customers, knowing full well the pain this causes Achamian. But she really has no choice: sooner or later, she realizes, Achamian will be called away. And yet she falls ever deeper in love with the hapless sorcerer, in part because of the respect he accords her and in part because of the worldly nature of his work. Though her sex has condemned her to sit half-naked in her window, the world beyond has always been her passion. The intrigues of the Great Factions, the machinations of the Consult: these are the things that quicken her soul!

Then disaster strikes: Achamian's informant, Inrau, is murdered, and the bereaved Schoolman is forced to travel to Momemn. Esmenet begs him to take her with him, but he refuses, and she finds herself once again marooned in her old life. Not long after, a threatening stranger comes to her room, demanding to know everything about Achamian. Twisting her desire against her, the man ravishes her, and Esmenet finds herself answering all his questions. Come morning he vanishes as suddenly as he appears, leaving only pools of black seed to mark his passing.

Horrified, Esmenet flees Sumna, determined to find Achamian and tell him what happened. In her bones she knows the stranger is somehow connected to the Consult. On her way to Momemn she pauses in a village, hoping to find someone to repair her broken sandal. When the villagers recognize the whore's tattoo on her hand they begin stoning her—the punishment the Tusk demands of prostitutes. Only the sudden appearance of a Shrial Knight named Sarcellus saves her, and she has the satisfaction of watching her tormentors humbled. Sarcellus takes her the rest of the way to Momemn, and Esmenet finds herself growing more and more infatuated with his wealth and aristocratic manner. He seems so free of the melancholy and indecision that plague Achamian.

Once they reach the Holy War, Esmenet stays with Sarcellus, even though she knows Achamian is only miles away. As the Shrial Knight continually reminds her, Schoolmen such as Achamian are forbidden to take wives. If she were to run to him, he says, it would be only a matter of time before he abandoned her again.

Weeks pass, and she finds herself esteeming Sarcellus less and pining for Achamian more and more. Finally, on the night before the Holy War is to march, she sets off in search of the portly sorcerer, determined to tell him everything that has happened. After a harrowing search she finally locates Xinemus's camp, only to find herself too ashamed to make her presence known. She hides in the darkness instead, waiting for Achamian to appear, and wondering at the strange collection of men and women about the fire. When dawn arrives without any sign of Achamian, Esmenet wanders across the abandoned site, only to see him trudging toward her. She holds out her arms to him, weeping with joy and sorrow ...

And he simply walks past her as though she were a stranger.

Heartbroken, she flees, determined to make her own way in the Holy War.

Cnaiür urs Skiötha is a Chieftain of the Utemot, a tribe of Scylvendi, who are feared across the Three Seas for their skill and ferocity in war. Because of the events surrounding the death of his father, Skiötha, thirty years previous, Cnaiür is despised by his own people, though none dare challenge him because of his savage strength and his cunning in war. Word arrives that the Emperor's nephew, Ikurei Conphas, has invaded the

Holy Steppe, and Cnaiür rides with the Utemot to join the Scylvendi horde on the distant Imperial frontier. Knowing Conphas's reputation, Cnaiür senses a trap, but his warnings go unheeded by Xunnurit, the chieftain elected King-of-Tribes for the coming battle. Cnaiür can only watch as the disaster unfolds.

Escaping the horde's destruction, Cnaiür returns to the pastures of the Utemot more anguished than ever. He flees the whispers and the looks of his fellow tribesmen and rides to the graves of his ancestors, where he finds a grievously wounded man sitting upon his dead father's barrow, surrounded by circles of dead Sranc. Warily approaching, Cnaiür nightmarishly realizes that he *recognizes* the man—or almost recognizes him. He resembles Anasûrimbor Moënghus in almost every respect, save that he is too young ...

Moënghus had been captured thirty years previous, when Cnaiür was little more than a stripling, and given to Cnaiür's father as a slave. He claimed to be Dûnyain, a people possessed of an extraordinary wisdom, and Cnaiür spent many hours with him, speaking of things forbidden to Scylvendi warriors. What happened afterward—the seduction, the murder of Skiötha, and Moënghus's subsequent escape—has tormented Cnaiür ever since. Though he once loved the man, he now hates him with a deranged intensity. If only he could kill Moënghus, he believes, his heart could be made whole.

Now, impossibly, this double has come to him, travelling the same path as the original.

Realizing the stranger could make possible his vengeance, Cnaiür takes him captive. The man, who calls himself Anasûrimbor Kellhus, claims to be Moënghus's son. The Dûnyain, he says, have sent him to assassinate his father in a faraway city called Shimeh. But as much as Cnaiür wants to believe this story, he's wary and troubled. After years of obsessively pondering Moënghus, he's come to understand that the Dûnyain are gifted with preternatural skills and intelligence. Their sole purpose, he now knows, is domination, though where others use force and fear, the Dûnyan use deceit and love.

The story Kellhus has told him, Cnaiür realizes, is precisely the story a Dûnyain seeking escape and safe passage across Scylvendi lands would provide. Nevertheless, he makes a bargain with the man, agreeing to accompany him on his quest. The two strike out across the Steppe, locked in a shadowy war of word and passion. Time and again Cnaiür finds himself drawn into Kellhus's insidious nets, only to recall himself at the last moment. Only his hatred of Moënghus and knowledge of the Dûnyain preserve him.

Near the Imperial frontier they encounter a party of hostile Scylvendi raiders. Kellhus's unearthly skill in battle both astounds and terrifies Cnaiür. In the battle's aftermath they find a captive concubine, a woman named Serwë, cowering among the raiders' chattel. Struck by her beauty, Cnaiür takes her as his prize, and through her he learns of Maithanet's Holy War for Shimeh, the city where Moënghus supposedly dwells ... Can this be a coincidence?

Coincidence or not, the Holy War forces Cnaiür to reconsider his original plan to travel around the Empire, where his Scylvendi heritage will mean almost certain death. With the Fanim rulers of Shimeh girding for war, the only possible way they can reach the holy city is to become Men of the Tusk. They have no choice, he realizes, but to join the Holy War, which according to Serwë, gathers about the city of Momemn in the heart of the Empire—the one place he cannot go. Now that they have safely crossed the Steppe, Cnaiür is convinced Kellhus will kill him: the Dûnyain brook no liabilities.

Descending the mountains into the Empire, Cnaiür confronts Kellhus, who claims he has use of him still. While Serwë watches in horror, the two men battle on the mountainous heights, and though Cnaiür is able to surprise Kellhus, the man easily overpowers him, holding him by the throat over a precipice. To prove his intent to keep their bargain, he spares Cnaiür's life. After so many years among world-born men, Kellhus claims, Moënghus will be far too powerful for him to face alone. They will need an army, he says, and unlike Cnaiür he knows nothing of war.

Despite his misgivings, Cnaiür believes him, and they resume their journey. As the days pass, Cnaiür watches Serwë become more and more infatuated with Kellhus. Though troubled by this, he refuses to admit as much, reminding himself that warriors care nothing for women, particularly those taken as the spoils of battle. What does it matter that she belongs to Kellhus during the day? She is Cnaiür's at night.

After a desperate journey and pursuit through the heart of the Empire, they at last find their way to Momemn and the Holy War, where they are taken before one of the Holy War's leaders, a Conriyan Prince named Nersei Proyas. In keeping with their plan, Cnaiür claims to be the last of the Utemot, travelling with Anasûrimbor Kellhus, a Prince of the northern city of Atrithau, who has dreamt of the Holy War from afar. Proyas, however, is far more interested in Cnaiür's knowledge of the Fanim and their way of battle. Obviously impressed by what he has to say, the Conriyan Prince takes Cnaiür and his companions under his protection.

Soon afterward, Proyas takes Cnaiür and Kellhus to a meeting of the Holy War's leaders and the Emperor, where the fate of the Holy War is to be decided. Ikurei Xerius III has refused to provision the Men of the Tusk unless they swear to return all the lands they wrest from the Fanim to the Empire. The Shriah, Maithanet, can force the Emperor to provision them, but he fears the Holy War lacks the leadership to overcome the Fanim. The Emperor offers his brilliant nephew, Ikurei Conphas, flush from his spectacular victory over the Scylvendi at Kiyuth, but only—once again—if the leaders of the Holy War pledge to surrender their future conquests. In a daring gambit, Proyas offers *Cnaiür* in Conphas's stead. A vicious war of words ensues, and Cnaiür manages to best the precocious Imperial Nephew. The Shriah's representative orders the Emperor to provision the Men of the Tusk. The Holy War will march.

In a mere matter of days, Cnaiür has gone from a fugitive to a leader of the greatest host ever assembled in the Three Seas. What does it mean for a Scylvendi to treat with outland princes, with peoples he is sworn to destroy? What must he surrender to see his vengeance through?

That night, he watches Serwë surrender to Kellhus body and soul, and he wonders at the horror he has delivered to the Holy War. What will Anasûrimbor Kellhus—a Dûnyain—make of these Men of the Tusk? No matter, he tells himself, the Holy War marches to distant Shimeh—to Moënghus and the promise of blood.

Anasûrimbor Kellhus is a monk sent by his order, the Dûnyain, to search for his father, Anasûrimbor Moënghus.

Since discovering the secret redoubt of the Kûniüric High Kings during the Apocalypse some two thousand years previous, the Dûnyain have concealed themselves, breeding for reflex and intellect, and continually training in the ways of limb, thought, and face—all for the sake of reason, the sacred Logos. In the effort to transform themselves into the perfect expression of the Logos, the Dûnyain have bent their entire existence to mastering the irrationalities that determine human thought: history, custom, and passion. In this way, they believe, they will eventually grasp what they call the Absolute, and so become true self-moving souls.

But their glorious isolation is at an end. After thirty years of exile, one of their number, Anasûrimbor Moënghus, has reappeared in their dreams, demanding they send to him his son. Knowing only that his father dwells in a distant city called Shimeh, Kellhus undertakes an arduous journey through lands long abandoned by men. While wintering with a trapper named Leweth, he discovers he can read the man's thoughts through the nuances of his expression. World-born men, he realizes, are little more than children in comparison with the Dûnyain. Experimenting, he finds that he can exact anything from Leweth—any love, any sacrifice—with mere words. So what of his father, who has spent thirty years among such men? What is the extent of Anasûrimbor Moënghus's power?

When a band of inhuman Sranc discovers Leweth's steading, the two men are forced to flee. Leweth is wounded, and Kellhus leaves him for the Sranc, feeling no remorse. The Sranc overtake him, and after driving them away, he battles their leader, a deranged Nonman, who nearly undoes him with *sorcery*. Kellhus flees, wracked by questions without answers: sorcery, he'd been taught, was nothing more than superstition. Could the Dûnyain have been wrong? What other facts had they over-looked or suppressed?

Eventually he finds refuge in the ancient city of Atrithau, where, using his Dûnyain abilities, he assembles an expedition to traverse the Sranc-infested plains of Suskara. After a harrowing trek, he crosses the frontier only to be captured by a mad Scylvendi Chieftain named Cnaiür urs Skiötha—a man who both knows and hates his father, Moënghus.

Though his knowledge of the Dûnyain renders Cnaiür immune to direct manipulation, Kellhus quickly realizes he can turn the man's thirst for vengeance to his advantage. Claiming to be an assassin sent to murder Moënghus, he asks the Scylvendi to join him on his quest. Overpowered by his hatred, Cnaiür reluctantly agrees, and the two men set out across the Jiünati Steppe. Time and again, Kellhus tries to secure the trust he needs to possess the man, but the barbarian continually rebuffs him. His hatred and penetration are too great.

Then, near the Imperial frontier, they find a concubine named Serwë, who informs them of a Holy War gathering about Momemn—a Holy War for *Shimeh*. The fact that his father has summoned him to Shimeh at the same time, Kellhus realizes, can be no coincidence. But what could Moënghus be planning?

They cross the mountains into the Empire, and Kellhus watches Cnaiür struggle with the growing conviction that he's outlived his usefulness. Thinking that murdering Kellhus is as close as he'll ever come to murdering Moënghus, Cnaiür attacks him, only to be defeated. To prove that he still needs him, Kellhus spares his life. He must, Kellhus knows, dominate the Holy War, but he as yet knows nothing of warfare. The variables are too many.

Though his knowledge of Moënghus and the Dûnyain renders him a liability, Cnaiür's skill in war makes him invaluable. To secure this knowledge, Kellhus starts seducing Serwë, using her and her beauty as detours to the barbarian's tormented heart.

Once in the Empire, they stumble across a patrol of Imperial cavalrymen; their journey to Momemn quickly becomes a desperate race. When they finally reach the encamped Holy War they find themselves before Nersei Proyas, the Crown Prince of Conriya. To secure a position of honour among the Men of the Tusk, Kellhus lies, and claims to be a Prince of Atrithau. To lay the groundwork for his future domination, he claims to have suffered dreams of the Holy War—implying, without saying as much, that they were godsent. Since Proyas is more concerned with Cnaiür and how he can use the barbarian's knowledge of battle to thwart the Emperor, these declarations are accepted without any real scrutiny. Only the Mandate Schoolman accompanying Proyas, Drusas Achamian, seems troubled by him—especially by his name.

The following evening, Kellhus dines with the sorcerer, disarming him with humour, flattering him with questions. He learns of the Apocalypse and the Consult and many other sundry things, and though he knows Achamian harbours some terror regarding the name "Anasûrimbor," he asks the melancholy man to become his teacher. The Dûnyain, Kellhus has come to realize, have been mistaken about many things, the existence of sorcery among them. There is so much he must know before he confronts his father ...

A final gathering is called to settle the issue between the lords of the Holy War, who want to march, and the Emperor, who refuses to provision them. With Cnaiür at his side, Kellhus charts the souls of all those present, calculating the ways he might bring them under his thrall. Among the Emperor's advisers, however, he observes an expression he cannot read. The man, he realizes, possesses a *false face*. While Ikurei Conphas and the Inrithi caste-nobles bicker, Kellhus studies the man, and determines that his name is Skeaös by reading the lips of his interlocutors. Could this Skeaös be an agent of his father?

Before he can draw any conclusions, however, his scrutiny is noticed by the Emperor himself, who has the adviser seized. Though the entire Holy War celebrates the Emperor's defeat, Kellhus is more perplexed than ever. Never has he undertaken a study so deep.

That night he consummates his relationship with Serwë, continuing the patient work of undoing Cnaiür—as all Men of the Tusk must be undone. Somewhere, a shadowy faction lurks behind faces of false skin. Far to the south in Shimeh, Anasûrimbor Moënghus awaits the coming storm.

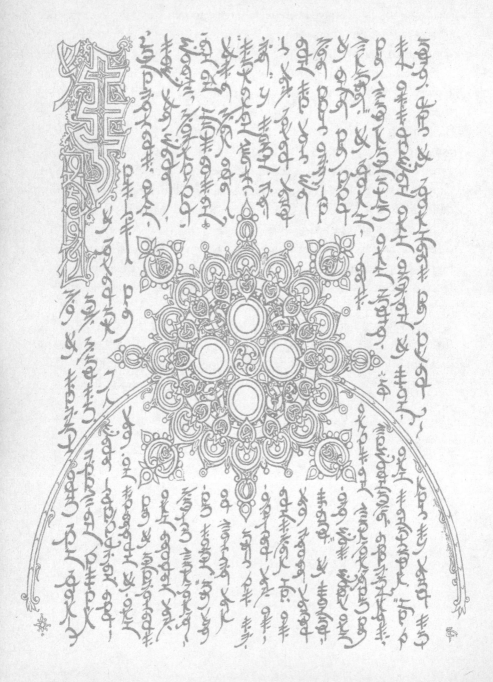

PART I:
The First March

HAPTER ONE

ANSERCA

Ignorance is trust.

—ANCIENT KÛNIÜRIC PROVERB

Late Spring, 4111 Year-of-the-Tusk, south of Momemn

Drusas Achamian sat cross-legged in the darkness of his tent, a silhouette rocking slowly to and fro, muttering dark words. Light spilled from his mouth. Though the moon-shining length of the Meneanor Sea lay between him and Atyersus, he walked the ancient halls of his School—walked among sleepers.

The dimensionless geometry of dreams never ceased to startle Achamian. There was something monstrous about a world where nothing was remote, where distances dissolved into a froth of words and competing passions. Something no knowledge could overcome.

Pitched from nightmare to nightmare, Achamian at last found the sleeping man he sought: Nautzera in his dream, seated on blood-muddied turf, cradling a dead king on his lap. "Our King is dead!" Nautzera cried in Seswatha's voice. "Anasûrimbor Celmomas is dead!"

An unearthly roar hammered his ears. Achamian whirled, raising his hands against a titanic shadow.

Wracu ... Dragon.

Billowing gusts staggered those standing, waved the arms of those

2

fallen. Cries of dismay and horror rifled the air, then a cataract of boiling gold engulfed Nautzera and the High King's attendants. There was no time for screams. Teeth cracked. Bodies tumbled like coals from a kicked fire.

Achamian turned and saw Nautzera amid a field of smoking husks. Shielded by his Wards, the sorcerer laid the dead king on the ground, whispering words Achamian could not hear but had dreamed innumerable times: "Turn your soul's eye from this world, dear friend ... Turn so that your heart might be broken no more."

With the force of a toppled tower, the dragon thundered to earth, his descent yanking smoke and ash into towering veils. Portcullis jaws clacked shut. Wings like war-galley sails stretched out. The light of burning corpses shimmered across iridescent scales of black.

"*Our Lord,*" the dragon grated, "*hath tasted thy King's passing, and he saith, 'It is done.'*"

Nautzera stood before the golden-horned abomination. "Not while I draw breath, Skafra!" he cried. "*Never!*"

Laughter, like the wheezing of a thousand consumptive men. The Great Dragon reared his bull-chest above the sorcerer, revealing a necklace of steaming human heads.

"*Thou art overthrown, sorcerer. Thy tribe hath perished, dashed like a potter's vessel by our fury. The earth is sown with thy nation's blood, and soon thine enemies will compass thee with bent bow and whetted bronze. Wilt thou not repent thy folly? Wilt thou not abase thyself before our Lord?*"

"As do you, mighty Skafra? As the exalted Tyrant of Cloud and Mountain abases himself?"

Membranes flickered across the dragon's quicksilver eyes. A blink. "*I am not a God.*"

Nautzera smiled grimly. Seswatha said, "Neither is your lord."

Great stamping limbs and the gnashing of iron teeth. A cry from furnace lungs, as deep as an ocean's moan and as piercing as an infant's shriek.

Uncowed by the dragon's thrashing bulk, Nautzera suddenly turned to Achamian, his face bewildered.

"Who are you?"

"One who shares your dreams ..."

For a moment they were like two men drowning, two souls kicking for sharp air ... Then darkness. The silent nowhere that housed men's souls.

Nautzera ... It is I.

A place of pure voice.

Achamian! That dream ... It plagues me so of late. Where are you? We feared you dead.

Concern? Nautzera betraying concern for him, the one Schoolman he despised above all others? But then Seswatha's Dreams had a way of sweeping aside petty enmities.

With the Holy War, Achamian replied. *The contest with the Emperor has been resolved. The Holy War marches on Kian.* Images accompanied these words: Proyas addressing rapt mobs of armoured Conriyans; the endless trains of armed lords and their households; the many-coloured banners of a thousand thanes and barons; a distant glimpse of the Nansur Columns, marching through vineyard and grove in perfect formation ...

So it begins, Nautzera said decisively. *And Maithanet? Were you able to learn anything more of him?*

I thought Proyas might assist me, but I was wrong. He belongs to the Thousand Temples ... To Maithanet.

What is it with your students, Achamian? Why do they all turn to our rivals, hmm? The ease with which Nautzera had recovered his sarcasm both stung and curiously relieved Achamian. The grand old sorcerer would need his wits for what followed.

I have seen them, Nautzera. A flash of Skeaös's naked body, chained and flailing like a holy shaker in the dust.

Seen whom?

The Consult. I've seen them. I know how they've eluded us for all these long years. A face unclenching, like a miser's fist from a golden ensolarii.

Are you drunk?

They're here, Nautzera. Among us. They've always been.

Pause. *What are you saying?*

The Consult still plies the Three Seas.

The Consult ...

Yes! Witness.

More images flashed, reconstructions of the madness that had occurred in the bowels of the Andiamine Heights. The hellish face unfolding, again and again.

Without sorcery, Nautzera. Do you understand? The onta was unmarked! We cannot see these skin-spies for what they are ...

Even though Inrau's death had intensified his hatred of Nautzera, Achamian had called him because he was a fanatic, the only man extreme enough in temper to soberly appraise the extremity of his revelation.

The Tekne, Nautzera said, and for the first time Achamian heard fear in the man's voice. *The Old Science ... It must be! The others must dream this, Achamian! Send this dream to the others!*

But ...

But what? There's more?

Far more. An Anasûrimbor had returned, a living descendent of the dead king Nautzera had just dreamed.

Nothing of significance, Achamian replied. Why had he said this? Why conceal Anasûrimbor Kellhus from the Mandate? Why protect—

Good. I can scarce digest this as it is ... Our ancient foe discovered at last! And behind faces of skin! If they could penetrate the sequestered heights of the Imperial Court, they could penetrate nearly any faction, Achamian. Any faction! Send this dream to the entire Quorum! All Atyersus trembles this night.

Daybreak seemed bold, and Achamian found himself wondering whether mornings always seemed such when greeted by a thousand spear points. Sunlight swept out from the edge of the purple earth, illuminating hillsides and tree lines with crisp morning brilliance. The Sogian Way, an old coastal road that predated the Ceneian Empire, shot straight to the southwest, bending only to the rise and fall of the distant hills. A long line of armed men trudged along it, knotted by baggage trains and flanked by companies of mounted knights. Where the sun touched them, it stretched their shadows far across the surrounding pasture.

The sight filled Achamian with wonder.

For so many years the concern of his days had been dwarfed by the horror of his nights. What he'd witnessed through Seswatha's eyes possessed no waking measure. Certainly the daylight world could still injure, could still kill, but it all seemed to happen at the scale of rats.

Until now.

Men of the Tusk, as far as the eye could see, scattered across the countryside, clustered about the road like ants on an apple peel. There a band of outriders following a faraway ridge line. Here a broken wain stranded amid streaming thickets of spears. Horsemen galloping through flowering groves. Local youths hollering from the tops of young birches. Such a sight! And it comprised only a fraction of their true might.

Shortly after leaving Momemn, the Holy War had splintered into disparate armies, each under one of the Great Names. According to Xinemus, this had been motivated in part by prudence—divided they could better forage if the Emperor fell short on his promise of provisions—and in part by stubbornness: the Inrithi lords simply could not agree on the best route to Asgilioch.

Proyas had struck for the coast, intending to follow the Sogian Way south to its terminus before turning west for Asgilioch. The other Great Names—Gothyelk with his Tydonni, Saubon and his Galeoth, Chepheramunni and the Ainoni, and Skaiyelt with his Thunyeri—had struck across the fields, vineyards, and orchards of the densely populated Kyranae Plain, thinking Proyas used a circle to travel in a straight line. With the ancient roads of Cenei little more than ruined tracks strewn across their homelands, they had no idea how much time the long way could save so long as it were paved.

At their present pace, Xinemus claimed, the Conriyan contingent would reach Asgilioch days before the others. And though Achamian worried—How could they win a war when simple marches defeated them?—Xinemus seemed convinced this was a good thing. Not only would it win glory for his nation and his prince, it would teach the others an important lesson. "Even the Scylvendi know roads are fucking better!" the Marshal had exclaimed.

Achamian plodded with his mule along the road's verge, surrounded by creaking wains. From the first day of the Holy War's march, he had taken to skulking in the baggage trains. If the columns of marching soldiery seemed like great rolling barracks, then the baggage trains seemed like great rolling barns. The smell of livestock, so like that of wet dogs. The groan and squeal of ungreased axles. The muttering of ham-fisted, ham-hearted men, punctuated now and again by the crack of whips.

He studied his feet—the pulp of trampled grasses had stained his toes green. For the first time, the question of why he shadowed the baggage trains struck him. Seswatha had always ridden at the right hand of kings, princes, and generals. So why didn't he do the same? Though Proyas maintained his veneer of indifference, Achamian knew he would accept his company—if only for Xinemus's sake. What student did not secretly crave their old teacher's presence in uncertain times?

So why did he march with the baggage? Was it habit? He was an aging spy, after all, and nothing concealed so well as humility in humble circumstances. Or was it nostalgia? For some reason, marching as he did reminded him of following his father to the boats as a child, his head thick with sleep, the sand cold, the sea dark and morning-warm. Always the same glance to the east, where cold grey promised a punishing sun. Always the heavy breath as he resigned himself to the inevitable, to the hardship become ritual that men called work.

But what comfort could such memories offer? Drudgery didn't soothe; it numbed.

Then Achamian realized: he marched with the beasts and baggage, not out of habit or nostalgia, but out of *aversion*.

I'm hiding, he thought. *Hiding from him …*

From Anasûrimbor Kellhus.

Achamian slowed, tugged his mule from the verge into the surrounding meadow. The dew-cold grasses made his feet ache. The wains continued to trundle by, an endless file.

Hiding …

More and more, it seemed, he caught himself doing things for obscure reasons. Retiring early, not because he was exhausted from the day's march—as he told himself—but because he feared the scrutiny of Xinemus, Kellhus, and the others. Staring at Serwë, not because she reminded him of Esmi—as he told himself—but because the way she stared at Kellhus worried him—as though she knew something …

And now this.

Am I going mad?

Several times now, he'd found himself cackling aloud for no apparent reason. Once or twice he'd raised a hand to his cheek to discover he'd been weeping. Each time he'd simply mumbled away his shock: few things are more familiar, he supposed, than finding oneself a stranger. Besides, what else could he do? Rediscovering the Consult was cause enough to go mad about the edges, certainly. But to suspect—no, to *know*—that the Second Apocalypse was beginning ... And to be *alone* with such knowledge!

How could someone like him bear such a weight?

The solution, of course, was to share the burden—to tell the Mandate about Kellhus.

Before, Achamian had merely *feared* that Kellhus augured the resurrection of the No-God. He'd omitted him from his reports because he'd known exactly what Nautzera and the others would have done. They would have seized him, then, like jackals with a boiled bone, they would have gnawed and gnawed until he cracked. But the incident beneath the Andiamine Heights had ... had ...

Things had changed. Changed irrevocably.

For so many years the Consult had been little more than an empty posit, an oppressive abstraction. What was it Inrau had called them? A father's sin ... But now—*now!*—they were as real as a knife's edge. And Achamian no longer feared that Kellhus augured the Apocalypse, he *knew*.

Knowing was so much worse.

So why continue concealing the man? An *Anasûrimbor* had returned. The Celmomian Prophecy had been fulfilled! Within the space of days, the Three Seas had assumed the same bloated dimensions as the world he suffered night after night. And yet he said nothing—*nothing!* Why? Some men, Achamian had observed, utterly refused to acknowledge things such as illness or infidelity, as though facts required acceptance to become real. Was this what he was doing? Did he think that keeping Kellhus a secret made the man less real somehow? That the end of the world could be prevented by covering his eyes?

It was too much. Too much. The Mandate simply *had* to know, no matter what the consequences.

I must tell them ... Tonight, I must tell them.

"Xinemus," a familiar voice said from behind, "told me I'd find you with the baggage."

"He did, did he?" Achamian replied, surprised by the levity of his tone.

Kellhus smiled down at him. "He said you preferred stepping in fresh shit over old."

Achamian shrugged, did his best to purge the phantoms from the small corners of his expression. "Keeps my toes warm ... Where's your Scylvendi friend?"

"He rides with Proyas and Ingiaban."

"Ah. So you've decided to slum with the likes of me." He glanced down at the Northerner's sandalled feet. "To the point of walking no less ..." Caste-nobles didn't march, they rode. Kellhus was a prince, though like Xinemus, he made it easy for others to forget his rank.

Kellhus winked. "I thought I'd let my ass ride me for a change."

Achamian laughed, feeling as though he'd been holding his breath and could only now exhale. Since that first evening outside Momemn, Kellhus had made him feel this way—as though he could breathe easy. When he'd mentioned this to Xinemus, the Marshal had shrugged and said, *"Everyone farts, sooner or later."*

"Besides," Kellhus continued, "you promised you'd instruct me."

"I did, did I?"

"You did."

Kellhus reached out and clasped the rope that swayed from his mule's crude bridle. Achamian looked at him quizzically. "What are you doing?"

"I'm your student," Kellhus said, checking the bindings on the mule's baggage. "Surely in your youth you led your master's mule."

Achamian answered with a dubious smile.

Kellhus ran a hand along the trunk of the beast's neck. "What's his name?" he asked.

For some reason the banality of the question shocked Achamian—to the point of horror. No one—no man, anyway—had cared to ask before. Not even Xinemus.

Kellhus frowned at his hesitation. "What's troubling you, Achamian?" *You ...*

He looked away, across the streaming queues of armed Inrithi. His ears both burned and roared. *He reads me like any scroll.*

"Is it so easy?" Achamian asked. "So easy to see?"

"What does it matter?"

"It matters," he said, blinking tears and turning to face Kellhus once again. *So I weep!* something desolate within him cried. *So I weep!*

"Ajencis," he continued, "once wrote that all men are frauds. Some, the wise, fool only others. Others, the foolish, fool only themselves. And a rare few fool both others and themselves—they are the rulers of Men ... But what about men like *me*, Kellhus? What about men who fool no one?"

And I call myself a spy!

Kellhus shrugged. "Perhaps they are less than fools and more than wise."

"Perhaps," Achamian replied, struggling to appear thoughtful.

"So what troubles you?"

You ...

"Daybreak," Achamian said, reaching out to scratch his mule's snout. "His name is Daybreak."

For a Mandate Schoolman, no name was more lucky.

Teaching always quickened something within Achamian. Like the black teas of Nilnamesh, it sometimes made his skin tingle and his soul race. There was the simple vanity of knowing, of course, the pride of seeing farther than another. And there was the joy of watching young eyes pop open in realization, of seeing someone *see*. To be a teacher was to be a student anew, to relive the intoxication of insight, and to be a prophet, to sketch the world down to its very foundation—not simply to tease sight from blindness, but to *demand* that another see.

And then there was the *trust* that was the counterpart of this demand, so reckless that it terrified Achamian whenever he considered it. The madness of one man saying to another, *"Please, judge me ..."*

To be a teacher was to be a father.

But none of this was true of teaching Kellhus. Over the ensuing days, as the Conriyan host marched ever farther south, they walked together, discussing everything imaginable, from the flora and fauna of the Three Seas to the philosophers, poets, and kings of Near and Far Antiquity.

Rather than follow any curriculum, which would have been impractical given the circumstances, Achamian adopted the Ajencian mode, and let Kellhus indulge his curiosity. He simply answered questions. And told stories.

Kellhus's questions, however, were more than perceptive—so much so that Achamian's respect for his intellect soon became awe. No matter what the issue, be it political, philosophical, or poetic, the Prince unerringly struck upon the matter's heart. When Achamian outlined the positions of the great Kûniüric thinker, Ingoswitu, Kellhus, following query upon query, actually arrived at the criticisms of Ajencis, though he claimed to have never read the ancient Kyranean's work. When Achamian described the Ceneian Empire's disarray at the end of the third millennium, Kellhus pressed him with questions—many of which Achamian couldn't answer—regarding trade, currency, and social structure. Within moments he was offering explanations and interpretations as fine as any Achamian had read.

"How?" Achamian blurted on one occasion.

"How what?" Kellhus replied.

"How is it that … that you see these things? No matter how deep I peer …"

"Ah," Kellhus laughed. "You're starting to sound like my father's tutors." He regarded Achamian in a manner that was at once submissive and strangely indulgent, as though he conceded something to an overbearing yet favoured son. The sunlight teased golden threads from his hair and beard. "It's simply a gift I have," he said. "Nothing more."

But such a gift! It was more than what the ancients called *noschi*—genius. There was something about the *way* Kellhus thought, an elusive mobility Achamian had never before encountered. Something that made him seem, at times, a man from a different age.

Most, by and large, were born narrow, and cared to see only that which flattered them. Almost without exception, they assumed their hatreds and yearnings to be correct, no matter what the contradictions, simply because they *felt* correct. Almost all men prized the familiar path over the true. That was the glory of the student, to step from the well-worn path and risk knowledge that oppressed, that horrified. Even still, Achamian, like all teachers, spent as much time uprooting prejudices as implanting truths. All souls were stubborn in the end.

Not so with Kellhus. Nothing was dismissed outright. Any possibility could be considered. It was as though his soul moved over something trackless. Only the truth led him to conclusions.

Question after question, all posed with precision, exploring this or that theme with gentle relentlessness, so thoroughly that Achamian was astonished by how much he himself knew. It was as though, prompted by Kellhus's patient interrogation, he'd undertaken an expedition through a life he'd largely forgotten. Kellhus would ask about Memgowa, the antique Zeumi sage who had recently become the rage among literate Inrithi caste-nobles, and Achamian would remember reading his *Celestial Aphorisms* by candlelight at Xinemus's coastal villa, savouring the exotic turn of his Zeumi sensibilities while listening to the wind scour the orchards outside the shuttered window, the plums thudding like iron spheres against the earth. Kellhus would question his interpretation of the Scholastic Wars, and Achamian would remember arguing with his own teacher, Simas, on the black parapets of Atyersus, thinking himself a prodigy, and cursing the inflexibility of old men. How he had hated those heights that day!

Question after question. Nothing repeated. No ground covered twice. And with each answer, it seemed to Achamian that he exchanged guesses for true insight, and abstractions for recovered moments of his life. Kellhus, he realized, was a student who taught even as he learned, and Achamian had never known another like him. Not Inrau, not even Proyas. The more he answered the man, the more Kellhus seemed to hold the answer to his own life.

Who am I? he would often think, listening to Kellhus's melodious voice. *What do you see?*

And then there were the questions regarding the Old Wars. Like most Mandate Schoolmen, Achamian found it easy to mention the Apocalypse and difficult to discuss it—very difficult. There was the pain of reliving the horror, of course. To speak of the Apocalypse was to wrestle heartbreak into words—an impossible task. And there was shame as well, as though he indulged some humiliating obsession. Too many men had laughed.

But with Kellhus the difficulty was compounded by the fact of the man's blood. He was an *Anasûrimbor*. How does one describe the end of the world to its unwitting messenger? At times, Achamian feared he might gag on the irony. And always he would think: *My School! Why do I betray my School?*

"Tell me of the No-God," Kellhus said one afternoon.

As often happened when they crossed flat pasture, the long lines had broken from the road, and men fanned across the grasses. Some even doffed their sandals and boots and danced, as though finding second wind in unburdened feet. Achamian, who'd been laughing at their antics, was caught entirely off guard.

Now he shuddered. Not so very long ago that name—the No-God— had referred to something distant and dead.

"You hail from Atrithau," Achamian replied, "and you want *me* to tell you of the No-God?"

Kellhus shrugged. "We read *The Sagas*, as you do. Our bards sing their innumerable lays, as do yours. But you ... You've *seen* these things."

No, Achamian wanted to say, *Seswatha has seen these things. Seswatha.*

Instead he studied the distance, gathering his thoughts. He clutched his hands, which felt as light as balsa.

You've seen these things. You ...

"He has, as you likely know, many names. The Men of ancient Kûniüri called him *Mog-Pharau,* from which we derive 'No-God.' In ancient Kyraneas, he was simply called *Tsurumah,* the 'Hated One.' The Nonmen of Ishoriol called him—with the peculiar poetry that belongs to all their names—*Cara-Sincurimoi,* the 'Angel of Endless Hunger' ... He is well named. Never has the world known a greater evil ... A greater peril."

"What is he, then? An unclean spirit?"

"No. Many demons have walked this world. If the rumours about the Scarlet Spires are true, some walk this world still. No, he is more and he is less ..."

Achamian fell silent.

"Perhaps," the Prince of Atrithau ventured, "we shouldn't speak—"

"I've *seen* him, Kellhus. As much as any man can, I've seen him ... Not far from here, at a place called the Plains of Mengedda, the shattered hosts of Kyraneas and her allies hoisted their pennants anew, determined to die grappling the Foe. That was two thousand years ago."

Achamian laughed bitterly, lowering his face. "I'd forgotten ..."

Kellhus watched him intently. "Forgotten what?"

"That the Holy War would be crossing the Plains of Mengedda. That I would soon trod earth that had witnessed the No-God's death ..." He looked to the southern hills. Soon the Unaras Spur, which marked the ends of the Inrithi world, would resolve from the horizon. And on the far side ...

"How could I've forgotten?"

"There's so much to remember," Kellhus said. "Too much."

"Which means too much has been forgotten," Achamian snapped, unwilling to absolve himself of this oversight. *I need my wits! The very world ...*

"You are too ..." Kellhus began, then trailed.

"Too what? Too harsh? You don't understand what it was like! Every infant stillborn for eleven years—for *eleven years,* Kellhus! Ever since the No-God's awakening, every womb a grave ... And you could *feel* him— no matter where you were. He was an ever-present horror in every heart. You need only look to the horizon, and you would *know* his direction. He was a shadow, an intimation of doom ...

"The High North had been laid waste—I need not recite that woe. Mehtsonc, the mighty capital of Kyraneas, had been overthrown the month before. Every hearthstone had been cracked. Every idol had been smashed. Every wife violated. All the great nations had fallen ... So little remained, Kellhus! So few survived!

"With their vassals and allies from the south, the Kyraneans awaited the Foe. Seswatha stood at the right hand of the Kyranean Great King, Anaxophus V. They'd become fast friends years before, when Celmomas had summoned all the lords of Eärwa to his Ordeal, the doomed Holy War meant to destroy the Consult before they could awaken Tsurumah. Together they watched his approach ..."

Tsuramah ...

Achamian abruptly stopped, turning to the north. "Imagine," he said, opening his arms to the sky. "The day wasn't unlike this, though the air smelled of wild blossoms ... Imagine! A great shroud of thunderheads, as broad as the horizon and as black as crow, boiling across *this* sky, spilling toward us like hot blood over glass. I remember threads of lightning flash-ing among the hills. And beneath the eaves of the storm, great cohorts of

Scylvendi galloping to the east and the west, intent on enveloping our flanks. And behind them, loping as fast as dogs, legions upon legions of Sranc, howling ... *howling* ..."

Kellhus placed a friendly hand upon his shoulder. "You needn't tell me this," he said.

Achamian stared at him blankly, blinking tears from his eyes. "No. I *need* to tell you this, Kellhus. I need you to *know*. For this, more than anything else, is who I am ... Do you understand?"

His eyes shining, Kellhus nodded.

"The dark swept over us," Achamian continued, "swallowed the sun. The Scylvendi struck first: mounted skirmishers harried our lines with archery, while divisions of bronze-armoured lancers swept into our flanks. When the screen of skirmishers thinned and withdrew, it seemed all the world had become Sranc. Masses of them, draped in human skins, bounding through the grasses, over hummocks. The Kyraneans lowered their spears and drew up their great shields.

"There are no words, Kellhus, for the dread and determination that moved us. We fought with reckless abandon, intent only on spitting our dying breath against the Foe. We sang no hymns, intoned no prayers— we'd forsworn these things. Instead, we sang our own dirges, bitter laments for our people, our race. We knew that after we passed only the toll we exacted from our foe would survive to sing for us!

"Then from nowhere, it seemed, dragons dropped from the clouds. *Dragons*, Kellhus! Wracu. Ancient Skafra, his hide scarred from a thousand battles; magnificent Skuthula, Skogma, Ghoset; all those who'd survived the arrows and sorceries of the High North. The Magi of Kyraneas and Shigek stepped into the sky and closed with the beasts."

Achamian stared into the vacant distance, overcome by images.

"Just south of here," he said, shaking his head. "Two thousand years ago."

"What happened next?"

Achamian stared at Kellhus. "The impossible. I ... no, *Seswatha* ... Seswatha himself struck down Skafra. Skuthula the Black was driven away, grievously wounded. The Kyraneans and their allies stood like breakers against a heaving sea, throwing back wave after black-hearted wave. For a moment, we almost dared rejoice. Almost ..."

"Then he came," Kellhus said.

Achamian nodded, swallowed. "Then he came … Mog-Pharau. In that much, the poet of *The Sagas* speaks true. The Scylvendi withdrew; the Sranc relented. A great rasping chatter passed through them, swelling into an impossible, keening roar. The Bashrag began beating the ground with their hammers. A churning blackness resolved on the horizon, a great whirlwind, like a black umbilicus joining earth and cloud. And everyone knew. Everyone simply *knew*.

"The No-God was coming. Mog-Pharau walked, and the world thundered. The Sranc began shrieking. Many cast themselves to the ground, scratching at their eyes, gouging … I remember having difficulty breathing … I had joined Anakka—Anaxophus—in his chariot, and I remember him gripping my shoulders. I remember him crying something I couldn't hear … Our horses reared in their harnesses, screaming. Men about us fell to their knees, clutching their ears. Great clouds of dust rolled over us …"

And then the voice, spoken through the throats of a hundred thousand Sranc.

WHAT DO YOU SEE?

I don't understand …

I MUST KNOW WHAT YOU SEE

Death. Wretched death!

TELL ME

Even you cannot hide from what you don't know! Even you!

WHAT AM I?

"Doomed," Seswatha whispered to the thunder. He clutched the Kyranean Great King by the shoulder. "Now, Anaxophus! Strike *now!*"

I CANNOT S—

A thread of silver light, swaying across the spiralling heights, flashing across the Carapace. A crack that made ears bleed. Everywhere, raining debris. The anguished wail of innumerable inhuman throats.

The whirlwind undone, like the smoke of a snuffed candle, spinning into oblivion.

Seswatha fell to his knees, weeping, crying out in grief and exultation. The impossible! The *impossible!* Beside him, Anaxophus dropped the Heron Spear, placed an arm about him.

"Are you okay, Achamian?"

Achamian? Who was Achamian?

"Come," Kellhus said. "Stand up."

A stranger's firm hands. Where was Anaxophus?

"Achamian?"

Again. It's happening again.

"Y-yes?"

"What is the Heron Spear?"

Achamian didn't answer. He couldn't. Rather, he walked silently for a long while, brooding over the moments before his tale had overwhelmed him, over the hideous loss of self and *now*—which seemed species of the same thing. Then he thought of Kellhus, who walked discreetly by his side. The overthrow of the No-God was a tale often referred to and rarely told by Mandate Schoolmen—in fact, Achamian couldn't remember *ever* telling it, not even to Xinemus. And yet he had yielded it to Kellhus thoughtlessly—even demanded that he hear it. Why?

He's doing something to me.

Stupefied, Achamian found himself staring at the man with the candour of a sleepy child.

Who are you?

Kellhus responded without embarrassment—such a thing seemed too small for him. He smiled as though Achamian were in fact a child, an innocent incapable of wishing him ill. The look reminded Achamian of Inrau, who'd so often seen him for what he wasn't: a good man.

Achamian looked away, his throat aching. *Must I give you up, too?*

A student like no other.

A handful of soldiers had started a hymn to the Latter Prophet, and the surrounding rumble of talk and laughter trailed into deep-throated song. Without warning, Kellhus stopped and knelt in the grasses.

"What are you doing?" Achamian asked, more sharply than he would have wished.

"Removing my sandals," the Prince of Atrithau said. "Come, let's bare our feet with the others."

Not sing with the others. Not rejoice with them. Just walk.

Lessons, Achamian would later realize. While Achamian taught, Kellhus continually gave lessons. He was almost certain of it, even though he had no inkling as to what those lessons might be. Intimations of trust, perhaps, of openness, possibly. Somehow, through the course of teaching Kellhus, Achamian had become a student of a different kind. And all he knew for sure was that his education was incomplete.

But as the days passed, this revelation simply complicated his anguish. One night he prepared the Cants of Calling no less than three times, only to have them collapse into mumbled curses and recriminations. The Mandate, his School—his *brothers*—must be told! An Anasûrimbor had returned! The Celmomian Prophecy was more than some backwater of Seswatha's Dreams. Many saw it as their culmination, as the very reason Seswatha had passed from life into his disciples' nightmares. The Great Warning. And yet he, Drusas Achamian, hesitated—no, more than hesitated, wagered. Sweet Sejenus ... He *wagered* his School, his race, his *world*, on a man he'd known no more than a fortnight.

Such madness! He played number-sticks with the end of the world! One man, frail and foolish—who was Drusas Achamian to take such risks? By what right had he shouldered such a burden? What right?

One more day, he told himself, pulling on his beard and his hair. *One more day* ...

Kellhus found him in the general exodus from the camp the morning after this resolution, and despite the man's good humour, hours passed before Achamian relented and began answering his questions. Too many things assailed him. Unspoken things.

"You worry about our fortunes," Kellhus finally said, his look solemn. "You fear that the Holy War won't succeed ..."

Of course Achamian feared for the Holy War. He'd witnessed too many defeats—in his dreams, anyway. But despite the thousands of armed men walking in his periphery, the Holy War was far from his thoughts. Even so, he pretended otherwise. He nodded without looking, as though making a painful admission. More unvoiced reproaches. More self-flagellation. With other men, small deceptions seemed both natural and necessary, but with Kellhus they ... they itched.

"Seswatha ..." Achamian began, hesitating. "Seswatha was little more than a boy when the first wars against Golgotterath were waged. In those early days, not even the wisest of the ancients understood what was at stake. And how could they? They were Norsirai, and the world was their dominion. Their barbaric kinsmen had been subdued. The Sranc had been driven into the mountains. Not even the Scylvendi dared their wrath. Their poetry, their sorcery, and their craft were sought across all of Eärwa, even by the Nonmen who had once tutored them. Foreign emissaries wept at the beauty of their cities. In courts as far away as Kyraneas and Shir men adopted their manner, their cuisine, their style of dress ...

"They were the very measure of their time—like us. Everything was less, and they were always more. Even after Shauriatas, the Grandmaster of the Mangaecca—the Consult—awakened the No-God, no one truly believed the end had come. Each heartbreak seemed more impossible than the last. Even the Fall of Kûniüri, the mightiest of their nations, barely shook the conviction that somehow, some way, the High North would prevail. Only as disaster piled upon disaster did they come to understand ..."

Shielding his eyes he looked into the Prince's face. "Glory doesn't vouchsafe glory. The unthinkable can always come to pass."

The end is coming ... I must decide.

Kellhus nodded, squinting against the sun. "Everything has its measure," he said. "Every man ..." He looked directly at Achamian. "Every decision."

For an instant Achamian feared his heart might stop. A *coincidence* ... *It has to be!*

Without warning, Kellhus bent and retrieved a small stone. He stared at the slope for several moments, as though searching for something, a bird or a hare, to kill. Then he threw it, the sleeve of his silk cassock snapping like leather. The stone whistled through the air, then skipped along the edge of a chapped-stone shelf. A rock teetered forward, then plummeted, cracking against steeper faces, releasing whole skirts of gravel, dust, and debris. Shouts of warning echoed from below.

"Did you intend that?" Achamian asked, his breath tight.

Kellhus shook his head. "No ..." He shot Achamian a quizzical look. "But then that was your point, wasn't it? The unforeseen, the catastrophic, follows hard upon all our actions."

Achamian wasn't so sure he'd even had a point. "And decisions," he said, as though speaking through a stranger's mouth.

"Yes," Kellhus replied. "Decisions."

That night Achamian prepared the Cants of Calling even though he knew he'd be unable to utter the first word. *What right have you?* he cried to himself. *What right? You who are so small* ... Kellhus was the Harbinger. The Messenger. Soon, Achamian knew, the horror of his nights would burst across the waking world. Soon the great cities—Momemn, Carythusal, Aöknyssus—would burn. Achamian had seen them burn before, many times. They would fall as their ancient sisters had fallen: Trysë, Mehtsonc, Myclai. Screaming. Wailing to smoke-shrouded skies ... They would be the new names of woe.

What right? What could justify such a decision?

"Who are you, Kellhus?" he murmured in the solitary darkness of his tent. "I risk everything for you ... Everything!" So why?

Because there was *something* ... something about him. Something that bid Achamian to wait. A sense of impossible becoming ... But what? What was he becoming? And was it *enough*? Enough to warrant betraying his School? Enough to throw the number-sticks of Apocalypse? Could *anything* be enough?

Other than the truth. The truth was always enough, wasn't it?

He looked at me and he knew. Throwing the stone, Achamian realized, had been another lesson. Another clue. But for what? That disaster would follow if he made the wrong decision? That disaster would follow no matter what his decision?

There was no end, it seemed, to his torment.

CHAPTER TWO

ANSERCA

Duty measures the distance between the animal and the divine.
—EKYANNUS I, 44 EPISTLES

*The days and weeks before battle are a strange thing. All the
contingents, the Conriyans, the Galeoth, the Nansur, the Thunyeri,
the Tydonni, the Ainoni, and the Scarlet Spires, marched to the
fortress of Asgilioch, to the Southron Gates and the heathen frontier.
And though many bent their thoughts to Skauras, the heathen
Sapatishah who would contest us, he was still woven of the same
cloth as a thousand other abstract concerns. One could still confuse
war with everyday living ...*
—DRUSAS ACHAMIAN, COMPENDIUM OF THE FIRST HOLY WAR

Late Spring, 4111 Year-of-the-Tusk, the province of Anserca

For the first few days of the march, everything had been confusion, especially at sunset, when the Inrithi scattered across field and hillside to
make camp. Unable to find Xinemus and too tired to care, Achamian had
even pitched his tent among strangers a couple of nights. As the
Conriyan host grew accustomed to itself as a host, however, collective
habit, combined with the gravity of fealty and familiarity, ensured that
the camp took more or less the same shape every evening. Soon

Achamian found himself sharing food and banter, not only with Xinemus and his senior officers, Iryssas, Dinchases, and Zenkappa, but with Kellhus, Serwë, and Cnaiür as well. Proyas visited them twice—difficult evenings for Achamian—but usually the Crown Prince would summon Xinemus, Kellhus, and Cnaiür to the Royal Pavilion, either for temple or for evening councils with the other great lords of the Conriyan contingent.

As a result, Achamian often found himself stranded with Iryssas, Dinchases, and Zenkappa. They made for awkward company, especially with a timid beauty such as Serwë in their midst. But Achamian soon began to appreciate these nights—particularly after spending his days marching with Kellhus. There would be the shyness of men meeting in the absence of their traditional brokers, then the rush of affable discourse, as though surprised and delighted they spoke the same language. It reminded him of the relief he and his childhood friends had felt whenever their older brothers had been called to the boats or the beaches. The fellowship of overshadowed souls was something Achamian could understand. Since leaving Momemn, it seemed the only moments of peace he found were with these men, even though they thought him damned.

One night, Xinemus took Kellhus and Serwë to join Proyas in celebration of Venicata, an Inrithi holy day. Iryssas and the others departed soon after to join their men, and for the first time Achamian found himself alone with the Scylvendi, Cnaiür urs Skiötha, the Last of the Utemot.

Even after several nights of sharing the same fire, the Scylvendi barbarian unnerved him. Sometimes, glimpsing him in his periphery, Achamian would involuntarily catch his breath. Like Kellhus, Cnaiür was a wraith from his dreams, a figure from a far more treacherous ground. Add to this his many-scarred arms and the Chorae he kept stuffed beneath his iron-plated girdle ...

But there were so many questions he needed to ask. Regarding Kellhus, mostly, but also regarding the Sranc clans to the north of his tribal lands. He even wanted to ask the man about Serwë—the way she doted on Kellhus yet followed Cnaiür to sleep had been noticed by all. On those nights the three retired early, Achamian could see the gossip in the looks exchanged by Iryssas and the others—though they had yet to share their speculations. When he'd asked Kellhus about her, the man had simply shrugged and said, "She's his prize."

For a time, Achamian and Cnaiür simply did their best to ignore each other. Shouts and cries echoed through the darkness, and shadowy clots of revellers filed along the unbounded edges of their firelight. Some stared—gawked even—but for the most part left them alone.

After scowling at a boisterous party of Conriyan knights, Achamian finally turned to Cnaiür and said, "I guess we're the heathens, eh, Scylvendi?"

An uncomfortable silence followed while Cnaiür continued gnawing at the bone he held. Achamian sipped his wine, thought of excuses he might use to withdraw to his tent. What did one say to a Scylvendi?

"So you teach him," Cnaiür suddenly said, spitting gristle into the fire. His eyes glittered from the shadow of his heavy brow, studying the flames.

"Yes," Achamian replied.

"Has he told you why?"

Achamian shrugged. "He seeks knowledge of the Three Seas … Why do you ask?"

But the Scylvendi was already standing, wiping greasy fingers against his breeches, then stretching his giant, sinuous frame. Without a word he strode off into the darkness, leaving Achamian baffled. Short of speaking, the man hadn't acknowledged him in any way.

Achamian resolved to mention the incident to Kellhus when he returned, but he quickly forgot the matter. Against the greater scheme of his fears, bad manners and enigmatic questions were of little consequence.

Achamian typically pitched his humble wedge tent beneath the weathered slopes of Xinemus's pavilion. Without exception, he would spend hours lying awake, his thoughts either choked by recriminations regarding Kellhus or smothered by the deranged enormity of his circumstances. And when these things passed into numbness, he would fret over Esmenet or worry about the Holy War. Too soon, it seemed, it would wander into Fanim lands—into battle.

The nightmares were becoming more unbearable. Scarcely a night passed where he didn't awaken long before the cockcrow horns, thrashing at his blankets or clawing his face, crying out to ancient comrades. Few Mandate Schoolmen enjoyed anything resembling peaceful slumber. Esmenet had once joked that he slept "like an old hound chasing rabbits."

"Try an old rabbit," he'd replied, "fleeing hounds."

But sleep—or the absolute, oblivious heart of it anyway—began to elude him altogether, until it seemed he simply shuffled from one clamour to another. He would crawl from his tent into the predawn darkness, hugging himself to still the tremors, and he would simply stand as the blackness resolved into a cold, colourless version of the vista he'd seen the previous evening, watching the sun's golden rim surface in the east, like a coal burning through painted paper. And it would seem he stood upon the very lip of the world, that if it tipped by the slightest measure, he would be cast into an endless black.

So alone, he would think. He would imagine Esmenet sleeping in their room in Sumna, one slender leg kicked from the covers, banded by threads of light as the same sun boiled through the cracks of her shutters. And he would pray that she was safe—pray to the Gods who'd damned them both.

One sun keeps us warm. One sun lets us see. One …

Then he would think of Anasûrimbor Kellhus—thoughts of anticipation and dread.

One evening, while listening to others argue about the Fanim, Achamian suddenly realized there was no reason to suffer his fears alone: he could tell Xinemus.

Achamian glanced across the fire at his old friend, who was arguing battles that had yet to be fought.

"Certainly Cnaiür knows the heathen!" the Marshal was protesting. "I never said otherwise. But until he sees us on the field, until he sees the *might of Conriya*, neither I—nor our Prince, I suspect—will take his word as scripture!"

Could he tell him?

The morning after the madness beneath the Emperor's palace had also been the morning the Holy War began its march. Everything had been confusion. Even still, Xinemus had made Achamian his priority, fairly interrogating him on the details of the previous night. Achamian had started with the truth, or a hollowed out version of it anyway, saying that the Emperor had required independent verification of certain claims made by his Imperial Saik. But what followed was pure fantasy—some story about finding the ciphers to an ensorcelled map. Achamian could no longer remember.

At the time, the lies had simply … happened. The events of that night and the revelations that followed had been too immediate and far too catastrophic in their implications. Even now, two weeks later, Achamian felt overmatched by their dread significance. Back then, he could only flounder. Stories, on the other hand, were something he could make sense of, something he could speak.

But how could he explain this to Xinemus? To the one man who believed. Who trusted.

Achamian watched and waited, glancing from face to illuminated face. He'd purposely unrolled his mat on the smoky side of the fire, hoping for a measure of solitude while he ate. Now it seemed that providence had placed him here, affording him a furtive glimpse of the whole.

There was Xinemus, of course, seated knees out and back upright like a Zeumi warlord, the hard set of his mouth betrayed by the laughter in his eyes and the crumbs in his square-cut beard. To his left, his cousin, Iryssas, rocked to and fro upon the trunk of a felled tree, so much like a big-pawed puppy in his exuberance, bullying as much as the patience of the others would allow. Sitting to his left, Dinchases, or "Bloody Dinch," held out his wine bowl for the slaves to refill, the X-shaped scar on his forehead inked black by the shadows. Zenkappa, as usual, sat by his side, his ebony skin shining in the firelight. For some reason, his manner and tone never ceased to remind Achamian of a mischievous wink. Kellhus sat cross-legged nearby, wearing a plain white tunic, and looking for all the world like a portrait plundered from some temple—at once meditative and attentive, remote and absorbed. Serwë leaned against him, her eyes shining beneath drowsy lids, a blanket pulled across her thighs. As always, the flawlessness of her face arrested, and the curves of her figure tugged. Close to her, but back farther from the fire, Cnaiür crouched in the shadows, gazing at the flames and tearing mouthful after mouthful of bread. Even eating he looked ready to break necks.

Such a strange tribe. His tribe.

Could they feel it? he wondered. Could they feel the end coming?

He had to share what he knew. If not with the Mandate, then with someone. He had to share or he would go mad. If only Esmi had come with … No. That way lay more pain.

He set down his bowl, stood, and before he realized it, found himself sitting next to his old friend, Krijates Xinemus, the Marshal of Attrempus.

"Zin ..."

"What is it, Akka?"

"I must speak with you," he said in a hushed voice. "There's ... there's ..."

Kellhus seemed distracted. Even still, Achamian couldn't shake the sense of being observed.

"That night," he continued, "that last night beneath Momemn's walls. Do you remember Ikurei Conphas coming for me, escorting me to the Emperor's palace?"

"How could I forget. I was worried sick!"

Achamian hesitated, glimpsed images of an old man—the Emperor's Prime Counsel—convulsing against chains. Glimpses of a face unclutching like hands and flexing outward, reaching ... A face that grasped, that seized.

Xinemus studied him by firelight, frowned. "What's wrong, Akka?"

"I'm a Schoolman, Zin, bound by oath and duty the same as y—"

"Lord Cousin!" Iryssas called over the flame. "You must listen to this! Tell him, Kellhus!"

"*Please*, Cousin," Xinemus replied sharply. "Can't you—"

"Pfah. Just listen to him! We're trying to understand what this means."

Xinemus began scolding the man, but it was already too late. Kellhus was speaking.

"It's just a parable," the Prince of Atrithau said. "Something I learned while among the Scylvendi ... It goes like this: A slender young bull and his harem of cows are shocked to discover that their owner has purchased another bull, far deeper of chest, far thicker of horn, and far more violent of temper. Even still, when the owner's sons drive the mighty newcomer to pasture, the young bull lowers his horns, begins snorting and stamping. 'No!' his cows cry. 'Please, don't risk your life for us!' 'Risk my life?' the young bull exclaims. 'I'm just making sure he knows I'm a *bull!*'"

A heartbeat of silence, then an explosion of laughter.

"A *Scylvendi* parable?" Xinemus cried out, laughing. "Are you—"

"This is my opinion!" Iryssas called through the uproar. "My interpretation! Listen! It means that our dignity—no, our *honour*—is worth more than anything, more than even our wives!"

"It means nothing," Xinemus said, wiping tears from his eyes. "It's a joke, nothing more."

"It is a parable of courage," Cnaiür grated, and everyone fell silent—shocked, Achamian supposed, that the taciturn barbarian had actually spoken. The man spat into the fire. "It is a fable that old men tell boys in order to shame them, to teach them that gestures are meaningless, that only death is real."

Looks were exchanged about the fire. Only Zenkappa dared laugh aloud.

Achamian leaned forward. "What do you say, Kellhus? What do you think it means?"

Kellhus shrugged, apparently surprised he held the answer so many had missed. He matched Achamian's gaze with friendly, yet utterly implacable, eyes. "It means that young bulls sometimes make good cows ..."

More gales of laughter, but Achamian could manage no more than a smile. Why was he so angry? "No," he called out. "What do you think it *really* means?"

Kellhus paused, clasped Serwë's right hand and looked from face to shining face. Achamian glanced at Serwë, only to look away. She was watching him—intently.

"It means," Kellhus said in a solemn and strangely touching voice, "that there are many kinds of courage, and many degrees of honour." He had a way of speaking that seemed to hush all else, even the surrounding Holy War. "It means that these things—courage, honour, even love—are *problems*, not absolutes. Questions."

Iryssas shook his head vigorously. He was one of those dull-witted men who continually confused ardour with insight. Watching him argue with Kellhus had become something of a sport.

"Courage, honour, love—these are problems? Then what are the solutions? Cowardice and depravity?"

"Iryssas ..." Xinemus said half-heartedly. "Cousin."

"No," Kellhus replied. "Cowardice and depravity are problems as well. As for the solutions? *You*, Iryssas—you're a solution. In fact, we're *all* solutions. Every life lived sketches a different answer, a different way ..."

"So are all solutions equal?" Achamian blurted. The bitterness of his tone startled him.

"A philosopher's question," Kellhus replied, and his smile swept away all awkwardness. "No. Of course not. Some lives are better lived than others—there can be no doubt. Why do you think we sing the lays we do? Why do you think we revere our scriptures? Or ponder the life of the Latter Prophet?"

Examples, Achamian realized. Examples of lives that enlightened, that *solved* ... He knew this but couldn't bring himself to say it. He was, after all, a sorcerer, an example of a life that solved nothing. Without a word, he rolled to his feet and strode into the darkness, not caring what the others thought. Suddenly, he needed darkness, solitude ...

Shelter from Kellhus.

He was kneeling to duck into his tent when he realized that Xinemus had yet to hear his confession, that he was still alone with what he knew.

Probably for the best.

Skin-spies in their midst. Kellhus the Harbinger of the world's end. Xinemus would just think him mad.

A woman's voice brought him up short. "I see the way you look at him."

Him—Kellhus. Achamian glanced over his shoulder, saw Serwë's willowy silhouette framed by the fire.

"And how's that?" he asked. She was angry—her tone had betrayed that much. Was she jealous? During the day, while he and Kellhus wandered the column, she walked with Xinemus's slaves.

"You needn't fear," she said.

Achamian swallowed at the sour taste in his mouth. Earlier, Xinemus had passed *perrapta* around instead of wine—wretched drink.

"Fear what?"

"Loving him."

Achamian licked his lips, cursed his racing heart.

"You dislike me, don't you?"

Even in the gloom of long shadows, she seemed too beautiful to be real, like something that had stepped between the cracks of the world—something wild and white-skinned. For the first time, Achamian realized how much he desired her.

"Only ..." She hesitated, studied the flattened grasses at her feet. She raised her face and for the briefest of instants looked at him with Esmenet's eyes. "Only because you refuse to see," she murmured.

See what? Achamian wanted to cry.

But she'd fled.

"Akka?" Kellhus called in the fading dark. "I heard someone weeping."

"It's nothing," Achamian croaked, his face still buried in his hands. At some point—he was no longer sure when—he'd crawled from his tent and huddled over the embers of their dying fire. Now dawn was coming.

"Is it the Dreams?"

Achamian rubbed his face, heaved cool air into his lungs.

Tell him!

"Y-yes ... The Dreams. That's it, the Dreams."

He could feel the man stare down at him, but lacked the heart to look up. He flinched when Kellhus placed a hand on his shoulder, but didn't pull away.

"But it isn't the Dreams, is it, Akka? It's something else ... Something more."

Hot tears parsed his cheeks, matted his beard. He said nothing.

"You haven't slept this night ... You haven't slept in many nights, have you?"

Achamian looked over the surrounding encampment, across the canvas-congested slopes and fields. Against a sky like cold iron, the pennants hung dead from their poles.

Then he looked to Kellhus. "I see his blood in your face, and it fills me with both hope and horror."

The Prince of Atrithau frowned. "So this is about me ... I feared as much."

Achamian swallowed, and without truly deciding to, threw the number-sticks. "Yes," he said. "But it's not so simple."

"Why? What do you mean?"

"Among the many dreams my brother Schoolmen and I suffer, there's one in particular that troubles us. It has to do with Anasûrimbor Celmomas II, the High King of Kûniüri—with his death on the Fields of Eleneöt in the year 2146." Achamian breathed deeply, rubbed angrily at his eyes. "You see, Celmomas was the first great foe of the Consult, and the first and most glorious victim of the No-God. The *first!* He died in my arms, Kellhus. He was my most hated, most cherished friend and he died in my arms!" He scowled, waved his hands in confusion. "I m-mean, I mean in S-Seswatha's arms ..."

"And this is what pains you? That I—"

"You don't understand! J-just listen ... He, Celmomas, spoke to me—to Seswatha—before he died. He spoke to all of us—" Achamian shook his head, cackled, pulled fingers through his beard. "In fact he *keeps* speaking, night after fucking night, dying time and again—and always for the first time! And-and he says ..."

Achamian looked up, suddenly unashamed of his tears. If he couldn't bare his soul before this man—so like Ajencis, so like *Inrau!*—then who?

"He says that an Anasûrimbor—an *Anasûrimbor*, Kellhus!—will return at the end of the world."

Kellhus's expression, normally so blessedly devoid of conflict, darkened. "What are you saying, Akka?"

"Don't you see?" Achamian whispered. "*You're the one*, Kellhus. The Harbinger! The fact you're here means that it's starting all over again ..."

Sweet Sejenus.

"The Second Apocalypse, Kellhus ... I'm talking about the Second Apocalypse. You are the sign!"

Kellhus's hand slipped from his shoulder. "But that doesn't make sense, Akka. The fact I'm here means nothing. *Nothing.* Now I'm here, and before I was in Atrithau. And if my bloodline reaches as far back as you say, then an Anasûrimbor has *always* been 'here,' wherever that might be ..."

The Prince of Atrithau's eyes lost their focus, wrestled with unseen things. For a moment, the glamour of absolute self-possession faltered, and he looked like any man overwhelmed by a precipitous turn of circumstance.

"It's just a ..." He paused, as if lacking the breath to continue.

"A coincidence," Achamian said, pressing himself to his feet. For some reason, he yearned to reach out, steady him with his embrace. "That's what I thought ... I admit I was shocked when I first met you, but I never thought ... It was just too mad! But then ..."

"Then what?"

"I found them. I found the Consult ... The night you and the others celebrated Proyas's victory over the Emperor, I was summoned to the

Andiamine Heights—by no less than Ikurei Conphas—and brought to the Imperial Catacombs. Apparently they'd found a spy in their midst, one that convinced the Emperor that sorcery simply *had* to be involved. But there was no sorcery, and the man they showed me was no ordinary spy ..."

"How so?"

"For one, he called me Chigra, which is Seswatha's name in *aghurzoi*, the perverted speech of the Sranc. Somehow he could see Seswatha's trace within me ... For another, he ..." Achamian pursed his lips and shook his head. "He *had no face*. He was an abomination of the flesh, Kellhus! A spy that can mimic the form of any man without sorcery or sorcery's Mark. Perfect spies!

"Somehow, somewhere, the Consult murdered the Emperor's Prime Counsel and had him *replaced*. These, these *things* could be anywhere! Here in the Holy War, in the courts of the Great Factions ... For all we know they could be Kings!"

Or Shriah ...

"But how does that make *me* the Harbinger?"

"Because it means the Consult has mastered the Old Science. Sranc, Bashrags, Dragons, all the abominations of the Inchoroi, are artifacts of the Tekne, the Old Science, created long, long ago, when the Nonmen still ruled Eärwa. It was thought destroyed when the Inchoroi were annihilated by Cû'jara-Cinmoi—before the Tusk was even written, Kellhus! But these, these skin-spies are *new*. New artifacts of the Old Science. And if the Consult has rediscovered the Old Science, there's a chance they know how to resurrect Mog-Pharau ..."

And that name stole his breath, winded him like a blow to the chest.

"The No-God," Kellhus said.

Achamian nodded, swallowing as though his throat were sore. "Yes, the No-God ..."

"And now that an Anasûrimbor has returned ..."

"That chance has become a near certainty."

Kellhus studied him for a stern moment, his expression utterly inscrutable. "So what will you do?"

"My mission," Achamian said, "is to observe the Holy War. But I've a decision to make ... One that claws my heart every waking moment."

"Which is?"

Achamian tried hard to weather his student's glare, but there seemed to be something in his eyes, something incomparable—terrifying even. "I haven't told them about you, Kellhus. I haven't told my brothers that the Celmomian Prophecy has been fulfilled. And so long as I don't tell them, I betray them, Seswatha, myself"—he cackled again—"maybe even the world ..."

"But why then?" Kellhus asked. "Why haven't you told them?"

Achamian took a deep breath. "Because when I do, they'll come for you, Kellhus."

"Perhaps they should."

"You don't know my brothers."

⊷∾⊶

Crouching naked in the pre-dawn gloom of the tent he shared with Kellhus, Cnaiür urs Skiötha peered at Serwë's sleeping face and used the tip of his knife to hook and draw away obscuring threads of her hair. The veil parted, he set aside the knife and ran two callused fingers along her cheek. She twitched and sighed, nestled deeper in her blanket. So beautiful. So like his forgotten wife.

Cnaiür watched her, as motionless and awake as she was motionless and asleep. All the while, he listened to the voices outside: Kellhus and the sorcerer, speaking nonsense.

In some ways it seemed a miracle. Not only had he traversed the length of the Empire, he'd spat at the feet of the Emperor, humiliated Ikurei Conphas before his peers, and attained the rights and privileges of an Inrithi Prince. Now he rode as a general in the greatest host he'd ever witnessed. A host that could crush cities, strike down nations, murder whole peoples. A host for memorialists' songs. A Holy War.

And it was bent on storming Shimeh, the stronghold of the Cishaurim. The Cishaurim!

Anasûrimbor Moënghus was Cishaurim.

Despite the deranged scale of its ambition, the Dûnyain's plan seemed to be working. In his dreams, Cnaiür had always come across Moënghus alone. Sometimes there would be words, sometimes not. There would always be bleeding. But now those dreams seemed little more than juvenile fantasies. Kellhus was right. After thirty years, Moënghus would be far more than someone who could be cut down in some alley; he would be a potentate. His would be an empire. And how could it be any other way? He was Dûnyain.

Like his son, Kellhus.

Who could say how far Moënghus's power reached? Certainly it encompassed the Cishaurim and the Kianene—the question was only one of degree. But was that power with them now, in the Holy War?

Did it include Kellhus?

Send them a son. What better way could a *Dûnyain* overthrow his enemies?

Already in their councils with Proyas, the Inrithi caste-nobles fell instantly silent at the sound of Kellhus's voice. Already they watched him when they thought him preoccupied, whispered when they thought he couldn't hear. And as pompous as they were, they *deferred* to him, not the way men accede to rank or station, but the way men yield to those who possess something they need. Somehow Kellhus had convinced them he stood outside the circle of the commonplace, outside even the extraordinary. It was more than just his claim to have dreamt of the Holy War from afar, more than the nefarious ways he spoke to them, as though he were a father playing upon the well-known conceits of his children. It was what he said as well, the *truths*.

"But the God favours the righteous!" Ingiaban, the Palatine of Kethantei, had cried one night at council. At Cnaiür's insistence, they'd been discussing various strategies the Sapatishah of Shigek, Skauras, might use to undo them. "Sejenus himself—"

"And you," Kellhus interrupted, "are you righteous?"

The air in the Royal Pavilion became tense with a strange, aimless expectation.

"*We* are the righteous, yes," the Palatine of Kethantei replied. "If not, then what in Juru's name are we doing *here*?"

"Indeed," Kellhus said. "What are we doing here?"

Cnaiür glimpsed Lord Gaidekki turning to Xinemus—a worried glance.

Wary, Ingiaban purchased time by sipping his anpoi. "Raising arms against the heathen. What else?"

"So we raise arms against the heathen because we're righteous?"

"And because they're wicked."

Kellhus smiled with stern compassion. "'He who's righteous is he who's not found wanting in the ways of the God ...' Isn't this what Sejenus himself writes?"

"Yes. Of course."

"And *who* finds men wanting in the ways of the God? Other men?"

The Palatine of Kethantei paled. "No," he said. "Only the God and his Prophets."

"So we're not righteous, then?"

"Yes ... I mean, no ..." Baffled, Ingiaban looked to Kellhus, a horrible frankness revealed in his face. "I mean ... I no longer know what I mean!"

Concessions. Always exacting concessions. Accumulating them.

"Then you understand," Kellhus said, his voice now deep and preternaturally resonant, a voice that seemingly spoke from everywhere. "A man can never judge himself righteous, Lord Palatine, he can only *hope*. And it's *this* that gives meaning to our actions. In raising arms against the heathen, we're not the priest before the altar, we're the *victim*. It means nothing to offer up another to the God, so we make offerings of ourselves. Make no mistake, all of you ... We wager our souls. We leap into the black. This pilgrimage is our sacrifice. Only afterward will we know whether we've been found wanting."

The mutter of startled, even wondrous assent.

"Well said, Kellhus," Proyas had declared. "Well said."

All men see from where they stand, and somehow Kellhus saw farther than any other man. He stood upon a different ground, greater, as though he occupied the heights of every soul. And though none of the Inrithi noblemen dared speak this intimation, they felt it—all of them. Cnaiür could see it in the cast of their eyes, hear it in the timbre of their voices: the first shadows of awe.

The wonder that made men small.

Cnaiür knew these secretive passions all too well. To watch Kellhus ply these men was to witness the shameful record of his own undoing at the hands of Moënghus. Sometimes the urge to cry out in warning almost overpowered him. Sometimes Kellhus seemed such an abomination that the gulf between Scylvendi and Inrithi threatened to disappear—particularly where Proyas was concerned. Moënghus had preyed upon the same vulnerabilities, the same conceits ... If Cnaiür shared these things with these men, how different could he be?

Sometimes crimes seemed crimes, no matter how ludicrous the victim. But only sometimes. For the most part Cnaiür merely watched with a numb kind of incredulity. He no longer heard Kellhus speak so much as observed him cut and carve, whittle and hew, as though the man had somehow shattered the glass of language and fashioned knives from the pieces. This word to anger so that word might open. This look to embarrass so that smile might reassure. This insight to remind so that truth might injure, heal, or astonish.

How easy it must have been for Moënghus! One stripling lad. One chieftain's wife.

Images, stark and dry, of the Steppe assailed him. The other women tearing at his mother's hair, clawing at her face, clubbing her with rocks, stabbing her with sticks. *Mother!* A bawling infant hoisted from her yaksh, tossed into the all-cleansing fire—his blond-haired half-brother. The stone faces of the men turning away from his look ...

How could he let it happen again? How could he stand by and watch? How could—

Still crouching next to Serwë, Cnaiür looked down, shocked to see that he'd been stabbing the ground with his knife. The bone-white reeds of the mat were snapped and severed about a small pit of black.

He shook his black mane, breathed as though punishing air. Always these thoughts—always!

Remorse? For outlanders? Concern for mewling peacocks? *Especially* Proyas!

"So long as what comes before remains shrouded," Kellhus had said on their trek across the Jiünati Steppe, "so long as men are already deceived, what does it matter?" And what did it matter, making fools of fools? What mattered was whether the man made a fool of *him*; this—*this!*—was the sharp edge upon which his every thought should bleed. Did the Dûnyain speak true? Was he truly his father's assassin?

I walk with the whirlwind!

He could never forget. He had only his hatred to preserve him.

And Serwë?

The voices from outside had trailed into silence. He could hear that weeping fool of a sorcerer clearing his nose outside. Then Kellhus pressed through the flap into the dim interior. His eyes flashed from Serwë to the knife to Cnaiür's face.

"You heard," he said in flawless Scylvendi. Even after all this time, hearing him speak thus made Cnaiür's skin prickle.

"This is a camp of war," he replied. "Many heard."

"No, they slept."

Cnaiür knew the futility of debate—he knew the Dûnyain—so he said nothing, rooted through his scattered belongings for his breeches.

Serwë complained and kicked at her blankets.

"Do you recall that first time we spoke in your yaksh?" Kellhus asked.

"Of course," Cnaiür replied, pulling on his breeches. "I curse that day with every waking breath."

"That witch stone you threw to me ..."

"You mean my father's Chorae?"

"Yes. Do you still have it?"

Cnaiür peered at him through the gloom. "But you know I do."

"And how would I know?"

"You know."

Cnaiür dressed in silence while Kellhus roused Serwë.

"But the *horrnns*," she complained, burying her head. "I haven't heard the horns ..."

Cnaiür laughed abruptly, deep and full-throated.

"Treacherous work," he said, now speaking in Sheyic.

"And what's that?" Kellhus replied—more for Serwë's benefit than anything, Cnaiür realized. The Dûnyain knew what he meant. He always knew.

"Killing sorcerers."

Just then, the horns sounded.

Late Spring, 4111 Year-of-the-Tusk, the Andiamine Heights

Xerius stood from the baths, walked up the marble steps to where the slaves waited with towels and scented oils. And for the first time in days he could feel it move him—harmony, the providence of auspicious deities ... He looked up with mild surprise when the Empress, his mother, appeared from the dark recesses of the chamber.

"Tell me Mother," he said without looking at her extravagant figure, "do you simply happen upon me at inopportune moments?" He turned to her as the slaves gently towelled his groin. "Or is this too something you measure?"

The Empress bowed her head slightly, as though she were Shriah, an equal. "I've brought you a gift, Xerius," she said, gesturing to the dark-haired girl at her side. With a flourish, her eunuch, the giant Pisulathas, opened the girl's robe and drew it away. Beneath, she was as white-skinned as a Galeoth—as naked as the Emperor, and almost as splendid.

Gifts from Mother—they underscored the treachery of gifts from those who were not one's tributaries. Such gifts weren't gifts at all, in fact. Such gifts always demanded exchange.

Xerius couldn't remember when Istriya had started bringing these men and women to him—these surrogates. She had the eye of a whore, his mother—he would grant her that. She knew, unerringly, what would please him. "You are a venal witch, Mother," he said, admiring the terrified girl. "Was there ever a son so fortunate as me?"

But Istriya said only, "Skeaös is dead."

Xerius looked at her momentarily, then returned his attention to the slaves, who'd begun rubbing him with oil. "*Something* is dead," he replied, suppressing a shudder. "We know not what."

"And why wasn't I told?"

"I knew you'd hear of it soon enough." He sat upon the chair brought for him, and his body slaves began combing his hair with more oils, filing his nails. "You always do," he added.

"The Cishaurim," Istriya said after a pause.

"But of course."

"Then they know. The Cishaurim know of your plans."

"It's of little consequence. They knew already."

"Have you become such a vulgar fool, Xerius? I thought that after this you would be ready to reconsider."

"Reconsider what, Mother?"

"This mad pact you have made with the heathen. What else?"

"Silence, Mother." Xerius glanced nervously at the girl, but it was plain that she didn't speak a word of Sheyic. "This isn't to be uttered aloud. Ever again. Do you hear me?"

"But the *Cishaurim*, Xerius! Think of it! At your bosom all these years, wearing the face of *Skeaös*! The Emperor's only confidant! That vile tongue clucking poison for counsel. *All these years*, Xerius! Sharing the hearth of your ambitions with an obscenity!"

Xerius had thought of this—had been able to think of little else these past days. At night he dreamed of faces—faces like fists. Of Gaenkelti, who had died so ... absurdly.

And then there was the *question*, the question that struck with such force it never failed to jar him from the tedium of his routines.

Are there others? Others like it ...

"You lecture the educated, Mother. You know that in all things there's a balance to be struck. An exchange of vulnerabilities for advantages. You taught me this."

But the Empress didn't relent. The old bitch never relented.

"The Cishaurim have had your *heart* in their clutches, Xerius. Through *you* they have supped on the very marrow of the Empire. And you would let *this*—an offence like no other—go unpunished *now*, when the Gods have delivered to you the instrument of your vengeance? You'd still pull the Holy War up short? If you spare *Shimeh*, Xerius, you spare the Cishaurim."

"*Silence!*" His scream pealed throughout the chamber.

Istriya laughed fiercely. "My naked son," she said. "My poor ... naked ... son."

Xerius leapt to his feet, shouldered past the circle of his slaves, his look wounded, quizzical.

"This isn't like you, Mother. You were never one to cower before damnation. Is it because you grow old, hmm? Tell me, what's it like to stand upon the precipice? To feel your womb wither, to watch the eyes of your lovers grow shy with hidden disgust ..."

He'd struck from impulse and found vanity—the only way he knew to injure his mother.

But there was no bruise in her reply. "There comes a time, Xerius, when you care nothing for your spectators. The spectacles of beauty are

like the baubles of ceremony—for the young, the stupid. The act, Xerius.
The act makes mere ornament of all things. You'll see."

"Then why the cosmetics, Mother? Why have your body slaves truss
you up like an old whore to the feast?"

She looked at him blankly. "Such a monstrous son ..." she whispered.

"As monstrous as his mother," Xerius added, laughing cruelly. "Tell
me ... Now that your debauched life is nearly spent, are you filled with
regret Mother?"

Istriya looked away, across the steaming bath waters. "Regret is
inevitable, Xerius."

These words struck him. "Perhaps ... perhaps it is," he replied, moved
for some reason to sudden pity. There had been a time when he and his
mother had been ... close. But Istriya could be intimate with only those
she possessed. She no longer possessed him.

The thought of this touched Xerius. To lose such a godlike son ...

"Always these savage exchanges, eh, Mother? I *do* repent them. I
would have you know that much." He looked at her pensively, chewed his
bottom lip. "But speak of Shimeh again and I will put your platitude to
the test. You *will* regret ... Do you understand this?"

"I understand, Xerius."

There was malice in her eyes when she met his gaze, but Xerius ignored
it. A concession, any concession, was a triumph when dealing with the
Empress.

Xerius studied the young girl instead, her taut breasts upswept like
swallow's wings, her soft weave of pubic hair. Aroused, he held out his
hand and she came to him, reluctantly. He led her to a nearby couch and
reclined, stretched out before her. "Do you know what to do child?" he
asked.

She opened her lithe legs, straddled him. Tears streamed down her
cheeks. Trembling, she lowered upon his member ...

Xerius gasped. It was like sinking into a warm, unbroken peach. If the
world harboured obscene things like the Cishaurim, it harboured also
such sweet fruits.

The old Empress turned to leave.

"Will you not stay, Mother?" Xerius called, his voice thick. "Watch
your son enjoy this gift of yours?"

Istriya hesitated. "No, Xerius."

"But you *will*, Mother. The Emperor is difficult to please. You must instruct her."

There was a pause, filled only by the girl's whimper.

"But certainly, my son," Istriya said at length, and walked grandly over to the couch. The rigid girl flinched when she grasped her hand and drew it down to Xerius's scrotum. "Gently, child," she cooed. "Shushh. No weeping …"

Xerius groaned and arched into her, laughed when she chirped in pain. He gazed into his mother's painted face suspended over the girl's shoulder, whiter even than the porcelain, Galeoth skin, and he *burned* with that old, illicit thrill. He felt a child again, careless. All was as it should be. The Gods were auspicious indeed …

"Tell me, Xerius," his mother said huskily, "how was it that you *discovered* Skeaös?"

# CHAPTER THREE

ASGILIOCH

The proposition "I am the centre" need never be uttered. It is the assumption upon which all certainty and all doubt turns.

—AJENCIS, THE THIRD ANALYTIC OF MEN

See your enemies content and your lovers melancholy.

—AINONI PROVERB

Early Summer, 4111 Year-of-the-Tusk, the fortress of Asgilioch

For the first time in living memory, an earthquake struck the Unaras Spur and the Inûnara Highlands. Hundreds of miles away the great bustling markets of Gielgath fell silent as wares swung on their hooks and mortar chipped down shivering walls. Mules kicked, their eyes rolling in fear. Dogs howled.

But in Asgilioch, the southern bulwark of the peoples of the Kyranae Plains since time immemorial, men were knocked to their knees, walls swayed like palm fronds, and the ancient citadel of Ruöm, which had survived the Kings of Shigek, the dragons of Tsurumah, and no less than three Fanim Jihads, collapsed in a mighty column of dust. As the survivors pulled bodies from the debris, they found themselves grieving the stone more than the flesh. "Hard-hearted Ruöm!" they cried out in disbelief. "The High Bull of Asgilioch has fallen!" For many in the

Empire, Ruöm was a totem. Not since the days of Ingusharotep II, the ancient God-King of Shigek, had the citadel of Asgilioch been destroyed—the last time the South ever conquered the peoples of the Kyranae Plains.

The first Men of the Tusk, a troop of hard-riding Galeoth horsemen under Coithus Saubon's nephew, Athjeäri, arrived four days following. To their dismay, they found Asgilioch in partial ruin, and her battered garrison convinced of the Holy War's doom. Nersei Proyas and his Conriyans arrived the day after, to be followed two days after that by Ikurei Conphas and his Imperial Columns, as well as the Shrial Knights under Incheiri Gotian. Where Proyas had taken the Sogian Way along the southern coast, then marched cross-country through the Inûnara Highlands, Conphas and Gotian had taken the so-called "Forbidden Road"—built by the Nansur to allow the quick deployment of their Columns between the Fanim and Scylvendi frontiers. Of those Great Names who struck through the heart of the province, Coithus Saubon and his Galeoth were the first to arrive—almost a full week after Conphas. Gothyelk and his Tydonni appeared shortly after, followed by Skaiyelt and his grim Thunyeri.

Of the Ainoni nothing was known, save that from the outset their host, perhaps hampered by its ponderous size or by the Scarlet Spires and their vast baggage trains, had trouble making half the daily distance of the other contingents. So the greater portion of the Holy War made camp on the barren slopes beneath Asgilioch's ramparts and waited, trading rumours and premonitions of disaster. To the sentries posted on Asgilioch's walls, they looked like a migrating nation—like something from the Tusk.

When it became apparent that days, perhaps weeks, might pass before the Ainoni joined them, Nersei Proyas called a Council of the Great and Lesser Names. Given the size of the assembly, they were forced to gather in Asgilioch's inner bailey, beneath the debris heaped about Ruöm's broken foundations. The Great Names took their places about a salvaged trestle table, while the others, dressed in the finery of a dozen nations, sat across the rubble slopes, making an amphitheatre of the ruin. They fairly shimmered in the bright sunlight.

They spent most of the morning observing the proper rituals and sacrifices: this was the first full Council since marching from Momemn. The afternoon they spent quarrelling, for the most part debating whether Ruöm's destruction portended catastrophe or nothing at all. Saubon claimed that the Holy War should break camp immediately, seize the passes of the Southron Gates, and march into Gedea. "This place oppresses us!" he cried, gesturing to the tiers of ruin. "We slumber and stir in the shadow of dread!" Ruöm, he insisted, was a Nansur superstition—a "shibboleth of the perfumed and the weak-hearted." The longer the Holy War loitered beneath its ruin, the more it would become their superstition.

If many saw sense in these arguments, many others saw madness. Without the Scarlet Spires, Ikurei Conphas reminded the Galeoth Prince, the Holy War would be at the mercy of the Cishaurim. "According to my uncle's spies, Skauras has assembled all the Grandees of Shigek and awaits us in Gedea. Who's to say the Cishaurim aren't waiting with him?" Proyas and his Scylvendi adviser, Cnaiür urs Skiötha, agreed: to march without the Ainoni was errant foolishness. But no amount of argument, it seemed, could sway Saubon and his confederates.

The sun smouldered over the western turrets, and they'd agreed on nothing save the obvious, such as dispatching riders to locate the Ainoni, or sending Athjeäri into Gedea to gather intelligence. Otherwise it seemed certain the Holy War, so recently reunited, would fracture once again. Proyas had fallen silent, his face buried in his hands. Only Conphas continued to argue with Saubon, if trading embittered insults could be called such.

Then Anasûrimbor Kellhus, the impoverished Prince of Atrithau, stood from his place among those watching and cried, "You mistake the meaning of what you see, all of you! The loss of Ruöm is no accident, but neither is it a curse!"

Saubon laughed, shouting, "Ruöm is a talisman against the heathen, is it not?"

"Yes," the Prince of Atrithau replied. "So long as the citadel stood, we could turn back. But now ... Don't you see? Just beyond these mountains, men congregate in the tabernacles of the False Prophet. We stand upon the heathen's shore. The heathen's *shore!*"

He paused, looked at each Great Name in turn.

"Without Ruöm there's no turning back ... The God has burned our ships."

Afterward it was decided: the Holy War would await the Ainoni and the Scarlet Spires.

Far from Asgilioch, in the centremost chamber of his great tent, Eleäzaras, Grandmaster of the Scarlet Spires, reclined in his chair, the one luxury he'd allowed himself for this mad journey. Beneath him, his body slaves washed his feet in steaming water. Three tripods illuminated the surrounding gloom. Smoke curled through the interior, casting shadows that resembled water-stained script along the bellied canvas.

The journey hadn't been as hard as he'd feared—thus far. Nevertheless, evenings such as this always seemed to occasion an almost shameful relief. At first he'd thought it was his age: more than twenty years had passed since his last journey abroad. Weary bones, he would think, watching his people labouring in evening light hoisting tent and pavilion to the very horizon. Weary old bones.

But when he recalled those years spent hiking from mission to mission, city to city, he realized that what he suffered now had nothing to do with weariness. He could remember lying beside his fire beneath the stars, no grand pavilion overhead, no silk pillows kissing his cheek, only hard ground and the humming exhaustion that comes when a traveller falls completely still. *That* had been weariness. But this? Borne on litters, surrounded by dozens of bare-chested slaves ...

The relief he experienced every evening, he realized, had nothing to do with fatigue, and everything to do with standing still ...

Which was to say, with Shimeh.

Great decisions, he reflected, were measured by their finality as much as by their consequences. Sometimes he could feel it like a palpable thing: the path not taken, that fork in history where the Scarlet Spires repudiated Maithanet's outrageous offer and watched the Holy War from afar. It didn't exist and yet it lingered, the way a night of passion might linger in the entreating look of a slave. He saw it everywhere: in nervous silences, in exchanged glances, in Iyokus's unrelenting cynicism, in General Setpanares's scowl. And it seemed to mock him with promise—just as the path he now walked mocked him with threat.

To join a Holy War! Eleäzaras dealt in unrealities; it was his trade. But the unreality of this, the Scarlet Spires *here*, was well nigh indigestible. The thought of it spawned ironies, not the ironies that cultured men— the Ainoni in particular—savoured, but rather the ironies that repro- duced themselves endlessly, that reduced all determination to shaking indecision.

Add to this the accumulation of complications: the House Ikurei plot- ting with the heathen; the Mandate playing some arcane Gnostic game every single Spires agent in Sumna uncovered and executed—even though they seemed secure enough *before* the Scarlet Spires set foot in the Empire. Even Maithanet, the Great Shriah of the Thousand Temples, worked some dark angle.

Small wonder Shimeh oppressed him. Small wonder each night seemed a respite.

Eleäzaras sighed as Myaza, his new favourite, kneaded his right foot with warmed oil.

No matter, he told himself. *Regret is the opiate of fools.*

He leaned his head back, watched the girl work through his eyelashes. "Myaza," he said softly, grinning at her modest smile. *"Mmmyassssaaa ..."*

"Hanamanu Eleäzarassss," she sighed in turn—daring wench! The other slaves gasped in shock, then broke into giggles. *Such a bad girl!* Eleäzaras thought. He leaned forward to scoop her into his arms. But the sight of a black-gowned Usher kneeling on the carpets halted him.

Someone wished to see him—obviously. Probably General Setpanares with more complaints about the host's sloth—which were really complaints about the Scarlet Spires' sloth. So the Ainoni would be the last to reach Asgilioch. What did it matter? Let them wait.

"What is it?" he snapped.

The young man raised his face. "A petitioner has come, Grandmaster."

"At this hour? Who?"

The Usher hesitated. "A magi of the Mysunsai School, Grandmaster. One Skalateas."

Mysunsai? Whores—all of them. "What does he want?" Eleäzaras asked. Something churned in his gut. More complications.

"He wouldn't say specifically," the Usher replied. "He says only that he's ridden hard from Momemn to speak with you on a matter of great urgency."

"Panderer," Eleäzaras spat. "Whore. Delay him momentarily, then send him in."

After the man withdrew, Eleäzaras had his body slaves dry his feet and bind his sandals. He then dismissed them. As the last slave hastened out, the man called Skalateas was escorted in by two armoured Javreh.

"Leave us," Eleäzaras said to the warrior-slaves. They bowed low, then also withdrew.

From his seat, he studied the mercenary, who was clean shaven in the Nansur fashion, dressed in the humble garments of a traveller: leggings, a plain brown smock, and leather sandals. He seemed to tremble, as well he should. He stood before no less than the Grandmaster of the Scarlet Spires.

"This is most impertinent, my mercenary brother," Eleäzaras said. "There are channels for this kind of transaction."

"Begging your pardon, Grandmaster, but there are no channels for what I have to ... to trade." In a rush he added, "I'm-I'm a White-Sash Peralogue of the Mysunsai Order, Grandmaster, contracted to the Imperial Family as an Auditor. The Emperor uses me, from time to time, to confirm certain determinations made by his Imperial Saik ..."

Eleäzaras digested this, decided to be accommodating. "Continue."

"Sh-should we, ah ... ah ..."

"Should we what?"

"Should we discuss the fee?"

A caste-menial, of course—suthenti. No appreciation of the game. But jnan, as the Ainoni were fond of saying, brooked no consent. If one man played, everyone played.

Rather than reply, Eleäzaras studied his long, painted nails, polished them absently against his breast. He looked up as though caught in a small indiscretion, then studied the fool like one burdened by determinations of life and death.

The conjunction of silence and scrutiny nearly undid the man. He clasped his shaking hands before him.

"F-forgive m-my eagerness, Grandmaster," Skalateas stammered, falling to his knees. "So often are knowledge and greed ... spurs to each other."

Well done. The man was not utterly devoid of wit.

"Spurs indeed," Eleäzaras said. "But perhaps you should let *me* decide which rides which."

"Of course, Grandmaster ... But ..."

"But nothing, whore. *Out* with it."

"Of course, Grandmaster," he said again. "It's the Fanim sorcerer-priests—the Cishaurim ... Th-they have a new kind of *spy*."

The dramatics were forgotten. Eleäzaras leaned forward.

"Tell me more."

"F-forgive me, Grandmaster," the man blurted. "B-but I would be paid before speaking any further!"

A fool after all. Time was ever the scholar's most precious commodity. Whore or not, the man should have known that. Eleäzaras sighed, then spoke the first impossible word. His mouth and eyes burned as bright as phosphor.

"*No!*" Skalateas cried. "Please! I'll speak! There's no need ..."

Eleäzaras paused, though his arcane muttering continued to echo, as though thrown by walls not found in this world. The silence, when it did come, felt absolute.

"On-on the eve b-before the Holy War marched from Momemn," the man began, "I was summoned to the Catacombs to observe what was supposed to be, they said, the interrogation of a spy. Apparently the Emperor's Prime Counsel—"

"Skeaös?" Eleäzaras exclaimed. "A *spy?*"

The Mysunsai hesitated, licked his lips. "Not Skeaös ... Someone masquerading as him. Or something ..."

Eleäzaras nodded. "You have my attention, Skalateas."

"The Emperor himself was present at the interrogation. He demanded, quite stridently, that I contradict the findings of the Saik, that I tell him sorcery was involved ... The Prime Counsel was—as you know—an old man, and yet he'd apparently killed or maimed several members of the Eothic Guard during his arrest—with his *bare hands*, they said. The Emperor was, well ... overwrought."

"So what did you see, Auditor? Did you see the Mark?"

"No. Nothing. He was unbruised. There was no sorcery whatsoever involved. But when I said as much to the Emperor, he accused me of conspiring with the Saik to overthrow him. Then the Mandate Schoolman arrived—escorted by Ikurei Conphas no—"

"Mandate Schoolman?" Eleäzaras said. "You mean Drusas Achamian?"

Skalateas swallowed. "You know him? We Mysunsai no longer bother with the Mandate. Does your Eminence maint—"

"Do you wish to sell knowledge, Skalateas, or trade it?"

The Mysunsai smiled nervously. "Sell it, of course."

"So then what happened next?"

"The Mandati confirmed my determination, and the Emperor accused him of lying as well. As I said, the Emperor was ... was ..."

"Overwrought."

"Yes. Even more so at this point. But the Mandati, Achamian, also seemed agitated. They argued—"

"Argued?" For some reason that didn't surprise Eleäzaras. "About what?"

The Mysunsai shook his head. "I can't remember. Something about fear, I think. Then the Prime Counsel began *speaking* to the Mandati—in some language I've never heard. He recognized him."

"Recognized? Are you sure?"

"Utterly ... Skeaös, or whatever it was, recognized Drusas Achamian. Then he—*it*—began shaking. We just stood gaping. Then it wrenched its chains from the wall ... Freed itself!"

"Did Drusas Achamian assist him?"

"No. He was as horrified as the rest of us—if not more so. In the uproar, it killed two or three men—I've never seen anything move so fast! That was when the Saik intervened, burned him ... Now that I think about it, burned him over the Mandati's objections. The man was wroth."

"Achamian tried to intercede?"

"To the point of sheltering the Prime Counsel with his own body."

"You're certain about that?"

"Absolutely. I'll never forget because that was when the Prime Counsel's face ... That was when his face ... *unpeeled*."

"Unpeeled ..."

"Or unfolded ... Its face just ... just opened, like *fingers* but ... I know of no other way to describe it."

"Like fingers?"

This can't be! He lies!

"You doubt me. You mustn't, your Eminence! This spy was a double, a mimic *without the Mark!* And that means he must be an artifact of the Psûkhe. The *Cishaurim*. It means they have spies *you cannot see*."

Numbness spilled like water from Eleäzaras's chest to his limbs. *I've wagered my School.*

"But their Art is too crude ..."

Skalateas looked curiously heartened. "Nevertheless, it's the only explanation. They've found some way of creating *perfect* spies ... Think! How long have they owned the Emperor's ear? The *Emperor!* Who knows how many ..." He paused, apparently wary of speaking too close to the heart of the matter. "But this is why I rode so hard to find you. To warn you."

Eleäzaras's mouth had become very dry. He tried to swallow. "You must stay with us, of course, so that we can ... interview you, further."

The man's face had become the very picture of dread. "I'm af-afraid that won't be possible, y-your Eminence. I'm expected back at the Imperial Court."

Eleäzaras clasped his hands to conceal the tremors. "You work for the Scarlet Spires, now, Skalateas. Your contract with House Ikurei is dissolved."

"Ah, y-your Eminence, as much as I abase myself before your glory and power—I am your slave!—I fear that Mysunsai contracts cannot be dissolved by fiat. N-not even yours. S-so if I c-could coll-collect my-my ..."

"Ah yes, your fee." Eleäzaras stared hard at the Mysunsai, smiled with deceptive mildness. *Poor fool. To think he'd underestimated the value of his information. This was worth far more than gold. Far more.*

The Mysunsai's face had gone blank. "I suppose I could delay my departure."

"You sup—"

At that point, Eleäzaras almost died. The man had started his Cant the instant of Eleäzaras's reply, purchasing a heartbeat's advantage—almost enough.

Lightning cut the air, skipped and thundered across the Grandmaster's reflexive Wards. Momentarily blinded, Eleäzaras tipped back in his chair and tumbled across the carpeted ground. He was singing before he found his knees.

The air danced with hammering lights. Flurries of burning sparrows ...

The fool cried out, sputtered as best he could, trying to reinforce his Wards. But for Hanumanu Eleäzaras, the Grandmaster of the Scarlet Spires, he was little more than a child's riddle, easily solved. Bird after fiery bird swept into him. Immolation after immolation, battering his Wards to ruin. Then chains flashed from corners of empty air, piercing limbs and shoulders, crossing as though looped between a child's fingers, until the man hung suspended. Threaded.

Skalateas screamed.

Javreh charged into the room, weapons drawn, only to halt, horror-stricken, before the spectacle of the Mysunsai. Eleäzaras barked at them to leave.

He glimpsed his Master of Spies, Iyokus, fighting his way past the retreating warrior-slaves. The chanv addict fairly tumbled across the carpets, his red-irised eyes wide, his bruised lips agog. Eleäzaras couldn't recall seeing such passion in the man's expression—at least not since the Cishaurim's fateful attack ten years before ...

Their declaration of war.

"Eli!" Iyokus cried, staring at Skalateas's impaled and writhing form. "What's this?"

The Grandmaster absently stamped at a small fire burning on the carpets. "A gift to you, old friend. Another enigma for you to interpret. Another threat ..."

"Threat?" the man cried. "What's the meaning of this, Eli? What's happened here?"

Eleäzaras studied the screaming Mysunsai—a scholar distracted by his work.

What do I do?

"That Mandate Schoolman," Eleäzaras snapped, turning to Iyokus. "Where's he now?"

"Marching with Proyas—or so I assume ... Eli? Tell me—"

"Drusas Achamian must be brought to me," Eleäzaras continued. "Brought to me or killed."

Iyokus's expression darkened.

"Something like that requires time ... planning ... He's a *Mandate Schoolman*, Eli! Not to mention the risk of reprisals ... What, do we war against both the Cishaurim and the Mandate? Either way, *nothing* will be done until I know what's going on. It is my right!"

Eleäzaras studied the man, matched his unsettling gaze. For perhaps the first time he felt comforted rather than chilled by his translucent skin. *Iyokus? It has to be you, doesn't it?*

"This must seem," he said, "irrational ..."

"Indeed. *Mad* even."

"Trust me, old friend. It's not. Need makes all things rational."

"Why this evasion?" Iyokus cried.

"Patience ..." Eleäzaras replied, gathering with his wind the dignity which behooved a Grandmaster. This was an occasion for control. Calculation. "First you must humour my madness, Iyokus ... And *then* let me recount the grounds that make it sane. First you must let me handle your face."

"And why's that?" the man asked. Astonishment.

From what seemed a distant place, Skalateas wailed.

"I must know that there are bones beneath ... *Proper* bones."

For the first time since leaving Momemn, Achamian found himself alone with the evening fire. Proyas was hosting a temple fete for the other Great Names, and everyone save the sorcerer and the slaves had been invited. So Achamian had decided to host a celebration of his own. He drank to the sun, which leaned against the shoulders of the Unaras Spur, to Asgilioch and her broken towers, and to the encamped Holy War, her innumerable fires glittering in the dusk. He drank until his head drooped before the flames, until his thoughts became a slurry of arguments, pleas, and regrets.

Telling Kellhus about his dilemma, he now knew, had been rash.

Two weeks had passed since his confession. During this time, the Conriyan contingent had abandoned the stone of the Sogian Way for the scrub and sandy slopes of the Inûnara Highlands. He had walked with Kellhus much as before, answering his questions, pondering his remarks—and wondering, always wondering, at the heart and intellect of the man. On the surface, everything was the same, save the lack of a road to follow. But beneath, everything had changed.

He'd thought sharing would ease his burden, that honesty would absolve his shame. How could he be such a fool, thinking that the *secrecy* of his dilemma had caused his anguish, rather than the dilemma? If anything, secrecy had been a balm. Now every time he and Kellhus exchanged glances, Achamian saw his anguish reflected and reproduced, until at times it seemed he couldn't breathe. Far from lessening his burden, he'd doubled it.

"What," Kellhus had subsequently asked, "will the Mandate do if you tell them?"

"Take you to Atyersus. Confine you. Interrogate you ... Now that they know the Consult runs amok, they'll do anything to exercise the semblance of control. For that reason alone, they'd never let you go."

"Then you mustn't tell them, Akka!" There had been an anger and an anxiousness to these words, a cross desperation that reminded him of Inrau.

"And the Second Apocalypse. What about that?"

"But are you *sure*? Sure enough to wager an entire life?"

A life for the world. Or the world for a life.

"You don't understand! The *stakes*, Kellhus! Think of what's at stake!"

"How," Kellhus had replied, "can I think of anything else?"

The Cultic priestesses of Yatwer, Achamian had once heard, always dragged *two* victims—usually spring lambs—to the sacrificial altar, one to pass under the knife, the other to witness the sacred passage. In this way, every beast thrown upon the altar always knew, in its dim way, what was about to happen. For the Yatwerians, ritual wasn't enough: the transformation of casual slaughter into true sacrifice required *recognition*. One lamb for ten bulls, a priestess had told him once, as though she possessed the calculus to measure such things.

One lamb for ten bulls. At the time, Achamian had laughed. Now he understood.

Before the dilemma had overwhelmed in a harried, flinching way, like some secret perversion. But now that Kellhus *knew*, it simply overwhelmed. Before Achamian could find respite, from time to time, in the man's remarkable company. He could pretend to be a simple teacher. But now, the dilemma had become something *between* them, something always *there* whether Achamian averted his eyes or not. There was no more pretending, no more "forgetting." Only the knife of inaction.

And wine. Sweet unwatered wine.

When they'd arrived at half-ruined Asgilioch, Achamian began, more out of desperation than anything else, teaching Kellhus algebra, geometry, and logic. What better way to impose clarity on soul-bruising confusion, certainty on rib-gnawing doubt? While the others watched from nearby, laughing, scratching their heads, or in the Scylvendi's case, glowering, Achamian and Kellhus spent hours scratching proofs across the bare earth. Within days the Prince of Atrithau was improvising new axioms, discovering theorems and formulae that Achamian had never imagined possible, let alone encountered in the classic texts. Kellhus even proved to him—proved!—that the logic of Ajencis as laid out in *The Syllogistics* was preceded by a *more basic logic*, one which used relations between entire sentences rather than subjects and predicates. Two thousand years of comprehension and insight overturned by the strokes of a stick across dust!

"How?" he'd cried. *"How?"*

Kellhus shrugged. "This is simply what I see."

He's here, Achamian had thought absurdly, *but he doesn't stand beside me ...* If all men saw from where they stood, then Kellhus stood somewhere else—that much was undeniable. But did he stand beyond the pale of Drusas Achamian's judgement?

Ah, the question. More drink was required.

Achamian rooted through his satchel, his only fireside companion, and withdrew the map he'd sketched—so long ago it now seemed— while journeying from Sumna to Momemn. He held it to the firelight, blinked several bleary times. All of them, every name scratched in black, was connected, except for

ANASÛRIMBOR KELLHUS

Relations. Like arithmetic or logic it all came down to relations. Achamian had inked those relations he knew without a doubt, such as the link between the Consult and the Emperor, and even those he simply assumed or feared, such as that between Maithanet and Inrau. Ink lines: one for the Consult infiltration of the Imperial Court, another for Inrau's murder, another for the Scarlet Spires' war against the Cishaurim, another for the Holy War's reconquest of Shimeh, and so on. Ink lines for relations. A thin skeleton of black.

But where did Kellhus fit? Where?

Achamian suddenly cackled, resisted the urge to throw the parchment into the fire. Smoke. Wasn't that what relations were in truth? Not ink, but smoke. Hard to see and impossible to grasp. And wasn't that the problem? The problem with everything?

The thought of smoke brought Achamian to his feet. He swayed for a moment, then bent to retrieve his satchel. Again he debated tossing the map into the flames, but thought better of it—he was a veteran of many drunken blunders—and stuffed the parchment back with his things.

With his satchel and Xinemus's wineskin slung over opposite shoulders, he stumbled off into the darkness, laughing to himself and thinking, *Yes, smoke ... I need smoke.* Hashish.

Why not? The world was about to end.

As the sun set behind the Unaras Spur, each point of firelight became a circle of illumination, until the encampment became gold coins scattered across black cloth. Among the first to arrive, the Conriyans had pitched their pavilions on the heights immediately below Asgilioch and its ready supply of water. As a result Achamian travelled down, always down, into what seemed an ever darker and more raucous underworld.

He walked and stumbled, exploring the shadowy arteries between pavilions. He passed many others: groups carousing from camp to camp, drunks searching for latrines, slaves on errands, even a Gilgallic priest chanting and swinging the carcass of a hawk from a leather string. From time to time he slowed, stared at the ruddy faces crowded about each fire, laughed at their antics or pondered their scowls. He watched them strut and posture, beat their breasts and bellow at the mountains. Soon they would descend upon the heathen. Soon they would close with their hated foe. "The God has burned our ships!" Achamian heard one bare-chested

Galeoth roar, first in Sheyic, then in his native tongue. "*Wossen het Votta grefearsa!*"

Periodically he paused to search the darkness behind him. Old habit.

After a time he found himself weary and nearly out of wine. He'd trusted Fate, Anagkë, to take him to the camp-followers; she was, after all, called "the Whore." But as with everything else, she'd led him astray—the fucking whore. He began daring the light to find directions.

"Wrong way, friend," an older man missing his front teeth told him at one camp. "Only mules rutting here. Oxen and mules."

"Good ..." Achamian said, clutching his groin in the familiar Tydonni manner, "at least the proportions will be right." The old man and his comrades burst into laughter. Achamian winked and tipped back his wineskin.

"Then that way," some wit called from the fire, pointing to the darkness beyond. "I hope your ass has deep pockets!"

Achamian coughed wine from his nose, then spent several moments bent over, hacking. The general merriment this caused won him a place by their fire. An inveterate traveller, Achamian was accustomed to the company of warlike strangers, and for a time he enjoyed their companionship, their wine, and his own anonymity. But when their questions became too pointed, he thanked them and took his leave.

Drawn by the throb of drums, Achamian crossed a portion of the camp that seemed deserted, then quite without warning found himself in the precincts of the camp-followers. Suddenly all the activity seemed concentrated between the fires. With every step he bumped some shoulder, pressed some back. In some places, he pressed through crowds in almost total darkness, with only heads, shoulders, and the odd face frosted by the Nail of Heaven's pale light. In others, torches had been hammered into the earth, either for musicians, merchants, or leather-panelled brothels. Several avenues even boasted hanging lanterns. He saw young Men of the Tusk—no more than boys, really—vomiting from too much drink. He saw ten-year-old girls drawing thick-waisted warriors behind curtained canopies. He even glimpsed a boy wearing smeared cosmetics, who watched with fearful promise as man after man passed. He saw craftsmen manning stalls, walked past more than a few impromptu smithies. Beneath the rambling canopies of an opium den, he saw men twitch as though beset by flies. He passed the gilded pavilions of the Cults: Gilgaöl, Yatwer, Momas, Ajokli, even elusive Onkis, who'd been Inrau's passion, as well as innumerable others. He waved away the ever-present beggars and laughed at the adepts who pressed clay blessing-tablets into his hands.

For tracts of his journey, Achamian saw no tents at all, only rough shelters improvised from sticks, twine, and painted leather, or in some cases, a simple mat. While wandering one alley, Achamian saw no less than a dozen couples, male and female or male and male, rutting in plain view. Once he paused to watch an improbably beautiful Norsirai girl gasp between the exertions of two men, only to be accosted by a black-toothed man with a stick, demanding coin. Afterward he watched an ancient, tattooed hermit try to force himself on a fat drab. He saw black-skinned Zeumi harlots dancing in their strange, puppet-limbed manner and dressed in gaudy gowns of false silk—caricatures of the ornate elegance that so characterized their faraway land.

The first woman found him more than the other way around. As he walked through a particularly gloomy alley between canvas shanties, he heard a rattle, then felt small hands groping for his groin from behind. When he turned and embraced her, she seemed shapely enough, though he could see little of her face in the dark. She was already rubbing his manhood through his robe, murmuring, "Jusht a copper, Lord. Jusht a copper for your sheed ..." He could sense her sour smile. "Two coppersh for my peach. Do you want my peach?"

Almost despite himself, he leaned into her whisking hands—gasped. Then a file of torch-bearing cavalrymen—Imperial Kidruhil—rumbled by, and he glimpsed her face: vacant eyes and ulcerated lips ...

He pressed her back, fumbling for his purse. He fished out a copper, meant to hand it to her, but fumbled it onto the ground instead. She fell to her knees, started combing the blackness, grunting ... Achamian fled.

A short time after, he found himself prowling the darkness, watching a group of prostitutes about their fire. They sang and clapped while a wanton, flat-chested Ketyai woman pranced around the flames, wearing only a blanket that reached her hips. This was a common custom, Achamian knew. They would each take turns, dancing lewdly and calling out into the surrounding blackness, declaring their wares and their station.

He reviewed the women from the shelter of darkness first, so as to avoid the embarrassment of choosing in their presence. The girl who danced didn't appeal to him—too much of a horse's mien. But the young Norsirai girl, who rolled her pretty face to the song like a child ... She sat on the ground with her knees haphazardly before her, the firelight chancing upon her inner thighs.

When he finally walked into their midst, they began shouting like slavers at auction, offering promises and praise that became mockery the instant he took the Galeoth girl by the hand. Despite the drink, he felt so nervous he could barely breathe. She looked so beautiful. So soft and unspoiled.

Picking a candle from a small row of votives, she pulled him into the blackness, led him to the last in a row of crude shelters. She shed her blanket and crawled beneath the stained leather. Achamian stood above her, panting, wanting to breathe deep the pale glory of her naked form. The far wall of her shelter, however, consisted of little more than rags knotted into ropes. Through it, he could see hundreds of people pressing in this direction and that through a shadowy thoroughfare.

"You want fuck me, yes?" she said as though nothing could be amiss.

"Oh, yes," he mumbled. Where had his breath gone?

Sweet Sejenus.

"Fuck me many time? Eh, Baswutt?"

He laughed nervously. Peered through the rag curtain once again. Two men were cursing at each other, scuffling near enough to make Achamian flinch.

"Many times," he replied, knowing this to be the polite way to discuss price. "How many do you think?"

"Think four ... Four silver times."

Silver? Obviously she'd confused his embarrassment for inexperience. Even still, what was money on a night like this? He celebrated, didn't he?

He shrugged, saying, "An old man like me?"

In this particular language, the man was forced to deride his own prowess in order to strike a fair bargain. If he was poor, he complained of being old, infirm, and so on. Arrogant men, Esmenet had told him once, usually fared poorly in these negotiations—which, of course, was the point. Harlots hated nothing more than men who arrived already believing the flattering lies they would tell them. Esmi called them the *simustarapari*, or "those-who-spit-twice."

The Galeoth girl studied him with nebulous eyes: she'd started petting herself in the gloom. "You so strong," she said, suddenly thick-tongued. "Like Baswutt ... Strong! *Two* silver times think?"

Achamian laughed, tried hard not to watch her fingers. The ground had started a slow spin. For an instant she looked pale and skinny in the dark, like an abused slave. The mat beneath her looked rough enough to cut her skin ... He'd drunk too much.

Not too much! Just enough ...

The ground steadied. He swallowed, nodded his agreement, then pulled the two coins from his purse. "What does 'Baswutt' mean?" he asked, slipping the silver into her small, waiting palm.

"Hmmm?" she replied, smiling triumphantly. She stashed the two white-shining talents with startling swiftness—What would she buy? he wondered—then looked back at him with large questioning eyes.

"What does that mean?" he repeated, more slowly. "Baswutt ..."

She frowned, then giggled. "For 'big bear' ..."

She was full-breasted, mature, but something about her manner reminded him of a little girl. The guileless smile. The rolling eyes and bouncing chin. The knees opening and closing like butterfly wings. Achamian half-expected a scolding mother to come barging between them. Was that part of the pantomime as well? Like the shameless banter?

His heart hammered.

He knelt where her toys should have been, between her legs. She squirmed and writhed, as though the threat of his mere presence would make her climax. "Fuck me, Baswutt," she gasped. "*Emmm*baswutt ... Fuck-me-fuck-me-fuck-me ... Mmmm, *pleassseee* ..."

He swayed, caught himself, chuckled. He began hitching up his robe, glanced nervously at the shadowy stream of passersby through the curtain. They walked so close he could spit on their shins.

He tried to ignore the smell. His smell.

"Oooh, such *big* bear," she cooed, stroking his cock.

Suddenly, his apprehension melted away, and some deranged part of him actually exulted in the thought of others watching. Let them watch! Let them *learn!*

Always the teacher ...

Cackling, he seized her narrow hips, pulled her across his thighs.

How he'd yearned for this moment! To have licence with a *stranger* ... It seemed there could be nothing so sweet as a fresh peach!

He was trembling! Trembling!

She moaned silver, cried gold. Faces turned in the passing crowd.

Through the knotted rags, Achamian saw Esmenet.

———— ❦ ————

"Esmi!" Achamian hollered, barrelling through arms and shoulders. The Galeoth girl was crying out something behind him—some gibberish.

He glimpsed Esmenet again, hurrying along a row of torches that fronted the canopies of a Yatwerian lazaret. A tall man, sporting the matted braids of a Thunyeri warrior, held her arm, but she seemed to be leading.

"Esmi!" he cried, jumping to be seen above the screens of people. She didn't turn. "Esmi! Stop!"

Why would she run? Had she seen him with the drab?

For that matter, what would she be doing *here?*

"Dammit, Esmenet! It's me! *Me!*"

Did she glance back? It was too dark to tell ...

For a heartbeat, he debated using sorcery: he could blind the entire quarter if he wished. But as always, he could sense the small points of death scattered throughout the surrounding crowds: Men of the Tusk, bearing their hereditary Chorae ...

He redoubled his efforts, began lunging through the mobs. Someone struck him, hard enough to leave his ears ringing, but he didn't care. "Esmi!"

He glimpsed her pulling the Thunyeri into an even darker byway. He stumbled free of what seemed the last thicket of people, then sprinted to the mouth of the alley. He hesitated before plunging into the blackness, struck by a sudden premonition of disaster. Esmenet here? In the Holy War? There was no way.

A *trap*. A thought like a knife.

The ground had resumed spinning.

If the Consult could fashion a Skeaös, couldn't they fashion an Esmenet as well? If they knew about Inrau, then they almost certainly knew about her ... What better way to gull a heartsick Schoolman than to ...

A *skin-spy? Do I chase a skin-spy?*

In his soul's eye, he saw Geshrunni's corpse pulled from the River Sayut. Murdered. Desecrated.

Sweet Sejenus, they took his face. Could the same have happened ...

"Esmi!" he cried, charging into the darkness. "Esmi! *Essmmii!*"

Miraculously, she paused with her escort in the light of a single torch, either alarmed by his cries or ...

Achamian staggered to a stop before her, utterly dumbstruck. He reeled.

It *wasn't* her—the brown eyes were smaller, the cheeks too high. Almost, but no ... Almost Esmenet.

"Another madman," the woman snorted to her companion.

"I-I thought ..." Achamian murmured. "I thought you were someone else."

"Poor girl," she sneered, turning her back.

"No, wait! Please ..."

"Please, what?"

Achamian blinked at his tears. She looked so ... so *close*. "I need you," he whispered. "I need your ... your comfort."

Without warning, the Thunyeri seized him by the throat, hammered him in the gut. *"Kundrout!"* the man bellowed. *"Parasafau ferautin kun dattas!"* Winded, Achamian coughed and clawed at the man's massive forearm. Panic. Then gravel and rock—ground—slammed against his chest and cheek. Concussion. Bright blackness. Someone screaming. The taste of blood. A dim image of the wild-haired warrior spitting on him.

He convulsed, rolled to his side. Sobbed, then pressed himself to his knees. Through tears he saw their retreating backs disappear in thickets of people.

"Esmi!" he bawled. "Esmenet, please!"

Such an old-fashioned name.

"Esssmmiiii!"

Come back ...

Then he felt the touch. Heard the voice.

"Still fetching sticks, I see ... Tired old dog."

———— ❦ ————

Glimpses of menace by torchlight.

Her slender arms bracing him, they stumbled through a gallery of darkling faces. She smelled of camphor and the oil of sesame—like a Fanim merchant. Could that be her smell?

"Sweet Seja, Akka, you're a mess."

"Esmi?"

"Yes ... It's me, Akka. Me."

"Your face ..."

"Some Galeoth ingrate." Bitter laugh. "That's the way it is with Men of the Tusk and their whores. If you can't fuck them, beat them."

"Oh, Esmi ..."

"Once the swelling starts I'll look a caste-noble virgin compared to you. Did you hear me scream when he-he kicked you in the face? What were you doing?"

"I'm-I'm not sure ... L-looking for you ..."

"Shush, Akka ... Shhhhh ... Not here. After."

"J-just say it ... M-my name. Just say it!"

"Drusas Achamian ... Akka."

And he wept, so hard that at first he didn't realize she wept with him.

———— ❦ ————

Perhaps driven by the same impulse, they retreated into the blackness behind a dark pavilion, fell to their knees and embraced.

"It's really you ..." Achamian murmured, seeing twin moons reflected in her wet eyes.

She laughed and sobbed. "Really me ..."

His lips burned with the salt of mingled tears. He pulled her left breast free of her hasas, began circling her nipple with his thumb. "Why did you leave Sumna?"

"I was afraid," she whispered, kissing his forehead and cheeks. "Why am I always afraid?"

"Because you breathe."

A passionate kiss. Hands fumbling in the blackness, tugging, clutching. The ground spun. He leaned back, and she hooked burning thighs about his waist. Then he was inside, and she gasped. They sat motionless for several heartbeats, throbbing together, exchanging shallow breaths.

"Never again," Achamian said.

"Promise?" She wiped at her face. Sniffled.

He began slowly rocking her. "Promise ... Nothing. No man, no School, no threat. Nothing will take you from me again."

"*Nothing ...*" she moaned.

For a time, they seemed one being, dancing about the same delirious burn, swaying from the same breathless centre. For a time, they felt no fear.

———— ⌾ ————

Afterward, they exchanged caresses and whispered sweet words in the darkness, apologies offered for things already forgiven. Eventually Achamian asked her where she kept her belongings.

"I've already been robbed," she said, trying to smile. "But I have a few things left. Not far from here."

"Will you stay with me?" he asked with tearful earnestness. "Can you?"

He watched her swallow, blink.

"I can."

He laughed, pushed himself to his feet. "Then let's get your things."

Even in the gloom he could see the terror in her eyes. She hugged her shoulders, as though reminding herself not to fly away, then slipped her hand into his waiting palm.

They walked slowly, like lovers strolling through a bazaar. Periodically, Achamian would stare into her eyes and laugh in disbelief.

"I thought you were gone," he said once.

"But I've always been here."

Rather than ask what she meant, Achamian simply smiled. For the moment, her mysteries didn't matter. He wasn't so fool drunk as to think nothing was amiss. Something had driven her from Sumna. Something had led her to the Holy War. Something had compelled her ... yes, to avoid him. But for the moment, none of this mattered. He cared only that she was *here*.

Just let this night last. Please ... Give me this one night.

They chatted effortlessly about effortless things, joking about this or that passerby, telling stories about the curious things they'd seen in the Holy War. The unspoken regions between them were well-marked, and for the moment, they steered each other clear of painful boundaries.

They paused to watch a mummer dip a leather rope into a basket filled with scorpions. When he pulled it clear, it seethed with chitinous limbs, pincers, and stabbing tails. This, the man proclaimed, was the famed Scorpion Braid, which the Kings of Nilnamesh still used to punish mortal crimes. When the audience encircled him, anxious for a closer look, he raised the Braid high for everyone to see, then suddenly began swinging it over their heads. Women screamed, men ducked or raised their hands, but not a single scorpion flew from the rope. The rope, the mummer cried over the commotion, was soaked in a poison that seized the scorpions' jaws. Without the antidote, he said, they would remain locked to the leather until they died.

For much of the demonstration, Achamian watched and delighted in Esmenet's expression, all the while wondering that she could seem so *new*. He found himself discovering things he'd never before noticed. The dusting of freckles across her nose and cheeks. The extraordinary white of her eyes. The smattering of auburn through her luxurious black hair. The athletic slope of her back and shoulders. Everything about her, it seemed, possessed a bewitching novelty.

I must always see her like this. As the stranger I love ...

Each time their glances met, they laughed as though celebrating a fortuitous reunion. But they always looked away, as though knowing their momentary bliss wouldn't bear examination. Then something, a flicker of anxiousness perhaps, passed between them, and they ceased looking at each other altogether. A sudden hollow opened in the heart of Achamian's elation. He clutched her hand for reassurance, but she left her fingers slack.

After several moments, Esmenet tugged him to a stop in the light of several bright burning pots. She stared into his face, expressionless save for the hard set of her jaw.

"Something's different," she said. "Before, you could always pretend. Even when Inrau died. But now ... something's different. What's happened?"

He shied from answering her. It was too soon.

"I'm a Mandate Schoolman," he said lamely. "What can I say? We all suffer ..."

She fixed him with a canny scowl. "Knowledge," she said. "You all suffer knowledge ... If you suffer more, it means you've learned more ... Is that it? Have you learned more?"

Achamian stared straight ahead, said nothing. It was too soon!

She looked past him, sorted through the shadowy crowds. "Would you like to hear what's happened to me?"

"Leave it be, Esmi."

She flinched, turned away, blinking. She pulled her hand free and resumed walking.

"Esmi ..." he said, following her.

"You know," she said, "it hasn't been bad, save the odd beating. Plenty of custom. Plenty of—"

"That's enough, Esmi."

She laughed, acted as if she were engaged in a different, more frank conversation. "I've even lain with *lords* ... Caste-nobles, Akka! Imagine. Even their cocks are bigger—Did you know that? I wouldn't know about the Ainoni—they seem to prefer boys. And the Conriyans, they flock about the Galeoth sluts—all that milk-white skin, you know. But the Columns, the Nansur, they like their peaches homegrown, though they rarely stray from the military brothels. And the Thunyeri! They can scarce bridle their seed when my knees flop open! Brutes though, especially when they're drunk. Stingy bastards, too. Oh, and the Galeoth— there's a treat. They complain I'm too skinny, but they love my skin. If it weren't for the guilt and anger afterward, they'd be my favourites. They're not accustomed to whores ... Not enough old cities in their country, I think. Not enough barter ..."

She studied Achamian, her look both bitter and shrewd. He walked, his eyes welded forward.

"Custom has been good," she said, looking away.

The old rage had returned, the one that had driven him from her arms months before. He clenched his fists, saw himself shaking her, striking her. *Fucking whore!* he wanted to scream.

Why tell him this? Why tell him what he couldn't bear to hear?

Especially when she had her own things to answer for ...

Why did you leave Sumna? How long have you been hiding from me? How long?

But before he could say anything, she veered from the armed throngs and walked toward a fire surrounded by painted faces—more harlots.

"Esmi!" a dark-haired woman called out in a brusque, even mannish, voice. "Who's your— " She paused, getting a better look, then laughed. "Who's your hapless friend?" She was stout-limbed and thick-waisted, but without being fat—the kind of woman, Esmi had told him once, prized by certain Norsirai men. Achamian immediately recognized her as someone who confused ill manners with daring.

Esmenet halted, hesitated long enough to make Achamian frown. "This is Akka."

The drab's heavy eyebrows popped up. "The infamous Drusas Achamian?" the woman said. "The *Schoolman?*"

Achamian looked to Esmenet. Who was this woman?

"This is *Yasellas*," Esmenet said, speaking the woman's name as though it explained everything. "Yassi."

Yasellas's appraising stare remained fixed on Achamian. "So what are you doing here, Akka?"

He shrugged, saying, "I follow the Holy War."

"The same as us!" Yasellas exclaimed. "Though you might say we march for a different Tusk ..." The other prostitutes burst out laughing— like men.

"*And* the little prophet," another said, her voice hoarse. "Good for only one sermon ..."

All the women howled, with the exception of Yassi, who only smiled.

More jokes followed, but Esmenet was already pulling him into the darkness, toward what must have been her shelter.

"All of us camp in bands," she said, pre-empting any questions or observations. "We watch out for one another."

"So I gathered ..."

"This is mine," she said, kneeling before the greased canvas flaps of a low wedge tent not so unlike his own. Achamian found himself relieved: without a word she crawled into the blackness. Achamian followed.

Within, there was barely enough room to sit upright. Beneath the incense, the air smelled of rutting—if only because Achamian couldn't stop imagining her with her men. She disrobed in the routine manner of a harlot, and he studied her lithe, small-breasted silhouette. She looked so frail in the remains of the firelight, so small and desolate. The thought of her pinioned here, night after night, beneath man after man ...

I must make this right!

"Do you have a candle?" he asked.

"Some ... But we'll be burned." Fire was the perennial fear of those raised in cities.

"No," he replied. "Never with me ..."

She withdrew a candle from a bundle in the corner, and Achamian ignited it with a word. In Sumna, she'd always marvelled at such tricks. Now, she simply regarded him with a kind of resigned wariness.

They both blinked in the light. She drew a stained blanket across her lap, stared vacantly at the snarl of coverings between them.

He swallowed. "Esmi? Why tell me ... all that."

"Because I had to know," she replied, looking down at her hands.

"Know what? What makes my hands shake? What makes my eyes dart in terror?"

Her shoulders hitched in the gloom; Achamian realized she was sobbing.

"You pretended I wasn't there," she whispered.

"I what?"

"That last night at Momemn ... I came to you. I watched your camp, your friends, only hidden because I was too afraid that I would ... that I would ... But you weren't there, Akka! So I waited and waited. Then I saw ... I saw *you* ... I wept with joy, Akka! Wept! I stood there, right before you, weeping! I held out my arms, and you ... and you ..." The anguished light in her eyes dulled, flickered out. She finished in a different voice—far colder.

"You pretended I wasn't there."

What was she talking about? Achamian pressed palms to his forehead, wrestled with the urge to lash out—to punish. She stood close enough to touch—after all this time!—and yet she receded ... He needed to understand.

"Esmi?" he said slowly, trying to collect his wine-addled wits. "What are you—"

"What was it, Akka?" she asked, rigid and cool. "Was I too polluted, too defiled? Too much a filthy whore?"

"No, Esmi, I—"

"Too bruised a *peach?*"

"*Esmenet*, listen to—"

She laughed bitterly. "So you're going to take me to your tent, you say? Add me to the bushel—"

He seized her by the shoulders, crying, "*You* speak of bushels to me? *You?*"

But he immediately repented, seeing his own savagery reflected in her terrified expression. She had even flinched, as though expecting a blow. He noticed, as though for the first time, the bruising about her left eye.

Who did this? Not me. Not me ...

"Look at us," he said, releasing her and carefully drawing back his hands. Both beaten. Both outcasts.

"Look at us," she mumbled, tears spilling down her cheeks.

"I can explain, Esmi ... Everything."

She nodded, rubbed her shoulders where he'd grabbed her. Female voices chimed in unison outside—they had started singing like the other harlots, promising soft thighs for hard silver. Firelight glittered through the open flaps, like gold through dark waters.

"That night you're talking about ... Sweet Sejenus, Esmi, if I didn't see you, it wasn't because I was *ashamed* of you! How could I be? How could anyone—let alone a *sorcerer!*—be ashamed of a woman such as you?"

She bit her lip, smiled through more tears. "Then why?"

Achamian rolled to his side and laid next to her, his eyes searching the dark canvas above.

"Because I *found them*, Esmi—that very night ... I found the Consult."

———— ∞ ————

"I remember nothing after that," he concluded. "I know I walked through the night, all the way from the Imperial Precincts to Xinemus's camp, but I remember none of it ..."

The words had splashed from him, an inarticulate rush, painting the horrific events that transpired that night beneath the Andiamine Heights. The unprecedented summons. The meeting with Ikurei Xerius III. The interrogation of Skeaös, his Prime Counsel. The face-that-was-not-a-face, unclenching like a woman's long-fingered fist. The dreadful conspiracy of skin. He told her about everything except Kellhus ...

Esmenet had curled into his arms to listen. Now she perched her chin on his chest.

"Did the Emperor believe you?"

"No ... I imagine he thinks the Cishaurim were responsible. Men prefer new loves and *old* enemies."

"And Atyersus? What of the Mandate?"

"Excited and dismayed in equal measure, or so I imagine ..." He licked his lips. "I'm not sure. I haven't contacted them since first reporting to Nautzera. They probably think I'm dead by now ... Murdered because of what I know."

"Then they haven't contacted you ..."

"That's not the way it works, remember?"

"Yes, yes ..." she replied, rolling her eyes and smirking. "How does it go? With the Cants of Calling, you need to know both the here, the individual, and the there, the location, to initiate contact. Since you march, they have no idea where you are ..."

"Exactly," he said, bracing himself for the inevitable question to follow.

Her eyes probed his, compassionate yet guarded.

"So then why haven't *you* contacted them?"

Achamian shuddered. He ran shaking fingers through her hair. "I'm so glad you're here," he murmured. "So glad you're safe ..."

"Akka, what is it? You're frightening me ..."

He closed his eyes, breathed deep. "I met someone. Someone whose coming was foretold two thousand years ago ..." He opened his eyes, and she was still there. "An Anasûrimbor."

"But that means ..." Esmenet frowned, stared into his chest. "You cried out that name in your sleep once, woke me ..." She looked up, peered into his face. "I remember asking you what it meant, 'Anasûrimbor,' and you said ... you said ..."

"I don't remember."

"You said that it named the last ruling dynasty of ancient Kûniüri, and ..." Her expression slackened in horror. "This isn't funny, Akka. You're really scaring me!"

She feared, Achamian realized, because she believed ... He gasped, blinked hot tears. Tears of joy.

She really believes ... All along she's believed!

"No, Akka!" Esmenet cried, clutching his chest. "This can't be happening!"

How could life be so perverse? That a Mandate Schoolman could celebrate the world's end.

With Esmenet pressed naked against him, he explained why he thought Kellhus, without any doubt, had to be the Harbinger. She listened without comment, watched him with a fearful expectancy.

"Don't you see?" he said, as much to the surrounding darkness as to her. "If I tell Nautzera and the others, they *will* take him ... No matter whose protection he enjoys."

"Will they kill him?"

Achamian blinked away disturbing images of past interrogations. "They'll break him, murder who he is ..."

"Even still," she said. "Akka, you must surrender him." There was no hesitation, no pause, only cold eyes and remorseless judgement. For women, it seemed, the scales of threat and love brooked no counterweights.

"But this is a *life*, Esmi."

"Exactly," she replied. "A life ... What difference does it make, the life of one man? So many die, Akka."

The hard logic of a hard world.

"It depends on the man, doesn't it?"

This gave her pause. "I suppose it does," she said. "So what kind of man is he? What kind of man is worth risking Apocalypse?"

Despite her sarcasm, he could tell she feared his answer. Certainty despised complications, and she needed to be certain. *She thinks she saves me*, he realized. *She needs me to be wrong for my sake ...*

"He's ..." Achamian swallowed. "He's unlike any other man."

"How so?" A prostitute's scepticism.

"It's difficult to explain." He hesitated, pondering his time with Kellhus. So many insights. So many instants of awe. "You know how it feels when you stand on someone else's ground—on their property?"

"I suppose … Like a trespasser or a guest."

"Somehow that's the way he makes you feel. Like a guest."

An expression of distaste. "I'm not sure I like the sound of that."

"Then it's not how it sounds." Achamian breathed deeply, groped for the proper words. "There's many … many *grounds* between men. Some are mutual, and some are not. When you and I speak of the Consult, for instance, you stand upon my ground, just as I stand upon your ground when you discuss your … your life. But with Kellhus, it makes no difference what you discuss or where you stand; somehow the ground beneath your feet *belongs to him*. I'm always his guest—always! Even when I teach him, Esmi!"

"You teach him? You've taken him as your student?"

Achamian frowned. She made it sound like a betrayal.

"Just the exoterics," he said with a shrug, "the world. Not the esoterics. He's not one of the Few …" Almost as an afterthought, he added, "Thank the God."

"Why do you say that?"

"Because of his intellect, Esmi! You've no idea! I've never met such a subtle soul, neither in life *nor in book* … Not even Ajencis, Esmi! *Ajencis!* If Kellhus possessed the ability to work sorcery, he'd be … he'd be …" Achamian caught his breath.

"What?"

"Another Seswatha … More than Seswatha …"

"Then I like him even less. He sounds *dangerous*, Akka. Let Nautzera and the others know. If they seize him, so be it. At least you can wash your hands of this madness!"

Fresh tears welled in his eyes. "But …"

"Akka," she pressed, "this burden isn't yours to bear!"

"But it is!"

Esmenet pushed herself from his chest, propping herself with an arm to lean over him. Her hair draped over her left shoulder, an impenetrable black in the candlelight. She seemed watchful, hesitant.

"Is it? I think you say this because of Inrau …"

Cold clasped his heart. Inrau. Sweet boy. Son.

"And why not?" he cried with sudden ferocity. "They killed him!"

"But they sent *you*! They sent you to Sumna to turn Inrau, and that's what you did, even though you knew exactly what would happen ... You told me this before you even contacted him!"

"So what are you saying? That *I killed Inrau?*"

"I'm saying that's what *you* think. You think you killed him."

Oh, Achamian, her tone said, *please ...*

"And what if I do? Does that mean I should relent a second time? Let those fools in Atyersus doom another man that I—"

"No, Achamian. It means you're not doing this—any of this!—to save this-this Anasûrimbor Kellhus. You're doing it to punish yourself."

He stared, dumbstruck. Was that what she thought?

"You say this," Achamian breathed, "because you know me so well ..." He reached out, traced the pale edge of her breast with a finger. "And Kellhus so little."

"No man is that remarkable ... I'm a whore, remember?"

"We'll see," he said, tugging her down. They kissed, long and deep.

"*We,*" she repeated, laughing as though both hurt and astounded. "It really is 'we' now, isn't it?"

With a shy, even scared, smile, she helped him pull free his weathered robes.

"When I can't find you," he said, "or even when you turn away, I feel ... I feel *hollow,* as though my heart's a thing of smoke ... Isn't that 'we'?"

She pressed him against the mat, straddled him.

"I recognize it," she replied, tears now streaming down her cheeks. "So it must be ..."

One lamb, Achamian thought, *for ten bulls.* Recognition.

He hardened against her, ached to know her again. As always, the images flickered, each as sharp as glass. Bloodied faces. The clash of bronze arms. Men consumed in billowing sorceries. Dragons with teeth of iron ... But she raised her hips, and with a single encompassing thrust, sheared away both past and future, sparing only the glorious pang of the present. He cried out.

She began grinding against him, not with the expertise of a harlot hoping to abbreviate her labour, but with the clumsy selfishness of a lover seeking surcease—a lover or a wife. Tonight she would take, and that, Achamian knew, was as much as any whore could give.

Wearing a harlot's face, it sat in the blackness, its ears pricked to the sounds of their lovemaking—glistening sounds—a mere arm's length away. And it thought of the weaknesses of the flesh, of all the *needs* that it was immune to, that made it powerful, deadly.

The air was suffused with their groaning scent, the heady perfume of unwashed bodies slapping in the night. It was not an unpleasant smell. Too devoid of fear perhaps.

The sound and smell of animals, aching animals.

But it knew something of their ache. Perhaps it knew far more. Appetite was direction, and its architects had given *it* direction—such exquisite hungers! Ah yes, the architects weren't fools.

There was ecstasy in a face. Rapture in deceit. Climax in the kill …

And certainty in the dark.

HAPTER FOUR

ASGILIOCH

No decision is so fine as to not bind us to its consequences.
No consequence is so unexpected as to absolve us of our decisions.
Not even death.

—XIUS, *THE TRUCIAN DRAMAS*

It seems a strange thing to recall these events, like waking to find I
had narrowly missed a fatal fall in the darkness. Whenever I think
back, I'm filled with wonder that I still live, and with horror that I
still travel by night.

—DRUSAS ACHAMIAN, *THE COMPENDIUM OF THE FIRST HOLY WAR*

Early Summer, 4111 Year-of-the-Tusk, the fortress of Asgilioch

Achamian and Esmenet awoke in each other's arms, sheepish with
memories of the previous night. They held each other tight to quell their
fears, then as the surrounding encampment slowly rumbled to life, they
made love with quiet urgency. Afterward, Esmenet fell silent, looked away
each time Achamian searched for her eyes. At first, he found himself
baffled and angered by this sudden change of demeanour, but then he
realized she was afraid. Last night she'd shared his tent. Today, she would
share his friends, his daily discourse—his *life*.

"Don't worry," he said, catching her eyes as she fussed with her hasas.

"I'm far more particular when it comes to my friends."

A frown crowded out the terror in her eyes. "More particular than what?"

He winked. "Than when it comes to my women."

She looked down, smiling and shaking her head. He heard her mutter some kind of curse. As he clambered from the tent she pinched his buttocks hard enough to make him howl.

Wrapping an arm around her waist, Achamian led Esmenet to Xinemus, who stood chatting with Bloody Dinch. When he introduced her, Xinemus merely offered her a perfunctory greeting, then pointed to a faint swath of smoke across the eastern horizon. The Fanim, he explained, had infiltrated the mountains and had struck across the highlands. Apparently a large village, a place called Tusam, had been taken unawares during the night and burned to the ground. Proyas wanted to survey the devastation first-hand—with his ranking officers.

The Marshal then left them, bawling orders to his men. Achamian and Esmenet retreated to the fire, where they sat wordlessly, watching long files of Attrempan horsemen pass into the deeper byways of the encampment. He could sense her apprehension, the certainty that she would shame him, but he could find no more words to amuse or comfort her. He could only watch as she watched, feeling excluded in the manner of slaves and cripples.

Then Kellhus joined them, peering as Xinemus had at the eastern horizon.

"So it starts," he said.

"What starts?" Achamian asked.

"The bloodshed."

With something of a bashful air, Achamian introduced Esmenet. He inwardly winced at the coldness of her tone and expression—at the bruising still visible on her cheek. But Kellhus, if he noticed, seemed unconcerned.

"Someone new," he said, smiling warmly. "Neither bearded nor haggard."

"Yet ..." Achamian added.

"I don't get haggard," Esmenet said in mock protest.

They laughed, and afterward Esmenet's hostility seemed to wane.

Serwë arrived shortly afterward, still wrapped in her blanket. From the first, she seemed to regard Esmenet with something between wonder and terror—more so the latter after seeing Esmenet talk rather than simply listen to the men. Achamian found this troubling, but remained certain they would become friends, if only to find respite from the masculine clamour that characterized their nights by the fire.

For some reason, he found the camp oppressive and sitting still impossible, so he suggested a trek into the mountains. Kellhus immediately agreed, saying that he'd yet to see the Holy War from afar. "Nothing is understood," he said, "until glimpsed from the heights." Serwë, who'd so often been abandoned throughout the day, was almost embarrassingly delighted to join them. Esmenet seemed happy simply to hold Achamian's hand.

The stout mountains of the Unaras Spur loomed large against azure skies, curving like a row of ancient molars toward the horizon. They searched all morning for a vantage that would let them see the Holy War entire, but the jumbled slopes confounded them, and the farther they walked, the more it seemed they could see only the outskirts of the vast encampment, hazed by the smoke of innumerable fires. They encountered several mounted patrols, who warned them of Fanim scouting parties. A band of Conriyan horsemen commanded by one of Xinemus's kinsmen insisted on providing an armed escort, but Kellhus ordered them away, invoking his status as an Inrithi Prince.

When Esmenet asked whether this was wise given the danger, Kellhus said only, "We walk with a Mandate Schoolman."

True enough, she supposed, but all this renewed talk of the heathen had unnerved her, reminded her the Holy War didn't march against abstractions. She found herself glancing to the east more and more often, as though expecting the heights they climbed to reveal the smouldering remains of Tusam.

How long had it been since she'd last sat in her window in Sumna? How long had she'd been walking?

Walking. The city whores called those who followed the Columns *peneditari*, the "long-walkers," a word that often became *pembeditari*, the "scratchers," because many believed camp-whores carried various infestations. Depending on who was asked, peneditari were either as worldly and thus as admirable as caste-noble courtesans, or as polluted and thus as despicable as the beggar-whores who laid with lepers. The truth, Esmenet would discover, lay somewhere in between.

She certainly felt like a peneditari. Never had she walked so much or so far. Even the nights, which she'd spent on her back or her knees, it seemed she'd walked, following a great army of capricious cocks and accusing eyes. Never had she pleasured so many men. Their ghosts still toiled upon her when she awoke in the morning. She would gather her things, join the march, and it would feel as though she fled rather than followed.

Even still, she'd found time to wonder, to learn. She studied the changing character of the lands they passed through. She watched her skin darken, her stomach flatten, her legs harden with muscle. She learned a smattering of Galeoth, enough to shock and delight her patrons. She taught herself how to swim by watching children thrashing in a canal. To be encompassed by cool water. To float!

To be cleansed all at once.

But every night was the same. The slap of pale loins, the crush of sunburned arms, the threats, the arguments, even the jokes she and the other whores shared about the fire—these things, it seemed, were *flattening* her, pounding her into a shape she could never fit into her previous life. As never before, she dreamed of faces, leering and whiskered.

Then, just the previous night, she had heard someone shouting her name. She whirled, surprised perhaps, but incredulous as well, thinking she'd misheard. Then she saw Achamian, obviously drunk, scuffling with a hulking Thunyeri.

She tried to flee, but she couldn't move. She could only watch, breathless, as the warrior threw him to the ground. She screamed when the boot came down, but she still couldn't move. Only when he pulled himself sobbing to his knees, cried out her name.

She ran to him—What choice did she have? In all the world, he had only her—*only her!* The outrage she'd thought she would feel was nowhere to be found. Instead, his touch, his smell, had exacted an almost perilous vulnerability, a sense of submission unlike any she'd ever known—and it was *good.* Sweet Sejenus, was it good! Like the small circle of a child's embrace, or the taste of peppered meat after a long hunger. It was like floating in cool, cleansing water.

No burdens, only flashing sunlight and slow-waving limbs, the smell of green ...

Now she was no longer peneditari; she was what the Galeoth called *"im hustwarra,"* a camp-wife. Now, at long last, she belonged to Drusas Achamian. At long last she was clean.

I could go to temple, she thought.

Esmenet had told him nothing of Sarcellus, nothing of that mad night in Sumna, nothing of what she suspected regarding Inrau. To speak of one, it seemed, would compel her to speak of the others. Instead, she said she'd left Sumna out of love for him, and that she'd joined the camp-followers after he'd repudiated her outside Momemn.

What could she do? *Risk everything* now that they'd found each other? Besides, she *had* left Sumna for him; she *had* joined the camp-followers because of him. Silence did not contradict truth.

Perhaps, if he'd been the same Achamian who had left her in Sumna ...

Achamian had always been ... weak, but it was a weakness born of honesty. Where other men became silent and remote, he spoke, and this gave him a curious kind of strength, one which set him apart from nearly every man Esmenet had known, and many women. But he was different now. More desperate.

In Sumna, she'd often accused him of resembling the madmen in the Ecosium Market who continually howled about iniquity and doom. Whenever they passed one, she'd say, "Look, another of your friends," just as he'd say, "Look, another one of your customers" when they glimpsed some dreadfully obese man. Now, she wouldn't dare. Achamian was still Achamian, but he'd acquired the same hollow, spent look of those madmen, the same stooped eyes, as though he perpetually watched some horror that walked between what everyone else could see.

What he said terrified her, of course—How couldn't she believe him?—but what terrified her more was the *way* he said it: the rambling, the erratic laughter, the spiteful vehemence, the bottomless remorse.

He was going mad. She knew this in her bones. But it wasn't, she understood, the discovery of the Consult, nor even the certainty of the

Second Apocalypse, that was breaking him, it was this man ... this Anasûrimbor Kellhus.

Such a stubborn fool! Why wouldn't he yield him to the Mandate? If Achamian weren't already a sorcerer, she'd say he'd been bewitched. No arguments would sway him. Nothing!

According to Achamian, women had no instinct for principle. For them everything was embodied ... How had he put it? Oh yes, that *existence preceded essence* for women. By nature, the tracks travelled by their souls ran parallel to those demanded by principle. The feminine soul was more yielding, more compassionate, more nurturing than the masculine. Consequently, principle became more difficult for them to see, like a staff in a thicket, which was why women were more likely to confuse selfishness for propriety—which, apparently, was what she was doing.

But for *men*, whose inclinations ranged so far and so violently, principle was an ever-present burden, a yoke they either toiled under or cast off altogether. Unlike women, men could always see what they *should* do, because it differed so drastically from what they *wanted*.

At first, Esmenet had almost believed him. How else could she explain his willingness to risk their love?

But then she realized it was *the principle that galled her*, not some dim-witted feminine confusion of hope and piety. Had she not given herself to him? Had she not relinquished her life, her talent?

Had she not finally relented?

And what was she asking him to relinquish in return? A man he'd known but a few weeks—a stranger! A man, moreover, that according to his own principles, he *should* surrender. "Perhaps yours is the womanish soul!" she'd wanted to cry. But for some reason, she couldn't. If men must spare women the world, then women must spare men the truth—as though each forever remained alternate halves of the same defenceless child.

Esmenet paused for breath, watched Achamian and Kellhus exchange some comment—something inaudible and humorous. Achamian laughed aloud. *I must show him. Somehow I must show him!*

Even when one floated, there was always a current ...

Always something to fight.

Serwë walked at her side, every so often casting nervous glances her way. Esmenet said nothing, though she knew the girl wanted to talk. She seemed harmless enough, given the circumstances. She was one of those rare women who could never be deflowered, never be despoiled. Had she been a fellow whore in Sumna, Esmenet would have secretly despised her. She would have resented her beauty, her youth, her blond hair, and her pale skin, but more than anything she would have resented her perpetual vulnerability.

"Akka has—" the girl blurted. She blushed, looked down to her feet. "Achamian's been teaching Kellhus wondrous things—*wondrous* things!"

Even her endearing accent. Resentment was ever the secret liquor of harlots.

Staring at nothing on the southern horizon, Esmenet said, "He has, has he?"

Perhaps that was the problem. Achamian had offered Kellhus the sanctuary of his instruction *before* he learned of the Consult skin-spies, which was to say, before he knew with certainty the man was the Harbinger—if he was in fact the Harbinger. Perhaps that was the obscure principle Achamian referred to, the bond ... Kellhus was *his student*, like Proyas or Inrau.

The thought made Esmenet want to spit.

Without warning, Serwë sprinted ahead, leaping over hummocks and through braces of weeds. "The flowers!" she cried. "They're so beautiful!"

Esmenet joined Achamian and Kellhus where they stood watching her. Several paces away, the girl kneeled before a bush freighted with extraordinary turquoise blooms.

"Ah," Achamian said, moving to join her, "*pemembis* ... Have you never seen them before?"

"Never," Serwë gasped.

Esmenet thought she could smell lilac.

"Never?" Achamian said, plucking a flower of his own. He glanced back at Esmenet, winked. "You mean you've never heard the legends?"

Esmenet waited next to Kellhus as Achamian related his story: something about an empress and her bloodthirsty paramours. Several uncomfortable moments passed. The man was tall, even for a Norsirai, and he possessed those muscular, long-armed proportions that would have sparked uncouth speculation among her old friends in Sumna. His eyes were striking blue, possessed of a clarity that recalled Achamian's stories of ancient northern kings. And there was something about his manner, a grace that didn't seem quite … earthly.

"So you lived among the Scylvendi?" she finally said.

Kellhus glanced at her as though at a distraction, then looked back to Serwë and Achamian. "For a time, yes."

"Tell me something about them."

"Such as …"

She shrugged. "Tell me about their scars … Are they trophies?"

Kellhus smiled, shook his head. "No."

"Then what are they?"

"That's not an easy question to answer … The Scylvendi believe only in actions, though they'd never say such. For them, only what men *do* is real. All else is smoke. They even call life *'syurtpiütha,'* or 'the smoke that moves.' For them a man's life isn't a *thing*, something that can be owned or exchanged, but rather a line or a track of actions. A man's line can be braided into one's own, as in the case of one's fellow tribesmen; herded, as in the case of slaves; or it can be stopped, as in the case of killing or murder. Since this latter is the action which *ends* action, the Scylvendi see it as the most significant, the most real, of all actions. The cornerstone of honour.

"But the scars, or swazond, don't *celebrate* the taking of life, as everyone in the Three Seas seems to assume. They mark the … intersection, you might say, between competing lines of action, the point where one life yields its momentum to another. The fact that Cnaiür, for instance, bears the scars of many means that he walks with the *momentum* of many. His swazond are far more than his trophies, they're the record of his reality. Seen through Scylvendi eyes, he's the single stone that has become an avalanche."

Esmenet stared in wonder. "But I thought the Scylvendi were uncouth … barbarians. Surely such beliefs are too subtle!"

Kellhus laughed. "All beliefs are too subtle." He held her with shining blue eyes. "And 'barbarity,' I fear, is simply a word for unfamiliarity that threatens."

Unsettled, Esmenet looked to the grasses thronging about her sandalled feet. She glanced at Achamian, saw him watching her from where he and Serwë crouched. He smiled knowingly, then continued expounding on the bobbing flowers.

He knew this would happen.

Then, from nowhere, Kellhus said, "So you were a whore."

She looked up in shock, reflexively covered the tattoo on the back of her left hand. "And what if I was?"

Kellhus shrugged. "Tell me something ..."

"Such as?" she snapped.

"What was it like, lying with men you didn't know?"

She *wanted* to be outraged, but there was a compelling innocence to his manner, a candour that left her baffled—and willing.

"Nice ... sometimes," she said. "Other times, unbearable. But one must feed to be fed. That's simply the way of things."

"No," Kellhus replied. "I asked you to tell me what it was *like* ..."

She cleared her throat, looked away in embarrassment. She saw Achamian brush Serwë's fingers, suppressed a pang of jealousy. She laughed nervously.

"Such a strange question ..."

"Have you never asked it?"

"No ... I mean yes, of course, but ..."

"So what was your answer?"

She paused, flustered, frightened, and curiously thrilled.

"Sometimes, after a heavy rain, the street beneath my window would be rutted by the wains, and I would ... I would watch them—the wheels creaking through the ruts—and I would think, *that's* what my life is like ..."

"A track worn by others."

Esmenet nodded, blinked away two tears.

"And other times?"

"Whores are mummers—you must understand that. We *perform* ..." She hesitated, searched his eyes as though they held the proper words. "I know the Tusk says we degrade ourselves, that we abuse the divinity of our sex ... and sometimes it feels that way. But not always ... Often, very often, I have these men upon me, these men who gasp like fish, thinking they've mastered me, *notched* me, and I feel pity for them—for *them*, not me. I become more ... more *thief* than whore. Fooling, duping, watching myself as though reflected across silver ... It feels like ... like ..."

"Like being free," Kellhus said.

Esmenet both smiled and frowned, troubled by the intimacy of the details she'd revealed, shocked by the poetry of her own insight, and somehow curiously relieved, as though she'd discharged a great burden. She almost trembled. And Kellhus seemed so ... *near*.

"Yes ..." She tried to swallow away the quaver in her voice. "But how—"

"So we've learned about holy pemembis," Achamian said, joining them with Serwë. "What have you learned?" He shot Esmenet a significant glance.

"What it's like to be who we are," Kellhus said.

Sometimes, though not often, Achamian would scan the distances and simply *know* that he'd walked the same or similar path two thousand years before. He would freeze, as though glimpsing a lion in the brush, and just look about in witless astonishment. It was a recognition that baffled, a knowing that could not be.

Seswatha had walked these same hills once, fleeing besieged Asgilioch, searching with a hundred other refugees for a way through the mountains, for a way to escape dread Tsuramah. Achamian found himself glancing over his shoulder, always northward, expecting to see black clouds massing on the horizon. He found himself clutching wounds he didn't have, blinking away images of a battle he hadn't fought: the Kyranean defeat at Mehsarunath. He found himself walking as though an automaton, gouged of all hope, of all aspiration save survival.

At some point Seswatha had abandoned the others to wander alone among the windswept rocks. Somewhere, not far, he'd found a small, shaded grotto, where he curled like a dog, hugging his knees, shrieking, wailing, imploring death ... When morning came, he had cursed the Gods for drawing breath.

Achamian found himself glancing at Kellhus, his hands shaking, his every thought turmoil.

Concerned, Esmenet asked him what was wrong.

"Nothing," he muttered brusquely.

She smiled, squeezed his hand as though she trusted him. But she knew. Twice he caught her casting terrified glances at the Prince of Atrithau.

As the afternoon waxed, Achamian slowly recollected himself. The farther they wandered from Seswatha's footsteps, it seemed, the more he could pretend. Without realizing, he'd led the others too far to return to the Holy War before dark, so he suggested they find a place to camp.

The mountain faces mellowed against violet clouds. As evening approached, they spied a stand of blooming ironwoods perched on a squat promontory. They hiked toward them, climbing the furrowed skirts of the mountain. Kellhus noticed the ruins first: the heaped remains of an old Inrithi chapel.

"Some kind of shrine?" Achamian asked no one in particular as they waded across scrub and grasses toward the foundations. The stand, he realized, was in fact an overgrown grove. The ironwoods stood in rows, their dark limbs knitted in purple and white, waving in the warm evening breeze.

They picked their way through blocks of stone, then clambered over the heaped walls, where they found a mosaic floor depicting Inri Sejenus, his head buried in debris, his two haloed hands outstretched. For a time all four of them simply milled about, exploring, trampling paths through the thronging weeds, wondering, Achamian supposed, at all that had been forgotten.

"No ash," Kellhus noted, after kicking at sandy earth. "It's as though the place simply fell in upon itself."

"So beautiful," Serwë said. "How could anyone let this happen?"

"After Gedea was lost to the Fanim," Achamian explained, "the Nansur abandoned these lands ... Too vulnerable to raids, I suppose ... Ruins like this probably dot the entire range."

They gathered dead scrub, and Achamian ignited their fire with a sorcerous word, realizing only afterward that he'd set the Latter Prophet's stomach aflame. Seated upon blocks on either side of the image, they continued talking, the firelight brightening in proportion to the gathering dark.

They drank unwatered wine, ate bread, leeks, and salted pork. Achamian translated those passages of text visible across the mosaic.

"The Marrucees," he said, studying a stylized seal written in High Sheyic. "This place once belonged to the Marrucees, an old College of the Thousand Temples ... If I remember aright, they were destroyed when the Fanim took Shimeh ... That means this place was abandoned long before the fall of Gedea."

Kellhus followed up with several questions regarding the Colleges—of course. Since Esmenet knew the ecclesiastical labyrinths of the Thousand Temples far better than he, Achamian let her answer. She had, after all, bedded priests from every college, sect, and cult imaginable ...

Fucked them.

He studied the pinch of sandal straps across his feet as he listened. He needed new ones, he realized. A profound sorrow seized him then, the hapless sorrow of a man persecuted by even the smallest of things. Where would he find sandals in the midst of this madness?

He excused himself, wandered into the collapsed byways beyond the fire.

He sat for a time at the ruin's edge, where the debris tumbled into the grove. All was black beneath the ironwoods, but their blooming crowns seemed otherworldly in the moonlight, slowly rocking to and fro in the breeze. The bittersweet scent reminded him of Xinemus's orchards.

"Moping again?" he heard Esmenet say from behind him.

He turned and saw her standing in gloom, painted in the same pale tones as the surrounding ruin. He wondered that night could make stone resemble skin and skin resemble stone. Then she was in his arms, kissing him, tugging at his linen robes. He pressed her backward, leaned her onto a cracked altar, his hands roaming across her thighs and buttocks. She groped for his cock, clutched it with both hands. They joined fires.

Afterward, brushing away grit from skin and clothes, they grinned knowing, shy grins.

"So what do you think?" Achamian asked.

Esmenet made a noise, something between a laugh and a sigh.

"Nothing," she said. "Nothing as tender, as wanton or delicious. Nothing as enchanted as this place ..."

"I meant Kellhus."

A flash of anger. "Is there nothing else you think about?"

His throat tightened. "How can I?"

She became remote and impenetrable. Serwë's laughter chimed across the ruins, and he found himself wondering what Kellhus had said.

"He *is* remarkable," Esmenet murmured, refusing to look at him.

So what should I do? Achamian wanted to cry.

Instead, he remained silent, tried to throttle the roar of inner voices.

"We *do* have each other," she suddenly said. "Don't we, Akka?"

"Of course we do. But what does—"

"What does anything matter, so long as we have each other?"

Always interrupting ...

"Sweet Sejenus, woman, *he's the Harbinger*."

"But we could flee! From the Mandate. From *him*. We could hide, just the two of us!"

"But Esmi ... The burden—"

"Isn't ours!" she hissed. "Why should *we* suffer it? Let's run away! Please, Akka! Leave all this madness behind!"

"This is foolishness, Esmenet. There's no hiding from the end of the world! Even if we could, I'd be a sorcerer without a school—a *wizard*, Esmi. Better to be a witch! They would hunt me. *All of them*, not just the Mandate. The Schools tolerate no wizards ..." He laughed bitterly. "We wouldn't even survive to be killed."

"But this is the *first time*," she said, her voice breaking. "The first time I've ever ..."

Something—the desolate stoop of her shoulders, perhaps, or the way she pressed her hands together, wrist to wrist—moved Achamian to hold her. But a panicked cry halted him. Serwë.

"Kellhus bids you come quickly!" she called from the dark. "There's torches in the distance! Riders!"

Achamian scowled. "Who'd be fool enough to ride mountain slopes at night?"

Esmenet didn't answer. She didn't need to ...

Fanim.

Esmenet cursed herself for a fool as they picked their way through the dark. Kellhus had kicked out their fire, transforming the mosaic of the

Latter Prophet into a constellation of scattered coals. They hastened across it, joined him on the grasses beyond the heaped debris.

"Look," the Prince of Atrithau said, pointing down the slopes.

If Achamian's words had winded her, then what she saw robbed her of all remaining breath. Strings of torches wound through the darkness below, following the mighty ramps of earth that composed the only approach to the ruined shrine. Hundreds of glittering points. Heathen, come to gut them. Or worse …

"They'll be upon us soon," Kellhus said.

Esmenet struggled with a sudden, panting terror. Anything could happen—even with men such as Achamian and Kellhus! The world was exceedingly cruel. "Perhaps if we hide …"

"They know we're here," Kellhus muttered. "Our fire. They followed our fire."

"Then we must see," Achamian said.

Shocked by his tone, Esmenet glanced in his direction, only to find herself stumbling backward in terror. White light flashed from his eyes and mouth, and words seemed to rumble down like thunder from the mountain faces. Then a line appeared from the earth between his outstretched arms, so brilliant she raised hands against its glare. It flashed upward, more perfect than any geometer's rule, taller than the brooding Unaras, striking through and illuminating clouds, on into the endless black …

The Bar of Heaven! she thought—a Cant from his stories of the First Apocalypse.

Shadows leapt across the far precipices. The tumbling landscape winked into existence as though exposed by a lightning flash. And Esmenet saw armoured horsemen, an entire column of them, shouting in alarm and struggling with their horses. She glimpsed astonished faces …

"Hold!" Kellhus shouted. "Hold!"

The light went out. Blackness.

"They're Galeoth," Kellhus said, placing a firm hand on her shoulder. "Men of the Tusk."

Esmenet blinked, clutched her breast. For among the riders, she'd seen Sarcellus.

A resonant voice shouted across the darkness: "We search for the Prince of Atrithau! Anasûrimbor Kellhus!"

The many-coloured tones were unknitted, combed into individual threads: sincerity, worry, outrage, hope ... And Kellhus knew there was no danger.

He's come for my counsel.

"Prince Saubon!" Kellhus called. "Come! The faithful are always welcome at our fire!"

"And sorcerers?" another voice cried. "Are blasphemers welcome as well?"

The indignation and sarcasm were plain, but the undertones defeated him. Who spoke? A Nansur, from Massentia perhaps, though his accent was strangely difficult to place. A hereditary caste-noble, with rank enough to ride with a prince ... One of the Emperor's generals?

"Indeed they are," Kellhus called back, "when they serve the faithful!"

"Forgive my friend!" Saubon shouted, laughing. "I fear he brought only one pair of breeches!" Hearty Galeoth cheer resounded across the slopes: laughter, catcalls, friendly jeers.

"What do they want?" Achamian asked in low tones. Even in the gloom, Kellhus could see the lines of recent pain through his present apprehension—remnants of some argument with Esmenet.

About him.

"Who knows?" Kellhus said. "At the Council, Saubon was first among those urging the others to march without the Ainoni and the Scarlet Spires. Perhaps with Proyas afield, he seeks further mischief ..."

Achamian shook his head. "He argued that the destruction of Ruöm threatened to demoralize the Men of the Tusk," the sorcerer amended. "Xinemus told me that *you* were the one who silenced him ... By reinterpreting the portent of the earthquake."

"You think he seeks reprisal?" Kellhus asked.

But it was too late. More and more horsemen were rumbling to a stop in the moonlight, dismounting, stretching weary limbs. Saubon and his entourage trotted toward them, flanked by torch-bearers. The Galeoth Prince reined his caparisoned charger to a halt, his eyes hidden in the shadows of his brow.

Kellhus lowered his head to the degree required by jnan—a bow between princes.

"We tracked you all afternoon," Saubon said, jumping from his saddle. He stood almost as tall as Kellhus, though slightly broader through the chest and shoulders. Like his men, he was geared for battle, wearing not only his chain hauberk, but his helm and gauntlets as well. A hasty Tusk had been stitched beneath the Red Lion embroidered across his surcoat—the mark of the Galeoth Royal House.

"And who is 'we'?" Kellhus asked, peering at the man's fellow riders.

Saubon made several introductions, starting with his grizzled groom, Kussalt, but Kellhus spared them little more than a cursory glance. The lone Shrial Knight, whom the Prince introduced as Cutias Sarcellus, dominated his attention ...

Another one. Another Skeaös ...

"At last," Sarcellus said. His large eyes glittered through the fingers of his fraudulent face. "The renowned Prince of Atrithau."

He bowed lower than his rank demanded.

What does this mean, Father?

So many variables.

After stationing pickets and dispersing his men about the edges of the grove, Saubon, along with his groom and the Shrial Knight, joined their fire in the ruined chapel's heart. Following the custom of the southern courts, the Galeoth Prince avoided all talk of his purpose, scrupulously awaiting what practitioners of jnan called the *memponti*, the "fortuitous turn" that would of its own accord lead to weightier matters. Saubon, Kellhus knew, thought the ways of his own people rude. With every breath he waged war with who he was.

But it was the Shrial Knight, Sarcellus, who commanded Kellhus's attention—and not just because of his missing face. Achamian had smoothed the shock from his expression, yet an apprehensive fury animated his eyes each time he looked at the Knight of the Tusk. Achamian not only recognized Sarcellus, Kellhus realized, he hated him. The Dûnyain monk could fairly *hear* movements of Achamian's soul: the seething resentment for some past slight, the wincing memories of being struck, the remorse ...

In Sumna, Kellhus realized, recalling to the last detail Achamian's every reference to his previous mission. *Something happened between him and Sarcellus in Sumna. Something involving Inrau ...*

Despite his hatred, the sorcerer obviously had no inkling that Sarcellus was another Skeaös ... Another Consult skin-spy.

And neither did Esmenet, though her reaction far eclipsed Achamian's. Shame. The fear of discovery. The treacherous hope ... *She thinks he's come to take her ... Take her from Achamian.*

She'd been the thing's lover.

But these mysteries paled before the greater question: What was it doing here? Not just in the Holy War, but *here*, this night, riding at Saubon's side ...

"How did you find us?" Achamian was asking.

Saubon ran fingers through his close-cropped hair.

"My friend, Sarcellus, here. He has an uncanny ability to track ..." He turned to the Knight-Commander. "How did you say you learned?"

"As a youth," Sarcellus lied, "on my father's western estates"—he pursed his lusty lips, as though restraining a smile—"tracking Scylvendi ..."

"Tracking *Scylvendi*," Saubon repeated, as though to say, *Only in the Nansurium* ... "I was ready to turn back at dusk, but he insisted you were near." Saubon opened his hands and shrugged.

Silence.

Esmenet sat rigid, covering her tattooed hand the way others might avoid smiling to conceal bad teeth. Achamian glanced at Kellhus, expecting him to brush away the awkwardness. Serwë, sensing the undercurrent of anxiety, clutched his thigh. The faceless beast stared into its bowl of wine.

Ordinarily, Kellhus would've said something. But for the moment he could provide little more than rote responses. His eyes watched, but they didn't focus. His expression merely mirrored those surrounding him. Self had vanished into *place*, a place of opening, where permutation after permutation was hunted to its merciless conclusion. Consequence and effect. Events like concentric ripples unfolding across the black waters of the future ... Each word, each look, a stone.

There was great peril here. The principles of this encounter had to be grasped. Only the Logos could illuminate the path ... Only the Logos.

"I followed your smell," Sarcellus was saying. He stared directly at Achamian, his eyes glittering with something incomprehensible. Humour?

The joke, Kellhus decided, was that this was no joke: the thing had tracked them like a dog. He needed to be exceedingly wary of these creatures. As of yet, he had no idea of their capabilities. *Do you know of these things, Father?*

Everything had transformed since he'd taken Drusas Achamian as his teacher. The ground of this world, he now knew, had concealed many, many secrets from his brethren. The Logos remained true, but its ways were far more devious, and far more spectacular, than the Dûnyain had ever conceived. And the Absolute ... the End of Ends was more distant than they'd ever imagined. So many obstacles. So many forks in the path ...

Despite his initial scepticism, Kellhus had come to believe much of what Achamian had claimed over the course of their discussions. He believed the stories of the First Apocalypse. He believed the faceless thing before him was an artifact of the Consult. But the Celmomian Prophecy? The coming of a Second Apocalypse? Such things were absurd. By definition, the future couldn't anticipate the present. What came after couldn't come before ...

Could it?

There was so much that must await his father ... So many questions.

His ignorance had already culminated in near disaster. The mere exchange of glances in the Emperor's Privy Garden had triggered several small catastrophes, including the events beneath the Andiamine Heights, which had convinced Achamian that Kellhus was in fact the Harbinger. If the man decided to tell his School that an Anasûrimbor had returned ...

There was great peril here.

Drusas Achamian had to remain ignorant—that much was certain. If he knew that Kellhus could *see* the very skin-spies that so terrified him, he wouldn't hesitate to contact his masters in Atyersus. So much depended on him remaining estranged from his School—isolated.

Which meant Kellhus must confront these things on his own.

"My groom," Saubon was saying to the Shrial Knight, "swears nothing short of sorcery led you to this place ... Kussalt fancies himself quite the tracker."

Did the Consult somehow *know* he'd revealed Skeaös in the Emperor's court? The Emperor had seen him studying his Prime Counsel, and more importantly, he'd remembered. Several times now, Kellhus had seen Imperial spies watching from a discreet distance, following. It was possible the Consult knew how Skeaös had been uncovered, perhaps even probable.

If they did know, then this Sarcellus could very well be a probe. They would need to discover whether Skeaös's unmasking had been an accident of the Emperor's paranoia, or whether this stranger from Atrithau had somehow *seen through his face.* They would watch him, ask discreet questions, and when this provided no answers, they would make contact ... Wouldn't they?

But there was also Achamian to consider. Doubtless the Consult would keep close watch on Mandate Schoolmen, the only individuals who believed they still existed. Sarcellus and Achamian had made contact before, both directly, as evident from the sorcerer's reaction, and indirectly via Esmenet, who obviously had been seduced at some point in the past. They were using her for some reason ... Perhaps they were testing *her,* sounding her capacity for deceit and treachery. She'd told Achamian nothing of Sarcellus; that much was apparent.

The study is so deep, Father.

A thousand possibilities, galloping across the trackless steppe of what was to come. A hundred scenarios flashing through his soul, some branching and branching, terminally deflected from his objectives, others flaring out in disaster ...

Direct confrontation. Accusations levelled before the Great Names. Acclaim for revealing the horror within. Mandate involvement. Open war with the Consult ... Unworkable. The Mandate couldn't be involved until they could be dominated. War against the Consult couldn't be risked. Not yet.

Indirect confrontation. Forays into the night. Throats cut. Attempted reprisals. A hidden war gradually revealed ... Also unworkable. If Sarcellus and the others were murdered, the Consult would know someone could see them. When they learned the details of Skeaös's discovery, if they hadn't already, they would realize it was Kellhus, and indirect confrontation would become open war.

Inaction. Watchful enemies. Appraisal. Sterile probes. Second guessing. Responses delayed by the need to know. Worry in the shadow of growing power ... Workable. Even if they learned the details surrounding Skeaös's discovery, the Consult would only have *suspicions*. If what Achamian claimed was true, they weren't so crude as to blot out potential threats without first *understanding* them. Confrontation was inevitable. The outcome depended only on how much time he had to prepare ...

He was one of the Conditioned, Dûnyain. Circumstances would yield. The mission must—

"*Kellhus*," Serwë was saying. "The Prince has asked you a question."

Kellhus blinked, smiled as though at his own foolishness. Without exception, everyone about the fire stared at him, some concerned, some puzzled.

"I'm-I'm sorry," he stammered. "I ..." He glanced nervously from watcher to watcher, exhaled, as though reconciling himself to his principles, no matter how embarrassing. "Sometimes I ... I *see* things ..."

Silence.

"Me too," Sarcellus said scathingly. "Though usually when my eyes are open."

Had he closed his eyes? He had no recollection of it. If so, it would be a troubling lapse. Not since—

"*Idiot*," Saubon snapped, turning to the Shrial Knight. "Fool! We sit about the man's fire and you *insult* him?"

"The Knight-Commander has caused no offence," Kellhus said. "You forget, Prince, that he's as much priest as warrior, and we've asked him to share a fire with a sorcerer ... It's like asking a midwife to break bread with a leper, isn't it?" A moment of nervous laughter, over-loud and over-brief. "No doubt," Kellhus added, "he's simply out of temper."

"No doubt," Sarcellus repeated. A mocking smile, bottomless, like all his expressions.

What does it want?

"Which begs the question," Kellhus continued, effortlessly grasping the "fortuitous turn" that had so far eluded Prince Saubon. "What brings a Shrial Knight to a sorcerer's fire?"

"I was sent by Gotian," Sarcellus said, "my Grandmaster ..." He glanced at Saubon, who watched stonefaced. "The Shrial Knights have sworn to be among the first who set foot upon heathen ground, and Prince Saubon proposes—"

But Saubon interrupted, blurting, "I would speak to you of this alone, Prince Kellhus."

———— ∞ ————

What would you have me do, Father?

So many possibilities. Incalculable possibilities.

Kellhus followed Saubon through the dark lanes of the ironwood grove. They paused at the edge of the cliff and looked out over the moonlit reaches of the Inûnara Highlands. Clear of the hissing leaves, the wind buffeted them. The long fall below was littered with fallen trees. Dead roots reached skyward. Some of the fallen still brandished great sockets of earth, like dusty fists raised against the survivors.

"You *do* see things, don't you?" Saubon finally said. "I mean, you *dreamed* of this Holy War from Atrithau."

Kellhus enclosed him in the circle of his senses. Heart rate. Blush reflex. The orbital muscles ringing his eyes ... *He fears me.*

"Why do you ask?"

"Because Proyas is a stubborn fool. Because those first to plate are those first to feast!"

The Prince of Galeoth was both daring and impatient. Though he appreciated subtlety, he preferred bold strokes in the end.

"You wish to march immediately," Kellhus said.

Saubon grimaced in the dark. "I would be in Gedea now," he snapped, "if it weren't for you!"

He spoke of the recent Council, where Kellhus's reinterpretation of Ruöm's destruction had amputated his arguments. But his resentment, Kellhus could see, was hollow. Though ruthless and mercenary, Coithus Saubon was not petty.

"Then why come to me now?"

"Because what you said ... about the God burning our ships ... It had the ring of truth."

He was a watcher of men, Kellhus realized, someone who continually measured. His whole life he'd thought himself a shrewd judge of character, prided himself on his honesty, his ability to punish flattery and reward criticism. But with Kellhus ... He had no yardstick, no carpenter's string. *He's told himself I'm a seer of some kind. But he fears I'm more ...*

"And that's what you seek? The truth?"

Though mercenary, Saubon did possess a kind of practical piety. For him faith was a game—a very serious game. Where other men begged and called it "prayer," he negotiated, haggled. By coming here, he thought he was giving the Gods their due ...

He's terrified of making a mistake. The Whore has given him but one chance.

"I need to know what you see!" the man cried. "I've fought many campaigns—all of them for my wretched father! I'm no fool when it comes to the field of war. I don't think I'd march into a Fanim tra—"

"But recall what Cnaiür said at Council," Kellhus interrupted. "The Fanim fight from horseback. They'd bring the trap to you. And remember the Cishaur—"

"Pfah! My nephew scouts Gedea as we speak, sends me messages daily. There's no Fanim host lurking in the shadow of these mountains. These skirmishers that Proyas chases are meant to fool us, delay us while the heathen gathers his might. Skauras is canny enough to know when he's overmatched. He's retreated to Shigek, barricaded himself in his cities on the Sempis, where he awaits the Padirajah and the Grandees of Kian. He's ceded Gedea to whoever has the courage to seize it!"

The Galeoth Prince clearly believed what he said, but could he *be* believed? His argument seemed sober enough. And Proyas himself had expressed nothing but respect for the man's martial acumen. Saubon had even fought Ikurei Conphas to a standstill just a few years previous ...

Cataracts of possibility. There was opportunity here ... And perhaps Sarcellus need not be confronted to be destroyed. But still.

I know so little of war. Too little ...

"So you *hope*." Kellhus said. "Skauras could—"

"So I *know!*"

"Then what does it matter, whether I sanction you or not? Truth is truth, regardless of who speaks it ..."

Desperation. "I ask only for your counsel, for what you see ... Nothing more."

Slackness about the eyes. Shortness of breath. Deadened timbre. *Another lie.*

"But I see many things ..." Kellhus said.

"Then tell me!"

Kellhus shook his head. "Only rarely do I glimpse the future. The hearts of men   *that is what they* ..." He paused, glanced nervously down the sheer drop, to the bleach-bone trees scattered and broken below. "That is what I'm moved to see."

Saubon had become guarded. "Then tell me ... What do you see in *my* heart?"

Expose him. Strip him of every lie, every pretense. When the shame passes ...

Kellhus held the man's eyes for a forlorn instant.

... he will think it proper to stand naked before me.

"A man and a child," Kellhus said, weaving deeper harmonics into his voice, transforming it into something palpable. "I see a man and a child ... The man is harrowed by the distance between the trappings of power and the impotence of his birthright. He would force what fate has denied him, and so, day by day lives in the midst of what he does not possess. *Avarice*, Saubon ... Not for gold, but for *witness*. Greed for the testimony of men—for them to look and say '*Here*, here is a King by his own hand!'"

Kellhus stared into the giddy void at his feet, his eyes glassy with the tumult of inner mysteries ...

Saubon watched with horror. "And the child? You said there was a child!"

"Cringes still beneath a father's hand. Awakens in the night and cries out, not for witness, but to be *known* ... No one knows him. No one loves."

Kellhus turned to him, his eyes shining with insight and unearthly compassion. "I could go on ..."

"No-no," Saubon stammered, as though waking from a trance. "Cease. That's enough ..."

But what was enough? Saubon yearned for pretexts; what would he give in return? When the variables were so many, everything was risk. Everything.

What if I choose wrong, Father?

"Did you hear that?" Kellhus cried, turning to Saubon in sudden terror.

The Galeoth Prince jumped back from the cliff's edge. "Hear what?"

Truth begat truth, even when it was a lie.

Kellhus swayed, staggered. Saubon leapt forward, pulled him from the long fall.

"*March,*" Kellhus gasped, close enough to kiss. "The Whore *will* be kind to you … But you must make certain the Shrial Knights are …" He opened his eyes in stunned wonder—as though to say, *This couldn't be their message!*

Some destinations couldn't be grasped in advance. Some paths had to be walked to be known. Risked.

"You must make certain the Shrial Knights are *punished.*"

With Kellhus and Saubon gone, Esmenet sat silently, staring into the fire, studying the mosaic image of the Latter Prophet reaching out beneath their feet. She pulled her toes from the circle of a haloed hand. It seemed sacrilege that they should trod upon him …

But then what did she care? She was damned. Never had that seemed more obvious than now.

Sarcellus here!

Affliction upon affliction. Why did the Gods hate her so? Why were they so cruel?

Resplendent in his silvered mail and white surcoat, Sarcellus chatted amiably with Serwë about Kellhus, asking where he came from, how they first met, and so on. Serwë basked in his attention; it was plain from her answers that she more than adored the Prince of Atrithau. She spoke as though she didn't exist outside her bond to him. Achamian watched, though for some reason it seemed he didn't listen.

Oh, Akka … Why do I know I'm going to lose you?

Not fear, *know*. Such was the cruelty of this world!

Murmuring excuses, Esmenet stood, then with slow, measured steps, fled from the fire.

Enfolded by darkness, she stopped, plopped down on the ruined stump of a pillar. The sounds of Saubon's men permeated the night: the rhythmic thwack of axes, deep-throated shouts, ribald laughter. Beneath the dark trees, warhorses snorted, stamped the earth.

What have I done? What if Akka finds out?

Looking back the way she'd come, she was shocked to discover she could still see Achamian, dusty orange before the fire. She smiled at the hapless look of him, at the five white streaks of his beard. He seemed to be talking to Serwë ...

Where had Sarcellus gone?

"It must be difficult being a woman in such a place," a voice called from behind her.

Esmenet jumped to her feet and whirled, her heart racing both with dismay and alarm. She saw Sarcellus strolling toward her. Of course ...

"So many pigs," he continued, "and only one trough."

Esmenet swallowed, stood rigid. She made no reply.

"I've seen you before too," he said, playing games with their pretense about the fire. "Haven't I?" He waved a mocking finger.

Deep breath. "No. I'm sure you haven't."

"But yes ... Yes! You're a ... harlot." He smiled winningly. "A *whore*."

Esmenet glanced around. "I have no idea what you're talking about."

"Sorcerers and whores ... It seems oddly appropriate, I suppose. With so many men licking your crotch, I imagine it serves to keep one with a magic tongue."

She struck him, or tried to. Somehow he caught her hand.

"Sarcellus," she whispered. "Sarcellus, please ..."

She felt a fingertip trace an impossible line along her inner thigh.

"Like I said," he muttered in a tone her body recognized. "One trough."

She glanced back toward the fire, saw Achamian peering after her with a frown. Of course he could see only blackness, such was the treachery of fire, which illuminated small circles by darkening the entire world. But what Achamian could or could not see did not matter.

"*No, Sarcellus,*" she hissed. "*Not ...*"

... here

"... while I live. Do you understand?"

She could feel the heat of him.

No-no-no-no ...

A different, more resonant voice called out. "Is there a problem?" Whirling, she saw Prince Kellhus stride from the shadows of the nearby grove.

"N-no. Nothing," Esmenet gasped, stunned to find her arm free. "Lord Sarcellus startled me, nothing more."

"She spooks easily," Sarcellus said. "But then most women do."

"You think so?" Kellhus replied, approaching until even Sarcellus had to look up. Kellhus stared at the man, his manner mild, even bemused, but there was an implacable constancy to his look that made Esmenet's heart race, that urged her limbs to run. Had he been listening? Had he heard?

"Perhaps you're right," Sarcellus said in an offhand manner. "Most men spook easy too."

There was a moment of uncomfortable silence. Something clawed at Esmenet to fill it, but she could find no breath to speak.

"I'll leave you two, then," Sarcellus declared. With a shallow bow, he turned and strode back to the fire.

Alone with Kellhus, Esmenet sighed in relief. The hands that had throttled her heart but moments before had vanished. She looked up to Kellhus, glimpsed the Nail of Heaven over his left shoulder. He seemed an apparition of gold and shadow. "Thank you," she whispered.

"You loved him, didn't you?"

Her ears burned. For some reason, saying no never occurred to her. One just didn't lie to Prince Anasûrimbor Kellhus. Instead, she said, "Please don't tell Akka."

Kellhus smiled, though his eyes seemed profoundly sad. He reached out, as though to touch her cheek, then dropped his hand.

"Come," he said. "Night waxes."

Clutching hands with the palm-to-palm urgency of young lovers, Esmenet and Achamian searched through the scrub and grasses for good sleeping ground. They found a flat area near the edge of the grove, not far from the cliff, and rolled out their mats. They laid down, groaning and puffing like an old man and woman. The ironwood nearest them had died some time ago, and it twined across the sky above them, like a thing of alabaster. Through smooth-forking branches, Esmenet studied the constellations, oppressed by the thought of Sarcellus and the angry memory of Achamian's earlier words ...

There's no hiding from the end of the world!

How could she be such a fool? A harlot who would place herself upon *his* scales? He was a Mandate Schoolman. Every night he lost loves greater than she could imagine, let alone *be*. She'd heard his cries. The frantic babbling in unknown tongues. The eyes lost in ancient hallucinations.

She knew this! How many times had she held him in the humid dark? Achamian loved her, sure, but Seswatha loved the dead.

"Did I ever tell you," she said, flinching from these thoughts, "that my mother read the stars?"

"Dangerous," he replied, "especially in the Nansurium. Didn't she know the penalties?"

The prohibitions against astrology were as severe as those against witchcraft. The future was too valuable to be shared with caste-menials. *"Better to be a whore, Esmi,"* her mother would say. *"Stones are nothing more than far-flung fists. Better to be beaten than to be burned ..."*

How old had she been? Eleven?

"She knew, which was why she refused to teach me ..."

"She was wise."

Meditative silence. Esmenet struggled with an unaccountable anger.

"Do you think they speak our future, Akka? The stars?"

A momentary pause. "No."

"Why?"

"The Nonmen believe the sky is endlessly empty, an infinite void ..."

"Empty? How could that be?"

"Even more, they think the stars are faraway suns."

Esmenet wanted to laugh, but then, as though suddenly seeing *through* her reflection across waters, she saw the plate of heaven dissolve into impossible depths, emptiness heaped upon emptiness, hollow upon hollow, with stars—no suns!—hanging like points of dust in a shaft of light. She caught her breath. Somehow the sky had become a vast, yawning pit. Without thinking, she clenched the grasses, as though she stood upon a ledge rather than lay across the ground.

"How could they believe such a thing?" she asked. "The sun moves in circles about the world. The stars move in circles about the Nail." The thought struck her that the Nail of Heaven itself might be another world, one with a thousand thousand suns. Such a sky that would be!

Achamian shrugged. "Supposedly that's what the Inchoroi told them. That they sailed here from stars that were suns."

"And you believe them, the Nonmen? That's why you don't think the stars weave our fate?"

"I believe them."

"But you still believe the future is written ..." The air became hard between them, the surrounding grasses as sharp as wire. "You believe Kellhus is the Harbinger."

She realized she'd been speaking of Kellhus all along. Prince Kellhus.

A heartbeat of silence. The sound of laughter over ruined walls—Kellhus and Serwë.

"Yes," Achamian said.

Esmenet held her breath. "What if he's more? More than the Harbinger ..."

Achamian rolled onto his side, propped his head on his palm. For the first time, Esmenet saw the tears coursing down his cheeks. He'd been crying all along, she realized. All along.

He suffers ... More than I can ever know.

"You understand," he said. "You see why he torments me, don't you?"

Her skin recalled the path of Sarcellus's finger along her inner thigh. She shuddered, thought she heard Serwë moaning in the dark, gasping ...

"*I asked you,*" Kellhus had said, "*to tell me what it was like.*"

She no longer wanted to run.

"The Mandate cannot know, Akka ... We must bear this burden alone."

Achamian pursed trembling lips. Swallowed. "We?"

Esmenet looked back to the stars. One more language she could not read.

"We."

CHAPTER FIVE

THE PLAINS OF MENGEDDA

Why must I conquer, you ask? War makes clear. Life or Death.
Freedom or Bondage. War strikes the sediment from the water
of life.

—TRIAMIS I, JOURNALS AND DIALOGUES

Early Summer, 4111 Year-of-the-Tusk, near the Plains of Mengedda

Cnaiür had known something was amiss long before sighting the fields of
trampled pasture and dead firepits: too little smoke on the horizon, and
too few scavenging birds in the sky. When he mentioned this to Proyas,
the Prince had blanched, as though he'd confirmed a festering concern.
When they crested the last of the hills and saw that only the Conriyans
and the Nansur remained beneath Asgilioch's walls, Proyas had fallen
into an apoplectic fury, fairly shrieking curses as he whipped his horse
down the slopes.

Cnaiür, Xinemus, and the other Conriyan caste-nobles comprising
their party chased him all the way to Conphas's headquarters, where the
Exalt-General explained, in his infuriatingly glib way, that the morning
of the day previous, Coithus Saubon had decided to make the most of
Proyas's absence. The Shrial Knights, of course, couldn't lay hoof or boot
in the tracks of another when it came to heathen land, and as for
Gothyelk, Skaiyelt, and their barbaric kinsmen, how could they be

expected to distinguish fools from wise men, what with all that hair in their eyes?

"Didn't you argue with them?" Proyas had cried. "Didn't you reason?"

"Saubon wasn't interested in reason," Conphas replied, speaking, as he always did, as though intellectually filing his nails. "He was listening to a louder voice—apparently."

"The God?" Proyas asked.

Conphas laughed. "I was going to say 'greed,' but, yes, I suppose 'the God' will do. He said your friend, the Prince of Atrithau, had a vision ..." He glanced at Cnaiür.

"You mean Kellhus?" Proyas cried. "*Kellhus* told him to march?"

"So the man said," Conphas replied. *Such is the madness of the world*, his tone added, though his eyes suggested something far different.

There was a moment of communal hesitation. Over the past weeks, the Dûnyain's name had gathered much weight among the Inrithi, as though it were a rock they held at arm's length. Cnaiür could see it in their faces: the look of beggars with gold sewn into their hems—or of drunkards with over-shy daughters ... What, Cnaiür wondered, would happen when the rock became too heavy?

Afterward, when Proyas confronted the Dûnyain at Xinemus's camp, Cnaiür could only think, *He makes mistakes!*

"What did you do?" Proyas asked the fiend, his voice quavering with rage.

Everyone, Serwë, Dinchases, even that babbling sorcerer and his shrew whore, sat stunned about the evening fire. No one spoke to Kellhus that way ... No one.

Cnaiür almost cackled aloud.

"What would you have me say?" the Dûnyain asked.

"What happened?" Proyas cried.

"Saubon came to us in the hills," Achamian said quickly, "while you were in Tus—"

"Silence!" the Prince cried, without so much as glancing at the Schoolman. "I have asked you—"

"You're not my better!" Kellhus thundered. All of them, Cnaiür included, jumped—and not merely in surprise. There was something in his tone. Something preternatural.

The Dûnyain had leapt to his feet, and though a length away, somehow seemed to loom over the Conriyan Prince. Proyas actually stepped backward. He looked as though he had remembered something unspoken between them.

"You're my *peer*, Proyas. Do not presume to be more."

From where Cnaiür stood, the ochre walls and turrets of squat Asgilioch framed the head and shoulders of the two men. Kellhus, his trim beard and long hair shining gold in the evening sun, stood a full head taller than the swarthy Conriyan Prince, but both men emanated grace and potency in equal measure. Proyas had recovered his angry glare.

"What I *presume*, Kellhus, is to be party to all decisions of moment regarding the Holy War."

"I made no decision. You know that. I told Saubon only ..." For a fleeting moment, a strange, almost lunatic vulnerability animated his expression. His lips parted. He seemed to look through the Conriyan Prince.

"Only what?"

The Dûnyain's eyes refocused, his stance hardened—everything about him ... *converged* somehow, as though he were somehow more *here* than anyone else. As though he stood among ghosts.

He speaks in hidden cues, Cnaiür reminded himself. *He wars against all of us!*

"Only what I see," Kellhus said.

"And just what is it you see?" The words sounded forced.

"Do you wish to know, Nersei Proyas? Do you *really* want me to tell you?"

Now Proyas hesitated. His eyes flickered to those surrounding, fell upon Cnaiür for a heartbeat, no more. Without expression he said, "You've doomed us." Then turning on his heel, he strode in the direction of his quarters.

Afterward, in the stuffy confines of their pavilion, Cnaiür set upon the Dûnyain in Scylvendi, demanding to know what had really happened. Serwë huddled in her watchful little corner, like a puppy beaten by two masters.

"I said what I said to secure our position," Kellhus asserted, his voice passionless, bottomless—the way it always was when he affected to reveal his "true self."

"And this is how you secure our position? By alienating our patron? By sending half the Holy War to its destruction? Trust me, Dûnyain, I have fought the Fanim; this Holy War, this ... this *migration*, or whatever it is, has precious little chance of overcoming them as it is—let alone conquering Shimeh! And you would *cut it in half*? By the Dead God, you *do* need me to teach you war, don't you?"

Kellhus, of course, was unmoved. "Alienating Proyas is to our advantage. He judges men harshly, holds all in suspicion. He opens himself only when he's moved to regret. And he will regret. As for Saubon, I told him only what he wanted to hear. Every man yearns to hear their flattering delusions confirmed. Every man. This is why they support—willingly—so many parasitic castes, such as augurs, priests, memorial—"

"Read my face, dog!" Cnaiür grated. "You will *not* convince me this is a success!"

Pause. Shining eyes blinking, watching. The intimation of a horrifying scrutiny.

"No," Kellhus said, "I suppose not."

More lies.

"I didn't," the monk continued, "anticipate the others—Gothyelk and Skaiyelt—would follow his lead. With just the Galeoth and the Shrial Knights, I deemed the risk acceptable. The Holy War could survive their loss, and given what you've said regarding the liabilities of unwieldy hosts, I though it might even profit. But without the Tydonni ..."

"Lies! You would have stopped them otherwise! You could have stopped them if you wished."

Kellhus shrugged. "Perhaps. But Saubon left us the very night he found us in the hills. He roused his men when he returned, and set out before dawn yesterday. Both Gothyelk and Skaiyelt had already followed him into the Southron Gates by the time we returned. It was too late."

"You believed him, didn't you? You believed all that tripe about Skauras fleeing Gedea. You *still* believe!"

"Saubon believed it. I merely think it probable."

"As you said," Cnaiür snarled with as much spite as he could muster, "every man yearns to hear their flattering delusions confirmed."

Another pause.

"First I require one Great Name," Kellhus said, "then the others will follow. If Gedea falls, then Prince Coithus Saubon will turn to me before making any decision of moment. We need this Holy War, Scylvendi. I deemed it worth the risk."

Such a fool! Cnaiür regarded Kellhus, even though he knew his expression would betray nothing, and his own, everything. He considered lecturing him on the treacherous ways of the Fanim, who invariably used feints and false informants, and who invariably gulled fools like Coithus Saubon. But then he glimpsed Serwë glaring at him from her corner, her eyes brimming with hatred, accusation, and terror. *This is always the way,* something within him said—something exhausted.

And suddenly he realized that he'd actually *believed* the Dûnyain, believed *that he had made a mistake.*

And yet it was often like this: believing and not believing. It reminded him of listening to old Haurut, the Utemot memorialist who'd taught him his verses as a child. One moment Cnaiür would be sweeping across the Steppe with a hero like the great Uthgai, the next he would be staring at a broken old man, drunk on gishrut, stumbling on phrases a thousand years old. When one believed, one's soul was *moved.* When one didn't, everything else moved.

"Not everything I say," the Dûnyain said, "can be a lie, Scylvendi. So why do you insist on thinking I deceive you in all things?"

"Because that way," Cnaiür grated, "you deceive me in nothing."

Riding on the flank to avoid the dust, Cnaiür glanced at Proyas and his entourage of caste-nobles and servants. Despite the lustre of their armour and dress, they looked grim. They had negotiated the Southron Gates through the Unaras, and at long last they rode across *heathen* land, across Gedea. But their mood was neither jubilant nor assured. Two days ago, Proyas had sent several advance parties of horsemen to search for Saubon, the Galeoth Prince. This morning, outriders belonging to Lord Ingiaban had found one of those parties dead.

Gedea, at least in the shadow of the Unaras, was a broken land, a jumble of gravel slopes and stunted promontories. Save for clutches of hardy cedars, the green of spring was growing tawny beneath the summer sun. The sky was a plate of turquoise, featureless, sere—so different from the cloudy depths of Nansur skies.

Vultures and jackdaws screeched into the air at their approach.

With a curse, Proyas reined to a halt. "So what does this mean?" he asked Cnaiür. "That Skauras has somehow positioned himself *behind* Saubon and the others? Have the Fanim encircled them?"

Cnaiür raised a hand against the sun. "Perhaps ..."

The bodies had been stripped where they'd fallen: some sixty or seventy dead men, bloating in the hot sun, scattered like things dropped in flight. Without warning, Cnaiür spurred ahead, forcing the Prince and his entourage to gallop after him.

"Sodhoras was my cousin," Proyas snapped, reining to a violent halt beside him. "My father will be furious!"

"*Another* cousin," Lord Ingiaban said darkly. He referred to Calmemunis and the Vulgar Holy War.

Cnaiür sniffed the air, contemplated the smell of rot. He'd almost forgotten what it was like: the scribbling flies, the swelling bellies, the eyes like painted cloth. He'd almost forgotten how holy.

War ... The very earth seemed to tingle.

Proyas dismounted and knelt over one of the dead. He waved away flies with his gauntlets. Turning to Cnaiür, he asked, "How about you? Do you still believe him?" He looked away, as though embarrassed by the honesty of his tone.

Him ... Kellhus.

"He ..." Cnaiür paused, spat when he should have shrugged. "He sees things."

Proyas snorted. "Your manner does little to reassure me." He stood, casting his shadow across the dead Conriyan, slapping the dust from the ornamental skirt he wore over his mail leggings. "This is always the way of it, I suppose."

"What do you mean, my Prince?" Xinemus asked.

"We think things will be more glorious than they are, that they'll unfold according to our hopes, our expectations ..." He unstopped his waterskin, took too long a drink. "The Nansur actually have a word for it," he continued. "We 'idealize.'"

Statements such as this, Cnaiür had decided, partially explained the awe and adoration Proyas roused in his men, including those who were names in their own right, such as Gaidekki and Ingiaban. The admixture of honesty and insight ...

Kellhus did much the same. Didn't he?

"So what do you think?" Proyas was asking. "What happened here?" He'd clambered back onto his horse.

"Hard to tell," Cnaiür replied, glancing once again over the dead.

"Pfah," Lord Gaidekki snorted. "Sodhoras was no fool. He was overwhelmed by numbers."

Cnaiür disagreed, but rather than dispute the man, he jerked his horse about and spurred toward the ridge. The soil was sandy, the turf shallow-rooted; his mount—a sleek, Conriyan black—stumbled several times before reaching the crest. Here he paused, leaning against his saddle's cantle to relieve a vagrant pain in his back. Before him, the far side sloped gradually down, lending the entire ridge the appearance of a titanic shoulder blade. To the immediate north, the bald heights of the Unaras Spur gathered in the haze.

Cnaiür followed the crest a short distance, studying the scuffed ground and counting the dead. Seventeen more, stripped like the others, their arms askew, their mouths teeming with flies. The sound of Proyas arguing with his Palatines wafted up from below.

Proyas was no fool, but his fervour made him impatient. Despite hours of listening to Cnaiür describe the resources and methods of the Kianene, he as yet possessed no clear understanding of their foe. His countrymen, on the other hand, possessed no understanding whatsoever. And when men who knew little argued with men who knew nothing, tempers were certain to be thrown out of joint.

Since the earliest days of the march, Cnaiür had harboured severe doubts regarding the Holy War and its churlish nobles. So far, nearly every measure he'd suggested in council had been either summarily rejected or openly scoffed at—the yapping fools!

In so many ways, the Holy War was the antithesis of a Scylvendi horde. The People brooked few if any followers. No pampering slaves, no priests or augurs, and certainly no women, which could always be had when one ranged enemy country. They carried little baggage over what a warrior and his mount could bear, even on the longest campaigns. If they exhausted their *amicut* and could secure no forage, they either let blood from their mounts or went hungry. Their horses, though small, unbecoming, and relatively slow, were bred to the land, not to the stable. The horse he now rode—a gift from Proyas—not only required grain over and above fodder, but enough to feed three men!

Madness.

The only thing Cnaiür had *not* protested was the very thing the dog-eyed idiots ceaselessly clucked and fretted over: the breakup of the Holy War into separate contingents. What was it with these Inrithi? Did brothers bed their sisters? Did they beat their children about the head? The larger the host, the slower the march. The slower the march, the more supplies the host consumed. It was that simple! The problem wasn't that the Holy War had divided. It simply had no choice: Gedea, by all accounts, was a lean country, scarcely cultivated and sparsely populated. The problem was that it had done so without *planning*, without advance intelligence of what to expect, without agreed-upon routes or secure communications.

But how to make them understand? And understand they must: the Holy War's survival depended on it. *Everything* depended on it ...

Cnaiür spat across the dust, listened to them bicker, watched them gesticulate.

Murdering Anasûrimbor Moënghus was all that mattered. It was the weight that drew all lines plumb.

Any indignity ... Anything!

"Lord Ingiaban," Cnaiür called down, startling them into silence. "Ride back to the main column and return with at least a hundred of your men. The Fanim are fond of surprising those who come to dispense with the dead."

When none of the milling nobles moved, Cnaiür cursed and urged his horse back down the slope. Proyas scowled as he approached, but said nothing.

He tests me.

"I care not if you think me impertinent," Cnaiür said. "I speak only of what must be done."

"I'll go," Xinemus offered, already drawing his horse around.

"No," Cnaiür said. "Lord Ingiaban goes."

Ingiaban grunted, ran fingers over the blue sparrows embroidered across his surcoat—the sign of his House. He glared at Cnaiür. "Of all the dogs who've dared piss on my leg," he said, "you're the first to aim higher than my knee." Several guffaws broke from the others, and the Count-Palatine of Kethantei grinned bitterly. "But before I change my leggings, Scylvendi, please tell me why you choose to piss on *me*."

Cnaiür wasn't amused. "Because your household is the closest. Because the life of your Prince is at stake."

The lantern-jawed Palatine paled.

"Do as he bids!" Xinemus cried.

"Watch yourself, Marshal," Ingiaban snarled. "Playing benjuka with our Prince doesn't make you my better."

"Which means, Zin," Lord Gaidekki quipped, "that you must piss no higher than his waist."

Another burst of laughter. Ingiaban ruefully shook his head. He paused before riding off, dipping his square-bearded chin to Scylvendi, but whether in conciliation or warning the Scylvendi couldn't tell.

An uncomfortable pause followed. The shadow of a vulture flickered across the group, and Proyas glanced skyward. "So, Cnaiür," he said, blinking away the sun, "what happened here? Were they overwhelmed by numbers?"

Cnaiür scowled. "They were outwitted, not outnumbered."

"How do you mean?" Proyas asked.

"Your cousin was a fool. He was accustomed to riding with his men in file, as horsemen must when using a road. They wound into this depression and began climbing the slope, some three or four abreast. The Kianene waited for them above, holding their horses to the ground."

"They were ambushed ..." Proyas raised a hand to better peer along the ridge line. "Do you think the heathen simply happened on them?"

Cnaiür shrugged. "Perhaps. Perhaps not. Since Sodhoras thought himself an outrider, he obviously saw no need to deploy scouts of his own. The Fanim are more canny. They could have tracked him for some time without his knowledge, judged that sooner or later he would come here ..." He brought his horse about and pointed to the group of bloating dead who littered the centre of the ridge line. They looked oddly peaceful, like eunuchs snoozing in the sun after bathing. "But this is moot. The Fanim attacked when the first men crested the ridge, Sodhoras among them—"

"How in hell," Lord Gaidekki blurted, "could you know wheth—"

"Because the horsemen below broke ranks to rush to their lord's defence, only to find the Fanim arrayed along the entire ridge line. Though it looks harmless, that slope is treacherous. Sand and gravel. Many were slain by arrows at close range as their horses floundered. Those few who gained the summit caused the Fanim quite some grief—I saw far more blood than bodies up there—but were eventually overwhelmed. The rest, some twenty or so more sober but hopelessly courageous men, realized the futility of saving their lord, and pulled back—there—perhaps intending to draw the Fanim down and exact some revenge."

Cnaiür glanced at Gaidekki, daring the brash Palatine to contradict him. But the man studied the disposition of the dead, like the others.

"The Kianene," Cnaiür continued, "remained on the crest ... They taunted the survivors, I think, by desecrating Sodhoras's corpse—someone was disembowelled. Then they tried to reduce your kinfolk with archery. Those Inrithi who fought them on the crest must have unnerved them, because they were taking no chances. Their arrows must have possessed little effect, even at that short range. At some point they began shooting their horses—something the Kianene are typically loath to do. This is something to remember ... Once Sodhoras's men were unhorsed, the Kianene simply rode them down."

War. The hairs rose on the nape of his neck ...

"They stripped the bodies," he added, "then rode off to the southwest."

Cnaiür wiped his palms across his thighs. The fools believed him—that much was plain from their stunned silence. Before this place had been a rebuke and a dread omen, but now ... Mystery made things titanic. Knowledge made small.

"Sweet Sejenus!" Gaidekki suddenly exclaimed. "He reads the dead like scripture!"

Proyas frowned at the man. "No blasphemy ... Please, Lord Palatine." He scratched his trim beard, his gaze wandering yet again over the dead. He seemed to be nodding. He fixed Cnaiür with a canny look.

"How many?"

"Fanim?" The Scylvendi shrugged. "Sixty, maybe seventy, lightly armoured horsemen. No more."

"And Saubon? Does this mean he's encircled?"

Cnaiür matched his gaze. "When one wars on foot against horse, one is always encircled."

"So the bastard may still live," Proyas said, his breathlessness betrayed by a faint quaver in his voice. The Holy War could survive the loss of one nation, but three? Saubon had gambled more than his own life on this rash gambit—far more—which was why Proyas, over Conphas's protestations, had ordered his people to march. Perhaps four nations could prevail where three could not.

"For all we know," Xinemus said, "the Galeoth bastard may be *right*. He could be fanning across Gedea as we speak, chasing Skauras's skirmishers to the sea."

"No," Cnaiür said. "His peril is great ... Skauras *has* assembled in Gedea. He awaits you with all his might."

"And how could you know that?" Gaidekki cried.

"Because the Fanim who killed your kinsman took a great risk."

Proyas nodded, his eyes at once narrow and apprehensive. "They attacked a larger and more heavily armed force ... Which means they were following orders—*strict* orders—to prevent any communication between isolated contingents."

Cnaiür lowered his head in deference—not to the man, but to the truth. At long last, Nersei Proyas was beginning to understand. Skauras had been watching, studying the Holy War since long before it had left Momemn's walls. He knew its weaknesses ... Knowledge. It all came down to knowledge.

Moënghus had taught him that.

"War is intellect," the Scylvendi chieftain said. "So long as you and your people insist on waging it with your hearts, you are doomed."

"*Akirea im Val!*" a thousand Galeoth throats boomed. "*Akirea im Val pa Valsa!*" Glory to the God. Glory to the God of Gods.

Startled from his reverie, Coithus Saubon looked down over the great, haphazard column that was his army, searching for some sign of

Kussalt, his groom, who'd ridden out to meet the scouts. He gnawed at his callused knuckles, as he always did when he was anxious. *Please*, he thought. *Please* ...

But there was no sign.

Pulling helm and coif from his head, he ran his fingers through his short, autumn-blond hair, squeezing out the sweat that kept nagging his eyes. He sat astride his horse, alone on a promontory overlooking a small but fast-running river not marked on any of his crude maps. Thankfully, the river was fordable, though not without difficulty. It had already claimed four wains and one life, as well as several precious hours; the valley was growing more and more congested as men and supplies gathered behind the ford. On the far side, warriors and followers alike shook water from their limbs, then fanned out, some following the banks to refill water-skins or, Saubon noted darkly, even to fish. Others trudged onward, their faces bovine with weariness, their packs swinging from pikes and spears.

To the south, the towering ridges that had everywhere obscured his view folded into the river vale, revealing the hazy contours of what was to come. There, beyond the failing hills, he could see it: a broad plain, blue with distance, reaching as far as the horizon. The Plains of Mengedda. The great Battleplain of legend.

His chest tightened. He thought of his older cousin, Tharschilka, whose bones mouldered with those of Calmemunis and the Vulgar Holy War among those distant grasses. He thought of Prince Kellhus ...

I own this land ... It belongs to me! It must!

They'd marched for an entire week, through the passes of the Southron Gates, then along a ruined Ceneian road which had inexplicably ended in a ravine. Here he and Gothyelk—the stubborn old bastard!—had quarrelled to the point of fisticuffs over which way they should continue. The jewel of Gedea, if it could be called such, was the city of Hinnereth to the southeast on the Meneanor Coast. Saubon wanted the city for himself, certainly, but the Holy War *needed* it to secure their flank as they continued south. For the great Hoga Gothyelk, however, Gedea was something to be crossed, not conquered. The fool spoke as though the lands between the Holy War and Shimeh were nothing more than strides on a sprinter's track. They'd bellowed at each other deep into the night, with Gotian trying time and again to find some common ground, and

Skaiyelt nodding off in his corner, pretending now and then to listen to his interpreter. In the end, they resolved to go their separate ways. Gotian, who like all Nansur caste-nobles had a thorough military education, elected to continue on to Hinnereth—he was no fool, at least. No one knew what Skaiyelt intended until the following day, when he struck southward with Gothyelk and his Tydonni.

Good riddance, Saubon had thought.

At the time, he'd still believed that Skauras had yielded Gedea.

"March," the Prince of Atrithau had said that night in the mountains. *"The Whore will be kind to you. Just make certain the Shrial Knights are punished."*

Never in his life had Saubon obsessed so long over so few words. They'd seemed straightforward enough at the time. But like those eerie, ancient Nonmen statues that looked benevolent or malicious, divine or demonic, depending upon where one stood, their meaning transformed with every passing day. Had Prince Kellhus in fact confirmed his beliefs? The Gods had given their assurances, certainly, and like the misers they were, they'd named their terms. But they'd said nothing about *Skauras yielding Gedea.* If anything, they had suggested the opposite ...

Battle. They suggested battle. How else was he to punish the Shrial Knights?

"Akirea im Val! Akirea im Val!"

Saubon glanced down for an instant, then resumed probing the southern horizon—the Battleplain. Flat, dark, and blue, it looked more an ocean than a great table of earth, like something that could swallow nations whole.

Skauras hadn't relinquished Gedea. He could feel it, like lead in his belly and bones. This realization, coming as it did hard on the heels of his feud with Gothyelk, had filled Saubon with terror—so much so that he'd refused to countenance it at first. He possessed the assurances of the Gods—the *Gods!* What did it matter whether he marched with Gothyelk and his Tydonni or no? The Whore *would* be kind to him. Gedea would be his!

So he told himself.

Then from nowhere, an inner voice had whispered, *Perhaps Prince Kellhus is a fraud ...*

Such was the madness of things—the perversity!—that one thought, one slight twitch of the soul, could overturn so much. Where before he need only collect the future like a tax farmer, now he threw number-sticks against the great black—for the lives of thousands, no less! Perhaps, for the entire Holy War.

One thought ... So frail was the balance between soul and world.

Dread overcame him, threatened him with despair. At night, he wept in the secrecy of his tent. Was this not always the way? Hadn't the Gods always taunted, frustrated, and humiliated him? First the fact of his birth—to be the *first* soul in the body of the *seventh* son! Then his father, who'd punished him beyond all reason, beat him for possessing his fire, his cunning! Then the wars against the Nansurium a few years previous ... Mere miles! So close he could see the smear of Momemn's smoke on the horizon! Only to be afflicted by Ikurei Conphas—to be bested by a stripling!

And now this ...

Why? Why cheat *him*? Hadn't he given? Hadn't he observed their petty statutes, slaked their obscene thirst for blood?

Then yesterday, both Athjeäri and Wanhail, whom Saubon had charged with scouting and securing the country in advance of the main body, had sighted large parties of heathen horsemen.

"Many-coloured, with thin, flowing coats," Wanhail, the Earl of Kurigald, had said at evening council. Despite their similar age and stature, Wanhail always struck Saubon as one of those men flung far from their natural station by the happenstance of birth: a tavern clown in the trappings of a caste-noble. "Worse than the Ainoni, even ... Like a troop of fucking dancers!"

There was a chorus of laughter.

"But fast," Athjeäri had added, his gaze fixed upon the fire. "*Very* fast." When he looked to the others, his expression was stern, his long-lashed eyes sober. "When we gave chase, they outstripped us with ease ..." He paused so the assembled earls and thanes could digest the significance of this. "And their archery! I've never seen the like. Somehow they can draw and release while they ride—fire backward at their pursuers!"

The assembled warlords were unimpressed: Inrithi caste-nobles, Norsirai or Ketyai, thought archery base and unmanly. Regarding the sightings themselves, the preponderance of opinion was that they meant little. "Of course they shadow us!" Wanhail argued. "The only surprise is that we haven't seen the bung-bangers before now." Even Gotian agreed, though with somewhat more decorum. "If Skauras wished to contest Gedea," he said, "then he would have defended the passes, no?" Only Athjeäri dissented. Afterward, he pulled Saubon aside and fairly hissed, "Something's amiss, Uncle."

Something *was* amiss, though Saubon had said nothing at the time. He'd learned long ago the virtue of suspending judgement in the company of his commanders—especially in situations where his authority was uncertain. Even though he could count on many men, mostly relatives or veterans of his previous campaigns, he was really only the titular head of the Galeoth contingent—a fact brought home by the number of caste-nobles who continually gambolled through the hills, hunting or hawking. The deference owed by earls to a lackland prince was largely ceremonial; his every command, it seemed, had to run a gauntlet of pride and whimsy.

So he pretended to deliberate, concealed the certainty that weighed so heavy against him. Concealed the truth.

They were alone, some forty or fifty thousand Galeoth and under nine thousand Shrial Knights, not to mention the uncounted thousands who followed, stranded in hostile country, wandering into the clutches of a ruthless, cunning, and determined foe. Gothyelk and his Tydonni were lost. Proyas and Conphas remained camped about Asgilioch. They were vastly outnumbered, if the estimates of Skauras's strength provided by Conphas could be trusted—and Gotian insisted they could. They had no real discipline, no real leader. And they had no sorcerers. No Scarlet Spires.

But he said the Whore would be kind … He said!

Saubon puzzled at the chorus of voices that continued to reverberate from below. "*Akirea im Val!*" Usually a patchwork of shouts, chants, and hymns characterized the march. Something had incited them. Once again, Saubon peered through the dust and massed men, searching for some sign of his groom. It had to be Kussalt …

Please …

There! Riding with a small party of horsemen. Saubon released a deep, shuddering breath, watched them pass through a screen of cheering

men-at-arms—Agmundrmen by the look of their teardrop shields—
before climbing the gravel incline to join him. His relief quickly evaporated. They bore lances, he realized. Lances capped with severed heads.

"*Akirea im Val pa Valsa!*"

Saubon clenched a fist, beat it against a mail-covered thigh. With
thumb and forefinger, he pinched a glimpse of Prince Kellhus from his
eyes.

No one knows you ...

Lances! They bore lances ... A traditional token, used by Galeoth
knights to warn their commanders of imminent battle.

"From Athjeäri?" he called out as Kussalt's horse gained the crest.

The old groom scowled, as though to say, *Who else?* Everything about
the man was dull: his mail, his ancient, dented battlecap, even the Red
Lion on Blue of his surcoat, which marked him as a member of the House
Coithus. Dull and dangerous. Kussalt cared nothing for his appearance,
and this made him appear all the more formidable. There was much
violence in that grizzled face. The only man Saubon had ever met with
eyes as implacable as Kussalt's had been Prince Kellhus.

"What does he say?" Saubon cried.

The old groom tossed the lance before reining to a halt. Saubon
snatched it—almost too late. He found himself face to face with a
severed head planted on its tip. Dark skin blanched and bloodless. The
braids of its goatee swaying. A Kianene noble, possessing the leathery
look of dead things left overlong in the sun. Even still, it seemed to gaze
at him, slack and heavy-lidded, like a man about to spill his seed.

His foe.

"War and apples," Kussalt said. "He said, 'War and apples.'" "Apples"
was common slang for decapitated heads among the Galeoth. In days of
yore, a tutor had once told Saubon, the Galeoth had stewed and stuffed
them, like the Thunyeri.

The others rumbled to the summit, hailing him. Gotian with his
second, Sarcellus. Anfirig, the Earl of Gesindal, with his groom. Several
thanes—representatives of different households. And four or five beard-
less adolescents ready to courier messages. With the exception of Kussalt
and Gotian, everyone carried a look somewhere between desperation
and exasperation.

The ensuing argument was as bitter as any Saubon had endured since parting ways with Gothyelk. Apparently Athjeäri and Wanhail had been fighting running battles since early morning. Athjeäri in particular, Kussalt said, was convinced that Skauras assembled nearby, most likely on the Plains of Mengedda. "He thinks the Sapatishah is trying to slow us with his pickets, keep us from reaching the Battleplain until he's prepared." But Gotian disagreed, insisting that Skauras had prepared long ago, that he was actually trying to *bait* them. "He knows your people are rash, that the promise of battle will bring them running." When Anfirig and the others began protesting, the Grandmaster screeched, "Don't you see? Don't you see?" over and over until everyone, including Saubon, fell silent.

"He wants to engage you as soon as possible on favourable ground! *As soon as possible!*"

"So?" Anfirig asked contemptuously. Whether directly or indirectly, Gotian was always lecturing them on the cunning and ferocity of the Fanim. As a result, many of the Galeoth thought he feared the heathen—thought he was craven—when what he truly feared, Saubon knew, was the reckless humour of his Norsirai allies.

"So, perhaps he knows something we don't! Something that necessitates closing with us quickly!"

The words struck Saubon breathless. "If Gedea is a broken country," he said numbly, "then the Battleplain would be the quickest means of crossing it ..." He glanced at Gotian, who nodded cautiously.

"What does—" Anfirig started.

"Think!" Saubon exclaimed. "Think, Anfi, think! Gothyelk! If Gothyelk wishes to cross Gedea as quickly as possible, *what path would he take?*"

The Earl of Gesindal was no fool, but then neither was he a prodigy. He lowered his greying, leonine head in concentration, then said, "You're saying he's *close*, that the Tydonni and Thunyeri have been marching parallel to us this entire time, making for the Battleplain, as we do ..." When he looked up, his eyes were bright with grudging admiration. As a close mead-friend of his oldest brother, Anfirig, Saubon knew, had always looked on him as the boy he'd so roundly teased in his youth.

"You're saying the Sapatishah is trying to prevent us from joining Gothyelk!"

"Exactly," Saubon replied. He glanced at Gotian once again, realized the Grandmaster had *given* him this insight. *He wants me to lead. Trusts me.*

But then the man didn't know him. No one did. No one—

What are these thoughts!

Save the Ainoni, the Tydonni comprised the largest contingent of the Holy War—some seventy thousand hard-bitten men. Add to that Skaiyelt's murderous twenty thousand, and they possessed nearly all the might of the Middle-North. The greatest Norsirai host since the fall of the Ancient North!

Ah, Skauras, my heathen friend …

Suddenly the severed head upon the lance no longer seemed a rebuke, a totem of their doom; it seemed a *sign*, the smoke that promised cleansing fire. With unaccountable certainty, Saubon realized that Skauras *was afraid …*

As well he should be.

His misapprehensions fell away, and the old exhilaration coursed like liquor through his veins, a sensation he had always attributed to Gilgaöl, One-Eyed War.

The Whore will be kind to you.

Saubon tossed the lance and its grisly trophy back to Kussalt, then began barking orders, dispatching multiple messengers to inform Athjeäri and Wanhail of the situation, charging Anfirig with the attempt to locate Gothyelk, bidding Gotian to send his knights throughout the column, urging restraint and discipline.

"Until we rejoin Gothyelk, we remain in the hills," he declared. "If Skauras wishes to close with us, either let him fight on foot or break a thousand necks!"

Then suddenly, he found himself alone with Kussalt, his ears buzzing, his face flushed.

It was happening, he realized. It was *beginning*. After years and months, the womanish war of words was finally over, and the real war was beginning. The others, like Proyas, had yearned to untangle the "holy" in "Holy War" from the Emperor's knots. Not Saubon. It was the "war" he was most interested in. This was what he told himself, anyway.

And not only was it happening, it was happening the way Prince Kellhus had said it would.

No one knows you. No one.

He glanced at the retreating forms of Gotian and Sarcellus as they thudded down the slope. The thought of sacrificing them—as Prince Kellhus, or the Gods, had demanded—suddenly deadened his heart.

Punish them. You must make sure the Shrial Knights are punished.

Something cold caught his throat, and as quickly as Gilgaöl had possessed him, the God fled.

"Is something wrong, m'Lord?" Kussalt asked. It was uncanny, the way the man could guess his moods. But then, he'd always been there. Saubon's earliest childhood memory was of Kussalt scooping him up into his arms and racing into the galleries of Moraör after a bee sting had nearly choked him.

Without realizing, Saubon resumed chewing on his knuckles.

"Kussalt?"

"Yes?"

Saubon hesitated, found himself looking away to the south, to the Battleplain. "I need a copy of *The Tractate* ... I need to search for ... something."

"What do you need to know?" the old groom said, his voice both shocked and curiously tender ...

Saubon glared at him. "What business—"

"I ask only because I carry *The Tractate* with me always ..." His chapped hand had wandered to his chest as he spoke; he laid his palm flat across his heart. "Here."

He'd memorized it, Saubon realized. For some reason this shocked him to the point of becoming faint. He'd always known Kussalt to be pious, and yet ...

"Kussalt ..." he began, but could think of nothing to say.

Those old, implacable eyes blinked, nothing more.

"I need ..." Saubon finally ventured, "I need to know what the Latter Prophet has to say regarding ... sacrifice."

The groom's bushy white brows knitted together. "Many things. Very many things ... I don't understand."

"What the Gods demand ... Is it proper because *they* demand it?"

"No," Kussalt said, still frowning.

For some reason, the thoughtless certainty of this answer angered him. What did the old fool know?

"You disbelieve me," Kussalt said, his voice thick with weariness. "But it's the glory of Inri Sej—"

"Enough of this prattle," Coithus Saubon snapped. He glanced at the severed head—at the apple—noticed the glint of a golden incisor between slack and battered lips. So this was their enemy ... Drawing his sword, he struck it from the lance, and the lance from Kussalt's fist.

"I believe what I need to," he grated.

CHAPTER SIX

THE PLAINS OF MENGEDDA

*One sorcerer, the ancients say, is worth a thousand warriors
in battle and ten thousand sinners in Hell.*
> —DRUSAS ACHAMIAN, *THE COMPENDIUM OF THE FIRST HOLY WAR*

*When shields become crutches, and swords become canes,
some hearts are put to rout.
When wives become plunder, and foes become thanes,
all hope has guttered out.*
> —ANONYMOUS, "LAMENT FOR THE CONQUERED"

Early Summer, 4111 Year-of-the-Tusk, near the Plains of Mengedda

Morning broke, and rough Galeoth and Tydonni horns pealed through the clear air, sounding, at the moment of their highest pitch, like a woman's shriek.

The call to battle.

Despite thousands of Fanim horsemen and dozens of small pitched battles, the day previous had witnessed the reunion of the Galeoth, Tydonni, and Thunyeri hosts in the hill country to the immediate north of the Battleplain. Reconciled, Coithus Saubon and Hoga Gothyelk agreed to march out onto the northern terminus of the plains that very evening, with the hope of pressing their advantage—if it could be called such. Here, they decided, their position would be as strong as anything they might hope to find. To the northeast, they could shelter their flank behind a series of salt marshes, whereas to the west, they could depend on the hills. A shallow ravine, guttered by a stream that fed the marshes, wound the entire length, from flank to flank. Here they had planned to draw up the common line. Its slopes were too shallow to break any charge, but it would force the heathen to scramble through the muck.

Now the wind came from the east, and men swore they could smell the sea. Some—a few—wondered at the ground beneath their feet. They asked others whether their sleep had been troubled, or whether they could hear a faint sound, like the hiss of foam in tidal pools.

The Great Earls of the Middle-North gathered their households and their client thanes, who in turn gathered their households. Majordomos hollered commands over the din. There were cheers and raucous laughter, the rolling thunder of hooves as bands of younger knights, already drunk, rushed southward, eager to be among the first to catch sight of the heathen. Milling on carpets of bruised and trampled grass, thousands made haste to ready themselves. Wives and concubines embraced their men. Shrial Priests led crowds of warriors and camp-followers alike in prayer. Thousands knelt upon the turf, muttering aloud from their ancestor scrolls, touching morning-cool earth to their lips. Cultic priests intoned ancient rites, anointed idols with blood and precious oils. Goshawks were sacrificed in the name of Gilgaöl. The shanks of butchered antelope were thrown across the godfires of the Dark Hunter, Husyelt.

Augurs cast their bones. Surgeons set knives upon the fire, readied their kits.

The sun rose bold on the horizon, bathing the turmoil in golden light. Standards waved listlessly in the breeze. Men-at-arms gathered in irregular masses, making for their places in the line. Mounted cohorts filed among them, their arms flashing, their shields bright with menacing totems and images of the Tusk.

Suddenly shouts broke out among those already gathered along the ravine. The entire horizon seemed to *move*, winked as though powdered by silver filings. The heathen. The Kianene Grandees of Gedea and Shigek.

Cursing, thundering commands, the Earls and Thanes of the Middle-North managed to draw up their thousands along the ravine's northern edge. The stream had already become a black, muddy basin, pocked and clotted with deep hoofprints. On the ravine's southern edge, before the massed lines of footmen, the Inrithi knights milled in great clots. Cries of dismay were raised when those ranging farther afield discovered bones among the weeds, bundled in rotted leather and cloth. The ruin of an earlier Holy War.

Many different hymns were taken up, particularly among the low-caste footmen, but they soon faltered, yielding to the cadences of one deep-throated paean. Soon the air thrummed with the chorus of thousands. The hornsmen began marking the refrains with sonorous peals. Even the caste-nobles, as they arranged themselves into long iron ranks, joined:

A warring we have come
A reaving we shall work.
And when the day is done,
In our eyes the Gods shall lurk!

It was a song as old as the Ancient North, a song from *The Sagas*. And as the Inrithi gave it voice once again, they felt the glory of their past flood through them, brace them. A thousand voices and one song. A thousand *years* and one song! Never had they felt so rooted, so certain. The words struck many with the force of revelation. Tears streamed down sunburned cheeks. Passions ignited, swept through the ranks, until men roared inarticulately and brandished their swords against the sky. They were thousands and they were one.

In our eyes the Gods shall lurk!

Taking the dawn as their armature, the Kianene rode out to answer them. They were a race born to the fierce sun, not to clouds and gloomy forests as the Norsirai, and it seemed to bless them with glory. Sunlight flashed across silvered battlecaps. The silk sleeves of their khalats glimmered, transformed their lines into a many-coloured horizon. Behind them the air resounded with pounding drums.

And the Inrithi sang,

In our eyes the Gods shall lurk!

Saubon, Gothyelk, and the other ranking nobles conferred for one last time before dispersing along the line. Despite their best efforts, it remained uneven, the ranks painfully shallow in some places, and pointlessly deep in others. Arguments broke out among clients of different lords. A man named Trondha, a client thane of Anfirig, had to be wrestled to the ground after attempting to knife one of his peers. But still, the song thundered, so loud some clasped their chests, fearing for the rhythm of their hearts.

A warring we have come
A reaving we shall work!

The Kianene drew closer, encompassing the grey-green plain, endless thousands of approaching horsemen—far more, it seemed, than the Inrithi leaders had supposed. Their drums thundered out across the open spaces, throbbing through an ocean of rumbling sound. The Galeoth longbowmen, Agmundrmen from the northern marches primarily, raised their yew bows and released. For a moment the sky was thatched, and a thin shadow plunged into the advancing heathen line—to little effect. The Fanim were closer now, and the Inrithi could see the polished bone of their bows, the iron points of their lances, their wide-sleeved coats fluttering in the breeze.

And they sang, the pious Knights of the Tusk, the blue-eyed warriors of Galeoth, Ce Tydonn, and Thunyerus. They sang, and the air shivered as though the skies were vaulted in stone.

And when the day is done,
In our eyes the Gods shall lurk!

Crying "Glory to the God!" Athjeäri and his thanes broke ranks, crouching forward on their mounts, slowly dipping their lances. More Houses abandoned the line and pounded toward the Kianene: Wanhail, Anfirig, Werijen Greatheart, and then old Gothyelk himself, bellowing,

"Heaven wills it!" Like an avalanche, House after House followed, until almost all the mail-clad might of the Middle-North cantered out to greet their foe. *"There!"* footmen on the line would cry, glimpsing the Red Lion of Saubon or the Black Stag of Gothyelk and his sons.

From a trot the massive warhorses were urged to a slow gallop. Nesting thrushes took flight, burst slapping into the sky. Everything became breath and iron, the rumble of brothers before, behind, and to the side. Then, like a cloud of locusts, arrows swept among them. There was a hellish racket punctuated by screaming horses and astonished shouts. Warhorses toppled and thrashed, yanking knights to the ground, breaking backs, crushing legs.

Then the madness fell away. Once again it was the pure thunder of the charge. The strange camaraderie of men bent to a single, fatal purpose. Hummocks, scrub, and the bones of the Vulgar Holy War's dead rushed beneath. The wind bled through chain links, tousled Thunyeri braids and Tydonni crests. Bright banners slapped against the sky. The heathen, wicked and foul, drew closer, ever closer. One last storm of arrows, these ones almost horizontal to the ground, punching against shield and armour. Some were struck from their saddles. Tongue tips were bitten off in the concussion of the fall. The unhorsed arched across the turf, screamed and swatted at the sky. Wounded mounts danced in frothing circles nearby. The rest thundered on, over grasses, through patches of blooming milkwort waving in the wind. They couched their lances, twenty thousand men draped in great mail hauberks over thick felt, with coifs across their faces and helms that swept down to their cheeks, riding chargers caparisoned in mail or iron plates. The fear dissolved into drunken speed, into the *momentum*, became so mingled with exhilaration as to be indistinguishable from it. They were addicted to the charge, the Men of the Tusk. Everything focused into the glittering tip of a lance. The target nearer, nearer ...

The rumble of hooves and drums drowned their kinsmen's song. They crashed through a thin screen of sumac ... Saw eyes whiten in sudden terror.

Then impact. The jarring splinter of wood as lances speared through shield, through armour. Suddenly the ground became still and solid beneath them, and the air rang with wails and shouts. Hands drew sword and axe. Everywhere figures grappled and hacked. Horses reared. Blades pitched blood into the sky.

And the Kianene fell, undone by their ferocity, crumpling beneath northern hands, dying beneath pale faces and merciless blue eyes. The heathen recoiled from the slaughter—and fled.

The Galeoth, the Tydonni, and the Thunyeri raised a mighty shout and spurred after them. But the Shrial Knights reined to a stop, seemed to mill in confusion.

The Inrithi knights spurred their warhorses, but the Fanim outdistanced them, peppered them with arrows as they fled. Suddenly they dissolved into an *advancing* tide of heathen horsemen, more heavily armoured. The two great lines crashed. Several desperate moments ensued. The orange and black standard of Earl Hagarond of Üsgald disappeared in the tumult, and the Galeoth lord was speared lifeless on the ground. A lance through the throat heaved Magga, cousin of Skaiyelt, from his horse and threw him into his kinsmen. Death came swirling down. Gothyelk himself was felled, and the roars of his sons pierced the din. The ululating cries of the Fanim reached a crescendo ...

But war was bloody work, and the iron men hammered their foes, split skulls through battlecaps, cracked wooden shields, broke the arms bearing them. Yalgrota Sranchammer beheaded a heathen horse with a single blow, tossed Fanim Grandees from their saddles as though they were children. Werijen Greatheart, Earl of Plaideöl, rallied his Tydonni and scattered the heathen who assailed Gothyelk. On the ground, Goken the Red, the Thunyeri Earl of Cern Auglai, butchered man and horse alike, and cut his way back to his struggling standard. Never had the Kianene encountered such men, such furious determination. Desert-dark faces howled against the turf. Hawkish eyes slackened with fear.

A moment of respite.

Householders dragged their wounded lords to pockets of safety. Injured in the arm, Earl Cynnea of Agmundr ranted at his kinsmen not to pull him away. Earl Othrain of Numaineiri wept as he lifted his family's ancient standard from the lifeless hands of his son and raised it once more. Prince Saubon bellowed for another horse. Across the stretch they had thundered across only moments before, men stumbled or crawled, fumbling to staunch their wounds. But many more roared in exultation, the madness of battle upon them, cruel Gilgaöl galloping through their hearts.

Their enemy was everywhere, before them, beside them, sweeping in on their flanks. Massive cohorts wheeled in the near distance, charged them from behind. Splendid in their silk khalats and golden corselets, the Grandees of Gedea and Shigek yet again assailed the iron men.

Beset on all sides, the Men of the Tusk died. Taken in the back by lances. Jerked by hooks from their saddles and ridden down. Pick-like axes punched through heavy hauberks. Arrows dropped proud warhorses. Dying men cried to their wives, their Gods. Familiar voices pierced the cacophony. A cousin. A mead-friend. A brother or father, shrieking. The crimson standard of Earl Kothwa of Gaethuni toppled, was raised once more, then disappeared forever, as did Kothwa and five hundred of his Tydonni. The Black Stag of Agansanor was also overcome, trampled into the turf. Gothyelk's householders tried to drag their wounded Earl away, but were cut down amid a flurry of Kianene horsemen. Only a frantic charge by his sons saved the old earl, though his eldest, Gotheras, was gored in the thigh.

Through the din, the Earls and Thanes of the Middle-North could hear horns desperately signalling retreat, but there was nowhere to withdraw. Jeering masses of heathen horsemen swirled about them, peppering them with arrows, rolling back their flanks, shrugging away their disjointed counter-charges. Everywhere they looked, they saw the silken standards of the Fanim, stitched in gold, bearing strange animal devices. And the endless, unearthly drums pounded out the rhythm of their dying.

Then suddenly, impossibly, the Kianene divisions blocking their retreat scattered, and lines of white-clad Shrial Knights swept into their midst, crying, "*Flee, brothers! Flee!*"

Panicked knights galloped, ran, or stumbled toward their countrymen. Bloodied bands tumbled through the ravine, careened into their own men. The Shrial Knights fought on for several moments, then wheeled, racing back, pursued by masses of heathen horsemen—a howling rush of lances, shields, dark faces, and frothing horses, as wide as the horizon. Limping across the Battleplain, hundreds of wounded were cut down within throwing distance of the common line. The Men of the Tusk could only watch, aghast. Their song was dead. They could hear only drums, pounding, pounding, pounding ...

Dread and the heathen were upon them.

"We had them ... Had them!" Saubon screamed, spitting blood.

Gotian seized him by both shoulders. "You had nothing, fool. Nothing! You knew the rule! When you break them, *return to the line!"*

After he'd skidded through the muck of the stream and pressed his way through the ranks, Gotian had sought out the Galeoth Prince, but had found a raving lunatic in his stead.

"But we *had* them!" Saubon cried.

There was a sudden shout, and Gotian reflexively raised his shield. Saubon simply continued to rave. "They *broke like children* before—" There was a clatter, like hail against a copper roof. Men screamed. "—like children! We hacked them *to the ground!"*

A heathen shaft stuck from the Galeoth's chest. For a moment, the Grandmaster thought the man was dead, but Saubon merely reached up and snapped it. It had pierced his hauberk, but had been stilled by the felt beneath.

"We fucking well had them!" Saubon continued to roar.

Gotian grabbed him again, shook him. *"Listen!"* he cried. "That's what they wanted you to think! The Kianene are too nimble, too pliable on the field and too fierce of heart to truly break. When you charge, you charge to bleed them, not to rout them!"

Saubon looked at him dully. "I've doomed us ..."

"Gather your wits, man!" Gotian roared. "We're not like the heathen. We're hard, but we're brittle. We *break!* Gothyelk is down. Wounded— perhaps mortally! *You must rally these men!"*

"Yes ... Rally ..." Abruptly, Saubon's eyes *shone,* as though some brighter fire now moved him. "The Whore would be kind!" the Prince cried. *"That's what he said!"*

Gotian could only stare, bewildered.

Coithus Saubon, a Prince of Galeoth, the seventh son of old evil Eryeat, hollered for his horse.

Great tides of Fanim lancers, countless thousands of them, crashed into the Inrithi line—and were stopped dead. Galeoth and Tydonni pikemen gutted their horses. Tattooed Nangaels from Ce Tydonn's northern marches cudgelled the fallen in the mud. Agmundrmen punched arrows through shield and corselet with their deadly yew bows. Auglishmen from the deep forests of Thunyerus broke ranks when the Fanim fled, hurling hatchets that buzzed like dragonflies.

At other points along the ravine, leather-armoured cohorts of Fanim swept parallel to the Inrithi ranks, loosing arrows and taunts, tossing the heads of those caste-nobles who'd fallen in the first charge. The Northmen would hunch beneath their kite shields, weather the barrage, and then, to the dismay of the heathen, throw those self-same heads back at them.

Soon the Fanim began flinching from sections of the Inrithi line—from the stouthearted Gesindalmen and Kurigalders of Galeoth, from the grim Numainerish and long-bearded Plaidolmen of Ce Tydonn—but they found none so fearsome as the flaxen-haired Thunyeri, whose great shields seemed walls of stone, and whose two-handed axes and broadswords could split iron-armoured men to the heart. Horseless, the giant Yalgrota Sranchammer stood before them, roaring curses and waving his axe wildly in the air. When the Kianene indulged him, he and his clansmen hacked them into bloody kindling.

Yet again and again, the Grandees of Gedea and Shigek spilled across the ravine and charged headlong into the iron men, besetting the Galeoth, then the Tydonni, searching for one ill-forged link. They need only break the Inrithi once, and this knowledge drove them to acts of fanatic desperation. Men with shattered scimitars, with spouting wounds, even men with their bowels hanging about their knees, surged forward, threw themselves at the Norsirai. But each time they became mired in melee, mud, and carnage before the howls of their lords sent them galloping for the safety of the open plain. In their wake the Men of the Tusk stumbled to their knees, crying out in bitter relief.

To the northeast, where the common line trailed into the salt marshes, the Padirajah's son, Crown Prince Fanayal, led the Coyauri, his father's elite heavy cavalry, against the Cuärwishmen of Ce Tydonn, who had crowded into the ranks of their neighbours to the west and were caught scrambling back to their positions. For several moments, all was chaos, and dozens of Cuärwishmen could be seen fleeing into the marshes. Broadswords and scimitars flashed in the sunlight. Suddenly bands of shimmering Coyauri began spilling behind the line, though the Fanayal's White Horse standard remained stalled near the ravine. Gothyelk's two younger sons charged the Coyauri with what horse that remained to them, and the Fanim, without the open ground their tactics favoured, were driven back with atrocious losses.

Heartened by this success, Prince Saubon of Galeoth mustered those knights still mounted, and the Inrithi began, with more and more confidence, answering Fanim assaults with counter-charges. They would crash into the seemingly amorphous masses, the Fanim would melt, then they would race to evade the darting masses trying to envelop their flanks. Breathless, they would tumble back into the common line, lances broken, swords notched, ranks thinned. Saubon himself lost three horses. Earl Othrain of Numaineiri was carried back by his household, mortally wounded. He soon joined his dead son.

The sun climbed high, and scoured the Battleplain with heat.

The Earls and Thanes of the Middle-North cursed and marvelled at the fluid tactics of the Kianene. They gazed with envy at their magnificent, glossy-coated horses, which the heathen riders seemed to guide with thought alone. They no longer scoffed that the heathen Grandees were proficient with the bow. Many shields were quilled with arrows. Broken shafts jutted from the hauberks of many men. In the Inrithi camp, thousands sprawled dead or wounded because of the heathen's archery.

The Fanim withdrew and reformed, and the Men of the Tusk raised a ragged cheer. Many infantrymen, suffocated by the heat, dashed into the corpse-strewn ravine and doused their heads with bloody and fouled water. Many others fell to their knees and shook, wracked by silent sobs. Body-slaves, priests, wives, and harlots walked among the men, salving wounds, offering water or beer to the common soldiers and wine to the caste-nobles. Small hymns were raised among pockets of exhausted warriors. Officers bawled commands, enlisting hundreds to hammer broken pikes, spears, even shards of wood to spike the incline before their lines.

Word arrived that the heathen had sent divisions of horsemen north into the hills in a bid to outflank the Inrithi position, where, anticipated by Prince Saubon, they had been utterly undone by the tactics and valour of Earl Athjeäri and his Gaenrish knights. More cheers swept through the common line, and for a short time, they waxed louder than the incessant thunder of Fanim drums.

But their jubilation was short-lived. Massed on the plains before them, the heathen had assembled beneath their triangular banners in long, staggered lines. The drums fell silent. For a moment, the Men of the Tusk could hear wind across the grasses, even bees as they meandered over the dead that choked the ravine. As they watched, a small party of horsemen trotted imperiously before the ranks of motionless Fanim, bearing the Black Jackal device of Skauras, the Kianene Sapatishah-Governor of Shigek. They heard a faint harangue, answered by resounding shouts in an unknown tongue.

Prince Saubon could be heard bellowing, offering fifty gold talents to the archer who could kill, and ten to the one who could wound, the Sapatishah. After testing the wind, individual Agmundrmen raised their yew bows to the sun and began taking potshots. Most of the missiles fell far short, but some few made the distance. The distant horsemen affected not to notice, until abruptly one began swatting at the back of his neck, then toppled to the turf.

The Men of the Tusk roared with jeering laughter. As one, they pounded their shields, hooting and yelling. The Sapatishah's entourage scattered, leaving one figure: a nobleman on a magnificent white caparisoned in black and gold, obviously unafraid, apparently unmoved by the derision booming across the plain. And to a man, the Inrithi realized they looked upon the great Skauras ab Nalajan, whom the Nansur called Sutis Sutadra, the Southern Jackal.

Arrows fletched in faraway Galeoth pocked the turf about him, but he didn't move. More and more shafts feathered the ground as Agmundrmen began finding the drift and distance. Facing the Inrithi, the remote Sapatishah pulled a knife from his crimson girdle—and began paring his nails.

Now the Fanim began to laugh and roar as well, beating their round shields with sun-flashing scimitars. The very earth seemed to shiver, so ferocious was the din. Two races, two faiths, willing hate and murder across the littered Battleplain.

Then Skauras raised a hand, and the drums resumed their implacable throbbing. The Fanim began advancing along the entirety of their line. The Men of the Tusk fell silent, butted their pikes and squared their shields with those of their neighbours. It was beginning again.

Trailing clouds of dust, the Kianene ponderously gathered speed. As though counting drumbeats, the forward ranks lowered their lances in unison, urged their horses to gallop. With a piercing cry, they threw themselves at the Inrithi, while mounted archers swept to either side, showering the Northmen with arrows. They came crashing in successive waves, deeper and more numerous than in the morning. Entire companies were sacrificed for mere lengths of earth. Here and there, against the Üsgalders of Galeoth, against the battered Cuärwishmen, the Nangaels and Warnutes of Ce Tydonn, the Kianene gained the crest of the ravine, pressed the iron men back. Pikes snapped, gouged faces, hooked harnesses. Curved scimitars cracked helms, snapped collarbones through iron mail. Maddened horses crashed through rank and shield. And just when the heathen's numbers and momentum seemed to fail, more waves resolved from the dust, leaping through the ravine, pounding over the dead, lancing into the staggered footmen. There was no time for tactics, no time for prayer, only the desperate scramble to kill and live.

At several points, the common line wavered, broke ...

Then, as though stepping out of the blinding sun, the Cishaurim revealed themselves.

⸙

Saubon even beat at several of the fleeing Üsgalders with the flat of his sword, but it was no use. Mad with panic, they scrambled from his warhorse's snorting path—and from the gold-armoured horsemen running them down.

"The God!" Saubon roared as he barrelled into the pursuing Coyauri. "The God wills it!" His black crashed against the mount of the heathen before him. The smaller charger stumbled, and Saubon punched his swordpoint clear through its astonished rider's neck. He wheeled and parried a heavy blow from a Kianene garbed in flowing crimson. His black stumbled sideways and screamed, throwing him thigh to thigh with the man—though Saubon towered higher. Saubon smashed down with his pommel and the man tumbled backward from his saddle, his face bloody ruin. From somewhere, a blade nicked Saubon's helm. He slashed the now riderless charger's hindquarters and it went dancing into the heathen dogs before him, then he swept his broadsword in a great backward arc, shearing off the jaw of his assailant's mount. The horse reared; its rider went down. Saubon reined his black to the left and trampled the shrieking blasphemer.

"*The God!*" he cried, hacking at another man, cracking the wood of his shield.

"*Wills!*" His second blow shattered the warding arm beneath.

"*It!*" The third cracked his silvered helm, halved his dark face.

The Coyauri beyond the slumping man hesitated. Those behind Saubon, however, did not. A lance scraped along his back, snagged his hauberk, almost throwing him from his saddle. Standing in his stirrups, he hacked again, snapping the lance. When his opponent reached back for his curved blade, Saubon plunged his sword into the joints of the man's harness. Another down. The heathen milled around him, bewildered.

"Craven," Saubon spat, and spurred into them with a crazed laugh. They recoiled in terror—that was the death of two more of them. But Saubon's black inexplicably reared and stumbled ... Another fucking horse! He slammed hard against the turf. Muddy thought—confusion. A stamping forest of legs and hooves. Inert bodies. Bruised weeds. *Up ... up ... must get up!* He kicked at his thrashing mount. A great, buoyant shadow loomed above. Iron-shod hooves chopped the turf about his head. He jammed his sword upward, felt the point skid along the horse's sternum, then plunge into soft brown belly. Flash of sunlight. Then he was clear, stumbling to his feet. But something shattered across his helm, knocking him back to his knees. Another concussion sent him face first into the ground.

By the God, his fury felt so *empty*, so frail against the earth! He reached out with his bare left hand and grabbed another hand—cold, heavily callused, leathery fingers and glass nails. A dead hand. He looked up across the matted grasses and stared at the dead man's face. An Inrithi. The features were flattened against the ground and partly sheathed in blood. The man had lost his helm, and sandy-blond hair jutted from his mail hood. The coif had fallen aside, pressed against his bottom lip. He seemed so heavy, so *stationary*—like more ground …

A nightmarish moment of recognition, too surreal to be terrifying.

It was *his* face! His *own hand* he held!

He tried to scream.

Nothing.

But there was the thunder of heavier hooves, shouts in familiar tongues. Saubon let slip the cold fingers, struggled to his hands and knees. Concerned voices. From nowhere it seemed, arms were hoisting him to his feet. He stared numbly at the bare turf, at the site where a moment before *his corpse* had been …

This ground … This ground is cursed!

"Here, take my arm," the voice was fatherly, as though to a son who'd just learned a hard lesson. "You're saved, my Prince." It was Kussalt.

Saved?

"Are you whole?"

Winded, Saubon spat blood and gasped, "Bruised only …"

Mere yards away, Shrial Knights and Coyauri jostled and hacked at one another. Swords rang, danced flashing across sun and sky. So beautiful. So impossibly remote, like a spectacle woven in cloth …

Saubon turned wordlessly to his groom. The old warrior looked haggard, beaten.

"You stemmed the breach," Kussalt said, his eyes strange with wonder, perhaps even pride.

Saubon blinked at the blood trickling into his left eye. An inexplicable cruelty overcame him. "You're old and slow … Give me your horse!"

Kussalt's look soured. Old lips tightened.

"This is no place to be thin-skinned, you old fool. *Now give me your fucking horse!*"

Kussalt jerked, as though something had popped within him, then slumped forward, staggering Saubon with his weight.

He fell backward with his groom, crashed on his rump.

"Kussalt!"

He dragged the man onto his thighs. An arrow shaft jutted from the small of Kussalt's back.

The groom gurgled, coughed dark, old-man's blood. His rolling eyes found Saubon's, and the old warrior laughed, coughed more blood. Saubon's skin pimpled with dread. How many times had he heard the man laugh? Three or four, over the course of his entire lifetime?

No-no-no-no …

"Kussalt!"

"*I would have you know …*" the old man wheezed, "*how much I hated you …*"

A convulsion, then he spat snotty blood. A long gasp, then he went utterly still.

Like more earth.

Saubon looked around the strange pocket of calm that held them. Everywhere, through the trampled grasses, dead eyes watched. And he understood.

Cursed.

The Coyauri had reeled away, fleeing through the guttered ravine. But instead of cheering, men screamed. Somewhere, lights flashed, so bright they threw shadows in the midday sun.

He never hated me …

How could he? Kussalt was the only one who …

Funny joke. Ha-ha, you old fool …

Someone was standing over him, shouting.

So tired. Had he ever been so tired?

"Cishaurim!" someone was screaming. "Cishaurim!"

Ah, the lights …

A slapping blow, torn links scoring his cheek. Where had his helm gone?

"Saubon! Saubon!" Incheiri Gotian was screaming. "*The Cishaurim!*"

Saubon pulled his fingers from his cheek. Saw blood.

Fucking ingrate. Fucking shit-skinned pick.

Make sure they're punished! Punish them! Punish!

Fucking picks.

"Charge them," the Galeoth Prince said mildly. He hugged his dead groom tight against his thighs and stomach. *What a joker.*

"You must charge the Cishaurim."

They walked to elude the companies of crossbowmen they knew the Inrithi kept behind their lines, armed with the Tears of God. Not one among their number could be risked, not with the Scarlet Spires girding for war—not for any reason. They were Cishaurim, Indara's Waterbearers, and their breath was more precious than the breath of thousands. They were oases among men.

Drawing their palms over grass, goldenrod, and white alyssum, they walked toward the common line, fourteen of them, their yellow silk cassocks whipped by wind and fiery convections, the five snakes about each of their throats outstretched, like the spokes of a candelabra, search-ing every direction. The desperate Northmen fired volley after volley of arrows, but the shafts burst into puffs of flame. The Cishaurim continued walking, sweeping their gouged eyes along the bristling Inrithi lines. Wherever they turned, blue-blinding light exploded among the Men of the Tusk, blistering skin, welding iron to flesh, charring hearts ...

Many Northmen held their position, dropping prone beneath their shields as they'd been taught. But many others were already fleeing—Üsgalders, Agmundrmen, and Gaenrish, Numaineirish and Plaidolmen—senseless to the rallying cries of their officers and lords. The Inrithi centre floundered, began to evaporate. Battle had become massacre.

Amid the tumult, Crown Prince Fanayal and his Coyauri fled the ravine, the Shrial Knights pursuing them through billowing dust and smoke—or so it seemed to all who watched. At first, the Fanim could scarce credit their eyes. Many cried out, not in fear or dismay, but in wonder at the deranged ferocity of the idolaters. When Fanayal wheeled away, Incheiri Gotian, some four thousand Shrial Knights massed behind him, continued galloping forward, crying—weeping—*"The God wills it!"*

They scattered across the Battleplain, unbloodied save for the morning's first disastrous charge, hurtling through the grasses, crouched low out of terror, crying out their fury, their defiance. They charged the fourteen Cishaurim, drove their mounts into the hellish lights that unspooled from their brows. And they died burning, like moths assailing coals in a fire's heart.

Filaments of blue incandescence, fanning out, glittering with unearthly beauty, burning limbs to cinders, bursting torsos, immolating men in their saddles. Amid the shrieks and wails, the rumble of hooves, the thunder of men howling *"The God wills it!"* Gotian was pitched breakneck from the charred remnants of his horse. Biaxi Scoulas, his leg burnt to a stump, toppled and was trampled to pulp by those pounding after him. The knight immediately before Cutias Sarcellus exploded, and sent a knife whistling through his windpipe. The First Knight-Commander collapsed, slapped face first onto the ground. Death came swirling down.

Brains boiled in skulls. Teeth snapped. Hundreds fell in the first thirty seconds. Hundreds more in the second. Scorching light materialized everywhere, like the cracks that dizzy glass. And still the Shrial Knights whipped their horses forward, leaping the smouldering ruin of their brothers, racing one another to their doom, thousands of them, howling, howling. The scrub and grasses ignited. Oily smoke bloomed skyward, drawn toward the Cishaurim by the wind.

Then a lone rider, a young adept, swept up to one of the sorcerer-priests—and took his head. When the nearest turned his sockets to regard him, only the boy's horse erupted in flame. The young knight tumbled and continued running, his cries shrill, his dead father's Chorae bound to the palm of his hand.

Only then did the Cishaurim realize their mistake—their arrogance. For several heartbeats they hesitated ...

And a tide of burnt and bloody knights broke from the rolling smoke, among them Grandmaster Gotian, hauling the Gold Tusk on White, his Order's sacred standard. In that final rush, hundreds more fell burning. But some didn't, and the Cishaurim rent the earth, desperately trying to bring those with Chorae down. But it was too late—the raving knights were upon them. One tried to flee by stepping into the sky, only to be felled by a crossbow bolt bearing a Tear of God. The others were cut down where they stood.

They were Cishaurim, Indara's Waterbearers, and their death was more precious than the death of thousands.

For an impossible moment, all was silent. The Shrial Knights, those few hundred who survived, began limping and staggering back to the battered ranks of their Inrithi brothers. Incheiri Gotian was among the last to reach safety, bearing a burnt youth slumped across his shoulders.

Skauras, knowing the Cishaurim had accomplished their task despite their deaths, roared at his Grandees to attack, but the shock of what they had witnessed weighed too heavily upon them. The Fanim withdrew, milling in confusion, while opposite a great swath of scorched earth and smoking dead, the Earls and Thanes of the Middle-North desperately reassembled the centre of the common line. By the time the Grandees of Shigek and Gedea renewed their assault, the iron men were again in position, their ranks thinned, their hearts hardened.

And they began singing anew their ancient paean, which now struck them as more prophecy than song:

> A *warring we have come*
> A *reaving we shall work.*
> And *when the day is done,*
> In *our eyes the Gods shall lurk!*

As the afternoon waxed, many more joined the fallen. Earl Wanhail of Kurigald was thrown from his horse in a counter-charge, and broke his back. Skaiyelt's youngest brother, Prince Narradha, was felled by an arrow in the eye. Among the living, some collapsed of heat exhaustion. Some went mad with grief, and had to be dragged, frothing, to the priests in the camp. But those who stood couldn't be broken. The iron men had rekindled their song, and the song had rekindled their violent fervour. The pounding of Fanim drums dimmed, then was drowned out altogether. Thousands of voices and one song. Thousands of years and one song.

> And *when the day is done,*
> In *our eyes the Gods shall lurk!*

As the sun lowered in the western skies, the Fanim flinched more and more from the Inrithi line, charged with ever greater trepidation. For they saw demons in the eyes of their idolatrous enemy.

Skaurus had already sounded the retreat when the banners of Proyas and his silver-masked Conriyans came snapping down the western hills. Without signal, the Galeoth, Tydonni, and Thunyeri ranks surged forward and ran booming across the Battleplain. Exhausted, heartbroken, the Fanim panicked; withdrawal degenerated into rout. The knights of Conriya swept into their midst, and the great Kianene host of Skaurus ab Nalajan, Sapatishah-Governor of Shigek, was massacred. Meanwhile, the Earls and Thanes of the Middle-North descended with what horse they had remaining on the vast Fanim encampment. Succumbing to licentious fury, the harrowed Northmen raped the women, murdered the slaves, and plundered the sumptuous pavilions of innumerable Grandees.

By sunset, the Vulgar Holy War had been avenged.

Over the following weeks, the Men of the Tusk would find thousands of bloated horses on the road to Hinnereth. They had been ridden to death, so mad were the heathen to escape the iron men of the Holy War.

Hunched on his saddle, Saubon watched files of weary men and women trudge across the moonlit grasses, no doubt eager to at last overtake Proyas and his knights. The Conriyan Prince, Saubon realized, must have pressed hard, perilously hard, to have so far outstripped his baggage and followers. He required no mirror to know how he looked: the horrified expressions of those walking from the darkness were reflection enough. Blood soaked his tattered surcoat. Gore clotted the links of his mail harness.

He waited until the man was almost immediately below before calling out to him ...

"Your friend. Where is he?"

The sorcerer, Achamian, shrank from his mounted form, clutching his woman. Small wonder, looming out of the dark like a bloodied apparition.

"You mean Kellhus?" the square-bearded Schoolman asked.

Saubon glowered. "Remember your place, dog. He's a prince."

"You mean, *Prince* Kellhus, then?"

Unaccountably chastised, Saubon paused, licked his swollen lips. "Yes ..."

The sorcerer shrugged. "I don't know. Proyas drove us like cattle to catch you. Everything's confused ... Besides, princes don't loiter with the likes of us in the wake of battle."

Saubon glared at the mealy-mouthed fool, wondering whether he should strike him for his impertinence. But the memory of seeing his own corpse on the field gave him pause. He shuddered, clutched his elbows. *That wasn't me!*

"Perhaps … Perhaps you can help me, then."

The sorcerer scowled in a bemused manner Saubon found offensive. "I'm at your disposal, my Prince."

"This ground … What is it about this ground?"

The sorcerer shrugged again. "This is the Battleplain … This is where the No-God died."

"I know the legends."

"I'm sure you do … Do you know what topoi are?"

Saubon grimaced. "No."

The attractive woman at his side yawned, rubbed her eyes. Without warning, a wave of fatigue crashed over the Galeoth Prince. He swayed in his saddle.

"You know the way you can see far from heights," the sorcerer was saying, "like towers or mountain summits?"

"I'm not a fool. Don't deal with me as one."

Pained smile. "Topoi are like heights, places where one can see far … But where heights are built with mounds of stone and earth, topoi are built with mounds of trauma and suffering. They are heights that let us see farther than this world … some say into the Outside. That's why this ground troubles you—you stand perilously high … This is the Battleplain. What you feel isn't so different from vertigo."

Saubon nodded, feeling his throat tighten. He understood, and for no apparent reason, that understanding roused an immeasurable relief. Two ferocious sobs wracked him. "Exhaustion," he croaked, wiping angrily at his eyes.

The sorcerer watched him, now with more regret than reproach. The woman stared at her feet.

Unable to look at the man, Saubon vaguely nodded in his direction, then made to ride off. The Schoolman's voice, however, brought him up short.

"Even among topoi," he called, "this place is … special." There was something different in his tone, a reluctance, perhaps, which struck Saubon like a winter gust across sweaty skin.

"How so?" he managed, looking into the dark night.

"Do you remember the line from *The Sagas*, '*Em yutiri Tir mauna, kim raussa raim*' ..."

Saubon blinked away tears, said nothing.

"'The soul that encounters Him,'" the Schoolman continued, "'passes no further.'"

"And just fucking what," the Galeoth Prince said, shocked by the savagery of his own voice, "is that supposed to fucking mean?"

The sorcerer looked out across the dark plains. "That in some way, *He's* out there somewhere ... Mog-Pharau." When he turned back to Saubon, there was real fear in his eyes.

"The dead do not escape the Battleplain, my Prince ... This place is cursed. The No-God died here."

Chapter Seven

Mengedda

Sleep, when deep enough, is indistinguishable from vigilance.
—SORAINAS, *THE BOOK OF CIRCLES AND SPIRALS*

Early Summer, 4111 Year-of-the-Tusk, the Plains of Mengedda

Broad black wings outstretched, the Synthese drifted on the early morning wind, just savouring the curious *familiarity* of it all. The eastern skyline gradually brightened, then suddenly the sun cracked the horizon, lancing between the hills, over the corpse-strewn expanse of the Battleplain, and out into the infinite black, where it would, eventually, trace a thread incomprehensibly long ...

Perhaps all the way home.

Who could blame it for indulging in nostalgia? To be here again after millennia, at the place where it had *almost happened*, where Men and Nonmen had almost flickered out forever. Almost. Alas ...

Soon enough. Soon enough.

It lowered its small human head and studied the patterns the innumerable dead had sketched across the plains, marvelling at the resemblances to certain sigils once prized by its species—back when they could actually be called such. Genera. Species. Race.

Inchoroi, the vermin had called them.

For a time it wondered at the sense of depth generated by the thousands of slow-circling vultures below, each sinking to the feast. Then it caught the scent it had been searching for ... that otherworldly fetor—so distinctive!—encoded in case of just such a contingency.

So Sarcellus was dead. Unfortunate.

At least the Holy War had prevailed—over the Cishaurim, no less!

Golgotterath would approve.

Smiling, or perhaps scowling, with tiny human lips, the Old Name swooped down to join the vultures in their ancient celebration.

The distances writhed, twisted with maggot-white forms draped in human skins—with Sranc, shrieking Sranc, thousands upon thousands of them, clawing black blood from their skin, gouging themselves blind. Blind! The whirlwind roared through their masses, tossing untold thousands into orbit about its churning black base.

Mog-Pharau walked.

The Great King of Kyraneas clutched Seswatha about the shoulders, but the sorcerer could not hear his cry. Instead he heard the voice, uttered through a hundred thousand Sranc throats, flaring like bright-burning coals packed into his skull ... The voice of the No-God.

WHAT DO YOU SEE?

See? What could he ...

I MUST KNOW WHAT YOU SEE

The Great King turned from him, reached for the Heron Spear.

TELL ME

Secrets ... Secrets! Not even the No-God could build walls against what was forgotten! Seswatha glimpsed the unholy Carapace shining in the whirlwind's heart, a nimil sarcophagus sheathed in choric script, hanging ...

WHAT AM—

Achamian woke with a howl, his hands cramped into claws before him, shaking.

But there was a tender voice, shushing, cooing reassurances. Soft hands caressed his face, stroked sweaty hair from his eyes, daubed tears from his cheek.

Esmi.

He lay in her arms for a long while, periodically shuddering, straining to keep his eyes open, to see what was here—now.

"I've been thinking of Kellhus," she said after his breathing had settled.

"Did you dream of him?" Achamian half-heartedly teased. He tried to clear his voice of phlegm.

Esmenet laughed. "No, you fool. I sa—"

WHAT DO YOU SEE?

A shrieking chorus, sharp and brief. He shook his head. "Sorry?" he said, laughing uneasily. "What did you say? I must have sleep in my eyes *and* ears ..."

"I said, *just thinking*."

"About what?"

Somehow, he could feel her cock her head, the way she always did when struggling to articulate something that eluded her. "About the way he speaks ... Haven't you—"

I CANNOT SEE

"No," he wheezed. "Never noticed." He coughed violently.

"*That*," she said, "is what you get sitting on the smoky side of the fire." One of her traditional admonitions.

"Old meat is better smoked." His traditional reply. He squeezed sweat from his eyes.

"Anyway, Kellhus ..." she continued, lowering her voice. Canvas was thin, and the camp crowded. "With everyone whispering about him because of the battle and what he said to Prince Saubon, it struck me—"

TELL ME

"—before falling asleep that almost everything he says is either, well ... either *near* or *far* ..."

Achamian swallowed, managed to say, "How do you mean?" He needed to piss.

Esmenet laughed. "I'm not sure ... Remember how I told you how he asked me what it was like to be a harlot—you know, to lie with strange men? When he talks that way, he seems near, *uncomfortably* near, until you realize how utterly honest and unassuming he is ... At the time, I thought he was just another rutting dog—"

WHAT AM I?

"The *point*, Esmi ..."

There was an annoyed pause. "Other times, he seems breathtakingly *far* when he talks, like he stands on some remote mountain and can see everything, or almost everything ..." She paused again, and from the length of it, Achamian knew he had bruised her feelings. He could feel her shrug. "The rest of us just talk in the middle somewhere, while he ... And now this, seeing what happened yesterday *before it happened*. With each day—"

I CANNOT SEE

"—he seems to talk *a little nearer and a little farther*. It makes me— Akka? You're trembling! Shaking!"

He gasped for breath. "I-I can't stay here, Esmi."

"What do you mean?"

"This place!" he cried. "I can't stay here!"

"Shhh. It'll be all right. I heard soldiers talking last night about moving come today. Away from the dead—from the chance of vapours and—"

TELL ME

Achamian cried out, struggled to retrieve his wits.

"Shhh, Akka, shhh ..."

"Did they say where?" he gasped.

Esmenet had kicked free her blankets to kneel naked over him, palms on his chest. She looked worried. Very worried. "They said something about ruins, I think."

"Ev-even worse."

"What do you mean?"

"This place is shaking me to pieces, Esmi. Echoes. *Echoes*. R-remember what I s-said to Saubon last night? The N-No-God ... His ... his echo is too strong here. Too strong! And the ruins, that would be the city of Mengedda. *Where it happened* ... Where the No-God was struck down. I know this sounds mad, but *I think this place—I think this place recognizes me* ... M-me or Seswatha within me."

"So what should we—"

TELL

"Leave ... Camp in the eastern hills overlooking the Battleplain. We can wait for the others there."

Her expression darkened with other worries. "Are you sure, Akka?"

"We'll be safe ... We just need to be far for a while."

With the accumulation of power, Achamian had once said, comes mystery. An old Nilnameshi proverb. When Kellhus had asked what the proverb meant, the Schoolman had said it referred to the paradox of power, that the more security one exacted from the world, the more insecure one became. At the time, Kellhus had thought the proverb yet another of Achamian's vacant generalizations, one that exploited the world-born propensity to confuse obscurity with profundity. Now he wasn't so sure.

Five days had passed since the battle. The last of the sun had boiled away among the western hills. The Great Names—including Conphas and Chepheramunni—had gathered with their retinues in an overgrown amphitheatre that had been excavated in ancient times from the side of a low hill. An enormous bonfire burned in its centre, transforming the stage into a hearth. The Great Names sat and conferred around the amphitheatre's lowest tier, while their advisers and caste-noble countrymen bickered and jested on the tiers above. Their ceremonial dress, much of it looted, glinted and shimmered in the firelight. Their faces shone pale orange. Before them, bare-chested slaves marched from the darkness to the stage, where they cast furniture, clothing, scrolls, and other worthless items from the Kianene camp onto the bonfire. A strange, iron-blue smoke whipped skyward from the flames. Its smell was offensive—reminiscent of the manural unguents used by the Yatwerian priestesses—but there was nothing else to burn on the Battleplain.

At long last, the Holy War was entire. Earlier in the afternoon, the Nansur and Ainoni hosts had filed across the plains and joined the vast encampment beneath the ruins of Mengedda—a once great city, Achamian had told Kellhus, destroyed during the early Age of Bronze. For the first time since faraway Momemn, a full Council of the Great and Lesser Names had been called. Even though his rank and notoriety had earned him a place among those sitting above the Great Names, Kellhus had elected to sit with the knights, men-at-arms, and followers massed on the heaped mounds of earth and rubble opposite the amphitheatre, where he could cultivate his reputation for humility and easily survey the expressions of all those he must conquer.

For the most part, their faces exhibited startling contrasts. Some bore marks—bandages, puckered wounds, and yellowing bruises—of the recent battle, while others bore no marks at all, particularly among the newly arrived Nansur and Ainoni. Some were flushed with celebratory cheer, for the back of the heathen had been broken. While others were ashen with horror and sleeplessness ...

Victory on the Battleplain, it seemed, had carried its own uncanny toll.

Ever since setting their pallets and mats across the Plains of Mengedda, various men and women of the Holy War had complained of suffering brutal nightmares. Each night, they claimed, they found themselves in desperate straits on the Battleplain, striving against and falling before foes they'd never before seen: archaic Nansur, true desert Kianene, Ceneian infantrymen, ancient Shigeki chariots, bronze-armoured Kyraneans, stirrupless Scylvendi, Sranc, Bashrags, and even, some had insisted, Wracu—dragons.

When the encampment was moved clear of the carrion winds to the ruins of Mengedda, the nightmares had only intensified. Some began claiming they'd dreamed of the recent battle against the Kianene, that they were burned anew by the Cishaurim, or that they fell to the battle-maddened Thunyeri. It was as though the ground had hoarded the final moments of the doomed, and counted and recounted them each night on the ledger of the living. Many tried to stop sleeping altogether, especially after a Tydonni thane was found dead one morning in his pallet. Some, like Achamian, had actually fled.

Then the pitted knives, coins, shattered helms, and bones started to appear, as though slowly vomited from the earth. At first here and there, found jutting from the turf in the morning, and in places men insisted they couldn't have been missed. Then more frequently. After stubbing his toe, one man allegedly found the skeleton of a child beneath the rushes of his tent.

Kellhus himself had dreamt nothing, but he'd seen the bones. According to Gotian, who'd explained the legends regarding the Battleplain in private council two days earlier, this ground had imbibed too much blood over the millennia, and now, like over-salted water, had to discharge the old to accommodate the new. The Battleplain was cursed, he said, but they needn't fear for their souls so long as they remained resolute in their faith. The curse was old and well understood. Proyas and Gothyelk, neither of whom suffered dreams, were loath to leave, both because the couriers they'd sent to Conphas and Chepheramunni had named Mengedda as their point of rendezvous, and because the streams running through the ruined city afforded the only expedient supply of water within a three-day march. Saubon also insisted they stay, though for reasons, Kellhus knew, entirely his own. Saubon *did* dream. Only Skaiyelt had demanded they leave.

Somehow, the very ground of battle had become their foe. Such contests, Xinemus had remarked one night about their fire, belonged to philosophers and priests, not warriors and harlots.

Such contests, Kellhus had thought, simply should not be ...

Ever since learning the desperate details of the Inrithi triumph, Kellhus had found himself beset with questions, quandaries, and enigmas.

Fate *had* been kind to Coithus Saubon, but only because the Galeoth Prince had dared punish the Shrial Knights. By all accounts, Gotian's catastrophic charge against the Cishaurim had saved the Earls and Thanes of the Middle-North. Events, in other words, had unfolded precisely as Kellhus had predicted. Precisely.

But the problem was that he hadn't predicted *anything*. He'd merely said what he'd needed to say to maximize the probabilities of securing Saubon and destroying Sarcellus. He'd taken a risk.

It simply *had* to be coincidence. At least this was what he'd told himself—at first. Fate was but one more world-born subterfuge, another lie men used to give meaning to their abject helplessness. That was why they thought the future a Whore, something who favoured no man over another. Something heartbreakingly *indifferent*.

What came *before* determined what came after ... *This* was the basis of the Probability Trance. *This* was the principle that made mastering circumstance, be it with word or sword, possible. *This* was what made him Dûnyain.

One of the Conditioned.

Then the earth began spitting up bones. Wasn't this proof that the ground *answered* to the tribulations of men, that it was *not* indifferent? And if earth—*earth!*—wasn't indifferent, then what of the future? Could what came *after* actually determine what came before? What if the line running between past and future was neither singular nor straight, but multiple and bent, capable of looping in ways that contradicted the Law of Before and After?

Could he be the Harbinger, as Achamian insisted?

Is this why you've summoned me, Father? To save these children?

But these were what he called primary questions. There were so many more immediate mysteries to be interrogated, so many more tangible threats. Such questions either belonged to philosophers and priests, as Xinemus had said, or to Anasûrimbor Moënghus.

Why haven't you contacted me, Father?

The bonfire waxed brighter, consuming a small library of scrolls the slaves had hauled from the darkness. Even though Kellhus sat apart, he could *feel* his position among the caste-nobles arrayed before him. It was like a palpable thing, as though he were a fisherman manning far-flung nets. Every glance, every watchful stare, was noted, categorized, and retained. Every face was deciphered.

A knowing look from a figure sitting among Proyas's caste-nobles ... Palatine Gaidekki.

He's discussed me at length with his peers, regards me as a puzzle, and thinks himself pessimistic as to the solution. But part of him wonders, even yearns.

A look from one of the Tydonni. A momentary meeting of eyes ... Earl Cerjulla.

He's heard the rumours, but remains too proud of his own battlefield deeds to concede anything to fate. He suffers the nightmares ...

A passing glance from behind Ikurei Conphas ... General Martemus.

He's heard much about me, but is too preoccupied to truly care.

From among the Thunyeri, a fiery-haired warrior, searching for someone among the crowd ... Earl Goken.

He's heard almost nothing of me. Too few Thunyeri speak different tongues.

A contemptuous glare from among the Conriyans ... Palatine Ingiaban.

He discusses me with Gaidekki, argues that I'm a fraud. My relationship to Cnaiür is what interests him. He too has stopped sleeping.

A steady, fixed look from among Gotian's diminished retinue ... *Sarcellus.*

One of what seemed a growing number of inscrutable faces. Skin-spies, Achamian had called them.

Why did he stare? Because of the rumours, like the others? Because of the horrific toll his words had exacted on the Shrial Knights? Gotian, Kellhus knew, struggled not to hate him ...

Or did he know that Kellhus could see him and had tried to kill him?

Kellhus matched the thing's unblinking gaze. Since his first encounter with Skeaös on the Andiamine Heights, he'd refined his understanding of their peculiar physiognomy. Where others saw blemished or beautiful faces, he saw eyes peering through clutched fingers. So far, he'd identified eleven of the creatures masquerading as various powerful personages, and he had no doubt there were more ...

He nodded amiably, but Sarcellus simply continued watching, expressionless, as though unaware or unconcerned that what he stared at was staring back ...

Something, Kellhus thought. *They suspect something.*

There was a small commotion in his periphery, and turning, Kellhus saw Earl Athjeäri pressing his way through the crowded spectators, climbing toward him. Kellhus bowed his head appropriately as the young caste-noble approached. The man reciprocated, though his declension fell slightly short.

"Afterward," Athjeäri said. "I need you to come with me afterward."

"Prince Saubon."

The striking, chestnut-haired man worked his jaw. Athjeäri was someone, Kellhus knew, who understood neither melancholy nor indecision, which was partly why he thought this errand demeaning. As much as he admired his uncle, he thought Saubon was making too much of this impoverished prince from Atrithau. Far too much.

So much pride.

"My uncle wants to meet," the Earl said, as though explaining a lapse. Without further word, he began pressing his way back to the amphitheatre. Kellhus looked out over the crowds below to the Great Names. He glimpsed Saubon nervously looking away.

His anguish grows. His fear deepens. For six nights now, the Galeoth Prince had assiduously avoided him, even in those councils where they shared seats about the same fire. Something had happened on the field, something more grievous than losing kinsmen or sending the Shrial Knights to their doom.

An opportunity.

Sarcellus, Kellhus noticed, had left his seat on the tiers, and now stood with a small party of Shrial Priests preparing to assist Gotian in the inaugural rites. The general rumble of voices trailed.

The Grandmaster began with a purificatory prayer Kellhus recognized from *The Tractate*. Then he spoke for some time of Inri Sejenus, the Latter Prophet, and what it meant for men to be Inrithi. "Whosoever repents the darkness in their heart," he quoted from the Book of Scholars, "let him raise high the Tusk and follow." To be Inrithi, he reminded them, was to be a follower of Inri Sejenus. And who followed more faithfully than those who walked in his Holy Steps?

"*Shimeh*," he said in a clear, far-travelling voice. "Shimeh is near, very near, for we have travelled farther in one day with our swords than we have in two years with our feet ..."

"Or our tongues!" some wit cried out.

Warm laughter.

"Four nights ago," Gotian declared, "I sent a scroll to Maithanet, our Most Holy Shriah, Exalted Father of our Holy War." He paused, and all was silence save the cracking of the bonfire. He still wore bandages about both hands, which had been burned by dragging the fallen through fiery grasses.

"Upon that scroll," he continued, "I wrote but one word—one word!— for my fingers still bled."

Sporadic shouts broke from the masses. The Charge of the Shrial Knights had already become legend.

"Triumph!" he cried.

"*Triumph!*"

The Men of the Tusk exploded in exultation, howling and wailing, some even weeping. Shadowy beneath the stars, the mounds and debris of surrounding Mengedda shivered.

But Kellhus remained silent. He glanced at Sarcellus, who had his back partially turned toward him, and noticed ... *discrepancies*. Smiling, resplendent in firelight and gold and white, Gotian waved for the masses to settle, then called on them to join him in the Temple Prayer.

Sweet God of Gods,
who walk among us,
innumerable are your holy names ...

Words uttered through a thousand human throats. The air thrummed with an impossible resonance. The ground itself spoke, or so it seemed ... But Kellhus saw only Sarcellus—saw only differences. His stance, his height and build, even the lustre of his black hair. All imperceptibly different.

A replacement.

The original copy had been killed, Kellhus realized, just as he'd hoped. The *position* of Sarcellus, however, had not. His death had gone unwitnessed, and they'd simply replaced him.

Strange that a man could be a position.

for your name is Truth,
which endures and endures,
for ever and ever.

After completing the purificatory rites, Gotian and Sarcellus withdrew. Stiff in their ornamental hauberks, the Gilgallic Priests then rose to declare the Battle-Celebrant, the man whom dread War had chosen as his vessel on the field five days previous. The masses fell silent in anticipation. The selection of the Battle-Celebrant, Xinemus had complained to Kellhus earlier that day, was the object of innumerable wagers, as though it were a lottery rather than a divine determination. An older man, his square-cut beard as white as hoarfrost, stepped to the forefront of the others: Cumor, the High Cultist of Gilgaöl. But before he could begin, Prince Skaiyelt leapt to his feet and cried, *"Weät firlik peor kaflang dau hara mausrot!"* He whirled from the Great and Lesser Names to those massed about Kellhus, his long blond hair and beard spilling from shoulder to shoulder. *"Weät dau hara mût keflinga! Keflinga!"*

Cumor sputtered something indignant and unintelligible, while everyone else turned to Skaiyelt's Thunyeri for explanation. His translators, it seemed, were nowhere to be found.

"He says," one of Gothyelk's men finally shouted in Sheyic from the higher tiers, "that we must first discuss leaving this place. That we *must* flee."

The humid air suddenly buzzed with competing shouts, some accusatory, others crying out assent. Skaiyelt's monstrous groom, Yalgrota, jumped to his feet and began beating his chest and roaring threats. The shrunken Sranc heads about his waist danced like tassels. Inexplicably, Skaiyelt began kicking at the ground. He crouched with his knife, then stood, raising something against the bonfire's glare. Hundreds gasped.

He held a skull, half choked with dirt, half crushed by some ancient blow.

"*Weät,*" he said slowly, "*dau hara mût keflinga.*"

The dead surfacing like the drowned ... *How,* Kellhus thought, *could this be possible?*

But he needed to stay focused on practical mysteries—not those pertaining to the ground.

Skaiyelt tossed the skull into the bonfire, glared at his fellow Great Names. The debate continued, and one by one they acquiesced, though Chepheramunni at first refused to credit the story. Even the Exalt-General conceded without complaint. Over the course of the debate, some looks wandered toward Kellhus, but no one solicited his opinion. After a short time, Proyas announced that the Holy War would leave Mengedda and her cursed plains come morning.

The Men of the Tusk rumbled in wonder and relief.

Attention was once again yielded to aging Cumor, who, either because he was flustered or dreaded further interruptions, dispensed with the Gilgallic rites altogether and came directly to stand over Saubon. The other priests seemed more than a little disconcerted.

"Kneel," the old man called out in a quavering voice.

Saubon did as he was told, but not before sputtering, "Gotian! He led the charge!"

"It is you, Coithus Saubon," Cumor replied, his tone so soft that few, Kellhus imagined, could hear him. "*You* ... Many saw it. Many saw *him*, the Shield-Breaker, glorious *Gilgaöl* ... He looked through your eyes! Fought with your limbs!"

"No ..."

Cumor smiled, then withdrew a circlet woven of thorns and olive sprigs from his voluminous right sleeve. Save for the odd cough, the gathered Inrithi fell absolutely silent. With an old man's unsteady gentleness, he placed the circlet upon Saubon's head. Then stepping back, the High Cultist of Gilgaöl cried, "Rise, Coithus Saubon, Prince of Galeoth ... Battle-Celebrant!"

Once again the assembly thundered in exultation. Saubon pressed himself to his feet, but slowly, like a man wearied by a near heartbreaking run. For a moment he looked about in disbelief, then without warning, he turned to Kellhus, his cheeks shining with tears in the firelight. His clean-shaven face still bore cuts and bruises from five days previous.

Why? his anguished look said. *I don't deserve this ...*

Kellhus smiled sadly, and bowed to the precise degree jnan demanded from all men in the presence of a Battle-Celebrant. He'd more than mastered their brute customs by now; he'd learned the subtle flourishes that transformed the seemly into the august. He knew their every cue.

The roaring redoubled. They'd all witnessed their exchanged look; they'd all heard the story of Saubon's pilgrimage to Kellhus at the ruined shrine.

It happens, Father. It happens.

But the thunderous cheering suddenly faltered, trailed into the rumble of questioning voices. Kellhus saw Ikurei Conphas standing before the bonfire not far from Saubon, his shouts only now becoming audible.

"—fools!" he railed. "Rank idiots! You'd *honour* this man? You'd acclaim acts that nearly doomed the entire Holy War?"

A tide of jeers and taunts swelled through the amphitheatre.

"Coithus Saubon, *Battle-Celebrant*," Conphas cried in derision, and somehow managed to silence the rumble. "*Fool-Celebrant*, I say! The man who nearly saw all of you killed on these cursed fields! And trust me, this is the one place where you *don't* want to die ..."

Saubon simply watched him, dumbstruck.

"You know what I mean," the Exalt-General said to him directly. "You know what you did was errant folly." Reflections of the bonfire curled like oil across his golden breastplate.

The masses had fallen utterly silent. He had no choice, Kellhus knew, but to intervene.

Conphas is too clever to—

"The craven see folly everywhere," a powerful voice boomed from the lower tiers. "All daring is rash in their eyes, because they would call their cowardice 'prudence.'" Cnaiür had stood from his place next to Xinemus.

Months had passed, and still the Scylvendi's penetration surprised him. Cnaiür saw the danger, Kellhus realized, knew that Saubon would be useless if he were discredited.

Conphas laughed. "So I'm a coward, am I, Scylvendi?" His right hand happened upon the pommel of his sword.

"In a manner," Cnaiür said. He wore black breeches and a grey thigh-length vest—plunder from the Kianene camp—that left both his chest and banded arms bare. Firelight shimmered across the vest's silk embroidery, flashed from his pale eyes. As always, the plainsman emanated a feral intensity that made others, Kellhus noted, stiffen in inarticulate alarm. Everything about him looked hard, like sinew one had to saw rather than slice.

"Since defeating the People," the Scylvendi continued, "much glory has been heaped upon your name. Because of this, you begrudge others that same glory. The valour and wisdom of Coithus Saubon have defeated Skauras—no mean thing, if what you said at your Emperor's knee was to be believed. But since this glory is not yours, you think it false. You call it foolishness, blind lu—"

"It *was* blind luck!" Conphas cried. "The Gods favour the drunk and the soft-of-head ... *That's* the only lesson we've learned."

"I cannot speak to what your gods favour," Cnaiür replied. "But you have learned much, very much. You have learned the Fanim cannot withstand a determined charge by Inrithi knights, nor can they break a determined defence by Inrithi footmen. You have learned the strengths and shortcomings of their tactics and their weapons against a heavily armoured foe. You have witnessed the limits of their patience. And you have *taught* as well—a very important lesson. You have taught them to *fear*. Even now, in the hills, they run like jackals before the wolf."

Cheers spread through the crowds, gradually growing into another deafening roar.

Stupefied, Conphas stared at the Scylvendi, his fingers kneading his pommel. He'd been roundly defeated. And so swiftly ...

"Time for another scar on your arms!" someone cried, and laughter boomed through the amphitheatre. Cnaiür graced the assembled Inrithi with a rare fierce grin.

Even from this distance, Kellhus knew the Exalt-General felt neither shame nor embarrassment: the man smiled as though a crowd of lepers had just insulted his beauty. For Conphas, the derision of thousands meant as little as the derision of one. The game was all that mattered.

Among those Kellhus needed to dominate, Ikurei Conphas was an especially problematic case. Not only did he suffer pride—almost lunatic in proportion—he possessed a pathological disregard for the estimations of other men. Moreover, like his uncle the Emperor, he believed that Kellhus himself was somehow connected to Skeaös—to the Cishaurim, if Achamian could be believed. Add to that a childhood surrounded by the labyrinthine intrigues of the Imperial Precincts, and the Exalt-General became almost as immune to Dûnyain techniques as the Scylvendi.

And he planned, Kellhus knew, something catastrophic for the Holy War ...

Another mystery. Another threat.

The Great Names moved on to bicker about further things. First Proyas, using arguments he'd rehearsed, Kellhus surmised, with Cnaiür, suggested they send a mounted force to Hinnereth with all dispatch, not to take the city but to secure its surrounding fields before they could be prematurely harvested and sheltered within its walls. The same, he declared, should be done for the entire coastline. Under torment, several Kianene captives had said that Skauras, as a contingency, had ordered all the winter grains in Gedea harvested as soon as they became milk-ripe. Swearing that the Imperial Fleet could supply the Holy War entire, Conphas argued against the plan, warning that Skauras yet possessed the strength and cunning to destroy any such force. Loath to depend on the Emperor in any way, the other Great Names were disinclined to believe him, however, and it was agreed: several thousand horsemen would be mustered and sent out on the morrow under Earl Athjeäri, Palatine Ingiaban, and Earl Werijen Greatheart.

Then the incendiary issue of the Ainoni host's sloth and the constant fragmentation of the Holy War was broached. Here masked

Chepheramunni, who had to answer to the Scarlet Spires, found a surprise ally in Proyas, who argued, with several provisos, that they actually should *continue* travelling in separate contingents. When the issue threatened to become intractable, he called on Cnaiür for support, but the Scylvendi's harsh assessment had little effect, and the argument dragged on.

The first Men of the Tusk continued shouting into the night, growing ever more drunk on the Sapatishah's sweet Eumarnan wines. And Kellhus studied them, glimpsed depths that would have terrified them had they known. Periodically, he revisited the thing called Sarcellus, who often gazed back, as though Kellhus were a boy with fine shanks that a wicked Shrial Knight might love. It taunted him. But such a look was merely a semblance, Kellhus knew, as surely as the expressions animating his own face.

Still, there could be no doubt—not any longer ... They knew Kellhus could see them.

I must move more quickly, Father.

The Nilnameshi had it wrong. Mysteries could be killed, if one possessed the power.

Lounging beneath the bellied crimson canvas of his pavilion, Ikurei Conphas spent the first hour verbally entertaining various scenarios involving the Scylvendi's murder. Martemus had said little, and in some infuriated corner of his thoughts Conphas suspected that the drab General not only secretly admired the barbarian but had thoroughly enjoyed the earlier fiasco in the amphitheatre. And yet, by and large, this bothered Conphas little, though he couldn't say why. Perhaps, assured of Martemus's actual loyalty, he cared nothing for the man's spiritual infidelities. Spiritual infidelities were as common as dirt.

Afterward, he spent another hour telling Martemus what was to happen at Hinnereth. This had lightened his mood greatly. Demonstrations of his brilliance always buoyed his spirits, and his plans for Hinnereth were nothing short of genius. How well it paid to be friends with one's enemies.

And so, feeling magnanimous, he decided to open a little door and allow Martemus—easily the most competent and trustworthy of all his generals—into some rather large halls. In the coming months, he would need confidants. All Emperors needed confidants.

But of course, prudence demanded certain assurances. Though Martemus was loyal by nature, loyalties were, as the Ainoni were fond of saying, like wives. One must always know where they lie—and with absolute certainty.

He leaned back into his canvas chair and peered past Martemus to the far side of the pavilion, where the crimson Standard of the Over-Army rested in its illumined shrine. His gaze lingered on the ancient Kyranean disc that glinted from the folds—supposedly once the chest piece of some Great King's harness. For some reason the figures stamped there—golden warriors with elongated limbs—had always arrested him. So familiar and yet so alien.

"Have you ever stared at it before, Martemus? I mean, truly *stared?*"

For a moment the General looked as though he might be too far into his cups, but only for a moment. The man never truly got drunk. "The Concubine?" he asked.

Conphas smiled pleasantly. Common soldiers commonly referred to the Over-Standard as the "Concubine" because tradition demanded it be quartered with the Exalt-General. Conphas had always found the name particularly amusing: he'd drawn his cock across that hallowed silk more than once ... A strange feeling, to spill one's seed on the sacred. Quite delicious. "Yes," he said, "the Concubine."

The General shrugged. "What officer hasn't?"

"And how about the Tusk? Have you ever laid eyes upon it?"

Martemus raised his brows. "Yes."

"Really?" Conphas exclaimed. He himself had never seen the Tusk. "When was that?"

"As a boy, back when Psailas II was Shriah. My father brought me with him to Sumna to visit his brother—my uncle—who for a time was an orderly in the Junriüma ... He took me to see it."

"Did he now? What did you think?"

The General stared into his wine bowl, which he held poised between his wonderfully thick fingers. "Hard to remember ... Awe, I think."

"Awe?"

"I remember my ears ringing. I shook, I know that ... My uncle told me I should be afraid, that the Tusk was *connected* to far bigger things." The General smiled, fixing Conphas with his clear brown eyes. "I asked him if he meant a mastodon and he swatted me—right there!—in the presence of the Holiest of Holies ..."

Conphas affected amusement. "Hmm, the Holiest of Holies ..." He took a long sip of his wine, savoured the warm, almost buzzing taste. Many years had passed since he'd last enjoyed Skauras's private stock. He could still scarcely believe the old jackal had been bested, and by *Coithus Saubon* ... He'd meant what he'd said earlier: the Gods *did* favour the soft-of-head. Men like Conphas, on the other hand, they tested. Men like themselves ...

"Tell me, Martemus, if you had to die defending one or the other, the Concubine or the Tusk, which would it be?"

"The Concubine," the General replied without a whisper of hesitation.

"And why's that?"

Again the General shrugged. "Habit."

Conphas fairly howled. Now *that* was funny. Habit. What more assurance could a man desire?

Dear man! Precious man!

He paused, collected himself for a moment, then said, "This man, Prince Kellhus of Atrithau ... What do you make of him?"

Martemus scowled, then leaned forward in his chair. Conphas had once made a game of this, leaning forward and back, and watching the way Martemus's pose answered his, as though some critical distance between their faces must always be observed. In some ways, Martemus was such a strange man.

"Intelligent," the General said after a moment, "well spoken, and utterly impoverished. Why do you ask?"

Still hesitant, Conphas appraised his subordinate for a moment. Martemus was unarmed, as was custom when conferring alone with members of the Imperial Family. He wore only a plain red smock. *He cares nothing about impressing me* ... This, Conphas reminded himself, was what made his opinion so invaluable.

"I think it's time I told you a little secret, Martemus ... Do you remember Skeaös?"

"The Emperor's Prime Counsel. What of him?"

"He was a spy, a *Cishaurim* spy … My uncle, ever keen to confirm his fears, noted that Prince Kellhus seemed peculiarly interested in Skeaös during that final gathering of the Great Names on the Andiamine Heights. Our Emperor, as you know, is not one to idly brood over his suspicions."

Martemus blanched with shock. For a moment, it looked his nose might fall off his face. Conphas could almost read his thoughts: *Skeaös a Cishaurim spy? This is a little secret?*

"So Skeaös admitted working for the Cishaurim?"

The Exalt-General shook his head. "He didn't need to … He was … He was some kind of abomination—a *faceless* abomination!—and of a species the Imperial Saik couldn't detect … Which means of course he *must* have been Cishaurim."

"Faceless?"

Conphas blinked, and for the thousandth time saw Skeaös's oh-so-familiar face … unclutch. "Don't ask me to explain. I cannot."

Fucking words.

"So you think this Prince Kellhus is a Cishaurim spy as well? A contact of some kind?

"He's *something*, Martemus. Just what remains to be seen."

The General's astonished expression suddenly hardened into something shrewd. "Like the Emperor, you're not one to harbour idle suspicions, Lord Exalt-General."

"True, Martemus. But unlike my uncle, I know the wisdom of staying my hand, of letting my enemies think I'm deceived. To observe, and to observe closely, is not to remain idle."

"But this is my point," Martemus said. "Surely you've purchased informants. Surely you've had the man watched … What have you learned so far?"

Surely. "Not much. He camps with the Scylvendi, seems to share a woman with him—quite a beauty, I'm told. He spends his days with a Schoolman named Drusas Achamian—the *same* Mandate fool my uncle contracted to corroborate the Imperial Saik regarding Skeaös, though whether this is anything more than a coincidence, I don't know. Supposedly they talk history and philosophy. He belongs, like the Scylvendi, to Proyas's inner circle, and he wields, as fairly the entire Holy War witnessed tonight, some kind of strange power over Saubon. Otherwise, the caste-menials seem to think he's a poor man's prophet—a seer or something."

"Not much?" Martemus exclaimed. "From your description, he sounds like a man of power to me—*frightful* power, if he belongs to the Cishaurim."

Conphas smiled. "Growing power ..." He leaned forward, and sure enough, Martemus leaned back. "Would you like to know what I think?"

"Of course."

"I think he's been sent by the Cishaurim to infiltrate and destroy the Holy War. Saubon's idiotic march and that nonsense about 'punishing the Shrial Knights' was simply his first attempt. Mark me, there *will* be another. He bewitches men, somehow, plays the prophet ..."

Martemus narrowed his eyes and shook his head. "But I've heard quite the opposite. They say he denies those who make more of him than he is."

Conphas laughed. "Is there any better way to posture as a prophet? People don't like the smell of presumption, Martemus. Even the pig castes have noses as keen as wolves when it comes to those who claim to be more. *Me*, on the other hand, I quite like the savoury stink of gall. I find it honest."

Martemus's face darkened. "Why are you telling me this?"

"Always to the quick, eh, General? Small wonder I find you so refreshing."

"Small wonder," the man repeated.

Such a dry wit, Martemus. Conphas reached for the decanter and refilled his bowl with more of the Sapatishah's wine. "I tell you this, Martemus, because I would have you play general in a different sort of war. Quite against all reason, you've become a man of power. If this Prince Kellhus collects followers to a purpose, if he *courts* the mighty, then you should prove well nigh irresistible."

A pained expression crept into Martemus's face. "You want me to play disciple?"

"Yes," Conphas replied. "I do not like the smell of this man."

"Then why not just have him killed?"

But of course ... How could he be so penetrating and so dense by turns?

The Exalt-General inclined his bowl and watched the blood-dark wine roll in the bottom. For an instant, its bouquet transported him back years, to his days as a hostage in Skauras's opulent court. He glanced once again to the Over-Standard behind its curtain of incense. His sweet Concubine.

"It's strange," Conphas said, "but I feel young."

CHAPTER EIGHT

MENGEDDA

All men are greater than dead men.

—AINONI PROVERB

*Every monumental work of the State is measured by cubits. Every
cubit is measured by the length of the Aspect-Emperor's arm. And
the Aspect-Emperor's arm, they say, stands beyond measure. But I
say the Aspect-Emperor's arm is measured by the length of a cubit,
and that all cubits are measured by the works of the State. Not even
the All stands beyond measure, for it is more than what lies within
it, and "more" is a kind of measure. Even the God has His cubits.*

—IMPARRHAS, *PSŪKALOGUES*

Early Summer, 4111 Year-of-the-Tusk, the Plains of Mengedda

"They celebrate my uncle's honour," Earl Athjeäri said as he led Kellhus
through carousing mobs of drunk Northmen. The Galeoth preferred
leather wedge tents with heavy wooden frames adorned by tusks and
crude animal totems. Without the need to stake guy ropes, they were able
to arrange them board to board, canvas to canvas, in large circular enclo-
sures about a central fire. Athjeäri led him through enclosure after enclosure, prompted by Kellhus's questions to explain the various peculiarities
of his people's appearance, customs, and traditions. Though annoyed at

first, the young Earl was soon beaming with wonder and pride, struck not only by the distinctiveness and nobility of his people, but by a new self-understanding as well. Like so many men, he'd never truly considered who or what he was.

Coithus Athjeäri, Kellhus knew, would never forget this walk.

At once so easy and so difficult …

Kellhus had taken the shortest path. He'd acquired crucial background knowledge concerning Saubon's heritage, and he'd gained the confidence and admiration of his precocious nephew, who hence would look on Prince Kellhus of Atrithau as a friend and more, as someone who made him wiser—*better*—than he was with other men.

Eventually, they shouldered their way into an enclosure far larger, and far drunker, than any of the others. On the far side Kellhus glimpsed the Red Lion banner of House Coithus rising above the shadowy congregation. Athjeäri began pushing his way toward it, cursing and berating his countrymen. But he paused when they neared the enclosure's centre, where a bonfire whisked sparks and smoke into the night sky.

"*This* will interest you," he said, grinning.

A large clearing had been opened before the fire, and two Galeoth, breathless and stripped to the waist, stood facing each other in its heart, holding what appeared to be two staffs between them. Each, Kellhus realized, had their wrists bound by leather straps to the end of each pole, so they were held from each other. Gripping the polished wood, they leaned each against the other, their white chests and sun-burned arms taut with veins and straining muscle. The onlookers hooped and roared.

Suddenly the nearer man pulled rather than pushed with his left, and his opponent stumbled forward. Then the two men fairly danced around the fire, heaving, yanking, shoving, thrusting, whatever it took to bring their opponent to the packed earth.

The larger man staggered, and for a moment looked as though he might lurch into the fire. The crowd gasped, then cheered as he caught himself just short of the fiery column. With a roar he jerked the smaller man into his long shadow, then drove him back, only to suddenly falter, shaking his head fiercely. A small flame puffed from his cropped mane, at the sight of which literally dozens doubled over with laughter. The man cried out, cursed. For an instant, it appeared he might panic, but someone sent what looked like beer or mead slapping across his scalp. More booming laughter, punctuated by cries of foul.

Athjeäri chortled, turned to Kellhus. "These two *really* hate each other," he called over the ruckus. "They want blood or burns more than silver!"

"What is this?"

"We call it *gandoki*, or 'shadows.' To beat your *gandoch*, your shadow, you must knock him to the ground." His laugh was relaxed and infectious, the laugh of a man utterly certain of his place among others. "The picks," he added, using the common derogatory term for non-Norsirai, "they think we Galeoth are a race without subtlety—and so women say of men! But gandoki proves that it's not entirely true."

Then suddenly, as though stepping through a door from nowhere, Sarcellus stood between them, wearing the same white and gold vestments as at the amphitheatre. "Prince," he said, bowing his head to Kellhus.

Athjeäri fairly whirled. "What are you doing here?"

The Shrial Knight laughed, fixing the Earl with large camel-lashed eyes. "The same as you, I suppose. I wished to confer with Prince Kellhus."

"You followed us," Athjeäri said.

"*Please* ..." the thing replied, pretending to be offended. "I knew I'd find him here, enjoying the largesse"—he looked sceptically at the surrounding crowds—"of the Battle-Celebrant."

Athjeäri glanced at Kellhus, his look, his heart rate, even the draw of his breath striking a note of scarcely concealed aversion. He thought Sarcellus vain and effete, Kellhus realized, a particularly repellent member of a species he'd long ago learned to despise. But then, that was likely what the original Cutias Sarcellus had been: a pompous caste-noble. Sarcellus, the *real* Sarcellus, was dead. What stood here in his stead was a beast of some kind, an exquisitely trained animal. It had wrenched Sarcellus from his place and had assumed all he once was. It had robbed him even of his death.

No murder could be more total.

"Well then," the young Earl said, looking off as though distracted.

"Allow me a few words with the Knight-Commander," Kellhus said.

Though he scowled as he spoke, Athjeäri agreed to meet him at Saubon's tent in a short time. "Run along," Sarcellus said, as the Earl impatiently shoved his way among his shouting kinsmen.

A keening shriek pealed through the air. Kellhus saw the larger gandoki player stumble and fall beneath the fists of several Galeoth who'd broken from the crowd. But the screaming came from his smaller opponent. Kellhus glimpsed the man between shadowy legs, blistered from the fire, smoking coals still embedded in his right shoulder and arm.

Others came rushing to the larger man's defence ... A knife flashed. Blood slopped across the packed ground.

Kellhus glanced at Sarcellus, who stood rigid, utterly absorbed by the mayhem unfolding before them. Pupils dilated. Arrested breath. Quickened pulse ...

It possesses involuntary responses.

Its right hand, Kellhus noted, lingered near his groin, as though straining against some overpowering masturbatory compulsion. Its thumb stroked its forefinger.

Another cry rang out.

The thing called Sarcellus fairly trembled with ardour. These things hungered, Kellhus realized. They *ached.*

Of all the rude animal impulses that coerced and battered the intellect, none possessed the subtlety or profundity of carnal lust. In some measure, it tinctured nearly every thought, impelled nearly every act. This was what made Serwë so invaluable. Without realizing, every man at Xinemus's fire—with the exception of the Scylvendi—knew they best wooed her by pandering to Kellhus. And they could do naught but woo her.

But Sarcellus, it was clear, ached for a different species of congress. One involving suffering and violence. Like the Sranc, these skin-spies continually yearned to rut with their knives. They shared the same maker, one who had harnessed the venal beast within their slaves, sharpened it as one might a spear point.

The Consult.

"Galeoth," Sarcellus remarked with an offhand grin, "are forever cutting their own throats, forever culling their own herd."

The brawl had been cut short by the ranting of Earl Anfirig. Carried hanging from arms and legs, three bloodied men were being hurried from the fire.

"'They strive,'" Kellhus said, quoting Inri Sejenus, "'for they know not what. So they cry villainy, and claim others stand in their way' ..."

Somehow the Consult knew he'd been instrumental to the Emperor's discovery of Skeaös. The question was whether his role had been incidental or otherwise. If they suspected he could somehow see their skin-spies, they would be forced to balance the immediate threat of exposure against the need to know *how* he could see them. *I must walk the line between, make myself a mystery they must solve ...*

Kellhus stared at the thing for a bold moment. When it feigned a scowl, he said, "No, please, indulge me ... There's something about you ... About your face."

"Is that why you watched me so in the amphitheatre?"

For a heartbeat, Kellhus opened himself to the legion within. He needed more information. He needed to know, which meant he needed a weakness, a vulnerability ...

This Sarcellus is new.

"Was I *that* indiscreet?" Kellhus said. "I apologize ... I was thinking of what you said to me that night in the Unaras at the ruined shrine ... You made quite an impression."

"And what did I say?"

It acknowledges its ignorance as any man would, any man with nothing to hide ... These things are well-trained.

"You don't recall?"

The imposter shrugged. "I say many things." With a smirk it added, "I have a beautiful voice ..."

Kellhus simulated a frown. "Are you playing with me? Playing some kind of game?"

The counterfeit face clenched into a scowl. "I assure you, I'm not. Just what did I say?"

"That something had happened," Kellhus began apprehensively, "that the endless ... *hunger*, I think you said ..."

Something like a twitch—too faint for world-born eyes—flickered across its expression.

"Yes," Kellhus continued. "The endless hunger ..."

"What about it?"

A near imperceptible tightening of pitch, quickening of cadence.

"You told me you weren't what you seemed. You told me you *weren't a Shrial Knight.*"

Another twitch, like a spider answering a shiver through its silk.

These things can be read.

"You deny this?" Kellhus pressed. "Are you telling me you don't remember?"

The face had become as impassive as a palm. "What else did I say?"

It's confused ... Uncertain as to what to do.

"Things I could scarcely credit at the time. You said you'd been assigned to coordinate observation of the Mandate Schoolman, and to that end you'd seduced his lover, Esmenet. You said that I was in great danger, that your masters thought I had some hand in some disaster in the Emperor's court. You said that you were prepared to help ..."

The creases and wrinkles of its expression jerked into a network of hairline cracks, as though sucking humid night air.

"Did I tell you why I confessed all this?"

"Because you'd hungered for it too ... But what's this? You really *don't remember,* do you?"

"I remember."

"Then *what is this?* Why have you become so ... so *coy?* You seem different."

"Perhaps I've reconsidered."

So much. In the span of moments, Kellhus had confirmed his hypotheses regarding the Consult's immediate interests, and he'd uncovered the rudiments of what he needed to read these creatures. But most important, he'd sown the threat of betrayal. How could Kellhus possibly know what he knew, they would ask, unless the original Sarcellus had actually told him? Whatever their ends, the Consult depended, through and through, upon total secrecy. One defection could undo everything. If they feared for the reliability of their field agents—these skin-spies—they would be forced to restrict their autonomy and to proceed with more caution.

In other words, they would be forced to yield the one commodity

Kellhus required more than any other: *time*. Time to dominate this Holy War. Time to find Anasûrimbor Moënghus.

He was one of the Conditioned, Dûnyain, and he followed the shortest path. The Logos.

The surrounding crowds had settled into rumbling conversations, and both Kellhus and Sarcellus looked to the bonfire. A towering Gesindalman, his hair bound into a war-knot, raised the gandoki sticks high against the night sky, crying out for more challengers. Laughing, the thing called Sarcellus seized Kellhus by the forearm and pulled him into the raucous circle. The crowd began thundering anew.

It believed me.

Did it improvise? Was it acting out of panic? Or was this its intent all along? There was no question of refusing the challenge, not in the company of warlike men. The resulting loss of face would be crippling.

Washed by the heat of the bonfire, they stripped, Kellhus to the linen kilt he wore beneath his blue-silk cassock, Sarcellus to nothing, in the fashion of Nansur athletes. The Galeoth howled in ridicule, but the thing called Sarcellus seemed oblivious. They stood a length apart, appraising each other while two Agmundrmen bound their wrists to the poles. The Gesindalman jerked each pole to ensure it was secure, then without a glance at either of them, he cried, "Gaaaan*doch!*"

Shadow.

Bare skin yellow in the firelight, they circled each other, lightly grasping the ends of their poles. Though still roaring, the crowds trailed into silence, fell away altogether, until there was only one figure, Sarcellus, occupying one *place* ...

Kellhus.

Sheets of muscle flexing beneath fire-shining skin, many anchored and connected in inhuman ways. Dilated eyes watching, *studying*, from a knuckled face. Steady pulse. Tumid phallus, hardening. A mouth made of gracile fingers, moving, speaking ...

"We are old, Anasûrimbor, very, very old. Age is power in this world."

He was bound to a beast, Kellhus realized, to something, according to Achamian, begot in the bowels of Golgotterath. An abomination of the Old Science, the Tekne ... Possibilities bloomed, like branches twining through the open air of the improbable.

"Very many," it hissed, "have thought to play the game you now play."

Losing was the simplest solution, but weakness incited contempt, invited aggression.

"We've had a thousand thousand foes through the millennia, and we've made shrieking agonies of their hearths, wildernesses of their nations, mantles of their skins ..."

But defeating this creature could render Kellhus too much a threat.

"All of them, Anasûrimbor, and you are no different."

He must strike some kind of balance. But how?

Kellhus thrust with his right, heaved with his left, tried to draw Sarcellus off-balance. Nothing. It was as though the poles had been harnessed to a bull. Preternatural reflexes. And strong—very strong.

Strategies revised. Alternatives revisited. The thing called Sarcellus grinned, his phallus now curved like a bow against his belly. To be aroused by battle or competition, Kellhus knew, occasioned great honour among the Nansur.

How strong is it?

Kellhus leaned into the poles, elbows back, as though holding a wheelbarrow, and *pushed*. Sarcellus adopted the same stance. Muscle strained, knotted, gleaming as though oiled. The ash poles creaked.

"Who are you?" Kellhus cried under his breath.

Sarcellus grunted, its fists shaking, sinking to its waist, then it yanked. Kellhus skidded forward. The instant of his imbalance, it jerked around, as though throwing a discus. Kellhus caught himself, heaved back on both poles. Then they were dancing around the clearing, jerking and thrusting, matching move with countermove, each the perfect shadow of the other ...

Between heartbeats, Kellhus tracked the shift and sway of its centre of balance, an abstract point marked by the peak of its erection. He observed repetitions, recognized patterns, tested anticipations, all the while analyzing the possibilities of the game, the manifold lines of move and consequence. He restricted himself to an elegant yet limited repertoire of moves, luring it into habits, reflexive responses ...

"What do you want?" he cried.

Then he improvised.

From a near crouch, he kicked down on the left pole while throwing up his left arm, and punching out with his right. Its right hand slammed to the earth, Sarcellus doubled forward and was thrown back. For an instant it resembled a man bound to a falling boulder ...

It kicked free of the ground, trying to somersault back to its feet. Kellhus yanked the poles backward, tried to slam it onto its stomach. Somehow it managed to pull its left leg, knee to chest, underneath in time. Its right foot scooped into the fire ...

A shower of ash and coals went streaming into the air, not to blind Kellhus, but to *obscure* the two of them, he realized, from the watching Galeoth ...

It jerked both arms back and out, thrust itself forward between the poles, kicked. Kellhus blocked with his own shin and ankle—once, twice ...

It means to kill me ... An unfortunate accident while playing a barbaric Galeoth game.

Kellhus jerked his arms inward and across, caught the thing's third kick with the bisecting poles. For a heartbeat, he held the advantage in balance. He thrust it backward, heaved it nude into the golden flames ...

Perhaps if I injure ...

Then yanked it forward.

A mistake. Unharmed, Sarcellus landed running, barrelled Kellhus backward with inhuman strength, slammed him into the packed Galeoth masses, bowling men over and forcing others to scramble clear. Once, twice, Kellhus almost fell, then his back slammed against something heavy—a tent frame. It collapsed with a crack and the wedge tent went down, under, and they were in the darkness beyond the enclosure—where the thing, Kellhus realized, hoped to kill.

This must end!

His feet caught hard earth. Bracing his legs, grasping the poles, he dipped and wrenched upward, wheeling Sarcellus high into the night air. The thing's astonishment lasted only a heartbeat, and it managed to crack one of the poles with a kick ... Kellhus slapped it to the ground like a flag.

The place became a man, slick with perspiration, breathing deep.

The first of the Galeoth sprinted over the demolished tent, calling for torches, stumbling in the sudden darkness. They saw Sarcellus pressing himself to his hands and knees at Kellhus's feet. As astounded as they were, they bawled out Kellhus's name, acclaiming him victor.

What have I done, Father?

As they unbound his wrists, slapping him on the back and swearing they'd never seen the like, Kellhus could only watch Sarcellus, who slowly pulled himself to his feet.

Bones should have been broken. But then, Kellhus now knew, it was a thing without bones, a thing of cartilage ...

Like a shark.

Saubon watched Athjeäri stare in horror at the bones scattered across the earthen floor. The tent was small, far smaller than the garish pavilions used by the other Great Names. Beneath the blue and red-dyed canvas, there was room enough only for a beaten field cot and a small camp table, where the Galeoth Prince sat, so very deep into his cups ...

Outside the revellers howled and laughed—the fools!

"But he's *here*, Uncle," the young Earl of Gaenri said. "He waits ..."

"Send him away!" Saubon cried. He loved his nephew, dearly, couldn't look at him without seeing his beloved sister's beautiful face. She'd protected him from Papa. She'd loved him before she died ...

But had she *known* him?

Kussalt knew—

"But Uncle, you asked—"

"I care not what I asked!"

"I don't understand ... What's happened to you?"

To be known by one man and to be *hated!* Saubon leapt from his seat, seized his nephew about the shoulders, cowed him the way only one of Eryeat's sons could. How he wanted to cry out the truth, to confess everything to this boy, this man with his sister's eyes—his sister's blood! But he wasn't her ... He didn't know him.

And he would despise him if he did.

"I cannot! I cannot have him see me like this! Can't you see?"

No one must know! No one!

"Like what?"

"*This!*" Saubon bawled, thrusting the young man back.

Athjeäri caught his balance and stood dumbstruck, openly hurt. He should have been outraged, Saubon thought. He was the Earl of Gaenri, one of the most powerful men in Galeoth. He should have been infuriated, not appalled ...

Kussalt's forever-murmuring lips. *"I would have you know how much I hate—"*

"Just send him away!" Saubon cried.

"As you wish," his nephew murmured. Glancing once again at the bones prodding through the earth, he withdrew through the leather flaps.

Bones. Like so many little tusks.

No one! Not even him!

Though it was late, sleep was out of the question. It seemed to Eleäzaras that he'd been asleep for weeks, now that High Ainon and the Scarlet Spires had finally rejoined the Holy War. For what was sleep, if not unconsciousness of the greater world? A profound ignorance.

To remedy this, Eleäzaras had set Iyokus, his Master of Spies, to work the instant their palanquins had set ground on the Plains of Mengedda. The battlefield of five days previous needed to be surveyed, and witnesses interviewed, to determine what tactics the Cishaurim had used, and how the Inrithi had bested them. The various informants and spies they'd placed throughout the Holy War also had to be contacted and questioned, both to ascertain how things stood in general now that they marched through heathen territory, and to pursue the matter of these new Cishaurim spies.

Faceless spies. Spies without the Mark.

He awaited Iyokus outside his pavilion, pacing by torchlight, while his secretaries and Javreh bodyguards watched from a discreet distance. After spending weeks entombed in his palanquin, he found himself despising enclosed spaces. Everything seemed to bind and constrict these days.

After a time, Iyokus emerged from the darkness, a ghoul in flashing crimson.

"Walk with me," he said to the chanv addict.

"Through the encampment?"

"You fear riots?" the Grandmaster asked somewhat incredulously. "After losing so many to the Cishaurim, I'd assumed they'd appreciate a few blasphemers in their midst."

"No ... I thought we might visit the ruins instead. They say Mengedda is older than Shir ..."

"Ah, Iyokus the Antiquarian," Eleäzaras laughed. "I keep forgetting ..." Though he personally had no interest in seeing the ruins—he thought antiquarianism a defect of character proper to Mandate Schoolmen— he felt curiously indulgent. Besides, the dead made for good company, he supposed, when planning one's very survival.

Instructing his bodyguards to remain behind, he strolled with Iyokus into the darkness.

"So what did you find?" he asked.

"After we illuminated the fields," Iyokus said, "things fell into place ..." Caught from the side by passing torchlight, his pigment-deprived eyes seemed to glow a momentary red. "Most unsettling, seeing the work of sorcery without the Mark. I had forgotten ..."

"One more reason for this outrageous risk, Iyokus: to stamp out the Psûkhe ..." A sorcery they couldn't see. A metaphysics they couldn't comprehend... What more did they need?

"Indeed," the linen-skinned man replied unconvincingly. "What we know is this: according to every report, Galeoth and non-Galeoth, Prince Saubon singlehandedly repulsed the Padirajah's Coyauri—"

"Impressive," Eleäzaras said.

"As impressive as it is unlikely," the ever-sceptical Master of Spies said. "But the point is moot. What matters is that the Fanim were then chased by the Shrial Knights. *That*, I think, was the decisive factor."

"How so?"

"The scorched turf corresponding to Gotian's charge doesn't begin at Saubon's lines along the ravine, where one might expect, but rather some seventy paces out ... I think the Coyauri, as they fled, actually screened the Shrial Knights from the Cishaurim ... They were only a hundred or so paces away when the psûkari began Scourging them."

"It was the Scourge they used, then?"

Iyokus nodded. "I would say so. And perhaps the Lash, as well."

"So they were Secondaries or Tertiaries?"

"Without question," the Master of Spies replied, "perhaps under one or two Primaries ... It's a pity we didn't have the foresight to post observers among the Norsirai: aside from what you and I witnessed ten years ago, we know next to nothing about their Concerts. And unfortunately no one seems to know just who any of them were—not even the higher ranking Kianene captives."

Eleäzaras nodded. "It would be nice to know who ... Even still, a dozen of them dead, Iyokus. A *dozen!*"

The Schoolmen of the Three Seas were called the "Few" for good reason. The Cishaurim, according to their informants in Shimeh and Nenciphon, could field at most one hundred to one hundred and twenty ranking psûkari, very near the number of sorcerers of rank the Scarlet Spires itself could field. When one counted in thousands, the loss of twelve scarcely seemed significant, and Eleäzaras had no doubt that many in the Holy War, among the Shrial Knights in particular, gnashed their teeth at the thought of how many they had lost for the sake of so few. But when one counted, as Schoolmen did, in *tens*, the loss of twelve was nothing short of catastrophic—or glorious.

"An astounding victory," Iyokus said. He gestured to the Men of the Tusk passing them in shadowy clots: spectators, Eleäzaras imagined, returning from the Council of Great and Lesser Names. "And from what I gather, the Men of the Tusk have only the dimmest notion."

So much the better, Eleäzaras thought. Strange, the way cruelty and jubilation could strike such sweet chords.

"This," he said with an air of declaration, "will be our strategy then. We conserve ourselves *at all costs*, allow these dogs to continue killing as many Cishaurim as they can." He paused to secure Iyokus's gaze. "We must save ourselves for Shimeh."

How many times had he, Iyokus, and the others debated this issue? Despite the sometimes unfathomable power of the Psûkhe, it remained, they all agreed, inferior to the Anagogis. The Scarlet Spires would win an open confrontation with the Cishaurim—there was no doubt. But how many of them would die? What power would the Scarlet Spires wield *after* destroying the Cishaurim? A triumph which saw them reduced to the status of a Minor School wouldn't be a triumph at all.

They must do more than defeat the Cishaurim, they must obliterate them. No matter how lunatic his thirst for vengeance, Eleäzaras would not gut his School.

"A wise course, Grandmaster," Iyokus said. "Yet I fear the Inrithi won't fare so well in a second encounter."

"And why's that?"

"The Cishaurim walked, probably to conceal themselves from Saubon's Chorae bowmen and crossbowmen, whom he'd positioned too far behind his forward ranks. The strange thing, however, is that they approached without a cavalry escort ..."

"They walked in the open? But I thought striking from opening waves of horsemen was their traditional tactic ..."

"So the Emperor's specialists claimed."

"Arrogance," Eleäzaras said. "Whenever they engage the Nansur, they face the Imperial Saik. This time they knew we were days away, still crossing the Southron Gates."

"So they waived precautions because they thought themselves invincible ..." Iyokus looked down, as though watching his sandalled feet and bruised toenails peep from the hem of his shining gown. "Possible," he finally said. "Their intent seems to have been to decimate the Inrithi centre, nothing more, to ensure it would collapse in the next assault. They probably thought themselves cautious ..."

They'd walked beyond the camp fires and embroidered round tents of their Ainoni countrymen to the perimeter of lost Mengedda. The ground sloped upward, breached by broad stone foundations—the remnants of some ancient wall, Eleäzaras realized. Taking care not to soil their gowns, they gained the stony summit. Around them stretched a great swath of debris fields, truncated walls, and on the skyline, an ancient acropolis crowned by a gallery of cyclopean pillars standing desolate beneath the constellation of Uroris.

Something broke the back of this place, Eleäzaras thought. *Something breaks the back of every place ...*

"What news of Drusas Achamian?" he asked. For some reason, he felt breathless.

The chanv addict stared into the night, lost in another of his annoying reveries. Who knew what happened in that spidery and methodical soul? Finally he said, "I fear you may be right about him ..."

"You *fear?*" Eleäzaras fairly snapped. "You concluded the interrogation of Skalateas yourself. You know what happened that night beneath the

Emperor's palace better than anyone—save the principals, perhaps. The abomination *recognized* Achamian, ergo, Achamian is somehow connected to the abomination. The abomination could only be a Cishaurim spy, ergo Achamian is connected to the Cishaurim."

Iyokus turned to him, his face as mild as milk. "But is the connection significant?"

"*That* is the very question we must answer."

"Indeed. And how do you propose we answer it?"

"How else? By seizing him. By interrogating him." Did he think the menace of these changelings didn't warrant such extreme measures? Eleäzaras couldn't imagine any greater threat!

"Just like Skalateas?"

Eleäzaras thought of the shallow grave they had left in Anserca, suppressed an uncharacteristic shudder.

"Just like Skalateas."

"And *that*," Iyokus said, "is precisely what I fear."

Suddenly Eleäzaras understood. "You think," he said, "that it would be useless to ply him ..."

Over the centuries, the Scarlet Spires had abducted dozens of Mandate Schoolmen, hoping to wrest from them the secrets of the Gnosis, the sorcery of the Ancient North. Not one of them had succumbed. Not one.

"I think plying him for *the Gnosis* would be useless," Iyokus said. "What I fear is that even under torment or the Compulsions, he'll simply insist the abomination that replaced Skeaös was a *Consult* and not a Cishaurim—"

"But we already know," Eleäzaras cried, "that the man plays a tune far different from the one he sings! Think of Geshrunni! Drusas Achamian *cut off his face* ... And then, a little over a year later, he's recognized by a *faceless* spy in the Emperor's dungeons? This is no mere coincidence!"

Eleäzaras glared at the man, clutched his shaking hands. He did not, he decided, like the reptilian way Iyokus *listened*.

"I know these arguments," Iyokus said. He turned to once again scrutinize the moonlit ruins, his expression translucent and unreadable. "I simply fear there's more to this ..."

"There's always more, Iyokus. Why else would men murder men?"

Esmenet had tried, many times since her daughter's death, to attend to the void within her.

She tried questioning it away by asking the priests she bedded, but they always said the same thing, that the God dwelt only in temples, and that she'd made a brothel of her body. Then they would brothel her again. For a time, she tried smearing it away by coupling with men for anything, half-coppers, bread, even a rotted onion—once. But men could never fill, only muddy.

So she turned to others like her, watching, observing. She studied the always-laughing whores, who somehow exulted in being guttered day for night, or the chirping slave girls, their faces anchored forward beneath their water-urns, smiling and rolling their eyes from side to side. She made their motions her motions, as though certainty were a kind of dance. And for a time she discovered comfort, as though habits of gesture and expression could drum for a deadened heart.

For a time she forgot the distance between a fact and a face.

She had never tried to love. If joy in gesture couldn't unseat desolation, then perhaps, joy in desperation.

For five days now, they'd camped together in the hills overlooking the Battleplain. Ranging ahead, Achamian had found a small stream, which they'd followed into the stony heights. They climbed into a band of pitch pine, whose massive cones rocked in slow circles in the wind, and found a pool of translucent green. They camped nearby, though the lack of forage for Achamian's mule, Daybreak, forced them to trek for an hour or so every day to gather fodder to supplement his grain.

Five days. Joking and brewing tea in the cool mornings, making love to the rush of dry wind through the trees, eating hare and squirrel—snared by Achamian, no less!—with their rations in the evening, touching each other's faces with wonder in the moonlight.

And swimming, floating. The crush of ardent heat in cool waters.

How she wished it would never end.

Esmenet pulled their sleeping mats from the tent, slapped them one after the other in the wind, then set them across warm rock. They'd pitched their tent across the soft ground beneath an ancient and massive pitch pine, a lone sentinel near the terminus of a broad shelf that terraced the north and eastern faces of the hill.

This, she thought, *is our place* ... Without visitors, without ruins, without *memories*, save for the animal bones they'd found curled beneath the tree when they'd first arrived.

She ducked back into the tent, pulled Achamian's worn leather satchel from the corner. It was musty, slick and damp where it had lain against the grasses. Powdery white mould had crept up the stitching.

She carried it out into the sunlight, sitting cross-legged on a soft but prickly carpet of pine needles. She pulled out various sheaves of vellum, and weighting them down with stones, set them out to dry. She found a small doll, human shaped, wooden, but with a simple silken nob for a head and a small rusty knife for a right hand. Humming an old tune from Sumna, she bounced it around, kicked its wooden legs in a little jig. After laughing at her foolishness, she set it out in the sun as well, crossing its legs and pressing its arms behind its head so that it looked like a daydreaming field-slave. What would Achamian be doing with a doll?

Then she pulled out a sheet that had been folded separate from the others. Opening it, she saw a series of brief, vertical scribbles arrayed across it, each joined to one, two, or several others by hastily scratched lines. Even though she couldn't read—she'd yet to meet a woman who could—she somehow knew this sheet was important. She resolved to ask Achamian when he returned.

After securing it under an axe-shaped flint, she turned to the stitching, began scratching away the mould with a twig.

Achamian emerged from the shadows of the deeper wood a short time afterward, bare to the waist, the firewood in his arms braced against his black-furred belly. He shot her a friendly frown as he walked past, glancing at his doll and papers. She grinned and snorted. She adored seeing him like this: a sorcerer playing woodsman, down to the breeches, no less. Even after all her time travelling with the Holy War, breeches still looked outlandish, barbaric—even curiously erotic. They were illegal in many Nansur cities.

"Do you know why the Nilnameshi think cats are more human than monkeys?" he asked, stacking his wood against the trunk of their great pine.

"No."

He turned toward her, slapping his palms against his breeches. "Curiosity. They think curiosity is what defines men." He walked up to her, grinning. "It certainly defines you."

"Curiosity has nothing to do with it," she replied, trying to sound cross. "Your bag smells like mouldy cheese."

"I always thought that was me."

"*You* smell like ass."

Achamian laughed, raised devilish brows. "But I washed my beard ..."

She tossed pine needles at his face, but the wind tugged them away. "And what's that for?" she asked, gesturing to the doll. "To lure little girls into your tent?"

He sat next to her on the ground. "*That*," he said, "is a Wathi Doll ... You'd make me throw it away if I told you more."

"I see ... And this," she continued, lifting the folded sheet. "What's this?"

His good humour evaporated.

"That's my map."

She held the parchment out between them, waved away a small wasp. "What's this writing? Names?"

"Individuals and different Factions. Everyone with some bearing on the Holy War ... The lines mark their interrelationships ... See," he said, pointing to a line of vertical script on the centre left edge, "that says, 'Maithanet.'"

"And below?"

"Inrau."

Without thinking she reached out and clutched his knee.

"What about the top corner, here," she said, a little too quickly.

"The Consult."

She listened to him recite the names, the Emperor, the Scarlet Spires, the Cishaurim, explaining their different intents and how he thought each might be related to the others. He said nothing that she hadn't heard before, but for some reason it suddenly seemed a powerful thing scratched in ink across this cured animal hide. It suddenly seemed horrifyingly *real* ... A world of implacable forces. Hidden. Violent ...

Chills pimpled her skin. Achamian, she realized, *didn't belong to her*—not truly. He never could. What was she compared with these mighty things?

I can't even read ...

"So why, Akka?" she found herself saying. "Why have you stopped?"

"What do you mean?" He stared fixedly at the sheet, as though absorbed.

"I know what you're supposed to *do*, Akka. In Sumna, you were constantly out, making inquiries, courting informants. Either that or you were waiting on some news. You were constantly *spying*. But not any more ... Not since you brought me to your tent."

"I thought it was only fair," he said breezily. "After all, you gave up—"

"Don't lie, Akka."

He sighed, and though sitting, assumed the stooping air of slaves who carried onerous burdens. She stared into his eyes. Clear, glistening brown. Need-nervous. Sad and wise. As always when she was this near to him, she yearned to comb her fingers through his beard, to probe the chin and jaw beneath.

How I love you.

"It's not you, Esmi," he said. "It's *him* ..." His gaze fell to the name nearest 'The Consult' on the parchment sheet, the only one he'd yet to decipher for her.

He didn't need to.

"Kellhus," she said.

They were silent for a time. A sudden gust whisked through the pine, and she glimpsed bits of fluff rolling away, up the granite slope and off into endless sky. For a moment she feared for the sheaves of parchment, but they were safe beneath their stones, their corners opening and closing like speechless mouths.

They'd ceased speaking of Kellhus aloud, ever since fleeing the Battleplain. Sometimes it seemed an unspoken accord, the kind lovers used to numb shared hurts. Other times it seemed a coincidence of aversions, like avoiding issues of fidelity or sex. But for the most part it just seemed unnecessary, as though any words they might use had been always already said.

For a time Kellhus had been a troubling figure, but he'd soon become intriguing, someone warm, welcoming, and mysterious—a man who promised pleasant surprises. Then at some point he'd become towering, someone who overshadowed all others—like a noble and indulgent father, or a great king breaking bread with his slaves. And now, even more so in his absence, he'd become a *shining* figure. A beacon of some kind. Something they must follow, if only because all else was so dark …

What is he? she wanted to say, but looked speechlessly to her lover instead.

To her husband.

They smiled at each other, shyly, as though just remembering they weren't strangers. They clasped dry, sun-warm hands. *Never have I been so happy.*

If only her daughter …

"Come," Achamian abruptly said, pressing himself to his feet. "I want to show you something."

She followed him from the matted humus onto the bare, sun-hot stone. She hissed and scampered to avoid burning her feet, climbing to the rounded ledge. With each step, the vast grey-green sweep of the Battleplain rose to brace the skies. Taking Achamian's proffered hand, she joined him on the ledge. She raised a hand to her brow, shielding her eyes from the sun's glare. Then she saw them …

"*Sweet Sejenus,*" she whispered.

Like the shadows of truly mountainous clouds, they darkened the plain, great columns of them, their arms winking like powdered diamond in the sunlight.

"The Holy War marches," Achamian said, rigid with what could only be awe.

Breathing hurt, or so it seemed. She glimpsed cohorts of knights, hundreds, even thousands, strong, and great files of infantrymen, as long as entire cities. She saw baggage-trains, rows of wains no bigger than grains of sand. And she saw banner after fluttering banner bearing the devices of a thousand Houses, each embroidered with silken Tusks …

"So many!" she exclaimed. What terror the Fanim must feel …

"More than two hundred and fifty thousand Inrithi warriors," Achamian said, "or so Zin claims …" For some reason, his voice came to her as though from the deeps of some cave. It sounded trapped and hollow. "And as many camp-followers, perhaps … No one knows for sure."

Thousands upon thousands. With the ponderousness of distant things, they encompassed the nearer reaches of the plain. They moved, she thought, like wine bleeding through wool.

How could so many be bent to one dreadful purpose? One place. One city.

Shimeh.

"Is it ..." she found herself gasping, "is it like something from your dreams?"

He paused, and though he neither swayed nor stumbled, Esmenet suddenly feared he was about to fall. She reached out, clutched his elbow.

"Like my dreams," he said.

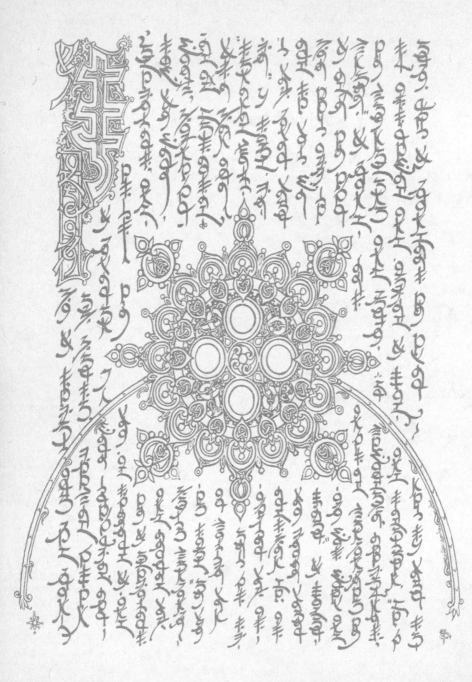

PART II:
The Second March

CHAPTER NINE

HINNERETH

One can look into the future, or one can look at the future. The latter is by far the more instructive.

—AJENCIS, THE THIRD ANALYTIC OF MEN

If one doubts that passion and unreason govern the fate of nations, one need only look to meetings between the Great. Kings and emperors are unused to treating with equals, and are often excessively relieved or repelled as a result. The Nilnameshi have a saying, "When princes meet, they find either brothers or themselves," which is to say, either peace or war.

—DRUSAS ACHAMIAN, THE COMPENDIUM OF THE FIRST HOLY WAR

Early Summer, 4111 Year-of-the-Tusk, Momemn

Song and myriad glittering torches greeted Ikurei Xerius III as he passed through curtains of wispy linen and into the palatial courtyard. Only in light must the Emperor be seen. There was a rustle of fabric as the throngs fell to their knees and pressed their powdered faces against the lawns. Only the tall Eothic Guardsmen remained standing. With child-slaves holding the hem of his gown, Xerius walked among the prostrated forms and savoured, as he always did, this loneliness. This godlike loneliness.

He summons me! Me! The insolence!

He mounted the wooden steps and climbed into the Imperial Chariot. A call was given for all to rise.

Xerius held out his white gloved hand, idly wondering whom Ngarau, his Grand Seneschal, had chosen to hand him the reins—an honour of great traditional significance, but beneath the Emperor's practical notice. Xerius trusted the judgement of his Grand Seneschal implicitly ... As he'd once trusted Skeaös.

A pang of horror. How long would that name cut like glass? *Skeaös.*

He barely noticed the boy who handed him the reins. Some young scion of House Kiskei? No matter. Xerius was typically graceful even when distracted—a trait inherited from his father. His father might have been a craven fool, but, oh, how he'd always looked the Great Emperor.

Xerius passed the reins to his Charioteer and numbly signalled the advance. The team started at the snap of the Captain's whip, then began prancing forward, drawing the gold-panelled chariot behind them. The censers affixed to the runners rattled, trailing streamers of blue incense. Jasmine and sweet sandalwood. The Emperor must be spared the disconcerting smells of his capital.

Observed by hundreds of painted and ingratiating faces, Xerius stared firmly forward, his stance statuary, his look remote and haughty. Only a select few received the nod of imperial acknowledgment: his bitchmother, Istriya; old General Kumuleus, whose support had assured him the Mantle after his father's death; and of course his favourite augur, Arithmeas. The intangible gold of Imperial favour was something Xerius hoarded jealously, and he was shrewd in its dispensation. Daring may be required to make the climb, but *thrift* was ever the key to holding the summit.

Another lesson Xerius had learned from his mother. The Empress had steeped him in the bloody history of his predecessors, tutored him with endless examples of past disaster. This one too trusting, that one too cruel, and so on. Surmante Skilura II, who'd kept a bowl of molten gold at his side to fling at those who displeased him, had been too cruel. Surmante Xatantius, on the other hand, had been too martial— conquest should enrich, not bankrupt. Zerxei Triamarius III had been too fat—so fat he needed slaves to brace his knees when he rode his horse. His death, Istriya had chortled, had been as much a matter of aesthetic decency as anything else. An emperor must look a God, not an overstuffed eunuch.

Too much of this and too much of that. "The world doesn't constrain us," the indomitable Empress had once explained, batting her harlot eyes, "so we must constrain ourselves—like the Gods ... Discipline, sweet Xerius. We must have *discipline*."

Something he possessed in abundance, or so Xerius thought.

Outside the courtyard, files of heavy cavalrymen, elite Kidruhil, positioned themselves before and after the Imperial Chariot, and flanked by running torch-bearers, the shining procession wound down the Andiamine Heights toward the dark and smoky troughs of Momemn. Moving slowly so the torch-bearers could keep pace, it clattered through the Imperial Precincts and onto the long, monumental avenue that joined the palace compounds to the temple-complex of Cmiral.

Numerous Momemnites stood in shadowy clots along the avenue, straining for a glimpse of their divine Emperor. Obviously word of his short pilgrimage had spread throughout the city. Turning left and right, Xerius smiled and raised his hand in salute after leisurely salute.

So he wants this to be public ...

At first, he could see little beyond the runners and their glittering torches, nor could he hear much over the sound of hooves clopping across cobble. The farther they travelled, however, the more congested the processional avenue became. Soon slaves and caste-menials jostled within spitting distance of the torch-bearers, their faces clearly illuminated, and Xerius realized that they actually jeered and laughed each time he saluted them. For a moment he feared his heart might stop. He clutched the shuddering runners to steady himself. That he could make such a fool of himself!

Despite the streaming censers, the air took on the distinct odour of shit.

Within moments, it seemed, hundreds had become thousands, and as their numbers grew, so did their gall. Soon the air shivered with the thunder of multitudes. Horrified, Xerius watched the torchlight sort through face after unwashed face, each turned to him, some watching in silent accusation or contempt, some sneering, others shouting or howling in spittle-flecked rage. The procession trundled on, as yet unimpeded, but the sense of bristling pageantry had evaporated. Xerius swallowed. Cold sweat snaked between his clothes and skin. He turned his eyes resolutely forward, to the stiff backs of his cavalrymen.

This is what he wants, he told himself. *Remember, be disciplined!*

Officers bawled urgent commands. The Kidruhil drew their clubs.

The procession found brief respite crossing the bridge over the Rat Canal. Xerius saw pleasure barges anchored in the black waters, drifting in torch-illumined fogs of incense. Rising from their cushions, caste-merchants and concubines lifted clay wafers, blessing-tablets to be broken in his name. But their looks, Xerius could not help but notice, turned away long before his passage was complete—to the awaiting mobs.

The unruly Momemnites once again engulfed the procession. Women, the old and the infirm, even children, all shouting now, all brandishing fists ... Glancing down, Xerius saw a poxed man rolling a rotted tooth on his tongue, which he spit as the Imperial Chariot passed. It fell somewhere beneath the wheels ...

They truly abhor me, Xerius realized. *They hate me ... Me!*

But this would change, he reminded himself. When all was finished, when the fruits of his labour had become manifest, they would hail him as no other emperor in living memory. They would rejoice as trains of heathen slaves bore tribute to the Home City, as blinded kings were dragged in chains to their Emperor's feet. And with shielded eyes they would gaze upon Ikurei Xerius III and they would know—*know!*—that he was indeed the *Aspect-Emperor,* returned from the ashes of Kyraneas and Cenei to compel the world, to force nation and tribe to bow and kiss his knee.

I will show them! They will see!

The immense plaza of Cmiral opened before him, and the thunder of Momemn's masses reached its crescendo, stealing his breath, numbing him with sound and implication. The forward Kidruhil halted, milled in momentary confusion. Xerius saw one cavalryman's horse rear. The Kidruhil who followed galloped ahead to secure the flanks. All flourished their clubs, waving them in warning, striking any who came too near. Beyond their small perimeter of gleaming armour and torchlight the world was dark riot. Impoverished humanity, roaring fields of them, from the temple-compounds to the left and right to the great basalt pillars of Xothei ahead.

Xerius clenched the chariot's forward rail until his knuckles whitened and his hands ached. All of them ... Over and over, crying *that name* ...

Dread, dizziness, and a sense of inner falling.

Has he incited them against me? Is this to be an assassination?

He watched as his Kidruhil clubbed first a sliver, then a wedge into the mobs. Suddenly he grinned, gritted his teeth in fierce pleasure. *This* was how the Gods affirmed themselves: with the blood of mortals! The crowd surged against the forward Kidruhil, and the thunder seemed redoubled. Several shining horsemen stumbled and vanished. More horsemen rushed forward. Clubs rose and fell. Swords were drawn.

The Charioteer steadied his team, glanced nervously at him.

You look an Emperor in the eye?

"Go!" Xerius roared. "Into them! Go!"

Laughing, he leaned from the runners and spat upon his people, upon those who cried another's name when Ikurei Xerius III stood godlike in their midst. If only he could spit molten gold!

Slowly, the chariot trundled ahead, lurching and throwing him forward as the wheels chipped over the fallen. His stomach burned with fear, his bowels felt loose, but there was a wildness in his thoughts, a delirium that exulted in death's proximity. One by one the torch-bearers were pulled under, but the Kidruhil stood fast, battling their way ever forward, hacking their way among the masses, their swords rising and falling, rising and falling, and it seemed to Xerius that he punished the mongrels with *his* arm, that it was *he* who reached forward and chopped them to the ground.

Laughing maniacally, the Emperor of Nansur passed among his people, toward the growing immensity of temple Xothei.

Finally the decimated procession reached the ranks of Eothic Guardsmen arrayed across Xothei's monumental steps. Deafened, afflicted by the torpor of dreams, Xerius was guided from the chariot onto the raised wooden walkway that led to the temple's great gate. The Emperor must always be seen standing above mere men. He viciously grabbed one of the captains by the arm.

"Send word to the barracks! Hack this place to silence! I want my chariot to skid across blood when I return!"

Discipline. He would teach them.

Then he strode toward Xothei's gate, stumbled for a moment on the hem of his gown, felt his heart stop beating for fury as laughter coloured the ambient roar. He glanced for an instant across what seemed an ocean of anger and rapture. Then, gathering his gown, he very nearly fled up the walkway. The temple's massive stonework encompassed him. Shelter.

The doors were ground shut behind him.

His legs folded beneath him. A moment of hushed bewilderment. The cold floor against his knees. He placed a trembling hand to his forehead, was surprised by the sweat that ran between his fingers.

Foolishness! What would Conphas think?

Ringing ears. Airy darkness. Around him, that *name* shivered up from the stone.

Maithanet.

A thousand thousand voices—or so it seemed—crying like a prayer the name that Xerius spat as a curse.

Maithanet.

Feeling winded, he walked unsteadily across the antechamber, paused. Few of the great lamp wheels had been set alight. Pale circles of light were thrown across the vast temple floor, across the rows of faded prayer tile. Columns as thick as netia pine soared into gloom. The hymnal galleries above were barely discernible in the dark. During times of official worship this floor would billow with clouds of incense, making the temple's recesses vague and ghostly, smearing the points of lamplight with haloes so that it seemed to the faithful that they stood at the very juncture of this world and the Outside. But now the place was cavernous and bare. Beneath the memory of myrrh, it smelled like a cellar. It was the juncture of nothing—only a pocket of peace purchased by dead stone.

In the distance, Xerius could see him, kneeling in the centre of the great hemisphere of idols.

There you are, he thought, feeling some solidity return to his hollow limbs. His slippers whispered as he walked across the floor. Unconsciously, his hands strayed across his vests and gown, smoothing, straightening. His eyes flitted across the friezes etched into the columns: kings, emperors, and gods, all rigid with the supernatural dignity of figures in stone. He came to a stop before the first tier of stairs. The tallest, centre dome gaped above him.

He stared for several moments at the Shriah's broad back.

Face your Emperor you fanatic ingrate!

"I'm pleased you've come," Maithanet said with his back still turned to him. The voice was rich, enfolding. There was no deference in the tone. Jnan held Shriah and Emperor equal.

"Why this, Maithanet? Why here?"

The broad back turned. Maithanet was wearing a plain white frock with sleeves that ended mid-arm. For an instant he appraised Xerius with glittering eyes, then he raised his head to the distant sound of the mob, as though it were the sound of rain prayed for and received. Xerius could see the strong chin beneath the black of his oiled beard. His face was broad, like that of a yeoman, and surprisingly youthful, though nothing about the man's manner spoke of youth. *How old are you?*

"*Listen!*" Maithanet hissed, raising his hands to the resonant sound of his name. *Maithanet-Maithanet-Maithanet* ...

"I am not a proud man, Ikurei Xerius, but it moves me to hear them call thus."

Despite the foolish dramatics, Xerius found himself awed by the man's presence. The giddiness of moments before revisited his limbs.

"I haven't the patience, Maithanet, for games of jnan."

The Shriah paused, then smiled winningly. He began walking down the steps. "I've come because of the Holy War ... I've come to look into your eyes."

These words further disconcerted the Emperor. Xerius had known, before coming here, that the stakes of this meeting could be high.

"Tell me," Maithanet said, "have you sealed a pact with the heathen? Have you vowed to betray the Holy War before it reaches the Sacred Land?"

Could he know?

"I assure you, Maithanet ... No."

"No?"

"I'm injured, Shriah, that you would—"

Maithanet's laughter was sudden, loud, reverberant enough to fill even the hollows of great Xothei.

Xerius fairly gasped. The Writ of Psata-Antyu, the code governing Shrial conduct, forbade laughing aloud as a carnal indulgence. Maithanet, he realized, was giving him a glimpse of his depths. But for what purpose? All of this—the mobs, the demand to meet here in Xothei, even the chanting of his name—was a demonstration of some kind, terrifying in its premeditated lack of subtlety.

I'll crush you, Maithanet was saying. *If the Holy War fails, you'll be destroyed.*

"Accept my apology, Emperor," Maithanet said lightly. "It would seem that even a holy war may be poisoned by"—a pained smile—"*false rumours, hmm?*"

He tries to cow me ... He knows nothing, so he tries to cow me!

Xerius remained silent, wrathful. He'd always possessed, he thought, a greater facility for hatred than Conphas. His precocious nephew could be vicious, savage even, but he inevitably slipped back into that glassy remoteness that so unnerved those in his company. For Xerius, hatred was something as enduring as it was implacable.

Such a strange habit, he suddenly realized, these momentary inquiries into his nephew's nature. When had Conphas become the rule he used to measure the cubits of his own heart?

"Come, Ikurei Xerius," the Shriah of the Thousand Temples solemnly said, as though the gravity of what would ensue might forever mark their lives. And for an brief instant, Xerius grasped the gift of character that had hurtled this man to such heights: the ability to impart sanctity to the moment, to touch people with awe as though it were bread drawn from his own basket.

"Come ... Listen to what I say to my people."

But over the course of this brief exchange, the sounds of thousands chanting Maithanet's name had transformed, hesitantly at first, but with greater certitude with each passing moment. Changed.

Into screams.

Obviously, the nameless Captain had executed his Emperor's instructions with blessed alacrity. Xerius grinned his own winning grin. At last he felt a match for this obscenely imposing man.

"Do you hear, Maithanet? Now they call out *my name*."

"Indeed they do," the Shriah said darkly. "Indeed they do."

Late Summer, 4111 Year-of-the-Tusk, Hinnereth, on the coast of Gedea

As though crowded by an antipathy to the sea, the land folded as it approached the broken coasts of Gedea. Since the coastal plains were narrow or nonexistent, save the alluvial flatlands surrounding Hinnereth, it seemed the land itself had conspired to bring the Holy War to the ancient city. As the first cohorts descended the terraced hills, Hinnereth sprawled before them, huddled against the Meneanor, a warren of mud and baked-brick structures enclosed by sandstone fortifications. The mournful wail of horns pierced the salty air, rang from hill to sea, and pronounced the city's doom. Column after column wound down from the hills: the turbulent swordsmen of the Middle-North, the long-skirted knights of Conriya and High Ainon, the veteran infantrymen of the Nansurium.

Hinnereth was an old prize. Like all lands falling between great, competing civilizations, Gedea had been a perpetual tributary, little more than an anecdote in the chronicles of her conquerors. Hinnereth, her only city of note, had seen innumerable foreign governors: Shigeki, Kyranean, Ceneian, Nansur, and most recently, Kianene. And now the Men of the Tusk would cut their names onto that list.

The Holy War dispersed into several different camps around the fields and groves outside of Hinnereth's walls. After conferring, the Great Names sent an embassy of thanes and barons to the gates demanding unconditional surrender. When the Fanim of Ansacer ab Salajka, the Kianene Sapatishah of Gedea, chased them away with arrows and ballistae, thousands were sent into the fields to harvest the wheat and millet secured the week previous by the advance forces of Earl Athjeäri, Palatine Ingiaban, and Earl Werijen Greatheart. Thousands more were sent into the hills to hew down trees for rams, towers, catapults, and mangonels.

The Siege of Hinnereth had begun.

After a week of preparations, the Men of the Tusk made their first assault. Clouds of arrows fell among them. Boiling oil poured down upon their mantlets. Men fell screaming from their ladders, or were cut down on the battlements. Fiery pitch transformed their siege towers into soaring pyres. They bled and burned beneath the walls of Hinnereth, and the Fanim mocked them from the heights.

In the wake of the disaster, some Great Names sent a delegation to the Scarlet Spires. Chepheramunni had already warned Saubon and the others that the Scarlet Schoolmen, short of Shimeh or a Cishaurim attack, had no intention of assisting the Men of the Tusk, so the decision was made to limit their demands. They asked for one breach in the walls, no more. Eleäzaras's refusal was scathing, as was the condemnation of Proyas and Gotian, who had forsworn the use of blasphemy unless absolutely necessary.

Another round of preparations followed. Some toiled in the hills, harvesting timber for more siege engines. Others hunched in the darkness of sappers' tunnels, dragging stone and sharp gravel out with blistered hands. Still others raised pyres of scrub and burned the dead. At night, they drank water carted down from the hills, ate bread, golden-red clusters of figs, roasted quail and goose—and cursed Hinnereth.

During this time, bands of Inrithi knights ranged south along the coasts, skirmishing with the remnants of Skauras's host, plundering fishing villages, and sacking those walled towns that failed to immediately throw open their gates. Earl Athjeäri struck inland, scouring the hills in search of battle and plunder. Near a small fortress called Dayrut, he surprised a detachment of several thousand Kianene and put them to rout with as many hundred thanes and knights. Returning to the fortress, he forced the locals to build a small catapult, which he then used to lob severed Kianene heads into the fortress one at a time. One hundred and thirty-one heads later, the terrified garrison threw open the gates and prostrated themselves in the dust. Each of them was asked: "Do you repudiate Fane and accept Inri Sejenus as the true voice of the manifold God?" Those who answered no were immediately beheaded. Those who answered yes were bound with ropes and sent back to Hinnereth, where they were sold to the slavers who followed the Holy War.

Other strongholds likewise fell, such was the general terror of the iron warriors. The old Nansur fortresses of Ebara and Kurrut, the half-ruined Ceneian fortress of Gunsae, the Kianene citadel of Am-Amidai, built when the populace had been still largely Inrithi—all of them, like so many coins swept into the mailed fist of the Holy War. Gedea would fall, it seemed, as quickly as the Inrithi could ride.

At Hinnereth, meanwhile, the Great Names had completed their preparations for a second assault, only to be awakened by shouts of astonishment. Men tumbled from their tents and pavilions. At first, most pointed to the great flotilla of war galleys and carracks anchored in the bay, hundreds of them, bearing the Black Sun pennants of Nansur. But soon, they all stared in disbelief at Hinnereth. The great forward gates of the city had been thrown open. All along the curtain walls, tiny figures pulled down the triangular banners of Ansacer, the infamous Black Gazelle, and raised the Black Sun of the Nansur Empire.

Some cheered. Others howled. Bands of half-naked horsemen could be seen galloping toward the towering gates, where they were halted by phalanxes of Nansur infantrymen. For a moment swords flashed in the distance.

But it was too late. Hinnereth had fallen, not to the Holy War, but to Emperor Ikurei Xerius III.

At first, Ikurei Conphas ignored the summons of the Council, and the daunting task of placating Saubon and Gothyelk fell to General Martemus. With the arrival of the Nansur fleet the previous night, he brusquely explained, the Gedean Sapatishah had seen the hopelessness of his position, and so sent Conphas the terms of his surrender. Martemus even produced a letter, dark with the cursive script of the Kianene, which he claimed was in Ansacer's own hand. The Sapatishah, he asserted, was deeply frightened of the fervour of the Inrithi, and would surrender only to the Nansur. In matters of mercy, Martemus said, a known enemy was always more preferable than an unknown. It had been the first instinct of the Exalt-General, he continued, to summon all the Great Names and present this letter for their appraisal, but Martemus himself had reminded the Exalt-General that the proffered capitulation of one's enemy was always a delicate thing, the result perhaps of passing apprehension rather than real resolution. Accordingly, the Exalt-General had decided to be decisive rather than democratic.

When the Great Names demanded to know why, if Conphas had truly acted in the interests of the Holy War, Hinnereth still remained closed to them, Martemus merely shrugged and informed them that those were the terms of the Sapatishah's surrender. Ansacer was a tender man, he said, and feared for the safety of his people. He had, moreover, great respect for the discipline of the Nansur.

In the end, only Saubon refused to accept Martemus's explanation. Hinnereth was his by right, he bellowed, just spoils of his victory on the Battleplain. When Conphas finally arrived the Galeoth Prince had to be physically restrained. Afterward, Gothyelk and Proyas reminded him that Gedea was an empty and impoverished land. Let the Emperor gloat over his first, hollow prize, they said. The Holy War would continue its march south. And ancient Shigek, a land of legendary wealth, awaited them.

⣗⣗⣗

"Stay with me, Zin," Proyas called out.

He'd dismissed the council only moments earlier. Now standing, he watched his people mill and make ready to leave. They filled the smoky interior of his pavilion, some pious, others mercenary, almost all of them proud to a fault. Gaidekki and Ingiaban continued to argue, as they always did, over things material and immaterial. Most of the others began filing from the chamber: Ganyatti, Kushigas, Imrothas, several high-ranking barons, and of course, Kellhus and Cnaiür. With the exception of the Scylvendi, they bowed one by one before vanishing through the blue silk curtains. Proyas acknowledged each with a curt nod.

Soon Xinemus was left standing alone. Slaves scurried through the surrounding gloom, gathering plates and sticky wine bowls, straightening rugs, and repositioning the myriad cushions.

"Something troubles you, my Prince?" the Marshal asked.

"I just have several questions ..."

"About?"

Proyas hesitated. Why should a prince shrink from speaking of any man?

"About Kellhus," he said.

Xinemus raised his eyebrows. "He troubles you?"

Proyas hooked a hand behind his neck, grimaced. "In all honesty, Zin, he's the least troubling man I've ever known."

"And that's what troubles you."

Many things troubled him, not the least of which was the recent disaster at Hinnereth. They'd been outmanoeuvred by Conphas and the Emperor. Never again.

He had no time and little patience for these ... personal matters.

"Tell me, what do you make of him?"

"He terrifies me," Xinemus said without an instant's hesitation.

Proyas frowned. "How so?"

The Marshal's eyes unfocused, as though searching for some text written within. "I've spilled many bowls with him," he said hesitantly. "I've broken much bread, and I cannot count the things he's shown me. Somehow, some way, his presence makes me ... makes me *better*."

Proyas looked to the ground, to the interleaved wings embroidered across the carpet at his feet. "He has that effect."

He could feel Xinemus study him in his cursed way: as though he saw past the fraudulent trappings of manhood to that sunken-chested boy who'd never left the training ground.

"He's only a man, my Prince. He says so himself ... Besides, we're past—"

"How is Achamian?" Proyas asked abruptly.

The stocky Marshal scowled. He buried two fingers between the plaits of his beard to scratch his chin. "I thought his name was forbidden."

"I merely ask."

Xinemus nodded warily. "Well. Very well, in fact. He's taken a woman, an old love of his from Sumna."

"Yes ... Esmenet is it? The one who was a whore."

"She's good for him," Xinemus said defensively. "I've never seen him so content, so happy."

"But you sound worried."

Xinemus narrowed his eyes an instant, then sighed heavily. "I suppose I do," he said, looking past Proyas. "For as long as I've known him, he's been a Mandate Schoolman. But now ... I don't know." He glanced up, matched his Prince's gaze. "He's almost stopped speaking of the Consult and his Dreams altogether ... You'd approve."

"So he's in love," Proyas said, shaking his head. "Love!" he exclaimed incredulously. "Are you sure?" A grin overpowered him.

Xinemus fairly cackled. "He's in love, all right. He's been stumbling after his pecker for weeks now."

Proyas laughed and looked to the ground. "So he has one of those, does he?" Akka in love. It seemed both impossible and strangely inevitable. *Men like him need love ... Men unlike me.*

"That he does. She seems exceedingly fond of it."

Proyas snorted. "He *is* a sorcerer after all."

Xinemus's eyes slackened for an instant. "That he is."

There was a moment of awkward silence. Proyas sighed heavily. With any man other than Xinemus, these questions would've come naturally, without uncertainty or reservation. How could Xinemus, his beloved Zin, be so mulish about something so obvious to other men?

"Does he still teach Kellhus?" Proyas asked.

"Every day." The Marshal smiled wanly, as though at his own foolishness. "That's what this is about, isn't it? You *want* to believe Kellhus is more, but—"

"He was right about Saubon!" Proyas exclaimed. "Even in the details, Zin! The *details!*"

"*And yet,*" Xinemus continued, frowning at the interruption, "he openly consorts with Achamian. With a *sorcerer* ..."

Xinemus mockingly had spoken the word as other men spoke it: like a thing smeared in shit.

Proyas turned to the table, poured himself a bowl of wine. It had tasted so sweet of late.

"So what do you think?" he asked.

"I think Kellhus simply sees what I see in Akka, and what *you* once saw ... That a man's soul can be good apart fro—"

"The Tusk says," Proyas snapped, "'Burn them, for they are Unclean!' Burn them! How much more clarity can there be? Kellhus consorts with an abomination. As do you."

The Marshal was shaking his head. "I can't believe that."

Proyas fixed him with his gaze. Why did he feel so cold?

"Then you cannot believe the Tusk."

The Marshal blanched, and for the first time the Conriyan Prince saw fear on his old sword-trainer's face—fear! He wanted to apologize, to unsay what he'd said, but the cold was so unyielding ...

So true.

I simply go by the Word!

If one couldn't trust the God's own voice, if one refused to listen—even for sentiment's sake!—then everything became scepticism and scholarly disputation. Xinemus listened to his heart, and this was at once his strength and his weakness. The heart recited no scripture.

"Well then," the Marshal said thinly. "You needn't worry about Kellhus any more than you worry about me ..."

Proyas narrowed his eyes and nodded.

⸻

There was constraint, there was direction, there was, most illuminating of all, a summoning together.

Night had fallen, and Kellhus sat alone upon a promontory, leaning against a solitary cedar. Drawn eastward by years of wind, the cedar's limbs swept across the starry heavens and forked downward. They seemed moored as though by strings to the panorama below: the encamped Holy War, Hinnereth behind her great belts of stone, and the Meneanor, her distant rollers silvered by moonlight.

But he saw none of this, not with his eyes ...

The promises and threats of what was came murmuring, and futures were discussed.

There was a world, Eärwa, enslaved by history, custom, and animal hunger, a world driven by the hammers of what came before.

There was Achamian and all he had uttered. The Apocalypse, the lineages of Emperors and Kings, the Houses and Schools of the Great Factions, the panoply of warring nations. And there was sorcery, the Gnosis, and the prospect of near limitless power.

There was Esmenet and slender thighs and piercing intellect.

There was Sarcellus and the Consult and a wary truce born of enigma and hesitation.

There was Saubon and torment pitched against lust for power.

There was Cnaiür and madness and martial genius and the growing threat of what he knew.

There was the Holy War and faith and hunger.

And there was Father.

What would you have me do?

Possible worlds blew through him, fanning and branching into a canopy of glimpses ...

Nameless Schoolmen climbing a steep, gravelly beach. A nipple pinched between fingers. A gasping climax. A severed head thrust against the burning sun. Apparitions marching out of morning mist.

A dead wife.

Kellhus exhaled, then breathed deep the bittersweet pinch of cedar, earth, and war.

There was revelation.

CHAPTER TEN

ATSUSHAN HIGHLANDS

Love is lust made meaningful. Hope is hunger made human.
                    —AJENCIS, *THE THIRD ANALYTIC OF MEN*

*How does one learn innocence? How does one teach ignorance? For to
be them is to know them not. And yet they are the immovable point
from which the compass of life swings, the measure of all crime and
compassion, the rule of all wisdom and folly. They are the Absolute.*
                    —ANONYMOUS, *THE IMPROMPTA*

Late Summer, 4111 Year-of-the-Tusk, Gedean interior

Peace had come.

Achamian had dreamed of war, more war than anyone save a Mandate
Schoolman could dream. He'd even witnessed war between nations—the
Three Seas bred quarrels as readily as did liquor. But he'd never belonged to
one. He had never marched as he marched now, sweating beneath the
Gedean sun, surrounded by thousands of iron-armoured Men, by the lowing
of oxen and the tramping of countless sandalled feet. War, in the smoke
darkening the horizon, in the braying of horns, in the great carnival of
encampment after encampment, in the blackened stone and whitened
dead. War, in past nightmares and future apprehensions. Everywhere, war.

And somehow, peace had come.

There was Kellhus, of course.

Since resolving not to inform the Mandate of his presence, Achamian's anguish had receded, then fallen away altogether. How this could be mystified him for the most part. The threat remained. Kellhus was, Achamian would remind himself from time to time, the Harbinger. Soon the sun would rise behind the No-God and cast his dread shadow across the Three Seas. Soon the Second Apocalypse would wrack the world. But when he thought of these things a queer elation warmed his horror, a drunken exhilaration. Achamian had always been incredulous of stories of men breaking ranks in battle to charge their foe. But now he thought he understood the impulse behind that heedless rush. Consequences lost all purchase when they became mad. And desperation, when pressed beyond anguish, became narcotic.

He was the fool who dashed alone into the spears of thousands. For Kellhus.

Achamian still taught him during the daylong march, though now both Esmenet and Serwë accompanied them, sometimes chatting to each other, but mostly just listening. Surrounding them, Men of the Tusk marched in their thousands, bent beneath their packs, sweating in the bright Gedean sun. Somehow, impossibly, Kellhus had exhausted everything Achamian knew of the Three Seas, so they talked of the Ancient North, of Seswatha and his world of bronze, Sranc, and Nonmen. Soon, Achamian realized from time to time, he would have nothing left to give Kellhus—save the Gnosis.

Which he could not give, of course. But he found it hard to resist wondering what Kellhus with his godlike intellect would make of it. Thankfully, the Gnosis was a language for which the Prince possessed no tongue.

The marches tumbled to a halt sometime between mid-afternoon and dusk, depending on the terrain and, most important, the availability of water. Gedea was a dry land, the Atsushan Highlands especially so. After the brisk routine of pitching camp, they gathered about Xinemus's fire, though Achamian often found himself eating alone with Esmenet, Serwë, and Xinemus's slaves. More and more, Xinemus, Cnaiür, and Kellhus supped with Proyas, who, under the Scylvendi's coarse tutelage, had become a man obsessed with strategy and planning. But usually they all found themselves about the fire for an hour or two before retiring to their pallets or mats.

And here, as everywhere else, Kellhus shone.

One night, shortly after the Holy War had left Hinnereth, they found themselves eating a contemplative meal of rice and lamb, which Cnaiür had secured for them the previous day. Commenting on the luxury of eating steaming meat, Esmenet asked the whereabouts of their provider.

"With Proyas," Xinemus said, "discussing war."

"What could they possibly talk about all the time?"

Caught mid-swallow, Kellhus held out a hand. "I've heard them," he said, his eyes wry and bright. "Their conversations sound something like this ..."

Esmenet was laughing already. Everyone else leaned forward eagerly. In addition to mischievous wit, Kellhus had an uncanny gift for voices. Serwë fairly chortled with excitement.

Kellhus assumed an imperious and warlike face. He spat between his feet, then in a voice that raised goose pimples, so near was it to Cnaiür's own, he said: "The People do not ride like sissies. They place one testicle to the left of the saddle, one testicle to the right, and they do not bounce, they are so heavy."

"I would," Kellhus-as-Proyas replied, "be spared your impudence, Scylvendi."

Xinemus coughed a mouthful of wine.

"That is because you do not understand the ways of war," Kellhus-as-Cnaiür continued. "They are hairy, and they are dark, like the cracks of unwashed wrestlers. War is where the sandal of the world meets the scrotum of men."

"I would be spared your blasphemy, Scylvendi."

Kellhus spat into the fire. "You think your ways are the ways of the People, but you are wrong. You are silly girls to us, and we would make love to your asses were they as muscular as those of our horses."

"I would be spared your *affections*, Scylvendi!"

"But you would live on," Esmenet cried out, "in the scars I cut into my arm!"

The camp fairly shrieked with laughter. Xinemus hung his head between his knees, shuddering and snorting. Esmenet rolled backward on her mat, screaming in her enticing and adorable way. Zenkappa and Dinchases leaned against each other, their shoulders jerking. Serwë had curled into a ball, and seemed to weep with joy as much as laugh. Kellhus merely smiled, looked about as though mystified by their hysterics.

When Cnaiür arrived later that night everyone fell silent, at once abashed and conspiratorial. Scowling, the Scylvendi paused before the fire, looked from face to grinning face. Achamian glanced at Serwë, was shocked by the malice in her smile.

Suddenly Esmenet burst out laughing. "You should have heard Kellhus," she cried. "You sounded hilarious!"

The Scylvendi's weathered face went blank. His murderous eyes became dull with ... Could it be? Then contempt regained the heights of his expression. He spat into the fire and strode off.

His spittle hissed.

Kellhus stood, apparently stricken with remorse.

"The man's a thin-skinned lout," Achamian said crossly. "Mockery is a gift between friends. A *gift*."

The Prince whirled. "Is it?" he cried. "Or is it an excuse?"

Achamian could only stare, dumbstruck. Kellhus had rebuked him. *Kellhus*. Achamian looked to the others, saw his shock mirrored in their faces, though not his dismay.

"Is it?" Kellhus demanded.

Achamian felt his face flush, his lips tremble. There was something about Kellhus's voice. So like Achamian's father's ...

Who's he to—

"Forgive me, Akka," the Prince said, lowering his head as though stunned by his own outburst. "I punish you for my own folly ... I act twice the fool."

Achamian swallowed. Shook his head. Forced a smile.

"No ... No, I apologize ..." His voice quavered. "I was too harsh."

Kellhus smiled, leaned to place a hand on his shoulder. At his touch, Achamian's entire side went numb. For some reason the Prince's smell, leather with a hint of rosewater, always flustered him.

"Then we're fools together," Kellhus said. There was delight, and the brief, uncanny sense that Kellhus was expecting something ...

"I've been saying that all along," Xinemus growled from the far side of the fire.

The Marshal's timing was impeccable—as usual. Esmenet led the charge of nervous laughter, and they recaptured something of their earlier cheer. Achamian found himself laughing as well.

All of them, at some point or another, inevitably ran afoul of one another's humour. Xinemus would complain of Iryssas, who would harp about Esmenet, who would gripe about Serwë, who would carp about Achamian, who would gripe about Xinemus. Too dense, too forward, too vain, too crude, and so on. All men were caste-merchants in some respect, haggling and trading, but without scales or touchstones to confirm the weight or purity of their coinage. They had only guesswork. Backbiting, petty jealousies, resentments, arguments, and third-party arbitrations simply belonged to the market of men.

But with Kellhus, it was different. Somehow he managed to browse the market without opening his purse. Almost from the beginning they'd recognized him as the Judge—including Xinemus, who was the titular head of their fire. No doubt there was an uncertainty about him, a capriciousness appropriate to his brilliance, but these were simply departures from a profound and immovable centre. Intelligence, as penetrating as any in near or far antiquity. Compassion, as broad as Inrau's and yet somehow far deeper—a benevolence born of *understanding* rather than forgiveness, as though he could see through the delinquent rush of thought and passion to the still point of innocence within each soul. And words! Analogies that seized reality and burned it from the inside out ...

He possessed, Achamian sometimes thought, what the poet Protathis claimed all men should strive for: the hand of Triamis, the intellect of Ajencis, and the heart of Sejenus.

And others thought this as well.

Every evening, after the dinner fires burned low, men and women from every nation, it seemed, began gathering round the perimeter of Xinemus's camp, sometimes calling out to Kellhus, but mostly keeping to themselves. A few in the beginning, then more and more, until they comprised a congregation of three dozen or so souls. Soon Xinemus's Attrempans were leaving large swaths of empty pasture between their round tents and their Marshal's pavilion. They would be supping with strangers otherwise.

For the first week or so everyone, including Kellhus, did their best to ignore them, thinking this would shortly drive them away. Who, they wondered, would sit unacknowledged night after night watching others—watching strangers—take their repose? But like little brothers with no resources of their own, they persisted. Their numbers even multiplied.

On a whim, Achamian took a seat among them one night, and watched as they watched, hoping to understand what it was that drew them to so demean themselves. At first, he merely saw familiar figures illumined by firelight against a greater dark. Cnaiür sitting cross-legged, his back as broad as an Ainoni fan and strapped with scarred muscle. Beyond him, on the far side of the fire, Xinemus upon his campstool, hands on his knees, his square-cut beard brushing his chest as he laughed in response to Esmenet, who knelt beside him, muttering something wicked about somebody, no doubt. Dinchases. Zenkappa. Iryssas. Serwë leaning back on her mat, bouncing her knees together, innocently exposing warm and promising shadows. And next to her, Kellhus, sitting serene and golden.

Achamian glanced at those seated throughout the surrounding darkness. He saw Men of the Tusk from every nation and caste. Some leaned together, talking amongst themselves. But most sat as he did, apart from their fellows, eyes sorting through the bright figures before them as though struggling to read by fading candlelight. They seemed ... ensorcelled, like fish drawn to a flashing lure. Compelled, not so much by the light as by the surrounding dark.

"Why do you do this?" he asked the man sitting nearest to him, a blond Tydonni with a soldier's forearms and a caste-noble's clear eyes.

"Can't you see?" the man replied, without so much as glancing in his direction.

"See what?"

"See *him*."

"You mean Prince Kellhus?"

The man turned to him, his smile at once beatific and filled with pity. "You're too close," he said. "That's why you can't see."

"See what?" Achamian asked. His breath felt pinched.

"He touched me once," the man inexplicably replied. "Before Asgilioch. I stumbled while marching and he caught me by the arm. He said, 'Doff your sandals and shod the earth.'"

Achamian chortled. "An old joke," he explained. "You must have cursed the ground when you stumbled."

"So?" the man replied. He was fairly trembling, Achamian realized, with indignant fury.

Achamian frowned, tried to smile, to reassure. "Well, it's an old saying—ancient, in fact—meant to remind people not to foist their failings on others."

"No," the man grated, "it's not."

Achamian paused. "Then what does it mean?"

Rather than answer, the man had turned away, as though wilfully consigning Achamian and his question to the oblivion of what he couldn't see. Achamian stared at him for a thick moment, bewildered and curiously dismayed. How could fury secure the truth?

He stood, slapped dust from his knees.

"It means," the man said from behind him, "that we must uproot the world. That we must destroy all that offends."

Achamian started, such was the hatred in the man's voice. He turned— to sneer or to scold, he wasn't sure which. Instead he simply stared, dumb-founded. For whatever reason, the man couldn't match his gaze; he scowled at the firelight instead. Achamian glanced from him to the other faces in the darkness. Most had turned to the sound of angry voices, but even as he watched they drifted back to Kellhus in the light. And somehow, the Schoolman simply knew these people wouldn't go away.

I'm no different, he thought, feeling the perplexing twinge of insights into things already known. *I simply sit closer to the fire ...*

Their reasons were *his* reasons. He knew this.

Their grounds were inchoate and innumerable: grief, temptation, remorse, confusion. They watched out of weariness, out of clandestine hope and fear, out of fascination and delight. But more than anything, they watched out of necessity.

They watched because they knew something was about to happen.

Without warning, the fire popped, belching a geyser of sparks, one of which floated toward Kellhus. Smiling, he glanced at Serwë, then reached out and pinched the point of orange light between thumb and forefinger. Extinguished it.

Several gasped in the darkness.

As the days passed, more and more watchers gathered. The situation became doubly uncomfortable, both because their camp had become a peculiar stage, an enclosure of light surrounded by shadowy watchers, and because of Kellhus's seething humour. The Prince of Atrithau had affected everyone who frequented Xinemus's fire, each according to their hopes and hurts, and to see the man who'd rewritten the ground of their understanding *angry* was troubling in the way of loved ones suddenly acting contrary to all expectations.

One night, for reasons peculiar to his own brooding humour, Xinemus finally blurted: "Dammit, Kellhus! Why don't you just *talk* to them?"

Stunned silence. Esmenet reached out, clutched Achamian's hand in the shadows between them. Only the Scylvendi continued eating, fingering gruel into his mouth. Achamian found himself repulsed, as though he witnessed something lewd and animal. A man too bent to the arch of his lust.

"Because," Kellhus said tightly, his eyes riveted upon the fire, "they make more of me than I am."

Do they? Achamian thought. He knew the others asked themselves the same question, even though they rarely spoke of Kellhus to one another. For some reason, a peculiar shyness afflicted them whenever the subject of Kellhus arose, as though they harboured suspicions too foolish or too hurtful to reveal. Achamian could only really speak of him to Esmenet, and even then ...

"So," Xinemus snapped. More than anyone, he seemed able to pretend that Kellhus was simply another face about their fire. "Go tell them."

Kellhus stared at the Marshal for several unblinking moments, then nodded. Without a word, he stood and strode off into the darkness.

And so began what Achamian came to call "The Imprompta," the nightly talks—almost sermons—Kellhus started giving to the Men of the Tusk. Not always, but often, he and Esmenet would join him, watch from nearby as he answered questions, discussed innumerable things. He told the two of them that their presence gave him heart, that they reminded him he was no more than those to whom he spoke. He confessed a growing conceit, a thought that terrified because he found it easier and easier to bear.

"So often when I speak," he said, "I don't recognize my voice."

Achamian couldn't remember ever clutching Esmenet's hand so fiercely.

The numbers attending began to swell, not so fast that Achamian could notice a difference between consecutive nights, but fast enough that several dozen had become hundreds by the time the Holy War neared Shigek. A handful of more devoted listeners would assemble a small wooden platform, upon which they would lay a mat between two iron braziers. Kellhus would sit cross-legged, poised and immobile between the shining flames. Usually he would wear a plain yellow cassock—looted, Serwë had told Achamian, from the Sapatishah's camp on the Plains of Mengedda. And somehow, whether by posture, bearing, or some trick of the light, he would look unearthly. Even glorious.

One evening, for reasons he couldn't fully articulate, Achamian followed Kellhus and Esmenet with a candle, his writing accoutrements, and a sheaf of parchment. The previous night Kellhus had spoken of trust and betrayal, telling the story of a fur trapper he'd known in the wastes north of Atrithau, a man who'd remained faithful to his dead wife by fostering a heartbreaking devotion to his dogs. "When one love dies," he'd said, "one must love another." Esmenet had openly wept.

It just seemed that such words *had* to be written.

With Esmenet, Achamian unrolled their mat to the left of Kellhus's platform. Torches had been staked across the small field. The atmosphere was sociable, though hushed by something more than respect and not quite reverence. Achamian glimpsed more than a few familiar faces in the crowd. Several high-ranking caste-nobles were present, including a square-jawed man wearing a Nansur general's blue cloak—General Sompas or Martemus, Achamian believed. Even Proyas sat in the dust with the others, though he seemed troubled. He looked away instead of acknowledging Achamian's gaze.

Kellhus took his place between the potted fires. The resulting silence seemed to hiss. For several moments he seemed unbearably *real*, like the sole living man, something raw and tumid in a world of smoky apparitions.

He smiled, and Achamian's chest, which had tightened like parched leather, relaxed to the point of feeling sodden. An unaccountable relief washed through him. Breathing deeply, he readied his quill, cursed as the first errant droplet of ink tapped onto the page.

"*Akka*," Esmenet chided.

As always, Kellhus searched the faces of those before him, his eyes glinting with compassion. After a few heartbeats his gaze settled upon one man—a Conriyan knight by the look of his tunic and the heft of his gold rings. Otherwise he looked haggard, as though he still slept upon the Battleplain. His beard was knotted with forgotten plaits.

"What happened?" Kellhus asked.

The nameless knight smiled, but there was a strange and subtle incongruence in his expression, something like glimpsing the difference between white eyes and yellow teeth.

"Three days ago," the man said, "our lord heard rumour of a village some miles to the west, so we rode out, hoping for plunder ..."

Kellhus nodded. "And what did you find?"

"Nothing ... I mean, no village. Our lord was wroth. He claims the others—"

"What did you find?"

The man blinked. Panic flashed from the stoic weariness of his expression. "A child," he said hoarsely. "A dead child ... We were following this trail, something worn by goatherds, I think, cutting across this hillside, and there was just this dead child, a girl, no more than five or six, lying in our path. Her throat had been cut ..."

"What happened next?"

"Nothing ... I mean, we simply ignored her, continued riding as though she were nothing more than discarded cloth ... a-a scrap of leather in the dust," he added, his voice breaking. He looked down to his callused palms.

"Guilt and shame wrack you by day," Kellhus said, "the feeling that you've committed some mortal crime. Nightmares wrack you by night ... She speaks to you."

The man's nod was almost comical in its desperation. He hadn't, Achamian realized, the nerve for war.

"But why?" he cried. "I mean, how many dead have we seen?"

"But not all seeing," Kellhus replied, "is *witness*."

"I don't understand ..."

"Witness is the seeing that *testifies*, that judges so that it may be judged. You saw, and you judged. A trespass had been committed, an innocent had been murdered. *You saw this*."

"Yes!" the man hissed. "A little girl. A *little girl!*"

"And now you suffer."

"But why?" he cried. "Why should I suffer? She's not mine. She was *heathen!*"

"Everywhere ... Everywhere we're surrounded by the blessed and the cursed, the sacred and the profane. But our hearts are like hands, they grow callous to the world. And yet, like our hands even the most callous heart will blister if overworked or chafed by something new. For some time we may feel the pinch, but we ignore it because we have so much work to do." Kellhus had looked down into his right hand. Suddenly he balled it into a fist, raised it high. "And then one *strike*, with a hammer or a sword, and the blister breaks, *our heart is torn*. And then we suffer, for we feel the ache for the blessed, the sting of the cursed. We no longer see, *we witness* ..."

His luminous eyes settled upon the nameless knight. Blue and wise.

"This is what has happened to you."

"Yes ... Yes! B-but what should I do?"

"Rejoice."

"Rejoice? But I *suffer!*"

"Yes, *rejoice!* The callused hand cannot feel the lover's cheek. When we witness, we *testify*, and when we testify *we make ourselves responsible for what we see*. And that—*that*—is what it means to belong."

Kellhus suddenly stood, leapt from the low platform, took two breathtaking steps into their midst. "Make no mistake," he continued, and the air thrummed with the resonance of his voice. "This world *owns* you. You *belong*, whether you want to or not. Why do we suffer? Why do the wretched take their own lives? Because the world, no matter how cursed, *owns us*. Because *we belong*.

"Should we celebrate suffering?" a challenging voice called. From somewhere ...

Prince Kellhus smiled, glancing into the darkness. "Then it's no longer suffering, is it?"

The small congregation laughed.

"No," Kellhus continued, "that's not what I mean. Celebrate the *meaning* of suffering. Rejoice that you *belong*, not that you suffer. Remember what the Latter Prophet teaches us: glory comes in joy and sorrow. Joy and sorrow ..."

"I s-see see the wisdom of you-your words, Prince," the nameless knight stammered. "I truly *see!* But ..."

And somehow, Achamian could *feel* his question ...

What is there to gain?

"I'm not asking you to see," Kellhus said. "I'm asking you to witness."

Blank face. Desolate eyes. The nameless knight blinked, and two tears silvered his cheek. Then he smiled, and nothing, it seemed, could be so glorious.

"To make myself ..." His voice quavered, broke. "To m-make ..."

"To be one with the world in which you dwell," Kellhus said. "To make a covenant of your life."

The world ... You will gain the world.

Achamian looked down to his parchment, realized he'd stopped writing. He turned, looked helplessly at Esmenet.

"Don't worry," she said. "I remember."

Of course she did.

Esmenet. The second pillar of his peace, and by far the mightier of the two.

It seemed at once strange and fitting to find something almost conjugal in the midst of the Holy War. Each evening they would walk exhausted from Kellhus's talks or from Xinemus's fire, holding hands like young lovers, ruminating or bickering or laughing about the evening's events. They would pick their way through the guy ropes, and Achamian would pull the canvas aside with mock gallantry. They would touch and brush as they disrobed, then hold each other in the dark—as though together they could be more than what they were.

A whore of word and a whore of body.

The greater world had receded into shadow. He thought of Inrau less and less over the days, and pondered the concerns of his life with Esmenet—and Kellhus—more and more. Even the threat of the Consult and the Second Apocalypse had become something banal and remote, like rumours of war among pale-skinned peoples. Seswatha's Dreams still came as fierce as ever, but they dissolved in the softness of her touch, in the consolation of her voice. "Hush, Akka," she would say, "it's only a dream," and like smoke, the images—straining, groaning, spitting, and shrieking—would twist into nothingness. For once in his life, Achamian was seized by the moment, by *now* ... By the small hurt in her eyes when he said something careless. By the way her hand drifted to his knee of its own accord whenever they sat together. By the nights they lay naked in the tent, her head upon his chest and her dark hair fanned across his shoulder and neck, speaking of those things only they knew.

"Everyone knows," she said one night after making love.

They'd retired early, and they could hear the others: first mock protests and uproarious laughter, then utter quiet bound by the magic of Kellhus's voice. The fire still burned, and they could see it, muted and blurred across the dark canvas.

"He's a prophet," she said.

Achamian felt something resembling panic. "What are you saying?"

She turned to study him. Her eyes seemed to glitter with their own light. "Only what you need to hear."

"And why would I need to hear that?" What had she said?

"Because you think it. Because you fear it ... But most of all, because you need it."

We are damned, her eyes said.

"I'm not amused, Esmi."

She frowned, but as though she'd noticed nothing more than a tear in one of her new Kianene silks. "How long has it been since you've contacted Atyersus? Weeks? Months?"

"What is it with—"

"You're waiting, Akka. You're waiting to see what he becomes."

"Kellhus?"

She turned her face away, lowered her ear to his heart. "He's a prophet."

She knew him. When Achamian thought back, it seemed that she'd always known him. He'd even thought her a witch when they met for the first time, not only because of the ever-so-faint Mark of the charmed whore's shell that she used as a contraceptive, but because

she guessed he was a sorcerer before he uttered scarcely five words.
From the very beginning, she seemed to have a talent for him. For
Drusas Achamian.

It was strange, to be known—truly known. To be awaited rather than
anticipated. To be accepted instead of believed. To be half another's elaborate habits. To see oneself continually foreshadowed in another's eyes.

And it was strange to know. Sometimes she laughed so hard she
belched. And when disappointed, her eyes dimmed like candles starved of
air. She liked the feel of knives between her toes. She loved to hold her
hand slack and motionless while his cock hardened beneath. "I do
nothing," she would whisper, "and yet you rise to me." She was frightened
of horses. She fondled her left armpit when deep in thought. She did not
hide her face when she cried. And she could say things of such beauty
that sometimes Achamian thought his heart might stop for having
listened.

Details. Simple enough in isolation, but terrifying and mysterious in
their sum. A mystery that he *knew* ...

Was that not love? To know, to trust a mystery ...

Once, on the night of Ishoiya, which Conriyans celebrated with
copious amounts of that foul and flammable liquor, perrapta, Achamian
asked Kellhus to describe the way he loved Serwë. Only he, Xinemus, and
Kellhus remained awake. They were all drunk.

"Not the way you love Esmenet," the Prince replied.

"And how is that? How do I love her?" He staggered to his feet, his
arms askew. He swayed before the smoke and fire. "Like a fish loves the
ocean? Like, like ..."

"Like a drunk loves his cask," Xinemus chortled. "Like my dog loves
your leg!"

Achamian granted him that, but it was Kellhus's answer he most
wanted to hear. It was always Kellhus's answer. "So, my Prince? How do I
love Esmenet?"

Somehow a note of anger had crept into his tone.

Kellhus smiled, raised his downcast eyes. Tears scored his cheek.

"Like a child," he said.

The words knocked Achamian from his feet. He crashed to his
buttocks with a grunt.

"Yes," Xinemus agreed. He looked forward into the night, smiling ... Smiling for his friend, Achamian realized.

"Like a child?" Achamian asked, feeling curiously childlike.

"Yes," Kellhus replied. "You ask no questions, Akka. It simply *is* ... Without reserve." He turned to him with the look Achamian knew so well, the look he so often yearned for when others occupied Kellhus's attention. The look of friend, father, student, and teacher. The look his heart could see.

"She's become your ground," Kellhus said.

"Yes ..." Achamian replied.

She's become my wife.

Such a thought! He beamed with a childish glee. He felt wonderfully drunk.

My wife!

But later that same night, he somehow found himself making love to Serwë.

Afterward he would scarcely remember, but he'd awakened on a reed mat by the remains of the fire. He'd been dreaming of the white turrets of Myclai and rumours of Mog-Pharau. Xinemus and Kellhus were gone, and the night sky seemed impossibly deep, the way it had looked that night he and Esmenet had slept out of doors at the ruined shrine. Like an endless pit. Serwë knelt above him, as flawless as ivory in the firelight, at once smiling and crying.

"What's wrong?" he gasped. But then he realized she'd hiked his robe to his waist, and was rolling his cock against his belly. He was already hard—insanely so, it seemed.

"*Serwë* ..." he managed to protest, but with each roll of her palm, bolts of rapture shuddered through him. He arched against the ground, straining to press himself into her hand. For some reason, it seemed that all he needed, all he'd ever needed, was to feel her fingers close about the head of his member.

"*No,*" he moaned, digging his heels into the turf, clawing at the grass. What was happening?

She released him, and he gasped at the kiss of cool air. He could feel his own fiery pulse ...

Something. He needed to say something! This couldn't be happening!

But she'd slipped free her hasas, and he trembled at the sight of her. So lithe. So smooth. White in shadow, burnished gold in firelight. Her peach hazed with tender blond. She no longer touched him, yet her beauty flailed at him, wrenched at his groin. He swallowed, struggled to breathe. Then she straddled him. He glimpsed the porcelain sway of her breasts, the hairless curve of her belly.

Is she with—

She encompassed him. He cried out, cursed.

"It is you!" she hissed, sobbing, staring desperately into his eyes. "I can see you. *I can see!*"

He turned his head aside in delirium, afraid he would climax too soon. This was Serwë ... Sweet Sejenus, *this was Serwë!*

Then he saw Esmenet, standing desolate in the dark. Watching ...

He closed his eyes, grimaced, and climaxed.

"*Guh ... g-guh ...*"

"I can *feel* you!" Serwë cried.

When he opened his eyes Esmenet was gone—if she had ever been.

Serwë continued to grind against him. The whole world had become a slurry of heat and wetness and thundering aching thrusting beauty. He surrendered to her abandon.

Somehow he awoke before the horns and sat for a time at the entrance to his tent, watching Esmenet sleep, feeling the pinch of dried seed on his thighs. When she awoke, he searched her eyes, but saw nothing. Through the hard, long march of the following day, she chastised him for drinking and nothing more. Serwë didn't so much as look at him. By the following evening he'd convinced himself it had been a dream. A delicious dream.

The perrapta. There could be no other explanation.

Fucking fish liquor, he thought, and tried to feel ruefully amused.

When he told Esmenet, she laughed and threatened to tell Kellhus. Afterward, alone, he actually wept in relief. Never, he realized, not even the night following the madness with the Emperor beneath the Andiamine Heights, had he felt a greater sense of doom. And he knew he belonged to Esmi—not the world.

She was his covenant. Esmenet was his wife.

The Holy War crept ever closer to Shigek, and still he ignored the Mandate. There were excuses he could assemble. He could ponder the

impossibility of making discreet inquiries, bribes, or dissembling sugges-
tions in an encampment of armed fanatics. He could remind himself of
what his School had done to Inrau. But ultimately they meant nothing.

He would rush the enemy ranks. He would see his heresy through. To
the end, no matter what horrors it might hold. For the first time in a long
and wandering life, Drusas Achamian had found happiness.

And peace had come.

<hr />

The day's march had been particularly trying, and Serwë sat by the fire,
rubbing her toes while staring across the flames at her love, Kellhus. If
only it could always be like this ...

Four days previous Proyas had sent the Scylvendi south with several
hundred knights—to learn the ways into Shigek, Kellhus had said. Four
days without chancing upon his famished glare. Four days without cringing in his iron shadow as he escorted her to their pavilion. Four days
without his dread savagery.

And each of them spent praying and praying, *Let him be killed!*

But this was the one prayer Kellhus wouldn't answer.

She stared and wondered and loved. His long blond hair flashed golden
in the firelight; his bearded features radiated good humour and understanding. He nodded as Achamian spoke to him about something—
sorcery perhaps. She paid scant attention to the Schoolman's words. She
was too busy listening to Kellhus's face.

Never had she seen such beauty. There was something inexplicable,
something godlike and surreal, about his appearance, as though a breathtaking elegance, an impossible grace, laid hidden within his expressions,
something that might flare at any moment and blind her with revelation.
A face that made each moment, each heartbeat ...

A gift.

She placed a hand on the gentle swell of her belly, and for an instant,
she thought she could feel the second heart within her—no larger than a
sparrow's—drumming through moment after thickening moment.

His child ... His.

So much had changed! She was wise, far more so, she knew, than a girl
of twenty summers should be. The world had chastened her, had shown

her the impotence of outrage. First the Gaunum sons and their cruel lusts. Then Panteruth and his unspeakable brutalities. Then Cnaiür and his iron-willed madness. What could the outrage of a soft-skinned concubine mean to a man such as him? Just one more thing to be broken. She knew the futility, that the animal within would grovel, shriek, would place soothing lips around any man's cock for a moment of mercy—that it would do anything, sate any hunger, to survive. She'd been enlightened.

Submission. Truth lay in submission.

"You've surrendered, Serwë," Kellhus had told her. "And by surrendering, you have conquered me!"

The days of nothing had passed. The world, Kellhus said, had prepared her for *him*. She, Serwë hil Keyalti, was to be his sacred consort.

She would bear the sons of the Warrior-Prophet.

What indignity, what suffering, could compare with this? Certainly, she wept when the Scylvendi struck her, clenched her teeth in fury and gagging shame when he used her. But afterward she *knew*, and Kellhus had taught her that knowing was exalted above *all other things*. Cnaiür was a totem of the old dark world, the ancient outrage made flesh. For every god, Kellhus had told her, there was a demon.

For every God ...

The priests, both those of her father and those of the Gaunum, had claimed the Gods moved the souls of men. But Serwë knew the Gods also moved *as* men. So often, watching Esmenet, Achamian, Xinemus, and the others about the fire, she would be amazed that they couldn't see, though sometimes she suspected that, in their heart of hearts, they knew and yet were stubborn.

But then, unlike her, they didn't couple with a god—and his guises.

They hadn't been taught how to forgive, how to submit, as she'd been taught, though they learned slowly. She often glimpsed the small, sometimes lonely ways in which he instructed them. And it was a wondrous thing, to watch a god instruct others.

Even now, he instructed them.

"No," Achamian was asserting. "We sorcerers are distinguished by our ability, you caste-nobles by your blood. What does it matter whether other men recognize us as such? We are what we are."

With smiling eyes, Kellhus said, "Are you sure?"

Serwë had seen this many times. The words would be simple, but the *way* would wrench at their hearts.

"What do you mean," Achamian said blankly.

Kellhus shrugged. "What if I were to tell you that I'm like you."

Xinemus's eyes flashed to Achamian, who laughed nervously.

"Like me?" the Schoolman asked. He licked his lips. "How so?"

"I can see the Mark, Akka ... I can see the bruise of your damnation."

"You jest," Achamian snapped, but his voice was strange ...

Kellhus had turned to Xinemus. "Do you see? A moment ago, I was no different from you. The distinction between us didn't exist until just—"

"It still doesn't exist," Achamian blurted, his voice rising. "I would have you prove this!"

Kellhus studied the man, his look careful and troubled. "How does one prove what one sees?"

Xinemus, who seemed unperturbed, chuckled. "What is it, Akka? There's many who see your blasphemy, but choose not to speak it. Think of the College of Luthymae ..."

But Achamian had jumped to his feet, his expression bewildered, even panicked. "It's just that ... that ..."

Serwë's thoughts leapt. *He knows, my love! Achamian knows what you are!*

She flushed at the memory of the sorcerer between her legs, but then reminded herself that it wasn't *Achamian* whom she remembered, it was Kellhus ...

"You must know me Serwë, in all my guises."

"There *is* a way to prove this!" the Schoolman exclaimed. He fixed them with a ludicrous stare, then without warning hurried off into the darkness.

Xinemus had begun muttering some joke, but just then Esmenet sat next to Serwë, smiling and frowning.

"Has Kellhus worked him into a frenzy again?" she asked, handing Serwë a steaming bowl of spiced tea.

"Again," Serwë said, and grasped the proffered bowl. She tipped a glittering drop to the earth before drinking. It tasted warm, coiled in her stomach like sun-hot silk. "Mmmm ... Thank you, Esmi."

Esmenet nodded, turned to Kellhus and Xinemus. The previous night, Serwë had cut Esmenet's black hair short—man short—so that now she resembled a beautiful boy. *Almost as beautiful as me*, Serwë thought.

She'd never known a woman like Esmenet before: bold, with a tongue as wicked as any man's. She frightened Serwë sometimes, with her ability to match the men word for word, joke for joke. Only Kellhus could best her. But she had always been considerate. Serwë had asked her once why she was so kind, and Esmenet had replied that the only peace she'd found as a harlot had been caring for those more vulnerable than her. When Serwë insisted she was neither a whore nor vulnerable, Esmenet had smiled sadly, saying, "We're all whores, Serchaa ..."

And Serwë had believed her. How couldn't she? It sounded so much like something Kellhus might say.

Esmenet turned to look at her. "Was the day's march hard on you, Serchaa?" She smiled the way Serwë's aunt had once smiled, with warmth and concern. But then her expression suddenly darkened, as though she'd glimpsed something disagreeable in Serwë's face. Her eyes became hooded.

"Esmi?" Serwë said. "Is something wrong?"

Esmenet's look became faraway. When it returned, her handsome face wrinkled into another smile—more sad, but just as genuine.

Serwë looked nervously to her hands, suddenly terrified that Esmenet somehow *knew*. In her soul's eye, she glimpsed the Scylvendi toiling above her in the dark.

But it wasn't him!

"The hills," she said quickly. "The hills are so hard ... Kellhus *says* he'll get me a mule."

Esmenet nodded. "Make sure he ..." She paused, frowned at the darkness. "What's he up to now?"

Achamian had returned from the darkness, bearing a small doll about as long as a forearm. He sat the doll down on the earth, with its back resting against the bonelike stone he'd been using as a seat moments earlier. With the exception of the head, it was carved from dark wood, with jointed limbs, a small rusty knife for a right hand, and engraved with rows of tiny text. The head, however, was a silken sack, shapeless, and no larger than a poor man's purse. Staring at it, it suddenly seemed a dreadful thing to Serwë. The firelight gleamed across its polished surfaces and gave the illusion that the words had been carved inches deep. The small shadow that framed it was black as pitch against the stone and shifted uneasily with the twining glitter of the flames. It looked like a little dead man propped before a towering fire.

"Does Achamian scare you, Serchaa?" Esmenet asked. Something wicked and mischievous glinted in her eyes.

Serwë thought about that night at the ruined shrine, when he'd sent light to the stars. She shook her head. "No," she replied. He was too sad to frighten.

"He will after this," Esmenet said.

"He leaves for proof," Xinemus jeered, "and he returns with a toy!"

"This is no 'toy,'" Achamian muttered, annoyed.

"He's right," Kellhus said seriously. "It is some kind of sorcerous artifact. I can see the Mark."

Achamian looked at Kellhus sharply, but said nothing. The fire crackled and hissed. He finished adjusting the doll, took two steps back. Suddenly, framed by the darkness and the shining fires of the greater encampment, he seemed less a weary scholar and more a Mandate Schoolman. Serwë shivered.

"This is called a 'Wathi Doll,'" he explained, "something I ... I purchased from a Sansori witch a couple of years ago ... There's a soul trapped in this doll."

Xinemus coughed wine through his nose. "*Akka*," he rasped, "I won't tolerate—"

"Humour me, Zin! Please ... Kellhus says he's one of the Few. This is the one way for him to prove it without damning himself—or you, Zin. Apparently for me, it's already too late."

"What should I do?" Kellhus asked.

Achamian knelt and fetched a twig from the ground at his feet. "I'll simply scratch two words into the earth, and you'll speak them, aloud. You won't be uttering a Cant, so you won't be marked by the blood-of-the-onta. No one will look at you and know you for a sorcerer. And you'll still be pure enough to handle Trinkets without discomfort. You'll just be uttering the artifact's cipher ... The doll will awaken only if you truly *are* one of the Few."

"Why's it bad that anyone recognize Kellhus as a sorcerer?" Bloody Dinch asked.

"Because he'd be *damned!*" Xinemus nearly shouted.

"That," Achamian acknowledged, "and he'd quickly be dead. He'd be a sorcerer without a school, a *wizard*, and the Schools don't brook wizards."

Achamian turned to Esmenet; they exchanged a quick, worried look. Then he walked over to Kellhus. Serwë could tell that a large part of him already regretted this spectacle.

With the twig, Achamian deftly scratched a line of signs in the earth before Kellhus's sandalled feet. Serwë assumed that they were two words, but she couldn't read. "I've written them in Kûniüric," he said, "to spare the others any indignity." He stepped back, nodded slowly. Despite the brown of innumerable days spent in the sun, he looked grey. "Speak them," he instructed.

Kellhus, his bearded face solemn, studied the words for a moment, then in a clear voice said, "*Skuni ari'sitwa ...*"

All eyes scrutinized the doll lying slack against the stone in the fire-light. Serwë held her breath. She'd expected that perhaps the limbs might twitch and then drawl into drunken life, as though the doll were a puppet, something that might prance on the end of invisible strings. But that didn't happen. The first thing to move, rather, was the stained, silk head—but it didn't loll with lazy life, or even slowly nod; instead, something moved from *within*. Serwë gasped in horror, realizing that a *tiny face*—nose, lips, brow, and eye sockets—now strained against the fabric ...

It was as though a narcotic haze had settled upon them, the torpor of bearing witness to the impossible. Serwë's heart hammered. Her thoughts wheeled ...

But she couldn't look away. A human face, small enough to palm, pressed against the silk. She could see tiny lips part in a soundless howl.

And then the limbs moved—suddenly, deftly, with none of the swaying stagger of a puppet. Whatever moved those limbs moved them from within, with the compact elegance of a body assured of its extremi-ties. And with half-panicked thoughts, Serwë understood that it was a soul, a *self-moving* soul ... In a single, languorous motion, it leaned forward, braced its arms against the earth, bent its knees, then came to its feet, casting a slender shadow across the earth, the shadow of man with a sack bound about his head.

"*By all that's holy* ..." Bloody Dinch hissed in a breathless voice.

The wooden man turned its eyeless face from side to side, studied the dumbstruck giants.

It raised the small, rusty blade it possessed in lieu of a right hand. The fire popped, and it jumped and whirled. A smoking coal bounced to a stop at its feet. Looking down, it knelt with the blade, flicked the coal back into the fire.

Achamian muttered something unspeakable, and it collapsed in a jumble of splayed limbs. He looked blankly at Kellhus, and in a voice as ashen as his expression, said, "So you're one of the Few ..."

Horror, Serwë thought. He was horrified. But why? Couldn't he see?

Without warning, Xinemus leapt to his feet. Before Achamian could even glance at him, the Marshal had seized his arm, yanked him violently about.

"Why do you do this?" Xinemus cried, his face both pained and enraged. "You *know* that it's difficult enough for me to ... to ... You *know!* And now *displays such as this? Blasphemy?*"

Stunned, Achamian looked at his friend aghast. "But Zin," he cried. "This is what I am."

"Perhaps Proyas was right," he snapped. With a growl he thrust Achamian away, then paced off into the darkness. Esmenet leapt from her place by Serwë and grasped one of Achamian's slack hands. But the sorcerer stared off into the blackness that had encompassed the Marshal of Attrempus. Serwë could hear Esmenet's insistent whisper: "*It's okay, Akka! Kellhus will speak to him. Show him his folly* ..." But Achamian, his face turned from those watching about the fire, pushed at her feebly.

Still bewildered, her skin still tingling in dread, Serwë looked to Kellhus beseechingly: *Please ... you must make this better!* Xinemus must forgive Achamian this. They must all learn to forgive!

Serwë didn't know when she'd begun speaking to him with her face, but she did it so often now that many times she couldn't sort what she'd told him from what she'd shown him. This was part of the infinite peace between them. Nothing was hidden.

And for some reason, his look reminded her of something he'd once said: "*I must reveal myself to them slowly Serwë, slowly. Otherwise they'll turn against me ...*"

Late that night, Serwë was awakened by voices—angry voices, just outside their tent. Reflexively she grasped for her belly. Her innards churned with fright. *Dear Gods ... Mercy! Please, mercy!*

The Scylvendi had returned.

As she knew he would. Nothing could kill Cnaiür urs Skiötha, not so long as Serwë remained alive.

Not again ... please-please ...

She could see nothing, but the menace of his presence already clutched at her, as though he were a wraith, something feral and malevolent bent upon consuming her, scraping out her heart the way Cepaloran women scrape pelts clean with sharpened oyster shells. She began to cry, softly, secretly, so he wouldn't hear ... Any moment, she knew, he would thrash into the tent, fill it with the stink of a man who'd just shed his hauberk, grip her about the throat and ...

Pleaasse! I know I'm supposed to be a good girl—I'll be a good girl! Please!

She heard his harsh voice, low so as not to be overheard, but fierce nonetheless.

"I tire of this, Dûnyain."

"*Nuta'tharo hirmuta,*" Kellhus replied with an impassiveness that unnerved her—until she realized: *He's cold because he hates him ... Hates him as I do!*

"I will not!" the Scylvendi spat.

"*Sta puth yura'gring?*"

"Because you ask me too! I tire hearing you defile my tongue. I tire of being mocked. I tire of these fools you ply. I tire of watching you defile my prize! *My prize!*"

A moment of silence. Buzzing ears.

"Both of us," Kellhus said in taut Sheyic, "have secured places of honour. Both of us have gained the ears of the great. What more could you want?"

"I want only one thing."

"And together, we walk the shortest path to—"

Kellhus abruptly halted. A hard moment passed between them.

"You intend to leave," Kellhus said.

Laughter, like a wolf's growl broken into fragments.

"There is no need to share the same yaksh."

Serwë gasped for air. The scar on her arm, the swazond the plainsman had given beneath the Hethanta Mountains, flared in sudden pain.

No-no-no-no-no ...

"Proyas ..." Kellhus said, his voice still blank. "You intend to camp with Proyas."

Please God noooo!

"I have come for my things," Cnaiür said. "I have come for my prize."

Never in all her violent life had Serwë felt herself pitched upon such a precipice. The breath was choked from her mid-sob, and she became very still. The silence shrieked. Three heartbeats it took Kellhus to answer, and for three heartbeats her very life hung as though from a gibbet between the voices of men. She would die for him, she knew, and she would die without him. It seemed she'd always known this, from the first clumsy days of her childhood. She almost gagged for fear.

And then Kellhus said: "No. Serwë stays with me."

Numb relief. Warm tears. The hard earth beneath her had become as fluid as the sea. Serwë very nearly swooned. And a voice that wasn't hers spoke through her anguish and her rapture and said: *Mercy ... At last mercy ...*

She heard nothing of their ensuing argument; succour and joy possessed their own thunder. But they didn't speak long, not with her weeping aloud. When Kellhus returned to his place beside her, she threw herself upon him, showered him with desperate kisses and held his strong body so tight she could scarcely breathe. And at last, when the great weariness of the unburdened overwhelmed her and she lay spinning on the threshold of sweet, childlike sleep, she could feel callused yet gentle fingers slowly caressing her cheek.

A God touched her. Watched over her with divine love.

———— ∞∞∞ ————

Its back to canvas, the thing called Sarcellus crouched, as still as stone. The musk of the Scylvendi's fury permeated the night air, sweet and sharp, heady with the promise of blood. The sound of the woman weeping tugged at its groin. She might have been worth its fancy, were it not for the smell of her fetus, which sickened ...

What passed for thought bolted through what passed for its soul.

CHAPTER ELEVEN

SHIGEK

If all human events possess purpose, then all human deeds possess purpose. And yet when men vie with men, the purpose of no man comes to fruition: the result always falls somewhere in between. The purpose of deeds, then, cannot derive from the purposes of men, because all men vie with all men. This means the deeds of men must be willed by something other than men. From this it follows that we are all slaves.

Who then is our Master?

—MEMGOWA, THE BOOK OF DIVINE ACTS

What is practicality but one moment betrayed for the next?

—TRIAMIS I, JOURNALS AND DIALOGUES

Late Summer, 4111 Year-of-the-Tusk, southern Gedea

Gedea didn't so much end as vanish. After dozens of skirmishes and petty sieges, Coithus Athjeäri and his knights raced south across the vast sandstone plateau of the Gedean interior. They followed ravines and ridge lines, always climbing. By day they hunted antelope for food and jackals for sport. At night they could smell the Great Desert on the wind. The grasses faltered, gave way to dust, gravel, and pungent-smelling scrub. After riding three full days without seeing so much as a goatherd, they finally sighted smoke on the southern horizon. They hastened up the slopes, only to rein their caparisoned mounts to a sudden and panicked halt. The ground plummeted a thousand feet or more. To either side great escarpments ramped into the hazy distances. Before them the long waters of the River Sempis snaked across a plain of verdant green, its back flashing opposite the sun.

Shigek.

The ancient Kyraneans had called her "Chemerat," the "Red Land," because of the copper-coloured silt the seasonal floods deposited across the plains. In far antiquity, she ruled an empire that extended from Sumna to Shimeh, and her God-Kings produced works unrivalled to this day, including the legendary Ziggurats. In near antiquity she was famed for the subtlety of her priests, the elegance of her perfumes, and the effectiveness of her poisons. For the Men of the Tusk, she was a land of curses, crypts, and uneasy ruins.

A place where the past became dread, it ran so deep.

Athjeäri and his knights descended the escarpments and wondered that sterile desert could so quickly become lush fields and heavy trees. Wary of ambush, they followed the ancient dikes, rode through one abandoned village then another. Finally they found one old man without fear, and with some difficulty determined that Skauras and all the Kianene had abandoned the North Bank. Hence the smoke they had seen from the escarpment. The Sapatishah was burning every boat he could find.

The young Earl of Gaenri sent word to the Great Names.

Two weeks later the first columns of the Holy War marched unopposed into the Sempis Valley. Bands of Inrithi spread across the floodplain, securing stores, occupying the villas and strongholds abandoned by the Kianene. There was little bloodshed—at first.

Along the river, the Men of the Tusk saw sacred ibis and heron wading among the reeds and great flocks of egret wheeling over the black waters. Some even glimpsed crocodiles and hippopotamuses, beasts which, they would learn, the Shigeki revered as holy. Away from the river, where small stands of various trees—eucalyptus and sycamore, date palm and fan palm—perpetually screened the distances, they were often surprised by ruined foundations, by pillars and walls bearing engravings of nameless kings and their forgotten conquests. Some of the ruins were truly colossal, the remains of palace or temple complexes once as great, it seemed to them, as the Andiamine Heights in Momemn or the Junriüma in Holy Sumna. Many of them wandered for a time, pondering things that may or may not have happened.

When they passed villages, walking along earthen banks meant to capture floodwaters for the fields, the inhabitants gathered to watch them, shushing children and holding tight barking dogs. In the centuries following the Kianene conquest the Shigeki had become devout Fanim, but they were an old race, tenants who had always outlived their landlords. They could no longer recognize themselves in the warlike images that glared from the broken walls. So beer, wine, and water were given to slake the invader's thirst. Onions, dates, and fresh-baked breads were furnished to sate his hunger. And, sometimes, daughters were offered to comfort his lust. Incredulous, the Men of the Tusk shook their heads and exclaimed that this was a land of marvels. And some were reminded of their first youthful visit to their father's ancestral home, of that strange sense of *returning* to a place where they had never been.

Shigek was oft named in *The Tractate*, the rumour of a distant tyrant, already ancient in those ancient days. As a result, some among the Inrithi found themselves troubled because the words seemed to overshoot the place. They urinated in the river, defecated in the trees, and slapped at the mosquitoes. The ground was old, melancholy, more fertile perhaps, but it was ground like any other ground. Most, however, found themselves struck by awe. No matter how sacred the text, the words merely dangled when the lands remained unseen. Each in their own way, they realized that pilgrimage was the work of stitching the world to scripture. They had taken their first true step.

And Holy Shimeh seemed so close.

Then Cerjulla, the Tydonni Earl of Warnute, encountered the walled town of Chiama. Fearing starvation because of a blight the previous year, the town elders demanded guarantees before throwing open their gates. Rather than negotiate, Cerjulla simply ordered his men to storm the walls, which were easily overcome. Once within, the Warnutishmen butchered everyone.

Two days afterward, there was another massacre at Jirux, the great river fortress opposite the South Bank city of Ammegnotis. Apparently the Shigeki garrison left there by Skauras had mutinied and murdered all their Kianene officers. When Uranyanka, the famed Ainoni Palatine of Moserothu, arrived with his knights, the mutineers threw open the gates only to be herded together and executed en masse. Heathens, Uranyanka would later tell Chepheramunni, he could tolerate, but treacherous heathens he could not forbear.

The following morning, Gaidekki, the tempestuous Palatine of Anplei, ordered the assault of a town called Huterat, not too far from the Old Dynasty city of Iothiah, presumably because his interpreter, a notorious drunkard, had mistranslated the town's terms of surrender. Once the gates were taken, his Conriyans ran amok through the streets, raping and murdering without discrimination.

Then, as though murder possessed its own unholy momentum, the Holy War's occupation of the North Bank degenerated into wanton carnage, though for what reason, no one knew. Perhaps it was the rumours of poisoned dates and pomegranates. Perhaps bloodshed simply begat bloodshed. Perhaps faith's certainty was as terrifying as it was beautiful. What could be more true than destroying the false?

Word of the Inrithi atrocities spread among the Shigeki. Before the altar and in the streets the Priests of Fane claimed that the Solitary God punished them for welcoming the idolaters. The Shigeki began barricading themselves in their great, domed tabernacles. With their wives and children they gathered wailing on the soft carpets, crying out their sins, begging for forgiveness. The thunder of rams at the doors would be their only answer. Then the rush of iron-eyed swordsmen.

Every tabernacle across the North Bank witnessed some kind of massacre. The Men of the Tusk hacked the screaming penitents into silence, then they kicked over the tripods, smashed the marmoreal altars, tore the tapestries from the walls and the grand kneeling rugs from the floors. Anything carrying the taint of Fanimry they heaved into colossal bonfires. Sometimes, beneath the rugs, they found the breathtaking mosaics of the Inrithi who had originally raised the temple, and the structure would be spared. Otherwise the great Fanim tabernacles of Shigek were burned. Beneath monstrous towers of smoke, dogs nosed the heaped dead and licked blood from the broad steps.

In Iothiah, which had thrown open her gates in terror, hundreds of Kerathotics, an Inrithi sect that had managed to survive centuries of Fanim oppression, saved themselves by singing the ancient hymns of the Thousand Temples. Men who had wailed in terror suddenly found themselves embracing the long lost brothers of their faith. That night the Kerathotics took to the streets, kicking down doors, murdering old competitors, unscrupulous tax-farmers, anyone they had begrudged under the Sapatishah's regime. Their grudges were many.

In red-walled Nagogris, the Men of the Tusk actually began slaughtering one another. Almost as soon as the Holy War had arrived in Shigek, the Shigeki potentates remaining in the city sent emissaries to Ikurei Conphas, offering to surrender to the Emperor in exchange for Imperial protection. Conphas promptly dispatched General Numemarius and a cohort of Kidruhil. Through some unexplained blunder, however, the gates were relinquished to a large force of Thunyeri, fierce Ingraulish and Skagwamen for the most part, who promptly began plundering the city. The Kidruhil attempted to intervene, and pitched battles broke out in the streets. When General Numemarius met with Yalgrota Sranchammer under flag of truce, the giant brained him. Disorganized by the death of their general and unnerved by the ferocity of the blond-bearded warriors, the Kidruhil withdrew from the city.

But none suffered more horribly than the Fanic priests.

At night, around fires of heathen reliquary, the Inrithi used them for drunken sport, slicing open their bellies, leading them like mules by their own entrails. Some were blinded, some strangled, some were forced to watch their wives and daughters raped. Others were flayed alive. A great many were burned as witches. Scarcely a village could be found without the mutilated corpse of some Fanic priest or functionary nailed to the vaulting limbs of a eucalyptus tree.

Two weeks passed, then suddenly, as though some precise measure had been exacted, the madness lifted. In the end, only a fraction of the Shigeki population had been killed, but no traveller could pass more than an hour without crossing paths with the dead. Instead of the humble boats of fishermen and traders, bloated corpses bobbed down the defiled waters of the Sempis and fanned out across the Meneanor Sea.

At long last, Shigek had been cleansed.

From the summit the ziggurat seemed far steeper than it had from the ground below. But then so did most things—after the fact.

Cresting the last of the treacherous steps, Kellhus turned to the surrounding vista. To the north and west, all was cultivation. He saw diked fields, lines of sycamore and ash, and villages that looked like mounds of shattered pottery in the distance. Several smaller ziggurats reared in the near distance, staunch and stolid, anchoring a network of channels and embankments that reached out to the hazy Gedean escarpments. To the south, past the shoulders of the ziggurat Achamian had called Palpothis, he saw stands of marsh gingkos standing like bent sentinels amid thickets of sandbar willows. The mighty Sempis glittered in the sunlight beyond. And to the east he saw lines of red through green—raised footpaths and ancient roadways—passing beneath shadowy copses and between sunny fields, all converging on Iothiah, which darkened the horizon with her walls and smoke.

Shigek. Yet another ancient land.

So old and so vast, Father ... Did you see it thus?

He glanced down the stair that formed a causeway across the ziggurat's mammoth back, saw Achamian still labouring up the steps. Sweat darkened the armpits and collar of his white linen tunic.

"I thought you said the ancients believed their gods lived atop these things," Kellhus called down. "Why do you tarry?"

Achamian paused, scowled up at the remaining distance. Gasping for breath, he struggled to smile through his grimace. "Because the ancients believed their gods lived atop these things ..."

Kellhus grinned, then turned to study the wrecked summit. The ancient godhouse lay in shambles: ruined walls and spilled blocks. He inspected sundered engravings and indecipherable pictograms. The remains of gods, he imagined, and their earthly invocations.

Faith. Faith had raised this black-stepped mountain—the beliefs of long dead men.

So much, Father, and all in the name of delusion.

It scarcely seemed possible. And yet the Holy War wasn't so different. In some ways it was a far greater, if more ephemeral, work.

In the months since arriving at Momemn, Kellhus had laid the foundation of his own ziggurat, insinuating himself into the confidence of the mighty, instilling the suspicion that he was more—far more—than the prince he claimed to be. With the reluctance proper to wisdom and humility, he'd finally assumed the role others had thrust upon him. Given the complexities involved, he had initially hoped to proceed with more caution, but his encounter with Sarcellus had forced him to accelerate his timetable, to take risks he would have otherwise avoided. Even now, he knew, the Consult watched him, studied him, and pondered his growing power. He had to seize the Holy War before their patience dwindled too far. He had to make a ziggurat of these men.

You saw them too, didn't you, Father? Is it you they hunt? Are they the reason you summoned me?

Looking across the near distance, he saw a man walking with his oxen along a raised pathway, flicking them with his switch every third or fourth step. He saw backs bent in neighbouring fields of millet. A half-mile away, he saw a party of Inrithi horsemen riding in single file through yellowing wheat.

Any one of them could be a Consult spy.

"Sweet Seja!" Achamian cried as he gained the summit.

What would the sorcerer do if he learned of his secret conflict with the Consult? The Mandate couldn't be involved, Kellhus knew, not until he possessed power enough to parley with them as equals.

Everything came to power.

"What's this called again?" Kellhus asked, though he forgot nothing.

"The Great Ziggurat of Xijoser," Achamian replied, still panting. "One of the mightiest works of the Old Dynasty ... Remarkable, isn't it?"

"Yes ..." Kellhus said with false forced enthusiasm.

He must feel shame.

"Something troubles you?" Achamian asked, leaning against his knees. He turned to spit over the summit's edge.

"Serwë ..." Kellhus said with an air of admission. "Tell me, would you think her capable of being ..." He feigned a nervous swallow.

Achamian looked away to the hazy landscape, but not before Kellhus glimpsed a fleeting expression of terror. Palms turning upward, nervous stroke of his beard, flaring heart rate ...

"Being what?" the sorcerer asked with sham disinterest.

Of all the souls Kellhus had mastered, few had proven as useful as Serwë. Lust and shame were ever the shortest paths to the hearts of world-born men. Ever since he'd sent her to Achamian the sorcerer had compensated for his half-remembered trespass in innumerable subtle ways. The old Conriyan proverb was true: no friend was more generous than the one who has seduced your wife ...

And generosity was precisely what he needed from Drusas Achamian.

"Nothing," Kellhus said with a shake of his head. "All men fear their women venal, I suppose." Some openings must be continually worked and worried, while others must be left to fester.

Avoiding his gaze, the Schoolman groaned and rubbed his lower back. "I'm getting too old for this," he said with anxious good humour. He cleared his throat and spit one final time. "How Esmi would crow ..."

Esmenet. She too had a part to play.

After so many weeks of prolonged contact, Kellhus had come to know Achamian far better than Achamian knew himself. Those who loved the Schoolman—Xinemus and Esmenet—often thought him weak. They softened hard words, pretended not to notice the unsteady hands or the fragile expressions, and they spoke with an almost parental defensiveness on his behalf. But Drusas Achamian, Kellhus knew, was stronger than anyone, especially Drusas Achamian, suspected. Some men frittered themselves away with incessant doubt and reflection until it seemed they had no shape they could grasp hold of. Some men had to be hewed by the crude axe of the world.

Tested.

"Tell me," Kellhus said, "how much must a teacher give?"

He knew that Achamian had long since stopped thinking himself his teacher, but the sorcerer was just vain enough not to disabuse him of this impression. The most powerful flatteries dwelt not in what was said but in the assumptions behind what was said.

"That," Achamian replied, daring his gaze once again, "depends upon the student ..."

"So the student must be known to prevent giving too little."

He must question himself.

"Or too much."

This was an intellectual habit of Achamian's: noting the importance of contrary and not so obvious things. He delighted in throwing aside the veil, in revealing the complexities that lurked beneath simple things. In this he was almost unique: world-born men, Kellhus had found, despised complexity as much as they cherished flattery. Most men would rather die in deception than live in uncertainty.

"Too much ..." Kellhus repeated. "You mean like Proyas?"

Achamian glanced to his sandalled feet.

"Yes. Like Proyas."

"What did you teach him?"

"What we call the exoterics ... Logic, History, Arithmetic—everything save the esoterics—sorcery."

"And that was too much?"

The sorcerer paused in puzzlement, suddenly unsure as to what he'd meant.

"No," he conceded after a moment. "I guess not. I *had* hoped to teach him doubt, tolerance, but the clamour of his faith was too great. Perhaps if they'd let me finish his education ... But he's lost. Another Man of the Tusk."

Now show him ease.

Kellhus snorted in a half laugh. "Like me."

"Exactly," the Mandate Schoolman said, grinning in the both sly and shy way that others, Kellhus had noted, found so endearing. "Another bloodthirsty fanatic."

Kellhus laughed Xinemus's laugh, then trailed, smiling. For some time he'd been mapping Achamian's responses to the finer nuances of his expression. Though Kellhus had never met Inrau, he knew—with startling exactitude—the peculiarities of the young man's manner and expression—so well that he could prompt Achamian to thoughts of Inrau with little more than a look or a smile.

Paro Inrau. The student Achamian had lost in Sumna. The student he'd failed.

"There's more than one kind of fanaticism," Kellhus said.

The sorcerer's eyes widened momentarily, then narrowed in anxious thoughts of Inrau and the events of the previous year—things he'd rather not remember.

The Mandate must become more than a hated master, they must become an enemy.

"But not all fanaticisms are equal," Achamian said.

"How do you mean? Not equal in principle, or not equal in consequence?"

Inrau was such a consequence, as were the countless thousands the Holy War had murdered over the past several days. *Your School*, Kellhus had suggested, *is no different.*

"The Truth," Achamian said. "The Truth distinguishes them. No matter what the fanaticism, Inrithi, Consult, or even Mandate, the consequences are the same: men die or suffer. The question is one of what they die or suffer *for* ..."

"So purpose—true purpose—justifies suffering, even death?"

"You must believe as much, otherwise you wouldn't be here."

Kellhus smiled as though abashed at having been exposed. "So it all comes to Truth. If one's purposes are true ..."

"Anything can be justified. Any torment, any murder ..."

Kellhus rounded his eyes the way he knew Inrau would. "Any betrayal," he said.

Achamian stared, his nimble face as stony as he could manage. But Kellhus saw past the dark skin, past the sheath of fine muscle, past even the soul that toiled beneath. He saw arcana and anguish, a yearning steeped in three thousand years of wisdom. He saw a child beaten and bullied by a drunken father. He saw a hundred generations of Nroni fishermen pinioned between hunger and the cruel sea. He saw Seswatha and the madness of war without hope. He saw ancient Ketyai tribesmen surge down mountain slopes. He saw the animal, rooting and rutting, reaching back to time out of memory.

He didn't see what came after; he saw what came before ...

"Any betrayal," the sorcerer repeated dully.

He is close.

"And your cause," Kellhus pressed. "The prevention of the Second Apocalypse."

"Is true. There can be no doubt."

"So in the name of that cause, you can commit any act, any betrayal?"

Achamian's eyes slackened in dread, and Kellhus glimpsed a worry too fleet to become a question. The Schoolman had become accustomed to the efficiency of their discourse: rarely had they ever wandered from question to question as they did now.

"It's strange," Achamian said, "the way things spoken with assurance by one can sound so outrageous when repeated by another ..."

An unanticipated turn, but an opportunity as well. *A shorter path.*

"It troubles," Kellhus said, "because it shows that conviction is as cheap as words. Any man can believe unto death. Any man can claim your claim."

"So you fear I'm no different from any other fanatic."

"Wouldn't you?"

How deep does his conviction go?

"You *are* the Harbinger, Kellhus. If you dreamed Seswatha's Dream as I did ..."

"But couldn't Proyas say the same of his fanaticism? Couldn't he say, 'If you spoke to Maithanet as I did'?"

How far would he follow it? To the death?

The sorcerer sighed and nodded. "That's always the dilemma, now isn't it?"

"But whose dilemma? Mine or yours?"

Would he follow it beyond?

Achamian laughed, but in the clipped manner of men who make light of what horrifies them.

"It's the *world's* dilemma, Kellhus."

"I need more than that, Akka—more than bald assertions."

Would he follow it all the way?

"I'm not sure—"

"What is it you want of me?" Kellhus exclaimed in sudden desperation. Inrau's indecision warbled through his voice. Inrau's horror pulled wide his eyes.

I must have it.

The sorcerer stared, horror-stricken. "Kellhus, I ..."

"Think of what you're telling me! Think, Akka, *think*! You're saying that I'm *the sign of the Second Apocalypse*, that I augur mankind's extinction!"

But of course Achamian thought him more ...

"No, Kellhus ... Not the end."

"Then what am I? Just what do you think I am?"

"I think ... I think you may be ..."

"What, Akka? What?"

"Everything has a *purpose!*" the Schoolman cried in exasperation. "You've come to me for a *reason*, even if you've yet to embrace it."

This, Kellhus knew, was false. For events to have purpose, their ends had to determine their beginnings, and this was impossible. Things were governed by their origins, not their destinations. What came before determined what came after; his manipulation of these world-born men was proof enough of that ... If the Dûnyain had been mistaken in their theorems, their axioms remained inviolate. The Logos had been complicated—nothing more. Even sorcery, from what he'd gleaned, followed laws.

"And what purpose is that?" Kellhus asked.

Achamian hesitated, and though he remained utterly silent, everything from his expression to his scent to his pulse howled in panic. He licked his lips ...

"I think ... to save the world."

Always it came to this. Always the same delusion.

"So *I'm* your cause?" Kellhus said incredulously. "I'm the *Truth* that justifies your fanaticism?"

Achamian could only stare in dread. Plundering the man's expression, Kellhus watched the inferences splash and trickle through his soul, drawn of their own weight to a single, inexorable conclusion.

Everything ... By his own admission, he must yield everything.

Even the Gnosis.

How powerful have you become, Father?

Without warning, Achamian stood and started down the monumental stair. He took each step with weary deliberation, as though counting them. The Shigeki wind tousled his shining black hair. When Kellhus called to him, he said only, "I tire of the heights."

As Kellhus had known he would.

General Martemus had always considered himself a practical man. He was someone who always clarified his tasks, then methodically set about achieving his goals. He had no birthright, no pampered childhood, to cloud his judgement. He simply saw, appraised, and acted. The world was not so complicated, he would tell his junior officers, so long as one remained clearheaded and ruthlessly practical.

See. Appraise. Act.

He had lived his life by this philosophy. How easily it had been defeated.

The task had seemed straightforward, if somewhat unusual, in the beginning. Watch Prince Anasûrimbor Kellhus of Atrithau, and attempt to gain his confidence. If the man collected followers to some insidious purpose, as Conphas suspected, then a Nansur General suffering a crisis of faith should have proven an irresistible opportunity.

It did not. Martemus had attended at least a dozen of his evening sermons, or "imprompta," as they were calling them, before the man had even acknowledged him with a single word.

Of course, Conphas, who always faulted his executors before his assumptions, had held Martemus responsible. There could be no doubt Kellhus was Cishaurim, because he was connected to Skeaös, who was indubitably Cishaurim. There could be no doubt the man played the prophet, not after the incident with Saubon. And there could be no way the man *knew* that Martemus was bait, since Conphas had told no one of his plan other than Martemus. Therefore, *Martemus* had failed, even if Martemus was too obstinate to see this for himself.

But this was merely one of innumerable petty injustices Conphas had foisted on him over the years. Even if Martemus had cared to take insult, which was unlikely, he was far too busy being afraid.

He wasn't quite sure when it happened, but at some point during the long march across Gedea, General Martemus, as eminently practical as he was, had ceased believing that Prince Kellhus *played* the prophet. This didn't mean he thought the man *was* in fact a prophet—Martemus remained practical in that respect—only that he no longer knew what he believed ...

But soon he would, and the prospect terrified him. Martemus was also an intensely loyal man, and he treasured his position as Ikurei Conphas's aide de camp. He often thought he'd been *born* to serve under the mercurial Exalt-General, to balance the man's undeniable brilliance with more sober, more dependable observations. *The prodigy must be reminded of the practical,* he would often think. No matter how delectable the spices, one could not do without salt.

But if Kellhus was in fact ... What happened to his loyalty then?

Martemus pondered this while sitting among the steaming thousands who'd gathered to hear Prince Kellhus's first sermon since the madness of reaching Shigek. Before him loomed ancient Xijoser, the Great Ziggurat, a mountain of corniced and polished black stone so massive it seemed he should cover his face and fall to his belly. The luxuriant plains of the Sempis Delta swept out in either direction, embellished by lesser ziggurats, waterways, reed marshes, and endless rice paddies. The sun flared white in desert skies.

Throughout the crowds, men and women talked and laughed. For a time Martemus watched the couple before him share a humble repast of onions and bread. Then he realized those sitting around him were taking care to avoid his look. His uniform and blue cloak probably frightened them, he thought, made him appear a caste-noble. He looked from neighbour to distracted neighbour, trying to think of something he might say to set them at ease. But he couldn't bring himself to utter the first word.

A profound loneliness struck him. He thought of Conphas once again.

Then he saw Prince Kellhus, small and distant, descending Xijoser's monumental stair. Martemus smiled, as though finding an old friend in a foreign market.

What will he say?

When he first started attending the imprompta, Martemus had assumed the talks would be either heretical or easily dismissed. They were neither. Indeed, Prince Kellhus recited the words of the Old Prophets and of Inri Sejenus as though they were his own. Nothing of what he said contradicted any of the innumerable sermons Martemus had heard over the course of his life—though those sermons often contradicted one another. It was as though the Prince pursued further truths, the unspoken implications of what all orthodox Inrithi already believed.

To listen to him, it seemed, was to learn what one already knew without knowing.

The Prince of God, some called him. He-who-sheds-light-within.

His white silk robes shining in the sunlight, Prince Kellhus paused on the ziggurat's lower steps and looked over the restless masses. There was something glorious about his aspect, as though he'd descended not from the heights but from the heavens. With a flutter of dread Martemus realized he never saw the man *ascend* the ziggurat, nor even step from the ruin of the ancient godhouse upon its summit. He had just ... noticed him.

The General cursed himself for a fool.

"The Prophet Angeshraël," Prince Kellhus called, "came down from his fast on Mount Eshki." The assembly fell absolutely silent, so much so that Martemus could hear the breeze buffet his ears. "Husyelt, the Tusk tells us, sent a hare to him, so he might eat at last. Angeshraël skinned the Hunter's gift and struck a fire so he might feast. When he had eaten and was content, sacred Husyelt, the Holy Stalker, joined him at his fire, for the Gods in those days had not left the world in the charge of Men. Angeshraël, recognizing the God as the God, fell immediately to his knees before the fire, not thinking where he would throw his face." The Prince suddenly grinned.

"Like a young man on his wedding night, he erred in his eagerness ..."

Martemus laughed with a thousand others. Somehow the sun flashed brighter.

"And the God said, 'Why does our Prophet fall to his knees only? Are not Prophets Men like other Men? Should they not throw their faces to the earth?' To which Angeshraël replied, 'I find my fire before me.' And peerless Husyelt said, 'The fire burns across earth, and what fire consumes becomes earth. I am your God. Throw your face to the earth.'"

The Prince paused.

"So Angeshraël, the Tusk tells us, bowed his head *into the flames*."

Despite the close, humid air, Martemus's skin pimpled. How many times, especially as a child, had he stared into some fire, struck by the errant thought of plunging his face into the flames—if only to feel what a Prophet once felt?

Angeshraël. The Burnt Prophet. *He lowered his face into fire! Fire!*

"Like Angeshraël," the Prince continued, "we find ourselves kneeling before just such a fire ..."

Martemus caught his breath. Heat flared through him, or so it seemed.

"Truth!" Prince Kellhus cried, as though calling out a name that every man recognized. "The fire of Truth. The Truth of who you are ..."

Somehow his voice had divided, become a chorus.

"You are frail. You are alone. Those who would love you know you not. You lust for obscene things. You fear even your *closest* brother. You understand far less than you pretend ...

"You—*you!*—are these things. Frail, alone, unknown, lusting, fearing, and uncomprehending. Even *now* you can feel these truths burn. Even now"—he raised a hand as though to further quiet silent men—"*they consume you.*"

He lowered his hand. "But you do not throw your face to the earth. You do not ..."

His glittering eyes fell upon Martemus, who felt his throat tighten, felt the small finishing-hammer of his heart tap-tap-tap blood to his face.

He sees through me. He witnesses ...

"But *why?*" the Prince asked, his timbre bruised by an old and baffling pain. "In the anguish of this fire lies the God. And in the God lies redemption. *Each* of you holds the key to your own redemption. You *already* kneel before it! But still you do not throw your face to the earth. You *are* frail. You *are* alone. Those who love you *know you not.* You lust for *obscene* things. You fear even your closest *brother.* And you understand far *less* than you pretend!"

Martemus grimaced. The words had drawn a pain from his bowels to the back of his throat and sent his thoughts reeling in giddy recognition of something at once familiar and estranged. *Me ... He speaks of me!*

"Is there any among you who would *deny* this?"

Silence. Somewhere, someone wept.

"But you *do* deny this!" Prince Kellhus cried, like a lover confronted by an impossible infidelity. "All of you! You kneel, but you also *cheat*—cheat the fire of your own heart! You give breath to lie after lie, clamour that this fire is *not* the Truth. That you are *strong.* That you are *not* alone. That those who love you *do* know you. That you lust *not* for obscene things. That you fear *not* your brother in any way. That you understand *everything!*"

How many times had Martemus lied thus? Martemus the practical man. Martemus the realistic man. How could he be these things if he *knew so well* of what Prince Kellhus spoke?

"But in the secret moments—yes, the *secret* moments—these denials ring hollow, do they not? In the secret moments you glimpse the anguish of Truth. In the secret moments you see that your life has been a mummer's farce. And you weep! And you ask what is wrong! And you cry out, 'Why cannot I be strong?'"

He leapt down several steps.

"Why cannot I be strong?"

Martemus's throat ached!—ached as though he himself had bawled these words.

"Because," the Prince said softly, "you lie."

And Martemus thought madly: *Skin and hair ... He's just a man!*

"You are frail because you *feign strength*." The voice was disembodied now, and it whispered secretly into a thousand flushed ears. "You are alone because *you lie ceaselessly*. Those who love you do not know you because you *are a mummer*. You lust for obscene things because you deny *that you lust*. You fear your brother, because you fear *what he sees*. You understand little because to learn you must admit *you know nothing*."

How could a life be cupped into a single palm?

"Do you see the tragedy?" the Prince implored. "The scriptures bid us to be godlike, to be *more* than what we are. And what are we? Frail men, with peevish hearts, envious hearts, choked by the shroud of our own lies. Men who *remain* frail because they cannot *confess their frailty*."

And this word, *frail*, seemed pitched down from the heavens, from the Outside, and for an instant, the man who'd spoken it was no longer a man but the earthly surface of something far greater. *Frail* ... Spoken not from the lips of a man, but from somewhere else ...

And Martemus understood.

I sit in the presence of the God.

Horror and bliss.

Chafing his eyes. Blinding his skin. Everywhere.

The presence of the God.

To at last be *still*, to be braced by that which braced the very world, and to see at long last how far one had plummeted. And it seemed to Martemus that he was *here* for the first time, as though one could only truly be oneself—*be here!*—in the clearing that was God.

Here ...

The impossibility of drawing sweet air through salty lips. The mystery of moving soul and furtive intellect. The grace of thronging passions. The impossibility.

The impossibility ...

The miracle of here.

"Kneel with me," a voice from nowhere said. *"Take my hand and do not fear. Throw your face into the furnace!"*

A place had been prepared for these final words, words that traced the scripture of his heart. A place of rapture.

The multitude cried out, and Martemus cried with them. Some openly wept, and Martemus wept with them. Others reached out as though trying to clutch his image. Martemus raised two fingers to brush his distant face.

How long Prince Kellhus spoke he couldn't say. But he spoke of many things, and upon whatever ground his words set foot, the world was transformed. *"What does it mean, to be a warrior? Is not war the fire? The furnace? Is not war the very truth of our frailty?"* He even taught them a hymn, which, he said, had come to him in a dream. And the song moved them the way only a song from the Outside could move them. A hymn sung by the very Gods. For the rest of his days, Martemus would awaken and hear that song.

And afterward, when the masses thronged about the Prince, fell to their knees and softly kissed the hem of his white robe, he bid them to stand, reminded them that he was just a man like other men. And at long last, when the crush of bodies delivered Martemus to him, the surreal blue eyes regarded him gently, glanced not at all at his golden cuirass, his blue cloak, or the insignia of his station.

"I have waited for you, General."

The excited rumble of others grew distant, as though the two of them had been submerged. Martemus could only stare, dumbstruck, overawed, and so gratified ...

"Conphas sent you. But that has changed now, hasn't it?"

And Martemus felt a child before his father, unable to lie, unable to speak the truth.

The Prophet nodded as though he had spoken. "What will happen to your loyalty, I wonder?"

Somewhere distant, almost too far to touch, men cried out. Martemus watched the Prophet turn his head, reach back with a golden-haloed hand, and seize a flying arm, which bore a fist, which gripped a long and silvery knife.

Assassination, he thought without concern.

The man before him couldn't be killed. He knew that now.

The mobs pummelled the assassin to the earth. Martemus glimpsed a bloodied, howling face.

The Prophet turned back to him.

"I would not divide your heart," he said. "Come to me again, when you are ready."

———— ❊ ————

"I'm warning you, Proyas. Something must be done about this man."

Ikurei Conphas had said this somewhat more emphatically than he'd intended. But then these were emphatic times.

The Conriyan Prince reclined in his camp chair and looked at him blandly. He picked at his trim beard with an absent hand. "What do you suggest?"

Finally.

"That we convene a full Council of the Greater and Lesser Names."

"And?"

"That we bring charges against him."

Proyas frowned. "Charges? What charges?"

"Under the auspices of the Tusk. The Old Law."

"Ah, I see. And what would you charge Prince Kellhus with?"

"With fomenting blasphemy. With pretensions to prophecy."

Proyas nodded. "In other words," he said scathingly, "with being a False Prophet."

Conphas laughed incredulously. He could remember once—long ago it now seemed—thinking he and Proyas would become fast and famous friends over the course of the Holy War. They were both handsome. They were close in age. And in their respective corners of the Three Seas, they were considered prodigies of similar promise—that was, until his obliteration of the Scylvendi at the Battle of Kiyuth.

I have no peers.

"Could any charge be more appropriate?" Conphas asked.

"I agreed," Proyas replied testily, "to discuss ways of surprising Skauras on the South Bank, not to discuss the piety of a man I consider to be my friend."

Although Proyas's pavilion was large and richly outfitted, it was both gloomy and intolerably hot. Unlike the others, who had traded their canvas for the marble of abandoned villas, Proyas maintained himself as though still on the march.

Only a fanatic.

"You've heard of these Sermons at Xijoser?" Conphas asked, thinking, *Martemus, you fool …*

But then, that was the problem. Martemus *wasn't* a fool. Conphas could scarce imagine anyone less foolish … That was precisely the problem.

"Yes, yes," Proyas replied with an exasperated breath. "I've been invited to attend on a number of occasions, but the field keeps me busy."

"I imagine … Did you know that many among the rank and file—my men, *your* men—refer to him as the Warrior-Prophet? The *Warrior-Prophet?*"

"Yes. I know this as well …" Proyas said this with the same air of indulgent impatience as before, but his brows knitted together, as if pinching a troubling thought.

"As it stands," Conphas said, speaking as though at the limits of his good humour, "this is the Holy War of the Latter Prophet … of *Inri Sejenus.* But if this fraud continues to gather followers, it will fast become the Holy War of the Warrior-Prophet. Do you understand?"

Dead prophets were useful, because one could rule in their name. But live prophets? *Cishaurim* prophets?

Perhaps I should tell him what happened with Skeaös …

Proyas shook his head in weary dismissal. "What would you have me do, eh, Conphas? Kellhus is … unlike other men. There's no doubt about that. And he does have these dreams. But he makes no claim to be a prophet. And he's angered when others call him so."

"So what? So he must first *admit* to being a False Prophet? Being a False Prophet in *fact* isn't enough?"

His expression pained, Proyas regarded him narrowly, looked him up and down as though assessing the appropriateness of his field armour.

"Why does this concern you so, Conphas? You're most assuredly not a pious man."

What would you have me do, Uncle? Should I tell him?

Conphas suppressed the urge to spit like the Scylvendi, ran his tongue over his teeth instead. He despised indecision.

"The question of my piety is not the concern here."

Proyas drew in and released a heavy breath. "I've sat long hours with the man, Conphas. Together, we've read aloud from *The Chronicle of the Tusk* and *The Tractate*, and not once, in all that time, have I detected the merest whisper of heresy. In fact, Kellhus is perhaps the most deeply pious man I've ever met. Now the fact that others have begun calling him Prophet is disturbing, I agree. But it is *not* his doing. People are weak, Conphas. Is it so surprising that they look to him and see his strength for more than what it is?"

Conphas felt sweet disdain unfold across his face. "Even *you* ... He's ensnared even you."

What kind of man? Though he was loath to admit it, his briefing with Martemus had shook him deeply. Somehow, over a matter of mere weeks, this Prince Kellhus had managed to reduce his most dependable man to a babbling idiot. Truth! The frailty of men! The furnace!

What nonsense! And yet nonsense that was seeping through the Holy War like blood through linen. This Prince Kellhus was a wound. And if he was in fact a Cishaurim spy as dear old Uncle Xerius feared, he could well prove mortal.

Proyas was angered, and answered disdain with disdain. "Ensnaring," he snorted. "Of course *you* would see it as such. Men of ambition never understand the pious. For them, goals must be worldly in order to be sensible. Solutions to base hungers."

There was something forced, Conphas decided, about these words.

I've planted a seed at least.

"There's much to be said for being well fed," Conphas snapped, then turned on his heel. He'd exceeded his daily ration of idiots.

Proyas's voice halted him before the curtains.

"One last thing, Exalt-General."

Conphas turned, lids low, eyebrows raised. "Yes?"

"You've heard of the attempt on Prince Kellhus's life?"

"You mean there's another sober man in this world?"

Proyas smiled sourly. For a moment, real hatred flashed in his eyes.

"Prince Kellhus tells me the man who tried to kill him was Nansur. One of your officers, in fact."

Conphas stared at the man blankly, realizing he'd been duped. All those questions ... Proyas had asked them in order to *implicate* him, to see whether he had motive. Conphas cursed himself for a fool. Fanatic or not, Nersei Proyas was not a man to be underestimated.

This is becoming a nightmare.

"What?" Conphas said. "You propose to arrest me?"

"You propose to arrest Prince Kellhus."

Conphas grinned. "You would find it hard to arrest an army."

"I see no army," Proyas said.

Conphas smiled. "But you do ..."

Of course there was nothing Proyas could do, even if the assassin had survived to name Conphas directly. The Holy War needed the Empire.

Even still, there was a lesson to be learned. War was intellect. Conphas would teach this Prince Kellhus that ...

His loitering Kidruhil snapped to attention as Conphas exited the pavilion. As a precaution he'd taken some two hundred of the heavily armoured cavalrymen as an escort. The Great Names were scattered from Nagogris on the edge of the Great Desert to Iothiah on the Sempis Delta, and Skauras had landed raiders on the North Bank to harry them. Risking death or capture clearing up a matter such as this wouldn't do. So far, the problem of Anasûrimbor Kellhus remained more theoretical than practical.

As his attendants fetched his horse, the Exalt-General looked for Martemus, found him milling among the troopers. Martemus had always preferred the company of common soldiers to that of officers, something that Conphas had once thought quaint, but now found annoying—even seditious.

Martemus ... What's happened to you?

Conphas mounted his black and rode over to him. The taciturn General watched him, apparently without apprehension.

Like a Scylvendi, Conphas spat on the earth beneath the shod hooves of Martemus's horse. Then he glanced back at Proyas's pavilion, at the embroidered eagles splayed in black across the weathered white canvas, and at the guards who eyed him and his men suspiciously. The Eagle and Tusk pennant of House Nersei lolled in the lazy breeze, framed by the faint escarpments of the South Bank.

He turned back to his wayward General.

"It appears," he said in a fierce voice that wouldn't carry, "that you aren't the only casualty of this spy's sorcery, Martemus ... When you kill this Warrior-Prophet, you'll be avenging many, very many."

CHAPTER TWELVE

IOTHIAH

... the ends of the earth shall be wracked by the howls of the wicked,
and the idols shall be cast down and shattered, stone against stone.
And the demons of the idolaters shall hold open their mouths, like
starving lepers, for no man living will answer their outrageous hunger.
—16:4:22 THE WITNESS OF FANE

Though you lose your soul, you shall win the world.
—MANDATE CATECHISM

Late Summer, 4111 Year-of-the-Tusk, Shigek

Xinemus didn't particularly like the man, and had never trusted him, but
he'd nonetheless been trapped into speaking with him. The man,
Therishut, a baron of dubious reputation from Conriya's frontier with
High Ainon, had intercepted him as Xinemus made his way from a planning session with Proyas. Upon seeing Xinemus, the man's thinly bearded
face had brightened with his best "oh-how-fortuitous" look. It was in
Xinemus's nature to be patient with even those he disliked, but distrust
was a different matter altogether. And yet, it was the small indignities
that the pious man must endure over all.

"I seem to remember, Lord Marshal," Therishut said, hastening to
match his pace, "that you have an affinity for books."

Ever polite, Xinemus nodded, and said: "An acquired taste."

"Then you must be excited that the famed Sareotic Library, in Iothiah, was taken intact by the Galeoth."

"The Galeoth? I thought it was the Ainoni."

"No," Therishut replied, drawing his lips into a strange upside-down smile. "I've heard that it was the Galeoth. Men of Saubon's own household in fact."

"Indeed," Xinemus said, impatiently. "Well enough then ..."

"I see you're busy, Lord Marshal. No bother ... I'll send one of my slaves to arrange an audience."

To bump into Therishut was annoying enough, but to actually suffer through a formal visit?

"I'm never too busy for a Baron of the Land, Therishut."

"Good!" the man nearly squealed. "Well then ... Not long ago, a friend of mine—well, I should say he's not yet my friend, but I ... I ..."

"He's someone you hope to curry favour with, Therishut?"

Therishut's face both brightened and soured. "Yes! Although that sounds rather indelicate, don't you think?"

Xinemus said nothing, but walked on, his eyes firmly fixed on the top of his pavilion amidst the jumble of others in the distance. Beyond, the hills of Gedea were pale in the haze. *Shigek*, he thought. *We've taken Shigek!* For some strange reason, the certainty that soon, impossibly soon, he'd set eyes on Holy Shimeh seized him. *It's happening ...* It was almost enough to make him be kind to Therishut. Almost.

"Well, this friend of mine who'd just returned from the Sareotic Library asked me what 'gnosis' was. And since you're the closest thing to a scholar I know, I thought you could help me help him. Do you know what 'gnosis' is?"

Xinemus stopped and eyed the small man carefully. "Gnosis," he said carefully, "is the name of the old sorcery of the Ancient North."

"Ah yes!" Therishut exclaimed. "That makes sense!"

"What interest does your friend have in libraries, Therishut?"

"Well, you know there's a rumour that Saubon might sell the books to raise more money."

Xinemus hadn't heard this rumour, and it troubled him. "I doubt the other Great Names would countenance that. So what, your friend has already begun taking inventory?"

"He's a most enterprising soul, Lord Marshal. A good man to know if one's interested in profits—if you know what I mean ..."

"Merchant-caste dog, no doubt," Xinemus said matter-of-factly. "Let me give you some advice, Therishut: heed your station."

But rather than take offence at this, Therishut smiled wickedly. "Surely, Lord Marshal," he said in a tone devoid of all deference, "*you* of all people."

Xinemus blinked, astonished more by his own hypocrisy than by Baron Therishut's insolence. A man who sups with a sorcerer castigating another for currying favour with a merchant? Suddenly the hushed rumble of the Conriyan camp seemed to buzz in his ears. With a fierceness that shocked him, the Marshal of Attrempus stared at Therishut, stared at him until, flustered, the fool mumbled insincere apologies and scurried away.

As he walked the remaining distance to his pavilion, Xinemus thought of Achamian, his dear friend of many, many years. And he thought of his caste, and was faintly shocked by the hollow of uneasiness that opened in his gut when he recollected Therishut's words: *You of all people.*

How many think this?

Their friendship had been strained of late, Xinemus knew. It would do them both some good if Achamian spent several days away.

In a library. Studying blasphemy.

"I don't understand," Esmenet said with more than a little anger.

He's leaving me ...

Achamian heaved a burlap sack of oats across his mule's back. His mule, Daybreak, regarded her solemnly. Beyond him, the largely deserted encampment crowded the slopes, pitched among and between small stands of black willows and cottonwoods. She could see the Sempis in the distance, shining like obsidian inlay beneath the punishing sun. Whenever she glanced at the hazy South Bank, dark with vegetation, she could feel the heathen watching.

"I don't understand, Akka," she repeated, plaintively this time.

"But, Esmi ..."

"But *what?*"

He turned to her, obviously irritated, distracted. "It's a *library*. A library!"

"So?" she said hotly. "The illiterate are not—"

"No," he snapped, scowling. "No! Look, I need some time alone. I need time to think. To think, Esmi, *think!*"

The desperation in his voice and expression shocked her into momentary silence.

"About Kellhus," she said. The skin beneath her scalp prickled.

"About Kellhus," he replied, turning back to his mule. He cleared his throat, spit into the dust.

"He's asked you, hasn't he?" Her chest tightened. Could it be?

Achamian said nothing, but there was a subtle heartlessness to his movements, and almost imperceptible blankness to his eyes. She was learning him, she realized, like a song sung many times. She knew him.

"Asked me what?" he said finally, tying his sleeping mat to the pack saddle.

"To teach him the Gnosis."

For the past three weeks, since following the Conriyan column into the Sempis Valley, through the madness of the occupation—ever since the night with the Wathi Doll—a strange rigidity had seemed to haunt Achamian, a tension that made it impossible for him to love or laugh for anything more than moments. But she'd assumed his argument with Xinemus and their subsequent estrangement had been the cause.

Several days earlier she'd confronted the Marshal on the issue, telling him of his friend's apprehensions. Yes, Achamian had committed an outrage, she explained, but he'd erred out of foolishness not disrespect. "He tries to forget, Zin, but he cannot. Every morning I cradle him as he cries out. Every morning I remind him the Apocalypse is over ... He thinks Kellhus is the Harbinger."

But Xinemus, she could tell, already knew this. He was patient in tone, word, manner—everything save his look. His eyes had never truly listened, and she'd known something deeper was wrong. A man like Xinemus, Achamian had told her once, risked much keeping a sorcerer as a friend.

She'd never pressed Achamian with anything more than warm reminders, like "He worries for you, you know." The hurts of men were brittle, volatile things. Achamian liked to claim that men were simple, that women need only feed, fuck, and flatter them to keep them happy. Perhaps this was true of certain men, perhaps not, but it certainly wasn't true of Drusas Achamian. So she'd waited, assuming that time and habit would return the two old friends to their old understanding.

For some reason, the notion that *Kellhus,* and not Xinemus, lay at the root of his distress never occurred to her. Kellhus was holy—she harboured absolutely no doubt about that now. He was a prophet, whether he himself believed it or not. And sorcery was unholy ...

What was it Achamian had said he would become?

A god-sorcerer.

Achamian continued to fuss over his baggage. He hadn't said anything. He didn't need to.

"But how could it be?" she asked.

Achamian paused, stared at nothing for several heartbeats. Then he turned to her, his face blank with hope and horror.

"How could a prophet speak blasphemy?" he said, and she knew that for him this was already an old and embittered question. "I asked him that ..."

"And what did he say?"

"He cursed and insisted he wasn't a prophet. He was offended ... hurt even."

I've a talent for that, his tone said.

A sudden desperation welled in Esmenet's throat. "You can't teach him, Akka! You mustn't teach him! Don't you see? *You're the temptation.* He must resist you and the promise of power you hold. He must deny you to become what he must become!"

"Is that what you think?" Achamian exclaimed. "That I'm King Shikol tempting Sejenus with worldly power like in *The Tractate?* Maybe he's *right,* Esmi, did you ever consider that? Maybe he's *not* a prophet!"

Esmenet stared at him, fearful, bewildered, but strangely exhilarated as well. How had she come so far? How could a whore from a Sumni slum stand *here,* so near the world's heart?

How had her life become scripture? For a moment, she couldn't believe ...

"The question, Akka, is what do *you* think?"

Achamian looked to the ground between them.

"What do I think?" he repeated pensively. He raised his eyes.

Esmenet said nothing, though she felt the hardness melt from her gaze.

Achamian shrugged and sighed. "That the Three Seas couldn't be more unprepared for a Second Apocalypse ... The Heron Spear is lost. Sranc roam half the world, in numbers a hundred—a thousand!—times greater than in Seswatha's day. And Men hold only a fraction of the Trinkets." He stared at her, and it seemed his eyes had never been so bright. "Though the Gods have damned me, damned us, I can't believe they would so abandon the world ..."

"Kellhus," she whispered.

Achamian nodded. "They've sent us more than a Harbinger ... That's what I think, or hope—I don't know ..."

"But *sorcery*, Akka ..."

"Is blasphemy, I know. But ask yourself, Esmi, *why* are sorcerers blasphemers? And why is a prophet a prophet?"

Her eyes opened horror-wide. "Because one sings the God's song," she replied, "and the other speaks the God's voice."

"Exactly," Achamian said. "Is it blasphemy for a *prophet* to utter sorcery?"

Esmenet stood staring, dumbstruck.

For the God to sing His own song ...

"Akka ..."

He turned back to his mule, bent to retrieve his satchel from the dust.

A sudden panic welled through her. "Please don't leave me, Akka."

"I told you, Esmi," he said, without turning his face to her, "I need to think."

But we think so well together!

He was wiser for her counsel. He *knew* this! Now he confronted a decision unlike any other ... So why would he leave her? Was there something else? Something more he was hiding?

She glimpsed him writhing beneath Serwë ... *He's found a younger whore*, something whispered.

"Why do you do this?" she asked, her voice far sharper than she had wished.

An exasperated pause. "Do what?"

"It's like a labyrinth with you, Akka. You throw open gates, invite me in, but refuse to show me the way. Why do you always hide?"

His eyes flashed with inexplicable anger.

"Me?" he laughed, turning back to his task. "*Hide*, you say?"

"Yes, hide. You're *so weak*, Akka, and you need not be. Think of what Kellhus has taught us!"

He glanced at her, his eyes poised between hurt and fury. "How about you? Let's talk about your daughter ... Remember her? How long has it been since you've—"

"That's different! She came before you! *Before* you!"

Why would he say this? Why would he *try* to hurt?

My girl! My baby girl is dead!

"Such fine discriminations," Achamian spat. "The past is never dead, Esmi." He laughed bitterly. "It's not even *past*."

"Then where's my daughter, Akka?"

For an instant he stood dumbstruck. She often baffled him like this.

Broken down fool!

Her fingers started shaking. Hot tears spilled across her cheeks. How could she think such things?

Because of what he said ... *How dare he!*

He gaped at her, as though somehow reading her soul. "I'm sorry, Esmi," he said vaguely. "I shouldn't have mentioned ... I shouldn't have said what I said."

His voice trailed away, and he again turned to his mule, began angrily cinching straps. "You don't understand what the Gnosis is to us," he added. "More than my pulse would be forfeit."

"Then teach me! Show me how to understand!"

This is Kellhus! We discovered him together!

"Esmi ... I can't talk to you about this. I can't ...."

"But why?"

"Because I know what you'll say!"

"No, Akka," she said, feeling the old whorish coldness. "You don't. You've no idea."

He caught the rough hemp cord hanging from his mule's crude bridle, momentarily fumbled it. For an instant, everything about him, his sandals, his baggage, his white-linen robe, seemed lonely and poor. Why did he always look so poor?

She thought of Sarcellus: bold, sleek, and perfumed.

Shabby cuckold!

"I'm not leaving you, Esmi," he said with a queer kind of finality. "I could never leave you. Not again."

"I see but one sleeping mat," she said.

He tried to smile, then turned, leading Daybreak away at an awkward gait. She watched him, her innards churning as though she dangled over unseen heights. He followed the path eastward, passing a row of weather-beaten round tents. He seemed so small so quickly. It was so strange, the way bright sun could make distant figures dark ...

"Akka!" she cried out, not caring who heard. "Akka!"

I love you.

The figure with the mule stopped, distant and for a moment, unrecognizable.

He waved.

Then he disappeared beneath a stand of black willows.

Intelligent people, Achamian had found, were typically less happy. The reason for this was simple: they were better able to rationalize their delusions. The ability to stomach Truth had little to do with intelligence— nothing, in fact. The intellect was far better at arguing away truths than at finding them. Which was why he had to flee Kellhus and Esmenet.

He led his mule along a path bounded to his right by the black expanse of the Sempis and to his left by a line of gigantic eucalyptus trees. Save for the odd flash of warmth between limbs, the half-canopy sheltered him from the sun. A breeze seeped through his white linen tunic. It was peaceful, he thought, to at long last be alone ...

When Xinemus had told him that certain books pertaining to the Gnosis had been found in the Sareotic Library, he could read the subtext well enough. *You should leave*, his friend had said without saying. Ever since the night with the Wathi Doll, Achamian had expected to be banished from his friend's fire, even if temporarily. Even more, he *needed* to be banished, to be forced from the company of those who overwhelmed him ...

But it cut nonetheless.

No matter, he told himself. Just another feud born of the awkwardness of their friendship. A caste-noble and a sorcerer. "There is no friend more difficult," one of the poets of the Tusk had written, "than a sinner."

And Achamian was nothing if not a sinner.

Unlike some sorcerers, he rarely pondered the fact of his damnation. For much the same reason, he imagined, men who beat their wives didn't ponder their fists ...

But there were other reasons. In his youth, he'd been one of those students who'd delighted in irreverence and impiousness, as though the mortal blasphemy he learned licensed any blasphemy, large and small. He and Sancla, his cellmate in Atyersus, used to actually read *The Tractate* aloud and laugh at its absurdities. The passages dealing with the circumcision of caste-priests. And of course the passages dealing with manural purification rites. But one passage, more than any other, would haunt him over the years: the famous "Expect Not Admonition" from the Book of Priests.

"Listen!" Sancla had cried from his pallet one night. "'And the Latter Prophet said: Piety is not the province of money-changers. Do not give food for food, shelter for shelter, love for love. Do not throw the Good upon the balance, but *give without expectation*. Give food for nothing, shelter for nothing, love for nothing. Yield unto him who trespasses against you. For these things alone, the wicked do not do. Expect not, and you shall find glory everlasting.'"

The older boy fixed Achamian with his dark, always-laughing eyes—eyes that would make them lovers for a time. "Can you believe it?"

"Believe what?" Achamian asked. He already laughed because he knew that whatever Sancla cooked up was certain to be deliriously funny. He was simply one of those people. His death in Aöknyssus three years later—he'd been killed by a drunken caste-noble with a Trinket—would crush Achamian.

Sancla tapped the scroll with his forefinger, something that would have earned him a beating in the scriptorium. "Essentially Sejenus is saying, 'Give without expectation of reward, and you can expect a huge reward!'"

Achamian frowned.

"Don't you see?" Sancla continued. "He's saying that piety consists of good acts in the absence of selfish expectation. He's saying you give nothing—nothing!—when you expect something in exchange ... You simply don't give."

Achamian caught his breath. "So the Inrithi who expect to be exalted in the Outside ..."

"Give nothing," Sancla had said, laughing in disbelief. "Nothing! But we, on the other hand, dedicate our lives to continuing Seswatha's battle ... We give everything, and we can expect only damnation as a result. We're the only ones, Akka!"

We're the only ones.

As tempting as those words were, as moving and as important as they'd been, Achamian had become too much a sceptic to trust them. They were too flattering, too self-aggrandizing, to be true. So instead, he'd thought it simply *had* to be enough to be a good man. And if it wasn't enough, then there was nothing good about those who measured good and evil.

Which was likely the case.

But of course Kellhus had changed everything. Achamian now pondered his damnation a great deal.

Before, the question of his damnation had merely seemed an excuse for self-torment. The Tusk and *The Tractate* couldn't be more clear, though Achamian had read many heretical works suggesting that the Scriptures' manifold and manifest contradictions proved that the prophets, olden day and latter, were simply men—which they were. "All Heaven," Protathis had once written, "cannot shine through a single crack."

So there *was* room to doubt his damnation. Perhaps, as Sancla had suggested, the damned were in fact the elect. Or perhaps, as Achamian was more inclined to believe, the *uncertain* were the Chosen Ones. He'd often thought the temptation to assume, to sham certainty, was the most narcotic and destructive of all temptations. To do good without certainty was to do good without expectation ... Perhaps *doubt itself* was the key.

But then of course the question could never be answered. If genuine doubt was in fact the condition of conditions, then only those ignorant of the answer could be redeemed. To ponder the question of his damnation, it had always seemed, was itself a kind of damnation.

So he didn't think of it.

But now ... Now *there could be an answer.* Every day he walked with its possibility, talked ...

Prince Anasûrimbor Kellhus.

It wasn't as though he thought Kellhus could simply tell him the answer, even if he could ever summon the courage to ask. Nor did he think that Kellhus somehow embodied or exemplified the answer. That would make him too small. He was not, in some mystic Nonmen fashion, the living sign of Drusas Achamian's fate. No. The question of his damnation or his exaltation, Achamian knew, depended on what *he himself was willing to sacrifice.* He himself would answer the question ...

With his actions.

And as much as this knowledge horrified him, it also filled him with an abiding and incredulous joy. The fear it engendered was old: for some time he'd feared the fate of the entire world depended on those selfsame actions. He'd grown numb to consequences of deranged proportions. But the joy was something new, something unexpected. Anasûrimbor Kellhus had made *salvation* a real possibility. Salvation.

Though you lose your soul, the Mandate catechism began, *you shall win the world.*

But it need not be! Achamian knew that now! Finally he could see how desolate, *how bereft of hope,* his prior life had been. Esmenet had taught him how to love. And Kellhus, Anasûrimbor Kellhus, had taught him how to hope.

And he would seize them, love and hope. He would seize them, and he would hold them fast.

He need only decide what to do ...

"Akka," Kellhus had said the previous night, "I need ask you something."

Only the two of them sat about the fire. They boiled water for some midnight tea.

"Anything, Kellhus," Achamian replied. "What troubles you?"

"I'm troubled by what I must ask ..."

Never had Achamian seen such a poignant expression, as though horror had been bent to the point where it kissed rapture. A mad urge to shield his eyes almost overcame him.

"What you *must* ask?"

Kellhus had nodded.

"Each day, Akka, I am less my self."

Such words! Their mere memory struck him breathless. Standing in an islet of sunlight, Achamian paused along the trail, pressed his palms to his chest. A cloud of birds erupted into the sky. Their shadows flickered across him, soundless. He blinked at the sun.

Do I teach him the Gnosis?

To his gut he balked at the notion—the mere thought of surrendering the Gnosis to someone outside his School made him blanch. He wasn't even sure he *could* teach Kellhus the Gnosis, even if he desired. His knowledge of the Gnosis was the one thing he shared with Seswatha, whose imprint owned every movement of his slumbering soul.

Will you let me? Do you see what I see?

Never—never!—in the history of their School had a sorcerer of rank betrayed the Gnosis. Only the Gnosis had allowed the Mandate to survive. Only the Gnosis had allowed them to carry Seswatha's war through the millennia. Lose it, and they became no more than a Minor School. His brothers, Achamian knew, would fight themselves to extinction to prevent that from happening. They would hunt both of them without relenting, and they would kill them if they could. They would not listen to reasons … And the name, Drusas Achamian, would become a curse in the dark halls of Atyersus.

But what was this other than greed or jealousy? The Second Apocalypse was imminent. Hadn't the time come to arm all the Three Seas? Hadn't Seswatha himself bid them share their arsenal before the shadow fell?

He had …

And wouldn't this make Achamian the most faithful of all Mandate Schoolmen?

He resumed walking, as though in a stupor.

In his bones he *knew* that Kellhus had been sent. The peril was too great, and the promise too breathtaking. He'd watched as Kellhus consumed a lifetime of knowledge in the space of months. He'd listened, breathless, as Kellhus voiced truths of thought more subtle than Ajencis, and truths of passion more profound than Sejenus. He'd sat in the dust gaping as the man extended the geometries of Muretetis beyond the limits of comprehension, as he *corrected* the ancient logic then drafted *new* logics the way a child might scribble spirals with a stick.

What would the Gnosis be to such a man? A plaything? What would he discover? What power would he wield?

Glimpses of Kellhus, striding as a god across fields of war, laying low host of Sranc, striking dragons from the sky, closing with the resurrected No-God, with dread Mog-Pharau ...

He's our saviour! I know it!

But what if Esmenet were right? What if Achamian were merely the test? Like old, evil Shikol in *The Tractate*, offering Inri Sejenus his thigh-bone sceptre, his army, his harem, everything save his crown, to stop preaching ...

Achamian halted once again, was bumped forward two steps by his mule, Daybreak. Stroking his snout, he smiled in the lonely way of men with hapless animals. A breeze swept across the shining reaches of the Sempis, hissed through the trees. He began trembling.

Prophet and sorcerer. The Tusk called such men Shaman. The word lay like a ziggurat in his thoughts, immovable.

Shaman.

No ... This is madness!

For two thousand years Mandate Schoolmen had kept the Gnosis safe. Two thousand years! Who was he to forsake such tradition?

Nearby, a crowd of young children was gathered beneath the sweep of a sycamore, chirping and jostling like sparrows over spilled bread. And Achamian saw two young boys, no more than four or five, making arm-waving declarations each with a hand firmly clasped in the hand of the other. The innocence of the act struck him, and he found himself wondering how old they would be when they saw the error of holding hands.

Or would they discover Kellhus?

A whining sound drew his eyes upward. He nearly cried out in shock.

A naked corpse had been nailed to the rafters of the tree above, purple and marbled with black-green. After the surprise passed he thought of kicking or cutting the man down, but then where would he carry him? To some nearby village? The Shigeki were so terrified of the Inrithi he'd be surprised if they looked at him, let alone touched him.

A pang of remorse struck him, and inexplicably, he thought of Esmenet. *Be safe*.

Leading Daybreak, Achamian continued past the children, through the sun-dappled shade and toward Iothiah, the ancient capital of the Shigeki God-Kings, whose walls wandered across the distance, belts of faint stone glimpsed through dark eucalyptus limbs. Achamian walked, and wrestled with impossibilities ...

The past was dead. The future, as black as a waiting grave.

Achamian wiped his tears on his shoulder. Something unimaginable was about to happen, something historians, philosophers, and theologians would argue for thousands of years—if years or anything else survived. And the acts of Drusas Achamian would loom so very large.

He would simply give. Without expectation.

His School. His calling. His life ...

The Gnosis would be his sacrifice.

Behind her mighty curtain walls, Iothiah was a warren of four-storey mud-brick buildings welded continuously together. The alleyways were narrow, screened from above by palm-leaf awnings, so that Achamian felt as though he walked through desert tunnels. He avoided the Kerothotics: he didn't like the look of triumph in their eyes. But when he encountered armed Men of the Tusk he would ask them for directions, and then pick his way through a further welter of alleys. The fact that most of the Inrithi he encountered were Ainoni concerned him. And once or twice, when the walls opened enough for him to spy the monuments of the city, he thought he could sense the deep bruise of the Scarlet Spires somewhere in the distance.

But then he encountered a troop of Norsirai horsemen—Galeoth, they said—and he was somewhat relieved. Yes, they knew how to find the Sareotic Library. Yes, the Library was in Galeoth hands. Achamian lied as he always lied, and told them that he was a scholar, come to chronicle the exploits of the Holy War. As always, their eyes brightened at the thought of finding some small mention in the annals of written history. They instructed him to follow as best he could, claiming they would pass the Library on their way to wherever it was they were stationed.

Noon saw him in the shadow of the Library, more apprehensive than ever.

If rumours of the existence of Gnostic texts had reached him, wouldn't they also have reached the Scarlet Spires? The thought of jostling for scrolls with the red-robed Schoolmen filled him with more than a little dread.

"What do you think?" he asked Daybreak, who snorted and nosed his palm.

The idea that Gnostic texts might have lain hidden here all this time wasn't as preposterous as it seemed. The Library was as old as the Thousand Temples, built and maintained by the Sareots, an esoteric College of priests dedicated to the preservation of knowledge. There was a time, during the Ceneian Empire, when it was law in Iothiah for all those entering the city in possession of a book to surrender it to the Sareots so that it might be copied. The problem, however, was that the Sareotic College was a religious institution, and as such, it necessarily forbade any of the Few from entering the famed Library.

When, many centuries later, the Sareots were massacred by the Fanim in the fall of Shigek, it was rumoured that the Padirajah himself had entered the Library. From his vest, the legend went, he pulled a slender, leather-bound copy of the *kipfa'aifan*, the *Witness of Fane*, bent to the shape of his breast. Holding it high in the airy gloom, he declared, "Here lies all written truth. Here lies the one path for all souls. Burn this wicked place." At that instant, it was said, a single scroll spilled from the racks and came rolling to his booted feet. When the Padirajah opened it he found a detailed map of all Gedea, which he later used to crush the Nansur in a number of desperate battles.

The Library was spared, but if it was closed to Schoolmen under the Sareots, it might well have ceased to exist under the Kianene.

There very well could be Gnostic texts in this Library, Achamian knew. They'd been discovered before. If there were any reason, aside from their dreams of the Old Wars, why the sorcerers of the Mandate were the most scholarly of the Schoolmen, it was their jealousy of the Gnosis. The Gnosis gave them a power far out of proportion to the size of their School. If a School like the Scarlet Spires were to come into its possession—who could say what might happen? Things wouldn't fare well with the Mandate, that much was certain.

But then, all that was about to change—now that an Anasûrimbor had returned.

Achamian led his mule into the middle of a small walled courtyard. The cobble had long ago been ground into red dust, save for the odd stones surfacing here and there like turtle shells. The Library itself presented the square front of a Ceneian temple, with columns soaring to brace a crumbling lintel pocked by figures that may have once been gods or men. Two large Galeoth swordsmen reclined in the shade against the two pillars flanking the entrance. They acknowledged him with bored stares as he approached.

"Greetings," he called, hoping they spoke Sheyic. "I am Drusas Istaphas, chronicler to Prince Nersei Proyas of Conriya."

When they failed to reply, he paused. Achamian found himself particularly unnerved by the one with a scar that dimpled his face from his hairline to his chin. These didn't seem like friendly men. But then, what cheer would a warrior find guarding something as useless as books?

Achamian cleared his throat. "Have there been many other visitors to the Library?"

"No," the scarless man replied, shrugging his shoulders beneath his hauberk. "Just a few thieving merchants, is all." The man spat something across the dust, and Achamian realized he'd been sucking on a peach pit.

"Well I can assure you I'm not of that caste. Assuredly not ..." Then, with a mixture of curiosity and deference: "Do I have your leave to enter?"

The man nodded to his mule. "Can't bring that thing," he said. "Can't have a donkey shitting in our hallowed halls now can we?" He smirked, and turned to his scarred friend, who continued to stare at Achamian. He looked like a bored boy deciding whether to poke a dead fish.

After gathering several things from his mule, Achamian rushed up the steps past the two guards. The great doors were gilded in tarnished bronze, and one of them lay ajar enough to admit a single man. As Achamian ducked into the gloom he heard one of the Galeoth—the scarred one, he thought—mutter "Filthy pick."

But the old Norsirai slur didn't bother him. Rather, he was *excited*. A sudden urge to cackle almost overcame him. Only now, it seemed, did the fact that this was the *Sareotic Library* fully strike him. The damned Sareots, hoarding text after text for over a thousand years. What might he find? Absolutely anything, and not just Gnostic works, might lie hidden within. *The Nine Classics*, the early *Dialogues of Inceruti*—even the lost works of Ajencis!

He passed through the darkness of a great vaulted antechamber, across a mosaic floor that once, he decided, had portrayed Inri Sejenus holding out haloed hands—at least before the Fanim, who'd obviously never used this place, had defaced it. He retrieved a candle from his saddlebag and ignited it with a secretive word. Holding the small point of light before him, he plunged into the hallowed halls of the Library.

⎯⎯⎯ ◌◌◌ ⎯⎯⎯

The Sareotic Library was a warren of pitch-black hallways that smelled of dust and the ghost of rotting books. Englobed by light, Achamian wandered through the blackness and filled his arms with treasures. Never had he seen such a collection. Never had he witnessed so many ruined thoughts.

Out of the thousands of volumes, and thousands upon thousands of scrolls, Achamian would be surprised if more than several hundred could be salvaged. He found nothing that even hinted at the Gnosis, but he did, nevertheless, find several things of peculiar interest.

He found one book by Ajencis he'd never seen before, but it was written in Vaparsi, an ancient Nilnameshi language he knew well enough only to decipher the title: *The Fourth Dialogue of the Movements of the Planets as They Pertain to* ... something or another. But the fact that this was a dialogue meant that it was exceedingly important. Very few of the great Kyranean philosopher's dialogues survived.

He found a heap of clay tablets written in the cuneiform script of ancient Shigek and draped by cobwebs woollen with dust. He retrieved one that seemed in good shape and decided he would try to smuggle it out, even though it might be a granary inventory for all he knew. It would make a good gift, he thought, for Xinemus.

And he found other tomes and scrolls—curiosities mostly. An account of the Age of Warring Cities by a historian he'd never encountered before. A strange, vellum-paged book, called *On the Temples and Their Iniquities*, which made him wonder if the Sareots might not have had heretical leanings. And some others.

After a time, both his excitement at finding things intact and his outrage at finding them destroyed flagged. He tired, and finding a stone bench in a niche, he arranged his discoveries and his humble belongings around him as though they were totems in a magic circle, then ate some stale bread and drank wine from his skin. He thought of Esmenet while he ate, cursed himself for his sudden longing.

He did his best not to think of Kellhus.

He replaced his sputtering candle and decided to read. *Alone with books, yet again.* Suddenly he smiled. *Again? No, at last ...*

A book was never "read." Here, as elsewhere, language betrayed the true nature of the activity. To say that a book was read was to make the same mistake as the gambler who crowed about winning as though he'd taken it by force of hand or resolve. To toss the number-sticks was to seize a moment of helplessness, nothing more. But to open a book was by far the more profound gamble. To open a book was not only to seize a moment of helplessness, not only to relinquish a jealous handful of heartbeats to the unpredictable mark of another man's quill, it was to allow oneself to be *written*. For what was a book if not a long consecutive surrender to the movements of another's soul?

Achamian could think of no abandonment of self more profound.

He read, and was moved to chuckle by ironies a thousand years dead, and to reflect pensively on claims and hopes that had far outlived the age of their import.

He wouldn't remember falling asleep.

There was a dragon in his dream, old, hoary, terrible—and malevolent beyond compare. Skuthula, whose limbs were like knotted iron, and whose black wings, when he descended, were broad enough to blot half the sky. The great fountain of luminescent fire that vomited from Skuthula's maw burnt the sand around his Wards to glass. And Seswatha fell to one knee, tasted blood, but the old sorcerer's head was thrown back, his white hair whipped into ribbons by the wind of beating dragon-wings, and the impossible words thundered like laughter from his incandescent mouth. Needles of piercing light filled the sky ...

But the corners of this scene were crimped, and then suddenly, as though dreams were painted across parchment, it crumpled and was tossed into blackness ...

The blackness of *open* eyes ... Gasping breath. Where was he? The Library, yes ... The candle must have gone out.

But then he realized just *what* had awakened him. His Wards of Exposure, which he'd maintained ever since joining the Holy—

Sweet Sejenus ... The Scarlet Spires.

He fumbled in the darkness, gathered his satchel. *Quickly, quickly ...* He stood in the blackness, and peered with different eyes.

The chamber was long, with low ceilings, and galleried by rows of racks and shelves. The intruders were somewhere near, hastening between queues of mouldering knowledge, closing on him from various points throughout the Library.

Did they come for the Gnosis? Knowledge ever found itself on the scales of greed, and no knowledge in the Three Seas, perhaps, was as valuable as the Gnosis. But to abduct a Mandate Schoolman in the midst of the Holy War? One would think the Scarlet Spires would have more pressing concerns—like the Cishaurim.

One would think ... But what of the skin-spies? What of the Consult?

They'd known he was bound to investigate even the rumour of a Gnostic text. And they had known a Library would be where he felt safest. Who would risk such treasures? Certainly not fellow Schoolmen, no matter how ill their will ...

The entire thing, he realized, was an outrageously extravagant trap—a trap that had included Xinemus. What better way to lull an ever suspicious Mandate Schoolman than to dangle the lure through the lips of his most trusted friend?

Xinemus? No. It couldn't be.

Sweet Sejenus ...

This was actually happening!

Achamian grabbed his satchel and lunged through the blackness, crashed into a heavy rack of scrolls, felt papyrus crumble in his fingers like the mud that skins the bottom of dried puddles. He thrust his satchel into the leafy debris. *Quickly, quickly.* Then he stumbled back in the direction he'd come.

They were closer now. Lights smeared the ceiling over the black shelves facing him.

He backed into the small alcove where he'd snoozed, then began uttering a series of Wards, short strings of impossible thoughts. Light flashed from his lips. Luminescence sheeted the air before him, like the glare of sunlight across mist.

Dark muttering from somewhere amid the teetering queues—skulking, insinuating words, like vermin gnawing at the walls of the world.

Then fierce light, transforming, for a heartbeat, the shelves before him into a dawn horizon ... Explosion. A geyser of ash and fire.

The concussion sucked the air from his lungs. The heat cracked the stone of the surrounding walls. But his Wards held.

Achamian blinked. A moment of relative darkness ...

"Yield Drusas Achamian ... You're overmatched!"

"Eleäzaras?" he cried. "How many times have you fools tried to wrest the Gnosis from us? Tried and failed!"

Shallow breath. Hammering heart.

"Eleäzaras?"

"You're doomed, Achamian! Would you doom the riches about you as well?"

As precious as they were, the words rolled and stacked about him meant nothing. Not now.

"Don't do this, Eleäzaras!" he cried in a breaking voice. *The stakes! The stakes!*

"It's already—"

But Achamian had whispered secrets to his first attacker. Five lines glittered along the gorge of blasted shelves, through smoke and wafting pages. Impact. The air cracked. His unseen foe cried out in astonishment—they always did at the first touch of the Gnosis. Achamian muttered more ancient words of power, more Cants. The Bisecting Planes of Mirseor, to continuously stress an opponent's Wards. The Odaini Concussion Cants, to stun him, break his concentration. Then the Cirroi Loom ...

Dazzling geometries leapt through the smoke, lines and parabolas of razor light, punching through wood and papyrus, shearing through stone. The Scarlet Schoolman screamed, tried to run. Achamian boiled him in his skin.

Darkness, save for glowering fires scattered through the ruin. Achamian could hear the other Schoolmen shouting to each other in shock and dismay. He could feel them scramble among the queues, hasten to assemble a Concert.

"Think on this, Eleäzaras! How many are you willing to sacrifice?"

Please. Don't be a—

The roar of flame. The thunder of toppling shelves. Fire broke like foaming surf about his Wards. A blinding flash, illuminating the vast chamber from corner to corner. The crack of thunder. Achamian stumbled to his knees. His Wards groaned in his thoughts.

He struck back with Inference and Abstraction. He was a Mandate Schoolman, a Gnostic Sorcerer-of-the-Rank, a War-Cant Master. He was as a mask held before the sun. And his voice slapped the distances into char and ruin.

The hoarded knowledge of the Sareots was blasted and burned. Convections whipped pages into fiery cyclones. Like leathery moths, books spiralled into the debris. Dragon's fire cascaded between the surviving shelves. Lightning spidered the air, crackled across his defences. The last queues fell, and across the ruin Achamian glimpsed his assailants: seven of them, like silk-scarlet dancers in a field of funeral pyres: the Schoolmen of the Scarlet Spires.

The glimpse of tempests disgorging bolts of blinding white. The heads of phantom dragons dipping and belching fire. The sweep of burning sparrows. The Great Analogies, shining and ponderous, crashing and thundering about his Wards. And through them, the Abstractions, glittering and instantaneous ...

The Seventh Quyan Theorem. The Ellipses of Thosolankis ... He yelled out the impossible words.

The leftmost Scarlet Schoolman screamed. The ghostly ramparts about him crumbled beneath an arcana of encircling lines. The Library walls behind him exploded outward, and he was puffed like paper into the evening sky.

For a moment, Achamian abandoned the Cants, began singing to save his Wards.

Cataracts of hellfire. The floor failed. Great ceilings of stone clapped about him like angry palms to prayer. He fell through fire and rolling, megalithic ruin. But still he *sang.*

He was a Scion of Seswatha, a Disciple of Noshainrau the White. He was the slayer of Skafra, mightiest of the Wracu. He had pitched his song against the dread heights of Golgotterath. He had stood proud and impenitent before Mog-Pharau himself ...

Jarring impact. Different footing, like the pitched deck of a ship. Shrugging slabs and heaped ruin away, tossing thundering stone into sky. Plunging through meaning after dark meaning, the hard matter of the world collapsing, falling away like lover's clothing, all in answer to his singing song.

And at last the sky, so water-cool when seen from the inferno's heart.

And there: the Nail of Heaven, silvering the breast of a rare cloud.

The Sareotic Library was a furnace in the husk of ragged, free-standing walls. And above, the Scarlet Magi hung as though from wires, and pummelled him with Cant after wicked Cant. The heads of ghostly dragons reared and vomited lakes of fire. Rising and spitting, wracking him with dazzling, bone-snapping fire. Sun after blinding sun set upon him.

On his knees, burned, bleeding from mouth and eyes, encircled by heaped stone and text, Achamian snarled Ward after Ward, but they cracked and shattered, were pinched away like rotted linen. The very firmament, it seemed, echoed the implacable chorus of the Scarlet Spires. Like angry smiths they punished the anvil.

And through the madness, Drusus Achamian glimpsed the setting sun, impossibly indifferent, framed by clouds piled rose and orange ...

It was, he thought, a good song.

Forgive me, Kellhus.

CHAPTER THIRTEEN

SHIGEK

Men are forever pointing at others, which is why I always follow the knuckle and not the nail.

—ONTILLAS, *ON THE FOLLY OF MEN*

A day with no noon,
A year with no fall,
Love is forever new,
Or love is not at all.

—ANONYMOUS, "ODE TO THE LOSS OF LOSSES"

Late Summer, 4111 Year-of-the-Tusk, Shigek

There was light.

"Esmi ..."

She stirred. What was her dream? Yes ... Swimming. The pool in the hills above the Battleplain.

A hand grasped her bare shoulder. A gentle squeeze.

"Esmi ... You must wake up."

But she was *so* warm ... She blinked, grimaced when she realized it was still night. Lamplight. Someone carried a lamp. What was Akka doing?

She rolled onto her back, saw Kellhus kneeling over her, his expression grave. Frowning, she pulled her blanket over her breasts.

"Wha—" she started, but paused to clear her throat. "What is it?"

"The Library of the Sareots," he said in a hollow voice. "It burns."

She could only blink at the lamplight.

"The Scarlet Spires have destroyed it, Esmi."

She turned, looking for Achamian.

❧

Something about Xinemus's expression struck Proyas to the marrow. He looked away, ran an idle thumb over the lip of his golden wine bowl, which lay empty on the table before him. He stared at the glister of the eagles stamped into its side.

"And just what would you have me do, Zin?"

Incredulity and impatience. "Everything in your power!"

The Marshal had informed him of Achamian's abduction two days previous—never had Proyas seen him so frantic with worry. At his behest, he'd issued orders for the arrest of Therishut, a baron from the southern marches he only vaguely remembered. Then, he'd ridden to Iothiah, where he demanded and received an audience with Eleäzaras himself. The Grandmaster had been accommodating, but he categorically denied the Marshal's accusations. He claimed his people had stumbled upon a hidden cell of Cishaurim while investigating the Sareotic Library. "We grieve the loss of two of our own," he said solemnly.

When Proyas asked, with all due courtesy, to view the Cishaurim remains, Eleäzaras said: "You can *take* them if you wish ... Have you a sack?"

You do see, his eyes had said, *the futility of what you do.*

But Proyas had seen the futility from the very beginning—even if they could find Therishut. Soon the Holy War would cross the River Sempis and assault Skauras on the South Bank. The Men of the Tusk needed the Scarlet Spires—desperately if what the Scylvendi said was true. What was the life of one man—a blasphemer no less—compared with that need? The God demanded sacrifices ...

Proyas could see the futility—he could scarce see anything else! The difficulty was one of making Xinemus see.

"Everything in my power?" the Prince repeated. "And what, pray tell, might that be, Zin? What power does a Prince of Conriya hold over the Scarlet Spires?"

He regretted the impatience in his tone, but it couldn't be helped.

Xinemus continued to stand at the ready, as though on parade. "You could call a Council ..."

"Yes, I could, but what purpose would that serve?"

"Purpose?" Xinemus repeated, obviously horrified. "What *purpose* would it serve?"

"Yes. It may be a hard question, but it's honest."

"Don't you understand?" Xinemus exclaimed. "Achamian isn't dead and gone! I'm not asking you to *avenge* him! *They've taken him*, Proyas. Even now, somewhere in Iothiah, they hold him. They ply him in ways you and I cannot imagine. The Scarlet Spires! *The Scarlet Spires have Achamian!*"

The Scarlet Spires. For those who lived in the High Ainon's shadow, they were the very name of dread. Proyas breathed deep. The God had decreed his priorities ...

Faith makes strong.

"Zin ... I know how this torments you. I know you feel responsible, but—"

"You ungrateful, arrogant, little pissant!" the Marshal exploded. He seized the corners of the table, leaned forward over the sheaves of parchment. Spittle flecked his beard. "Did you learn so little from him? Or was your heart flint in childhood as well? This is *Achamian*, Proyas. *Akka!* The man who doted on you! Who cherished you! The man who made you into *who* you are!"

"Remember yourself Marshal! I will toler—"

"You will hear me out!" Xinemus roared, pounding the table with his fist. The golden wine bowl bounced and rolled off the edge.

"As inflexible as you are," the Marshal grated, "you know how these things work. Remember what you said on the Andiamine Heights? 'The game is without beginning or end.' I'm not asking you to storm Eleäzaras's compound, Proyas, I'm simply asking you *to play the game!* Make them think you'll stop at nothing to see Akka safe, that you're willing to declare open war against them if he should be killed. If they believe you're willing to forsake anything, even Holy Shimeh, to recover Achamian, they will yield. They *will* yield!"

Proyas stood, retreated from his old sword-trainer's furious aspect. He *did* know how "these things" worked. He *had* threatened Eleäzaras with war.

He laughed bitterly.

"Are you *mad*, Zin? Are you truly asking me to put my old boyhood tutor before my God? To put a *sorcerer* before my God?"

Xinemus released the table, stood upright. "After all these years, you still don't understand, do you?"

"What's there to understand?" Proyas cried. "How many times must we have this conversation? Achamian is Unclean! *Unclean!*" A heady sense of conviction seized him, an incontestable *making* certain, as though knowing possessed its own fury. "If blasphemers kill blasphemers, then we're saved oil and wood."

Xinemus flinched as though struck.

"So you will do nothing."

"And *neither will you*, Marshal. We prepare to march against the South Bank. The Padirajah has summoned every Sapatishah from Girgash to Eumarna. All Kian assembles!"

"Then I resign as Marshal of Attrempus," Xinemus declared in a stiff voice. "What is more, I repudiate you, your father, and my oath to House Nersei. No longer shall I call myself a Knight of Conriya."

Proyas felt a numbness through his face and hands. This was impossible.

"Think about this, Zin," he said breathlessly. "Everything ... Your estates, your chattel, the sanctions of your caste ... Everything you have, *everything you are*, will be forfeit."

"No, Prosha," he said, turning for the curtains. "It's you who surrender everything."

Then he was gone.

The reed wick of his oil lamp sputtered and fizzled. The gloom deepened.

So much! The endless battles with his peers. The heathen. The burdens—the innumerable burdens! The never-ending fear of what might come. And Xinemus had always been there. He'd always been the *one!* The one who understood, who made clear what vexed, who shouldered what was beyond bearing ...

Akka.

Sweet Seja ... What had he done?

Nersei Proyas fell to his knees, clutched at a knifing pang in his stomach. But the tears wouldn't come.

I know you test me! I know you test me!

Two bodies, one warmth.

Wasn't that what Kellhus had said of love?

Esmenet watched Xinemus sit hesitantly, as though unsure of his welcome. He ran a heavy hand across his face. She could see the desperation in his eyes.

"I've made," he said leadenly, "what inquiries I could."

He meant there had been talk, the chatter of men who must make certain sounds, preserve certain semblances.

"*No!* You *must* make more! You can't give up, Zin. Not after ..."

The pain in his eyes completed her sentence.

"The Holy War assaults the South Bank in a matter of days, Esmi ..." He pursed his lips.

He meant the issue of Drusas Achamian had been conveniently forgotten, as all intractable and embarrassing matters must be. How? How could one know Drusas Achamian, wander through his precincts, and then pull away, whisked like sheets across dry skin? But they were men. Men were dry on the outside, and wet only within. They couldn't commingle, weld their life to another in the ambiguity of fluids. Not truly.

"Perhaps ..." she said, wiping tears and trying hard, very hard, to smile. "Perhaps Proyas is-is lonely ... Perhaps he n-needs to take his ease with—"

"No, Esmi. No."

Hot tears. She shook her head slowly, her face slack.

No ... I must do something! There must be something I can do!

Xinemus looked past her to the sunny earth, as though searching for lost words.

"Why won't you stay with Kellhus and Serwë?" he asked.

So much had changed in such a short time. Xinemus's camp had dissolved with his station. Kellhus had taken Serwë to join Proyas, something that had dismayed her even though she understood his reasons. As much as Kellhus loved Akka, all men were his province now. But how she'd begged! Grovelled! She had even tried, at the pitch of shameful desperation, to seduce him, though he would have none of it.

The Holy War. The Holy War. Everything was about the fucking Holy War!

What about *Achamian?*

But Kellhus couldn't cross Fate. He had a far greater whore to answer to ...

"And if Akka comes back?" she sobbed. "What if he comes back and can't find me?"

Though everyone had left, her tent—*Akka's* tent—hadn't moved. She lingered in the gap where her joy had been. Now under the command of Iryssas, the Attrempans treated her with deference and respect. The "sorcerer's woman" they called her ...

"It's not good for you to stay here alone," Xinemus said. "Iryssas will march with Proyas soon, and the Shigeki ... There could be reprisals."

"I'll manage," she croaked. "I've spent my life alone, Zin."

Xinemus pressed himself to his feet. He held a hand to her cheek, pinched away a tear with a gentle thumb. "Stay safe, Esmi."

"What are you going to do?"

He glanced into the distance behind her, perhaps at the hazy ziggurats, perhaps at nothing.

"Search," he said in a hopeless voice.

"I'll ride with you," she exclaimed, jumping to her feet.

I'm coming, Akka! I'm coming!

Xinemus strode wordlessly to his horse, climbed into his saddle. He drew a knife from his girdle, then tossed it high in the air. It thudded into the bare earth between her feet.

"Take it," he said. "Be safe, Esmi."

For the first time Esmenet noticed Dinchases and Zenkappa in the distance, also mounted, waiting for their former lord. They waved before falling in behind him. She fell to her seat, burst into further sobs. She buried her face in hot arms.

When she looked up, they were gone.

Helplessness. If women were hope's oldest companions, it was due to helplessness. Certainly women often exercised dreadful power over a single hearth, but the world between hearths belonged to men. And it was into this world that Achamian had disappeared: the cold darkness between firepits.

All she could do was wait ... What greater anguish could there be than waiting? Nothing etched the shape of one's impotence with more galling meticulousness than the blank passage of time. Moment after moment, some dull with disbelief, others taut with voiceless shrieks. Moment after gnashing moment. Bright with the flare of agonized questions: *Where is he? What will I do without him?* Dark with the exhaustion of hope: *He's dead. I am alone.*

Waiting. This was what tradition said a woman *should* do. To wait at the hearth's edge. To peer and peer and yet always be stared down. To haggle endlessly with nothing. To think without hope of insight. To repeat words said and words implied. To chase hints into incantations, as though by their tumbling precision and the sheer pitch of their pain the movements of her soul might seize the world at some deeper level, and force it to yield.

As the days passed, it seemed she'd become a still point in the ponderous wheel of events, the only structure to remain after the floodwaters retreated. The tents and pavilions fell like shrouds unfurled across the dead. The vast baggage trains were loaded. Armoured men on horse chopped to and fro from the horizon, bearing arcane missives, onerous commands. Great columns were formed up across the pasture, and with shouts and hymns, they passed away.

Like a season.

And Esmenet sat alone in the midst of their absence. She watched the breeze tease threads free of trampled grasses. She watched bees dart like black buzzing dots across the bruised reaches. She felt embalmed by the silence. She was held motionless by the false peace of passing commotion.

Sitting before Achamian's tent, her back turned to their pathetic possessions, her every surface exposed to gaping, sun-bright spaces, she wept—called out his name as though he might lie hidden behind some copse of black willows, whose verdant branches waved each independent of the other, as though beneath the tug of different skies.

She could almost see him, crouched behind that shade-black trunk.

Come out, Akka ... They've all left. It's safe now, my love ...

Day. Night.

Esmenet would make her own silent inquiries, an interrogation without hope of answer. She would think much of her dead daughter, and make forbidden comparisons between that cold world and this one. She would walk down to the Sempis and stare at its black waters, not knowing whether she wanted to drink or drown. She would glimpse herself in the distance, arms waving ...

One body, no warmth.

Day. Night. Moment by moment.

Esmenet had been a whore, and whores knew how to wait. Patience through the long succession of lusts, her days lined up as though words on a scroll as long as life, each whispering the same thing.

It's safe now, my love. Come out.

It is safe.

Since leaving Xinemus's camp, Cnaiür passed his days much as before, either conferring with Proyas or discharging his requests. Skauras had wasted little time in the weeks following his defeat on the Battleplain. He'd ceded what land he couldn't hold, which included the entire North Bank of the Sempis. He burned every boat he could find to prevent any mass crossing, raised makeshift watch towers along the entire South Bank, and gathered the remnants of his army. Fortunately for the Shigeki and their new Inrithi warlords, he hadn't burned the granaries or scorched the fields and orchards as he withdrew. In Council, Saubon claimed this was due to the heathen's haste, which in turn was due to their terror. But Cnaiür knew better. There had been nothing haphazard about the Kianene evacuation of the North Bank. They knew Hinnereth would delay the Men of the Tusk. Even at Zirkirta, where the Scylvendi had crushed the heathen eight years before, the Kianene had recovered quickly from their initial rout. They were a tenacious and resourceful race.

Skauras had spared the North Bank, Cnaiür knew, because he intended to reclaim it.

This wasn't a fact Inrithi stomachs found easy to digest. Even Proyas, who'd set aside the many conceits of his caste and had embraced Cnaiür's tutelage, couldn't believe the Kianene still posed any real threat.

"Are you assured of your victory?" Cnaiür asked one night while supping with the Prince in private.

"Assured?" Proyas replied. "But of course."

"Why?"

"Because my God has willed it."

"And Skauras? Would he not give much the same answer?"

Proyas's eyebrows jumped up, then knitted into a frown. "But that's not to the point, Scylvendi. How many thousands have we killed? How much terror have we struck into their hearts?"

"Too few thousands, and far, far too little terror."

Cnaiür explained the way the memorialists recited verses dedicated to each of the Nansur Columns, stories that described their devices, their arms, and their mettle in battle so that when the Tribes went on pilgrimage or to war, they could read the Nansur battle line. "This was why the People lost at Kiyuth," he said. "Conphas switched his Columns' devices, told us a false story ..."

"Any fool knows how to read his opponent's line!" Proyas spat.

Cnaiür shrugged. "Then tell me," he said, "what story did you read on the Battleplain?"

Proyas blanched. "How in the blazes am I supposed to know? I recognized only a handful ..."

"I recognized all of them," Cnaiür asserted. "Of all the great Kianene Houses, and there are many, only two-thirds rode against us on the Plains of Mengedda. Of those, several were likely token contingents, depending on how many enemies Skauras entertains among his peers. After the massacre of the Vulgar Holy War, many among the heathen, including the Padirajah, were no doubt contemptuous of the Holy War's threat ..."

"But now ..." Proyas said.

"They will not repeat their mistake. They will strike treaties with Girgash and Nilnamesh. They will empty every barracks, saddle every horse, arm every son ... Make no mistake, even now they ride toward Shigek in their thousands. They will answer Holy War with Jihad."

Following this exchange, Proyas out and out capitulated to his admonishments. At the next Council, after the other Great Names, with the exception of Conphas, scoffed at Cnaiür and his warnings, Proyas had captives secured in cross-river raids dragged before them. They confirmed everything Cnaiür had predicted. For over a week, the wretches said, Grandees from as far away as Seleukara and Nenciphon had been riding out of the southern deserts. Some names even the Norsirai seemed to recognize: Cinganjehoi, the far-famed Sapatishah of Eumarna, Imbeyan, the Sapatishah of Enathpaneah, even Dunjoksha, the tyrannical Sapatishah who ruled the governorate of Amoteu from Shimeh.

It was agreed. The Holy War had to cross the River Sempis as soon as humanly possible.

"To think," Proyas confided to him afterward, "that I thought you no more than an effective ruse to employ against the Emperor. Now you're our general in all but name. You realize that?"

"I have said or offered nothing that Conphas himself could not say or offer."

Proyas laughed. "Save trust, Scylvendi. Save trust."

Though Cnaiür grinned, these words cut him for some reason. What did it matter, the trust of dogs and cattle?

Cnaiür had been born for war, as much as he'd been bred for it. This, and this alone, was the one certainty of his life. So he bent himself to the problem of assaulting the South Bank with relish and uncommon zeal. While the Great Names directed the construction of rafts and barges in great enough numbers to convey the entire Holy War across the Sempis, Cnaiür supervised the Conriyan effort to find the ideal place to land. He led his war parties on night raids against the South Bank, even bringing cartographers to map the terrain. If one thing impressed him about the Inrithi manner of making war, it was their use of maps. He directed the questioning of captives, and even taught several traditional Scylvendi techniques to Proyas's interrogators. He questioned those, such as Earl Athjeäri, who raided the South Bank to plunder and harry, about what they'd seen. And he held council with others, like Earl Cerjulla, General Biaxi Sompas, and Palatine Uranyanka, who shared his task.

Except for Proyas's councils, he neither saw nor spoke to Kellhus. The Dûnyain was little more than a rumour.

Cnaiür's days were much the same as before. But his nights ...

They were far different.

He never pitched his tent on the same ground. Most evenings, after sunset or after supping with Proyas and his caste-nobles, he rode from the Conriyan camp, past the sentries and out into the fields. He struck his own fire, listened to the night wind roar through the trees. Sometimes, when he could see it, he stared at the Conriyan encampment and counted fires like an idiot child. "Always number your foemen," his father had once told him, "by the glitter of their fires." Sometimes he gazed at the stars and wondered if they too were his enemies. Every so often, he imagined he camped across the lonely Steppe. The Holy Steppe.

He often brooded over Serwë and Kellhus. He found himself continually rehearsing his reasons for abandoning her to the Dûnyain. He was a warrior—a Scylvendi warrior! What need had he, man-killing Cnaiür, of a woman?

But no matter how obvious his reasons, he still couldn't help but think of her. The globes of her breasts. The wandering line of her hips. So perfect. How he'd burned for her, burned the way a warrior, a man, should! She was his prize—his proof!

He remembered pretending to sleep while listening to her sob in the darkness. He remembered the remorse, as heavy as spring snow, pressing him breathless with its cold. What a fool he'd been! He thought of the apologies, of the desperate pleas that might soften her hatred, that might let her see. He thought of kissing the gentle swell of her belly. And he thought of Anissi, the first wife of his heart, slumbering in the flickering gloom of their faraway hearth, holding tight their daughter, Sanathi, as though sheltering her from the terror of womanhood.

And he thought of Proyas.

On the worst nights he hugged himself in the blackness of his tent, screaming and sobbing. He beat the earth with his fists, stabbed holes with his knife, then fucked them. He cursed the world. He cursed the heavens. He cursed Anasûrimbor Moënghus and his monstrous son.

He thought, *So be it.*

On the best nights he made no camp at all, but instead rode to the nearest Shigeki village, where he would kick in doors and glory in screams. On a whim, he avoided those doors marked with what he imagined was lamb's blood. But when he found all the doors so marked, he ceased to discriminate. "*Murder me!*" he would roar at them. "*Murder me and it stops!*"

Bawling men. Shrieking girls and silent women.

He would take what compensation he could.

A week passed before Cnaiür found the Holy War's best point of purchase on the South Bank: the shallow tidal marshes along the southern edge of the Sempis Delta. Of course all the Great Names, with the exception of Proyas and Conphas, balked at the news, especially after their own people returned with descriptions of the terrain. They were knights, through and through, trained and bred to the charge, and from all accounts, no horse could do more than thrash its way forward through the marsh.

But of course that was the point.

At a Council held in Iothiah, Proyas bid him to explain his plan to the assembled Inrithi. He unrolled a large map of the southern Delta across the table occupied by the Great Names.

"At Mengedda," he declared, "you learned the Kianene were faster. This means no matter where you assemble to cross the Sempis, Skauras will assemble first. But at Mengedda you also learned the strength of your footmen. And more important, you *taught*. These marshes are shallow. A man, even a heavily armed man, can easily walk through them, but horses must be led. As much as you pride your mounts, the Kianene pride theirs more. They will refuse to dismount, and they will not send their conscripts to contest you. What could conscripts do against men who can break a Grandee's charge? No. Skauras will yield the entirety of the marsh ..."

He jabbed a chapped finger at the map, some distance to the south of the marsh.

"He will draw back here, to the fortress of Anwurat. He will give you all this pasture to assemble. He will cede you both ground and your horses."

"How can you be so certain?" Gothyelk cried. Of all the Great Names, the old Earl of Agansanor seemed the most troubled by Cnaiür's savage heritage—with the exception of Conphas, of course.

"Because Skauras," Cnaiür said evenly, "is not a fool."

Gothyelk hammered a fist down on the table. But before Proyas could intervene, the Exalt-General stood from his seat and said, "He's right!"

Stunned, the Great Names turned to him. Since the debacle at Hinnereth, Conphas had largely kept his counsel. His was no longer a welcome voice. But to hear him confirm the Scylvendi on something as daring as this ...

"The dog's right, as much as it pains me to say it." He looked at Cnaiür with eyes that both laughed and hated. "He's found our purchase on the South Bank."

Cnaiür imagined cutting his pampered throat.

After this, the Scylvendi Chieftan's reputation was secured. He even became something of a fashion among certain Inrithi caste-nobility, particularly the Ainoni and their wives. Proyas had warned him this might happen. "They will be drawn to you," he explained, "the way old leches are drawn to young boys." Cnaiür found himself beset with invitations and propositions. One woman, through sheer perseverance, even found him at his camp. He stopped short of strangling her.

As the far-flung Holy War began gathering near Iothiah, Cnaiür troubled himself with thoughts of Skauras, much the way he'd once troubled himself with thoughts of Conphas before the Battle of Kiyuth. The man was obviously fearless. The story of him standing alone paring his nails while Saubon's Agmundrmen archers feathered the surrounding turf had become something of a legend. And from his interrogations of Kianene captives Cnaiür had learned other details: that he was a severe disciplinarian, that he possessed a gift for organization, and that he commanded the respect of even those who otherwise outranked him, such as the Padirajah's son, Fanayal, or his famed son-in-law, Imbeyan. Cnaiür had also, quite inadvertently, learned much from Conphas, who occasionally recollected incidents from his youth as a hostage of the Sapatishah. If his stories could be believed, Skauras was an exceedingly canny and strangely mischievous man.

Of all these characteristics, it was this latter, mischievousness, that struck Cnaiür the most. Apparently Skauras liked to drug his unwitting guest's wine with a variety of Ainoni and Nilnameshi narcotics—even with chanv on occasion. "All those who drink with me," Conphas once quoted him as claiming, "drink with themselves as well." When Cnaiür had first heard this story, he'd thought it simply more proof of the way luxury drowned manly sense. But now he wasn't so sure. The point of the narcotics, Cnaiür realized, was to make his guests *other* to themselves, strangers with whom they could tip bowls.

Which meant the wily Sapatishah not only liked to trick and deceive, he liked to show, to *prove* ...

For Skauras, the imminent battle would be more than a contest, it would be a demonstration. The man had underestimated the Inrithi at Mengedda, seeing only his strengths and his opponent's weaknesses, much as Xunnurit had underestimated Conphas at Kiyuth. He wouldn't try to overpower the Men of the Tusk; he was not a man to repeat his mistakes. Rather, he would try to outwit them, to show them fools ...

So what would the wily old warrior do?

Cnaiür shared his apprehensions with Proyas.

"You must be sure," he told the Prince, "that the Scarlet Spires remains with the host at all points."

Proyas had pressed a hand to his forehead. "Eleäzaras will resist," he said wearily. "He's already said he will follow only *after* the Holy War has crossed. Apparently his spies have told him the Cishaurim remain in Shimeh ..."

Cnaiür scowled and spat. "Then we have the advantage!"

"The Scarlet Spires, I fear, conserve themselves for the Cishaurim."

"They must accompany us," Cnaiür insisted, "even if they remain hidden. There must be something you can offer."

The Prince smiled mirthlessly. "Or someone," he said with uncommon grief.

At least once daily, Cnaiür rode to the river to view the preparations. The floodplains surrounding Iothiah had been denuded of trees, as had the banks of the Sempis, where thousands of barebacked Inrithi toiled over felled trunks, hacking, pounding, binding. He could ride for miles, breathing deep the smell of sweat, pitch, and hewn wood, before glimpsing the end of them. Hundreds hailed him as he passed, saluting him with cries of "Scylvendi!"—as though his ancestry had become his fame and title.

Cnaiür need only peer across the Sempis to know that Skauras awaited them on the far bank. As tiny as mites in the distance, Fanim horsemen continuously patrolled the shoreline—entire divisions of them. Sometimes he heard their thousand-throated jeers across the water, sometimes the throb of their drums.

As a precaution, squadrons of Imperial war galleys were stationed in the river.

The Holy War began embarking long before dawn. Hundreds of crude barges and thousands of rafts were first poled then paddled into the Sempis. By the time the morning sun enamelled the waters much of the vast flotilla was underway, packed with anxious men and horses.

Cnaiür crossed with Proyas and his immediate entourage. Xinemus was absent, which Cnaiür thought strange, until he realized that the Marshal had his own men to watch over. But of course Kellhus was in attendance, and the Prince stood at his side for some time. They traded avid words, and periodically Proyas laughed with an uneasiness that tickled to hear.

Cnaiür had watched the Dûnyain's influence grow. He'd watched as he gradually bridled all those about Xinemus's fire, working their hearts the way saddle makers worked leather, tanning, gouging, shaping. He'd watched as he lured more and more Men of the Tusk with the grain of his deceit. He'd watched him yoke thousands—*thousands!*—with simple words and bottomless looks. He'd watched him minister to Serwë ...

He'd watched until he could bear watching no more.

Cnaiür had always known Kellhus's capabilities, had always known the Holy War would yield to him. But knowing and witnessing were two different things. He cared nothing for the Inrithi. And yet, watching Kellhus's lies spread like cancer across an old woman's skin, he found himself *fearing* for them—fearing, even as he scorned them! How they fell over themselves, fawning, wheedling, grovelling. How they degraded themselves, youthful fools and inveterate warriors alike. Imploring looks and beseeching expressions. Oh, Kellhus ... Oh, *Kellhus* ... Staggering drunks! Unmanly ingrates! How *easily* they surrendered.

And none more so than Serwë. To watch her succumb, again and again. To see his hand drift deep between Dûnyain thighs ...

Fickle, treacherous, whorish bitch! How many times must he strike her? How many times must he take her? How many times must he stare, dumbfounded by her beauty?

Cnaiür sat cross-legged on the prow, watching the far embankment, probing the shadows beneath the trees. He could see clots of horsemen, what seemed thousands of them, tracking their slow drift down river.

The air was dank. Nervous voices rang across the waters: Inrithi calling to each other between crafts, jokes mostly. Cnaiür saw far too many bare asses.

"Look at the assholes!" some wit cried out, watching the Kianene crowding the opposite bank.

"I resent that!" someone bawled from a nearby raft.

"What are you? Heathen?"

"Nay, I'm an *asshole!*"

For a time, it seemed the Sempis itself thundered with laughter.

But the mood turned when one fool stumbled into the river. Cnaiür actually saw it happen. The man hit the water face first, and thanks to his armour, simply continued dropping until obscured by the reflections of his horrified comrades. Jeers and catcalls thundered from the southern shore. Proyas cursed, and soundly upbraided all those floating within earshot.

Afterward, the Prince left Kellhus and jostled his way to Cnaiür on the prow, his eyes shining in that peculiar way—the way they always shone after he spoke with Kellhus. The way, in fact, everyone's eyes shone, as though they just had awakened from a nightmare and found their families intact.

But there was more to his manner, a too-forward camaraderie that spoke of dread.

"You avoid Kellhus like the plague, you know that?"

Cnaiür snorted.

Proyas watched him, his smile fading. "Such things are difficult," he said. His eyes darted from Cnaiür to the heathen streaming and massing along the southern shore.

"What things are difficult?" Cnaiür asked.

Proyas grimaced, scratched the back of his head. "Kellhus told me ..."

"Told you what?"

"About Serwë."

Cnaiür nodded, spat into the water rolling beneath the prow. Of course the Dûnyain had told him. What better way to explain their estrangement? What better way to explain the estrangement between any men? A woman.

Serwë ... His prize. His proof.

The perfect explanation. Simple. Plausible. Certain to discourage further questions ...

The Dûnyain explanation.

A moment of silence passed, awkward with misgivings and small misapprehensions.

"Tell me, Cnaiür," Proyas finally said. "What do the Scylvendi believe? What are their Laws?"

"What do I believe?"

"Yes ... Of course."

"I believe your ancestors killed my God. I believe your race bears the blood-guilt of that crime."

His voice didn't quaver. His expression didn't break. But as always, he could hear the infernal chorus.

"So you worship vengeance ..."

"I worship vengeance."

"And that's why the Scylvendi call themselves the People of War."

"Yes. To war is to avenge."

The proper answer. So why the throng of questions?

"To take back what has been taken," Proyas said, his eyes at once troubled and bright. "Like our Holy War for Shimeh."

"No," Cnaiür replied. "To murder the taker."

Proyas shot him an alarmed look, then glanced away. With an air of admission that Cnaiür found effeminate, he said, "I like you much better, Scylvendi, when I forget who you are."

But Cnaiür had turned away, searching the southern banks for sight of more men who would kill him, if they could. What Proyas remembered or forgot mattered nothing to him. He was what he was.

I am of the People!

In a long drifting column, the Inrithi flotilla entered the first of the Delta channels. Cnaiür couldn't help but wonder what Skauras would think when his watchers reported they'd lost sight of the Holy War. Had he anticipated this? Or had he simply feared it? Even now the Emperor's warships would be taking positions along the southernmost navigable channels. The Sapatishah would know soon enough where the Holy War intended to land.

As it happened, they were harassed only by mosquitoes. The morning, then the afternoon, took on the strange character of lulls before imminent battle. It was always the same. For some reason, the air would become leaden, the moments would drop like stones, and a restless boredom unlike any other would weigh and weigh, making necks stiff and heads ache. Every man, no matter how terrified on the morn, would find himself *yearning* for the battle, as though the violence of its promise burdened far more than the violence of its consummation.

Night passed in discomfort and the delirium of almost sleep.

They reached the salt marshes around noon the following day: a deep-green sea of reeds reaching to either horizon. Suddenly the torpor lifted, and Cnaiür felt a sudden frenzy akin to that of the charge. He waded with the others through the morass, dragging the barge as far forward as possible, hacking with his sword at the towering papyrus. Soon he found himself one of thousands stamping forward, levelling the reeds into a vast swampy plain. Eventually inroads were cut to the hard ground of the South Bank. With Proyas, Kellhus, Ingiaban, and a party of knights, Cnaiür slogged forward to see what awaited them. As always the Dûnyain's presence made his heart itch, like the threat of a blow from unseen quarters.

To the east they glimpsed the distant breakers of the Meneanor. Before them, to the south, the land climbed in stony heaps, becoming a mass of iron-coloured hills. To the west they saw a broad swath of pasture, creased like a brooding man's forehead, darkened by distant orchards. On a lone hill, barely distinguishable for the haze, they could see the squat ramparts of Anwurat. Small bands of horsemen trotted across the intervening distance, but nothing more.

Skauras had yielded the South Bank. As Cnaiür had predicted.

Proyas fairly howled in celebration.

"What fools!" Ingiaban cried. "What fools!"

Ignoring the torrent of acclamation, Cnaiür glanced at Kellhus, wasn't surprised to see him watching, studying. Cnaiür spat and looked away, knowing full well what the Dûnyain had seen.

It was too easy.

The Holy War spent the entire afternoon stumping out from the swamp. Most pitched their tents in the failing light of dusk. Cnaiür heard the Inrithi sing, scoffed as he always scoffed. He watched them kneel in prayer, congregate around their priests and idols. He listened to them laugh and cavort, and he wondered that their merriment could sound genuine rather than forced, as it should on the eve before battle. War for them wasn't holy. War for them was a means, not an end. A track to their destination.

Shimeh.

But the darkness snuffed their celebratory mood. To the south and to the west the entire horizon twinkled with lights, like embers kicked across folds of blue wool. Camp fires, innumerable thousands of them, tended by the leather-hearted warriors of Kian. The beat of drums rolled down the hillsides.

At the Council of Great and Lesser Names, the Men of the Tusk, dazzled by the bloodless success of their landing, acclaimed Cnaiür their King-of-Tribes—what they called their Battlemaster. Followed by his generals and lesser officers, Ikurei Conphas stormed from the Council in a fury. Cnaiür wordlessly accepted, too conflicted to feel either pride or embarrassment. Slaves were given the task of stitching his own battlefield standard, something the Inrithi held sacred.

Afterward, Cnaiür found Proyas standing alone in the darkness, staring at the countless heathen fires.

"So many," the Prince said softly. "Eh, Battlemaster?"

Proyas hitched his lips into a smile, but Cnaiür could see him wring his hands in the moonlight. The barbarian was struck by how young the man looked, how frail ... For the first time, it seemed, Cnaiür understood the catastrophic dimensions of what would soon happen. Nations, faiths, and races.

Where did this young man, this boy, belong in all of this? How would he fare?

He could be my son.

"I shall overcome them," Cnaiür said.

But afterward, as he walked toward his solitary camp on the windy shores of the Meneanor, he fumed over these words. Who was he to give assurances to an Inrithi prince? What did it matter to him who died and who lived? What did it matter so long as he was party to the killing?

I am of the People!

Cnaiür urs Skiötha, the most violent of all men.

Later that night, he squatted before the churning surf and washed his broadsword in the sea, thinking of how he'd once crouched on the misty shores of the faraway Jorua Sea with his father, doing much the same. He listened to the thunder of distant breakers, to the hiss of water washing through sand and gravel. He looked across the Meneanor's shining reaches and pondered its tracklessness. A different kind of steppe.

What was it his father had said of the sea?

Afterward, as he sat sharpening his blade for the morrow's worship, Kellhus stepped soundlessly from the blackness. The wind twisted his hair into flaxen tails.

Cnaiür grinned wolfishly. For some reason he wasn't surprised.

"What brings you here, Dûnyain?"

Kellhus studied his face by firelight, and for the first time Cnaiür didn't care.

I know you lie.

"Do you think the Holy War will prevail?" Kellhus asked.

"The great prophet," Cnaiür snorted. "Have others come to you with that same question?"

"They have," Kellhus replied.

Cnaiür spat into the fire. "How fares my prize?"

"Serwë is well ... Why do you avoid my question?"

Cnaiür sneered, turned back to his blade. "Why do you ask questions when you know the answer?"

Kellhus said nothing, but stood like something otherworldly against the darkness. The wind whipped smoke about him. The sea thundered and hissed.

"You think something has broken within me," Cnaiür continued, drawing out his whetstone to the stars. "But you are wrong ... You think I have become more erratic, more unpredictable, and therefore more a threat to your mission ..."

He turned from his broadsword and matched the Dûnyain's bottomless gaze.

"But you are wrong."

Kellhus nodded, and Cnaiür cared not at all.

"When this battle comes," the Dûnyain said, "you must instruct me ... You must teach me War."

"I would sooner cut my throat."

A gust assailed his fire, blowing sparks over the strand. It felt good, like a woman's fingers through his hair.

"I'll give you Serwë," Kellhus said.

The sword fell with a clang to Cnaiür's feet. For an instant, it seemed he gagged on ice.

"Why," he spat contemptuously, "would I want your pregnant whore?"

"She's your prize," Kellhus said. "She bears your child."

Why did he long for her so? She was a vain, shallow-witted waif—nothing more! Cnaiür had seen the way Kellhus used her, the way he dressed her. He'd heard the words he bid her speak. No tool was too small for a Dûnyain, no word too plain, no blink too brief. He'd utilized the chisel of her beauty, the hammer of her peach ... Cnaiür had seen this!

So how could he contemplate ...

All I have is war!

The Meneanor crashed and surged across the beaches. The wind smelled of brine. Cnaiür stared at the Dûnyain for what seemed a thousand heartbeats. Then at last he nodded, even though he knew he relinquished the last remnant of his hold on the abomination. After this he would have nothing but the word of a Dûnyain ...

He would have nothing.

But when he closed his eyes he saw her, felt her soft and supple, crushed beneath his frame. She was his prize! His proof!

Tomorrow, after worship ...

He would take what compensation he could.

CHAPTER FOURTEEN

ANWURAT

It is the difference in knowledge that commands respect. This is why the true test of every student lies in the humiliation of his master.
— GOTAGGA, THE PRIMA ARCANATA

The children here play with bones instead of sticks, and whenever I see them, I cannot but wonder whether the humeri they brandish are faithful or heathen.

Heathen, I should think, for the bones seem bent.
— ANONYMOUS, LETTER FROM ANWURAT

Late Summer, 4111 Year-of-the-Tusk, Shigek

Reviewing the latest intelligence reports, Ikurei Conphas let Martemus stand unacknowledged for several moments. The canvas walls of his command pavilion had been rolled up and bound to facilitate traffic. Officers, messengers, secretaries, and scribes shuttled back and forth between the lamp-illumined interior and the surrounding darkness of the Nansur encampment. Men called out and muttered in deliberation, their faces almost uniformly blank, their eyes slack with the wary expectancy of battle. They were Nansur, and no people had lost more sons to the Fanim.

Such a battle! And he—he! the Lion of Kiyuth!—would be little more than a subaltern ...

No matter, it would be salt for the honey, as the Ainoni were fond of saying. The bitterness that made vengeance sweet.

"When dawn breaks and the Scylvendi dog leads us into battle," Conphas said, still studying the documents fanned across the table before him, "I've decided that you, Martemus, will be my representative."

"Do you have any specific instructions?" the General asked stiffly.

Conphas looked up, appraised the hard-jawed man for several condescending moments. Why had he allowed him to keep his blue general's cloak? He should have sold the fool to the slavers.

"You think I give you this charge because I trust you to the degree I distrust the Scylvendi ... But you're wrong. As much as I despise the savage, as much as I intend to see him dead, I do in fact trust him in matters of war ..." And well he should, Conphas mused. As strange as it seemed, the barbarian had been his student for quite some time. Since the Battle of Kiyuth, if not longer ...

No wonder they called Fate a whore.

"But you, Martemus," Conphas continued. "You I scarcely trust at all."

"Then why give me such an assignment?"

No protestations of innocence, no hurt looks or clenched fists ... Only stoic curiosity. For all his failings, Conphas realized, Martemus remained a remarkable man. It would be such a waste.

"Because you've unfinished business." Conphas handed several sheets to his secretary, then looked down as though to study the next sheaf of parchment. "I've just been told the Prince of Atrithau accompanies the Scylvendi." He graced the General with a dazzling smile.

Martemus said nothing for a stone-faced moment.

"But I told you ... He's ... he's ..."

"Please," Conphas snapped. "How long has it been since you've drawn your sword, hmm? If I doubt your loyalty, I laugh at your prowess ... No. You'll only observe."

"Then who—"

But Conphas had already waved the three men forward: the assassins dispatched by his uncle. The two, who were obviously Nansur, weren't all that imposing, perhaps—but the third, the black-skinned Zeumi, drew nervous glances from even the most distracted of Conphas's officers. He towered a full head above the surrounding mob, bull-chested and yellow-eyed. He wore the red-striped tunic and iron-scale harness of an imperial auxiliary, though a great tulwar hung across his back.

A Zeumi sword-dancer. The Emperor had been generous indeed.

"These men," Conphas said, staring hard at the General, "will do the work ..." He leaned forward, lowering his voice so as not to be overheard. "But *you*, Martemus, you'll be the one who brings me Anasûrimbor Kellhus's head."

Was that horror he saw in the man's eyes? Or was it hope?

Conphas fell back into his chair. "You can use your cloak as a sack."

The long howl of Inrithi horns pierced the predawn gloom, and the Men of the Tusk arose certain of their triumph. They stood on the South Bank. They had met their enemy before and had crushed him. They would enter battle with all of their assembled might. And most importantly, the God *himself* walked among them—they could see Him in thousands of bright eyes. Spears and lances had become, it seemed to them, markers of the Tusk.

The air was rifled by the commanding cries of thanes, barons, and their majordomos. Men hastened into their gear. Horsemen streamed between the tents. Armoured men knelt in circles, praying. Wine was passed, bread hastily broken and devoured. Bands of men drifted to their places in the line, some singing, some watchful. Small groups of wives and prostitutes waved hands and coloured scarfs at passing troops of mounted warriors. Priests intoned the most profound benedictions.

By the time the sun gilded the Meneanor, the Inrithi had assembled in rank after glorious rank across the fields. Several hundred paces away an immense arc of silvered armour, brilliant coats, and stamping horses awaited them. From the southern heights to the dark Sempis, the Fanim encompassed the horizon. Great divisions of horsemen trotted across the northern pastures. Arms flashed from the walls and turrets of Anwurat. Deep formations of spearmen darkened the shallow embankments to the south. More horsemen massed across the southern hilltops, following the heights to the sea. Every distance, it seemed, bristled with heathen.

The Inrithi line seethed with the habits and hatreds of its constituent nations. The unruly Galeoth, hurling insults and jeering reminders of earlier slaughter. The magnificent knights of Conriya, hollering curses through silvered war masks. The glaring Thunyeri, swearing oaths of blood to their shield-brothers. The disciplined Nansur, standing immobile, keen to the calls of their officers. The Shrial Knights, eyeing the skies, their lips tight with fervent prayer. The haughty Ainoni, anxious and impassive behind the white cosmetics of war. The black-armoured ranks of Tydonni, taking sullen measure of the mongrels they were about to kill.

A hundred hundred banners fluttered in the morning wind.

What was this trade he had made? War for a woman ...

With Kellhus at his side, Cnaiür led a small army of officers, observers, and field messengers up turf and gravel ramps to the summit of a small hillock dominating the central pastures. Proyas had provided him slaves, and they hastened to prepare his command, unloading trestles from the wains, pitching canopies, and laying mats upon the ground. They raised his ad hoc standard: two bolts of white silk, each banded with lateral stripes of red and flanked by horsetails that swished in the sea-borne breeze.

The Inrithi were already calling it the "Swazond Standard." The mark of their Battlemaster.

Cnaiür rode to the summit's edge and stared in wonder.

Beneath him, sweeping out in either direction, the Holy War darkened the woollen distances: great squares and mobs of infantrymen, files and lines of burnished knights. Facing them, the heathen ranks scrawled along the hills and opposing fields, twinkling in the morning sun. Just small enough to obscure with two fingers, the fortress of Anwurat reared in the near distance, its walls and parapets adorned with long saffron banners.

The air thrummed with the din of innumerable shouts. The faint peal of faraway battlehorns was overpowered by the strident blare of those more near. Cnaiür breathed deep, smelled sea, desert, and dank river—nothing of the absurd spectacle before him. If he closed his eyes and covered his ears, he thought, he could pretend he was alone ...

I am of the Land!

He dismounted, contemptuously thrust his reins to the Dûnyain. Staring across the plains, he searched for weaknesses in the Inrithi disposition. Beyond a mile, their standards became little more than snags in the tatting of their ranks, so he could only assume the farther Great Names had arrayed their formations as discussed. The Ainoni especially, on the extreme south, looked little more than dark fields aligned along the lower slopes of the coastal hills.

He pinched his eyes, stiffened in sudden awareness of Kellhus at his side. The man wore a white samite robe, cinched into a tail in the Conriyan style, which is to say at the small of his back, so that his waist and legs remained unencumbered. Beneath he sported a corselet of Kianene manufacture—probably looted from the Battleplain—and the pleated kilt of a Conriyan knight. His battlecap was Nansur, open faced, without so much as a nose bar. As always, the long pommel of his sword jutted above his left shoulder. Two crude-looking knives, their hilts worked with Thunyeri animal devices, had been thrust into his leather girdle. On the right breast of his robe, someone had embroidered the Red Tusk of the Holy War.

Cnaiür's skin prickled at the nearness of him.

What was this trade he had made?

Never had Cnaiür suffered a night like the night previous. Why? he'd screamed at the Meneanor. Why had he agreed to teach the Dûnyain war? War! For Serwë? For a bauble found on the Steppe?

For nothing?

He'd traded many things over the past months. Honour for the promise of vengeance. Leather for effeminate silks. His yaksh for a prince's pavilion. The Utemot in their unwashed hundreds, for the Inrithi in their hundreds of thousands ...

Battlemaster ... King-of-Tribes!

Part of him reeled in drunken exultation at the thought. Such a host! From the river to the hills, a distance of almost seven miles, and still the ranks ran deep! The People could never assemble such a horde, not if they emptied every yaksh, saddled every boy. And here *he*, Cnaiür urs Skiötha, breaker-of-horses-and-men, commanded. Outland princes, earls and palatines, thanes and barons in their thousands, even an Exalt-General answered to him! *Ikurei Conphas*, the hated author of Kiyuth!

What would the People think? Would they call this glory? Or would they spit and curse his name, give him to the torments of the aged and infirm?

But wasn't all war, all battle, holy? Wasn't victory the mark of the righteous? If he crushed the Fanim, ground them beneath the heel of his boot, what would the People think of his trade then? Would they finally say, "This man, this many-blooded man, is truly of the land"?

Or would they whisper as they always whispered? Would they laugh as they always laughed?

"Yours is the name of our shame!"

What if he made a gift of the Inrithi? What if he delivered *them* to destruction? What if he rode home with Ikurei Conphas's head in a sack?

"Scylvendi," Moënghus said from his side.

That voice!

Cnaiür looked to Kellhus, blinking.

Skauras! the Dûnyain's look shouted. *Skauras is our foe here!*

Cnaiür turned to the expectant Inrithi behind him. He could hear them muttering. With the exception of Proyas, each of the Great Names had sent representatives—to keep watch as much as to dispense advice, Cnaiür imagined. He recognized many of them from the Councils of the Great and Lesser Names: Thane Ganrikka, General Martemus, Baron Mimaripal, others. For some reason, a great hollow opened in his belly ...

I must concentrate! Skauras is the foe here!

He spat across the dusty grass. Everything was at the ready. The Inrithi had assembled with a swiftness and exactitude that heartened. Skauras had deployed precisely as Cnaiür had expected. There was nothing more to be done, yet ...

More time! I need more time!

But he had no time. War had come, and he'd agreed to yield its secrets in exchange for Serwë. He'd agreed to surrender the last shred of leverage he possessed. After this he would have nothing to secure his vengeance. Nothing! After this, there would be no reason for Kellhus to keep him alive.

I'm a threat to him. The only man who knows his secret ...

So what was she, that he'd doom himself for her? What was she, that he would trade *war*?

Something is wrong with me … Something.

No! Nothing! Nothing!

"Signal the general advance," he barked, turning back to the field. A chorus of excited voices erupted behind him. Horns soon clawed at the sky.

Kellhus fixed him with shining, empty eyes.

But Cnaiür had already looked away, back to the sweep of the west and to the great lines and squares of the Holy War sprawled across it. Long rows of armoured horsemen were beginning to trot forward, followed by deeper ranks of footmen, walking with the speed with which one might greet a friend. Perhaps half a mile distant, the Fanim awaited them across the depths and the heights, holding tight their stamping thoroughbreds, hunching behind shield and spear. The pounding of their drums rumbled down from the hills.

The Dûnyain loomed in his periphery, as sharp as a mortal rebuke.

What was this trade he had made? A woman for war.

Something is wrong …

Behind him, the Inrithi lords began singing.

Along the entirety of the line, the Inrithi knights quickly outpaced the men-at-arms. Hares darted from copses, raced across the parched turf. Shod hooves made hash of desiccated weeds. Soon the Men of the Tusk sailed across the uneven pasture, trailing immense skirts of dust. The sky was darkened by heathen arrows. Horses shrieked, tumbled. Armoured men rolled across the turf and were trampled by their kin. But the Men of the Tusk combed the fields with thundering hooves. Bobbing lance tips sketched circles around the nearing wall of heathen, who barbed the distance like a hedge of silvered thorns. Hatred clamped tooth to tooth. War shouts became howls of ecstasy. Heart and limb hummed with rapture. Could anything be so clear, so pure? Outstretched like great, fluid arms the holy warriors embraced their enemy.

The sermon was simple.

Break.

Die.

Serwë was utterly alone. She'd avoided the company of the priests and other women who'd gathered in prayer at various points throughout the encampment. She'd already prayed to her God. She'd kissed him, and had wept as he'd ridden off to join the Scylvendi.

She sat before their firepit, boiling water for the tea prescribed by Proyas's physician-priest. Her tanned arms and shoulders burned in the rising sun. There was sand beneath the thin grass, and she could feel its grit chafe the soft skin behind her knees. The pavilion billowed and snapped like a ship's sail in the wind—a strange song, with random crescendo and meaningless pause. She wasn't afraid, but she was afflicted by competing confusions.

Why must he risk himself?

The loss of Achamian had filled her with pity for Esmenet and with fear for herself. Until his disappearance it hadn't seemed she lived in the midst of a war. It had been more like a pilgrimage—not one where the faithful travel to visit something sacred, but rather one where people travel to *deliver* something holy.

To deliver Kellhus.

But if Achamian, a great sorcerer, could vanish, become a casualty, might not Kellhus vanish also?

But this thought didn't so much frighten her—the possibility was too unthinkable—as it confused her. One cannot fear for a God, but one can be baffled over whether one *should.*

Gods could die. The Scylvendi worshipped a dead god.

Does Kellhus fear?

That too, was unimaginable.

She thought she heard something—a shadow—behind her, but her water had begun to boil. She stood to retrieve the crude kettle with clumsy sticks. How she missed Xinemus's slaves! She managed to set it on the turf without burning herself—a minor miracle. She stood, sighing and rubbing her lower back, when a warm hand reached around her and clutched her growing belly. Kellhus!

Smiling, she half-turned, pressed her cheek to his chest and hooked a hand about his neck.

"What are you doing?" she laughed—and frowned. He seemed shorter. Did he stand in a hole?

"Warring is hungry business, Serwë. Certain appetites must be attended."
Serwë blushed and wondered yet again that he had chosen her—*her!*
I bear his child.

"Now?" she murmured. "What of the battle? Don't you worry?"

His eyes laughing, he drew her toward the entrance of their pavilion.
"I worry for you."

His Inrithi retinue chattered and cheered behind him. Different voices
cried, "Look! Look!"

Everywhere Cnaiür turned, he saw glory and horror. To his right, waves
of Galeoth and Tydonni galloped across the northern pastures into masses
of Kianene horsemen. Before him, thousands of Conriyan knights raced
beneath the peril of Anwurat's heights. To his immediate left, the
Thunyeri, and beyond them, the Nansur Columns, marched inexorably
westward. Only the extreme south, obscured by curtains of dust, remained
inscrutable.

His heart quickened. His breath sharpened. *Too fast! Everything happens
too fast!*

Saubon and Gothyelk scattered the Fanim, pursued them hard through
swirling grit.

Proyas, flanked by hundreds of mail-armoured knights, crashed into
the bristling ranks of an immense Shigeki phalanx. His footmen had
charged into his wake, and now thronged about Anwurat's southern
bastions, bearing mantlets and great iron-headed ladders. Archers raked
the parapets in volleys, while trains of men and oxen dragged assorted
siege engines into position.

Skaiyelt and Conphas advanced across the pasture to the south,
holding their horses in reserve. A series of earthen embankments, shallow
but too sharp for charging horses, stepped the fields before them. As
Cnaiür had guessed, the Sapatishah had massed his Shigeki conscripts
along them. The position might have rendered Skauras's entire centre
immune to attack had not Cnaiür ordered several hundred rafts dragged
from the marshes and dispersed among the Thunyeri and Nansur. Even
now, in a hail of spears and javelins, the Nansur were raising the first of
them as improvised ramps.

General Setpanares and his tens of thousands of Ainoni knights remained hidden. Cnaiür could see the rearmost infantry phalanxes—they were little more than the shadows of squares at this distance—but nothing more.

Already the dogs gnaw at my gut!

He glanced at Kellhus. "Since Skauras has secured his flanks using the land," he explained, "this battle will be one of *yetrut*, penetration, not one of *unswaza*, envelopment. Hosts, like men, prefer to face their enemy. Circumvent or break their lines, assault them from the flank or the rear ..."

He let his voice trail. The wind had thinned the dust to near transparency across the southern hills. Peering, he could see threads of what must be Ainoni knights withdrawing all along their two-mile section of line. They seemed to be reforming on the slopes. Behind them, the many bars and squares of Ainoni infantry had stalled.

The Kianene still held the heights.

I should have given the Ainoni the centre! Who has Skauras positioned there? Imbeyan? Swarjuka?

"And this," Kellhus asked, "is how you crush your foe?"

"What?"

"By assaulting their flank or rear ..."

Cnaiür shook his black mane. "No. This is how you convince your foe."

"Convince?"

Cnaiür snorted. "*This war*," he snapped in Scylvendi, "*is simply your war made honest.*"

Kellhus acknowledged nothing. "Belief ... You're saying battle is a disputation of belief ... An argument."

Cnaiür squinted, peered once more toward the south.

"The memorialists call battle *otgai wutmaga*, a great quarrel. Both hosts take the field believing they are the victors. One host must be disabused of that belief. Attacking his flank or his rear, overawing him, bewildering him, shocking him, killing him: these are all arguments, meant to convince your foe he is defeated. He who believes he is defeated is defeated."

"So in battle," Kellhus said, "conviction makes true."

"As I said, it is honest."

Skauras! I must concentrate upon Skauras!

Overcome by a sudden restlessness, Cnaiür tugged at his mail harness as though plagued by a pinch. Barking several brief commands, he dispatched a rider to General Setpanares. He needed to know who'd beaten the Ainoni back from the hilltops—though by the time the man returned, Cnaiür knew, the battle would likely be decided. Then he ordered the Hornsman to remind the General to secure his flanks. Out of expediency, they'd adopted the Nansur mode of communication, with batteries of trumpeters stationed about the field, relaying coded numbers that corresponded to a handful of different warnings and commands. Though the Ainoni General struck him as solid, his King-Regent, Chepheramunni, was a rank fool.

And the Ainoni were a vain and effeminate race—something Skauras wouldn't overlook.

Cnaiür glanced at the Nansur and the Thunyeri. The farther Columns, those adjacent to the Ainoni, appeared to be storming up their ramps already. Closer, where he could actually distinguish individual men, the first of the rafts were slamming into place. Wherever they fell, several Shigeki vanished—crushed. The first of the Thunyeri charged forward, howling …

Meanwhile Proyas and his stalwarts waded through disintegrating ranks of Shigeki. Sunlight flashed from their threshing swords. But farther west, beyond the mud-brick village and dark orchards to the immediate rear of the Shigeki, Cnaiür could see distant lines of approaching horsemen: Skauras's reserves, he imagined. He couldn't discern any of their devices through the haze, but their numbers looked worrisome … He dispatched a messenger to warn the Conriyans.

Everything goes to plan … Cnaiür had known the Shigeki flanking Anwurat would collapse before the fury of Proyas's charge. And Skauras, he assumed, had also known: the question was one of *whom* the Sapatishah would send into the breach …

Probably Imbeyan.

Then he glanced to the north, to the open fields, where the Fanim horsemen had fallen back before Gothyelk and Saubon, taking high-walled Anwurat as their implacable hinge.

"See how Skauras frustrates Saubon?" he said.

Kellhus searched the pastures and nodded. "He doesn't contest so much as delay."

"He concedes the north. The Galeoth and Tydonni knights possess the advantage of *gaiwut*, of shock. But the Kianene possess the advantages of *utmurzu*, cohesion, and *fira*, speed. Though the Fanim cannot withstand the Inrithi charge, they are quick enough and cohesive enough to execute the *malk unswaza*, the defensive envelopment."

Even as he said this, he saw streamers of hard-riding Kianene sluice around the Northmen.

Kellhus nodded, his eyes fixed on the distant drama. "When the attacker over-commits on the charge, he risks exposing his flanks."

"Which the Inrithi usually do. Only their superior *angotma*, heart, saves them."

Inrithi knights stood their ground, suddenly beset on all sides. Some distance away, the Galeoth and Tydonni infantry continued to trudge forward.

"Their conviction," Kellhus said.

Cnaiür nodded. "When the memorialists counsel the Chieftains before battle, they bid them recall that in conflict all men are bound to one another, some by chains, some by ropes, and some by strings, all of different lengths. They call these bindings the *mayutafüri*, the ligaments of war. These are just ways of describing the strength and flexibility of a formation's *angotma*. Those Kianene the People would call *trutu garothut*, men of the long chain. They can be thrown apart, but they will pull themselves together. The Galeoth and Tydonni we would call *trutu hirothut*, men of the short chain. Left alone, such men would battle and battle. Only disaster or *utgirkoy*, attrition, can break the chains of such men."

As they watched, the Fanim scattered before the long swords of the Norsirai knights, drawing back to reform even farther to the west.

"The leader," Cnaiür continued, "must continually appraise and reappraise the string, rope, and chain of his enemy and his men."

"So the north doesn't worry you."

"No ..."

Cnaiür whirled southward, struck by an inexplicable apprehension of doom. The Ainoni knights appeared to have retired for some reason, though too much dust still obscured the heights to be certain. The

306 THE SECOND MARCH

infantry had resumed their climb, all along the line. He dispatched messengers to Conphas, bidding him to send his Kidruhil to the Ainoni rear. He ordered the Hornsman to signal Gotian ...

"There," he said to Kellhus. "Do you see the Ainoni infantry advance?"

"Yes ... Certain formations seem to drift ... to the right."

"Without knowing, men will lean into the shield of the man to their right, seeking protection. When the Fanim charge to meet them, they will concentrate on those units, watch ..."

"Because they betray weaknesses in discipline."

"Yes, depending on who leads. If Conphas were directing them, I would say they drift right purposefully, to draw the Kianene away from his less experienced formations."

"Deception."

Cnaiür clutched his iron-plated girdle tight. A tremor had passed through his hands.

Everything goes to plan!

"Know what your enemy knows," he said, hiding his face in the distance. "The ligaments must be defended as fiercely as they are attacked. Use knowledge of your enemy, deception, terrain, even harangues or examples of valour to guard and guard vigorously. Tolerate no disbelief. Fortify your host against it, and punish all instances with torture and death."

What's Setpanares doing?

"Because it spreads," Kellhus said.

"The People," Cnaiür replied, "have many stories of Nansur Columns perishing to the man ... The hearts of some men never break. But most look to others for what to believe ..."

"And this is rout, the loss of all conviction? What we witnessed on the Battleplain?"

Cnaiür nodded. "This is why *cnamturu*, vigilance, is a leader's greatest virtue. The field must be continually read. The signs must be judged and rejudged. The *gobozkoy* must not be missed!"

"The moment of decision."

Cnaiür scowled, remembering that he'd mentioned the term in passing months ago, at the fateful Council with the Emperor on the Andiamine Heights. "The moment of decision," he repeated.

He continued staring at the coastal hills, watching the long line of faint infantry squares ascend the distant slopes. General Setpanares *had* withdrawn his horse ... But why?

Save the south, the Fanim relented on every front. What plagued him so?

Cnaiür glanced at Kellhus, saw his shining eyes study the distances the way they so often scrutinized souls. A gust cast his hair forward across his lower face.

"I fear," the Dûnyain said, "the moment has already passed."

⸺◦◦◦⸺

Between her cries, Serwë heard the peal of battlehorns.

"How?" she gasped.

She lay on her side, her face buried in the cushions where Kellhus had thrust it. He plumbed her from behind, his chest a furnace across her back, his hand holding her knee high. How *different* he felt!

"How what, sweet Serwë?"

He pressed deep and she moaned. "So different," she breathed. "You feel so different."

"For you, sweet Serwë ... For you ..."

For her! She ground against him, savoured his difference. "*Yessss,*" she hissed.

He rolled onto his back, pulling her onto him. He traced the ivory summit of her belly with his haloed left hand, then reached down to make her cry out. With his right, he yanked her head up by her hair, turned her so he could mutter in her ear. Never had he used her like this!

"Talk to me, sweet Serwë. Your voice is as sweet as your peach."

"W-what?" she panted. "What would you have me say?"

He reached down, lifted her buttocks from his hips—effortlessly, as though she were a coin. He began thrusting, slow and deep.

"Speak of me ..."

"Kellhhhhussss," she moaned. "I love you ... I *worship* you! I do, I do, I do!"

"And why, sweet Serwë?"

"Because you're the God incarnate! Because you've been sent!"

He fell absolutely still, knowing he'd delivered her to the humming brink.

She gasped for air upon him, felt his heart pound against her spine and through his member, thrum like a bowstring. Through fluttering lashes, she gazed up at the geometry of canvas creases, watched the lines bend and refract through joyous tears.

She encompassed him. To his foundation, he was hers! The mere thought made the air between her thighs thicken, until every draft seemed palpable, like something twitching.

She cried out. Such rapture! Such sweet rapture!

Sejenus ...

"And the Scylvendi," he purred, his voice moist with promise. "Why does he despise me so?"

"Because he fears you," she mumbled, squirming against him. "Because he knows you'll punish him!"

He began moving again, but with infernal wariness. She squealed, clenched her teeth, marvelled at the wonder of his difference. He even *smelled* different.

Like ... Like ...

His hand closed about the back of her neck ... How she loved this game!

"And why does he call me *Dûnyain?*"

"What do you mean?" Cnaiür said to the Dûnyain. "Nothing has been decided. Nothing!"

He tries to deceive me! To undermine me before these outlanders!

Kellhus regarded him with utter dispassion. "I've studied *The Book of Devices*, the Nansur manual describing the various personages and their signs in the Kianene order of—"

"As have I!"

The illuminated pages, anyway. Cnaiür couldn't read.

"Most of the devices lie too far to be seen," Kellhus continued, "but I've been able to infer the identity of most ..."

Lies! Lies! He fears I grow too powerful!

"How?" Cnaiür fairly cried.

"Differing shapes. The manual includes lists of each Sapatishah's client Grandees ... I simply counted."

Cnaiür swept out his hand as though beating the air of flies.

"Then who faces the Ainoni?"

"Overlooking the Meneanor, Imbeyan with the Grandees of Enathpaneah. Swarjuka of Jurisada occupies the remaining heights. Dunjoksha and the Grandees of Holy Amoteu hold the descending ground opposite the Ainoni right and Nansur left. The Shigeki, the centre. Even though Skauras's standard flies from Anwurat, I believe his Grandees, along with Ansacer and the other survivors of the Battleplain, contest the northern pastures. Those horsemen beyond the village, the ones about to descend upon Proyas, likely belong to Cuäxaji and the Grandees of Khemema. Others ride with him, auxiliaries or allies of some kind ... Likely the Khirgwi. Many ride camels."

Cnaiür stared incredulously at the man, his jaw working. "But that is impossible ..."

Where was Crown Prince Fanayal and the feared Coyauri? Where was dread Cinganjehoi and the famed Ten Thousand Grandees of Eumarna?

"It's fact," Kellhus said. "Only a fraction of Kian stands before us."

Cnaiür jerked his gaze yet again to the southern hills and knew, from heart to marrow, that the Dûnyain spoke true. Suddenly he saw the field through Kianene eyes. The fleet Grandees of Shigek and Gedea drawing the Tydonni and Galeoth ever farther west. The Shigeki multitude dying as they should, and fleeing as everyone knew they would. Anwurat, an immovable point threatening the Inrithi rear. Then the southern hills ...

"He shows us," Cnaiür murmured. "Skauras shows us ..."

"Two armies," Kellhus said without hesitation. "One defending, one concealed, the same as on the Battleplain."

Just then, Cnaiür saw the first long threads of Kianene horsemen descend the faraway southern slopes. Skirts of dust billowed behind them, obscuring the threads that followed. Even from here he could see the Ainoni infantrymen bracing ... Miles of them.

The Nansur and Thunyeri, meanwhile, had charged and hacked their way past the final embankments. The Shigeki ranks dissolved before their onslaught. Innumerable thousands already fled westward, pursued by

battle-crazed Thunyeri. The Inrithi officers and caste-nobles behind
Cnaiür and Kellhus broke into full-throated cheers.

The fools.

Skauras need not fight a battle of penetration along a single line. He
had speed and cohesion, *fira* and *utmurzu*. The Shigeki were simply a ruse,
a brilliantly monstrous sacrifice—a way to scatter the Inrithi across the
broken plains. Too much conviction, the wily old Sapatishah knew, could
be as deadly as too little.

A great ache filled Cnaiür's chest. Only Kellhus's strong grip saved him
the humiliation of falling to his knees.

Always the same ...

Never had he been so conflicted. Never had he been so confused.

Throughout the battle, while the others had gawked, exclaimed,
and pointed, General Martemus had watched the Scylvendi and
Prince Kellhus, straining to hear their banter. The barbarian wore a
harness of polished scale, the sleeves hacked short to reveal his many-
scarred forearms. A leather girdle set with iron plates strapped his
stomach and waist. A pointed Kianene battlecap, its silvering chipped
in innumerable places, protected his head. Long black hair whipped
about his shoulders.

Martemus could've recognized him from miles distant. He was
Scylvendi filth. As impressive as he'd found the man both in Council and
in the field, the outrage of a Scylvendi—a *Scylvendi!*—overseeing the
Holy War in battle was almost too much to bear. How could the others
not see the disgusting truth of his heritage? The man's every scar argued
his assassination! Martemus would've gladly—*gladly!*—sacrificed his life
to avenge those the savage had butchered.

Why, then, had Conphas ordered him to murder the *other* man standing next to the Scylvendi?

Because, General, he's a Cishaurim spy ...

But no spy could speak such words.

That's his sorcery! Always remember—

No! Not sorcery, truth!

As I said, General. That is his sorcery ...

Martemus watched, unmoved by the prattle around him.

But no matter how mortal his mission, he couldn't ignore glory in the field. No soldier could. Drawn by shouts of genuine triumph, Martemus turned to see the heathen's entire centre collapse. Across miles, from Anwurat to the southern hills, Shigeki formations crumbled and scattered westward, pursued by charging ranks of Nansur and Thunyeri footmen. Martemus cheered with the others. For a moment, he felt only pride for his countrymen, relief that victory had come at so slight a cost. Conphas had conquered again!

Then he glanced back at the Scylvendi.

He'd been a soldier too long not to recognize the stink of disaster—even beneath the perfume of apparent victory. Something had gone catastrophically wrong ...

The barbarian screamed at the Hornsman to signal the retreat. For a moment, those about Martemus could only stare in astonishment. Then everything erupted in tumult and confusion. The Tydonni thane, Ganrikki, accused the Scylvendi of treachery. Weapons were drawn, brandished. The deranged barbarian kept roaring at them to peer south, but nothing could be seen for the dust. Even still, the violence of the Scylvendi's protestations had unsettled many. Several began shouting for the Hornsman, including Prince Kellhus. But the Scylvendi had had enough. He barrelled through the astonished onlookers and leapt onto his horse. Within heartbeats, it seemed, he was racing southeast, trailing a long banderole of dust.

Then the horns sounded, cracking the air.

Others started running to their horses as well. Martemus turned back, looked to the three men Conphas had given him. One, the towering black-skinned Zeumi, met his eyes, nodded, then glanced past him to the Prince of Atrithau. They would run nowhere.

Unfortunate, Martemus thought. Running had been his first truly practical thought in a long time.

For a heartbeat, Prince Kellhus caught his look. His smile held such sorrow that Martemus nearly gasped. Then the Prophet turned to the distances seething beneath his feet.

Vast waves of Kianene horsemen, their corselets flashing from their many-coloured coats, charged down the slopes and slammed into the astonished Ainoni. The forward ranks hunched behind their shields, struggled to brace their long spears on the incline, while above them scimitars flashed in the morning sun. Dust swept across the arid slopes. Horns brayed in panic. The air thundered with shouts, rumbling hooves, and the pulse of Fanim drums. More heathen lancers crashed into and through the Ainoni ranks.

The tributary Sansori under Prince Garsahadutha were the first to break, scattering before none other than fierce Cinganjehoi himself, the famed Tiger of Eumarna. Within moments, it seemed, the Grandees of Eumarna were pounding into the rear of the forward phalanxes. Soon every phalanx on the Ainoni left, with the exception of the elite Kishyati under Palatine Soter, was either stranded or routed. Withdrawing in order, the Kishyati fought off charge after charge, purchasing precious time for the Ainoni knights below.

The whole world, it seemed, was obscured by wind-drawn curtains of dust. Stiff in their elaborate armour, the knights of Karyoti, Hinnant, and Moserothu, Antanamera, Eshkalas, and Eshganax, thundered up the slopes, charging through the thousands who fled. They met the Fanim in an ochre haze. Lances cracked and horses shrieked. Men cried out to the hidden heavens.

Swinging his great two-handed mace, Uranyanka, Palatine of humid Moserothu, upended heathen after heathen. Sepherathindor, Count-Palatine of Hinnant, led his painted knights on a rampage, hewing men like wood. Prince Garsahadutha and his Sansori stalwarts continued charging forward, searching for the holy standards of their kinsmen. The Kianene horsemen broke and fled before them, and the Ainoni bellowed in exultation.

The wind began to clear the haze.

Then Garsahadutha, several hundred paces ahead of his peers, stumbled into Crown Prince Fanayal and his Coyauri. Skewered through the eye socket, the Sansori Prince crashed from his saddle, and death came swirling down. Within moments, all six hundred and forty-three knights of Sansor had been either unhorsed or killed. Unable to see more than several paces, many of the Ainoni knights below simply charged the sound of battle—vanished into the saffron fog. Others milled about their barons and palatines, waiting for the wind.

Horse archers appeared on their flanks and to their rear.

Serwë huddled, wracked by sobs, struggling to cover herself with her blanket.

"What have I done?" she bawled. "What have I done to displease you?"

A haloed hand struck her, and she slammed against the carpets.

"I love you!" she shrieked. "*Kellhuuuus!*"

The Warrior-Prophet laughed.

"Tell me, sweet, sweet Serwë, what have I planned for the Holy War?"

The Swazond Standard leaned in a gust, the bolts of white billowing and snapping like sails. Martemus had already resolved to kick the abomination to the ground—afterward ... Everyone had abandoned the hillock, save himself, Prince Kellhus, and Conphas's three assassins.

Though more dust than ever plumed along the southern hills, Martemus could see what had to be Ainoni infantry fleeing the pale clouds. He'd long since lost sight of the Scylvendi across the broken pasture. To the west of the looming disaster, he could see the Columns of his countrymen reforming. Soon, Martemus knew, Conphas would have them marching double-time toward the marshes. The Nansur were old hands when it came to surviving Fanim catastrophes.

Prince Kellhus sat with his back to the four of them, his feet sole to sole and his palms flat upon his knees. Beyond him, men climbed and toppled from fortress walls, lines of knights galloped across dusty pastures, northmen axed hapless Shigeki to the ground ...

The Prophet seemed to be ... listening.

No. Bearing witness.

Not him, Martemus thought. *I cannot do this.*

The first of the assassins approached.

CHAPTER FIFTEEN

ANWURAT

Where the holy take men for fools, the mad take the world.
—PROTATHIS, *THE GOAT'S HEART*

Late Summer, 4111 Year-of-the-Tusk, Shigek

A dried riverbed creased the heart of the plain, and for a time Cnaiür raced through it, climbing out only when the course began winding like an old man's veins. He jerked his black to a stamping halt on the bank. The coastal hills piled above him, their heights and seaward reaches still skirted in chalklike dust. To the west, the remaining Ainoni phalanxes were withdrawing down the slopes. To the east, innumerable thousands sprinted across the broken pasture. Not far, on a small knoll, he saw a clot of infantrymen dressed in long black leather kilts stitched with iron rings, but without helms or weapons. Some sat, others stood, stripping off their armour. Save those who wept, all watched the shrouded hills with a look of stunned horror.

Where were the Ainoni knights?

To the extreme east, where the turquoise and aquamarine band of the Meneanor disappeared behind the dun foundations of the hills, he saw a great cataract of Kianene horsemen spill across the strand. He need not see their devices to know: Cinganjehoi and the Grandees of Eumarna, pounding across uncontested ground ...

Where were the reserves? Gotian and his Shrial Knights, Gaidekki, Werijen Greatheart, Athjeäri, and the others?

Cnaiür felt a sharp pang in his throat. He clenched his teeth.

It's happening again ...

Kiyuth.

Only this time *he* was Xunnurit. *He* was the arrogant mule!

He pinched sweat from his eyes, watched the Fanim gallop behind a screen of distant scrub and stunted trees—an endless tide ...

The encampment. They ride for the encampment ...

With a yell he spurred his horse to the east.

Serwë.

Masses of warring men animated the horizon, crashing into stubborn ranks, churning in melee. The air didn't so much thunder as *hiss* with the sound of distant battle, like a sea heard through a conch shell, Martemus thought—an angry sea. Winded, he watched the first of Conphas's assassins stride up behind Prince Kellhus, raise his short-sword ...

There was an impossible moment—a sharp intake of breath.

The Prophet simply turned and caught the descending blade between his thumb and forefinger. "No," he said, then swept around, knocking the man to the turf with an unbelievable kick. Somehow the assassin's sword found its way into his left hand. Still crouched, the Prophet drove it down through the assassin's throat, nailing him to the turf.

A mere heartbeat had passed.

The second Nansur assassin rushed forward, striking. Another kick from a crouch, and the man's head snapped backward, his blade flew from senseless fingers. He slumped to the earth like a cast-off robe—obviously dead.

The Zeumi sword-dancer lowered his great tulwar and laughed.

"A civilized man," he said, his voice deep.

Without warning, he sent the tulwar whooshing through the air around him. Sunlight flashed as though from the silvered spokes of a chariot wheel.

Now standing, the Prophet drew his strange, long-pommelled sword from his shoulder sheath. Holding it in his right hand, he lowered its tip to the ground before his booted feet. He flicked a clot of dirt into the sword-dancer's eyes. The sword-dancer stumbled back, cursing. The Prophet lunged, buried his sword point deep into the assassin's palate. He guided the towering corpse to the earth.

He stood alone against a vista of strife and woe, his beard and hair boiling in the wind. He turned to Martemus, stepped over the sword-dancer's body ...

Illuminated by the morning sun. A striding vision. A walking aspect ...

Something too terrible. Too bright.

The General stumbled backward, struggled to draw his sword.

"Martemus," the vision said. It reached out and clasped the wrist of his frantic sword arm.

"Prophet," Martemus gasped.

The vision smiled, saying: "Skauras knows the Scylvendi leads us. He's seen the Swazond Standard ..."

General Martemus stared, uncomprehending.

The Warrior-Prophet turned, nodded toward the sweeping landscape.

No recognizable lines remained. Martemus saw Proyas and his Conriyan knights first, stranded about the mud-brick warren of the distant village. Erupting from the shadow of the orchards, several thousand Kianene horsemen swept about their flank, led by the triangular standard of Cuäxaji, the Sapatishah of Khemema. The Conriyans were doomed, Martemus thought, but otherwise he didn't understand what the Warrior-Prophet meant ... Then he glanced toward Anwurat.

"Khirgwi," the General murmured. Thousands of them, mounted on tall loping camels, plowing into the hastily drawn ranks of Conriyan infantry, spilling around their flanks, racing toward the hillock, toward the Swazond Standard ...

Toward them.

Their unnerving, ululating war cries permeated the din.

"We must flee!" he cried.

"No," the Warrior-Prophet said. "The Swazond Standard cannot fall."

"But it will!" Martemus exclaimed. "It already has!"

The Warrior-Prophet smiled, and his eyes glittered with something fierce and unconquerable. *"Conviction,* General Martemus ..." He gripped his shoulder with a haloed hand.

"War is conviction."

Confusion and terror ruled the hearts of the Ainoni knights. Disoriented in the dust, they hailed one another, trying to determine some course of action. Cohorts of fleet archers swept about them, shooting their caparisoned horses out from beneath him. Knights cursed and hunched behind arrow-studded shields. Every time Uranyanka, Sepherathindor, and the others charged, the Kianene scattered, outdistanced them while sending more knights crashing into the sun-baked turf. Many of the Ainoni lost their way and were stranded, harassed from all sides. Kusjeter, the Count-Palatine of Gekas, blundered onto the summit of the slopes and found himself trapped between the spiked earthworks that had defeated the initial Ainoni charges and the ruthless lances of the Coyauri below. Time and again he fought off the elite Kianene cavalrymen, only to be unhorsed and taken for dead by his own men. His knights panicked, and he was trampled in their flight. Death came swirling down ...

Meanwhile the Sapatishah of Eumarna, Cinganjehoi, charged across the pastures below. Most of his Grandees fanned northward, eager to visit ruin on the Inrithi encampment. The Tiger himself struck westward, riding hard with his household through fields of bolting Ainoni infantrymen. He stormed the command of General Setpanares, overrunning it. The General himself was killed, but Chepheramunni, the King-Regent of High Ainon, managed a miraculous escape.

Far to the northwest, the command of Cnaiür urs Skiötha, Battlemaster of the Holy War, dissolved in confusion and accusations of treachery. The masses of Shigeki conscripts composing Skauras's centre had utterly folded before the combined might of the Nansur, Thunyeri, and the flanking charge of Proyas and his Conriyan knights. Believing the Holy War victorious, the Inrithi had dashed forward in pursuit, abandoning their formations. The battle line broke into disordered masses separated by glaring expanses of open pasture. Many actually fell to their knees on the parched turf, crying out thanks to the God. Very few heard the horns signalling a

general retreat, largely because very few horns carried the call. Most trumpeters had refused to believe the command was real.

Not once did the thundering drums of the heathen falter.

The Grandees of Khemema and tens of thousands of camel-mounted
Khirgwi, ferocious tribesmen from the southern deserts, materialized
out of the masses of fleeing Shigeki and charged headlong into the
scattered Men of the Tusk. Cut off from his infantry, Proyas withdrew
to the mud-brick alleys of a nearby village, crying out to both the God
and his men. Falling into shield-wall circles across the pastures, the
Thunyeri fought with stubborn astonishment, shocked to encounter an
enemy whose fury matched their own. Prince Skaiyelt desperately
called for his Earls and their knights, but they were frustrated by the
embankments.

One great battle had become dozens of lesser ones—more desperate
and far more dreadful. Everywhere the Great Names looked, cohorts of
Fanim rode hard across the open pasture. Where the heathen outnumbered, they charged and overwhelmed. Where they could not grapple,
they circled and harried with deadly archery.

Overcome by dismay, many knights charged alone, only to be unhorsed
by arrows and trampled into the dust.

⸎

Cnaiür rode hard, cursing himself for losing his way among the endless
alleys and avenues of the camp. He reined to a halt in an enclosure of
heavy-framed Galeoth tents, searched the northern distances for the
distinctive peaks of the round tents favoured by the Conriyans. From
nowhere it seemed, three woman dashed northward across the enclosure,
then vanished past the tents on the far side. A moment later, another
followed, black-haired, screaming something unintelligible in some
Ketyai tongue. He looked to the south, saw dozens of plumes of black
smoke. The wind faltered for a moment, and the surrounding canvas fell
silent.

Cnaiür glimpsed a blue surcoat abandoned next to a smoking firepit.
Someone had been stitching a red tusk across its breast ...

He heard screams—thousands of them.

Where was she?

He knew what was happening, and more importantly, he knew *how* it would happen. The first fires had been set as a signal to those Inrithi in the field—to convince them they were truly overthrown. Otherwise the encampment would be closely inventoried before it was destroyed. Even now, Kianene would be encircling the camp, loath to lose any plunder, especially the kind that wriggled and screamed. If he didn't find Serwë soon ...

He spurred off to the northeast.

Yanking his black tight around a pavilion panelled with embroidered animal totems, he broke along a winding corridor, saw three Kianene sitting upon their caparisoned mounts. They turned at the sound of his approach, but at once looked away, as though mistaking him for one of their own. They seemed to be arguing. Drawing his broadsword, Cnaiür spurred to a gallop. He killed two on his first pass. Though their orange-coated comrade had called out at the last instant, they hadn't so much as looked at him. Cnaiür reined to a halt, wheeled to make a second pass, but the remaining Fanim fled. Cnaiür ignored him and struck due east, at last recognizing—or so he thought—where he stood in the encampment.

A skin-pimpling shriek, no more than a hundred paces away, brought him to a momentary trot. Standing in his stirrups, he caught fleeting glimpses of figures dashing between crowded shelters. More screams rifled the air, breathless and very near. Suddenly a horde of camp-followers burst sprinting from between the panoply of surrounding tents and pavilions. Wives, whores, slaves, scribes, and priests, either crying or blank-faced, simply rushing where everyone else seemed to rush. Some screamed at the sight of him and scrambled either to the left or the right. Others ignored him, either realizing he wasn't Fanim or knowing he could only strike so many. After a moment their numbers thinned. The young and the hale became the old and the infirm. Cnaiür glimpsed Cumor, the aging high priest of Gilgaöl, urged forward by his adepts. He saw dozens of frantic mothers hauling terrified children. Some distance away, a group of twenty or so bandaged warriors—Galeoth by the look of them—had abandoned their flight and now prepared to make a stand. They started singing ...

Cnaiür heard a growing chorus of harsh and triumphant cries, the snort and rumble of horses ...

He reined to a halt, drew his broadsword.

Then he saw them, jostling and barrelling among the tents, looking for a moment like a host wading through crashing surf. The Kianene of Eumarna ...

Cnaiür looked down, startled. A young woman, her leg slicked in blood, an infant strapped to her back, clutched his knee, beseeching him in some unknown tongue. He raised his boot to kick her, then unaccountably lowered it. He leaned forward and hoisted her before him onto his saddle. She fairly shrieked tears. He wheeled his black around and spurred after the fleeing camp-followers.

He heard an arrow buzz by his ear.

His golden hair fanned in the wind. His white samite robe billowed.

"Keep down!" the Prophet commanded.

But Martemus could only stand dumbfounded. The fields beneath seethed with dust and shadowy files of Khirgwi. Before them, the Warrior-Prophet jerked first one shoulder back, then the other. He ducked his head, swayed back from the waist, crouched, then bounced upright. It was a curious dance, at once random and premeditated, leisurely and breathtakingly quick ... It wasn't until one struck Martemus in the thigh that he realized the Prophet danced about the path of arrows.

The General fell to the ground, clutching his leg. The whole world howled, clamoured.

Through tears of pain he glimpsed the Swazond Standard against the sun's flashing glare.

Sweet Sejenus. I'm going to die.

"Run!" he cried. "You must run!"

His black snorted spittle, gasped, and screamed. Tent after tent whisked by, canvas stained and striped, leather painted, tusks and more tusks. The nameless woman in his arms trembled, tried vainly to look at her baby. The Kianene thundered ever closer, galloping in files down the narrow alleys, fanning across the rare openings. He could hear them trade shouts, cry out tactics. "*Skafadi!*" they cried. "*Jara til Skafadi!*" Soon many were pounding along parallel alleyways. Twice he had to crush the woman and her child against the neck of his horse as arrows hissed about them.

He spurred more blood from his black's flanks. He heard screams, realized he'd overtaken the mass of fleeing camp-followers. Suddenly everywhere he looked he saw frantic, hobbling men, wailing mothers, and ashen-faced children. He jerked his mount to the left, knowing the Kianene followed him. He was the famed Skafadi Captain who rode with the idolaters. Every captive he'd interrogated had heard of him. He broke into one of the immense squares the Nansur used for drills, and his black leapt forward with renewed fury. He drew his bow, notched a shaft, and killed the nearest Kianene pounding through the dust behind him. His second shaft found the neck of the horse following, and an entire cluster of Fanim toppled in a plume of dust.

"*Zirkirtaaaaa!*" he howled.

The woman shrieked in terror. He glanced forward, saw dozens of Fanim horsemen streaming into the western entrance of the field.

Fucking Kianene.

He brought his ailing black about and spurred toward the northern entrance, thanking the Nansur and their slavish devotion to the compass. The sky rang with distant screams and raw-throated shouts of "*Ût-ût-ût-ût!*" The nameless woman wept in terror.

Nansur barrack tents hedged the north like a row of filed teeth. The gap between them bounced nearer, nearer. The woman alternately looked forward, then yanked her head backward to the Kianene—as did, absurdly, her black-haired infant. Strange, Cnaiür thought, the way infants knew when to be calm. Suddenly Fanim horsemen erupted through the northern entrance as well. He swerved to the right, galloped along the airy white tents, searching for a way to barge between. When he saw none, he raced for the corner. More and more Kianene thundered through the eastern entrance, fanning across the field. Those behind pounded nearer. Several more arrows whisked through the air about them. He wheeled his black about, knocked the woman face first onto the dusty turf. The babe finally started screeching. He tossed her a knife—to cut through canvas …

The air thrummed with hooves and heathen shouts.

"Run!" he barked at her. "*Run!*"

Veils of dust swept over him.

He turned, laughing.

Drawing his broadsword, he ducked a sweeping scimitar, then jabbed his assailant in the armpit. He swept his sword about and shattered the blade of the next, splitting the man's cheek. When the fool reached up, Cnaiür punched through his silvered corselet. Blood fountained like wine from a punctured skin. He caught the shield of the next, swinging his sword like a mace. The man toppled backward over his horse's rump, somehow landed on his hands and knees. His helm bounced from his head, between stamping hooves. Flipping his grip, Cnaiür stabbed down through the back of his skull.

He stood in his stirrups, swung the blood from his blade into the faces of the astonished Kianene.

"Who?" he roared in his sacred tongue.

He hacked at the riderless horses barring him from his foe. One went down thrashing. Another screamed and bucked into the knotted heathen ranks.

"I am Cnaiür urs Skiötha," he bellowed, "most violent of all men!"

His heaving black stepped forward.

"I bear your fathers and your brothers upon my arms!"

Heathen eyes flashed white from the shadows of their silvered helms. Several cried out.

"*Who,*" Cnaiür roared, so fiercely all his skin seemed throat, "*will murder me?*"

A piercing, feminine cry. Cnaiür glanced back, saw the nameless woman swaying at the entrance of the nearest tent. She gripped the knife he'd thrown her, gestured with it for him to follow. For an instant, it seemed he'd always known her, that they'd been lovers for long years. He saw sunlight flash through the far side of the tent where she'd cut open the canvas. Then he glimpsed a shadow from above, heard something not quite ...

Several Kianene cried out—a different terror.

Cnaiür thrust his left hand beneath his girdle, clutched tight his father's Trinket.

For an instant he met the woman's wide uncomprehending eyes, and over her shoulder, those of her baby boy as well ... Somehow he knew that now—that he was a son.

He tried to cry out.

They became shadows in a cataract of shimmering flame.

⸺ ⧟ ⸺

One space.

And the crossings were infinite.

Kellhus had been five when he'd first set foot outside Ishuäl. Pragma Uän had gathered him and the others his age, bid them all hang onto a long rope. Then without explanation he led them down the terraces, out the Fallow Gate, and into the forest, stopping only when he reached a grove of mighty oaks. He allowed them to wander for a time—to sensitize themselves, Kellhus now knew. To the chattering of one hundred and seventeen birds. To the smells of moss along bark, of humus wheezing beneath little sandals. To the colours and the shapes: white bands of sunlight against copper gloom, black roots.

But for all this roaring and remarkable newness, Kellhus could think of nothing save the Pragma. In fact, he fairly trembled with anticipation. Everyone had seen Pragma Uän with the older boys. Everyone knew he taught what the older boys called the ways of limb ...

Of battle.

"What do you see?" the old man finally asked, looking to the canopy above them.

There were many eager answers. Leaves. Branches. Sun.

But Kellhus saw more. He noticed the dead limbs, the scrum of competing branch and twig. He saw slender trees, mere striplings, ailing in the shadow of giants.

"Conflict," he said.

"And how is that, young Kellhus?"

Terror and exultation—the passions of a child. "The tr-trees, Pragma," he stammered. "They war for ... for *space*."

"Indeed," Pragma Uän replied, his manner devoid of anything save confirmation. "And this, children, is what I shall teach you. How to be a tree. How to war for space ..."

"But trees don't move," another said.

"They move," the Pragma replied, "but they are slow. A tree's heart beats but once every spring, so it must war in all directions at once. It must branch and branch until it obscures the sky. But you, your hearts beat many, many times, you need only war in one direction at a time. This is how men seize space."

As old as he was, the Pragma seemed to pop to his feet. He brandished a stick.

"Come," he said, "all of you. Try to touch my knees."

And Kellhus rushed with the others through the dappled sunlight. He squealed with frustration and delight each time the stick thwacked or poked him back. He watched in wonder as the old man danced and swirled, sent children flopping onto their rumps or rolling like badgers through the leaves. Not one touched his legs. Not one so much as stepped into the circle described by his stick.

Pragma Uän had been a triumphant tree. The absolute owner of one space.

Wrapped in tattered brown cloth, bearing shields of lacquered camel hides, the Khirgwi beat their lurching camels forward, brandished their wild scimitars. The air screamed with their ululations.

Kellhus raised his Dûnyain steel.

They laughed and sneered. Desert dark faces, so certain ...

They came galloping toward the circle described by his sword.

Cnaiür kicked at his saddle and the blasted hulk of his horse. He pushed himself from the ash, blinked stinging smoke from his eyes. Ringing. Aside from smoke and the stink of scorched meat, the whole world was ringing. He could hear nothing else.

He found the burnt husks that had been the nameless woman and her child. He retrieved his knife, holding it gingerly by its charred grip.

It burned and did not burn, in the strange way sorcerous heat seeped into the real.

He began walking northward, passing among the sagging, curse-embroidered pavilions of the Ainoni. Pictogram banners fluttered in the wind. Behind him, Scarlet Schoolmen strode across the sky. Pillars of fire whooshed soundlessly. Lightning sheeted the distances. It seemed that men should shriek.

And he thought, *Serwë* ...

People, elated, terrified, bewildered, crowded about him. Though their mouths opened and their tongues flapped against their teeth, Cnaiür heard only ringing. He pressed them aside with hollow arms, continued walking.

Something ached in his left hand. He opened it, saw his father's Chorae. Dull even in sunlight, cluttered with senseless script, a grimy iron eyeball. Twice it had saved him.

He pressed it back beneath his girdle.

Then he heard the crack of lightning. The ringing faded into a piercing whine—almost inaudible. He paused, closed his eyes. Screams and shouts, this one far, that one near, very near. They etched the distances, sweeping out to the horizon of his hearing, finally vanishing in the ambient roar of battle and sea ...

After a time he found Proyas's elaborate pavilion occupying a small knoll. How weathered it now looked, he thought, and sadness welled through him. Everything seemed so tired.

He found the old pavilion he'd shared with Kellhus nearby, creaking and flapping in the wind. A kettle sat next to the blackened pit. Smoke spiralled across the ground, raced between neighbouring tents.

Cnaiür's heart hammered. Had she gathered with the other followers to watch the battle from the southwestern edge of the encampment? Had the Kianene taken her? A beauty such as hers was sure to be taken, pregnant or not. She was a plaything of princes. An extraordinary gift!

A prize!

The sound of her voice made him jump. A shriek ...

For a moment he stood dumbfounded, unable to move. He heard a masculine voice, soft, cajoling, and yet somehow insanely cruel ...

The ground dipped at Cnaiür's feet. He stumbled backward. One step. Two. His skin prickled to the point of stinging.

The Dûnyain.

"Please!" Serwë screamed. "*Pleasssse!*"

The Dûnyain!

How?

Cnaiür crept forward. His ribs seemed rock. He couldn't breathe! The knife trembled in his hand. He reached out, used the dagger's shaking tip to part the canvas flap.

The interior was too dark to see at first. He glimpsed shadows, heard Serwë's hitching sobs ...

Then he saw her, kneeling naked before a towering shadow. One eye swelled shut, blood pulsing from her scalp and nose, sheeting her neck and her breasts.

What?

Without thinking, Cnaiür slipped into the gloom of the pavilion. The air reeked of foul rutting. The Dûnyain whirled, as naked as Serwë, a bloody hand clamped about his engorged member.

"The Scylvendi," Kellhus drawled, his eyes blazing with lurid rapture. "I didn't smell you."

Cnaiür struck at his heart. Somehow the bloody hand flickered up, grazed his wrist. The knife dug deep just below the Dûnyain's collar bone.

Kellhus staggered back, raised his face to the bellied canvas, and screamed what seemed a hundred screams, a hundred voices bound to one inhuman throat. And Cnaiür saw his face *open*, as though the joints of his mouth were legion and ran from his scalp to his neck. Through steepled features, he saw lidless eyes, gums without lips ...

The thing struck him, and he fell to one knee. He yanked his broadsword clear.

But it had vanished through the flap, leaping like some kind of beast.

<hr>

With their horses dying beneath them, the scattered masses of Ainoni knights soon had no choice but to stand their ground. More and more, the Kianene rode howling into their midst, making targets of their white-painted faces in the sunny murk. Blood clotted luxurious square-cut beards. Pictogram standards were toppled and trampled. Dust transformed sweat into grime. Seriously wounded, Sepherathindor was carried from the forward ranks, where he "laughed with Sarothesser," as all Ainoni caste-nobles strove to do when certain of death.

Some, like Galgota, Palatine of Eshganax, charged down the slopes to escape, abandoning those kinsmen and clients who'd been unhorsed. Some, like cruel Zursodda, bled his people with reckless counter-attacks until scarcely a mounted man remained. But others, like hard-hearted Uranyanka, or fair Chinjosa, the Count-Palatine of Antanamera, simply awaited each heathen onslaught. They bellowed encouragement to their men, disputed every dusty step. Again and again the Kianene charged. Horses screamed. Lances cracked. Men yelled and wailed. Scimitars and longswords rang across the slopes. And each time the Fanim reeled back, astounded by these defeated men who refused to be defeated.

To the northwest, the Khirgwi assaulted the Inrithi with relentless and sometimes deranged fury. Many actually leapt from their taller camels to tackle dumbstruck knights from their saddles. Kushigas, the Conriyan Palatine of Annand, was killed this way, as was Inskarra, the Thunyeri Earl of Skagwa. Proyas was encircled, as were thousands of Thunyeri behind their shield-walls. The Khirgwi swept about Anwurat and descended on the fortress's Conriyan besiegers, putting them to rout. And they charged the rambling hillock where the Battlemaster had planted his Swazond Standard.

The Grandees of Eumarna, meanwhile, stormed through the winding alleys and long avenues of the Inrithi encampment, setting tent and pavilion alight, cutting down priests, dragging screaming wives to the ground and violating them. At the sight of smoke pluming from the distant camp, many men in Skauras's staff fell to their knees and wept, giving praise to the Solitary God. Several hailed the Sapatishah, kissing the ground near his feet.

Then glittering lights filled the eastern sky. Cinganjehoi's glorious horsemen had blundered upon the Scarlet Spires ... And catastrophe.

Those who survived the Schoolmen's initial assault fled in their thousands, most along the broad beaches along the Meneanor, where they were caught by Grandmaster Gotian, Earl Cerjulla, and Earl Athjeäri, leading the Holy War's reserves. Some nine thousand Inrithi knights descended upon them, hacking them to the sand, driving them back into the crashing surf. Very few escaped.

The Imperial Kidruhil, meanwhile, broke the bristling collar about the knights of High Ainon. Imbeyan and the Grandees of Enathpaneah were driven back. For the first time there was pause in what would be called the Battle of the Slopes. The dust began to clear ... When the situation on the pastures below became clear, shouts of exultation broke from the long and ragged lines of Ainoni knights. With the Kidruhil, they charged as one toward the heights.

To the north, the ferocious momentum of the Khirgwi was first blunted by the miraculous stand of Prince Kellhus of Atrithau beneath the Swazond Standard, then stopped altogether by the flanking charges of the black-armoured Auglish and Ingraulish knights of Earl Goken and Earl Ganbrota.

Then the drums of the Fanim fell silent. Far to the northwest, Prince Saubon and Earl Gothyelk had finally broken the Grandees of Shigek and Gedea, whom they chased along the banks of the Sempis. Though vastly outnumbered, Earl Finaöl and his Canutish knights charged the Padirajic Guardsmen protecting the sacred drums. Earl Finaöl himself was speared in the armpit, but his kinsmen won through, and cut down the fleeing drummers. Soon breathless Galeoth and Tydonni footmen were chasing women and slaves through the sprawling Kianene encampment.

The great Fanim host disintegrated. Crown Prince Fanayal and his Coyauri fled due south, pursued by the Kidruhil along the never-ending beaches. Imbeyan surrendered the heights to the spattered Ainoni and attempted to withdraw through the hills. But Ikurei Conphas had anticipated him, and he was forced to flee with a handful of householders while his Grandees bled themselves charging the hard-bitten veterans of the Selial Column. Though General Bogras was killed by a stray Kianene arrow, the Nansur did not break, and the Enathpaneans were cut down to a man. The Khirgwi fled southwest, pursued by the iron men into the trackless desert.

Hundreds of Inrithi would be lost for following the tribesmen too far.

Cnaiür saw his charred knife on the mats.

Clutching a bloodstained blanket, Serwë staggered after Kellhus, screaming like a lunatic. When Cnaiür restrained her, she began clawing at his eyes. He pushed her to the ground.

"He neeeeds me," she wailed. *"He's hurt!"*

"It wasn't him," Cnaiür murmured.

"You killed him! You killed him!"

"It wasn't him!"

"You're sick! You're mad!"

Somehow the old rage swamped his disbelief. He grabbed her by the arm and wrenched her through the flaps. "I'm taking you! You're my prize!"

"You're mad!" she shrieked. "He's told me everything about you! Everything!"

He struck her to the ground.

"What has he said?"

She wiped blood from her lip, and for the first time didn't seem afraid. "Why you beat me. Why your thoughts never stray far from me, but return, always return to me in fury. He's told me *everything!*"

Something trembled through him. He raised his fist but his fingers would not clench.

"What has he said?"

"That I'm nothing but a sign, a token. That you strike not me, but yourself!"

"I will strangle you! I will snap your neck like a cat's! I will beat blood from your womb!"

"Then do it!" she shrieked. "Do it, and be done with it!"

"You are my prize! My prize! To do with as I please!"

"No! No! I'm not your prize! I'm your shame! He told me this!"

"Shame? What shame? What has he said?"

"That you beat me for surrendering as you surrendered! For fucking him the way *you fucked his father!*"

She still lay on the ground, legs askew. So beautiful. Even beaten and broken. How could anything human be so beautiful?

"What has he said?" he asked blankly.

He. The Dûnyain.

She was sobbing now. Somehow the knife had appeared in her hands. She held it to her throat, and he could see the perfect curve of her neck reflected. He glimpsed the single swazond upon her forearm.

She has killed!

"You're mad!" she wept. "I'll kill myself! I'll kill myself! I'm not your prize! I'm his! HIS!"

Serwë ...

Her fist hooked inward. The blade parted flesh.

But somehow he'd captured her wrist. He wrenched the knife from her hand.

He left her weeping outside the Dûnyain's pavilion. He stared out over the trackless Meneanor as he wandered between the tents, through the growing crowds of jubilant Inrithi.

So unnatural, he thought, the sea …

⊗∽∾⊗

When Conphas found Martemus, the sun was an orb smouldering in the cloudless skies of the west, gold across pale blue—colours stamped into every man's heart. With a small cadre of bodyguards and officers, the Exalt-General had ridden to the hillock where the accursed Scylvendi had established his command. On the summit, he found the General sitting cross-legged beneath the Scylvendi's leaning standard, surrounded by ever widening circles of Khirgwi dead. The man stared at the sunset as though he hoped to go blind. He had removed his helmet, and his short, silvered hair fluttered in the breeze. The man looked at once younger, Conphas thought, and yet more fatherly without his helmet.

Conphas dismissed his entourage, then dismounted. Without a word he strode to the General, drew his longsword, then hacked at the Swazond Standard's wooden pole. Once, twice … With a crack, the wind bore the obscene banner slowly down.

Satisfied, Conphas stood over his wayward General, gazing out to the sunset as though to share in whatever nonsense Martemus thought he saw.

"He's not dead," Martemus said.

"Pity."

Martemus said nothing.

"Do you remember," Conphas asked, "that time we rode across the fields of dead Scylvendi after Kiyuth?"

Martemus's eyes flickered to him. He nodded.

"Do you recall what I said to you?"

"You said war was intellect."

"Are you a casualty of that war, Martemus?"

The sturdy General frowned, pursed his lips. He shook his head. "No."

"I worry that you are, Martemus."

Martemus turned away from the sun and studied him with pinched eyes. "I worried too … But no longer."

"No longer … Why so, Martemus?"

"I watched," the General said. "I saw him kill all these heathen. He killed and he killed until they fled in terror." Martemus turned back to the sunset. "He's not human."

"Neither was Skeaös," Conphas replied.

Martemus looked to his callused palms.

"I am a practical man, Lord Exalt-General."

Conphas studied the sun-burnished carnage, the open mouths and unclosed eyes, the hands like good-luck monkey paws. He followed the smoke pluming from Anwurat—not so far away. Not so far.

He gazed back into Martemus's sun. There was such a difference, he thought, between the beauty that illuminated, and the beauty that was illuminated.

"You are at that, Martemus. You are at that."

Skauras ab Nalajan had dismissed his subordinates, servants, and slaves, the long train of men that defined any station of power, and sat alone at a polished mahogany table drinking Shigeki wine. For the first time, it seemed, he truly tasted the sweetness of those things he had lost.

Though old, the Sapatishah-Governor was still hale. His white hair, oiled to his scalp in the Kianene fashion, was as thick as that of any younger man. He had a distinguished face, made severe and wise by his long moustaches and thin braided beard. His eyes glittered dark beneath a brooding brow.

He sat in a high turret room of Anwurat's citadel. Through the narrow window he could hear the sounds of desperate battle below, the voices of beloved friends and followers crying out.

Though he was a pious man, Skauras had committed many wicked acts in his life—wicked acts were ever the inescapable accessories of power. He contemplated them with regret and pined for a simpler life, one with fewer pleasures, surely, but with fewer burdens as well. Certainly nothing so crushing as this ...

I have doomed my people ... my faith.

It had been a good plan, he reflected. Give the idolaters the illusion of a single fixed line. Convince them he would fight their battle. Draw their right into the north. Break their line, not through punishing and futile charges, but by *breaking*—or appearing to—in the centre. Then crush their left with Cinganjehoi and Fanayal.

How glorious it should have been.

Who could have guessed such a plan? Who could have anticipated him?

Probably Conphas.

Old enemy. Old friend—if such a man could be anyone's friend.

Skauras reached beneath his jackal-embroidered coat and withdrew the parchment the Nansur Emperor had sent him. For months it had pressed against his breast, and now, after the day's disaster, it was perhaps the only remaining hope of stopping the idolaters. Sweat had rounded it to the curve of his body, had rendered it cloth-soft. The word of Ikurei Xerius III, the Emperor of Nansur.

Old foe. Old friend.

Skauras didn't read it. He didn't need to. But the idolaters—they must never read it.

He placed its corner in the brilliant teardrop of his lamp. Watched it curl and ignite. Watched the spindly threads of smoke rise before they were yanked out the window.

By the Solitary God, it was still daylight!

"And they looked up, and saw that lo, the day had not gone, and that their shame lay open, for all to see ..."

The Prophet's words. May he grant them mercy.

He let the parchment go as fluttering wings of flame engulfed it. It thrashed feebly, like a living thing. The finish of the table blistered and blackened beneath.

A fitting mark, the Sapatishah-Governor supposed. A hint. A small oracle to future doom.

Skauras drank more wine. Already the idolaters were ramming the door. Quick, deadly men.

Are we all dead? he wondered.

No. Only me.

In the depths of his final, most pious prayer to the Solitary God, he didn't hear the fibrous snapping of wood. Only the final crash and the sound of kindling skating across the tiled floor told him that the time had come to draw his sword.

He turned to face the rush of strapping, battle-crazed infidels.

It would be a short battle.

She awoke with her head cradled in his lap. He wiped her cheeks and brow with a wetted cloth. His eyes glittered with tears in the lantern light.

"The baby?" she gasped.

Kellhus closed his eyes and nodded. "Is fine."

She smiled and began weeping. "Why? How have I angered you?"

"It wasn't me, Serwë."

"But it was you! I saw you!"

"No ... You saw a demon. A counterfeit with my face ..."

And suddenly she *knew*. What had been familiar became alien. What had been inexplicable became clear.

A demon visited me! A demon ...

She looked to him. More hot tears spilled across her cheeks. How long could she cry?

But I ... He ...

Kellhus blinked slowly. *He took you.*

She gagged. She rolled her cheek onto his thigh. Convulsions wracked her, but no vomit would come.

"I ..." she sobbed. "I ..."

"You were faithful."

She turned to him, her face crumpling.

But it wasn't you!

"You were deceived. You were faithful."

He wiped at her tears, and she glimpsed blood on his cloth. They lay silently for a time, simply staring into each other's eyes. She felt her stinging skin soothed, her hurts fade into a strange buzzing ache. How long, she wondered, could she stare into those eyes? How long could her heart bask in their all-knowing sight?

Forever?

Yes, forever.

"The Scylvendi came," she finally said. "He tried to take me."

"I know," Kellhus replied. "I told him he could."

And somehow she knew this too.

But why?

He smiled glory.

"Because I knew you wouldn't let him."

───────── ⊂⊃⊃⊃ ─────────

How much have they learned?

In the lonely light of a single lantern, Kellhus talked to Serwë in cooing tones, matching her rhythms, heartbeat for heartbeat, breath for breath. With a patience no world-born man could fathom, he slowly lured her into the trance the Dûnyain called the Whelming, to the place where voice could overwrite voice. Eliciting a long string of automatic responses, he reviewed her interrogation at the hands of the skin-spy. Then he gradually scraped the thing's assault from the parchment of her soul. Come morning, she would awaken puzzled by her cuts and bruises, nothing more. Come morning, she would awaken cleansed.

Afterward, he pressed through the raucous and celebratory alleys of the encampment, walking toward the Meneanor, toward the Scylvendi's seaside camp. He ignored all those who hailed him, adopting an air of brooding distraction that wasn't so far from the truth ... Those who persisted shrank from his angry glare.

He had one task remaining.

Of all his studies, none had been so deep or so perilous as the Scylvendi. There was the man's pride, which like Proyas and the other Great Names had made him exceedingly sensitive to relations of dominance. And there was his preternatural intelligence, his ability not only to grasp and penetrate but to reflect on the movements of his own soul— to ask after the origins of his own thoughts.

But more than anything there was his *knowledge*—his knowledge of the Dûnyain. Moënghus had yielded too much truth in his effort to escape the Utemot those many years ago. He'd underestimated what Cnaiür would make of the fragments he'd revealed. Through his obsessive rehearsal of the events surrounding his father's death, the plainsman had come to many troubling conclusions. And now, of all world-born men, he alone knew the truth of the Dûnyain. Of all world-born men, Cnaiür urs Skiötha was awake ...

Which was why he had to die.

Almost to a man, the Men of Eärwa adhered without thought or knowledge to the customs of their people. A Conriyan didn't shave because bare cheeks were effeminate. A Nansur didn't wear leggings because they were crude. A Tydonni didn't consort with dark-skinned peoples—or picks, as they called them—because they were polluted. For world-born men, such customs simply *were*. They gave precious food to statues of dead stone. They kissed the knees of weaker men. They lived in terror of their wanton hearts. They each thought themselves the absolute measure of all others. They felt shame, disgust, esteem, reverence ...

And they never asked why.

Not so with Cnaiür. Where others adhered out of ignorance of the alternatives, he was continually forced to choose, and more importantly, to *affirm* one thought from the infinite field of possible thoughts, one act from the infinite field of possible acts. Why upbraid a wife for weeping? Why not strike her instead? Why not laugh, ignore, or console? Why not weep *with* her? What made one response more true than another? Was it one's blood? Was it another's words of reason? Was it one's God?

Or was it, as Moënghus had claimed, one's *goal?*

Encircled by his people, born of them and destined to die among them, Cnaiür had chosen his blood. For thirty years he tried to beat his thoughts and passions down the narrow tracks of the Utemot. But despite his brutal persistence, despite his native gifts, his fellow tribesmen could always smell a wrongness about him. In the intercourse between men, every move was constrained by others' expectations; it was a kind of dance, and as such, it brooked no hesitation. The Utemot glimpsed his flickering doubts. They understood that he *tried*, and they knew that whoever tried to be of the People couldn't be of the People.

So they punished him with whispers and guarded eyes—for more than a hundred seasons ...

Thirty years of shame and denial. Thirty years of torment and terror. A lifetime of cannibal hatred ... In the end, Cnaiür had cut a trail of his own making, a solitary track of madness and murder.

He had made blood his cleansing waters. If war was worship, then Cnaiür would be the most pious of the Scylvendi—not simply *of* the

People, but the greatest among them as well. He told himself his arms were his glory. He was Cnaiür urs Skiötha, the most violent of all men.

And so he continued telling himself, even though his every swazond marked not his honour, but the death of Anasûrimbor Moënghus. For what was madness, if not a kind of overpowering *impatience*, a need to seize at once what the world denied? Moënghus not only had to die, he had to die *now*—whether he was Moënghus or not.

In his fury, Cnaiür had made all the world his surrogate. And he avenged himself upon it.

Despite the accuracy of this analysis, it availed Kellhus little in his attempts to possess the Utemot Chieftain. Always the man's knowledge of the Dûnyain barred his passage. For a time, Kellhus even considered the possibility that Cnaiür would never succumb.

Then they found Serwë—a surrogate of a different kind.

From the very beginning, the Scylvendi had made her his track, his proof that he followed the ways of the People. Serwë was the erasure of Moënghus, whose presence Kellhus's resemblance so recalled. She was the incantation that would undo Moënghus's curse. And Cnaiür fell in love, not with her, but with the *idea* of loving her. Because if he loved her, he couldn't love Anasûrimbor Moënghus ...

Or his son.

What followed had been almost elementary.

Kellhus began seducing Serwë, knowing that he showed the barbarian his own seduction at the hands of Moënghus some thirty years previous. Soon, she became both the erasure *and the repetition* of Cnaiür's heart-breaking hate. The plainsman began beating her, not simply to prove his Scylvendi contempt for women, but to better beat himself. He punished her for repeating *his* sins, even though he at once loved her and despised love as weakness ...

And so as Kellhus intended, contradiction piled upon contradiction. World-born men, he'd discovered, possessed a peculiar vulnerability to contradictions, particularly those that provoked conflicting passions. Nothing, it seemed, so anchored their hearts. Nothing so obsessed.

Once Cnaiür had utterly succumbed to the girl, Kellhus simply took her away, knowing the man would trade anything for her return, and that he would do so without even understanding why.

And now the usefulness of Cnaiür urs Skiötha was at an end.

The monk climbed the sparsely grassed pate of a dune. The wind whipped through his hair, yanked his white samite robe about his waist. Before him, the Meneanor swept out to where the earth seemed to spill into the great void of the night. Immediately below, he saw the Scylvendi's simple round tent; it had been kicked down and trampled. No fire burned before it.

For a moment Kellhus thought he was too late, then he heard raw shouts on the wind, glimpsed a figure amid the heaving waves. He walked through the ruined camp to the water's edge, felt the crunch of shells and gravel beneath his sandalled feet. Moonlight silvered the rolling waters. Gulls cried out, hanging like kites in the night wind.

Kellhus watched the waves batter the Scylvendi's nude form.

"There are no tracks!" the man screamed, beating the surf with his fists. "Where are the—"

Without warning, he went rigid. Dark water swelled about him, engulfed him almost to his shoulders, then tumbled forward in clouds of crystalline foam. He turned his head, and Kellhus saw his weathered face, framed by long tails of sodden black hair. There was no expression.

Absolutely no expression.

Cnaiür began wading to shore; the surf broke about him, as insubstantial as smoke.

"I did everything you asked," he called over the surrounding thunder. "I shamed my father into battling you. I betrayed him, my tribe, my race …"

The water dropped from his massive chest to the concave plane of his stomach and groin. A wave crashed about his white thighs, tugged upon his long phallus. Kellhus filtered out the Meneanor's clamour, bound his every sense to the approaching barbarian. Steady pulse. Bloodless skin. Slack face …

Dead eyes.

And Kellhus realized: *I cannot read this man.*

"I followed you across the trackless Steppe."

The slap of bare feet across waterlogged sand. Cnaiür paused before him, his great frame glistening as though enamelled in the moonlight.

"I loved you."

Kellhus reached back, drew his Dûnyain sword, levelled it before him. "Kneel," he said.

The Scylvendi fell to his knees. He held out his arms, trailing fingers through the sand. He bent his face back to the stars, exposing his throat. The Meneanor surged and seethed behind him.

Kellhus stood motionless above him.

What is this, Father? Pity?

He gazed at the abject Scylvendi warrior. From what darkness had this passion come?

"Strike!" the man cried. The great scarred body trembled in terror and exultation.

But still, Kellhus couldn't move.

"Kill me!" Cnaiür shouted to the bowl of the night. With uncanny swiftness he seized Kellhus's blade, jerked its point to his throat. "Kill! Kill!"

"No," Kellhus said. A wave crashed, and the wind whipped cold spray across them.

Leaning forward, he gently pried his blade from the man's heavy grip.

Cnaiür's arms snapped about either side of his head, wrenched him to the cool sand.

Kellhus remained motionless. Whether by luck or instinct, the barbarian had yanked him within a coin's edge of death. The merest twitch, Kellhus knew, could break his neck.

Cnaiür drew him close enough for him to feel his humid body heat.

"*I loved you!*" he both whispered and screamed. Then he thrust Kellhus backward, nearly tossing him back to his feet. Wary now, Kellhus rolled his chin to straighten a kink from his neck. Cnaiür stared at him in hope and horror ...

Kellhus sheathed his sword.

The Scylvendi swayed backward, raising his fists to his head. He clutched handfuls of hair, wrested them from his scalp.

"But you said!" he raved, holding out bloody shocks of hair. "*You said!*"

Kellhus watched, utterly unmoved. There were other uses.

There were always other uses.

The thing called Sarcellus followed a narrow track along the embankments between fields. Despite the uncharacteristic humidity, it was a clear night, and the moon etched the surrounding clots of eucalytpus and sycamore in blue. He slowed as he passed the first ruins, and guided his mount between a long gallery of columns that jutted from a collection of grassy mounds. Beyond the columns, the Sempis lay as still as any lake, bearing the white moon and the shadowy line of the northern escarpments upon its mirror back. Sarcellus dismounted.

This place had once belonged to the ancient city of Girgilioth, but that mattered little to the thing called Sarcellus. He was a creature of the moment. What mattered was that it was a landmark, and landmarks were good places for spies to confer with their handlers—human or otherwise.

Sarcellus sat with his back against one of the columns, lost in thoughts both predatory and impenetrable. Cylindrical friezes of leopards standing like men soared across the moon-pale column above. The flutter of wings stirred him from his reverie and he looked up with his large brown eyes, reminded of different pillars.

A bird the size of a raven alighted upon his knee—a bird like any raven save for its white head.

White, human head.

The face twitched with bird-nervousness, regarded Sarcellus with tiny turquoise eyes.

"I smell blood," it said in a thin voice.

Sarcellus nodded. "The Scylvendi … He interrupted my interrogation of the girl."

"Your effectiveness?"

"Is unimpaired. I heal."

A tiny blink. "Good. Then what have you learned?"

"He's not Cishaurim." The thing had spoken this softly, as though to preserve tiny eardrums.

A cat-curious turn of the head. "Indeed," the Synthese said after a moment. "Then what is he?"

"Dûnyain."

Tiny grimace. Small, glistening teeth, like grains of rice, flashed between its lips. "All games end with me, Gaörtha. All games."

Sarcellus became very still. "I play no game. This man is Dûnyain. That's what the Scylvendi calls him. She said there's no doubt."

"But there's no order called 'Dûnyain' in Atrithau."

"No. But then we know that he's not a Prince of Atrithau."

The Old Name paused, as though to cycle large human thoughts through a small bird intellect.

"Perhaps," it eventually said, "it's no coincidence that this order takes its name from ancient Kûniüric. Perhaps this man's name, Anasûrimbor, is not a clumsy Cishaurim lie after all. Perhaps he *is* of the Old Seed."

"Could the Nonmen have trained him?"

"Perhaps ... But we have spies—even in Ishterebinth. There is little that Nin-Ciljiras does that we don't know. Very little."

The small face cackled. It folded and unfolded its obsidian wings.

"No," it continued, its small brow furrowed, "this Dûnyain is not a ward of the Nonmen ... When the light of ancient Kûniüri was stamped out, many stubborn embers survived. The Mandate is just such an ember. Perhaps the Dûnyain is another, just as stubborn ..."

The blue eyes flickered—another blink. "But far more secretive."

Sarcellus said nothing. Speculation on such matters was beyond his warrant, beyond his making.

The tiny teeth clicked, once, twice, as though the Old Name tested their mettle.

"Yes ... An *ember* ... in the very shadow of Holy Golgotterath no less ..."

"He's told the woman the Holy War will be his."

"And he's not Cishaurim! Such a mystery, Gaörtha! Who are the Dûnyain? What do they want with the Holy War? And how, my pretty pretty child, can this man see through your face?"

"But we don't—"

"He sees *enough* ... Yes, more than enough ..."

It bent its head to the right, blinked, then straightened.

"Indulge this Prince Kellhus for a while yet, Gaörtha. With the Mandate sorcerer removed from the game he's become less of a threat. Indulge him ... We must learn more about this 'Dûnyain.'"

"But even now he grows in power. More and more these Men call him

'Warrior-Prophet' or 'Prince of God.' If he continues, he will become very difficult to remove."

"Warrior-Prophet ..." The Synthese cackled. "Very cunning, this Dûnyain. He leashes these fanatics with leather of their own making ... What is his sermon, Gaörtha? Does it in any way threaten the Holy War?"

"No. Not yet, Consult Father."

"Measure him, then do as you see fit. If it seems he might call the Holy War to kennel, you must silence him—no matter what the cost. He is but a curiosity. The Cishaurim are our foe!"

"Yes, Old Father."

Gleaming like wet marble, the white head bobbed twice, as though in answer to some overriding instinct. A wing dropped to Sarcellus's knee, dipped between his shadowy thighs ... Gaörtha went rigid.

"Are you badly hurt, my sweet child?"

"Yessss," the thing called Sarcellus gasped.

The small head tilted backward. Heavy-lidded eyes watched the wingtip circle and stroke, stroke and circle. "Ah, but imagine ... Imagine a world where no womb quickens, where no soul hopes!"

Sarcellus sucked drool in delight.

CHAPTER SIXTEEN

SHIGEK

Men never resemble one another so much as when asleep or dead.

—OPPARITHA, ON THE CARNAL

The arrogance of the Inrithi waxed bright in the days following Anwurat. Though the sober-minded demanded they press the attack, the great majority clamoured for respite. They thought the Fanim doomed, just as they thought them doomed after Mengedda. But while the Men of the Tusk tarried, the Padirajah plotted. He would make the world his shield.

—DRUSAS ACHAMIAN, THE COMPENDIUM OF THE FIRST HOLY WAR

Early Autumn, 4111 Year-of-the-Tusk, Iothiah

Achamian suffered dreams …

Dreams drawn from the sheath.

Drizzle hazed the distances, obscuring the Ring Mountains behind drapes of woollen grey, granting the madness before him the span of all visible creation. Masses of Sranc, bristling with black-bronze weapons. Ranks of Bashrag, beating the mud with their massive hammers. And beyond them, the high ramparts of Golgotterath. Misty barbicans above precipitous cliffs, the two great horns of the Ark rearing into murky obscurity, curved and golden against the endless grey, trailing skirts of unguttered water.

Hoary Golgotterath, raised about the greatest terror ever to fall from the heavens.

Soon to yield ...

A great yawing rumbled from the parapets out and across the dreary plains.

Like a tide of spiders, the Sranc surged forward, howling through pools, sprinting through mud. They crashed into the phalanxes of the warlike Aörsi, the long-haired bulwark of the North; they seethed against the shining ranks of the Kûniüri, the high tide of Norsirai glory. The Chieftain-Princes of the High Norsirai whipped their chariots forward and all perished before them. The standards of Ishterebinth, last of the Nonmen Mansions, charged deep into a sea of abominations, leaving black-blooded ruin in their wake. Great Nil'gikas stood like a point of brilliant sunlight amid smoke and violent shadow. And Nymeric sounded the Worldhorn, over and over, until the Sranc could hear nothing but the peal of their doom.

Seswatha, Grandmaster of the Sohonc, raised his face to the rain and tasted sweet joy, for it was happening, truly happening! Unholy Golgotterath, ancient Min-Uroikas, was about to fall. He had warned them in time!

Achamian would relive all eighteen years of that delusion.

Dreams drawn from the knife's sheath.

And when he awakened, to the sound of harsh shouts or to the patter of cold water across his face, it would seem that one horror had merely replaced another. He would blink against torchlight, would dully note the bite of chains, a mouth stuffed with rank cloth, and the dark, scarlet-robed figures that surrounded him. And he would think, before succumbing to the Dreams once again, *It comes ... the Apocalypse comes ...*

"Strange, isn't it, Iyokus?"

"And what is that?"

"That men can be rendered so helpless so easily."

"Men *and* Schools ..."

"What are you implying?"

"Nothing, Grandmaster."

"Look! He watches!"

"Yes ... He does that from time to time. But he must recover more of his strength before we can begin."

Esmenet cried out when she saw them walking their mounts across the field toward her. Kellhus and Serwë, haggard from long and sleepless travel. Suddenly she was running across the uneven pasture, as though drawn by a long irresistible line. Toward them. No, not them—*toward him.*

She flew to him, clutched him harder than she thought her limbs capable. He smelt of dust and scented oils. His beard and hair kissed her bare skin with soft curls. She could feel her tears roll from her cheek to his neck in continuous lines.

"Kellhus," she sobbed. "Oh, Kellhus ... I think I'm going *mad!*"

"No, Esmi ... It is grief."

He seemed a pillar of comfort. His square chest flattening her breasts. His long warding arms about her back and narrow waist.

He pressed her back, and she turned to Serwë, who was also crying. They hugged, then together walked back to the lonely tent on the slope. Kellhus led their horses.

"We *missed* you, Esmi," Serwë said, strangely flustered.

Esmenet regarded the girl with sorrow. Her left eye was bruised black and cherry and an angry red cut poked from beneath her hairline. Even if Esmenet had the heart—and she had none—she would wait for Serwë to explain rather than ask what had happened. With such marks, asking demanded lies, and silence afforded truth. That was the lot of women— especially when they were wanton ...

Aside from her face, the girl appeared healthy, almost aglow. Beneath her hasas, her belly had swelled in the narrow-hipped manner Esmenet could only envy. A hundred questions assailed Esmenet. How was her back? How often did she pee? Had there been any bleeding? Suddenly she realized how terrified the girl must be—even with Kellhus. Esmenet could remember her own joyous terror. But then, she'd been alone. Absolutely alone.

"You must be famished!" she exclaimed.

Serwë shook her head in feeble denial, and both Esmenet and Kellhus laughed. Serwë was always hungry—as a pregnant woman should be.

For a moment, Esmenet felt the old sunshine flash from her eyes. "It's so good to see you," she said. "I've mourned more than the loss of Achamian."

Dusk had come, so she began drawing wood—mostly bone-coloured flotsam she'd found along the river—to throw into the fire. Kellhus sat cross-legged before the dwindling flames. Serwë leaned her head against his shoulder, her hair nearly bleached white by the sun, her nose red and peeling as always.

"This is the same fire," Kellhus said. "The one we struck after first coming to Shigek."

Esmenet paused, her arms wrapped about her wood.

"It is!" Serwë exclaimed. She looked around the bare slopes, turned to the dark band of the river in the near distance. "But everything's gone ... All the tents. All the people ..."

Esmenet fed the fire piece by elaborate piece. She'd obsessed over her fires of late. There was no one else to tend.

She could feel Kellhus's gentle scrutiny.

"Some hearths can't be rekindled," he said.

"It burns well enough," Esmenet murmured. She blinked tears, sniffled and wiped at her nose.

"But what makes a hearth, Esmi? Is it the fire, or the family that keeps it?"

"The family," she finally said. A strange blankness had overcome her.

"*We're* that family ... You know that." Kellhus had bent his head sideways to look into her downturned face. "And Achamian knows that too."

Her legs became strangers, and she stumbled, fell onto her rump. She began weeping yet again.

"B-but I-I have to-to stay ... I-I have-have t-to wait for him ... for him to come *home*."

Kellhus knelt beside her, lifted her chin. She glimpsed a tear's shining track across his left cheek.

"*We* are that home," he said, and somehow that was the end of it.

Over the course of dinner, Kellhus explained all that had happened the previous week. He was a most extraordinary storyteller—he always had been—and for a time Esmenet found herself lost in the Battle of Anwurat and its wrenching intricacies. Her heart pounded in her throat when he described the burning of the encampment and the charge of the Khirgwi, and she clapped and laughed every bit as hard as Serwë when he described his defence of the Swazond Standard, which according to him consisted of no more than a succession of outlandishly lucky blunders. And she found herself wondering that such a miraculous man—a prophet! for he could be nothing else—concerned himself with *her*, Esmenet, a caste-menial whore from the slums of Sumna.

"Ah, Esmi," he said, "it brings such peace to my heart to see you smile." She bit her lip, laughed through a crying face.

He continued, more seriously, to explain the events following the battle. How the heathens had been chased into the desert. How Gotian had held Skauras's severed head before their victory fires. How even now the Holy War secured the South Bank. From the Delta to the deep desert, tabernacles burned ...

Esmenet had seen the smoke.

They sat silently for a while, listening to the fire gorge on her wood. As always the sky was desert clear, and the vault of stars seemed endless. Moonlight silvered the eternal Sempis.

How many nights had she pondered these things? Sky and sweeping landscape. Dwarfing her, terrifying her with their monstrous indifference, reminding her that hearts were no more than fluttering rags. Too much wind, and they were tossed into the great black. Too little, and they fell slack.

What chance did Akka have?

"I received word from Xinemus," Kellhus finally said. "He still searches ..."

"So there's hope?"

"There's always hope," he said in a voice that at once encouraged and deadened her heart. "We can only wait and see what he finds."

Esmenet couldn't speak. She glanced at Serwë, but the girl avoided her eyes.

They think he's dead.

She knew better than to hope. This was the world. But *dead* seemed such an impossible thought. How could one think the end of thinking?

Akka would—

"Come," Kellhus said, in the quick and open manner of someone assured of his new course. He strode around her small fire, sat with his knees in his hands next to her. With a stick he scratched an oddly familiar sign into the bare earth before them. "In the meantime, let's teach you how to read."

It seemed all crying had been wrung from her, but somehow ...

Esmenet looked to Kellhus and smiled through her tears. Her voice felt small and broken.

"I've always wanted to read."

⌘

The seamless transition of agonies—from Seswatha's torture in the bowels of Dagliash two thousand years before to *now* ... The pain of puckered burns, chafed wrists, joints contorted by the wrong distribution of his body's weight. At first Achamian didn't realize he was awake. It merely seemed that Mekeritrig's face had transformed into that of Eleäzaras—the inhumanly beautiful face of the Mantraitor had become that of the Grandmaster, rutted and whiskered.

"Ah, Achamian," Eleäzaras said, "it's good to see you *seeing*—things in this world at least. For some time we feared you wouldn't awaken at all. You were very nearly killed, you know. The Library was absolutely ruined ... All those books ash, simply because of your stubbornness. How the Sareots must howl in the Outside. All their poor books."

Achamian was gagged, naked, and chained, wrists above his head and ankle to ankle, so that he hung suspended over a great mosaic floor. The chamber was vaulted, but he couldn't see the ceiling's peak, nor could he see the terminus of the walls that framed the silk-gowned entourage before him. The surrounding spaces were lost in gloom. Three glowering tripods provided light, and only he, hanging in the confluence of their circles of illumination, was bright.

"Ah yes ..." Eleäzaras continued, watching him with a thin smile. "This place. It's always good to have a sense of one's prison, no? An old Inrithi chapel, by the looks of it. Built by the Ceneians, I suppose."

Suddenly he understood.

The Scarlet Spires! I'm dead ... I'm dead.

Tears welled down his cheeks. His body, beaten, numb from hanging, betrayed him, and he felt the rush of urine and bowel along his naked legs, heard mud slap across the mosaic serpents at his feet.

Nooo! This can't be happening!

Eleäzaras laughed, a thin, wicked thing. "And now," he said, his tone jnanic and droll, "some long-dead Ceneian architect also howls."

There was uneasy laughter from his retinue.

Seized by animal panic, Achamian writhed against his chains, hacked against the cloth in his throat. Spasms struck and he went limp. He swung in small circles, punished by wave after wave of pain.

Esmi ...

"There's much *certainty* here," Eleäzaras said, holding a kerchief to his face, "don't you think, Achamian? You know *why* you've been taken. And you also know the inevitable outcome. We'll ply you for the Gnosis, and you, conditioned by years of Mandate training, will frustrate our every attempt. You'll die in agony, your secrets clutched close to your heart, and we'll be left with yet another useless Mandate corpse. This is the way that it's *supposed* to happen, no?"

Achamian simply stared in blank horror, an anguished pendulum slowly swinging to and fro, to and fro ...

What Eleäzaras said was true. He was supposed to die for his knowledge, for the Gnosis.

Think, Achamian, think! Please-please-dear-God-you-must-think!

Without the guidance of the Nonmen Quya, the Anagogic Schools of the Three Seas had never learned how to surpass what were called the Analogies. All their sorcery, no matter how powerful or ingenious, arose through the power of arcane associations, through the resonances between words and *concrete* events. They required detours—dragons, lightnings, suns—to burn the world. They could not, like Achamian, conjure the *essence* of these things, the Burning itself. They knew nothing of the Abstractions.

Where they were poets, he was a *philosopher*. They were mere bronze to his iron, and he would show them.

Achamian snorted air through his nostrils. Through bleary eyes, he glared at the Grandmaster.

I will see you burn! I will see you burn!

"But *here*," Eleäzaras was saying, "in these tumultuous times, the past need not be our tyrant. Here, your torment, your death, isn't assured ... Here, nothing is for certain."

Eleäzaras walked from the others—five graceful, measured steps—and came to a stop very near to Achamian.

"To prove this to you, I'll have your gag removed. I'll actually let you *speak*, rather than ply you, as we have your fellow Schoolmen in the past, with endless Compulsions. But I warn you, Achamian, it will be fruitless to try to assail us." He produced a slender hand from the cuff of his glyph-embroidered sleeve, gestured to the mosaic floor.

Achamian saw a broad circle, painted in red, across the stylized animals of the mosaic floor: the representation of a snake scaled by pictograms and devouring its own tail.

"As you can see," Eleäzaras said mildly, "you're chained above a Uroborian Circle ... To even begin a Cant will invite immeasurable pain, I assure you. I've witnessed it before."

So had Achamian. The Scarlet Spires, it seemed, possessed many potent poetic devices.

The Grandmaster retreated, and a lumbering eunuch appeared from the shadows. With fat but nimble fingers, he withdrew the gag. Achamian sucked air through his mouth, tasted the stink of his body's earlier treachery. He hung his head forward, spit as best he could.

The Scarlet Schoolmen watched him expectantly, even apprehensively.

"Well?" Eleäzaras asked.

Achamian blinked, cocked his neck against the pain. "Where are we?" he croaked.

A broad smile split the Grandmaster's thin grey goatee.

"Why, Iothiah of course."

Achamian grimaced and nodded. He looked down to the Uroborian Circle beneath, saw his urine trickle along the grout between mosaic tiles ...

It didn't seem a matter of courage, only a giddy instant of disconnection, a wilful ignorance of the consequences.

He said two words.

Agony.

Enough to shriek, to empty bowels once again.

Threads of incandescence, winding, forking beneath his skin, as though he possessed sunlight for blood.

Shriek and shriek until it seemed that eyes must rupture, that teeth must crack, spill to mosaic floor, clicking like porcelain against porcelain.

And then back to nightmares of a far older, and far less momentary, torment.

⁂

When the shrieking stopped, Eleäzaras stared at the unconscious figure. Even chained and naked, his shrivelled phallus prodding from black pubic hair, the man seemed ... threatening.

"Stubborn," Iyokus said, in a tone that insolently asked, *What did you expect?*

"Indeed," Eleäzaras replied, and fumed. Delay after delay. The Gnosis would be such a lovely thing to wrest from this quivering dog, but it would be an unexpected gift. What he *needed* to know is what happened that night in the Imperial Catacombs beneath the Andiamine Heights. He needed to know what this man knew of the Cishaurim skin-spies.

The Cishaurim!

Directly or indirectly, this one Mandate dog had undone whatever advantage they'd gained at the Battle of Mengedda. First, by killing two sorcerers of rank at the Sareotic Library, among them Yutirames, an old and powerful ally of Eleäzaras's. Then, by providing that fanatic Proyas with leverage. If it hadn't been for the man's threats of avenging his "dear old tutor," Eleäzaras would never have allowed the Scarlet Spires to join the Holy War on the South Bank. Six! Six sorcerers of rank fell to Fanim bowmen armed with Chorae at the Battle of Anwurat. Ukrummu, Calasthenes, Naïn ...

Six!

And this, Eleäzaras knew, was precisely what the Cishaurim wanted ... To bleed them while jealously guarding their own blood!

Oh, he did covet the Gnosis. So much that it almost proved a counter-weight to that other word—"Cishaurim." Almost. That evening at the Sareotic Library, watching this one man resist eight sorcerers of rank with glittering, abstract lights, Eleäzaras had envied as he'd never envied before. Such miraculous power. Such purity of dispensation. *How?* he had thought. *How?*

Fucking Mandate pigs.

After he learned what he needed about the Cishaurim, he would see this dog plied in the old way. All things in the world were a lottery, and who knew, seizing this man might prove an act as significant as destroying the Cishaurim—in the end.

That, Eleäzaras decided, was Iyokus's problem. He could not fathom the fact that certain rewards made even the most desperate gambles worthwhile. He knew nothing of hope.

Chanv addicts never seemed to know anything of hope.

The Sempis seemed more than a river in the crossing.

Esmenet had ridden behind Serwë to a nearby Inrithi ferry, both terrified of floating on a beast's back, and amazed by the girl's native ability to ride. She was Cepaloran, Serwë explained. She'd been born astride a saddle.

Which meant, Esmenet thought in a moment of uncommon bitterness, with her legs spread wide.

Afterward, standing in the shade of hissing leaves, she looked across the river to the denuded North Bank. The barrenness saddened her, reminded her of her heart and why she had to leave. But the distance ... A terrifying sense of finality seized her, a certainty that the Sempis, whose waters she'd thought kind, was in fact ruthlessly vindictive, and would brook no return.

I can swim ... I know how to swim!

Kellhus clasped her about the shoulder. "The world looks south," he said.

Returning to the Conriyan encampment was far less difficult than she feared. Proyas had pitched camp beyond the high walls of Ammegnotis, the only great city on the South Bank. Because of this they found themselves part of a great stream of market-bound traffic: bands of horsemen, wains, barefooted penitents, all crowding the side of the road where the shade of palms was deepest. But rather than vanishing into the crowd, they found themselves beset by people, mostly Men of the Tusk but some camp-followers as well, all begging to be touched or blessed by the Warrior-Prophet. Word of his stand against the Khirgwi, Serwë explained, had further confirmed him in the hearts of many people. They were fairly mobbed by the time they reached the camp.

"He no longer rebukes them," Esmenet said, watching in astonishment.

Serwë laughed. "Isn't it wonderful?"

And it was—*it was!* There was Kellhus, the man who had teased her so many times about their fire, walking among adoring masses, smiling, touching cheeks, uttering warm and encouraging words. There was *Kellhus!*

The Warrior-Prophet.

He looked up to them, grinned and winked. Pressed against the girl's back in the saddle, Esmenet could feel Serwë shiver in delight, and for an instant she experienced a pang of savage jealousy. Why did she always lose? Why did the Gods hate her so? Why not someone else, someone *deserving?* Why not Serwë?

But shame followed hard on these thoughts. Kellhus had come for *her.* Kellhus! This man whom others worshipped had come out of concern for her.

He does this for Achamian. For his teacher ...

Proyas had posted pickets around the outskirts of the Conriyan camp—primarily because of the furor surrounding Kellhus, Serwë explained—and they soon found themselves walking unmolested through long canvas alleys.

Esmenet had told herself she feared returning because it would stir too many recollections. But losing those recollections was what she truly feared. Her refusal to leave their old camp had been rash, desperate, pathetic ... Kellhus had shown her that. But remaining *had* fortified her somehow—or so it seemed when she thought about it. There was the clutching sense of defensiveness, the certainty that she must protect Achamian's surroundings. She'd even refused to touch the chipped clay bowl he'd used for his tea that final morning. By describing his absence in such heartbreaking detail, such things had become, it seemed to her, fetishes, charms that would secure his return. And there was the sense of desolate pride. Everyone had fled, but she remained—*she remained!* She would look across the abandoned fields, at the firepits becoming earthen, at the paths scuffed through the grasses, and all the world would seem a ghost. Only her loss would seem real ... Only Achamian. Wasn't there some glory, some grace in that?

Now she was moving on—no matter what Kellhus said about hearth and family. Did that mean she was leaving Akka behind as well?

She wept while Kellhus helped her pitch Achamian's tent, so small and threadbare, in the shadow of the grand brocaded pavilion he shared with Serwë. But she was grateful. So very grateful.

She had assumed the first few nights would be awkward, but she was wrong. Kellhus was too generous, and Serwë too innocent, for her to feel anything other than welcome. From time to time, Kellhus would make her laugh, simply to remind her, Esmenet suspected, that she could still feel joy. Otherwise, he would either share her sorrow, or withdraw, so she might suffer in seclusion.

Serwë was ... well, Serwë. Sometimes she would seem utterly oblivious to Esmenet's grief and act as though nothing had changed, as though Achamian might at any moment come strolling down the winding alley, laughing or quarrelling with Xinemus. And though Esmenet found the *thought* of this offensive, she found it peculiarly comforting in practice. It was nice to pretend.

Other times, Serwë would seem absolutely devastated, for her, for Achamian, as well as for herself. Part of this was the pregnancy, Esmenet knew—she herself had wept and laughed like a madwoman while carrying her daughter—but Esmenet found it particularly difficult to bear. She would dutifully ask Serwë what was wrong, would always be gentle, but her thoughts would fill her with shame. If Serwë said she cried for Achamian, Esmenet would wonder why. Had they been lovers for more than one night? If Serwë said she cried for *her*, Esmenet would be indignant. What? Was she that pathetic? And if Serwë simply seemed to wallow, Esmenet would find herself disgusted. How could anyone be so selfish?

Afterward, Esmenet would berate herself. What would Achamian think of such bitter, spiteful thoughts? How disappointed he'd be! "Esmi!" he'd say. "Esmi, *please* ..." And she'd spend watch after sleepless watch remembering all her horrid words, all her petty cruelties, and begging the Gods for forgiveness. She didn't *mean* them. How could she?

On her third night, she heard a soft tapping against her tent flap. When she pulled it aside, Serwë pressed in, smelling of smoke, oranges, and jasmine. The half-naked girl knelt in the gloom crying. Esmenet already knew Kellhus hadn't returned, because she'd been listening. He had his councils and, of course, his growing congregation.

"Serchaa?" she asked, overcome by the motherly weariness of having to console those who suffered far less than herself. "What is it, Serchaa?"

"Please, Esmi. Please, I beg you!"

"Please *what*, Serchaa? What do you mean?"

The girl hesitated. Her eyes were little more than glittering points in the gloom.

"Don't steal him!" Serwë suddenly cried. "Don't steal him from me!"

Esmenet laughed, but softly so as not to bruise the girl's feelings.

"Steal Kellhus," she said.

"Please, Esmi! Y-you're so beautiful ... Almost as beautiful as me! But you're smart too! You speak to him the way other men speak to him! I've heard you!"

"Serchaa ... I love *Akka*. I love Kellhus too, but not ... not the way you fear. Please, you mustn't fear! I couldn't bear it if you feared me, Serchaa!"

Esmenet had thought herself sincere, but afterward, as she nestled against Serwë's slender back, she found herself exulting in the thought of Serwë's fear. She curled the girl's blond hair between her fingers, thinking of the way Serwë had swept it across Achamian's chest ... How easy, she wondered, would it yank from her scalp?

Why did you lie with Akka? Why?

The following morning, Esmenet awoke stricken with remorse. Hatred, as the Sumni said, was a rapacious houseguest, and lingered only in hearts fat with pride. Esmenet's heart had grown very thin. She stared at the girl in the tinted light. Serwë had rolled in her sleep, and now lay with her angelic face turned to Esmenet. Her right hand cupped the bulge of her stomach. She breathed quiet as a babe.

How could such beauty dwell in a slumbering face? For a time, Esmenet pondered what it was she thought she saw. There was a peculiar sense of *sneakiness*, the thrill of one-sided witness so familiar to children. This was what made Esmenet grin. But there was far more: the aura of dormant life, the premonition of death, the wonder of seeing the unruly carnival of

human expression enclosed in the stillness of a single point. There was a
sense of truth, a recognition that *all faces* held this one point in common.
This, Esmenet knew, was *her* face, as it was Achamian's, or even Kellhus's.
But more than anything, there was a glorious vulnerability. The sleeping
throat, the Nilnameshi proverb went, was easily cut.

Was this not love? To be watched while you slept …

She was crying when Serwë awoke. She watched the girl blink, focus,
and frown.

"Why?" Serwë asked.

Esmenet smiled. "Because you're so beautiful," she said. "So perfect."

Serwë's eyes flashed with joy. She rolled onto her back, stretching her
arms into the stuffy air.

"I *know!*" she cried, rolling her shoulders in a little jig. She looked to
Esmenet, bounced her eyebrows up and down. "Everybody wants me!" she
laughed. "Even you!"

"Little bitch!" Esmenet gasped, raising her hands as though to claw at
her eyes.

Kellhus was already at the fire when they tumbled from the tent,
laughing and squealing. He shook his head—as perhaps a man should.

From that day, Esmenet found herself tending to Serwë with even
greater kindness. It was so strange, so confusing, the friendship she'd
found with this girl, this pregnant child who had taken a prophet as a
lover.

Even before Achamian had left for the Library, she'd wondered what it
was Kellhus saw in Serwë. Certainly it had to be more than her beauty—
which was, Esmenet often thought, nothing short of otherworldly.
Kellhus saw *hearts*, not skin, no matter how smooth or marble white. And
Serwë's heart had seemed so flawed. Joyous and open, certainly, but also
vain, petulant, peevish, and wanton.

But now Esmenet wondered whether these very flaws held the secret
of her heart's perfection. For she'd glimpsed that perfection while
watching her sleep. For an instant, she'd glimpsed what only Kellhus
could see … The beauty of frailty. The splendour of imperfection.

She had *witnessed*, she realized. Witnessed truth.

She could find no proper words, but she felt better for it, revived
somehow. That morning Kellhus had looked at her and had nodded in a

frank, admiring manner that reminded her of Xinemus. He said nothing because nothing needed to be said—or so it seemed. Perhaps, she thought, truth wasn't unlike sorcery. Perhaps those who see truth simply see each other.

Later, before she left with Serwë to scrounge through the half-abandoned bazaars of Ammegnotis, Kellhus assisted her with her reading. Despite her protestations, he'd given her *The Chronicle of the Tusk* as a primer. Simply holding the leather-bound manuscript filled her with dread. The look of it, the smell of it, even the rasping creak of its spine spoke of righteousness and irrevocable judgement. The pages seemed inked in iron. Every word she sounded out possessed an anxiousness all its own. Every bird-track column threatened the next.

"I need not," she told Kellhus, "read the warrant of my own damnation!"

"What does it say?" Kellhus asked, ignoring her tantrum.

"That I'm filth!"

"What does it *say*, Esmi."

She returned to the exhausting trial of wrestling sounds from marks, and words from sounds.

The day was desert hot, particularly in the city, where the stone and the mud brick soaked up the sun and seemed to redouble its heat. Esmenet retired early that night, and for the first time in many days, fell asleep without crying for Achamian.

She awoke to what the Nansur called "fool's morning." Her eyes simply fluttered open, and she found herself alert, even though the darkness and the temperature told her the morning lay many watches away. She frowned at the entrance to the tent, which had been pulled open. Her bare feet jutted from her blankets. Moonlight bathed them and the sandalled feet of a man ...

"Such interesting company you keep," Sarcellus said.

Screaming never occurred to her. For a heartbeat or two, his presence seemed as *proper* as it seemed impossible. He lay beside her, his head propped on his elbow, his large brown eyes glittering with amusement. Beneath white, gold-floriated vestments, he wore a Shrial gown with a Tusk embroidered across its chest. He smelled of sandalwood and other ritual incenses she couldn't identify.

"Sarcellus," she murmured. How long had he been watching her?

"You never did tell the sorcerer about me, did you?"

"No."

He shook his head in rueful mockery. "Naughty whore."

The sense of unreality drained away, and the first true pang of fear struck her.

"What do you want, Sarcellus?"

"You."

"Leave ..."

"Your prophet isn't what you think he is ... You do know that."

Fear had become terror. She knew full well how cruel he could be to those who fell outside the narrow circle of his respect, but she'd always thought herself within that circle—even after she'd left his tent. But something had happened ... Somehow, she understood she meant nothing, absolutely *nothing,* to the man now gazing upon her.

"Leave now, Sarcellus."

The Knight-Commander laughed. "But I need you, Esmi. I need your help ... There's gold ..."

"I'll scream. I'm warning—"

"There's life!" Sarcellus snarled. Somehow his hand had clamped about her mouth. She didn't need to feel the prick to know he held a knife to her throat.

"Listen, whore. You've made a habit of begging at the wrong table. The sorcerer's dead. Your prophet will soon follow. Now I ask, where does that leave you?"

He swept the covers away, exposed her to the warm night air. She flinched, sobbed as the knifepoint swizzled across her moonlit skin.

"Eh, *old* whore? What will you do when your peach loses its pucker, hmm? Whom will you bed then? How will you end, I wonder? Will you be fucking lepers? Or will you be sucking scared little boys for scraps of bread?"

She wet herself in terror.

Sarcellus breathed deep, as though savouring the bouquet of her humiliation. His eyes laughed. "Is that *understanding* I smell?"

Esmenet, sobbing, nodded against the iron fingers.

Sarcellus smirked, removed his hand.

She shrieked, screamed until it seemed her throat must bleed.

Then Kellhus held her, and she was drawn from the tent to the glowing coals of the firepit. She heard shouts, saw men crowding about them with torches, heard voices rumbling in Conriyan. Somehow she explained what happened, shuddering and sobbing within the frame of Kellhus's strong arms. After what seemed both heartbeats and days, the commotion passed. People returned to what sleep remained to them. The terror receded, replaced by the exhausted throb of embarrassment. Kellhus told her he would complain to Gotian, but that there would be very little anyone could do.

"Sarcellus is a Knight-Commander," Kellhus said.

And she was just a dead sorcerer's whore.

Naughty whore.

Esmenet refused Serwë's offer to stay with her and Kellhus in their pavilion, but accepted her offer to wash with her laver. Afterward, Kellhus followed her to her tent.

"Serwë cleaned it for you," he said. "She replaced your bedding."

Esmenet started crying yet again. When had she become so weak? So pathetic?

How could you leave me? Why did you leave me?

She crawled into the tent as though diving into a burrow. She hid her face in clean woollen blankets. She smelled sandalwood ...

Bearing his lantern, Kellhus followed, sat cross-legged over her. "He's gone, Esmenet ... Sarcellus won't return. Not after tonight. Even if nothing happens, the questions will embarrass him. What man doesn't suspect other men of acting on their own lusts?"

"You don't understand," she gasped. How could she tell him? All this time fearing for Achamian, even daring to mourn him, and still ... "I lied to him!" she exclaimed. "I *lied to Akka!*"

Kellhus frowned. "What do you mean?"

"After he left me in Sumna the Consult came to me, the *Consult* Kellhus! And I knew that Inrau's death had been no suicide. I knew it! But I never told Akka. Sweet Sejenus, *I never told him!* And now he's gone, Kellhus! Gone!"

"Breathe, Esmi. *Breathe* ... What does this have to do with Sarcellus?"

"I don't know ... That's the mad part. I don't know!"

"You were lovers," Kellhus said, and she went still, like a child confronted by a wolf. Kellhus had always known her secret, since that night at the Shrine above Asgilioch when he'd interrupted her and Sarcellus. So why her terror now?

"For a time you thought you loved Sarcellus," Kellhus continued. "You even judged Achamian against him ... You judged and found Achamian wanting."

"I was a fool!" she cried. "A fool!" How could she be such a fool?

No man is your equal, love! No man!

"Achamian was weak," Kellhus said.

"But I loved him *for* those weaknesses! Don't you see? That's why I loved him!"

I loved him in truth!

"And that's why you could never go to him ... To go to him while you shared Sarcellus's bed would be to accuse him of those very weaknesses he couldn't bear. So you stayed away, fooled yourself into thinking you searched for him when you were hiding all the while."

"How can you know these things?" she sobbed.

"But no matter how much you lied to yourself, you *knew* ... And that's why you could never tell Achamian about what happened in Sumna—no matter how much he needed to know! Because you knew he wouldn't understand, and you feared what he would *see* ..."

Despicable, selfish, hateful ...

Polluted.

But Kellhus could see ... He'd always seen.

"Don't look at me!" she cried.

Look at me ...

"But I do, Esmi. I do look. And what I see fills me with *wonder*."

And these narcotic words, so warm and so close—so very close!—stilled her. Her pillow ached against her cheek, and the hard earth beneath her mat bruised, but all was warm and all was safe. He blew out his lantern, then quietly withdrew from her tent. The warm memory of his fingers continued to comb her hair.

Obviously famished, Serwë had started eating early. A pot of rice boiled on the fire, which Kellhus periodically opened and closed, adding onions, spices, and Shigeki pepper. Ordinarily Esmenet would have cooked, but

Kellhus had her reading aloud from *The Chronicle of the Tusk*, laughing at her rare fumbles and showering her with encouragement.

She was reading the Canticles, the old "Tusk Laws," many of which the Latter Prophet had rescinded in *The Tractate*. Together they wondered that children were stoned to death for striking their parents, or that when a man murdered some other man's brother, his *own* brother was executed.

Then she read, "'Suffer not a ...'"

She recognized the words because of sheer repetition. Sounding out the following word, she said, "'whore ...'" and stopped. She glanced at Kellhus and angrily recited, "'Suffer not a whore to live, for she maketh a pit of her womb ...'" Her ears burned. She squelched a sudden urge to cast the book into the flames.

Kellhus gazed back, utterly unsurprised.

He's been waiting for me to reach this passage. All along ...

"Give me the book," he said, his tone unreadable.

She did as she was told.

In a fluid, almost thoughtless motion, he pulled his knife from the ceremonial sheath he wore about his waist. Pinching the blade near the tip, he proceeded to scratch the ink of the offending statement from the vellum. For several heartbeats, Esmenet couldn't comprehend what he was doing. She simply stared, a petrified witness.

Once the column was clean, he leaned back to survey his handiwork.

"Better," he said, as though he'd just scraped mould from bread. He turned to pass the book back.

Esmenet couldn't bring herself to touch it. "But ... But you can't do that!"

"No?"

He pressed the book into her hands. She fairly tossed it into the dust on her far side.

"That's *Scripture*, Kellhus. The Tusk. The Holy Tusk!"

"I know. The warrant of your damnation."

Esmenet gawked like a fool. "But ..."

Kellhus scowled and shook his head, as though astonished she could be so dense.

"Just who, Esmi, do you think I am?"

Serwë chirped with laughter, even clapped her hands.

"Wh-who?" Esmenet stammered. It was the most she could manage. Other than in rare anger or jest, she'd never heard Kelhus speak with ... with such *presumption*.

"Yes," Kellhus repeated, *"who?"* His voice seemed satin thunder. He looked as eternal as a circle.

Then Esmenet glimpsed it: the shining gold about his hands ... Without thinking, she rolled to her knees before him, pressed her face into the dust.

Please! Please! I'm nothing!

Then Serwë hiccuped. Suddenly, absurdly, it was just Kellhus before her, laughing, drawing her up from the dust, bidding her to eat her supper.

"Better?" he said as she numbly resumed her place beside him. Her whole skin burned and prickled. He nodded toward the open book while filling his mouth with rice.

Bewildered, flustered, she blushed and looked down. She nodded to her bowl.

I knew this! I always knew this!

The difference was that Kellhus now knew as well. His presence burned in her periphery. How, she breathlessly wondered, how could she ever look into his eyes again?

Throughout her entire life she'd looked upon things and people that stood apart. She was Esmenet, and that was her bowl, the Emperor's silver, the Shriah's man, the God's ground, and so on. She stood here, and those things *there*. No longer. Everything, it seemed, radiated the warmth of his skin. The ground beneath her bare feet. The mat beneath her buttocks. And for a mad instant, she was certain that if she raised her fingers to her cheek, she would feel the soft curls of a flaxen beard, that if she turned to her left, she would see *Esmenet* hovering motionless over her rice bowl.

Somehow, everything had become *here*, and everything here had become *him*.

Kellhus!

She breathed in. Her heart battered her breast.

He scraped the passage clean!

In a single exhalation, it seemed, a lifetime of condemnation slipped from her, and she felt shriven, *truly shriven*. One breath and she was absolved! She experienced a kind of lucidity, as though her thoughts had been cleansed like water strained through bright white cloth. She thought she *should* cry, but the sunlight was too sharp, the air too clear for weeping.

Everything was so *certain*.

He scraped the passage clean!

Then she thought of Achamian.

The air smelled of wine and vomit and armpits. Torches flared through the murk, painting mud-brick walls in oranges and blacks, illuminating slivers of the drunken warriors who crowded the dark: a bearded jaw line here, a furrowed brow there, a glistening eye, a bloody fist upon a pommel. Cnaiür urs Skiötha walked among them, through the tight alleys of the Heppa, Ammegnotis's ancient district of revels. He shouldered his way forward, moving intently, as though he had a destination. Laughter and light boomed through wide-thrown doors. Shigeki girls giggled, called out in mangled Sheyic. Children hawked stolen oranges.

Laughing, he thought. *All of them laughing ...*

You're not of the land!

"You!" he heard someone cry.

Weeper! Faggot weeper!

"*You*," a young Galeoth man at his side said. Where had he come from? His eyes flashed in wonder, but something about the broken light made his face lurid. His lips looked wanton and feminine, the black hollow of his mouth promising. "You travelled with him. You're his first disciple! His first!"

"Who?"

"Him. The Warrior-Prophet."

You beat me, old Bannut, his father's brother, cried, *for fucking him the way you fucked his father!"*

Cnaiür seized the man, yanked him close. "*Who?*"

"Prince Kellhus of Atrithau ... You're the Scylvendi who found him on the Steppe. Who delivered him to us!"

Yes ... The *Dûnyain.* Somehow he'd forgotten about him. He glimpsed a face blow open, like Steppe grasses in a gust. He felt a palm, warm and tender upon his thigh. He began shaking.

You're more ... More than the People!

"I am of the People!" he grated.

The man wrenched ineffectually at his wrists. "Pleease!" he hissed. "I thought ... I thought ..."

Cnaiür tossed him to the ground, glared at the shadowy procession of passersby. Did they laugh?

I watched you that night! I saw the way you looked at him!

How did he find himself on this track? Where was he riding?

"What did you call me?" he screamed at the prostrate man.

He remembered running as hard as he could, away from the black paths worn through the grasses, away from the yaksh and his father's all-knowing wrath. He found a clutch of sumacs and cleared a hollow in their hidden heart. The weave of green grasses through grey. The smell of earth, of beetles crawling through damp and dark grottoes. The smell of solitude and secrecy, under the sky but sheltered from the wind. He pulled the broken pieces from his belt and spread them in breathless wonder. He reassembled them. She was so sad. And so beautiful. Impossibly beautiful.

Someone. He was forgetting to hate someone.

CHAPTER SEVENTEEN

SHIGEK

*In terror, all men throw up their hands and turn aside their faces.
Remember, Tratta, always preserve the face! For that is where
you are.*

—THROSEANIS, *TRIAMIS IMPERATOR*

*The Poet will yield up his stylus only when the Geometer can
explain how Life can at once be a point and a line. How can all
time, all creation, come to the now? Make no mistake: this moment,
the instant of this very breath, is the frail thread from which all
creation hangs.*
    That men dare to be thoughtless …

—TERES ANSANSIUS, *THE CITY OF MEN*

Early Autumn, 4111 Year-of-the-Tusk, Shigek

One day, returning from the river with their laundered clothes, Esmenet overheard several Men of the Tusk discussing the Holy War's preparations for their continuing march. Kellhus spent part of the afternoon with her and Serwë, explaining how the Kianene, before retreating across the desert, had slaughtered every camel on the South Bank, just as they'd burned every boat before retreating across the Sempis. Since then, forays into the deserts of Khemema to the south had found every well poisoned.

"The Padirajah," Kellhus said, "hopes to make of the desert what Skauras hoped to make of the Sempis."

The Great Names, of course, were undeterred. They planned to march along the coastal hills followed by the Imperial Fleet, which would provide them with all the water they would need. The road would be laborious—they would have to send parties of thousands through the hills to collect the water—but it would see them safely to Enathpaneah, to the very marches of the Sacred Land, long before the Padirajah could possibly recover from his defeat at Anwurat.

"Soon you two will be shuffling through sand," Kellhus said in the warm teasing manner that Esmenet had learned to love long ago. "It'll be hard for you, Serwë, heavy with child, carrying our pavilion on your back."

The girl shot him a look, at once scolding and delighted.

Esmenet laughed, at the same time realizing she'd be travelling even farther from Achamian ...

She wanted to ask Kellhus if he'd heard any word from Xinemus, but she was too frightened. Besides, she knew Kellhus would tell her as soon as any news arrived. And she knew what that news would be. She'd glimpsed it in Kellhus's eyes many, many times.

Once again they'd gathered about the same side of the fire to avoid the winding smoke, Kellhus in the centre, Serwë on his right, and Esmenet on his left. They were cooking small pieces of lamb on sticks, which they ate with small pieces of bread and cheese. This had become a favourite treat of theirs—one of many little things that had kept the promise of family.

Kellhus leaned past her to grab more bread, still teasing Serwë.

"Have you ever pitched a pavilion across sand before?"

"Kell-*hussss*," Serwë complained and exulted.

Esmenet breathed deeply his dry, salty smell. She couldn't help herself.

"They say it takes *forever*," he chided, withdrawing his hand and accidentally brushing Esmenet's right breast.

The tingle of inadvertent intimacy. The flush of a body suddenly thick with a wisdom that transcended intellect.

For the remainder of the afternoon, Esmenet found her eyes plagued by a nagging waywardness. Where before her look had confined itself to

Kellhus's face, it now roamed over his entire form. It was as though her eyes had become brokers, intermediaries between his body and her own. When she saw his chest, her breasts tingled with the prospect of being crushed. When she glimpsed his narrow hips and deep buttocks, her inner thighs hummed with expectant warmth. Sometimes her palms literally itched!

Of course this was madness. Esmenet needed only to catch Serwë's watchful eyes to recall herself.

Later that night, after Kellhus had left, the two of them stretched across their mats, their heads almost touching, their bodies angled to either side of the fire. They often did this when Kellhus was away. They stared endlessly into the flames, sometimes talking, but mostly saying nothing at all, save yelping when the fire spat coals.

"Esmi?" Serwë asked in a peculiar, brooding tone.

"Yes, Serchaa?"

"I *would*, you know."

Esmenet's heart fluttered. "You would what?"

"Share him," the girl said.

Esmenet swallowed. "No ... Never, Serwë ... I told you not to worry."

"But that's what I'm saying ... I don't fear losing him, not any more, and not to anyone. All I want is what *he* wants. He's everything ..."

Esmenet lay breathless, staring between legs of wood at the pulsing furnace of coals.

"Are you saying ... Are you saying that he ..."

wants me ...

Serwë laughed softly. "Of course not," she said.

"Of course not," Esmenet repeated. With an inner shrug, she shook away these mad and maddening thoughts. What was she doing? He was Kellhus. *Kellhus.*

She thought of Akka, blinked two burning tears.

"Never, Serwë."

Kellhus didn't return until the following night, when he rode into their little camp accompanied by Proyas himself. The Conriyan Prince looked particularly travel-worn and haggard. He was dressed in a simple blue tunic—his riding clothes, Esmenet supposed. Only the gold-embroidered intricacy of his hems spoke to his station. His beard, which he usually kept clipped close to his jaw, had grown out, so that it more resembled the square-cut beards of his caste-nobles.

At first Esmenet kept her gaze averted, worried Proyas might guess the intensity of her hatred if he glimpsed her eyes. How couldn't she hate him? He'd not only refused to help Achamian, he'd refused to allow Xinemus to help as well, and had divested the Marshal of his rank and station when he insisted. But something in his voice, a high-born desperation, perhaps, made her watchful. He seemed uncomfortable—even forlorn—as he took his place beside Kellhus at the fire, so much so that she found her dislike faltering. He too had loved Achamian once. Xinemus had told her as much.

Perhaps that's why he suffered. Perhaps he wasn't so unlike her.

That, she knew, was what Kellhus would say.

After pouring everyone watered wine, and serving the men the remnants of the meal she'd prepared for herself and Serwë, Esmenet took a seat on the far side of the fire.

The men discussed matters of war as they ate, and Esmenet was struck by the contradiction between the way Proyas deferred to Kellhus and the general reserve of his manner. Suddenly she understood why Kellhus forbade his followers from joining their camp. Men like Proyas, like any of the Great Names, she supposed, would be troubled by Kellhus. Those at the centre of things were always more inflexible, always more invested, than those at the edges. And Kellhus promised a new centre ...

It was easy to move from edge to edge.

The men fell silent to finish their lamb, onions, and bread. Proyas set aside his plate, washed his palette with a sip of wine. He glanced at Esmenet, inadvertently it seemed, then stared off into the distance. Esmenet suddenly found the quiet suffocating.

"How fares the Scylvendi?" she asked, uncertain of what else to say.

He glanced back to her. For an instant, his eyes lingered on her tattooed hand ...

"I see him but rarely," the handsome man replied, staring into the flames.

"But I thought he counselled ..." She paused, suddenly uncertain as to the propriety of her words. Achamian had always complained of her forward manner with caste-nobles ...

"Counselled me on war?" Proyas shook his head, and for a brief instant she could see why Achamian had loved him. It was so strange, being with those he'd once known. Somehow it made his absence at once palpable and easier to bear.

He was real. He had left his mark. The world remembered.

"After Kellhus explained what happened at Anwurat," the Prince continued, "the Council hailed Cnaiür as the author of our victory. The Priests of Gilgaöl even declared him Battle-Celebrant. But he would have nothing of it …"

The Prince took another deep draught of wine. "He finds it unbearable, I think …"

"As a Scylvendi among Inrithi?"

Proyas shook his head, set his empty bowl curiously close to his right foot.

"Liking us," he said.

Without further word he stood and excused himself. He bowed to Kellhus, thanked Serwë for the wine and her gracious company, then without so much as glancing at Esmenet, strode off into the darkness.

Serwë stared at her feet. Kellhus seemed lost in otherworldly ruminations. Esmenet sat silently for a time, her face burning, her limbs and thoughts itching with a peculiar hum. It was always peculiar, even though she knew it as well as the taste of her own mouth.

Shame.

Everywhere she went. It was her characteristic stink.

"I'm sorry," she said to the two of them.

What was she doing here? What could she offer other than humiliation? She was polluted—polluted! And here she stayed with Kellhus? With *Kellhus?* What kind of fool was she? She couldn't change who she was, no sooner than she could wash the tattoo from the back of her hand! The seed she could rinse away, but not the sin! Not the sin!

And he was … He was …

"I'm sorry," she sobbed. "I'm sorry!"

Esmenet fled the fire, crawled into the solitary darkness of her tent. Of *his* tent! *Akka's!*

Kellhus came to her not long after, and she cursed herself for hoping he would.

"I wish I were dead," she whispered, lying face first against the ground. "So do many."

Always implacable honesty. Could she follow where he led? Had she the strength?

"I've only loved two people in my life, Kellhus ..."

The Prince never looked away. "And they're both dead."

She nodded, blinked tears.

"You don't know my sins, Kellhus. You don't know the darknesses I harbour in my heart."

"Then tell me."

They talked long into the night, and a strange dispassion moved her, rendering the extremities of her life—death, loss, humiliation—curiously inert.

Whore. How many men had embraced her? How many gritty chins against her cheek? Always something to be endured. All of them punishing her for their need. Monotony had made them seem laughable, a long queue of the weak, the hopeful, the ashamed, the angered, the dangerous. How easily one grunting body replaced the next, until they became abstract things, moments of a ludicrous ceremony, spilling bowel-hot libations upon her, smearing her with their meaningless paint. One no different from the next.

They punished her for that as well.

How old had she been, when her father had sold her to the first of his friends? Eleven? Twelve? When had the punishment begun? When had he first lain with her? She could remember her mother weeping in the corner ... but not much more.

And her daughter ... How old had she been?

She had thought her father's thoughts, she explained. Another mouth. Let it feed itself. The monotony had numbed her to the horror, had made degradation a laughable thing. To trade flashing silver for milky seed— the fools. Let Mimara be schooled in the foolishness of men. Clumsy, rutting animals. One need only pay with a little patience, mimic their passion, wait, and soon it would be over. In the morning, one could buy food ... Food from fools, Mimara. Can't you see child? Shush. Stop weeping. Look! Food from fools!

"That was her name?" Kellhus asked. "Mimara?"

"Yes," Esmenet said. Why could she say that name now, when she could never utter it with Achamian? Strange, the way long sorrow could silence the pang of unspeakable things.

The first sobs surprised her. Without thinking, she leaned into Kellhus, and his arms enclosed her. She wailed and beat softly against his chest, heaved and cried. He smelled of wool and sunburned skin.

They were dead. The only ones she'd ever loved.

After her breathing settled, Kellhus pressed her back, and her hands fell slack to his lap. Over the course of several heartbeats, she felt him harden against the back of her wrist, as though a serpent flexed beneath wool. She neither breathed nor moved.

The air, as silent as a candle, roared …

She pulled her hands away.

Why? Why would she poison a night such as this?

Kellhus shook his head, softly laughed. "Intimacy begets intimacy, Esmi. So long as we remember ourselves, there's no reason for shame. All of us are frail."

She looked down to her palms, her wrists. Smiled.

"I remember … Thank you, Kellhus."

He raised his hand to her cheek, then ducked from her little tent.

She rolled to her side, squeezed her hands palm to palm between her knees, and murmured curses until she fell asleep.

The message had arrived by sea, the man said. He was Galeoth, and from the look of his surcoat, a member of Saubon's own household.

Proyas weighed the ivory scroll-case in his hand. It was small, cold to the touch, and finely worked with tiny Tusks. Clever workmanship, Proyas thought. Innumerable tiny representations, each figure defined by further figures, so that there was no blank ground to throw each into relief, only tusks and more tusks. There was a sermon, Proyas mused, even in the container of this message.

But then that was Maithanet: sermons all the way down.

The Conriyan Prince thanked and dismissed the man, then returned to his chair by his field table. It was hot and humid in his pavilion, so much so he found himself resenting the lamps for their added heat. He'd stripped down to a thin, white linen tunic and had already decided that he would sleep naked—after he investigated this letter.

With his knife he carefully broke the canister's wax seal. He tipped it, and the small scroll slid out, fastened by yet another seal, this one bearing the Shriah's own mark.

What could he want?

Proyas brooded for a moment on the privilege of receiving such letters from such a man. Then he snapped the wax seal, peeled open the parchment roll.

Lord Prince Nersei Proyas,

> *May the Gods of the God shelter you, and keep you.*
> *Your last missive ...*

Proyas paused, struck by a sense of guilt and mortification. Months ago, he'd written Maithanet at Achamian's behest, asking about the death of a former student of his—Paro Inrau. At the time, he hadn't believed he would actually send it. He'd been certain that writing the letter would make sending it impossible. What better way to at once discharge and dispose of an obligation? *Dear Maithanet, a sorcerer friend of mine wants me to ask whether you killed one of his spies ...* It was madness. There was no way he could send such a letter ...

And yet.

How could he not feel a sense of kinship to this Inrau, this other student Achamian had loved? How could he not remember everything about the blasphemous fool, the wry smile, the twinkling eyes, the lazy afternoons doing drills in the gardens? How could he not pity him, a good man, a kind man, hunting fables and wives' tales to his everlasting damnation?

Proyas had sent the letter, thinking that at long last the matter of his Mandate tutor could be put to rest. He'd never expected a reply—not truly. But he was a Prince, an heir apparent, and Maithanet was the Shriah of the Thousand Temples. Letters between such men somehow found their way, no matter how fierce the world between them.

Proyas continued reading, holding his breath to numb the shame. Shame at having sent such a trivial matter to the man who would cleanse the Three Seas. Shame at having written this to a man at whose feet he'd wept. And shame for feeling shame at having fulfilled an old teacher's request.

Lord Prince Nersei Proyas,

> May the Gods of the God shelter you, and keep you.
>
> Your last missive, we are afraid, left us deeply perplexed, until we recalled that you yourself once maintained several—How should we put it?—dubious associations. We had been informed that the death of this young priest, Paro Inrau, had been a suicide. The College of Luthymae, the priests charged with the investigation of this matter, reported that this Inrau had once been a student of Mandate sorcery, and that he had recently been seen in the company of one Drusas Achamian, his old teacher. They believed that this Achamian had been sent to pressure Inrau into performing various services for his School; in short, to be a spy. They believe that, as a result, the young priest found himself in an untenable position. Tribes 4:8: "He wearies of breath, who has no place he might breathe."
>
> The responsibility for this young man's unfortunate death, we fear, lies with this blasphemer, Achamian. There is nothing more to it. May the God have mercy on his soul. Canticles 6:22: "The earth weeps at words which know not the Gods' wrath."
>
> But as your missive left us perplexed, we fear that this missive shall leave you equally baffled. By allying the Holy War with the Scarlet Spires, we have already asked much in the way of Compromise from pious men. But in this it has been clear, we pray, that Necessity forced our hand. Without the Scarlet Spires, the Holy War could not hope to prevail against the Cishaurim. "Answer not blasphemy with blasphemy," our Prophet says, and this verse has been oft repeated by our enemies. But in answering the charges of the Cultic Priests, the Prophet also says: "Many are those who are cleansed by way of iniquity. For the Light must ever follow upon the dark, if it is to be Light, and the Holy must ever follow upon the wicked, if it is to be Holy." So it is that

the Holy War must follow upon the Scarlet Spires, if it is to be Holy.
Scholars 1:3: "Let Sun follow Night, according to the arch of
Heaven."

Now we must ask a further Compromise of you, Lord Nersei
Proyas. You must do everything in your power to assist this Mandate
Schoolman. Perhaps this might not be as difficult as we fear, since this
man was once your teacher in Aöknyssus. But we know the depth of
your piety, and unlike the greater Compromise we have forced upon
you with the Scarlet Spires, there is no Necessity that we can cite that
might give comfort to a heart made restless by the company of sin.
Hintarates 28:4: "I ask of you, is there any friend more difficult than
the friend who sins?"

Assist Drusas Achamian, Proyas, though he is a blasphemer, for in
this wickedness, the Holy shall also follow. Everything shall be made clear,
in the end. And it shall be glorious. Scholars 22:36: "For the warring
heart becomes weary and will turn to sweeter labours. And the peace of
dawn's rising shall accompany Men throughout the toils of the day."

May the God and all His Aspects shelter you and keep you.

Maithanet

Proyas lowered the letter to his lap.

"*Assist Drusas Achamian ...*"

What could the Shriah possibly mean? What could be at stake, for him
to make such a request?

And what was he to do with such a request, now that it was too late?
Now that Achamian was gone.

I killed him ...

And Proyas suddenly realized that he'd used his old teacher as a
marker, as a measure of his own piety. What greater evidence could there
be of righteousness than the willingness to sacrifice a loved one? Wasn't
this the lesson of Angeshraël on Mount Kinsureah? And what better way
to sacrifice a loved one than by hating?

Or delivering him to his enemies ...

He thought of the whore at Kellhus's fire—Achamian's lover, Esmenet
... How desolate she'd seemed. How frightened. Had he authored that
look?

She's just a whore!

And Achamian was just a sorcerer. Just.

All men were not equal. Certainly the Gods favoured whom they would, but there was more. *Actions* determined the worth of any pulse. Life was the God's question to men, and actions were their answers. And like all answers they were either right or wrong, blessed or cursed. Achamian had condemned himself, had damned himself by his own actions! And so had the whore ... This wasn't the judgement of Nersei Proyas, this was the judgement of the Tusk, of the Latter Prophet!

Inri Sejenus ...

Then why this shame? This anguish? Why this relentless, heart-mauling doubt?

Doubt. In a sense, that had been Achamian's single lesson. Geometry, logic, history, mathematics using Nilnameshi numbers, even philoso-phy!—all these things were dross, Achamian would argue, in the face of doubt. Doubt had made them, and doubt would unmake them.

Doubt, he would say, set men free ... *Doubt,* not truth!

Beliefs were the foundation of actions. Those who believed without doubting, he would say, acted without thinking. And those who acted without thinking were enslaved.

That was what Achamian would say.

Once, after listening to his beloved older brother, Tirummas, describe his harrowing pilgrimage to the Sacred Land, Proyas had told Achamian how he wished to become a Shrial Knight.

"Why?" the portly Schoolman had exclaimed.

They'd been strolling through the gardens—Proyas could remember bounding from leaf to fallen leaf just to hear them crackle beneath his sandals. They stopped near the immense iron oak that dominated the garden's heart.

"So I can kill heathens on the Empire's frontier!"

Achamian tossed his hands skyward in dismay. "Foolish boy! How many faiths are there? How many competing beliefs? And you would *murder* another on the slender hope that yours is somehow the *only* one?"

"Yes! I have *faith!*"

"Faith," the Schoolman repeated, as though recalling the name of a hated foe. "Ask yourself, Prosha ... What if the choice isn't between certainties, between this faith and that, but between faith and *doubt?* Between renouncing the mystery and embracing it?"

"But doubt is weakness!" Proyas cried. "Faith is strength! Strength!" Never, he was convinced, had he felt so holy as at that moment. The sunlight seemed to shine straight through him, to bathe his heart.

"Is it? Have you looked around you, Prosha? Pay attention, boy. Watch and tell me how many men, out of weakness, *lapse* into the practice of doubt. Listen to those around you, and tell me what you see ..."

He did exactly as Achamian had asked. For several days, he watched and listened. He saw much hesitation, but he wasn't so foolish as to confuse that with doubt. He heard the caste-nobles squabble and the hereditary priests complain. He eavesdropped on the soldiers and the knights. He observed embassy after embassy posture before his father, making claim after florid claim. He listened to the slaves joke as they laundered, or bicker as they ate. And in the midst of innumerable boasts, declarations, and accusations, only rarely did he hear those words Achamian had made so familiar, so commonplace ... The words Proyas himself found so difficult! And even then, they belonged most to those Proyas considered wise, even-handed, compassionate, and least to those he thought stupid or malicious.

"I don't know."

Why were these words so difficult?

"Because men want to murder," Achamian had explained afterward. "Because men want their gold and their glory. Because they want beliefs that *answer* to their fears, their hatreds, and their hungers."

Proyas could remember the heart-pounding wonder, the exhilaration of straying ...

"Akka?" He took a deep, daring breath. "Are you saying the Tusk *lies?*"

A look of dread. "I don't know ..."

Difficult words, so difficult they would see Achamian banished from Aöknyssus and Proyas tutored by Charamemas, the famed Shrial scholar. And Achamian had known this would happen ... Proyas could see that now.

Why? Why would Achamian, who was already damned, sacrifice so much for so few words?

He thought he was giving me something ... Something important.

Drusas Achamian had loved him. What was more, he'd loved him so deeply he'd imperilled his position, his reputation—even his vocation, if what Xinemus had said was true. Achamian had given without hope of reward.

He wanted me to be free.

And Proyas had given him away, thinking only of rewards.

The thought was too much to bear.

I did it for the Holy War! For Shimeh!

And now this letter—from Maithanet.

He snatched up the parchment, scanned it once again, as though the Shriah's manly script might offer some answer ...

"Assist Drusas Achamian ..."

What had happened? The Scarlet Spires he could understand, but what use could the Shriah of the Thousand Temples have with a Schoolman? And with a *Mandate* Schoolman, no less ...

A sudden chill dropped through him. Beneath the black walls of Momemn, Achamian had once argued that the Holy War wasn't what it seemed ... Was this letter proof of that fact?

Something had frightened, or at least concerned, Maithanet. But what?

Had he heard rumours of Prince Kellhus? For weeks now, Proyas had meant to write the Shriah regarding the Prince of Atrithau, but for some reason he couldn't bring himself to put ink to parchment. Something compelled him to wait, but whether it was hope or fear he couldn't determine. Kellhus simply struck him as one of those mysteries that could only be resolved through patience. And besides, what would he say? That the Holy War *for* the Latter Prophet was witnessing the birth of a *Latter* Latter Prophet?

As much as he was loath to admit it, Conphas was right: the notion was simply too absurd!

No. If the Holy Shriah harboured reservations concerning Prince Kellhus, Proyas was fairly confident he would've simply asked. As it was, there wasn't so much as a hint, let alone mention, of the Prince of Atrithau in the letter. Chances were Maithanet had no inkling of Kellhus's existence, let alone his growing stature.

No, Proyas decided. It must be something else ... Something the

Shriah thought beyond his tolerance or his ken. Otherwise, why not explain his reasons?

Could it be the Consult?

"The Dreams," Achamian had said at Momemn. "They've been so forceful of late."

"Ah, back to the nightmares again ..."

"Something is happening, Proyas. I know it. I *feel* it!"

Never had he looked so desperate.

Could it be?

No. It was too absurd. Even if they did exist, how could the Shriah find them when the Mandate themselves couldn't?

No ... It had to be the *Scarlet Spires*. After all, that had been Achamian's mission, hadn't it? Watch the Scarlet Spires ...

Proyas yanked at his hair and snarled under his breath.

Why?

Why couldn't this one thing be pure? Why must everything holy— *everything!*—be riddled by tawdry and despicable intent?

He sat very still, drawing breath after shuddering breath. He imagined drawing his sword, slashing and hacking wildly through his chambers, howling and shrieking ... Then he collected himself to the beat of his own pulse.

Nothing pure ... Love transformed into betrayal. Prayers bent into accusations.

This was Maithanet's point, wasn't it? The holy followed upon the wicked.

Proyas had thought himself the moral leader of the Holy War. But now he knew better. Now he knew he was merely one more piece upon the benjuka plate. The players were perhaps known to him—the Thousand Temples, House Ikurei, the Scarlet Spires, the Cishaurim, and perhaps even Kellhus—but the *rules*, which were the most treacherous element of any game of benjuka, were definitely not known.

I don't know. I don't know anything.

The Holy War had only triumphed, and yet never had he felt so desperate.

So weak.

I told you, old tutor. I told you ...

As though stirring from a stupor, Proyas called for Algari, his old Cironji body-slave, and bid the man to bring him his writing chest. As tired as he was, he had no choice but to answer the Shriah now. Tomorrow the Holy War marched into the desert.

For some reason, after unlatching the small mahogany and ivory chest and running his fingers over the quill and curled parchment, Nersei Proyas felt like a young boy once again, about to begin his writing drills under Achamian's hawkish but all-forgiving eyes. He could almost feel the sorcerer's friendly shadow, looming watchfully over his boy-slender shoulders.

"*That House Nersei could produce a boy so daft!*"

"*That the School of Mandate could send a tutor so blind!*"

Proyas almost laughed his tutor's world-wise laugh.

And tears clotted his eyes as he completed the first line of his baffled reply to Maithanet.

... but it would seem, Your Eminence, that Drusas Achamian is dead.

Esmenet smiled, and Kellhus saw through her olive skin, through the play of muscles over bone, all the way to the abstract point that described her soul.

She knows I see her, Father.

The campsite bustled with activity and rumbled with open-hearted conversation. The Holy War was about to march across the deserts of Khemema, and Kellhus had invited all fourteen of his senior Zaudunyani, which meant "the Tribe of Truth" in Kûniüric, to his fire. They already knew their mission; Kellhus need only remind them of what he promised. Beliefs alone didn't control the actions of men. There was also *desire*, and these men, his apostles, must shine with that desire.

The Thanes of the Warrior-Prophet.

Esmenet sat across from him on the far side of the fire, laughing and chatting with her neighbours, Arweal and Persommas, her face flushed with a joy she wouldn't have dared imagine and couldn't yet dare admit. Kellhus winked at her, then looked to the others, smiling, laughing, calling out ...

Scrutinizing. Dominating.

Each was a riotous font of significance. The downcast eyes, quickened heart, and fumbling words of Ottma spoke to the overpowering presence of Serwë, who blithely gossiped at his side. The momentary sneer the instant before Ulnarta smiled meant he still disapproved of Tshuma because he feared the blackness of his skin. The way Kasalla, Gayamakri, and Hilderath oriented their shoulders toward Werjau, even while speaking to others, meant they still considered him to be first among them. And indeed, the way Werjau tended to call across the fire more and more, leaning forward with his palms down, while the others generally restricted their conversation to those beside them, spoke to the assertion of unconscious relations of dominance and submission. Werjau even thrust out his chin ...

"Tell me, Werjau," Kellhus called out. "What is it you see within your heart?"

Such interventions were inevitable. These were world-born men.

"Joy," Werjau said, smiling. Faint deadening about the eyes. Flare in pulse. Blush reflex.

He sees, and he doesn't see.

Kellhus compressed his lips, rueful and forbearing. "And what is it I see?"

This he knows ...

The sound of other voices trailed into silence.

Werjau lowered his eyes.

"Pride," the young Galeoth said. "You see pride, Master."

Kellhus grinned, and the anxiety was swept from them.

"Not," he said, "with that face, Werjau."

All of them, including Serwë and Esmenet, howled with laughter, and Kellhus glanced around the fire, satisfied. He could tolerate no posturing among them. It was the utter absence of presumption that made his company so utterly unique, that made their hearts leap and their stomachs giddy at the prospect of seeing him. The weight of sin was found in secrecy and condemnation. Strip these away, deny men their deceptions and their judgements, and their self-sense of shame and worthlessness simply vanished.

They felt greater in his presence, both pure and *chosen*.

———— ✬ ————

Pragma Meigon stared through young Kellhus's face, saw his fear. "They're harmless," he said.

"What are they, Pragma?"

"Exemplary defectives … Specimens. We retain them for purposes of education." The Pragma simulated a smile. "For students such as you, Kellhus."

They stood deep beneath Ishuäl, in a hexagonal room within the mighty galleries of the Thousand Thousand Halls. Save for the entrance, staggered racks of knobbed and runnelled candles covered the surrounding walls, shedding a light without shadows and as bright and clear as the noonday sun's. This alone made the room extraordinary—light was otherwise forbidden in the Labyrinth—but what made the room astonishing were the many men shackled in its sunken centre.

Each of them was naked, linen pale, and bound with greening copper straps to boards that leaned gently backward. The boards themselves had been arranged in a broad circle, with each man lying fixed within arm's reach of his comrades and positioned at the edge of the floor's central depression, so that a boy Kellhus's height could stand at the lip of the surrounding floor and look the specimens directly in the face …

Had they possessed faces.

Their heads were drawn forward into open iron frames, where they were held motionless by bracketing bars. Behind their heads, wires had been fixed to the base of each frame. These swept forward in a radial fashion, ending in tiny silver hooks that anchored the obscuring skin. Slick muscle gleamed in the light. To Kellhus, it looked as though each man had thrust his head into a spider web that had peeled away his face.

Pragma Meigon had called it the Unmasking Room.

"To begin," the old man said, "you'll study and memorize each of their faces. Then you'll reproduce what you've seen on parchment." He nodded to a battery of worn scrivening tables along the southern walls.

His limbs as light as autumn leaves, Kellhus stepped forward. He heard the masticating of pasty mouths, a chorus of voiceless grunts and gaspings.

"Their larynxes have been removed," Pragma Meigon explained. "To assist concentration."

Kellhus paused before the first specimen.

"The face possesses forty-four muscles," the Pragma continued. "Operating in concert, they are capable of signifying every permutation of passion. All those permutations, young Kellhus, derive from the fifty-seven base and base-remove types found here in this room."

Despite the absence of skin, Kellhus immediately recognized horror in the flayed face of the specimen strapped before him. Like warring flatworms, the fine muscles about his eyes strained outward and inward at the same time. The larger, rat-sized muscles about his lower face yanked his mouth into a perpetual fear-grin. Lidless eyes stared. Rapid breaths hissed ...

"You're wondering how he can maintain that particular expressive configuration," the Pragma said. "Centuries ago we found we could limit the range of behaviours by probing the brain with needles—with what we now call neuropuncture."

Kellhus stood transfixed. Without warning, an attendant loomed over him, holding a narrow reed between his teeth. He dipped the reed into the bowl of fluid he carried, then blowing, sprayed the specimen with a fine orangish mist. He then continued on to the next.

"Neuropuncture," the Pragma continued, "made possible the rehabilitation of defectives for instructional purposes. The specimen before you, for instance, always displays fear at a base-remove of two."

"Horror?" Kellhus asked.

"Precisely."

Kellhus felt the childishness of his own horror fade in understanding. He looked to either side, saw the specimens curving out of sight, rows of white eyes set in shining red musculatures. They were only defectives—nothing more. He returned his gaze to the man before him, to fear base-remove two, and committed what he saw to memory. Then he moved on to the next gasping skein of muscles.

"Good," Pragma Meigon had said from his periphery. "Very good."

Kellhus turned once more to Esmenet, peeled away her face with the hooks of his gaze.

She'd already made two trips from the fire to her tent—promenades to draw his attention and covertly gauge his interest. She periodically looked from side to side, feigning amusement in things elsewhere to see if he watched her. Twice he let her catch him. Each time he grinned with boyish good nature. Each time she looked down, blushing, pupils dilated, eyes blinking rapidly, her body radiating the musk of nascent arousal. Though Esmenet had not yet come to his bed, part of her ached for him, even wooed him. And she knew it not.

For all her native gifts, Esmenet remained a world-born woman. And for all world-born men and women, two souls shared the same body, face, and eyes. The animal and the intellect. Everyone was two.

Defective.

One Esmenet had already renounced Drusas Achamian. The other would soon follow.

Esmenet blinked against the turquoise sky, held a hand against the sun. No matter how many times she witnessed it, she was dumbstruck.

The Holy War.

She'd paused with Kellhus and Serwë on the summit of a rise so that Serwë could readjust her pack. Fields of Inrithi warriors and camp-followers walked past them, toward the crumbling cliffs of the southern escarpment. Esmenet looked from man to armoured man, each farther than the next, past clots and through thickening screens, until losing them in the teeming distances, where they winked in the sunlight like metal filings. She turned, saw the sand-coloured walls of Ammegnotis behind them, dwindling against the black and green of the river and her verdant banks.

Shigek.

Goodbye, Akka.

Teary-eyed, she deliberately struck out on her own, simply waving a hand when Kellhus called out to her.

She walked among strangers, feeling the aim of hooded eyes and muttered words—as she so often did. Some men actually accosted her, but she ignored them. One even angrily grabbed her tattooed hand, as though to remind her of something she owed all men. The parched grasses became thinner and thinner, leaving gravel that burned toes and cooked air. She sweat and suffered and somehow knew it was only the beginning.

That evening she found Kellhus and Serwë without much difficulty. Though they had little fuel, they managed dinner with a small fire. The air cooled as quickly as the sun descended, and they enjoyed their first desert dusk. The ground radiated warmth like a stone drawn from a hearth. To the east, sterile hills ringed the distance, obscuring the sea. To the south and west, beyond the riot of the encampment, the horizon formed a perfect shale line that thickened into red as it approached the sun. To the north, Shigek could still be glimpsed between the tents, its green becoming black in the growing twilight.

Serwë was already snoozing, curled across her mat close to the little lapping tongue of their fire.

"So how was your walk?" Kellhus asked.

"I'm sorry," she said, shamefaced. "I—"

"There's no need to apologize, Esmi ... You walk where you choose."

She looked down, feeling both relieved and grief-stricken.

"So?" Kellhus repeated. "How was your walk?"

"Men," she said leadenly. "Too many men."

"And you call yourself a harlot," Kellhus said, grinning.

Esmenet continued staring at her dusty feet. A shy smile stole across her face.

"Things change ..."

"Perhaps," he said in a manner that reminded Esmenet of an axe biting into wood. "Have you ever wondered why the Gods hold men higher than women?"

Esmenet shrugged. "We stand in the shadow of men," she replied, "just as men stand in the shadow of the Gods."

"So you think *you* stand in the shadow of men?"

She smiled. There was no deception with Kellhus, no matter how petty. That was his wonder.

"*Some* men, yes ..."

"But not many?"

She laughed, caught in an honest conceit. "Not many at all," she admitted. Not even, she breathlessly realized, Akka ...

Only you.

"And what of other men? Aren't all men overshadowed in some respect?"

"Yes, I suppose ..."

Kellhus turned his palms upward—a curiously disarming gesture. "So what makes you less than a man?"

Esmenet laughed again, certain he played some game. "Because everywhere I've been—every place I've *heard* of for that matter—women serve men. That's simply the way. Most women are like ..." She paused, troubled by the course of her thoughts. She glanced at Serwë, her perfect face illuminated by the wavering light of the fire.

"Like her," Kellhus said.

"Yes," Esmenet replied, her eyes forced to the ground by a strange defensiveness. "Like her ... Most women are simple."

"And most men?"

"Well, certainly more men than women are learned ... Wise."

"And is this because men are *more* than women?"

Esmenet stared at him, dumbfounded.

"Or is it," he continued, "because men are *granted* more than women in this world?"

She stared, her thoughts spinning. She breathed deeply, set her palms carefully upon her knees. "You're saying women are ... are actually *equal?*"

Kellhus hoisted his brows in pained amusement. "Why," he asked, "are men willing to exchange gold to lie with women?"

"Because they desire us ... They lust."

"And is it lawful for men to purchase pleasure from a woman?"

"No ..."

"So why do they?"

"They can't help themselves," Esmenet replied. She lifted a rueful eyebrow. "They're *men.*"

"So they have no control over their desire?"

She grinned in her old way. "Witness the well-fed harlot sitting before you."

Kellhus laughed, but softly, and in a manner that effortlessly sorted her pain from her humour.

"So why," he said, "do men herd cattle?"

"Cattle?" Esmenet scowled. Where had all these absurd thoughts come from? "Well ... to slaughter for ..."

She trailed in sudden understanding. Her skin pimpled. Once again she sat in shadow, and Kellhus hoarded the failing sun, looking for all the world like a bronze idol. The sun always seemed to relinquish him last ...

"Men," Kellhus said, "cannot dominate their hunger, so they dominate, domesticate, the *objects* of their hunger. Be it cattle ..."

"Or women," she said breathlessly.

The air prickled with understanding.

"When one race," Kellhus continued, "is tributary to another, as the Cepalorans are to the Nansur, whose tongue do both races speak?"

"The tongue of the conqueror."

"And whose tongue do you speak?"

She swallowed. "The tongue of men."

With every blink, it seemed, she saw man after man, arched over her like dogs ...

"You see yourself," Kellhus said, "as men see you. You fear growing old, because men hunger for girls. You dress shamelessly, because men hunger for your skin. You cringe when you speak, because men hunger for your silence. You pander. You posture. You primp and preen. You twist your thoughts and warp your heart. You break and remake, cut and cut and cut, all so you might answer in your conqueror's tongue!"

Never, it seemed, had she been so motionless. The air within her throat, even the blood within her heart, seemed absolutely still ... Kellhus had become a voice falling from somewhere between tears and firelight.

"You say, 'Let me shame myself for you. Let me suffer you! I beg you, *please!*'"

And somehow, Esmenet knew where these words must lead, so she thought of other things, like how parched skin and cloth seemed so clean ...

Filth, she realized, needed water the same as men.

"And you tell yourself," Kellhus continued, "'These tracks I will not follow!' Perhaps you refuse certain perversities. Perhaps you refuse to kiss. You pretend to scruple, to discriminate, though the world has forced you onto trackless ground. The coins! The coins! Coins for everything, and everything for coins! For the landlord. For the apparati, when they come for their bribes. For the vendors who feed you. For the toughs with scabbed knuckles. And secretly, you ask yourself, 'What could be unthinkable when I'm already damned? What act lies beyond me, when I have no dignity?'

"'What love lies beyond sacrifice?'"

Her face was wet. When she drew her hand from her cheek, the whorls of her fingertips were black.

"You speak the tongue of your conquerors ..." Kellhus whispered. "You say, Mimara, come with me child."

A shiver passed through her, as though she were a drumskin ...

"And you take her ..."

"She's dead!" some woman cried. "She's *dead!*"

"To the slavers in the harbour ..."

"*Stop!*" the woman hissed. "*I say, no!*"

Gasping, like knives.

"And you sell her."

She remembered his arms enclosing her. She remembered following him to his pavilion. She remembered lying at his side, weeping and weeping, while his voice made her anguish plain, while Serwë stroked tears from her cheeks, ran cool fingers through her hair. She remembered telling them what had happened. About the hungry summer, when she had swallowed men for free just for their seed. About hating the little girl—the filthy little bitch!—who wept and demanded and demanded, who ate her food, who sent her into the streets, all because of love! About the hollow-eyed madness. Who could understand starvation? About the slavers, their larders growing fat because of the famine. About Mimara shrieking, her little girl shrieking! About the poison coins ... Less than a week! They had lasted less than a week!

She remembered shrieking.

And she remembered weeping as she'd never wept before, because she'd spoken, and *he had heard*. She remembered drifting in his confidence, in his poetry, in his godlike knowledge of what was right and true ...

In his absolution.

"You are forgiven, Esmenet."

Who are you to forgive?

"Mimara."

———— ∞∞∞ ————

She awoke with her head upon his arm. There was no confusion, though it seemed there should be. She knew where she was, and though part of her quailed, part of her exulted as well.

She lay with Kellhus.

I didn't couple with him ... I only wept.

Her face felt bruised from the previous evening. The night had been hot, and they'd slept without blankets. For what seemed a long time, she lay motionless, simply savouring his white-skinned nearness. She placed a hand upon his bare chest. He was warm and smooth. She could feel the slow drum of his heart. Her fingers tingled, as though she touched an iron-smith's anvil as he hammered. She thought of the weight of him, flushed ...

"Kellhus ..." she said. She looked up to the profile of his face, somehow knowing he was awake.

He turned and looked at her, his eyes smiling.

She snorted in embarrassment, then looked away.

Kellhus said, "It's strange, isn't it, lying so close ..."

"Yes," she replied smiling, looking up, then out and away. "Very strange."

He rolled to face her. Esmenet heard Serwë groan and complain from his far side, still asleep.

"Shhh," he said laughing softly. "She loves sleep more than me."

Esmenet looked at him and laughed, shaking her head, beaming with incredulous excitement.

"This is so strange!" she hissed. Never had her eyes felt so bright.

She pressed her knees together in nervousness. He was so close!

He leaned toward her, and her mouth slackened, her eyes became heavy-lidded.

"No," she gasped.

Kellhus shot her a friendly frown. "My loin cloth just bunched," he said.

"Oh," she replied. They both burst into laughter.

Again she could sense the weight of him ...

He was a man who dwarfed her, as a man should.

Then his hand was beneath her hasas, sliding between her thighs, and she found herself moaning into his sweet lips. And when he entered her, pinned her the way the Nail of Heaven pinned the skies, tears brimmed and spilled from her eyes, and she could only think, *At last! At last he takes me!*

And it did not seem, it *was*.

No one would call her harlot any more.

PART III:
The Third March

CHAPTER EIGHTEEN

KHEMEMA

To piss across water is to piss across your reflection.

—KHIRGWI PROVERB

Early Autumn, 4111 Year-of-the-Tusk, southern Shigek

Sweating beneath the sun, the Men of the Tusk struck south, winding up the staggered escarpments of the South Bank, and onto the furnace plains of the Carathay Desert, or as the Khirgwi called it, Ej'ulkiyah, the "Great Thirst." The first night, they stopped near Tamiznai, a caravan entrepôt that had been sacked by the retreating Fanim.

Shortly afterward, Athjeäri, who'd been sent to reconnoitre the route to Enathpaneah, returned from the southern waste, his men hollow-eyed with thirst and exhaustion. His mood was black. He told the Great Names that he'd found no unpolluted wells, and that he'd been forced to travel by night, the heat was so intense. The heathen, he said, had retreated to the far side of Hell. The Great Names told him of the endless trains of mules they'd brought, and of the Emperor's fleet that would follow them loaded with fresh Sempis water. They explained their elaborate plans for transporting that water across the coastal hills.

"You know not," the young Earl of Gaenri said, "the lands you risk."

The following evening, the horns of Galeoth, Nansur, Thunyerus, Conriya, Ce Tydonn, and High Ainon pealed through the arid air.

Pavilions were torn down amid the shouts of soldiers and slaves. Mules were loaded and beaten into long files. The Cultic Priests of Gilgaöl cast a goshawk onto their godfire, then released another to the evening sun. Infantrymen swung their packs from their spears, joking and complaining about the prospect of marching through the night. Hymns resolved and faded from the rumble of busy thousands.

The air cooled, and the first columns set across the western shoulders of Khemema's coastal hills.

The first Khirgwi came after midnight, howling from the backs of loping camels, bearing the truth of the Solitary God and His Prophet on the edges of sharp knives. The attacks were both brief and vicious. They fell upon stragglers, soaked the sands with red waters. They evaded the Inrithi pickets and swept howling into the baggage trains, where they sliced open the precious bladders of water wherever they found them. Sometimes, especially when they strayed onto hard gravel flats, they were overtaken and cut down in furious melees. Otherwise, they outdistanced their pursuers and vanished into the moonlit sands.

The next day, the first mule trains crawled through the coastal hills to the Meneanor and found a bay, quicksilver in the sun and peppered by the red-sailed ships of the Nansur fleet. There were hearty greetings as the first boatloads of water were dragged ashore. Songs were raised as the onerous work of transferring the water to the mules began. Men stripped to their waist, and many plunged into the rolling waves to relieve themselves of the heat. And that evening, when the Holy War stirred from suffocating tents, they were greeted by fresh Sempis water.

The Holy War continued its nocturnal march. Despite the blood-curdling raids, many found themselves awed by the beauty of the Carathay. There were no insects, save the odd crazed beetle rolling its ball of dung across the sands. The Inrithi laughed at these, called them "shit chasers." And there were no animals, except of course the vultures circling endlessly above. Where there was no water, there was no life, and apart from the heavy skins draped about the shoulders of the Holy War, there was no water in the Carathay. It was as if the sun had burnt the whole world to sterile bone. The Men of the Tusk stood apart from the sun, stone, and sand, and it was beautiful, like a haunting nightmare described by another. It was beautiful because they need not suffer the consequences of what they witnessed.

On the seventh assigned meeting between the Holy War and the Imperial Fleet, the Men of the Tusk picked their way through dry gorges and gathered across the beaches. They looked across the Meneanor, which was marbled by vast curls of lime and turquoise, and saw no ships. The rising sun gilded the sea in white. They could see the distant breakers, like lines of foaming diamonds. But no ships.

They waited. Messengers were sent back to the encampment. Saubon and Conphas soon joined them, bathed in the sea water for a time, spent an hour arguing, and then rode back to the Holy War. A Council was called and the Great and Lesser Names squabbled until dusk, trying to decide what to do. Accusations were levelled against Conphas, but were quickly dropped when the Exalt-General pointed out that his life was as much at stake as theirs.

The Holy War waited a night and a day, and when the Emperor's fleet still failed to arrive, they decided to continue their march. Many theories were aired. Perhaps, Ikurei Conphas suggested, the fleet had been beset by a squall and had decided to sail south to the next designated meeting point to conserve time. Or perhaps, Prince Kellhus suggested, there was a *reason* why the Kianene had waited so long to contest the seas. Perhaps the camels had been slaughtered and the fleet hidden to lure the Holy War into the Carathay.

Perhaps Khemema was a trap.

Two days later, the bulk of the Great and Lesser Names accompanied the mule trains across the hills to the sea, and stared dumbfounded at its empty beauty. When they returned from the hills, they no longer walked apart from the desert. Sun, stone, and sand beckoned to them.

All water was severely rationed according to caste. Anyone caught hoarding or exceeding their ration, it was declared, would be executed.

In Council, Ikurei Conphas unfurled maps inked by Imperial Cartographers in the days when Khemema had belonged to the Empire, and jabbed his finger at a place called Subis. The oasis of Subis, he insisted, was far too large for the heathens to poison. With the water remaining, the Holy War could reach Subis intact, but only if everything—mules, slaves, camp-followers—was left behind ...

"Leave behind …" Proyas said. "How do you propose we do that?"

Even though orders were dispatched with the utmost secrecy, word spread quickly through the drowsing encampment. Many fled to their doom in the open desert. Some took up arms. The rest simply waited to be cut down: body-slaves, camp whores, caste-merchants, even slavers. Screams echoed over the dunes.

Several riots and mutinies broke out among the Inrithi. At first, many refused to kill their own. The Holy War, the Great Names explained to their men, had to survive. *They* had to survive. In the end, countless thousands were murdered by the grief-stricken Men of the Tusk. Only priests, wives, and useful tradesmen were spared.

That night the Inrithi marched blank-eyed through what seemed a cooling oven—away from the horror behind them, toward the promise of Subis … Men-at-arms, warhorses, and hearts had become beasts of burden.

When the Khirgwi found the fields of heaped bodies and strewn belongings, they fell to their knees and cried out in exultation to the Solitary God. The trial of the idolaters had begun.

The enormous column of the Holy War drifted and scattered in the rush southward. The Khirgwi massacred hundreds of stragglers. Several tribes cut to the heart of the column, wreaking what havoc they could before fleeing into the waste. One group of raiders actually stumbled upon the Scarlet Spires, and were burnt into oblivion.

The following morning the Great and Lesser Names met in desperation. Water, they knew, had to lie all about them; the Khirgwi couldn't harass them otherwise. So where were their wells? They called forward the more successful raiders among them—Athjeäri, Thampis, Detnammi, and others—and charged them with taking the battle to the desert tribes with the goal of finding their hidden wells. Leading thousands of Inrithi knights, these men rode over the long dunes and disappeared into the wavering distances.

With the exception of Detnammi, the Ainoni Palatine of Eshkalas, they all returned the following night, beaten back by the ferocity of the Khirgwi and the merciless heat of the Carathay. No wells had been found. Even if they had, Athjeäri said, he had no idea how they might be found twice, so featureless was the desert.

Meanwhile, the water had almost run out. With Subis nowhere in sight, the Great Names decided to put down all horses save those belonging to caste-nobility. Several thousand Cengemi footmen, Ketyai tributaries of the Tydonni, mutinied, demanding that *all* horses be slaughtered and the excess rations be divided equally among all Men of the Tusk. Gothyelk and the other Earls of Ce Tydonn responded with ruthless alacrity. The leaders of the mutiny were arrested, gutted, then hung from pikes above the sand.

Very little water remained the ensuing night, and the Men of the Tusk, their skin like parchment, overcome by irritability and fatigue, began casting away their food. They no longer hungered. They *thirsted*, thirsted as they'd never thirsted before. Hundreds of horses collapsed and were left to snort their final breaths in the dust. A strange apathy descended upon the men. When the Khirgwi assailed them, many simply continued to walk, not hearing or not caring that their kinsmen perished behind them.

Subis, they would think, and that name became more fraught with hope than the name of any God.

When dawn arose and they still hadn't reached Subis, the decision was made to continue. The world became a hazy furnace of baked stone and dunes tanned and curved like a harlot's lovely skin. The distances shimmered with hallucinatory lakes, and many perpetually ran, convinced they saw the promised oasis, promised Subis.

Subis ... A lover's name.

The Men of the Tusk stumbled down long, flinty slopes, filed between sandstone outcroppings that resembled towering mushrooms on thin stems. They climbed mountainous dunes.

The village looked like a many-chambered fossil unearthed by the wind. The deep green and sun silver of the oasis beckoned with its impossibility ...

Subis.

Ragged ranks surged across the sun-hammered sands. Men charged through the abandoned village, between date palms trailing skirts of dead fronds and acacias freighted with weaver's nests. They jostled, skidded across the packed dust, toppled splashing and laughing into the glittering waters ...

Where they found Detnammi.

Dead, bloated, floating in the crystal green, with all four hundred and fifty-nine of his men.

The promise of Subis had been poisoned. The Khirgwi had found a way.

But the Men of the Tusk were beyond caring. They gulped water and retched, then gulped more. Thousands upon thousands roared down the dunes and descended upon the oasis. They pushed and heaved at the masses before them only to find themselves engulfed. Hundreds were crushed to death. Hundreds more actually drowned as men were shouldered into the pool's centre. Some time passed before the Great Names could impose order. Thanes and knights warded men from the oasis at sword point. They were forced to make more than a few examples. Eventually, vast relays were organized to fill and distribute waterskins. Swimmers began removing the dead from the pool. Bodies were heaped in the sun.

The Great Names denied Detnammi and his men funeral rites, realizing he'd struck south for Subis instead of searching for Khirgwi wells— obviously to save himself. Chepheramunni, the King-Regent of High Ainon, denounced the Palatine of Eshkalas, posthumously stripped him of his rank and station. Ritual Ainoni curses were cut into his body, which was laid out for the vultures.

Meanwhile, the Men of the Tusk drank their fill. Many retired to the shade beneath the palms, leaning against trunks and wondering that fronds could so resemble vulture's wings. Their thirst slaked, they began to worry about sickness. The Cultic physician-priests of dread Pestilence, Akkeägni, were called before the Great Names, and they named those sicknesses associated with drinking water fouled by the dead. Otherwise, their pharmaka and their reliquary abandoned to the desert, they could do little more than mutter pre-emptive prayers.

The God would not be satisfied.

Everyone was afflicted somehow—chills, cramps, nausea—but thousands became severely ill, stricken by convulsive vomiting and diarrhea. By the following morning, the worst were doubled over with abdominal pain, their skin blotched by angry red spots.

In Council, the Great Names stared and stared at Ikurei Conphas's maps. Enathpaneah, they knew, was simply too far. They sent several dozen parties to various points on the Meneanor coast, hoping against hope they might find the Imperial Fleet. Accusations were levelled against the Emperor, and twice Conphas and Saubon had to be physically restrained. When the search parties returned from the hills empty-handed, the Great Names solemnly agreed to continue their southward march.

Either way, Prince Kellhus said, the God would see to them.

The Men of the Tusk abandoned Subis the following evening, their waterskins brimming with polluted water. Several hundred, those too sick to walk, remained behind, waiting for the Khirgwi.

Sickness spread among the men, and those without friends or kin were abandoned. The Holy War became a vast army of shuffling men and stumbling horses, marching across blue vistas of sun-cracked stone and flint-strewn sand. About the Nail of Heaven, clouds of stars wheeled above them, numbering their dead. Those too sick to keep pace fell behind, wept in the dust like broken men, dreading the morrow's sun as much as the Khirgwi.

"Enathpaneah," the walkers said to one another, for the Great Names had lied, telling them Enathpaneah was only three days distant when it was more than six. "The God will show us to Enathpaneah."

A name like a promise … Like Shimeh.

For those afflicted by diarrhea, the ration of water simply wasn't enough. Already weakened, they collapsed, panting against the cool sands. Many of the sickest died this way—thousands of them.

After two days, the water began to run out. The thirst returned. Lips cracked, eyes grew curiously soft, and skin tightened, became as dry as papyrus and cracked around joints.

There were some, very few, who seemed impossibly strong during this trial. Nersei Proyas was one of the few caste-nobles who refused to water his horse while his men died. He walked among the steadfast knights and soldiers of Conriya, giving words of encouragement, reminding them that before all, faith was a matter of trial.

Followed by two beautiful women, Prince Kellhus also spread words of strength. They didn't merely suffer, he told men, they suffered *for* … For Shimeh. For the Truth. For the God! And to suffer for the God was to secure glory in the Outside. Many would be broken in this furnace, that was true, but those who survived would know the temper of their own hearts. They would be, he claimed, unlike other men. They would be *more* ...

The Chosen.

Wherever Prince Kellhus and his two women went, men crowded about them, begging to be touched, to be cured, to be forgiven. Stained by dust into the colour of the desert, his face bronzed and his flowing hair almost bleached white, he seemed the very incarnation of sun, stone, and sand. He, and he alone, could stare into the endless Carathay and *laugh,* hold out his arms to the Nail of Heaven and give thanks for their suffering.

"The God chooses!" he would cry, "The God!"

And the words he spoke were like *water.*

On the third night, he halted in a vast bowl between dunes. He marked a place across the trampled sands, and bid several of his closest adherents, his Zaudunyani, to begin digging. When they despaired of finding anything, he commanded them to continue. Very soon they felt *moisture* in the sand ... Then he walked farther and bid those rushing past to dig more holes at various places. Others he organized into an armed perimeter. Held back by hedges of levelled spears, wondering thousands crowded around the lip of the depression, curious to see what happened. After several watches, some fourteen pools of dark water glittered in the moonlight. Spring-fed wells ...

The waters were muddy, but they were sweet, and unfouled by the taste of dead men.

When the first of the Great Names at last beat and hollered their way to the floor of the depression, they found Prince Kellhus at the bottom of a pit, standing knee-deep in waters with a dozen others, hoisting brimming skins to the groping hands above.

"He showed me," he laughed, when they hailed them. "The God showed me!"

More wells were dug at the behest of the Great Names, and water relays were once again organized. Since most of the Holy War had suffered severe dehydration, the Great Names decided to linger for several days. The remaining horses were butchered and eaten raw for lack of fuel. In the Councils, Prince Kellhus was congratulated for his discovery, but little more. Many in the Holy War, especially the caste-menials, openly hailed him as the Warrior-Prophet. In closed meetings the Great Names argued over the Prince of Atrithau, but they could find no consensus. The desert, Ikurei Conphas warned, had made a False Prophet of Fane as well.

Meanwhile, the Khirgwi tribes gathered in the deep desert, thinking the Holy War, like a jackal, had found its place to die. The following night they attacked en masse, a wild rush of thousands spilling from the crests of dunes, confident they would ride down more corpses than men. Though surprised, the Men of the Tusk, their flesh revived, their faith renewed, encircled and slaughtered the desert tribesmen. Entire tribes, who'd bled much through the endless skirmishes across Khemema, were extinguished. The survivors withdrew to their hidden oasis homes.

The last of the food gave out. Waterskins were once again filled and heaped across strong backs. Songs were raised across the dark, desert landscape, many of them hymns to the Warrior-Prophet. The Holy War resumed its southward march, unconquered and defiant. Between Mengedda, Anwurat, and the desert, they had lost almost a third of their number, but still their great columns spanned the horizon.

They crossed deep wadis, cut by the infrequent winter rains, and climbed rolling dunes. They laughed once again at the shit-chasers scurrying with their dung across the sands. Day came, and they perched their canvas sheets against the punishing sun so they might sleep through the merciless heat.

As evening fell on the second day, and the encampment once again made ready to march, many noticed clouds across the western sky—the first clouds they'd seen, it seemed to them, since Gedea. They were smeared across the horizon, deep purple, and they folded around the setting sun so that it seemed the iris of an angry red eye. Without their omen-texts, the priests could only guess at the meaning.

The air still shimmered with heat, rolled like water over the sun-baked distances. And it was still—very still. A hush fell across the reaches of the Holy War. Men peered at the horizon, looked nervously at the wrathful eye, realizing the clouds belonged to the *ground* not the sky. And then they understood.

Sandstorm.

With the sluggish elegance of a scarf coiling in the wind, pummelling clouds of dust rolled toward them from the west. Old Carathay could still hate. The Great Thirst could still punish.

Skin-serrating blasts. Gusts with a million stinging teeth. The Men of the Tusk howled to one another without being heard. They tried to look, perhaps glimpsed the shadowy figures of others through the brown haze, but were then blinded. They huddled in clots beneath the biting wind, felt the sand suck at them as it heaped around their limbs. Their makeshift shelters were torn away, thrashed like paper through mountainous gusts. A new calligraphy of dunes was scrawled about them. Forgotten waterskins were buried.

The sandstorm raged until dawn, and when the winds receded, the Men of the Tusk wandered like stunned children across a transformed land. They salvaged what they could of their remaining baggage, found several dead men buried beneath the sands. The Great and Lesser Names met in Council. They hadn't enough shelter from the sun, they realized, to remain through the day. They must march—that much was clear. But where? Most argued that they should return to the well discovered by Prince Kellhus—as he was still called in the Councils, as much by his own insistence as by the loathing some had taken to the name "Warrior-Prophet." At least they had enough water to make it that far.

But the dissenters, led by Ikurei Conphas, insisted the well was likely lost to the sands. They pointed to the surrounding dunes, so bright in the sun they sheared one's eyes, and insisted the land around the wells was certain to have been just as disfigured if not more. If the Holy War used its remaining water to march *away* from Enathpaneah, and the wells couldn't be found, then it was doomed. As it stood, Conphas claimed, once again relying upon his map, the Holy War was within two days march of water. If they marched now they would suffer, certainly, but they would survive.

To the surprise of some, Prince Kellhus agreed. "Surely," he said, "it's better to wager suffering to avoid death than to wager death to avoid suffering."

The Holy War marched toward Enathpaneah.

They passed beyond the sea of dunes and entered land like a burning plate, a flat stone expanse where the air fairly hissed with heat. Once again the water was strictly rationed. Men became dizzy with thirst, and some began casting away armour, weapons, and clothes, walking like naked madmen until they fell, their skin blackened by thirst and blistered by sun. The last of the horses died, and the footmen, ever resentful that their lords tended to their mounts more faithfully than to their men, would curse and kick gravel at the wooden corpses as they passed. Old Gothyelk collapsed and was strapped to a litter made by his sons, who shared their rations of water with him. Lord Ganyatti, the Conriyan Palatine of Ankirioth, whose bald head looked so much like a blistered thumb jutting from a torn glove, was bound like a sack to his horse.

When night had at last fallen, the Holy War continued its march south, once again stumbling along the backs of sandy dunes. The Men of the Tusk walked and walked, but the cool desert night provided little relief. None talked. They formed an endless procession of silent wraiths, passing across Carathay's folds. Dusty, harrowed, hollow-eyed, and with drunken limbs, they walked. Like a pinch of mud dropped in water they crumbled, wandered from one another, until the Holy War became a cloud of disconnected figures, feet scraping across gravel and dust.

The morning sun was a shrill rebuke, for still the desert had not ended. The Holy War had become an army of ghosts. Dead and dying men lay scattered in their thousands behind it, and as the sun rose still more fell. Some simply lost the will, and fell seated in the dust, their thoughts and bodies buzzing with thirst and fatigue. Others pressed themselves until their wracked bodies betrayed them. They struggled feebly across the sand, waving their heads like worms, perhaps croaking for help, for succour.

But only death would come swirling down.

Tongues swelled in mouths. Parchment skin went black and tightened until it split about purple flesh, rendering the dying unrecognizable. Legs buckled, folded, refused one's will as surely as if one's spine had been broken. And the sun beat them, scorching chapped skin, cooking lips to hoary leather.

There was no weeping, no wails or astonished shouts. Brothers abandoned brothers and husbands abandoned wives. Each man had become a solitary circle of misery that walked and walked.

Gone was the promise of sweet Sempis water. Gone was the promise of Enathpaneah …

Gone was the voice of the Warrior-Prophet.

Only the trial remained, drawing out warm, thrumming hearts into an agonized line, desert thin—desert simple. Frail heartbeats stranded in the wastes, pounding with receding fury at seeping, water-starved blood.

Men died in the thousands, gasping, each breath more improbable than the last, at furnace air, sucking final moments of anguished, dreamlike life through throats of charred wood. Heat like a cool wind. Black fingers twitching through searing sands. Flat, waxy eyes raised to blinding sun.

Whining silence and endless loneliness.

⸺⧆⸺

Esmenet stumbled by his side, kicking sand and fiery gravel with feet she could no longer feel. Above her, the sun shrieked and shrieked, but she'd long ceased worrying how light could make sound.

He carried Serwë in his arms, and it seemed to Esmenet that she'd never witnessed anything so triumphant.

Then he stopped before a deep and dark vista.

She swayed and the wailing sun twirled above her, but somehow he was there, beside her, bracing her. She tried licking cracked lips, but her tongue was too swollen. She looked to him, and he grinned, impossibly hale …

He leaned back and cried out to the hazy roll and pitch of distant green, to the wandering crease of a flashing river. And his words resounded across the compass of the horizon.

"Father! We come, Father!"

⸺⧆⸺

Early Autumn, 4111 Year-of-the-Tusk, Iothiah

Xinemus's fierce scowl silenced him, and the three men retreated into a grotto of darkness where the wall pinched one of the compound's structures. They dragged the warrior-slave's corpse with them.

"I always thought these bastards were tough," Bloody Dinch whispered, his eyes still wild from his kill.

"They are," Xinemus replied softly. He scanned the gloomy courtyard below them—a puzzle-box of open spaces, bare walls, and elaborate facades. "The Scarlet Spires purchase their Javreh from the Sranc Pits. They are hard men, and you'd do well to remember it."

Zenkappa smirked in the dark and added, "You got lucky, Dinch."

"By the Prophet's Balls!" Bloody Dinch hissed, "I—"

"*Shhht!*" Xinemus spat. Both Dinch and Zenkappa were good men, fierce men, Xinemus knew, but they were bred to battle in open fields, not to slink through shadows as they did now. And it bruised Xinemus in some strange way that they seemed incapable of grasping the importance of what they attempted. Achamian's life meant little to them, he realized. He was a sorcerer, an abomination. Achamian's disappearance, the Marshal imagined, was a matter of no small relief to the two of them. There was no place for blasphemers in the company of pious men.

But if they failed to grasp the importance of their task, they were well aware of its lethality. To skulk like thieves among armed men was harrowing enough, but in the midst of the *Scarlet Spires* ...

Both were frightened, Xinemus realized—thus the forced humour and empty bravado.

Xinemus pointed to a nearby building across a narrow portion of the courtyard. The bottom floor consisted of a long row of colonnades framing the pitch-black of its hollow interior.

"Those abandoned stables," he said. "With any luck, they'll be connected to those barracks."

"*Empty* barracks, I hope," Dinch whispered, studying the dark confusion of buildings.

"So they look."

I'll save you Achamian ... Undo what I've done.

The Scarlet Spires had taken up residence in a vast, semi-fortified complex that looked as though it dated back to the age of Cenei—the sturdy palace of some long-dead Ceneian Governor, Xinemus supposed. They had watched the compound for over a fortnight, waited as the great trains of armed men, supplies, and slave-borne litters wound from the narrow gates into Iothiah's labyrinthine streets to join the march across Khemema. Xinemus had no definite idea of the size of the Scarlet Spires' contingent, but he reckoned it numbered in the thousands. This meant the compound itself must be immense, a warren of barracks, kitchens, storerooms, apartments, and official chambers. And this meant that when the bulk of the School travelled south, those few remaining would find it difficult to defend against intruders.

This was good ... If in fact Achamian was actually imprisoned here.

The Scarlet Spires wouldn't dare take Achamian with them; Xinemus was sure of that much. The road was no place to interrogate a Mandate sorcerer, especially when one marched with a prince such as Proyas. And the fact that the Scarlet Spires had actually left a *mission* here meant that the School had unfinished business to attend to in Iothiah. Xinemus had wagered that Achamian was that unfinished business.

If he wasn't here, then he was very likely dead.

He's here! I feel it!

When the three men reached the interior of the stables, Xinemus clutched at the Trinket about his neck as though it were holier than the small golden Tusk that clicked at its side. The Tears of God. Their only hope against sorcerers. Xinemus had inherited three Trinkets when his father had died, and this was the reason he attempted this with only Dinchases and Zenkappa. Three Trinkets for three men about to wander into a den of abominations. But Xinemus prayed they wouldn't need them. Whatever their sins, sorcerers were men, and men slept.

"Hold them in your bare fists," Xinemus commanded. "Remember, they must be touching your skin to afford you any protection. Whatever you do, *don't* let it go ... This place is sure to be protected by Wards, and if the Trinket leaves your skin, even for a moment, we'll be undone ..." He ripped his own Trinket from about his neck, and felt comforted by the cold weight of its iron, the imprint of its deep runes against his palm.

The stalls hadn't been mucked, and the stable smelled of dried horse-shit and straw. After several moments of fumbling they found a passage-way that led them into the abandoned barracks.

Then their nightmarish journey through the maze began. The complex was as huge as Xinemus had both hoped and feared, and as much as he was relieved by the endless series of *empty* rooms and corridors, he despaired of ever finding Achamian. Once or twice they heard distant voices speaking Ainoni, and they would crouch in pitch shadows or behind exotic Kianene furniture. They passed through dusty audience halls, filled with enough moonlight that they might wonder at the grand, geometric frescoes across the vaulted ceilings. They skulked by sculleries and kitchens, and heard slaves snoring in the humid dark. They crept up stairs and down halls lined by apartments. Each door they opened seemed hinged upon a precipice: either Achamian or certain death lay on the far side. Every instant, every breath seemed an impossible gamble.

And everywhere they imagined the ghosts of the Scarlet Magi, holding arcane conferences, summoning demons, or studying blasphemous tomes in the very rooms they glided past.

Where were they holding him?

After some time, Xinemus began to feel bold. Was this how a thief or a rat felt, prowling at the edges of what others could see or know? There was exhilaration, and strangely enough, *comfort* in lurking unseen in the marrow of your enemy's bones. Xinemus was overcome by a sudden certainty:

We're going to do this! We're going to save him!

"We should check the cellars …" Dinch hissed. A sheen of sweat covered his grizzled face and his grey square-cut beard was matted. "They'd put him someplace where his screams couldn't be heard by visitors, wouldn't they?"

Xinemus grimaced, both at the loudness of the old majordomo's voice and at the truth of what he said. Achamian had been tortured and tortured long … It was an unbearable thought.

Akka …

They returned to a stone stairwell they'd passed, descended down into pitch blackness.

"We need some light!" Zenkappa exclaimed. "We won't be able to find our hands down here!"

They stumbled blindly into a carpeted corridor, packed close enough together to smell the sweat of one another's fear. Xinemus despaired. This was hopeless!

But then they saw a light, and a small sphere of illuminated hallway, *moving* …

The corridor where they found themselves was narrow with a low rounded ceiling—they could see this now—and exceedingly long, as though it ran the greater length of the compound.

A sorcerer walked through it.

The figure was thin, but dressed in voluminous scarlet silk robes, with deep sleeves embroidered with golden herons. His face was the clearest, because it was bathed in impossible light. Rutted cheeks lost in the slick curls of a lavishly braided beard, bulbous eyes, bored by the tedium of walking from place to place, all illuminated by a teardrop of candlelight suspended a cubit before his forehead, *without any candle.*

Xinemus could hear Dinch's breath hiss through clenched teeth.

The figure and the ghostly light paused at a juncture in the corridor, as if he had stumbled across a peculiar smell. The old face scowled for a moment, and the sorcerer seemed to peer into the darkness *at* them. They stood as still as three pillars of salt. Three heartbeats ... It was as though the eyes of Death itself sought them.

The man's scowl lapsed back into boredom, and he turned down the juncture, trailing a momentary skirt of illuminated stonework and scrolled carpet in his wake. And then blackness. Sanctuary.

"Dear, sweet Sejenus ..." Dinch gasped.

"We must follow him," Xinemus whispered, feeling his nerves gradually calm.

Witnessing the face, the sorcerous light, now made their every step sing with peril. The only thing keeping Dinchases and Zenkappa behind him, Xinemus knew, was a loyalty that transcended fear of death. But here, in this place, in the bowels of a Scarlet Spires stronghold, that loyalty was being tested as it had never been tested before, even in the heart of their most desperate battles. Not only did they gamble with the obscenely unholy, there were no *rules* here, and this, added to mortal fear, was enough to break any man.

They found the juncture but could see no light down the other corridor, so they inched blindly forward as they had before, following the limestone walls with their fingers.

They came to a heavy door. Xinemus could see no light seep around it. He grasped the iron latch, hesitated.

He's close! I'm sure of it!

Xinemus pulled open the door.

From the drafts across their humid skin they could tell the door opened upon a large chamber, but the darkness was still impenetrable. They felt as though they were entombed in dread night.

Holding a hand before him, Xinemus stepped into open blackness, hissed at the others to follow.

A voice cracked the silence, stilled their hearts.

"But this will not do."

Then lights, blinding, stinging bright and bewildering. Xinemus yanked free his sword.

Blinked, and squinting, focused on the figures congregated about them. A half-circle of a dozen Javreh, fully geared for war beneath blue and red coats. Six of them with levelled crossbows.

Stunned, his thoughts reeling in panic, Xinemus lowered his father's great sword.

We're undone ...

Behind stood three of the Scarlet Magi. The one they'd seen earlier, another much like him but with a beard dyed in yellow henna, and a third, who from his very bearing Xinemus knew had to be the senior.

Against his crimson gown the man was more than pale; he was devoid of pigment. A chanv addict, no doubt. One small obscenity to heap upon all the others. About his waist he wore a broad blue sash, and over it, a golden belt pulled low to his groin by a heavy pendant that hung between his thighs—serpents coiled about a crow.

The red-irised eyes studied them, pained by amusement.

"Tsk, tsk, tsk ..." From lips as translucent as drowned worms.

Do something! I must do something! But for the first time in his life, Xinemus was paralyzed by terror.

"Those things," the sorcerer-addict continued, "that you clutch to protect yourselves against us ... Those Trinkets. We *can* feel them, you know ... Especially when they grow near. Hard sensation to describe, really ... Kind of like a stone marble, pitting a thin sheet of cloth. The more marbles, the deeper the pit ..."

The flicker of translucent eyelids. "It was almost as though we could *smell* you."

Xinemus managed to sound defiant. "Where's Drusas Achamian?"

"Wrong question, my friend. If I were you, I should rather ask, 'What have I done?'"

Xinemus felt the flare of righteous anger. "I'm warning you, sorcerer. Surrender Achamian."

"Warn *me?*" Droll laughter. The man's cheeks fluted like fish gills. "Unless you're speaking of inclement weather, Lord Marshal, I think there's very little you could warn me about. Your Prince has marched into the wastes of Khemema. I assure you, you're quite alone here."

"But I still bear his writ."

"No, you don't. You were stripped of your rank and station. But either way, the fact is you *trespass*, my friend. We Schoolmen look very seriously upon trespass, and care nothing for the writ of Princes."

Humid dread. Xinemus felt his hackles rise. This had been a fool's errand ...

But my path is righteous ...

The sorcerer smiled thinly. "Tell your clients to drop their Trinkets. Of course, you may drop yours as well, Lord Marshal ... Carefully."

Xinemus glanced apprehensively at the levelled bolts, at the stone-faced Javreh who aimed them, and felt as though his life was held from a string.

"Immediately!" the mage snapped.

All three Trinkets thudded like plums against the carpets.

"Good ... We're fond of collecting Chorae. It's a good thing to know where they are ..."

Then the man uttered something that turned his crimson irises into twin suns.

Xinemus was thrown to his knees by a blast of heat from behind him. He could hear shrieking ...

Dinch and Zenkappa shrieking.

By the time he turned, Dinch had already fallen, a heap of writhing char and incandescent flame. Zenkappa flailed and continued to shriek, immolated in a column of blowing fire. He stumbled two steps into the dark corridor and collapsed onto the floor. The shrieks trailed into the sound of sizzling grease.

On his knees, Xinemus stared at the two fires. Without knowing, he'd brought his hands up to cover his ears.

My path …

He felt gauntleted hands clench him, powerful limbs pin him to his knees. He was wrenched around to face the chanv addict. The sorcerer was very near now, near enough that the Marshal could smell his Ainoni perfumes.

"Our people tell us," the addict said, in a tone which suggested that untoward things were best not mentioned in polite company, "that you're Achamian's closest friend—from the days when you both tutored Proyas."

Like a man unable to fully rouse himself from a nightmare, Xinemus simply stared, slack-faced. Tears streamed down his broad cheeks.

I've failed you again, Akka.

"You see, Lord Marshal, we worry that Drusas Achamian tells us lies. First we'll see if what he's told you corresponds with what he's been telling us. And then we shall see if he values the Gnosis over his closest friend. If he values knowledge over life *and* love …"

The translucent face paused, as though happening across a delicious thought.

"You're a pious man, Marshal. You already know what it means to be an instrument of the truth, no?"

Yes. He knew.

To suffer.

⦿

Heaps of masonry nested in ashes.

Truncated walls, hedged by rubble, sketching random lines against night sky.

Cracks forked like blind branches chasing elusive sun.

Spilled columns, halved by moonlight.

Scorched stone.

The Library of the long-dead Sareots, ruined by the avarice of the Scarlet Schoolmen.

Silent, save for the small sound of scraping, like a bored child playing with a spoon.

How long had it scuttled like a rat through the hollows, crawled through the labyrinthine galleries hewn by the random plunge of cement and stone? Past entombed texts, wood-blackened and crocodile-scaled by fire, and once a lifeless human hand. Through a tiny mine, whose only ore was the debris of knowledge. Upward, always upward, digging, burrowing, crawling. How long? Days? Weeks?

It knew very little of time.

It shrugged its way through torn, animal-skin pages pinched by massive surfaces of stone. It heaved aside a palm-sized brick, raised a silky face to the clouds of stars. Then it climbed and climbed, and at last lifted its small, puppet body upon the summit of the ruin.

Raised a little knife, no bigger than a cat's tongue.

As though to touch the Nail of Heaven.

A Wathi Doll, stolen from a dead Sansori witch ...

Someone had spoken its name.

HAPTER NINETEEN

ENATHPANEAH

Late Autumn, 4111 Year-of-the-Tusk, Enathpaneah

The first sound Proyas heard was the rush of wind through leaves, the sound of openness. Then, impossibly, he heard gurgling water—the sound of life.

The desert ...

He awoke with a start, blinked sunlight from eyes that teared in pain. It seemed a coal flared red-hot behind his forehead. He tried to call out for Algari, his body-slave, but could do no more than whisper. His lips stung, burned as though bleeding.

"Your slave is dead."

Proyas remembered something … A great bloodletting across the sands.

He turned to the sound of the voice, saw Cnaiür crouched nearby, bent over what looked to be a belt. The man was shirtless, and Proyas noted the blistered skin of his massive shoulders, the stinging red of his scarred arms. His normally sensual lips were swollen and cracked. Behind him, a brook sloshed through a groove that wandered between earth and stone. The green of living things blurred the distance.

"Scylvendi?"

Cnaiür looked up, and for the first time Proyas noticed his age: the branching of wrinkles about his snow-blue eyes, the first greying hairs in his black mane. The barbarian was, he realized, not so much younger than his father.

"What happened?" Proyas croaked.

The Scylvendi resumed digging at the leather wrapped about his scarred knuckles. "You collapsed," he said. "In the desert …"

"You … You saved me?"

Cnaiür paused without looking up. Then continued working.

They drifted like reavers come from the furnace, men hard-bitten by the trials of the sun, and they fell upon the villages and stormed the hillside forts and villas of northern Enathpaneah. Every structure they burned. Every man they smote with the edge of the sword, until none were left breathing. So too, every woman and child they found hidden they put to the sharp knife.

There were no innocents. This was the secret they carried away from the desert.

All were guilty.

They wandered southward, scattered bands of wayfarers, come from the plains of death to harrow the land as they'd been harrowed, to deliver suffering as they'd suffered. The horrors of the desert were reflected in their ghastly eyes. The cruelty of blasted lands was written into their gaunt frames. And their swords were their judgement.

Some three hundred thousand souls, perhaps three-fifths of them combatants, had marched under the Tusk into Khemema. Only one hundred thousand, almost all of them combatants, would leave. Despite these losses, with the exception of Palatine Detnammi, none of the Great had died. Using the Inrithi caste-nobles as compass points, Death had drawn circles, each one more narrow than the last, taking the slaves and the camp-followers, then the indentured caste-menial soldiers, and so on. Life had been rationed according to caste and station. Two hundred thousand corpses marked the Holy War's march from the oasis of Subis to the frontier of Enathpaneah. Two hundred thousand dead, beat into black leather by the sun.

For generations the Khirgwi would call their route *saka'ilrait*, "the Trail of Skulls."

The desert road had sharpened their souls into knives. The Men of the Tusk would lay the keel of another road, just as appalling, and far more furious.

Late Autumn, 4111 Year-of-the-Tusk, Iothiah

How long had they plied him?

How much misery had he endured?

But no matter how they tormented him, with crude pokers or with the subtlest of sorcerous deceits, he could not be broken. He shrieked and shrieked, until it had seemed his howls were a faraway thing, the torment of some stranger carried upon the wind. But he did not break.

It had nothing to do with strength. Achamian wasn't strong.

But Seswatha …

How many times had Achamian survived the Wall of Torment in Dagliash? How many times had he bolted from the anguish of his sleep, weeping because his wrists were free, because no nails pierced his arms? In the ways of torture, the Scarlet Spires were mere understudies compared with the Consult.

No. Achamian wasn't strong.

For all their merciless cunning, what the Scarlet Magi never understood was that they plied *two* men, not one. Hanging naked from the chains, his face slack against shoulder and chest, Achamian could see the foremost of his diffuse shadows fan across the mosaic floor. And no matter how violent the agonies that shuddered through him, the shadow remained firm, untouched. It whispered to him, whether he wailed or gagged ...

Whatever they do, I remain untouched. The heart of a great tree never burns. The heart of a great tree never burns.

Two men, like a circle and its shadow. The torture, the Cants of Compulsion, the narcotics—everything had failed because there were two men for them to compel, and the one, Seswatha, stood far outside the circle of the present. Whatever the affliction, no matter how obscene, his shadow whispered, *But I've suffered more ...*

Time passed, misery piled upon misery, then the chanv addict, Iyokus, dragged a man before him, thrust him to his knees just beyond the Uroborian Circle, arms bound behind his back, naked save for his chains. A face, broken and bearded, looked up to him, seemed to weep and laugh.

"Akka!" the stranger cried out, his mouth mealy with blood. Spittle trailed from his lips. "Bease, Akka! *Beease tell them!*"

There was something about him, an irksome familiarity ...

"We've exhausted the conventional methods," Iyokus said, "as I suspected we would. You've proven yourself as stubborn as your predecessors." The red-irised eyes darted to the stranger. "The time has come to break new ground ..."

"I can bear no more," the man sobbed. "No more ..."

The Master of Spies pursed his bloodless lips in mock remorse. "He came hoping to save you, you know."

Achamian peered at the man as though he were something accidentally glimpsed—something merely there.

No.

It couldn't be. He wouldn't permit it.

"So the question is," Iyokus was saying, "how far does your indifference extend? Will it bear the mutilation of loved ones?"

No!

"I find dramatic gestures are more effective at the beginning, before a subject becomes too accustomed ... So I thought we would start by putting out his eyes."

He made a circling gesture with his index finger. One of the slave-soldiers behind Xinemus grabbed a fistful of hair, yanked his head back, then raised a shining knife.

Iyokus glanced at Achamian, then nodded to his Javreh. The man stabbed downward, almost gingerly, as though skewering a plum from a platter.

Xinemus shrieked, the pit of his eye cramped about polished steel.

Achamian gasped at the impossibility. That so familiar and so cherished face, crinkling into a thousand friendly frowns, splitting into a thousand rueful grins, asylum amid so much condemnation, now, now ...

The Javreh lifted his knife.

"ZIN!" Achamian screeched.

But there was his hanging shadow, smeared across mortared glass, whispering,

I know not this man.

Iyokus was speaking. "Achamian. Achamian! I need you to listen to me carefully, Achamian, as one Schoolman to another. You and I both know you'll never leave this room alive. But your friend, here, Krijates Xinemus ..."

"Beaassee!" the Marshal wailed. *"Beeaaaaseee!"*

"I am," Iyokus continued, "the Master of Spies for the Scarlet Spires. No more and no less. I bear neither you nor your friend the slightest ill will. Unlike some, I need not hate my subjects to do what I do. You and your suffering are simply a means to an end. If you give me what my School needs, Achamian, your friend will become useless to me. I'll order his chains removed, and set him free. You have my word as a Schoolman on that ..."

Achamian believed him, and would have given anything if he could. But a sorcerer two thousand years dead looked from his eyes, watched with a horrific detachment ...

Iyokus studied him, his membranous skin moist in the unsteady light. He hissed and shook his head.

"Such fanatic stubbornness! Such strength!"

The red-gowned sorcerer whirled, nodded to the slave-soldier holding Xinemus.

"Nooooo!" a piteous voice howled.

A stranger convulsed in sightless agony, soiling himself.

I know not this man.

The nameless orange tabby froze, crouched, his ears pricked forward, his eyes fastened on the debris-strewn alleyway before him. Something crept through the shadows, slow like a lizard in the cold ... Suddenly it dashed across dusty sunlight. The tabby jumped.

For five years he'd skulked the alleys and gutters of Iothiah, feeding on mice, preying on rats, and when he could, scavenging rare scraps discarded by men. Once he'd even eaten from the corpse of a fellow cat that some boys had thrown from a rooftop.

Only recently had he started dining on dead men.

Every day, with a piety born of his blood, he padded, crept, and prowled along the same circuit. Through the alleys behind the Agnotum Market, where the rats nosed garbage, along the ruined wall, where the dead weeds and thistles beckoned mice, behind the eateries on the Pannas, across the temple ruins, then through the labyrinthine slots between the crumbling Ceneian tenements, where sometimes a child might scratch his ears.

For some time now, dead men had started appearing along his track.

And now this ...

Slinking around obstacles, he crawled to the nest of shadows where the running thing had disappeared. He wasn't hungry. He just needed to see.

Besides, he longed for the taste of living, *bleeding* prey ...

Hunched against a burnt-brick wall, he craned his head around a corner. He halted, absolutely still, the world before his face murmuring through his whiskers ...

No heartbeat, no whistling rat squeals that only he could hear.

But something moved ...

He leapt at a shadowy form, claws extended. He bore the figure down, burying claws into its back, teeth into its soft fabric of its throat. The taste was wrong. The smell was wrong. He felt the first cut, then the second. He wrenched at the throat, seeking meat, the gorgeous rush of hot blood.

But there was nothing.

Another cut.

The tabby released the thing, tried to scramble away, but his hind-quarters flailed, faltered. He yowled and shrieked, scratching at the scabbed cobble.

Little doll arms closed about the tabby's throat.

The taste of blood.

Late Autumn, 4111 Year-of-the-Tusk, Caraskand

Positioned on the great land route linking the nations south of the Carathay to Shigek and Nansur, Caraskand was an ancient and strategic way station. All those goods that merchants were loath to trust to the capricious seas—Zeumi silks, the cinnamon, pepper, and magnificent tapestries of Nilnamesh, Galeoth wool and fine Nansur wine—passed through the great bazaars of Caraskand, and had done so for thousands of years.

A Shigeki outpost in the days of the Old Dynasty, Caraskand had grown with the passing centuries, and for brief periods between the ascendancy of greater nations, had ruled her own small empire. Enathpaneah was a semimountainous land, sharing in both the arid summers of the Carathay and the rain-drenched winters of Eumarna. Caraskand sprawled across nine hills in her heart. Her great curtain walls had been raised by Triamis I, the greatest of the Ceneian Aspect-Emperors. The vast markets had been cleared by Emperor Boksarias when Caraskand had been one of the wealthiest governorates in the Ceneian Empire. The hazy towers and vast barracks of the Citadel of the Dog, which could be seen from any of the city's nine heights, had been raised by the warlike Xatantius, Emperor of Nansur, who'd used Caraskand as his proxy capital for his endless wars against Nilnamesh. And the white-marble magnificence of the Sapatishah's Palace, which made an acropolis of the Kneeling Heights, had been raised by Pherokar I, the fiercest and most pious of Kian's early Padirajahs.

Although tributary, Caraskand was a great city in the way of Momemn, Nenciphon, or even Carythusal. And though she'd been the prize of innumerable wars, she was proud.

Proud cities do not yield.

Despite the proclamations of the Padirajah, the Holy War had somehow survived Khemema. The Men of the Tusk were no longer a terrifying rumour from the north. Their approach could be measured by the plumes of smoke that marred the northern horizon. Refugees crowded the gates, speaking of butchery at the hands of inhuman men. The Holy War, they said, was the wrath of the Solitary God, who'd sent the idolaters to punish them for their iniquities.

Panic seized Caraskand, and not even the reassurances of their glorious Sapatishah-Governor, Imbeyan the All-Conquering, could calm the city. Hadn't Imbeyan fled like a beaten dog from Anwurat? Hadn't the idolaters killed three-quarters of the Grandees of Enathpaneah? Strange names were traded in the streets. Saubon, the blond beast of barbaric Galeoth, who could loosen men's bowels with a look. Conphas, the great tactician who had crushed even the Scylvendi with genius in arms. Athjeäri, more wolf than man, who ranged the hillsides and plundered all of hope. The Scarlet Spires, the obscene sorcerers from whom even the Cishaurim fled. And Kellhus, the Demon who walked among them as a False Prophet, inciting them to mad and diabolical acts. These names were repeated often, and carefully, as are all sounds of doom, like the gongs that marked the evening executions.

But there was no talk of submission in the streets and bazaars of Caraskand. Very few fled. A silent consensus had grown among them: the idolaters must be resisted, that was the Solitary God's will. One didn't flee God's wrath, no more than a child fled the raised hand of his father.

To be punished was the lot of the faithful.

They crowded the interiors of their grand tabernacles. They wept and prayed, for themselves, for their possessions, for their city.

The Holy War was coming ...

Late Autumn, 4111 Year-of-the-Tusk, Iothiah

They'd left him in the chapel for some time, hanging from the chains, slowly suffocating. The tripods had grown dim, reduced to beds of glowering coals, so that the surrounding darkness was shaped by lines and faint surfaces of orange stone. Achamian wasn't aware that Iyokus had joined him until the chanv addict spoke.

"You're curious, no doubt, to know how the Holy War fares."

Achamian didn't move his head from his chest.

"Curious?" he croaked.

The linen-skinned sorcerer was little more than a voice in his periphery.

"The Padirajah, it seems, is a very cunning man. Rather than simply assume victory, he'd made plans beyond the Battle of Anwurat. This is the sign of intellect, you know. The ability to plan *against* your hopes. He knew the Holy War must cross the wastes of Khemema to continue its march on Shimeh."

A small cough.

"Yes ... I know."

"Well, there was some question, back when the Holy War besieged Hinnereth, as to why the Padirajah refused to give battle at sea. The Kianene fleet scarce rules the Meneanor, but it's far from impotent. The question was raised again when we took Shigek, then forgotten. Everyone assumed Kascamandri thought his fleet overmatched—and why not? For all Kian's victories against the Empire over the centuries, very few have been at sea ... It turns out everyone assumed wrong."

"What do you mean?"

"The Holy War decided to march across Khemema using the Imperial Fleet to bear their water. It now appears the Padirajah had anticipated this. Once the Holy War had marched far enough into the desert that it couldn't turn back, the Kianene fleet fell upon the Nansur ..."

Iyokus grinned with sardonic bitterness.

"They used the Cishaurim."

Achamian blinked, saw red-sailed ships burning in the mad lights of the Psûkhe. A sudden flare of concern—he was beyond fear now—bid him raise his head and stare at the Scarlet Schoolman. The man seemed a ghost against shimmering white silks.

"The Holy War?" Achamian croaked.

"Nearly destroyed. Innumerable dead lie across the sands of Khemema."

Esmenet? He hadn't thought her name for a long while. In the beginning, it had been a refuge for him, reprieve in the sweet sound of a name, but once they brought Xinemus to their sessions, once they started using his love as an instrument of torment, he'd stopped thinking of her. He'd withdrawn from all love ...

To things more profound.

"It seems," Iyokus continued, "that my brother Schoolmen have suffered grievously as well. Our mission here has been recalled."

Achamian stared down at him, unaware that tears had wet his swollen cheeks. Iyokus watched him carefully, standing just beyond the edge of the accursed Uroborian Circle.

"What does that mean?" Achamian rasped. *Esmenet? My love ...*

"It means your torment is at an end ..." Hesitant pause. "I would have you know, Drusas Achamian, that I was against seizing you. I've presided over the interrogation of Mandate Schoolmen before, and know them to be both tedious and futile ... And distasteful ... most distasteful."

Achamian stared, said nothing, felt nothing.

"You know," Iyokus continued, "I wasn't surprised when the Marshal of Attrempus corroborated your version of the events beneath the Andiamine Heights. You truly believe that the Emperor's adviser, Skcaös, was a Consult spy, don't you?"

Achamian swallowed painfully. "I know he was. And someday soon, so will you."

"Perhaps. Perhaps ... But for now, my Grandmaster has decided these spies must be Cishaurim. One cannot substitute legends for what is known."

"You substitute what you fear for what you don't know, Iyokus."

Iyokus regarded him narrowly, as though surprised that one so helpless, so degraded, could still say fierce things. "Perhaps. But regardless, our time together is at an end. Even now we make preparations to join our brethren beyond Khemema ..."

Hanging like a sack from the chains, his body numb from remembered agony, Achamian looked upon the sorcerer as though from an immovable place, from some hold deep within the beaten ship of his body. A place not at sea.

Iyokus had become anxious.

"I know our kind isn't given to ... religious inclinations," he said, "but I thought I'd extend this one courtesy at least. Within a matter of days, a slave will be sent down to the cellars bearing a Trinket and a knife. The Trinket will be for you, and the knife for your friend ... You have that long to prepare yourself for your journey."

Such strange words for a Scarlet Schoolman. For some reason, Achamian knew this wasn't another sadistic game. "Will you tell this to Xinemus as well?"

The translucent face turned to him sharply, but then unaccountably softened. "I suppose I will," Iyokus said. "He at least might be assured a place in the Afterlife ..."

The sorcerer turned, then strode pale into the blackness. A distant door opened onto an illuminated corridor, and Achamian glimpsed the profile of Iyokus's face. For an instant, he looked like any other man.

Achamian thought of swaying breasts, the kiss of skin to skin in lovemaking.

Survive, sweet Esmi. Survive me.

Late Autumn, 4111 Year-of-the-Tusk, Caraskand

Flushed by their atrocities, the southward-wandering Men of the Tusk gathered about the great walls of Caraskand. In immense trains, they filed down from the heights and found their fury tempered by towering fortifications. The ramparts scrawled across the surrounding hills, immense sandstone belts the colour of copper, rising and falling across the haze of distant slopes.

Unlike the walls of Shigek's great cities, these, the Inrithi found, were defended.

Standards were planted in rocky soil. Client nobles, who'd been flung far afield by the suffering of the desert, found their patron lords. Makeshift tents and pavilions were raised. Shrial and Cultic priests gathered the faithful, and long dirges were raised for those countless thousands claimed by the desert. The Councils of the Great and Lesser Names were held, and after long rites of benediction for their survival of Khemema, the investiture of Caraskand was planned.

Nersei Proyas rode out to meet with Imbeyan at the Ivory Gate, so named because its immense barbican was constructed of white limestone rather than the reddish rock of Enathpaneah's quarries. Through an interpreter, the Conriyan Prince demanded the Sapatishah's surrender and made promises regarding the release of Imbeyan's household and the lives of the city's inhabitants. Dressed in magnificent coats of blue and yellow, Imbeyan laughed and said that what the desert had started, the stubborn walls of Caraskand would see completed.

Raised upon steep slopes for the most part, Caraskand's walls met level ground only along their northeastern sections, where the hills yielded to several miles of alluvial flatland, choked with field and grove and peppered with abandoned farms and estates—the Tertae Plain. Here, the Inrithi built their largest camps and prepared to storm the gates.

Sappers began dredging their tunnels. Teams of oxen and men were sent into the hills to fell timber for siege engines. Outriders were dispatched to scout and plunder the surrounding countryside. Blistered faces healed. Desert-gnawed limbs were thickened with hard work and the hearty spoils of Enathpaneah. The Inrithi once again began singing their songs. Priests led processions around the vast circuit of Caraskand's walls, brushing the ground before them with rushes and cursing the stone of the fortifications. From the walls, the heathens would jeer and cast missiles, but they were little heeded.

For the first time in months, the Inrithi saw clouds, real clouds, curling through the sky like milk in water.

At night, when the Inrithi gathered about their fires, the tales of woe and redemption in Khemema were gradually replaced by remarks of wonder at their survival and ceaseless speculation about *Shimeh*. Caraskand was a name often mentioned in *The Tractate*, enough that it seemed the great gate to the Sacred Land. Blessed Amoteu, the country of the Latter Prophet, was very near.

"After Caraskand," they said, "we shall cleanse Shimeh."

Shimeh. In speaking this holy name, the fervour of the Holy War was rekindled.

Masses trekked into the hillsides to hear the sermons of the Warrior-Prophet, who many believed had delivered the Holy War from the desert. Thousands scarred their arms with tusks and became his Zaudunyani. In the Councils of the Great and Lesser Names, the lords of the Holy War listened to his counsel with trepidation. The Prince of Atrithau had joined the Holy War impoverished, but he now commanded a contingent as great as any.

Then, as the Men of the Tusk prepared their first assault against Caraskand's turrets, the skies darkened, and it began to rain. Three hundred Tydonni were killed in a flash flood south of the city. Dozens more when a sapper's tunnel collapsed. Dried stream beds became torrents. It rained and rained, so that parched leather began to rot and mail hauberks had to be continually rolled in barrels of gravel to defeat the rust. In many places the earth became as soft and slick as rotten pears, and when the Inrithi attempted to bring up their great siege towers they found them immovable.

The winter rains had come.

The first man to die of the plague was a Kianene captive. Afterward his body was launched from a catapult over the city's walls—as would be those who followed.

<hr />

Late Autumn, 4111 Year-of-the-Tusk, Iothiah

Mamaradda had decided he would kill the sorcerer first. Though he wasn't sure why, the Javreh Captain found the idea of killing a *sorcerer* thrilling to the point of arousal. That this might have anything to do with the fact that his masters were also sorcerers never occurred to him.

He entered the chapel briskly, clenching and unclenching the Trinket his masters had given him. The sorcerer hung like some huntsman's prize at the far end of the chamber, his battered form bathed in the orange glow of the three tripods flanking him. As Mamaradda approached he noticed that the man swayed gently to and fro, as though in some gentle draft. Then he heard the sound of scraping, high-pitched, like iron against glass.

He paused midway beneath the airy vaults, instinctively peered at the floor beneath the sorcerer—at the black-red calligraphy of the Uroborian Circle.

He saw something small crouched at the edge of the Circle ... A cat? Scratching to bury piss? He swallowed, squinted. The rapid scrape-scrape-scrape whined bright in his ears, as though someone filed his teeth with a rusty knife. What?

It was a *tiny man*, he realized. A tiny man bent over the Uroborian Circle, scraping at the arcane paint ...

A doll?

Mamaradda hissed in sudden terror, clutched for his knife.

The scraping stopped. The hanging sorcerer raised his bleary, bearded face, fixed Mamaradda with glittering eyes. A heartbeat of abject horror.

The Circle is broken!

There was an impossible muttering ...

Sunlight sparkled from the sorcerer's mouth and eyes.

Impossible lights, curved like Khirgwi blades, pranced like spider's legs around him. Geysers of dust and shards spat from the mosaic floor. The very air seemed to *crack*.

Mamaradda raised his arms and howled, was blinded by a flurry of unearthly incandescence.

But then the lights were gone, and he was untouched—*unharmed* ...

He remembered the Trinket clenched fast in his fist. Mamaradda, Shield Captain of the Javreh, laughed.

The tripods spilled, as though kicked over by shadows. A shower of coals took Mamaradda in the face. Several found his mouth, cracked his teeth with their heat. He dropped his Trinket, screamed over the muttering ...

His heart exploded in his chest. Fire boiled outward, flaring through his orifices and his fingernails. Mamaradda fell, little more than wet skin about char.

Vengeance roamed the halls of the compound—like a God.

And he sang his song with a beast's blind fury, parting wall from foundation, blowing ceiling into sky, as though the works of man were things of sand.

And when he found *them*, cowering beneath their Analogies, he sheared through their Wards like a rapist through a cotton shift. He beat them with hammering lights, held their shrieking bodies as though they were curious things, the idiot thrashing of an insect between thumb and forefinger ...

Death came swirling down.

He felt them scramble through the corridors, desperate to organize some kind of concerted defence. He knew that the sound of agony and blasted stone reminded them of their deeds. Their horror would be the horror of the *guilty*. Glittering death had come to redress their trespasses.

Suspended over the carpeted floors, encompassed by hissing Wards, he blasted his own ruined halls. He encountered a cohort of Javreh. Their frantic bolts were winked into ash by the play of lights before him. Then they were screaming, clawing at eyes that had become burning coals. He strode past them, leaving only smeared meat and charred bone. He encountered a dip in the fabric of the onta, and he knew that more awaited his approach armed with the Tears of God.

He brought the building down upon them.

And he laughed more mad words, drunk with destruction. Fiery lights shivered across his defences and he turned, seething with dark crackling humour, and spoke to the two Scarlet Magi who assailed him, uttered intimate truths, fatal Abstractions, and the world about them was wracked to the pith.

He clawed away their flimsy Anagogic defences, raised them from the ruin like shrieking dolls, and dashed them against bone-breaking stone.

Seswatha was free, and he walked the ways of the present bearing tokens of ancient doom.

He would show them the Gnosis.

When the first shiver passed through the foundations, Iyokus thought, *I should've known.*

His next thought, unaccountably, was of Eleäzaras.

I told him ill would come of this.

For the completion of their task, Eleäzaras had left him only six Schoolmen, three of them sorcerers of rank, and some two hundred and fifty Javreh. Worse yet, they were scattered throughout the compound. Once he might have thought this would be more than enough to manage a Mandate sorcerer, but after the fury of the Sareotic Library he was no longer sure ... Even had they been prepared.

We're doomed.

Over the long years of his life, the chanv had rendered his passions as colourless as his skin. What he felt now was more the memory of a passion rather than the passion itself. The memory of fear.

But there was hope yet. The Javreh possessed at least a dozen Trinkets, and moreover, *he*, Heramari Iyokus, was here.

Like his brethren, he envied the Mandate the Gnosis, but unlike them, he did not hate. If anything, Iyokus respected the Mandate. He understood the pride of secret knowledge.

Sorcery was nothing if not a great labyrinth, and for a thousand years the Scarlet Spires had charted it, delving, always delving, mining knowledge both dread and disastrous. And even though they'd yet to discover the glorious precincts of the Gnosis, there were certain branches, certain forks, which they *alone* had mapped. Iyokus was a scholar of these forbidden forks, a student of the Daimos.

A Daimotic sorcerer.

In their darkest conferences, they sometimes wondered: How would the War-Cants of the Ancient North fare against the Daimos?

The sound of screams percolated through the halls. The walls thrummed with the reverberations of nearing blasts. Iyokus, who was wan and calculating even in circumstances as dreadful as these, understood the time had come to answer that question.

He threw aside the brilliant carpets and painted the circles across the tiles with deft, practised strokes. Light spilled from his colourless lips as he muttered the Daimotic Cants. And, as the tempest approached, he at last completed his interminable song. He dared speak the Ciphrang's *name*.

"Ankaryotis! Heed me!"

From the safety of his circle of symbols, Iyokus gazed in wonder at the sheeted lights of the Outside. He looked upon a writhing abomination, scales like knives, limbs like iron pillars ...

"Does it hurt?" he asked against the thunder of its wail.

What hast thou done, mortal?

Ankaryotis, a fury of the deep, a Ciphrang summoned from the Abyss.

"I have bound you!"

Thou art damned! Dost thou not recognize he who shall keepeth thee for Eternity?

A demon ...

"Either way," Iyokus cried, "such is my fate!"

The Javreh leapt like flaming dancers, screaming, stumbling, thrashing across the lavish Kianene carpets.

Battered, naked, Achamian walked between them.

"IYOKUS!" he thundered.

Sheets of falling stucco flashed into smoke against his Wards.

"IYOKUS!"

Dust shivered in the air.

With words, he tore the walls before him away. He walked over empty space, across a collapsed floor. Masonry crashed from the ceilings. He peered through the billowing clouds of powdered brick ...

And was engulfed in brilliant dragon fire.

He turned to the chanv addict, laughed. Encircled by ghostly walls, the Master of Spies crouched on a floating fragment of floor, his pale face working to his staccato song ... Vultures brighter than sunlight swept into Achamian's defences. Shimmering lava exploded from beneath, washed across his Wards. Lightning danced from the room's four dark corners ...

"YOU ARE OVERMATCHED, IYOKUS!"

He struck with a Cirroi Loom, grasping the addict's Wards with geometries of light.

Then he was falling, borne down by a raving demon, perched upon his Wards, hammering with great nailed fists.

With each blow he coughed blood.

He crashed into heaped debris, struck with an Odaini Concussion Cant, throwing the Ciphrang backward through shadowy ruin. He glanced up, searching for Iyokus. He glimpsed him scrambling through a breach in the far wall. He sung a Weära Comb, and a thousand lines of light flashed outward. The wall collapsed, riddled with innumerable holes, as did the ceiling beyond. Incandescent threads fanned across Iothiah and into the night sky.

He pushed himself to his feet.

"IYOKUS!"

Howling, the demon once again leapt upon him, blazing with hellish light.

———— ✦ ————

Achamian charred its crocodile hide, ribboned its otherworldly flesh, smote its elephantine skull with ponderous cudgels of stone, and it bled fire from a hundred wounds. But still it refused to fall. It howled obscenities that cracked rock and rifled the ground with chasms. More floors collapsed, and they grappled through dark cellars made bright by flickering fury.

Sorcerer and demon.

Unholy Ciphrang, a tormented soul thrust into the agony of the World, harnessed by words like a lion by strings, yoked to the task that would see it freed.

Achamian endured its unearthly violence, heaped injury after injury upon its agony.

And in the end it grovelled beneath his song, cringed like a beaten animal, then faded into the blackness ...

Achamian wandered naked through the smoking ruins, a husk animated by numb purpose. He stumbled down slopes of debris and wondered that he'd been the catastrophe that had wrought this devastation. He saw the mutilated corpses of those he'd burned and broken. He spat upon them in sudden memory of his hate.

The night was cool and he savoured the kiss of air across his skin. The stone bit his bare feet.

He passed blankly into the intact structures, like a ghost returning to where memories burn brightest. It took some time, but at last he found Xinemus, chained, huddled in his own excrement, and weeping as he clutched arms and knees over his nakedness. For a while Achamian simply sat next to him ...

"I can't see!" the Marshal wailed. "Sweet Sejenus, I can't see!"

He groped for, then seized, Achamian's cheeks.

"I'm so sorry, Akka. I'm so sorry ..."

But the only words Achamian could remember were those that killed. That damned.

When they finally hobbled from the ruined compound of the Scarlet Spires into the alleys of Iothiah, the astonished onlookers—Shigeki, armed Kerathotics, and the few Inrithi who garrisoned the city—gaped in both wonder and horror. But they dared not ask them anything. Nor did they follow the two men as they shuffled into the darkness of the city.

CHAPTER TWENTY

CARASKAND

*The vulgar think the God by analogy to man and so worship Him
in the form of the Gods. The learned think the God by analogy to
principles and so worship Him in the form of Love or Truth. But
the wise think the God not at all. They know that thought, which
is finite, can only do violence to the God, who is infinite.*

It is enough, they say, that the God thinks them.

—MEMGOWA, THE BOOK OF DIVINE ACTS

*... for the sin of the idolater is not that he worships stone, but that he
worships one stone over others.*

—8:9:4 THE WITNESS OF FANE

Early Winter, 4111 Year-of-the-Tusk, Caraskand

Immense timber and hide siege towers trundled toward Caraskand's western
walls, driven by vast teams of mud-splattered oxen and exhausted men.
Catapults hurled stone and flaming pitch. Inrithi archers raked the parapets.
From flanking towers and the streets beyond the wall, heathens released
soaring clouds of arrows. Throughout the packed ranks of Inrithi, men cried
out, rolled in the muck clutching wounded limbs. The towers groaned
nearer, their sides sheeted in flaming tar. The men massed on their peaks
hunched behind their shields, peered through smoke, waiting for the signal.

428

A horn blared through the din.

The timber bridges slammed onto the battlements. Iron-armoured knights surged across, crying "Die or conquer!" Swinging great broadswords, they leapt into the spears and scimitars of the Kianene. On the ground below, thousands more rushed forward, raising great iron-hooked ladders. Stones and corpses crashed down upon them. Blistering oil sent men screaming from the rungs. But somehow, they gained the summits, heaved themselves between the battlements and fell upon the Fanim. Pitched battles were fought against woollen skies. Faithful and heathen alike toppled from the heights.

The Nangaels, the Anpleians, and the dour Gesindalmen all managed to seize sections of the wall. More and more Inrithi spilled from the siege towers or clambered over the parapets, pausing only to glance in wonder at the great city exposed below. Some charged the nearest tower. Others were forced to crouch behind their teardrop shields as heathen bowmen began scouring the heights from nearby rooftops. Shafts flashed overhead, buzzing like dragonflies. Pots of burning pitch exploded among them. Men fell shrieking, trailing streamers of smoke. One of the siege towers erupted into an inferno. The other smoked so intensely that dozens of Nangaelish knights fell from the bridge, urged to rush blind by those choking behind.

Then Imbeyan and his Grandees charged from the towers. Men grappled, hacked, and roared.

Denied their siege towers and exposed to a whistling barrage of missiles from the city side of the wall, the Inrithi began falling more quickly than the ladders could replace them. Within moments, it seemed, every man boasted a dozen arrows jutting from his shield or armour. The knights striving against Imbeyan found themselves pressed back through the screams and corpses of their kinsmen. At last Earl Iyengar, seeing the mortal desperation in the eyes of his knights, signalled the retreat. The survivors fell back to the ladders. Very few reached the ground alive.

Twice more the Inrithi stormed the walls of Caraskand over the following weeks, and twice more the ferocity and craft of the Kianene drove them back with atrocious losses.

The siege wore on through the rains and pestilence.

Within days of identifying the sickness that caste-menials called "the hollows" and caste-nobles "hemoplexy," the physician-priests found themselves overwhelmed with hundreds complaining of headaches and chills. When Hepma Scaralla, the ranking High Priest of Akkeägni, Disease, informed the Great Names that the rumours were true, that the dread God indeed groped among them with his hemoplectic Hand, panic seized the Holy War. Even after Gotian threatened deserters with Shrial Censure, hundreds fled into the Enathpanean hills, such was the terror of hemoplexy.

While the healthy warred and died beneath Caraskand's walls, thousands remained within their sodden, makeshift tents, vomiting spittle, burning with fever, wracked by convulsive chills. After a day or two, eyes would dull, and aside from bouts of delirious ranting, men would be robbed of all spirit. After four or five days, skin would discolour—welts raised by the God's Hand, the physician-priests explained. The fevers would peak after the first week, then rage for another, robbing even iron-limbed men of all remaining strength. Either it broke, or the invalid fell into a deathlike sleep from which very few ever awakened.

Throughout the encampments the physician-priests organized lazarets for those without retinues or comrades to care for them. The surviving priestesses of Yatwer, Anagke, Onkis, even Gierra, as well as other cultic servants of the Hundred Gods, attended to pallet after pallet of prostrate sick. And no matter how much aromatic wood they burned, the stench of death and bowel gagged passersby. Nowhere, it seemed, could a man walk without hearing delirious shrieks or smelling hemoplectic putrescence. The stench was such that many Men of the Tusk took to walking through the encampment holding urine-soaked rags to their faces—as was the Ainoni custom during times of pestilence.

The plague intensified, and Disease's Hand spared no one, not even members of the blessed castes. Cumor, Proyas, Chepheramunni, and Skaiyelt all succumbed within days of one another. At times, it seemed the sick outnumbered the healthy. Shrial Priests wandered through the wretched alleyways of the encampment, stumping through mud from tent to tent, searching for the dead. The funeral pyres burned continuously. In one grievous night three hundred Inrithi died, among them Imrothus, the Conriyan Palatine of Aderot.

And the miserable rains waxed on and on, rotting canvas, hemp, and hope.

Then the Earl of Gaenri returned, bearing news of doom.

Ever impatient, Athjeäri had abandoned Caraskand in the early days of the siege, charging through Enathpaneah with his Gaenrish knights and some thousand more Kurigalders and Agmundrmen given to him by his uncle, Prince Saubon. He stormed the old Ceneian fortress of Bokae on the western frontier of Enathpaneah, taking it with few losses. Then he ranged southward, crushing those local Grandees who dared take the field against him and raiding the northern frontiers of Eumarna, where his knights were heartened to find good, green land.

For a time he besieged the immense fortress of Misarat, but withdrew once word came that Cinganjehoi himself had set out to relieve the fortress. Athjeäri struck northeast. He evaded the Tiger in the cedar-wooded ravines of the Betmulla Mountains, then descended into Xerash, where he met and routed the small army of Utgarangi, the Sapatishah of Xerash. The Sapatishah proved a compliant captive, and in exchange for five hundred horses and intelligence, Athjeäri delivered him unharmed to his ancient capital, Gerotha, the city reviled in *The Tractate* as the "harlot of Xerash." Then he rode hard for Caraskand.

What he found dismayed him.

He recounted his journey for those Great Names fit to attend Council, moving quickly to the intelligence offered by Utgarangi. According to the Sapatishah, the Padirajah himself, the great Kascamandri, marched from Nenciphon with the survivors of Anwurat, the Grandees of Chianadyni—the homeland of the Kianene—and the warlike Girgash, the Fanim of Nilnamesh.

That night Prince Skaiyelt died, and the Thunyeri filled the showering sky with their uncanny dirges. The following day, word arrived that Cerjulla, the Tydonni Earl of Warnute, had also fallen, encamped about the walls of nearby Joktha. Not long after, Sepherathindor, the Ainoni Count-Palatine of Hinnant, stopped breathing. And according to the physician-priests, Proyas and Chepheramunni would soon follow ...

A great fear seized the surviving leaders of the Holy War. Caraskand continued to rebuke them, Akkeägni oppressed them with misery and death, and the Padirajah himself marched upon them with yet another heathen host.

They were far from home, among hostile lands and wicked peoples, and the God had turned his face from them. They were desperate.

And for such men questions of why, sooner or later always became questions of *who* ...

The rain drummed down across his pavilion, filling it with a humid, ambient roar.

"So just what," Ikurei Conphas asked, "do you want, Knight-Commander?" He frowned. "Sarcellus is it?"

Though Sarcellus often accompanied Gotian at council, Conphas had never been introduced to him—not formally. The man's dark hair matted his scalp, bled rainwater across what in childhood must have been a lovely and brattish face. The white surcoat over his hauberk was improbably clean, so much so that he looked an anachronism, a throwback to the days when the Holy War still camped beneath Momemn. Everyone else, Conphas included, had been reduced to rags or plundered Kianene attire.

The Shrial Knight nodded without breaking eye contact. "Merely to speak about troubling things, Exalt-General."

"I'm always keen for troubling news, Knight-Commander, let me assure you." Conphas grinned, adding, "I'm something of a masochist, or have you noticed?"

Sarcellus smiled winsomely. "The Councils have made this fact exceedingly clear, Exalt-General."

Conphas had never trusted Shrial Knights. Too much devotion. Too much renunciation ... Self-sacrifice, he'd always thought, was more madness than foolishness.

He'd come to this conclusion in his adolescence, after perceiving just how often—and how happily—others injured or destroyed themselves in the name of faith or sentiment. It was as though, he realized, everyone took instructions from a voice he couldn't hear—a voice from nowhere. They committed suicide when dishonoured, sold themselves into slavery to feed their children. They acted as though the world possessed fates *worse* than death or enslavement, as though they couldn't live with themselves if harm befell others …

Wrack his intellect as he might, Conphas could neither fathom the sense nor imagine the sensation. Of course there was the God, the Scriptures, and all that rubbish. *That* voice he could understand. The threat of eternal damnation could wring reason out of the most ludicrous sacrifice. *That* voice came from somewhere. But this other voice …

Hearing voices made one mad. One need only stroll through a local agora, listen to the hermits cry, "What? What?" to confirm that fact. And for Shrial Knights, hearing voices made one fanatic as well.

"So what's your trouble?" Conphas asked.

"This man they call the Warrior-Prophet."

"Prince Kellhus," Conphas said.

He leaned forward in his camp chair, gestured for Sarcellus to take a seat. He could smell mustiness beneath the aromatic steam of his pavilion's censers. The rain had trailed, and now merely drummed fingers across the canvas slopes above.

"Yes … Prince Kellhus," Sarcellus said, squeezing water from his hair.

"What about him?"

"We know tha—"

"We?"

The Shrial Knight blinked in irritation. Despite his pious appearance, there was, Conphas thought, something about his bearing, some whiff of conceit perhaps, that belied the gold-embroidered tusk across his breast … Perhaps he'd misjudged this Sarcellus.

Perhaps he's a man of reason.

"Yes," the man continued. "Myself, and a handful of my brothers …"

"But not Gotian?"

Sarcellus grimaced in a fashion that Conphas found most agreeable. "No, not Gotian … Not yet, anyway."

Conphas nodded. "By all means, continue …"

"We know you've tried to assassinate Prince Kellhus."

The Exalt-General snorted, at once amused and offended. The man was either exceedingly bold or insufferably impertinent. "You *know*, do you?"

"We *think* …" Sarcellus amended. "Whatever … What's important is that you realize *we share your sentiment*. Especially after the madness of the desert ..."

Conphas frowned. He knew what the man meant: Prince Kellhus had walked from the Carathay commanding the worship of thousands, and the wonder of everyone, it sometimes seemed, save himself. But Conphas would've expected a Shrial Knight to argue signs and omens, not power ...

The desert *had* been madness. At first Conphas had shambled through the sands no different from the rest, cursing that damned fool Sassotian, whom he'd installed as General of the Imperial Fleet, and pondering, endlessly pondering, mad scenarios that would see him saved. Then, after he burned through the hope that fuelled these ruminations, he found himself harassed by a peculiar disbelief. For a while, the prospect of death seemed something he merely indulged for decorum's sake, like the fatuous assurances caste-merchants heaped onto their wares. "Yes, yes, you will die! I guarantee!"

Please, he thought. *Who do you think I am?*

Then, with the shadowy lassitude that characterized so much of that march, his doubt flipped into certainty, and he felt an almost intellectual wonder—the wonder of finding the conclusion to one's life. There was no final page, he realized, no last cubit to the scroll. The ink simply gave out, and all was blank and desert white.

So here, he thought, looking across the wind-rippled dunes, *lies my life's destination. This is the place that has waited for me, waited since before I was born* ...

But then he'd found *him*, Prince Kellhus, scooping up water in that sandy pit—*wading* while he, Ikurei Conphas, died of thirst! Of all the deranged possibilities he'd considered, none seemed quite as mad as this: saved by the man he'd failed to kill. What could be more galling? More ludicrous?

But at the time ... At the time, his heart had caught—it still fluttered at the memory!—and for an instant, Conphas had wondered if Martemus had been right ... Perhaps there *was* more to this man. This Warrior-Prophet.

Indeed. The desert had been madness.

Conphas fixed the Shrial Knight with an appraising stare. "But he saved the Holy War," he said. "Your life ... My life ..."

Sarcellus nodded. "Indeed, and *that*, I would say, is the problem."

"How so?" Conphas snapped, even though he knew exactly what the man meant.

The Knight-Commander shrugged. "Before the desert, Prince Kellhus was simply another zealot with some claim to the Sight. But now ... *Especially* now with the Dread God walking among us ..." He sighed and leaned forward, his hands folded together, his forearms against his knees. "I fear for the Holy War, Exalt-General. *We* fear for the Holy War. Half of our brothers acclaim this fraud as another Inri Sejenus, as our salvation, while the other half decry him as an anathema, as the cause of our misery."

"Why are you telling me this?" Conphas asked mildly. "Why are you *here*, Knight-Commander?"

Sarcellus's grin was crooked. "Because there'll be mass mutinies, riots, perhaps even open warfare ... We need someone with the skill and power to minimize or forestall such eventualities, someone who yet commands the loyalty of his men. We need someone who can preserve the Holy War."

"After you've killed Prince Kellhus ..." Conphas said derisively. He shook his head, as though disappointed by his own lack of surprise. "He camps with his followers now, and they guard him as though he were the Tusk. They say that in the desert a hundred of them surrendered their water—their lives—to him and his women. And now another hundred have stepped forward as his bodyguard, each of them sworn to die for the Warrior-Prophet. Not even the Emperor could claim such protection! And still you think you can kill him."

A drowsy blink, which made Conphas certain—absurdly—that Sarcellus had beautiful sisters.

"Not think, Exalt-General ... Know."

Serwë's scream was like an animal thing, as much a grunt as a wail. Esmenet bent over her, combing her fingers through the girl's sweaty hair. Rain pulsed across the bellied ceiling of their makeshift pavilion, and here and there a trickle of water glittered in the gloom, slapping against plaited mats. For Esmenet, it seemed they crouched in the illuminated heart of a cave, littered by musty cloth and rotting reeds.

The Kianene woman Kellhus had summoned cooed to Serwë in a tongue only Kellhus seemed to understand. Esmenet found the throaty sound of the woman's voice soothing. They stood, she realized, in a place where differences of language and faith no longer mattered.

Serwë was about to give birth.

The midwife sat cross-legged between Serwë's opened knees, Esmenet knelt over her anguished face, and Kellhus stood above them, his expression watchful, wise, and sad. Esmenet looked to him, worried. *All will be as it should be*, his eyes said. But his smile did not sweep her apprehension away.

There's more, she reminded herself. *More than me.*

How long had it been since Achamian had left her?

Not that long, perhaps, but the desert lay between them.

No walk, it seemed, could be longer. The Carathay had ravished her, fumbling with knot and clasp, thrusting leathery hands beneath her robe, running polished fingertips across her breasts and thighs. It had stripped her past her skin, to the wood of her bones. It had spilled and raked her across the sand, like seashells.

It had offered her up to Kellhus.

At first she'd barely noticed the desert. She'd been too drunk, too juvenile, with joy. When Kellhus walked with her and Serwë, she'd laughed and talked much as she always had, but it'd seemed a pretense somehow, a way to disguise the wondrous intimacies they now shared. She'd forgotten what it'd been like in her adolescence, before whoring had placed nakedness and coupling beyond the circle of private, secret things. Making love to Kellhus—and Serwë—had taken what was once brazen and made it demure. She felt hidden and she felt whole.

When Kellhus walked with his Zaudunyani, she and Serwë marched hand in hand, discussing everything and anything so long as it returned to him. They giggled and blushed, used jokes to plot pleasures. They confessed resentments and fears, knowing the bed they shared brooked no deceit. They dreamed of palaces, of armies of slaves. Like little boys, they boasted of kings kissing the earth beneath their feet.

But in all that time, she hadn't so much walked through as *around* the Carathay. Dunes, like the tangle of tanned harem bodies. Plains hissing with sunlight. The desert had seemed little more than a fitting ground for her love and the nearing ascendancy of the Warrior-Prophet. Only when the water began to fail, when they massacred the slaves and the camp-followers ... Only then did she truly cross the Great Thirst.

The past crumbled, and the future evaporated. Her every heartbeat belonged, it seemed, to a different heart. She could remember the accumulating signs of death, wasting, as though her body were a candle notched with the watches—a light to read by. She could remember wondering at Serwë, who'd become a stranger in Kellhus's arms. She could remember wondering at the stranger who walked with her own limbs.

Nothing branched in the Carathay. Everything roamed without root or source. The death of trees: this, she had thought, was the secret of the desert.

Then Kellhus asked her to surrender her water.

Serwë. She'll lose the baby ...

His clear eyes reminded her of who she was: Esmenet. She drew up her waterskin and extended it with unwavering hands. She watched him pour her muddy life into a stranger's mouth. And when the last of it trailed like spittle, she understood—she *apprehended*—and with a brilliance no less ruthless than the sun.

There's more than me.

Kellhus tossed her waterskin into the dust.

You are the first, his eyes said, and his look was like water—like life.

Her feet scalded by gravel. Her hair feathered by dust. Her lips cracked by the sun. Every breath like burning wool in her throat and chest. And then, impossibly, they came to good, green earth. To Enathpaneah. They stumbled into a rivered valley, into the shade of strange willows. While Serwë dozed he undressed Esmenet, carried her into the transparent waters. He bathed her, washed the velvet dust from her skin.

You are my wife, he said. *You, Esmi ...*

She blinked, and the sun glittered through her water-beaded lashes.

We crossed the desert, he said.

And I, she thought, *am your wife.*

He laughed, pawed at her face as though embarrassed, and she caught and kissed his sun-haloed palm ... The waters that trailed from the flaxen ringlets of his hair and beard had been brown—the colour of dried blood.

Kellhus built a shelter of stone and branches for Serwë. He snared rabbits, rooted for tubers, and made fire by spinning sticks into sticks. For a time, it seemed they alone survived, that all mankind and not just the Holy War had perished. They alone spoke. They alone gazed and understood *that* they gazed. They alone loved, across all lands and all waters, to the world's very pale. It seemed all passion, all knowing, was *here*, ringing in one penultimate note. There was no way to explain or to fathom the sensation. It wasn't like a flower. It wasn't like a child's careless laugh.

They had become the measure ... Absolute. Unconditioned.

When they made love in the river, it seemed they sanctified the sea.

You, Esmenet, are my wife.

Burning, submerged in clear waters—in each other ... The anchoring ache.

The desert had changed everything.

"Kellhuuus!" Serwë panted between contractions. "Kellhus, I'm afraid!" She groaned and cried out. "Something's wrong! Something's wrong!"

Kellhus exchanged several words with the Kianene matron, who rinsed Serwë's inner thighs with steaming water, nodded and grinned. He glanced at Esmenet, then knelt beside the prostrate girl, cupped her shining cheek. She seized his hand and pressed her gasping mouth against it, her blond brows knitted in panic, her look desperate, beseeching.

"Kelluuussss!"

"Everything," he said, his eyes bright with wonder, "is as it should be, Serwë."

"You," the girl exclaimed, gulping air. *"You!"*

He nodded, as though hearing far more than one enigmatic word. Smiling, he wiped tears from her cheek with the flat of his thumb.

"Me," he whispered.

For a heartbeat, Esmenet glimpsed herself as though from afar. How could she not catch her breath? She knelt with *him*, the Warrior-Prophet, over the woman giving birth to his first child ...

The world had its habits. Sometimes events would pinch, tickle, or caress—occasionally they would batter—but somehow they always funnelled into the monotony of the half-expected. So many dim happenings! So many moments that shed no light, that marked no turn, that signalled nothing at all, save elemental loss. For her entire life, Esmenet had felt like a child being led by the hand of a stranger, passing through this crowd and that, heading somewhere she knew she shouldn't go, but fearing too much to ask or to fight.

Where are you taking me?

She had never dared ask this, not because she feared the answer, but because she feared what the answer would make of her life.

Nowhere. Nowhere good.

But now, after the desert, after the waters of Enathpaneah, she knew the answer. Every man she'd bedded, she had bedded for him. Every sin she'd committed, she had committed for him. Every bowl she'd chipped. Every heart she'd bruised. Even Mimara. Even *Achamian*. Without knowing, Esmenet had lived her entire life for him—for Anasûrimbor Kellhus.

Grief for his compassion. Delusion for his revelation. Sin so he might forgive. Degradation so he might raise her high. *He* was the origin. *He* was the destination. He was the *from where* and the *to which*, and he was here!

Here!

It was mad, it was impossible, it was true.

When she reflected on it, Esmenet could only laugh in joyous wonder. How distant the holy had always seemed, like the faces of kings and emperors on the coins she'd so coveted. Before Kellhus, all she knew of the holy was that it somehow always found her at the pitch of her misery and humiliation. Like her father, it came in the small hours of the night, whispering threats, demanding submission, promising brevity, solace, and providing only interminable horror and shame.

How could she not hate it? How could she not fear it?

She'd been a whore in *Sumna*, and being a whore in a holy city was no mean thing. Some of the others jokingly referred to themselves as "cutpurses at the gates to Heaven." They traded endless, mocking stories about the pilgrims who so frequently wept in their arms. "All that work to see the Tusk," old Pirasha had once quipped, "and they end up *showing* it instead!"

And Esmenet had laughed with them, even though she knew those pilgrims wept because they'd failed, because they'd sacrificed crops, savings, and the company of loved ones to come to Sumna. No low-caste man was so foolish as to *aspire* to wealth or joy—the world was far too capricious. Only redemption, only holiness, lay within their grasp. And there she was swinging her knees in her window, like one of those mad lepers who, for no more reason than spite, threw themselves upon the unafflicted.

How distant that woman now seemed—that *whore*. How near the Holy ...

Serwë wailed and shrieked, her body cramped about the agony of her womb.

The Kianene woman cried out encouragement, grimaced and smiled. Serwë threw her head back into Esmenet's knees, puffing air, staring with crazed eyes, screaming. Esmenet watched, breathless, her limbs numbed by wonder, her thoughts troubled that something so miraculous could fit so seamlessly into the moment-to-moment banality of life.

"*Heba serrisa!*" the Kianene woman cried. "*Heba serrisa!*"

The babe sucked its first breath, gave voice to its first, wailing prayer.

Esmenet stared at the newborn, realizing it was the spoils of her surrendered water. She had suffered so that Serwë might drink, and now there was this squalling babe, this son of the Warrior-Prophet.

There had been branches after all ...

Crying, she looked down at Serwë. "A son, Serchaa. You have a son! And he isn't blue!"

Biting her lip, Serwë smiled, sobbed and laughed. They shared a wise and joyous look no man save Kellhus could understand.

Laughing aloud, he lifted the screeching babe from the midwife's arms, peered at it searchingly. It quieted, and for a moment seemed to study Kellhus in turn, dumbfounded as only an infant can be. He raised it beneath a glittering thread of water, rinsed the blood and mucus from its face. When it began squalling once again, he cried out in mock surprise, turned to Serwë with tender eyes.

For an instant, just an instant, Esmenet thought she'd heard the voice of someone hated.

He lowered the child and delivered it to Serwë, who cradled it and continued to cry. A sudden grief overcame Esmenet, the rebuke of another's joy. Keeping her face lowered, she stood, then wordlessly rushed out of the pavilion.

Outside, the men of the Hundred Pillars, Kellhus's sacred bodyguard, stared in iron-eyed alarm, but made no move to stop her. Even still, she wandered only a short distance among the ad hoc shelters, knowing that some fretting adherent would harass her otherwise. The Zaudunyani, the faithful, maintained an armed perimeter about the encampment at all times—as much to guard against their fellow Men of the Tusk, Kellhus had admitted, as against heathen sorties.

Another thing the desert had changed ...

The rain had stopped, and the air was cool and hard with dripping things. The clouds had parted and she could see the Nail of Heaven, like a glittering navel revealed by raised woollen robes. If she lifted her face and stared only at the Nail, she knew she could imagine herself anyplace: Sumna, Shigek, the desert, or even in one of Achamian's sorcerous Dreams. The Nail of Heaven was the one thing, she thought, that cared nothing for where or when.

Two men—Galeoth by the look of them—trudged toward her through darkness and muck. "Truth shines," one of them, his face still puckered from what had to be bad desert burns, muttered as they neared. Then they recognized her ...

"Truth shines," Esmenet replied, lowering her face.

She avoided their flustered looks as they passed. "*Lady* ..." one of them whispered, as though choked by wonder. More and more they acted shamefaced and servile in her presence, as though she herself were becoming more and more. Though it made her uncomfortable, their obeisance also thrilled her. And with the passing of the days, it seemed to embarrass her less and please her more. It was no dream.

Notes rasped from the dark horizon. Somewhere, she knew, the Shrial Priests blew their prayer horns, and the orthodox Inrithi knelt before their makeshift shrines. For a moment the sound reminded her of Serwë's cries, heard from afar.

Her grief tumbled into regret. Why couldn't she give this moment of joy to Serwë, when in the desert she'd willingly given her her water, when she'd very nearly given her her life? Was it jealousy she felt? No. Jealousy pursed one's lips into a bitter line. She hadn't felt bitter ...

Had she?

Kellhus is right ... We know not what moves us. There was more, always more.

The mud felt cool beneath her toes—so different from furnace sands.

Cries from a nearby tent startled her. It was someone suffering the hollows, she realized. Even as she backed away, she battled the urge to see who it might be, to offer comfort.

"Pleeassse ..." a thin voice gasped. "I need ... I need ..."

"I cannot," she said, staring in horror at the shadowy, leather and branch hut housing the voice. Kellhus had cloistered the sick, allowing only the survivors of earlier outbreaks to attend those still ailing. The Dread God, he said, communicated the disease through lice.

"I roll about in my own excrement!"

"I can't ..."

"How?" the wretched voice asked. "How?"

"Please," Esmenet softly cried. "You must understand. It's forbidden."

"He can't hear you ..."

Kellhus. Hearing his voice seemed an inevitable thing. She felt his arms encompass her, his silky beard comb across her bare neck. These didn't seem inevitable; they almost surprised ...

"They hear only their own suffering," he explained.

"Like me," Esmenet replied, suddenly overcome with remorse. Why had she run?

"You must be strong, Esmenet."

"Sometimes I feel strong. Sometimes I feel *new*, but then ..."

"You *are* new. My Father has remade all of us. But your past remains your past, Esmenet. Who you once were, remains who you once were. Forgiveness between strangers takes time."

How could he do this? How could he so effortlessly speak her heart?

But she knew the answer to that question—or so she thought.

Men, Kellhus had once told her, were like coins: they had two sides. Where one side of them *saw*, the other side of them *was seen*, and though all men were both at once, men could only truly know the side of themselves that saw and the side of others that was seen—they could only truly know the inner half of themselves and the outer half of others.

At first Esmenet thought this foolish. Was not the inner half the *whole*, what was only imperfectly apprehended by others? But Kellhus bid her to think of everything she'd witnessed in others. How many unwitting mistakes? How many flaws of character? Conceits couched in passing remarks. Fears posed as judgements ...

The shortcomings of men—their limits—were written in the eyes of those who watched them. And this was why everyone seemed so desperate to secure the good opinion of others—why everyone played the mummer. They knew without knowing that what they saw of themselves was only half of who they were. And they were desperate to be whole.

The measure of wisdom, Kellhus had said, was found in the distance between these two selves.

Only afterward had she thought of *Kellhus* in these terms. With a kind of surpriseless shock, she realized that not once—not once!—had she glimpsed shortcomings in his words or actions. And this, she understood, was why he seemed limitless, like the ground, which extended from the small circle about her feet to the great circle about the sky. He had become her horizon.

For Kellhus, there was no distance between seeing and being seen. He alone was whole. And what was more, he somehow stood from without and *saw from within*. He *made* whole ...

She bent her head back and gazed up into his eyes.

You're here, aren't you? You're with me ... inside.

"Yes," Kellhus said, and it seemed a god looked upon her.

She blinked two wondrous tears.

I am your wife! Your wife!

"And you must be strong," he said over the piteous voice of the invalid. "The God purges the Holy War, purifies us for the march on Shimeh."

"But you said we needn't fear the disease."

"Not the disease—the Great Names. Many of them are beginning to fear me ... Some think the God punishes the Holy War because of me. Others fear for their power and privilege."

Did he fear an attack, a war within the Holy War?

"Then you must speak to them, Kellhus. You must make them see!"

He shook his head. "Men praise what flatters and mock what rebukes— you know that. Before, when it was just the slaves and the men-at-arms, they could afford to overlook me. But now that their most trusted advisers and clients take the Whelming, they're beginning to understand the truth of their power, and with it, their vulnerability."

He holds me! This man holds me!

"And what's that?"

"Belief."

Esmenet looked hard into his eyes.

"You and Serwë," he continued, "aren't to travel unaccompanied under any circumstances. They would use you against me if they could ..."

"Have things become so desperate?"

"Not yet. But they could very soon. So long as Caraskand continues to resist us ..."

Sudden, bottomless horror. In her soul's eye she glimpsed assassins dispatched in the black of night, gold-adorned conspirators scowling by candlelight. "They'll try to kill you?"

"Yes."

"Then you must kill them!"

The thoughtless ferocity of these words shocked her. But she didn't repent them.

Kellhus laughed. "To say such things on such a night!" he chided.

Her earlier remorse came rushing back. Serwë had given birth tonight! Kellhus had a son! And all she could do was wallow in her own lacks and losses. *Why did you leave me, Akka?*

An aching sob welled through her. "Kellhus," she murmured. "Kellhus, I feel so ashamed! I envied her! I so envied her!"

He chuckled and nuzzled her scalp.

"You, Esmenet, are the lens through which I'll burn. *You* ... You're the womb of tribes and nations, the begetting fire. You're immortality, hope, and history. You're more than myth, more than scripture. You're the mother of these things! You, Esmenet, are the mother of more ..."

Breathing deep the dark, rainy world, she clutched his arms tight against her. She'd known this, ever since the earliest days of the desert, she'd known this. It was why she'd cast her whore's shell, the contraceptive charm the witches sell, across the sands.

You are the begetting fire ...

No more would she turn aside seed from her womb.

Early Winter, 4111 Year-of-the-Tusk, the Meneanor coast, near Iothiah

TELL ME ...

A towering whirlwind, joining armed earth to hoary heavens, belching dust and Sranc into the skies.

WHAT DO YOU SEE?

Achamian awoke without crying out. He lay still, searching for his breath. He blinked tears, but he did not weep. Sunlight shone through his fretted window, illuminating the banded crimson carpet in the room's heart. He nestled deep into the warm sockets of his sheets, wondering at the peace of his mornings.

The luxury alone seemed impossible. Somehow, after the destruction of the Scarlet Spires compound in Iothiah, he and Xinemus had found themselves honoured guests of Baron Shanipal, the representative Proyas had left behind in Shigek. Apparently one of the Baron's client knights had found them wandering naked through the city. Recognizing Xinemus, he'd delivered them to Shanipal, who'd brought them here—a luxurious Kianene villa on the Meneanor coast—to convalesce.

For weeks now, they'd enjoyed the Baron's protection and hospitality, long enough to forget their wonder at having escaped and to begin obsessing over their losses. Survival, Achamian was fast learning, was itself something to be survived.

He coughed and kicked his feet free of his covers. His Shigeki attendant, one of two slaves Baron Shanipal had assigned him, appeared from behind a floral-brocaded partition. The Baron, who was one of those odd men whose graciousness or viciousness depended on how convincingly one catered to his eccentricities, had determined they must live like the dead Grandees who once owned this villa. Apparently, the Kianene slept with slaves in their rooms—like the Norsirai with their dogs.

After bathing and dressing, Achamian prowled the halls of the villa, searching for Xinemus, who obviously hadn't returned to his room the previous night. The Kianene had left enough behind—mahogany-veneered furniture, soft-brushed rugs, and cerulean wall hangings—that Achamian could almost believe he was the guest of a true Fanim Grandee instead of an Inrithi Baron who happened to dress and live like one.

He found himself cursing the Marshal as he searched the rooms. The healthy always begrudged the sick: being shackled by another's incapacities was no easy thing. But the resentment Achamian suffered was curiously ingrown, almost labyrinthine in its complexity. With Xinemus, every day seemed more difficult than the last.

In so many ways, the Marshal was his oldest and truest friend—this alone made Achamian responsible. The fact the man had sacrificed what he'd sacrificed, suffered what he'd suffered, to *save* Achamian simply compounded this responsibility. But Xinemus still suffered. Despite the sunlight, despite the silk and submissive slaves, he still screamed in those basements, he still betrayed secrets, he still cracked teeth in anguish ... Every day it seemed, he lost his eyes anew. And because of this, he didn't simply hold Achamian accountable, he *accused* ...

"Look at the wages of my devotion!" he'd once shouted. "Do the sockets weep, for my cheek feels dry. Do the lids wither, eh, Akka? Describe them to me, for I can no longer see!"

"No one asked you to save me!" Achamian had cried. How long must he repay unwanted favours? "No one asked you for your folly!"

"Esmi," Xinemus had replied. "Esmi asked."

No matter how hard Achamian tried to forgive these tantrums, their poison struck deep. He often found himself mulling the limits of his responsibility, as though they were a matter for debate. What exactly did he owe? Sometimes he told himself that Xinemus, the true Xinemus, had died, and that this blind tyrant was no more than a stranger. Let him beg with the others in the gutter! Other times he convinced himself that Xinemus *needed* to be abandoned, if only to scrub him of his cursed caste-noble pride.

"You hold fast what you must relinquish," he once told the Marshal, "and you relinquish what you must hold fast ... This cannot go on, Zin. You must remember who you are!"

And yet Xinemus wasn't alone. Achamian had changed also—irrevocably.

Not once had he wept for his friend. He, the weeper ... Nor had he cried out upon awakening from the Dreams—not since escaping. For some reason, he just did not feel ... capable. He could remember the sensations, the roaring ears, the burning eyes and panged throat, but they seemed rootless, abstract, like something read rather than known.

What was strange was that Xinemus seemed to *need* his tears, as though worse than the torments, worse than blindness even, was the fact that *he*, and not Achamian, had become the weak one. Stranger still, the more Xinemus seemed to need his tears, the farther they slipped from Achamian's grasp. Often it seemed they wrestled when they spoke, as though Xinemus were the failing father who continually shamed himself by trying to assert ascendency over his son.

"I'm the strong one!" he'd once bawled in a drunken stupor. "Me!"

Watching, Achamian could muster no more than breathless pity.

He could mourn, he could feel, but he couldn't weep for his friend. Did this mean he too had been gouged of something essential? Or had he recovered something? He felt neither strong nor decisive, and yet he somehow knew he'd become these things. "Torment teaches," the poet Protathis wrote, "what love has forgotten." Had this been the gift of the Scarlet Spires? Had they burned some lesson into him?

Or had they simply beaten him numb?

Whatever the answer, he would see them burn—especially Iyokus. He would show them the wages of his newfound certainty.

Perhaps that had been their gift. Hatred.

After querying several slaves, he found Xinemus drinking alone on one of the terraces overlooking the sea. The morning sun promised hot skin in cool air—a sensation Achamian had always found heartening. The crash of breakers and the smell of brine tickled him with memories of his youth. The Meneanor swept out to the horizon, the turquoise of the shallows dropping into bottomless blue.

Drawing a deep breath, he approached the Marshal, who reclined with a bowl in his hands, his feet kicked upon the glazed brick railing. The previous night Shanipal had offered to pay their way by ship to Joktha, the port city of Caraskand. Achamian intended—no, *needed*—to leave as soon as possible, but he couldn't do so without Xinemus. For some reason, he knew Xinemus would die if he left him behind. Grief and bitterness had killed greater men.

He paused, mustering his arguments, steeling his nerves …

Without warning, Xinemus exclaimed, "All this dark!"

He was drunk, Achamian realized, noticing the pale red stains across the breast of his white linen tunic. Dead drunk.

Achamian opened his mouth, but no words came. What could he say? That Proyas needed him? Proyas had stripped him of his land and titles. That the Holy War needed him? He would only be a burden—he knew that ...

Shimeh! He came to see—

Xinemus pulled his feet down, leaned forward in his chair.

"Where do you lead, eh, Dark? What do you *mean*?"

Achamian stared at his friend, studied the planes of sunlight across his bearded profile. As always, he caught his breath at the sight of his empty eye sockets. It was as though Xinemus would forever have knives jutting from his eyes.

The Marshal pressed a palm outward to the sun, as though reassuring himself of some fact of distance. "Eh, Dark? Were you always like this? Were you always *here*?"

Achamian looked down, stricken with remorse. *Say something!*

But the words would not come. What was he to say? That he had no choice but to find Esmenet?

Then go! Go find your whore! Just leave me be!

Xinemus cackled, stumbling as drunks often do from one passion to another.

"Do I sound bitter, Dark? Oh, I know you're not so bad. You spare me the indignity of Akka's face! And when I piss, I need not convince myself my hands are big! To think ..."

At first, Achamian had been desperate for news regarding the Holy War, so much so he could scarcely grieve for Xinemus and his loss. For the entirety of his torment, Esmenet had seemed unthinkable, as though some part of him had understood the vulnerability she represented. But from the moment he recovered his senses, he could think of no one else—save perhaps Kellhus. What he would give to hold her in his arms, to smother her with laughter, tears, and kisses! What joy he would find in her joy, in her weeping disbelief!

He could see it all so clearly ... How it would be.

"I just want to know," Xinemus cried in a drunk's cajoling manner, "*who you fucking are!*"

Though at first he had only cause to fear the worst, Achamian *knew* she lived. According to the rumours, the Holy War had almost perished crossing Khemema. But according to Xinemus, she travelled with *Kellhus*, and he could imagine no place safer. Kellhus *couldn't die*, could he? He was the *Harbinger*, sent to save humanity from the Second Apocalypse.

Yet another certainty born of his torment.

"You feel like wind!" Xinemus cried, his voice growing more shrill. "You smell like sea!"

Kellhus would save the world. And he, Drusas Achamian, would be his counsellor, his guide.

"Open your eyes, Zin!" the Marshal cried, his voice cracking. Achamian glimpsed spittle flash in the sunlight. "Open your *fucking eyes!*"

A powerful breaker exploded across the black rocks below. Salty mist hazed the air.

Xinemus dropped his wine bowl, slapped madly at the sky, crying, "Huhh! Huhh!"

Achamian dashed forward two steps. Paused.

"Every sound," the Marshal gasped. "Every sound makes me cringe! Never have I suffered such fear! Never have I suffered such fear! Please, God ... Please!"

"Zin," Achamian whispered.

"I've been good! So good!"

"Zin!"

The Marshal fell absolutely still.

"Akka?" His arms fell inward, and he clutched at himself, as though trying to squeeze into the darkness only he could see. "Akka, no! No!"

Without thinking, Achamian hastened to him, embraced him.

"You're the cause of this!" Xinemus screeched into his chest. "*This is your doing!*"

Achamian held tight his sobbing friend. The broadness of Xinemus's shoulders surprised his outstretched arms.

"We need to leave," he murmured. "We must find the others."

"I know," the Marshal of Attrempus gasped. "We must find Kellhus!"

Achamian lowered his jaw against his friend's scalp. He wondered that his cheeks were dry.

"Yes ... Kellhus."

---∽∾∽---

Early Winter, 4111 Year-of-the-Tusk, near Caraskand

The hub of the abandoned estate had been built by the ancient Ceneians. On his first visit, Conphas had amused himself by touring the structures according to their historical provenance, finishing with the small marble tabernacle some Kianene Grandee had raised generations past. He despised not knowing the layout of the buildings that housed him. It was a general's habit, he supposed, to think of all places as battlefields.

The Inrithi caste-nobles began arriving in the afternoon, troops of mounted men cloaked against the interminable drizzle. Standing with Martemus in the gloom of a covered veranda, Conphas watched them hasten across the courtyard. They'd changed so much, it seemed, since that afternoon in his uncle's Privy Garden. If he closed his eyes he could still see them, scattered among the ornamental cypresses and tamarisks, their faces hopeful and unguarded, their manner arrogant and theatrical, their finery reflecting the peculiarities of their respective nations. Looking back, everything about them seemed so ... *untested.* And now, after months of war, desert, and disease, they looked grim and hard, like those infantrymen in the Columns who continually renewed their terms—the flint-hearted veterans that recruits admired and young officers mortally feared. They seemed a separate people, a new race, as though the differences that distinguished Conriyans from Galeoth, Ainoni from Tydonni, had been hammered out of them, like impurities from steel.

And of course they all rode Kianene horses, all wore Kianene clothes ... One must not overlook the superficial; it ran too deep.

Conphas glanced at Martemus. "They look more heathen than the heathen."

"The desert made the Kianene," the General said, shrugging, "and it has remade us."

Conphas regarded the man thoughtfully, troubled for some reason. "No doubt you're right."

Martemus fixed him with a bland stare. "Will you tell me what this is about? Why summon the Great and Lesser Names secretly?"

The Exalt-General turned to the black, rain-curtained hills of Enathpaneah. "To save the Holy War, of course."

"I thought we cared only for the Empire."

Once again Conphas scrutinized his subordinate, trying to decipher the man more than the remark. Since the debacle with Prince Kellhus, he continuously found himself *wanting* to suspect the General of treachery. He begrudged Martemus much for what had happened in Shigek. But not, strangely enough, his company.

"The Empire and the Holy War travel the same road, Martemus." Though soon—he found himself thinking, they would part ways. It would be so very tragic ...

First Caraskand, then Prince Kellhus. The Holy War must wait. Order must be observed in all things.

Martemus had not so much as blinked. "And if—"

"Come," Conphas interrupted. "Time to tease the lions."

The Exalt-General had instructed his attendants—after the desert he'd been forced to enlist soldiers to do the work of slaves—to take the Inrithi caste-nobles to a large indoor riding room adjacent to the stables. Conphas and Martemus found them spread in clots throughout the airy gloom, warming themselves over the orange glow of coal braziers, muttering in the low voices of sodden men—some fifty or sixty of them all told. For an instant, no one noticed their arrival, and Conphas stood motionless beneath the arched entranceway, studying them, from their eyes, which seemed desert bright in the grey light, to the straw clinging to their wet boots.

How much, he idly wondered, would the Padirajah pay for this room?

The voices trailed as more and more men noticed his presence.

"Where's the Anasûrimbor?" Palatine Gaidekki called out, his look as sharp and as cynical as always.

Conphas grinned. "Oh, he's here, Palatine. In *theme* if not in body."

"More than Prince Kellhus is missing," Earl Gothyelk said. "So is Saubon, Athjeäri ... Proyas is sick, of course, but I see none of Kellhus's more ardent defenders here ..."

"A felicitous coincidence, I am sure ..."

"I thought this was about Caraskand," Palatine Uranyanka said.

"But of course! Caraskand resists us. We're here to ask *why*."

"So why does she resist us?" Gotian asked, his tone contemptuous.

Not for the first time Conphas realized that they despised him—almost to a man. All men hate their betters.

He opened his arms and walked into their midst. "Why?" he called out, glaring at them, challenging them. "This is the question, isn't it? Why do the rains keep falling, rotting our feet, our tents, our *hearts?* Why does the hemoplexy strike us down indiscriminately? Why do so many of us die thrashing in our own bowel?" He laughed as though in astonishment. "And all this *after* the desert! As if the Carathay weren't woe enough! So *why?* Need we ask old Cumor to consult his omen-texts?"

"No," Gotian said tightly. "It is plain. The anger of the God burns against us."

Conphas inwardly smiled. Sarcellus had insisted the so-called Warrior-Prophet would be dead within days. But whether he succeeded or not— and Conphas suspected not—they would need allies following the attempt. No one knew precisely how many "Zaudunyani" Prince Kellhus commanded, but they numbered in the tens of thousands at least … The more the Men of the Tusk suffered, it seemed, the more they turned to the fiend.

But then, as the saying went, no dog so loved its master as when it was beaten.

Conphas glared at the assembled lords, pausing in the best oratorical fashion. "Who could disagree? The anger of the God *does* burn against us. And well it should …"

He swept his gaze across them.

"Given that we harbour and abet a False Prophet."

Howls erupted from among them, more in protest than in assent. But Conphas had expected as much. At this juncture, the important thing was to get these fools *talking*. Their bigotries would do the rest.

Chapter Twenty-one

Caraskand

And We will give over all of them, slain, to the Children of Eänna; you shall hamstring their horses and burn their chariots with fire. You shall bathe your feet in the blood of the wicked.

—TRIBES 21:13, THE CHRONICLE OF THE TUSK

Winter, 4111 Year-of-the-Tusk, Caraskand

Coithus Saubon bound through the rain, skidded across a section of slop, leapt a small ravine, and climbed the far side. He raised his face to the grey sky and laughed.

It's mine! By the Gods it will be mine!

Realizing that this moment demanded a certain modicum of jnan, composure at the very least, he reduced his gait, walking briskly through the clusters of ad hoc shelters. When finally he spied Proyas's pavilion near a copse of rain-dreary sycamores, he hastened toward it.

King! Yes I shall be King!

The Galeoth Prince halted before the pavilion, puzzled by the absence of guards. Proyas was somewhat soft-hearted with his men—perhaps he'd bid them stay within, out of the fucking rain. All around, muddy ground sizzled with waters. The turf was moated with flooded ruts and puddles. The rain drummed across the sagging canvas before him.

King of Caraskand!

"Proyas!" he shouted through the ambient roar. He could feel the rain at long last soak through the heavy felt beneath his hauberk. It felt like a warm kiss against his skin. "Proyas! Blast you man, I need to talk! I know you're in there!"

At length he heard a muffled voice cursing from within. When the flap was at last pulled aside, Saubon was taken aback. Proyas stood before him, thin, haggard, a dark wool blanket wrapped about his shivering frame.

"They said you'd recovered," Saubon said, embarrassed.

"Of course I'm recovered, you idiot. I stand."

"Where are your guards? Your physician?"

A gravelly cough wracked the ailing Prince. He cleared his throat, blew strings of sputum from his mouth. "Sent them all away," he said, wiping his lip with a sleeve. "Needed to sleep," he added, raising a pained brow.

Saubon roared with laughter, almost grabbed the man in his mailed arms. "You won't be able to sleep now, my pious friend!"

"Saubon. Prince. Please, to the point if you will. I'm grievously sick."

"I've come to ask a question, Proyas ... One question only."

"Ask it then."

Saubon suddenly calmed, became very serious.

"If I deliver Caraskand, will you support my bid to be its King?"

"What do you mean 'deliver'?"

"I mean throw open its gates to the Holy War," the Galeoth Prince replied, fixing him with a penetrating, blue-eyed stare.

Proyas's whole bearing seemed transformed. The pallor fell from his face. His dark eyes became lucid and attentive. "You're serious about this."

Saubon cackled like a greedy old man. "Never have I been so serious."

The Conriyan Prince scrutinized him for several moments, as though gauging the alternatives.

"I like not this game you—"

"Just answer the question, damn you! Will you support my bid to be crowned King of Caraskand?"

Proyas was silent for a moment, but then slowly nodded. "Yes ... You deliver Caraskand, and I assure you, you'll be its King."

Saubon raised his face and his arms to the menacing sky and howled out his battle cry. The rains plummeted upon him, rinsed him in soothing cold, fell between his lips and teeth and tasted of honey. He'd tumbled in the breakers of circumstance, so violently that mere months ago he'd thought he would die. Then he'd met Kellhus, the Warrior-Prophet, the man who'd set him onto the path toward his own heart, and he'd survived calamities that could break ten lesser men. And now this, the lifelong moment come at last. It seemed a giddy, impossible thing.

It seemed a gift.

Rain, so heartbreakingly sweet after Khemema. Beads pattered against his forehead, cheeks, and closed eyes. He shook water from his matted hair.

King ... I will be King at long last.

"Where," Proyas asked, "have all these hard silences come from?"

Cnaiür regarded him from the pavilion's gloomy heart. The Conriyan Prince, he realized, hadn't been idle during his convalescence. He'd been thinking.

"I don't understand," Cnaiür said.

"But you do, Scylvendi ... Something happened to you at Anwurat. I need to know what."

Proyas was still sick—grievously so, it appeared. He sat bundled beneath wool blankets in a camp chair, his normally hale face drawn and pale. In any other man, Cnaiür would have found such weakness disgusting, but Proyas wasn't any other man. Over the months the young prince had come to command something troubling within him, a respect not fit for a fellow Scylvendi, let alone an outlander. Even sick he seemed regal.

He's just another Inrithi dog!

"Nothing happened at Anwurat," Cnaiür said.

"What do you mean, *nothing*? Why did you run? Why did you disappear?"

Cnaiür scowled. What was he supposed to say?

That he went mad?

He'd spent many sleepless nights trying to wring sense from Anwurat. He could remember the battle slipping from his grasp. He could remember murdering a Kellhus who wasn't Kellhus. He could remember sitting on the strand, watching the Meneanor hammer the shore with fists of foaming white. He could remember a thousand different things, but they all seemed stolen, like stories told by a childhood friend.

Cnaiür had lived the greater part of his life with madness. He heard the way his brothers spoke, he understood how they thought, but despite endless recriminations, despite years of roaring shame, he couldn't make those words and thoughts his own. His was a fractious and mutinous soul. Always one thought, one hunger, too many! But no matter how far his soul wandered from the tracks of the proper, he'd always borne witness to its treachery—he'd always *known* the measure of his depravity. His confusion had been that of one who watches the madness of another. *How?* he would cry. *How could these thoughts be mine?*

He had always owned his madness.

But at Anwurat, that had changed. The watcher within had collapsed, and for the first time his madness had owned him. For weeks he'd been little more than a corpse bound to a maddened horse. How his soul had galloped!

"What does it matter to you, my comings and goings?" Cnaiür fairly cried. He hooked his thumbs in his iron-plated girdle. "I am not your client."

Proyas's expression darkened. "No ... But you stand high among my advisers." He looked up, his eyes hesitant. "Especially since Xinemus ..."

Cnaiür grimaced. "You make too mu—"

"You saved me in the desert," Proyas said.

Cnaiür quashed the sudden yearning that filled him. For some reason, he *missed* the desert—far more so than the Steppe. What was it? Was it the anonymity of footsteps, the impossibility of leaving track or trail? Was it respect? The Carathay had killed far more than he ... Or had his heart recognized itself in her desolation?

So many cursed questions! Shut up! Shut—

"Of course I saved you," Cnaiür said. "What prestige I hold, remember, I hold through you." Almost instantly he regretted the remark. He had meant it as a dismissal, but it had sounded like an admission.

For a moment, Proyas looked as though he might cry out in frustration. He lowered his face instead, studied the mats beneath his bare white feet. When he looked up, his expression was at once plaintive and challenging.

"Did you know that Conphas recently called a secret council to discuss Kellhus?"

Cnaiür shook his head. "No."

Proyas was watching him very closely.

"So you and Kellhus still don't speak."

"No." Cnaiür blinked, glimpsed an image of the Dûnyain, his face cracking open as he screamed. A memory? When had it happened?

"And why's that, Scylvendi?"

Cnaiür struggled to hide his sneer. "Because of the woman."

"You mean Serwë?"

He could remember Serwë shrieking, covered in blood. Had that happened at Anwurat as well? Had it happened at all?

She was my mistake.

What had possessed him to take her that day he and Kellhus had killed the Munuäti? What had possessed him to take a woman—a *woman!*—on the trail? Was it her beauty? She was a prize—there could be no doubt about that. Lesser chieftains would have flaunted her at every opportunity, would have entertained offers just to see how many cattle she could fetch, all the while knowing she was beyond bartering.

But still, it was *Moënghus* he hunted! Moënghus!

No. The answer was plain: he'd taken her because of Kellhus. Hadn't he?

She was my proof.

Before finding her, he'd spent weeks alone with the man—weeks alone with a *Dûnyain*. Now, after watching the inhuman fiend devour heart after Inrithi heart, it scarcely seemed possible he'd survived. The bottomless scrutiny. The narcotic voice. The demonic truths ... How could he *not* take Serwë after enduring such an ordeal? Besides beautiful, she was simple, honest, passionate—everything Kellhus wasn't. He warred against a spider. How could he not crave the company of flies?

Yes ... That was it! He'd taken her as a *landmark*, as a reminder of what was human. He should've known she'd become a battleground instead.

He used her to drive me mad!

"You must pardon my scepticism," Proyas was saying. "Many men are strange when it comes to women ... But you?"

Cnaiür bristled. What was he saying?

Proyas looked down to the sheafs on the table next to him, their corners curling in the wet. He absently tried to straighten one with thumb and forefinger. "All this madness with Kellhus has set me thinking," he said. "Especially about *you*. By the thousands they flock to him, they abase themselves before him. By the *thousands* ... And yet you, the one man who knows him best, can't abide his company. Why is that, Cnaiür?"

"As I said, because of the woman. He stole my prize."

"You loved her?"

Men, the memorialists said, often strike their sons to bruise their fathers. But then why did they strike their wives? Their lovers?

Why had he beaten Serwë? To bruise Kellhus? To injure a Dûnyain?

Where Kellhus caressed, Cnaiür had slapped. Where Kellhus whispered, Cnaiür had screamed. The more the Dûnyain compelled love, the more he exacted terror, and without any true understanding of what he did. At the time, she had simply *deserved* his fury. *Wayward bitch!* he would think. *How could you? How could you?*

Did he love her? Could he?

Perhaps in a world without Moënghus ...

Cnaiür spat across the Prince's matted floor. "I owned her! She was mine!"

"And this is all?" Proyas asked. "This is the sum of your grudge against Kellhus?"

The sum of his grudge ... Cnaiür nearly cackled aloud. There was no sum for what he felt.

"I find your silence unnerving," Proyas said.

Cnaiür spat once again. "And I find your interrogation offensive. You presume too much, Proyas."

The drawn yet handsome face flinched. "Perhaps," the Prince said, sighing deeply. "Perhaps not ... Nevertheless, Cnaiür, I would have your answer. I must know the truth!"

The truth? What would these dogs make of the truth? How would Proyas react?

He eats you, and you know it not. And when he's done, there will be only bones ...

"And what truth would that be?" Cnaiür snapped. "Whether Kellhus is truly an Inrithi Prophet? You think that is a question I can answer?"

Proyas had leaned forward in agitation; he now collapsed back in his chair.

"No," he gasped, drawing a hand to his forehead. "I merely hoped that ..." He trailed, shaking his head wearily. "But none of this is to the point. I called you here to discuss other matters."

Cnaiür watched the man closely, found himself troubled by the evasiveness of his eyes.

Conphas has approached him ... They plan to move against Kellhus.

Why should he continue lying for the Dûnyain? He no longer believed the man would honour their pact ...

So just what did he believe?

"Saubon has come to me," Proyas continued. "He's exchanged missives—and now even hostages—with a Kianene officer named Kepfet ab Tanaj. Apparently, Kepfet and his fellows hate Imbeyan so fiercely they're prepared to sacrifice anything just to see him dead."

"Caraskand," Cnaiür said. "He offers Caraskand."

"A section of her walls, to be more precise. To the west, near a small postern gate."

"So you want my counsel? Even after Anwurat?"

Proyas shook his head. "I want more than your counsel, Scylvendi. You're always saying we Inrithi carve up honour the way others carve up stags, and this is no different. We have suffered much. Whoever breaks Caraskand will be immortalized ..."

"And you are too sick."

The Conriyan Prince snorted. "First you spit at my feet, now you call out my infirmities ... Sometimes I wonder whether you earned those scars murdering manners instead of men!"

Cnaiür felt like spitting, but refrained.

"I earned these scars murdering fools."

Proyas started laughing but finished hacking phlegm from his lungs. He leaned back and blew strings of mucus into a spittoon set in the shadows behind his chair. Its brass rim gleamed in the uncertain light.

"Why me?" Cnaiür asked. "Why not Gaidekki or Ingiaban?"

Proyas groaned and shuddered beneath his blankets. He leaned forward, elbows on knees, and clutched his head. Clearing his throat, he raised his face to Cnaiür. Two tears, relics of his coughing fit, fell across his cheek.

"Because you're"—he swallowed—"more capable."

Cnaiür stiffened, felt a snarl twitch across his lips. *He means more disposable!*

"I know you think that I lie," Proyas said quickly. "But I don't. If Xinemus were still ... still ..." He blinked, shook his head. "I would've asked him."

Cnaiür studied him closely. "You fear this may be a trap ... That Saubon might be deceived."

Proyas chewed at the inside of his cheek, nodded. "An entire city for the life of one man? No hatred could be so great."

Cnaiür did not bother contradicting him.

There was a hate that eclipsed the hater, a hunger that encompassed the very ground of appetite.

Bent low, his broadsword before him, Cnaiür urs Skiötha stole across the heights of the wall toward the postern gate, thinking of Kellhus, Moënghus, and murder.

Need me ... I must find some way to make him need me!

Yes ... The madness was lifting.

Cnaiür paused, pressed his armoured back against the wet stone. Saubon crowded close behind him, followed by some fifty other hand-picked men. Drawing long even breaths, Cnaiür tried to calm the anxiousness of his limbs. He glanced across the great weave of moonlit structures below. It was strange, seeing the city that had bitterly denied them so exposed, almost like lifting the skirts of a sleeping woman.

A heavy hand fell upon his shoulder, and Cnaiür turned to see Saubon in the gloom, his hard, grinning face framed by his mail hood. Moonlight rimmed his battle helm. Though he respected the Galeoth Prince's prowess on the field, Cnaiür neither liked nor trusted him. The man had, after all, kennelled with the Dûnyain's other dogs.

"She looks almost wanton ..." Saubon whispered, nodding toward the city below. He looked back, his eyes bright. "Do you still doubt me?"

"I never doubted you. Only your faith in this Kepfet."

The Galeoth Prince's grin broadened. "Truth shines," he said.

Cnaiür squashed the urge to sneer. "So do pigs' teeth."

He spat across the ancient stonework. There was no escaping the Dûnyain—not any more. It sometimes seemed the abomination spoke from every mouth, watched from all eyes. And it was only getting worse.

Something ... There must be something I can do!

But what? Their pact to murder Moënghus was a farce. The Dûnyain honoured nothing for its own sake. For them only the ends mattered, and everything else, from warlike nations to shy glances, was a tool—something to be used. And Cnaiür possessed nothing of use—not any more. He'd squandered his every advantage. He couldn't even offer his reputation among the Great Names, not after the degradation of Anwurat ...

No. There was nothing Kellhus needed from him. Nothing except ...

Cnaiür actually gasped aloud.

Except my silence.

In his periphery, he glimpsed Saubon turn to him in alarm.

"What's wrong?"

Cnaiür glanced at him contemptuously. "Nothing," he said.

The madness was lifting.

Cursing in Galeoth, Saubon started past him, crawling beneath the pitted battlements. Cnaiür followed, his breath rasping over-loud in his ears. Rainwater had pooled through the joints between flagstones, reflecting moonlight. He splashed through them, his fingers aching with cold. The farther they crept along the parapet, the more the balance of vulnerability seemed to shift. Before Caraskand had seemed exposed, but now, as the towers of the postern gate loomed nearer, they seemed the vulnerable ones. Torches glittered along the tower's crest.

They paused before an iron-strapped door, looked to one another apprehensively, as though realizing this would be the definitive test of Kepfet and his unlikely hatred. Saubon looked almost terrified in the pallid light. Cnaiür scowled and yanked on the iron handle.

It grated open.

The Galeoth Prince hissed, laughed as though amused by his momentary doubt. Whispering "Die or conquer!" he slipped around the masonry into the black maw. Cnaiür glanced one last time at Caraskand's moonlit expanse, then followed, his heart thundering.

Moving in dark, deadly files, they spilled through the corridors and down the stairwells. As Proyas had bidden him, Cnaiür stayed close to

Saubon, jostling behind him through narrow hallways. He knew the layout of the gate must be simple, but tension and urgency made it seem a maze.

Saubon's outstretched hand stopped him in the blackness, pulled him to the chapped wall. The Galeoth Prince had halted before a door. Threads of golden light traced its outline in the dark. Cnaiür's skin prickled at the sound of muted shouts.

"The God," Saubon whispered, "has given me this place, Scylvendi. Caraskand will be mine!"

Cnaiür peered at him in the darkness. "How do you know?"

"I know!"

The Dûnyain had told him. Cnaiür was certain of it.

"You brought Kepfet to Kellhus ... Didn't you?"

He let the Dûnyain read his face.

Saubon grinned and snorted. Without answering, he turned his back to Cnaiür, rapped the door with the pommel of his sword.

Wood scraped against stone—the sound of someone pushing back a chair. There was a muffled laugh, voices speaking Kianene. If the Norsirai sounded like grunting pigs, Cnaiür thought, the Kianene sounded like honking geese.

Saubon swung his broadsword around, gripping it like a dagger and raising it high. For a mad instant, he resembled a boy preparing to spear fish in a stream. The door jerked open; a human face surfaced ...

Saubon snatched the man's braided goatee, stabbed downward with his sword. The Kianene was dead before he clanked to the ground. Howling, the Galeoth Prince leapt into airy light beyond the door.

Cnaiür tumbled after him with the others, found himself in a narrow, candle-lit room. A great wheeled spool loomed before him, wrought in ancient wood, wrapped by chains that dropped from chutes in the fluted ceiling. Beyond, he glimpsed several red-jacketed Kianene soldiers scrambling for their weapons. Two simply sat dumbstruck, one with bread in hand, at a rough-hewn table set in the far corner.

Saubon hacked into their midst. One fell shrieking, clutching his face.

Cnaiür leapt into the fray, crying out in Scylvendi. He hammered the sword from the slack, panicked hand of the heathen guardsman before him: a stoop-shouldered adolescent sporting no more than wisps of a goatee. Cnaiür crouched and hacked at the legs of a second guardsman rushing his flank. The man toppled, and Cnaiür whirled back to the boy, only to see him vanish through a far door. A Galeoth knight he didn't recognize speared the man he'd felled.

Nearby, Saubon hacked at two Kianene, brandishing his sword like a pipe, grunting obscenities with each swing. He'd lost his helm; blood matted his shaggy blond hair. Cnaiür charged to his side. With his first blow, he cracked the round, yellow and black shield of the nearest guardsman. The heathen skidded on blood, and as his arms reflexively opened, Cnaiür punched his sword through the man's ring harness. His scream was a convulsive, gurgling thing. Glancing to his left, he saw Saubon shear off his foeman's lower jaw. Hot blood sprayed across Cnaiür's face. The heathen stumbled, flailed. Saubon silenced him with a blow that almost severed his head.

"Raise the gate!" the Galeoth Prince roared. "Raise the gate!"

Inrithi warriors, mostly ruddy-faced Galeoth, now packed the room. Several fell upon the wooden wheels. The sound of chains grating across stone drowned out their excited muttering.

The air reeked of pierced entrails.

Saubon's captains and thanes had assembled about him. "Hortha! Fire the signal! Meärji, storm the second tower! You must take it, son! You must make your ancestors proud!" The radiant blue eyes found Cnaiür. Despite the blood threading his face, there was a majesty to his look, a paternal confidence that chilled Cnaiür's heart. Coithus Saubon was already king, and he belonged to Kellhus.

"Secure the murder room," the Galeoth Prince said. "Take as many men as you need ..." His eyes swept across all those assembled. "Caraskand falls, my brothers! By the God, *Caraskand falls!*"

Cheers resounded through the room, fading into hoarse shouts and the sound of boots making muck of the glossy pools of red across the floor. "Die or conquer!" men cried. "Die or conquer!"

After crowding through a far hallway, Cnaiür barged through a likely door and found the murder room, though the gloom was so deep it took several moments for his eyes to adjust. Not far, a single point of candle-light sputtered in circles. He could hear the portcullis creaking up into the ancient machinery of the chamber. He could smell the humid cold of outside, feel air wash upward from his feet. He was standing upon a large grate, he realized, set over the passage between the two gates. Things and surfaces resolved from the gloom: wood stacked against the walls; rows of amphorae, no doubt filled with oil to pour through the grate; two ovens no higher than his knee, each stocked with kindling, furnished with bellows, and bearing iron pots for cooking the oil ...

Then he saw the Kianene boy he'd disarmed earlier, huddled against the far wall, his brown eyes as wide as silver talents. For a heartbeat, Cnaiür couldn't look away. The sound of screams and shouts echoed through unseen corridors.

"*P-pouäda t'fada,*" the adolescent sobbed. "*Os-osmah ... Pipiri osmah!*"

Cnaiür swallowed.

From nowhere it seemed, a Galeoth thane—someone Cnaiür didn't recognize—strode past him toward the boy, his sword raised. Just then, light glittered up from the passage below, and through the grate at his feet, Cnaiür saw a band of torch-bearing Galeoth rush toward the outer doors of the postern gate. He glanced up, saw the thane swing his sword downward as though clubbing an unwanted whelp. The boy had raised warding hands. The blade glanced from his wrist and struck along the bone of his forearm, slicing back a shank of meat the size of a fish. The boy screamed.

The doors burst open beneath. Exultant cries pealed through the room, followed by cold air and shining torchlight. The first of the thousands Saubon had concealed on the broken slopes beneath the gate began rushing through the passageway beneath. The thane hacked at the adolescent, once, twice ...

The screams stopped.

Squares of light raced across the thane's blood-spattered form. The blue-eyed man gazed in wonder at the spectacle beneath. He glanced at Cnaiür, grinned, and pawed at his teary cheeks.

"Truth shines!" he convulsively cried. "Truth shines!"

His eyes shouted glory.

Without thinking, Cnaiür dropped his sword and seized him, almost hoisted him from his feet. For a heartbeat, they grappled. Then Cnaiür smashed his forehead into the thane's face. The man's broadsword fell from senseless fingers. His head lolled backward. Cnaiür slammed his forehead down again, felt teeth snap. Shouts and clamour reverberated up through the iron grate. With each rushing torch lattices of shadow swept up and over them. Again, bone hammering against bone, face breaking beneath face. The bridge of the man's nose collapsed, then his left cheek. Again and again, smashing his face into slurry.

I am stronger!

The twitching thing slouched to the ground, drained across the Men of the Tusk.

Cnaiür stood, his chest heaving, blood streaming in rivulets across the iron scales of his harness. The very world seemed to move, so great was the rush of arms and men beneath him.

Yes, the madness was lifting.

Horns pealed across the great city. War horns.

There was no rain in the morning, but a thin fog wearied the distances, drained Caraskand's reaches of contrast and colour, rendering the far quarters ghostlike. Though overcast, one could feel the sun burning behind the clouds.

The Fanim, both native Enathpaneans and Kianene, crowded onto roofs and strained to see what was happening. As they watched a growing pall of smoke rise from the eastern quarters of the city, women clasped crying children tight, ashen-faced men scored their forearms with finger-nails, and old mothers wailed into the sky. Below them, Kianene horse-men beat their way through the tight streets, riding down their own people, struggling to answer the call of the Sapatishah's drums and make their way to the towering fortress in the city's northwest, the Citadel of the Dog. And then, after a time, the terrified watchers could actually see, in those distant streets where the angles allowed them, the Men of the Tusk—small, wicked shadows through the smoke. Iron-draped figures rushed through the streets, swords rose and fell, and tiny, hapless forms collapsed beneath them. Some of the onlookers were so terror-stricken they became sick. Some rushed down into the congested streets to join in the mad, hopeless attempt to escape. Others remained, and watched the approaching columns of smoke. They prayed to the Solitary God, tore at their beards and their clothes, and thought panicked thoughts about everything they were about to lose.

Saubon had gathered his men and struck through the streets toward the mighty Gate of Horns. The massive barbican fell after fierce fighting, but the Galeoth had found themselves sorely pressed by those Fanim horsemen the Sapatishah's officers had been able to muster. In the narrow streets, clots of men joined in dozens of small, pitched battles. Even with the constant string of reinforcements arriving from the postern gate, the Galeoth found themselves stubbornly giving ground.

But the mighty Gate of Horns was finally thrown open, and Athjeäri with his Gaenrish knights pounded into the city on their stolen horses, followed by rank after rank of Conriyans, invincible and inhuman behind their godlike masks. In their wake, their Prince, the ailing Nersei Proyas, was borne into Caraskand on a litter.

The Kianene were routed by this new onslaught, and their last chance to save their city was lost. Organized resistance crumbled and became confined to small pockets scattered throughout Caraskand. The Inrithi broke into roaming bands and began to pillage the city.

Houses were ransacked. Entire families were put to the sharp knife. Black-skinned Nilnameshi slave girls were dragged sobbing from their hiding places by the hair, violated, and then put to the sword. Tapestries were torn from the walls, rolled, or tied into sacks into which plates, statuary, and other articles of gold and silver were swept. The Men of the Tusk rifled through ancient Caraskand, leaving behind them scattered clothes and broken chests, death and fire. In some places the scattered looters were slaughtered and chased away by armed bands of Kianene, or held at bay until some thane or baron rallied enough men to close with the heathen.

The hard battles were fought across Caraskand's great market squares and through the more magnificent of the buildings. Only the Great Names were able to hold enough men together to batter open the tall doors and then fight their way down the long, carpeted corridors. But in these places, the spoils were the greatest—cool cellars filled with Eumarnan and Jurisadi wines, golden reliquary behind fretted shrines, alabaster and jade statues of lions and desert wolves, intricate plaques of clear chalcedony. Their coarse shouts echoed beneath airy domes. They tracked blood and filth across broad, white-tiled floors. Men sheathed their weapons and fumbled with their breeches, strolling into the marmoreal recesses of some dead Grandee's harem.

The doors of the great tabernacles were battered down, and the Men of the Tusk waded among masses of kneeling Fanim, hacking and clubbing until the tiled floors were matted with the dead and dying. They smashed down the doors of the adjoining compounds, wandered into the dim, carpeted interiors. Soft shadows and strange scents greeted them. Light rained down through tiny windows of coloured glass. At first they were fearful. These were the dens of the Unholy, where the monstrous Cishaurim worked their abominations. They walked quietly, numbed by their dread. But eventually the drunkenness of the screaming streets would return to them. Someone would reach out and spill a book from an ivory lectern, and when nothing happened the aura of foreboding would dissolve, replaced by sudden, righteous fury. They would laugh, cry out the names of Inri Sejenus and the Gods as they plundered the inner sanctums of the False Prophet. They tortured Fanic priests for their secrets. They set glorious, many-pillared tabernacles of Caraskand aflame.

The Men of the Tusk cast the bodies from the rooftops. They rifled the pockets of the dead, tugging rings from grey fingers, or just sawing at the knuckles to save time. Shrieking children were torn from their mothers, tossed across rooms and caught on sword point. The mothers were beaten and raped while their gutted husbands wailed about their entrails. The Inrithi were like wild-eyed beasts, drunk with howling murder. Moved by the God's own fury, they utterly destroyed all in the city, both men and women, young and old, oxen, sheep, and asses, with the edge of the sharp sword.

The anger of the God burned bright against the people of Caraskand.

Sunlight broke across the city, cold and brilliant against a dark horizon. Wings outstretched, the Old Name floated on hot western winds. Caraskand pitched and yawed beneath him, a vista of flat-roofed structures, encrusting hillsides, enveloping distances in mud-brick confusion, opening about broad agoras and monumental complexes.

Fires burned in the east, screening the far quarters. He soared around mountainous plumes.

He saw Caraskandi crowding the rooftop gardens of the merchant quarter, howling in disbelief. He saw packs of armed Inrithi ranging through abandoned streets, dispersing into buildings. He saw the first of the domed tabernacles burning. From so far, they looked like bowls upended over firepits. He saw horsemen charging across the great market squares, and phalanxes of footmen battling down broad avenues toward the hazy blue ramparts of the Citadel of the Dog.

And he saw the man who called himself Dûnyain, fleeing across ramshackle rooftops, running like the wind, pursued by the jump and tumble of Gaörta and the others. He watched the man leap and pirouette onto a third floor, sprint, then vault beyond the far edge of the adjacent two-storey structure. He landed in a crouch amid a clot of Kianene footmen, then bounced away, taking four lives with him. The soldiers had scarcely drawn their swords when Gaörta and his brothers descended upon them.

What was this man? Who were the Dûnyain?

These were questions that needed to be answered. According to Gaörta, the man's Zaudunyani, his "tribe of truth," numbered in the tens of thousands. It was only a matter of weeks, Gaörta insisted, before the Holy War succumbed to him entirely. But the questions these facts raised were overmatched by the perils. Nothing could interfere with the Holy War's mission. Shimeh must be taken. The Cishaurim must be destroyed!

Despite the questions, the man's existence could no longer be tolerated. He had to die, and for reasons that transcended their war against the Cishaurim. More troubling than his preternatural abilities, more troubling than even his slow conquest of the Holy War, was the man's *name*. An Anasûrimbor had returned—an *Anasûrimbor*! And though Golgotterath had long scoffed at the Mandate and their prattle regarding the Celmomian Prophecy, how could they afford to take chances? They were so near! So close! Soon the Children would gather, and they would rain ruin upon this despicable world! The End of Ends was coming ...

One did not gamble with such things. They would kill this Anasûrimbor Kellhus, then they would seize the others, the Scylvendi and the women, to learn what they needed to know.

The Dûnyain's distant figure dashed into some kind of compound—disappeared. The Synthese craned its small human neck, banked against the sweeping sky, watched his slaves disappear after him.

Good. Gaörta and his brothers were closing ...

The Warrior-Prophet ... The Old Name had already decided he would couple with his corpse.

———— ∞∞ ————

The percussive slap of sandals, the rhythmic pant of tireless, animal lungs, the slap of fabric about hooking arms.

They're too fast!

Kellhus ran. As fleet as memories, chambers rushed past him, each possessing the spare elegance of desert peoples. Behind him, Sarcellus and the others fanned through the surrounding corridors. Kellhus kicked through a door, rolled down a stone stair, came to his feet in the gloom. They followed, mere heartbeats behind. He heard steel whisk against wood—a sheath. He ducked right and rolled. A knife flashed to his left, chipped dim stone, clattered to the floor. Kellhus plunged down another stair, into pitch blackness. He blundered through a brittle wooden door, felt the air bloom into emptiness about him, smelled stale cistern waters.

The skin-spies hesitated.

All eyes need light.

Kellhus spun about the room, his every surface alive, reading the warp and weft of drafts, the crunch and rasp of his sandals scuffing stone, the flutter of his clothing. His outstretched fingers touched table, chair, brick oven, a hundred different surfaces in a handful of instants. He fell into stance in the room's far corner. Drew his sword.

Motionless.

Somewhere in the pitch, a wood splinter snapped.

He could feel them slip through the entrance, one after the other. They spread across the far wall, their hearts thudding in competing rhythms. Kellhus could smell their musk roll through the room.

"I've tasted both of your peaches," the one called Sarcellus said—to mask the sounds of the others, Kellhus realized. "I tasted them long and hard—did you know that? I made them squeal ..."

"You lie!" Kellhus cried in mimicry of desperate fury. He heard the skin-spies pause, then close on the corner where he'd thrown his voice.

"Both were sweet," Sarcellus called, "and so very juicy ... The man, they say, ripens the peach."

Kellhus had punched his sword point through the ear of the creature that glided before him, lowered it as soundlessly as he could to the ground.

"Eh, Dûnyain?" Sarcellus asked. "That makes you twice the cuckold!"

One bumped into a chair.

Kellhus leapt, gutted it, rolled under the table as it squealed and shrieked.

"He plays us!" one cried. "*Unza, pophara tokuk!*"

"*Smell* him!" the thing called Sarcellus shouted. "Cut anything that smells his smell!"

The disembowelled creature flopped and flailed, screaming in demonic voices—as Kellhus had hoped. He ducked from under the table, backed to the wall to the left of the entrance. He pulled free his samite robe, tossed it onto the back of a chair he couldn't see—but remembered ...

Kellhus stood motionless. The drafts came to him, murmuring. He could feel their bestial heartbeats, taste the feral heat of their bodies. Two leapt at his robe before him. Swords swooped and cracked into the chair. Lunging, he skewered the one to the left in the throat, only to have his blade wrenched from him as the creature toppled backward. Kellhus leaned back and to the left, felt steel whip the air. He caught an arm, exploded the elbow, blocked the knife-bearing fist that hooked about. He reached into its throat and jerked out its windpipe.

He jumped backward. Sarcellus's sword whistled through the blackness. Twisting into a handstand, Kellhus caught the back of a chair and vaulted to a crouch at the far edge of the trestle table.

The gutted skin-spy thrashed immediately below him. Even still, he heard the thing called Sarcellus bound out of the cellar. Flee ...

For several moments Kellhus remained still, drawing long deep breaths. Inhuman screaming resounded through the blackness. It sounded like something—many somethings—burning alive.

How are such creatures possible? What do you know of them, Father?

Retrieving his long-pommelled sword, Kellhus struck off the living skin-spy's head. Sudden silence. He wrapped it, still streaming blood, in his slashed robe.

Then he climbed back toward slaughter and daylight.

The great black fortress the Men of the Tusk called the Citadel of the Dog dominated the easternmost of Caraskand's nine hills. They called her such because the way her inner and outer curtain walls enclosed the towering central keep vaguely resembled a dog curled about his master's leg. The Fanim simply called her "Il'huda," "the Bulwark." Raised by the great Xatantius, the most warlike of the early Nansur emperors, the Citadel of the Dog reflected the scale and ingenuity of a people who'd managed to flourish in the shadow of the Scylvendi: round towers, massive barbicans, offset inner and outer gates. The fortress's defences were tiered, so that each concentric ring overshadowed the next. And her outer walls were shelled in a glossy, well-nigh impenetrable, basalt.

Knowing that the fortress—which the Nansur called "Insarum," her original name—was the key to the city, Ikurei Conphas had assailed it almost immediately, hoping to storm the walls before Imbeyan could organize any concerted defence. The men of the Selial Column gained the southern heights only to be thrown back after horrifying losses. Soon the Galeoth were on the steep slopes with them, and then the Tydonni: Saubon and Gothyelk were not so foolish as to leave such a prize to the Exalt-General. Siege engines constructed to assail Caraskand's curtain walls were drawn up. Mangonels hurled burning tar over the fortifications. Trebuchets rained granite boulders and Fanim bodies. Tall, iron-hooked ladders were pressed against the walls, and the Kianene hefted rocks and boiling oil over the battlements to crush and burn those that climbed them. Protected by hide mantlets, an iron-headed battering ram was brought under the immense barbican and beneath a hail of fire and missiles began hammering at the gate. Clouds of arrows reached into the sky. Saubon himself was carried down with a Kianene arrow in his thigh.

Sheer numbers and ferocity gained the Warnutishmen of Ce Tydonn the western wall. Tall, bearded knights, clients of the dead Earl Cerjulla, hacked through the crowds of heathen who swarmed up to dislodge them. They were pelted by archers from the inner compound, but the arrows, if they could punch through the heavy mail, were merely embedded in the thick layers of felt beneath. Many roared and fought with several shafts jutting from their backs. The dead and dying were thrown headlong from the walls to crash onto the rocks or the men teeming below. The Tydonni planted their feet and refused to give ground, while behind them, more of their cousins, Agansi under Gothyelk's youngest son, Gurnyau, gained the summit. Under the direction of the wounded Saubon, the longbowmen of Agmundr raked the heights of the inner wall, forcing the Enathpanean and Kianene archers to shelter behind crenellations. Someone raised the Mark of Agansanor, the Black Stag, upon one of the outer towers. A great shout was raised by the Inrithi encircling the heights.

Then came a light more blinding than the sun. Men cried out, pointing to mad, saffron-robed figures hanging between the towers of the black keep. Eyeless Cishaurim, each with two snakes wrapped about their throats.

Threads of unholy incandescence waved across the outer wall like ropes in water. Stone cracked beneath the flashing heat. Hauberks were welded to skin. The Tydonni crouched beneath their great tear-shaped shields, leaning against the light, shouting in horror and outrage before being swept away. The Agmundrmen fired vainly at the floating abominations. Teams of Chorae Crossbowmen watched bolt after bolt whistle wide because of the range.

The tall knights of Ce Tydonn were decimated. Many, seeing the hopelessness of their plight, brandished their longswords, howled curses until the end. Others ran. Those who could scrambled down the ladders. Several warriors leapt from the battlements, their beards and hair aflame. An unholy torrent consumed Gothyelk's Standard.

Then the lights flickered out.

For a moment all was silent save for those left screaming upon the heights. Then the Kianene upon the walls burst into cheers. They rushed across the stolen summits, cast those Tydonni still living from the wall, including Gothyelk's youngest son, Gurnyau. Mad with grief, the old Earl had to be dragged away.

The Men of the Tusk withdrew in turmoil. Riders were dispatched, charged with finding the Scarlet Spires, who'd yet to enter Caraskand. They bore but one message: "Cishaurim defend the Citadel of the Dog."

Still bearing his trophy, Kellhus strode out onto the terrace of an abandoned palatial compound. He passed through a small garden of winter blooms and sculpted shrubs. The body of a dead woman, her gown hiked over her head, lay motionless between two junipers. Stepping over her, Kellhus walked out across the shining marble to the terrace balustrade. The breeze carried a bouquet of foul and sweet odours—the smell of precious things burning.

The Citadel of the Dog dominated the near distance, black and hazy, rising mountainous from the welter of walls and roofs crowding the valley below. He glimpsed tiny Kianene soldiers rushing along the heights, their silvered helms winking as they passed between battlements. He saw Inrithi bodies dumped from the walls.

To the north and to the south, Caraskand continued to die. Peering through screens of smoke, he studied the riot of distant buildings, glimpsed dozens of miniature dramas: pitched battles, petty atrocities, bodies being stripped, women wailing, even a child jumping from a rooftop. A sudden shriek drew his eyes downward, and he saw a band of black-armoured Thunyeri rushing through the enclosed garden of the compound immediately below the terrace. He quickly lost sight of them. Harsh laughter wafted up through the breeze.

He looked past the Citadel, south to the hills beyond Caraskand's far-wandering walls. To Shimeh.

I grow near, Father. Very near.

He swung the bloody sack he'd made of his robe from his shoulder, and the thing's severed head tumbled across the marmoreal floor. He studied its face, which seemed little more than a tangle of snakes with human-skin. A lidless eye gleamed in the shadows beneath. Kellhus already knew these creatures weren't sorcerous artifacts; he'd learned enough from Achamian to conclude they were worldly weapons, fashioned by the ancient Inchoroi the way swords were fashioned by Men. But with their faces undone, this fact seemed all the more remarkable.

Weapons. And the Consult had finally wielded them.

Wars within wars. It has finally come to this.

Kellhus had already encountered several of his Zaudunyani. Even now his instructions were spreading through the city. Serwë and Esmenet would be evacuated from the camp. Soon his Hundred Pillars would be securing this nameless merchant palace. The Zaudunyani he'd charged with watching the skin-spies he'd so far identified were being sought. If he could organize before the chaos ended ...

The Holy War must be purged.

Just then, light flared across the Citadel. A crack boomed over the city, like thunder rising out from the ground. A chorus of unsettling disharmonies reverberated in its wake. More flashes of light, and Kellhus saw sheets of masonry crash down the Citadel's foundations. Debris tumbled down the hillside.

Hanging in the air, the sorcerers of the Scarlet Spires had formed a great semicircle about the Citadel's immense barbican. Through a dark hail of arrows, glittering fire washed over the turrets, and even from this distance Kellhus could see burning Fanim leap into the baileys. Lightning leapt from phantom clouds, exploding stonework and limbs alike. Flocks of incandescent sparrows swarmed over the battlements, plummeting into face after howling face.

Despite the destruction, one Scarlet Schoolman, then another, and then another still, plunged to the rooftops below, struck into salt by heathen Chorae. His eye drawn by a blinding flash, Kellhus saw one sorcerer crash into the hillside, where he broke and tumbled like a thing of stone. Hellish lights scourged the ramparts. Tower tops exploded in flame. All living things were consumed.

The song of the Scarlet Schoolmen trailed. The thunder rumbled into the distances. For several heartbeats, all Caraskand stood still.

The fortress walls steamed with the smoke of burning flesh.

Several of the sorcerers strode forward. Achamian had told Kellhus once that no sorcerer truly flew, but rather walked a surface that wasn't a surface—the ground's echo in the sky. The Schoolmen advanced through the curtains of smoke until they dangled over the narrow baileys of the inner keep. Kellhus glimpsed the outline of their ghostly Wards. They seemed to be waiting ... or searching.

Suddenly, from various points across the Citadel, seven lines of piercing blue swept across smoke and sky, intersecting on the centremost Schoolman ...

Cishaurim, Kellhus realized. *Cishaurim shelter in the Citadel.*

The ring of crimson figures, mere specks in the distance, answered their hidden foe. Kellhus raised a hand against the brilliance. The air shivered with concussions. A western tower buckled beneath the weight of fire, then ponderously toppled. Breaking over the outer curtain wall, it plunged to slopes below, where it collapsed into an avalanche of rubble and pluming dust.

Kellhus watched, wondering at the spectacle and at the promise of deeper dimensions of understanding. Sorcery was the only unconquered knowledge, the last remaining bastion of world-born secrets. He was one of the Few—as Achamian had both feared and hoped. What kind of power would he wield?

And his father, who was Cishaurim, what kind of power did he *already* wield?

The Scarlet Schoolmen pummelled the Citadel without pause or remorse. There was no sign of the Cishaurim who'd attacked moments earlier. Smoke and dust billowed and plumed, encompassing the black-walled heights. Sorcerous lights flashed through what clear air remained; otherwise they flickered and pulsed as though through veils of black gossamer.

Uncanny hymns ached in Kellhus's ears. How could such things be said? How could words come before?

Another tower collapsed in the south, crashing upon its foundations, swelling into a black cloud that rolled down over the surrounding tenements. Watching Men of the Tusk flee through the streets, Kellhus glimpsed a figure in yellow silks soar free of the surging eclipse, arms to his side, sandalled feet pointing downward. The Inrithi warriors scattered beneath him.

A surviving Cishaurim.

Kellhus watched the figure glide low over the stepped rooftops, dip into avenues. For a moment he thought the man might escape—smoke and dust had all but engulfed the Scarlet Schoolmen. Then he realized ...

The Cishaurim was turning in his direction.

Rather than continuing south, the figure hooked westward, using what structures he could to cover his passage from the far-seeing Schoolmen. Kellhus tracked his progress as he zigzagged through the streets, averaging the mean of his sudden turns to determine his true trajectory. As improbable—as impossible—as it seemed, there could be no doubt: the man was coming toward him. Could it be?

Father?

Kellhus backed away from the balustrade, bent to rewrap the skin-spy's severed head in his ruined robe. Then he gripped one of two Chorae his Zaudunyani had given him ... According to Achamian, it offered immunity to the Psûkhe as much as it did sorcery.

The Cishaurim was climbing the slopes to the terrace, kicking loose leaves as he skimmed the odd tree-top. Birds burst into the air in his wake. Kellhus could see the black pits of his eyes, the two distended snakes about his neck, one looking forward, the other scanning the Citadel's continuing destruction.

A dragon's howl gouged the distances, followed by another thunderclap. The marble tingled beneath his feet. More clouds of black bloomed about the Citadel ...

Father? This cannot be!

The Cishaurim glided low over the compound where Kellhus had seen the Thunyeri a short time earlier, then swooped upward. Kellhus actually heard the flutter of his silken robes.

He leapt backward, drawing his sword. The sorcerer-priest sailed over the balustrade, his hands pressed together, fingertip to fingertip.

"Anasûrimbor Kellhus!" the descending figure called.

Meeting his reflection, the Cishaurim came to a jarring halt. Flecks of debris chattered across the polished marble.

Kellhus stood motionless, holding tight his Chorae.

He's too young—

"I am Hifanat ab Tunukri," the eyeless man said breathlessly, "a Dionoratë of the tribe Indara-Kishauri ... I bear a message from your Father. He says, 'You walk the Shortest Path. Soon you will grasp the Thousandfold Thought.'"

Father?

Sheathing his sword, Kellhus opened himself to every outward sign the man offered. He saw desperation and purpose. *Purpose above all ...*

"How did you find me?"

"We see you. All of us." Behind the man, the smoke rising from the Citadel opened like a great velvet rose.

"Us?"

"All of us who serve *him*—the Possessors of the Third Sight."

Him ... Father. He controlled a faction within the Cishaurim ...

"I must," Kellhus said emphatically, "know what he intends."

"He told me nothing ... Even if he had, there wouldn't be time."

Though battle stress and the absence of eyes complicated his reading, Kellhus could see the man spoke sincerely. But why, after summoning him from so far, would his father now leave him in the dark?

He knows the Pragma have sent me as an assassin ... He needs to be certain of me first.

"I must warn you," Hifanat was saying. "The Padirajah himself comes with the South. Even now his outriders ponder the smoke they see on the horizon."

There had been rumours of the Padirajah's march ... Could he be so close? Contingencies, probabilities, and alternatives lanced through Kellhus's intellect—to no avail. The Padirajah coming. The Consult attacking. The Great Names plotting ...

"Too much happens ... You must tell my father!"

"There's no—"

The snake watching the Citadel abruptly reared and hissed. Kellhus glimpsed three Scarlet Schoolmen striding across the empty sky. Though threadbare, their crimson gowns flashed in the sunlight.

"The Whores come," the eyeless man said. "You must kill me."

In a single motion Kellhus drew his blade. Though the man seemed oblivious, the closer asp reared as though drawn back by a string.

"The Logos," Hifanat said, his voice quavering, "is without beginning or end."

Kellhus beheaded the Cishaurim. The body slumped to the side; the head lopped backward. Halved, one of the snakes flailed against the floor. Still whole, the other wormed swiftly into the garden.

Rising where the Citadel of the Dog had been, a great black pillar of smoke loomed over the sacked city, reaching, it seemed, to the very heavens.

Every quarter of Caraskand burned now, from the "Bowl"—so named because of its position between five of Caraskand's nine hills—to the Old

City, marked by the gravelly fragments of the Kyranean wall that had once enclosed ancient Caraskand. Columns of smoke hazed and plumed the distances—none so great as the tower of ash that dominated the southeast.

From a hilltop far to the south, Kascamandri ab Tepherokar, the High Padirajah of Kian and all the Cleansed Lands, watched the smoke with tears in his otherwise hard eyes. When his scouts had first come to him with news of the disaster, Kascamandri had refused to believe it, insisting that Imbeyan, his always resourceful and ferocious son-in-law, simply signalled them. But there was no denying his eyes. Caraskand, a city that rivalled white-walled Seleukara, had fallen to the cursed idolaters.

He had arrived too late.

"What we cannot deliver," he told his shining Grandees, "we must avenge."

Even as Kascamandri wondered what he would tell his daughter, a troop of Shrial Knights caught Imbeyan and his retinue trying to flee the city. That evening Gotian directed his fellow Great Names to set their booted feet upon the man's cheek, saying, "Cherish the power the God has given us over our enemies." It was an ancient ritual, first practised in the days of the Tusk.

Afterward, they hung the Sapatishah from a tree.

"Kellhus!" Esmenet cried, running through a gallery of black marble pilasters. Never had she set foot in a structure as vast or luxurious. "Kellhus!"

He turned from the warriors who congregated around him, smiled with the wry, touching camaraderie that always sent a pang from her throat to her heart. Such a wild, reckless love!

She flew to him. His arms wrapped her shoulders, enveloped her in an almost narcotic sense of security. He seemed so strong, the one immovable thing ...

The day had been one of doubt and horror—both for her and Serwë. Their joy at Caraskand's fall had been swiftly knocked from them. First, they'd heard news of the assassination attempt. Devils, several wild-eyed

Zaudunyani had claimed, had set upon Kellhus in the city. Not long after, men of the Hundred Pillars had come to evacuate the camp. No one, not even Werjau or Gayamakri, seemed to know whether Kellhus still lived. Then they'd witnessed horror after horror racing through the ransacked city. Unspeakable things. Women. Children ... She'd been forced to leave Serwë in the courtyard. The girl was inconsolable.

"They said you'd been attacked by demons!" she cried into his chest.

"No," he chuckled. "Not demons."

"What happens?"

Kellhus gently pushed her back. "We've endured much," he said, stroking her cheek. He seemed to be watching more than looking ... She understood the implied question: *How strong are you?*

"Kellhus?"

"The trial is about to begin, Esmi. The true trial."

A horror like no other shuddered through her. *Not you!* she inwardly cried. *Never you!*

He had sounded afraid.

Winter, 4111 Year-of-the-Tusk, the Bay of Trantis

Even though the wind still buffeted the sails in fits and starts, the bay was preternaturally calm. One could balance a Chorae on an upturned shield, the *Amortanea* was so steady.

"What is it?" Xinemus asked, turning his face to and fro in the sunlight. "What is it everyone sees?"

Achamian glanced to his friend, then back to the wrecked shore.

A gull cried out, as gulls always do, in mock agony.

Throughout his life moments like this would visit him—moments of quiet wonder. He thought of them as "visitations" because they always seemed to arise of their own volition. A pause would descend upon him, a sense of detachment, sometimes warm, sometimes cold, and he would think, *How is it I live this life?* For the span of several heartbeats, the nearest things—the feel of wind through the hairs of his arm, the pose of Esmenet's shoulders as she fussed over their meagre belongings—would seem very far. And the world, from the taste of his teeth to the unseen horizon, would seem scarcely possible. *How?* he would silently murmur. *How could this be?*

Aside from the wonder, there was never any answer.

Ajencis had called this experience *umresthei om aumreton*, "possessing in dispossession." In his most famed work, *The Third Analytic of Men*, he claimed it to be the heart of wisdom, the most reliable mark of an enlightened soul. The same as true possession required loss and recovery, true existence, he argued, required *umresthei om aumreton*. Otherwise one simply stumbled through a dream …

"Ships," Achamian said to Xinemus. "Burnt ships."

The great irony, of course, was that *umresthei om aumreton* rendered everything dreamlike—or nightmarish, as the case might be.

The lifeless heights of Khemema's coastal hills walled the circumference of the bay. Beneath tiered escarpments, a series of narrow beaches rimmed the shoreline. The sands were linen white, but for as far as the eye could see, a rind of blackened debris marred the slopes, like the salt ringing the armpits of a field-slave's tunic. Everywhere, Achamian saw ships and the remains of ships, all gutted by fire. There were hundreds of them, covered in legions of red-throated gulls.

Shouts echoed across the deck of the *Amortanea*. The Captain, a Nansur named Meümaras, had called anchor.

Some ways from the shore, several half-burned derelicts conferred on a sandbar—triremes by the look of them. Beyond them, a dozen or so prows reared from the water, their iron rams browning with rust, their bright-painted eyes chapped and peeling. The majority of ships packed the strand, beached like diseased whales, obviously cast up by some forgotten storm. A few were little more than blackened ribs about a keel. Others were entire hulks, stumped on their side or overturned entirely. Batteries of broken oars jutted skyward. Seaweed hung in hairy ropes from the bulwarks. And everywhere Achamian looked he saw gulls, swinging through the air above, squabbling over lesser wreckage, and crowding the upturned bellies of ship after harrowed ship.

"This is where the Kianene destroyed the Imperial Fleet," Achamian explained. "Where the Padirajah nearly destroyed the Holy War …" He remembered Iyokus describing the disaster while he'd hung helpless in the cellars of the Scarlet Spires' compound. That was when he'd stopped fearing for himself and had started fearing for Esmenet.

Kellhus. Kellhus has kept her safe.

"The Bay of Trantis," Xinemus said sombrely. By now, the whole world knew of this place. The Battle of Trantis had been the greatest naval defeat in the Empire's history. After luring the Men of the Tusk deep into the desert, the Padirajah had attacked their only source of water, the Imperial Fleet. Though no one knew exactly what had happened, it was generally accepted that Kascamandri had managed to secrete a great number of Cishaurim aboard his own fleet. According to rumour, the Kianene had returned from the battle short only two galleys, both of which they'd lost to a squall.

"What do you see?" Xinemus pressed. "What does it look like?"

"The Cishaurim burned everything," Achamian replied.

He paused, almost overcome by a visceral reluctance to say anything more. It seemed blasphemous, somehow, rendering a thing like this in words—a sacrilege. But then such was the case whenever one described another's loss. There was no way around words.

"There's charred ships everywhere … They look like seals, sunning on the shore. And there's gulls—thousands of gulls … What we call *gopas* in Nron. You know, the ones that look like they've had their throats cut. Ill-mannered brutes they are."

Just then, the *Amortanea*'s Captain, Meümaras, walked from his men to join them on the railing. From their first meeting in Iothiah, Achamian had found himself liking the man. He was what the Nansur called a *tesperari*, a private contractor who'd once commanded a war galley. His hair was short and patrician-silver, and his face, though leathered by the sea, possessed a thoughtful delicacy. He was clean-shaven, of course, which made him seem boyish. But then all Nansur seemed boyish.

"It's out of our way, I know," the man explained. "But I had to see for myself."

"You lost someone," Achamian said, noting his swollen eyes.

The Captain nodded, looked nervously to the charred hollows strewn across the beach. "My brother."

"You're certain he's dead?"

A party of gulls screeched overhead. An embassy, offering terms.

"Others," Meümaras said, "acquaintances of mine who've gone ashore, say that bones and dried carcasses litter the strand for miles— north and south. As catastrophic as the Kianene attack was, thousands, perhaps tens of thousands, survived because General Sassotian had moored so close to shore ... Don't you smell it?" he asked, glancing at Xinemus. "The dust ... like bitter chalk. We stand at the edge of the Great Carathay."

The Captain turned to Achamian, held his gaze with firm brown eyes. "No one survived."

Achamian stiffened, struck by what was now an old fear. Despite the desert air, a clamminess crept over his skin. "The Holy War survived," he said.

The Captain frowned, as though put off by something in Achamian's tone. He opened his mouth in retort, but then paused, his eyes suddenly thoughtful.

"You fear you've lost someone as well." He glanced yet again at Xinemus.

"No," Achamian said. *She's alive! Kellhus has saved her!*

Meümaras sighed, looked away in pity and embarrassment. "I wish you luck," he said to the lapping waters. "I truly do. But this Holy War ..." He fell into cryptic silence.

"What about the Holy War?" Achamian asked.

"I'm an old sailor. I've seen enough voyages blown off course, enough vessels founder, to know the God gives no guarantees, no matter who the captain or what the cargo." He looked back to Achamian. "There's only one thing certain about this Holy War: there's never been a greater bloodletting."

Achamian knew different, but refrained from saying as much. He resumed his study of the obliterated fleet, suddenly resenting the Captain's company.

"Why would you say that?" Xinemus asked. As always when he spoke, he turned his face from side to side. For some reason, Achamian found the sight of this increasingly difficult to bear. "What have you heard?"

Meümaras shrugged. "Craziness, for the most part. There's talk of hemoplexy, of disastrous defeats, of the Padirajah marshalling all his remaining strength."

"Pfah," Xinemus spat with uncharacteristic bitterness. "Everyone knows as much."

Achamian now heard dread in Xinemus's every word. It was as though something horrific loomed in the blackness, something he feared might recognize the sound of his voice. As the weeks passed it was becoming more and more apparent: the Scarlet Spires had taken more than his eyes; they had taken the light and devilry that had once filled them as well. With the Cants of Compulsion, Iyokus had moved Xinemus's soul in perverse ways, had forced him to betray both dignity and love. Achamian had tried to explain that it wasn't *he* who'd thought those thoughts, who'd uttered those words, but it didn't matter. As Kellhus said, men couldn't see what moved them. The frailties Xinemus had witnessed were his frailties. Confronted by the true dimensions of wickedness, he'd held his own infirmity accountable.

"And then," the Captain continued, apparently untroubled by Xinemus's cholic, "there's the stories of the new prophet."

Achamian jerked his head about so fast he wrenched his neck. "What about him?" he asked carefully. "Who told you this?"

It simply had to be Kellhus. And if Kellhus survived ...

Please, Esmi. Please be safe!

"The carrack we exchanged berths with in Iothiah," Meümaras said. "Her captain had just returned from Joktha. He said the Men of the Tusk are turning to someone called Kelah, a miracle worker who can wring water from desert sand."

Achamian found his hand pressed against his chest. His heart hammered.

"Akka?" Xinemus murmured.

"It's him, Zin ... It has to be him."

"You know him?" Meümaras asked with an incredulous grin. Gossip was a kind of gold among seamen.

But Achamian couldn't speak. He clung to the wooden rail instead, battling a sudden, queerly euphoric dizziness.

Esmenet was alive. *She lives!*

But his relief, he realized, went even deeper ... His heart leapt at the thought of Kellhus as well.

"Easy!" the Captain cried, seizing Achamian by the shoulders.

Achamian stared at the man dully. He'd nearly swooned ...

Kellhus. What was it the man stirred within him? To be more than what he was? But who, if not a sorcerer, knew the taste of those things that transcended men? If sorcerers sneered at men of faith, they did so because faith had rendered them pariahs, and because faith, it seemed to them, knew nothing of the very transcendence it claimed to monopolize. Why submit when one could yoke?

"Here," Meümaras was saying. "Sit for a moment."

Achamian fended away the man's fatherly hands. "I'm okay," he gasped.

Esmenet and Kellhus. They lived! The woman who could save his heart, and the man who could save the world ...

He felt different, stronger hands brace his shoulders. Xinemus.

"Leave him be," he heard the Marshal saying. "This voyage has been but a fraction of our journey."

"Zin!" he exclaimed. He wanted to chortle, but the pang in his throat forbade it.

The Captain retreated, whether out of compassion or embarrassment, Achamian would never know.

"She lives," Xinemus said. "Think of her joy!"

For some reason, these words struck the breath from him. That Xinemus, who suffered more than he could imagine, had set aside his hurt to ...

His hurt. Achamian swallowed, tried to squeeze away an image of Iyokus, his red-irised eyes slack with indolent regret.

He reached out, clutched his friend's hand. They squeezed, each according to his desperation.

"There will be fire when I return, Zin."

He swept his dry eyes across the wrecked warships of the Imperial Fleet. Suddenly they looked more a transition and less an end—like the carapaces of monstrous beetles.

The red-throated gulls kept jealous watch.

"Fire," he said.

CHAPTER TWENTY-TWO

CARASKAND

For all things there is a toll. We pay in breaths, and our purse is soon empty.

—SONGS 57:3, THE CHRONICLE OF THE TUSK

Like many old tyrants, I dote upon my grandchildren. I delight in their tantrums, their squealing laughter, their peculiar fancies. I wilfully spoil them with honey sticks. And I find myself wondering at their blessed ignorance of the world and its million grinning teeth. Should I, like my grandfather, knock such childishness from them? Or should I indulge their delusions? Even now, as death's shadowy pickets gather about me, I ask, Why should innocence answer to the world? Perhaps the world should answer to innocence ...

Yes, I rather like that. I tire of bearing the blame.

—STAJANAS II, RUMINATIONS

Winter, 4111 Year-of-the-Tusk, Caraskand

The following morning a pall of smoke lay over Caraskand. The city quilted the distance, pocked here and there by great, gutted structures. The dead lay everywhere, piled beneath smoking tabernacles, sprawled through sacked palaces, scattered across the reaches of Caraskand's famed bazaars. Cats lapped blood from the grouting. Crows pecked at sightless eyes.

A single horn echoed mournfully across the rooftops. Still groggy from the previous day's debauch, the Men of the Tusk stirred, anticipating a day of repentance and sombre celebration. But from various quarters of the city more horns blared out, sounding the call to arms. Iron-mailed knights clacked down streets, crying out frantic alarums.

Those who climbed the southern walls saw divisions of many-coloured horsemen spilling across ridge lines and down sparsely wooded hills. At long last, Kascamandri I, the Padirajah of Kian, had taken the field against the Inrithi. The Great Names desperately tried to muster their thanes and barons, but with their men scattered throughout the city, it was hopeless. Gothyelk, still distraught over the loss of his youngest, Gurnyau, couldn't be roused, and the Tydonni refused to leave the city without the beloved Earl of Agansanor. With the recent death of Prince Skaiyelt, the long-haired Thunyeri had disintegrated into clannish mobs, and, unaccountably, had renewed their bloody sack of the city. And the Ainoni Palatines, with Chepheramunni on his death bed, had fallen to feuding amongst themselves. The horns called and called, but far too few answered.

The Fanim horsemen descended so quickly that most of the Holy War's siege camps had to be abandoned, along with the war engines and the food supplies amassed within them. Retreating knights set several of the camps ablaze to prevent them from falling into the heathen's hands. Hundreds of those too sick to flee the camps were left to be massacred. Those bands of Inrithi knights who dared contest the Padirajah's advance were quickly thrown back or overrun, encompassed by waves of ululating horsemen. By mid-morning the Great Names frantically recalled those remaining outside Caraskand and bent themselves to defending the vast circuit of the city's walls.

Celebration had turned to terror and disbelief. They were imprisoned in a city that had already been besieged for weeks. The Great Names ordered hasty surveys of the remaining food stores. They despaired after learning that Imbeyan had burned the city's granaries when he realized he'd lost Caraskand. And of course, the vast storerooms of the city's final redoubt, the Citadel of the Dog, had been destroyed by the Scarlet Spires. The broken fortress burned still, a beacon on Caraskand's easternmost hill.

Seated upon a lavish settee, surrounded by his counsellors and his many children, Kascamandri ab Tepherokar watched from the terrace of a hillside villa as the great horns of his army inexorably closed about Caraskand. Propped against his whale-like belly, his lovely girls peppered him with questions about what happened. For months he'd followed the Holy War from the fleshpot sanctuaries of the Korasha, the exalted White-Sun Palace in Nenciphon. He'd trusted the sagacity and warlike temper of his subordinates. And he'd scorned the idolatrous Inrithi, thinking them barbarous and hapless in the ways of war.

No longer.

To redress his negligence, he'd raised a host worthy of his jihadic fathers: the survivors of Anwurat, some sixty thousand strong, under the peerless Cinganjehoi, who had set aside his enmity to his Padirajah; the Grandees of Chianadyni, the Kianene homeland, with some forty thousand horsemen under Kascamandri's own ruthless and brilliant son, Fanayal; and Kascamandri's old tributary, King Pilasakanda of Girgash, whose vassal Hetmen marched with thirty thousand black-skinned Fanim and one hundred mastodons from pagan Nilnamesh. These last, in particular, caused the Padirajah to take pride, for the lumbering beasts made his daughters gape and giggle.

As evening fell, the Padirajah ordered an assault on Caraskand's walls, hoping to use the disarray of the idolaters to his advantage. Ladders made by Inrithi carpenters were drawn up, as well as the single siege tower they'd captured intact, and there was fierce fighting along the walls around the Ivory Gates. The mastodons were yoked to a mighty iron-headed ram made by the Men of the Tusk, and soon drumming thunder and elephant screams could be heard above the roar of battling men. But the iron men refused to yield the heights, and the Kianene and Girgashi suffered horrendous losses—including some fourteen mastodons, burned alive by flaming pitch. Kascamandri's youngest daughter, beautiful Sirol, wept.

When the sun finally set, the Men of the Tusk greeted the darkness with both relief and horror. For they were saved and they were doomed.

———⋙⋘———

The deep, staccato thunder of drums.

With Cnaiür standing behind him, Proyas leaned against a limestone battlement on the summit of the Gate of Horns, peering through an embrasure at the muddy plains below. Kianene teemed across the landscape, dragging Inrithi wares and shelters to immense bonfires, pitching bright pavilions, reinforcing palisades and earthworks. Bands of silver-helmed horsemen patrolled the ridge lines, galloped through orchards or across fields between byres.

The Inrithi had chosen the same plains to launch their assaults: the burned hulk of a siege tower stood no more than a stone's throw from where Proyas had positioned himself. He squeezed shut his burning eyes. *This can't be happening! Not this!*

First the euphoria—the rapture!—of Caraskand's fall. Then the Padirajah, who'd for so long been little more than a rumour of terrible power to the south, had materialized in the hills above the city. At first Proyas could only think that someone had made a catastrophic mistake, that everything would resolve itself once the chaos of the city's ransacking passed. Those silk-cowled divisions couldn't be Kianene horsemen ... The heathen had been mortally wounded at Anwurat—undone! The Holy War had taken mighty Caraskand, the great gate of Xerash and Amoteu, and now stood poised to march into the Sacred Lands! They were *so close* ...

So close that Shimeh, he was certain, could see Caraskand's smoke on the horizon.

But the horsemen *had* been Kianene. Riding beneath the White Padirajic Lion, they streamed about the great circuit of the city's walls, burning the impoverished Inrithi camps, slaughtering the sick, and riding down those foolish enough to resist their advance. Kascamandri had come; both the God—and hope—had forsaken them.

"How many do you estimate?" Proyas asked the Scylvendi, who stood, his scarred arms folded across his scale harness.

"Does it matter?" the barbarian replied.

Unnerved by the man's turquoise gaze, Proyas turned back to the smoke-grey vista. Yesterday, while the dimensions of the disaster slowly unfolded, he'd found himself asking why over and over again. Like a wronged child, his thoughts had stamped about the fact of his piety. Who among the Great Names had toiled as he'd toiled? Who'd burned more sacrifices, intoned more prayers? But now he no longer dared ask these questions.

Thoughts of Achamian and Xinemus had seen to that.

"It is you," the Marshal of Attrempus had said, *"who surrender everything ..."*

But in the God's name! For the God's glory!

"Of course it matters," Proyas hissed. He knew the Scylvendi would bristle at his tone, but he neither worried nor cared. "We must find some way out!"

"Exactly," Cnaiür said, apparently unperturbed. "We must find some way out ... No matter how large the Padirajah's host."

Scowling, Proyas turned back to the embrasure. He was in no mood to be corrected.

"What of Conphas?" he asked. "Is there any chance he lies about the food?"

The barbarian shrugged his massive shoulders. "The Nansur are good counters."

"And they're good liars as well!" Proyas exclaimed. Why couldn't the man just answer his questions? "Do you think Conphas tells the truth?"

Cnaiür spat across the ancient stonework. "We'll have to wait ... See if he stays fat while we grow thin."

Curse the man! How could he bait him at such a time, in such straits?

"You are besieged," the Scylvendi warrior continued, "within the very city you have spent weeks starving. Even if Conphas does hoard food, it would not be of consequence. You have only one alternative, and one alternative only. The Scarlet Spires must be roused, now, before the Padirajah can assemble his Cishaurim. The Holy War must take to the field."

"You think I disagree?" Proyas cried. "I've already petitioned Eleäzaras—and do you know what he says? He says, 'The Scarlet Spires have already suffered too many needless losses ...' Needless losses! What? Some dozen or so dead at Anwurat—if that! A handful more in the desert—not bad compared to a hundred thousand *faithful* souls lost! And what? Five or so struck by Chorae yesterday—heaven forfend! Killed while destroying the only remaining stores of food in Caraskand ... All wars should be so bloodless!"

Proyas paused, realized he was panting. He felt crazed and confused, as though he suffered some residue of the fevers. The great, age-worn stones of the barbican seemed to wheel about him. If only, he thought madly, Triamis had built these walls with bread!

The Scylvendi watched him without passion. "Then you are doomed," he said.

Proyas raised his hands to his face, scratched his cheeks. *It can't be! Something ... I'm missing something!*

"We're cursed," he murmured. "They're right ... The God does punish us!"

"What are you saying?"

"That maybe Conphas and the others are right about him!"

The brutal face hardened into a scowl. "Him?"

"Kellhus," Proyas exclaimed. He clutched trembling hands, ground one palm against the other.

I falter ... I fail!

Proyas had read many accounts of other men floundering in times of crisis, and absurdly, he realized that this—this!—was *his* moment of weakness. But contrary to his expectation, there was no strength to be drawn from this knowledge. If anything, knowing he faltered threatened to hasten his collapse. He was too sick ... Too tired.

"They rail against him," he explained, his voice raw. "First Conphas, but now even Gothyelk and Gotian." Proyas released a shuddering breath. "They claim he's a False Prophet."

"This is no rumour? They've told you this themselves?"

Proyas nodded. "With my support, they think they can openly move against him."

"You would risk a war *within* these walls? Inrithi against Inrithi?"

Proyas swallowed, struggled to shore up his gaze. "If that's what the God demands of me."

"And how does one know what your God demands?"

Proyas stared at the Scylvendi in horror.

"I just ..." A pang welled against the back of his throat. Hot tears flooded across his cheek. He inwardly cursed, opened his mouth again, sobbed instead of spoke ...

Please God!

It had been too long. The burden had been too great. Everything! Every day, every word a battle! And the sacrifices—they had cut too deep. The desert, even the hemoplexy, had been nothing. But Achamian—ah, that was something! And Xinemus, whom he'd abandoned. The two men he respected most in the world, given up in the name of Holy War ... And still it wasn't enough!

Nothing ... Never good enough!

"Tell me, Cnaiür," he croaked. A strange tooth-baring smile seized his face, and he sobbed again. He covered his eyes and cheeks with his hands, crumpled against the parapet. "Please!" he cried to the stone. "Cnaiür ... You must tell me what to do!"

Now it was the Scylvendi who looked horrified.

"Go to Kellhus," the barbarian said. "But I warn you"—he raised a mighty, battle-scarred fist—"secure your heart. Seal it tight!" He lowered his chin and glared, the way a wolf might ...

"Go, Proyas. Go ask the man yourself."

Like something carved out of living rock, the bed rose from a black dais set in the chamber's heart. The veils, which usually trailed between the bed's five stone posts, had been pinned to the emerald and gold canopy. Lying with one leg kicked free of the sheets, Kellhus stroked Esmenet's cheek, saw past her flushed skin, beyond her beating heart, following the telltale markers all the way to her womb.

Our blood, Father ... In a world of maladroit and bovine souls, nothing could be more precious.

The House of Anasûrimbor.

The Dûnyain not only saw deep, they saw far. Even if the Holy War survived Caraskand, even if Shimeh was reconquered, the wars were only beginning ... Achamian had taught him that much.

And in the end, only sons could conquer death.

Was this why you summoned me? Do you die?

"What is it?" Esmenet asked, drawing sheets up to her breast.

Kellhus had jerked forward, sitting cross-legged upon the bed. He peered across the candle-lit gloom, tracking the muffled sounds of some commotion beyond the doors. *What does he—*

Without warning, the double doors burst open, and Kellhus saw Proyas, still weak from his convalescence, struggling with two of the Hundred Pillars.

"Kellhus!" the Conriyan Prince barked. "Tell your dogs to kennel, or by the God there'll be blood!"

At a word, the bodyguards released him, assumed positions at either side of the door. The man stood, his chest heaving, his eyes searching through the shadows of the lavish bedchamber. Kellhus encircled him with his senses ... The man shouted desperation from every pore, but the wildness of his passion made the specifics difficult to ascertain. He feared the Holy War was lost, as did all men, and that Kellhus was somehow to blame—as did many.

He needs to know what I am.

"What happens, Proyas? What ails you, that you'd commit such an outrage?"

But the Prince's eyes had found Esmenet, rigid with shock. Kellhus instantly saw the peril.

He searches for excuses.

An interior porch had been raised about the doors; Proyas took an unsteady step toward the railing. "What's she doing?" He blinked in confusion. "Why's she *in your bed?*"

He doesn't want to understand.

"She's my wife ... What business—"

"Wife?" Proyas exclaimed. He raised a half-opened hand to his brow. "She's your *wife?*"

He's heard the stories ... But all this time he's afforded me his doubt.

"The desert, Proyas. The desert marked us all."

He shook his head. "Fie on the desert," he murmured, then looked up in sudden fury. "Fie on the desert! She's ... She's ... Akka loved her! *Akka!* Don't you recall? Your *friend* ..."

Kellhus lowered his eyes in penitent sadness. "We thought he would want this."

"Want? Want his best friend fucking the wo—"

"Who," Esmenet spat, "are you to speak of Akka to me!"

"What do you say?" Proyas said, blanching. "What do you mean?" His lips pursed; his eyes slackened. His right hand fell to his chest.

Horror had opened a still point in the throng of his passions—an opportunity ...

"But you already know," Kellhus said. "Of all people, you've no right to judge."

The Conriyan Prince flinched. "What do you mean?"

Now ... Offer him truce. Show him understanding. Make stark his trespasses ...

"Please," Kellhus said, reaching out with word, tone, and every nuance of expression. "You let your despair rule you ... And me, I succumb to ill manners. Proyas! You're among my dearest friends ..." He cast aside the sheets, swung his feet to the floor. "Come, let us drink and talk."

But Proyas had fastened on his earlier comment—as Kellhus had intended. "I would know why I've no right to judge. What's that supposed to mean, 'dear friend'?"

Kellhus drew his lips into a pained line. "It means that *you*, Proyas, not we, have betrayed Achamian."

The handsome face slackened in horror. His pulse drummed.

I must move carefully.

"No," Proyas said.

Kellhus closed his eyes as though in disappointment. "Yes. You accuse us because you hold yourself accountable."

"Accountable? Accountable for what?" He snorted like a frightened adolescent. "I did nothing."

"But you did everything, Proyas. You needed the Scarlet Spires, and the Scarlet Spires needed Achamian."

"No one knows what happened to Achamian!"

"But *you* know ... I can see this knowledge within you."

The Conriyan Prince stumbled backward. "You see nothing!"

So close ...

"Of course I do, Proyas. How, after all this time, could you still doubt?"

But as he watched, something happened: an unforeseen flare of recognition, a cascade of inferences, too quick to silence. *That word ...*

"Doubt?" Proyas fairly cried. "How could I not doubt? The Holy War stands upon the precipice, Kellhus!"

Kellhus smiled the way Xinemus had once smiled at things both touching and foolish.

"The God *tries* us, Proyas. He's yet to pass sentence! Tell me, how can there be trial without doubt?"

"He tries us ..." Proyas repeated, his face blank.

"Of *course*," Kellhus said plaintively. "Simply open your heart and you'll see!"

"Open my ..." Proyas trailed, his eyes brimming with incredulous dread. "He told me!" he abruptly whispered. "This is what he meant!" The yearning in his look, the ache that had warred against his misgivings, suddenly collapsed into suspicion and disbelief.

Someone has warned him ... The Scylvendi? Has he wandered so far?

"Proyas ..."

I should have killed him.

"And how about you, *Kellhus?*" Proyas spat. "Do you doubt? Does the great Warrior-Prophet fear for the future?"

Kellhus looked to Esmenet, saw that she wept. He reached out and clasped her cold hands.

"No," he said.

I do not fear.

Proyas was already backing out the double doors, into the brighter light of the antechamber.

"You will."

For over a thousand years Caraskand's great limestone walls had stared across the broken countryside of Enathpaneah. When Triamis I, perhaps the greatest of the Aspect-Emperors, had raised them, his detractors in Imperial Cenei had scoffed at the expenditure, claiming that he who conquers all foes has no need of walls. Triamis, the chroniclers write, had dismissed them by saying, "No man can conquer the future." And indeed, over the ensuing centuries Caraskand's "Triamic Walls," as they were called, would blunt the rush of history many times, if not redirect it altogether. And sometimes, they would cage it.

Day after day, it seemed, Inrithi horns blared from the high towers, calling the Men of the Tusk to the ramparts, for the Padirajah threw his people at Triamis's mighty fortifications with reckless fury, each time convinced the strength of the starving idolaters would fail. Haggard and hungry, Galeoth, Conriyans, and Tydonni manned the war engines abandoned by Caraskand's erstwhile defenders, casting pots of flaming pitch from mangonels, great iron bolts from ballistae. Thunyeri, Nansur, and Ainoni gathered on the walls, crowding beneath the battlements and huddling beneath shields to avoid volleys of arrows that at times darkened the sun. And day after day, it seemed, they beat the heathen back.

Even as they cursed them, the Kianene could only marvel at their desperate fury. Twice young Athjeäri led daring sorties across the rutted plain, once seizing the sappers' trenches and collapsing their tunnels, once charging over slovenly earthworks and sacking an isolated encampment. All the world could see they were doomed, and yet they fought as though they knew it not.

But they knew—as only men stalked by famine could know.

The hemoplexy, or the hollows, was running its course. Many, such as Chepheramunni, the King-Regent of High Ainon, lingered on death's marches, while others, such as Zursodda, Palatine-Governor of Koraphea, or Cynnea, Earl of Agmundr, finally succumbed. The funeral pyres still burned, but more and more they took casualties, and not the sick, as their fuel. As the flames consumed the Earl of Agmundr, his famed longbowmen launched burning arrows over the walls, and the Kianene wondered at the madness of the idolaters. Cynnea would be among the last of the great Inrithi lords to perish in the grip of the Disease.

But even as the plague waned, the threat of starvation waxed. Dread Famine, Bukris, the God who devoured men and vomited up skin and bones, walked the streets and halls of Caraskand.

Throughout the city, men began hunting cats, dogs, and finally even rats for sustenance. Poorer caste-nobles had taken to opening veins in their mounts. The horses themselves quickly consumed what thatched roofs could be found. Many bands began holding lotteries to see who would butcher their horse. Those without horses scratched through the dirt, looking for tubers. They boiled grapevines and even thistles to quiet the nagging madness of their bellies. Leather—from saddles, jerkins, or elsewhere—was also boiled and consumed. When the horns sounded the harnesses of many would swing like skirts, having lost their straps and buckles to some steaming pot. Gaunt men roamed the streets, looking for anything to eat, their faces blank, their movements sluggish, as though they walked through sand. Rumours circulated of men feasting on the bloated corpses of the Kianene, or committing murder in the dead of night to quiet their mad hunger.

In the wake of Famine, foul Disease returned, preying on the weak. Men, particularly among the caste-menials, began losing teeth to scurvy. Dysentery punished others with cramps and bloody diarrhea. In many quarters, one could find warriors wandering without their breeches, wallowing, as some are wont to do, in their degradation.

During this time, the furor surrounding Kellhus, Prince of Atrithau, and the tensions between those who acclaimed him and those who condemned him, escalated. In Council, Conphas, Gothyelk, and even Gotian relentlessly denounced him, claiming he was a False Prophet, a cancer that must be excised from the Holy War. Who could doubt the God punished them? The Holy War, they insisted, could have only one Prophet, and his name was Inri Sejenus. Proyas, who'd once eloquently defended Kellhus, withdrew from all such debates, and refused to say anything. Only Saubon still spoke in his favour, though he did so half-heartedly, not wishing to alienate those whose approval he needed to secure his claim to Caraskand.

Despite this, none dared move against the so-called Warrior-Prophet. His followers, the Zaudunyani, numbered in the tens of thousands, though they were less numerous among the upper castes. Many still remembered the Miracle of Water in the desert, how Kellhus had saved the Holy War, including those miscreants who now called him anathema. Strife and riot broke out, and for the first time Inrithi swords shed Inrithi blood. Knights repudiated their lords. Brothers forsook brothers. Countrymen turned upon one another. Only Gotian and Conphas, it seemed, were able to command the loyalty of their men.

Nevertheless, when the horns sounded, the Inrithi forgot their differences. They roused themselves from the torpor of disease and sickness, and they battled with a fervour only those truly wracked by the God could know. And to the heathens who assailed them, it seemed dead men defended the walls. Safe about their fires, the Kianene whispered tales of wights and damned souls, of a Holy War that had already perished, but fought on, such was its hate.

Caraskand, it seemed, named not a city, but misery's own precinct. Her very walls—walls raised by Triamis the Great—seemed to groan.

———— ∝∞∞ ————

The luxury of the place reminded Serwë of her indolent days as a concubine in House Gaunum. Through the open colonnade on the far side of the room she could see Caraskand wander across the hills beneath the sky. She was reclined on a green couch, her arms drawn out of her gown's shoulders so that it hung from the gorgeous sash about her waist. Her pink son squirmed against her naked chest, and she had just begun feeding when she heard the latch drawn. She had expected it to be one of the Kianene house slaves, so she gasped in surprise and delight when she felt the Warrior-Prophet's hand about her bare neck. The other brushed her bare breast as he reached to draw a gentle finger along the infant's chubby back.

"What are you doing here?" she asked, as she raised her lips through his beard to give him a kiss.

"Much happens," he said gently. "I wanted to know you were safe ... Where's Esmi?"

It always seemed so strange to hear him ask such simple questions. It reminded her that the God was still a man. "Kellhus," she asked pensively, "what's your father's name?"

"Moënghus."

Serwë furrowed her brow. "I thought his name was ... Aethel, or something like that."

"Aethelarius," the Warrior-Prophet said. "In Atrithau, Kings take a great ancestor's name when they ascend the throne. Moënghus is his true name."

"Then," she said, running fingers over the fuzz of the infant's pale scalp, "that's what his name will be when he's anointed: *Moënghus*." This wasn't an assertion. In the Warrior-Prophet's presence all declarations became questions.

Kellhus grinned. "That's what we shall name our child."

"What kind of man is your father, my Prophet?"

"A most mysterious one, Serwë."

Serwë laughed softly. "Does he know that he fathered the voice of the God?"

Kellhus pursed his lips in mock concentration. "Perhaps."

Serwë, who'd grown accustomed to cryptic conversations such as this, smiled. She blinked at the tears in her eyes. With her child warm against her breast, and the breath of the Prophet warmer still across her neck, the World seemed a closed circle, as though woe had been exiled from joy at long last. No longer taxed by cruel and distant things, the hearth now answered to the heart.

A sudden pang of guilt struck her. "I know that you grieve," she said. "So many suffer ..."

He lowered his face. Said nothing.

"But I've never been so happy," she continued. "So whole ... Is that a sin? To find rapture where others suffer?"

"Not for you, Serwë. Not for you."

Serwë gasped and looked down at her suckling babe.

"Moënghus is hungry," she laughed.

Glad to have concluded their long search, Rash and Wrigga paused along the crest of the wall. Dropping his shield, Rash sat with his back to the parapet, while Wrigga stood, leaning against the stonework, staring through an embrasure at the fires of the enemy across the Tertae Plain. Neither man paid heed to the shadowy figure crouched beneath the battlements farther down.

"I saw the child," Wrigga said, still staring into the dark.

"Did you?" Rash asked with genuine interest. "Where?"

"Before the lower gates of the Fama Palace. The Anointing was public ... You didn't know, did you?"

"Because no one tells me anything!"

Wrigga resumed his scrutiny of the night. "Surprisingly dark, I thought."

"What?"

"The child. The child seemed so dark."

Rash snorted. "Birth hair ... It'll soon fall out. I swear my second daughter had sideburns!"

Friendly laughter. "Someday, when all this is over, I'll come and woo your hairy daughters."

"Please ... Start with my hairy wife!"

More laughter, choked by a sudden realization. "Oh ho! So that's how you got your nickname!"

"Saucy bastard!" Rash cried. "*No,* my skin's just—"

"The child's name," a voice grated from the darkness. "What is it?"

Both men started, turned to the towering spectre of the Scylvendi. They'd seen the man before—few Men of the Tusk hadn't—but neither had ever found themselves so close to the barbarian. Even in moonlight, his aspect was unnerving. The wild black hair. The fuming brow above eyes like chips of ice. The powerful shoulders, faintly stooped, as though bent by the preternatural strength of his back. The lean, adolescent waist. And the arms, thatched by scars both ritual and incidental, strapped by unfatted muscle. He seemed a thing of stone, ancient and famished.

"Wh-what's this?" Rash stammered.

"The name!" Cnaiür snarled. "What did they name it?"

"Moënghus!" Wrigga blurted. "They anointed him by the name, Moënghus ..."

The air of menace suddenly vanished. The barbarian became curiously blank, motionless to the point where he seemed inanimate. His manic eyes looked through them, to places far and forbidding.

A taut moment passed, then without a word, the Scylvendi turned and walked into the darkness.

Sighing, the two men looked to each other for what seemed a long time, then just to be certain, they resumed their fabricated conversation. As they'd been instructed.

———❦———

Some other way, Father. There must be.

No one came to the Citadel of the Dog, not even the most desperate of the rat eaters.

Standing high upon the crest of a ruined wall, Kellhus gazed across the dark expanse of Caraskand with her thousand points of smouldering light. Beyond the walls, particularly across the plains to the north, he could see the innumerable fires of the Padirajah's army.

The path, Father ... Where's the path?

No matter how many times he submitted to the rigours of the Probability Trance, all the lines were extinguished, either by disaster or by the weight of excessive permutations. The variables were too many, the possibilities too precipitous.

Over the past weeks he'd exerted whatever influence he'd possessed, hoping to circumvent what now seemed more and more inevitable. Of the Great Names, only Saubon still openly supported him. Though Proyas had so far refused to join Conphas's coalition of caste-nobles, the Conriyan Prince continued to rebuff Kellhus's every overture. Among the lesser Men of the Tusk, the divisions between the Zaudunyani and the Orthodox, as they were now calling themselves, were deepening. And the threat of further, more determined attacks by the Consult made it impossible for him to move freely among them—as he must to secure those he already possessed and to conquer those he did not.

Meanwhile, the Holy War died.

You told me mine was the Shortest Path ... He'd relived his brief encounter with the Cishaurim messenger a thousand times, analyzing, evaluating, weighing alternate interpretations—all for naught. Every step was darkness now, no matter what his father said. Every word was risk. In so many ways, it seemed, he was no different from these world-born men ...

What is the Thousandfold Thought?

He heard the rattle of rock against rock, then a small cascade of gravel and grit. He peered through the shadows amassed about the ruin's roots. The blasted walls formed a roofless labyrinth beyond the Nail of Heaven's pale reach. A darker shadow clambered across heaped debris. He glimpsed a round face in starlight ...

He called down. "Esmenet? How did you find me?"

Her grin was pure mischief, though Kellhus could see the concern beneath.

She's never loved another as she loves me. Not even Achamian.

"Werjau told me," she said, picking her way up and along the truncated wall.

"Ah, yes," Kellhus said, understanding immediately. "He fears women."

Esmenet wobbled for a moment, threw out her arms. She caught herself, but not before Kellhus found himself puzzled by a sudden shortness of breath. The fall would have been fatal.

"No ..." She concentrated for a moment, her tongue between her lips. Then she danced up the remaining length. "He fears *me!*" She threw herself into his arms, laughing. They held each other tight on the dark and windy heights, surrounded by a city and a world—by Caraskand and the Three Seas.

She knows ... She knows I struggle.

"We all fear you," Kellhus said, wondering at the clamminess of his skin.

She comes to comfort.

"You tell such delicious lies," she murmured, raising her lips to his.

⊙≈⊙

They arrived shortly after dusk, the nine Nascenti, the senior disciples of the Warrior-Prophet. A grand teak-and-mahogany table, no higher than their knees, had been pulled onto the terrace of the merchant palace Kellhus had taken as their base and refuge in Caraskand. Standing unnoticed in the shadows of the garden, Esmenet watched them as they knelt or sat cross-legged upon the cushions set about the table. These days worry lined the faces of most everyone, but the nine of them seemed particularly upset. The Nascenti spent their time in the city, organizing the Zaudunyani, consecrating new Judges, and laying the foundation of the Ministrate. They knew better than most, she imagined, the straits of the Holy War.

Raised about the northern face of the Heights of the Bull, the terrace overlooked a greater part of the city. The labyrinthine streets and byways of the Bowl, which formed the heart of Caraskand, ascended into the distance, hanging from the surrounding heights like a cloth draped between five stumps. The ruined shell of the Citadel reared to the east, the wandering lines of her blasted walls etched in moonlight. To the northwest, the Sapatishah's Palace sprawled across the Kneeling Heights, which were low enough to afford glimpses of lamp-lit figures over rose marble walls. The night sky was rutted by black clouds, but the Nail of Heaven was clear, brilliant, sparkling from the dark depths of the firmament.

A sudden hush fell across the Nascenti; as one they lowered their chins to their breast. Turning, Esmenet saw Kellhus stride from the golden interior of the adjacent apartments. He cast a fan of shadows before him as he walked past a row of flaming braziers. Two bare-chested Kianene boys flanked him, bearing censers that boiled with steely blue smoke. Serwë followed in his train, along with several men in hauberks and battle helms.

Esmenet cursed herself for catching her breath. How could he make her heart pound so? Glancing down, she realized she'd folded her right hand over the tattoo marring the back of her left.

Those days are over.

She stepped from the garden and greeted him at the head of the table. He smiled, and holding the fingers of her left hand, seated her to his immediate right. His white silk robe swayed in the breeze that touched them all, and for some reason, the Twin Scimitars embroidered about its hems and cuffs did not seem incongruous in the least. Someone, Serwë likely, had knotted his hair into a Galeoth war braid. His beard, which he now wore plaited and square-cut like the Ainoni, gleamed bronze in the light of nearby braziers. As always, the long pommel of his sword jutted high over his left shoulder. Enshoiya, the Zaudunyani now called it: Certainty.

His eyes twinkled beneath heavy brows. When he smiled, nets of wrinkles flexed about the corners of his eyes and mouth—a gift of the desert sun.

"You," he said, "are branches of me." His voice was deep and many-timbred, and somehow seemed to speak from her breast. "Of all peoples only you know what comes before. Only you, the Thanes of the Warrior-Prophet, know what moves you."

While he briefed the Nascenti on those matters he and she had already discussed, Esmenet found herself thinking about Xinemus's camp, about the differences between those gatherings and these. Mere months had passed, and yet it seemed she'd lived an entire life in the interim. She frowned at the strangeness of it: Xinemus holding court, calling out in mirth and mischief; Achamian squeezing her hand too tightly, as he sometimes did, searching for her eyes too often; and Kellhus with Serwë ... still little more than a promise, though it seemed Esmenet had loved him even then—secretly.

For some strange reason, she was overcome by a sudden yen to see the Marshal's wry Captain, Bloody Dench. She remembered her final glimpse of him, as he waited with Zenkappa for Xinemus to rejoin them, his short-cropped hair silver in the Shigeki sun. How black those days now seemed. How heartless and cruel.

What had happened to Dinchases? And Xinemus ...

Had he found Achamian?

She suffered a moment of gaping horror ... Kellhus's melodic voice retrieved her.

"If anything should happen," he was saying, "you shall hearken to Esmenet as you hearken to me ..."

For I'm his vessel.

The words triggered an exchange of worried looks. Esmenet could read the sentiment well enough: what could the Master mean, placing a woman before his Holy Thanes? Even after all this time, they still struggled with the darkness of their origins. They had not utterly embraced him, as she had ...

Old bigotries die hard, she thought with more than a little resentment.

"But Master," Werjau, the boldest among them, said, "you speak as though you might be taken from us!"

A heartbeat passed before she realized her mistake: what worried them was what his words *implied*, not the prospect of subordinating themselves to his Consort.

Kellhus was silent for a long moment. He looked gravely from face to face. "War is upon us," he said finally, "from both without and within."

Even though she and Kellhus had already discussed the danger he spoke of, chills pimpled her skin. Cries erupted around the table. Esmenet felt Serwë's hands clasp about her own. She turned to reassure the girl, only to realize that Serwë had reached to reassure *her. Just listen,* the girl's beautiful eyes said. The lunatic dimensions of Serwë's belief had always baffled and troubled Esmenet. The girl's conviction was more than monumental—it seemed continuous with the ground, it was so immovable.

She let me into her bed, Esmenet thought. *For love of him.*

"Who assails us?" Gayamakri was crying.

"Conphas," Werjau spat. "Who else? He's been working against us since Shigek ..."

"Then we must strike!" white-haired Kasaumki shouted. "The Holy War must be cleansed before the siege can be broken! Cleansed!"

"Errant madness!" Hilderuth barked. "We must negotiate ... You must go to them, Master."

Kellhus silenced them with little more than a look.

It frightened her, sometimes, the way he effortlessly commanded these men. But then it could be no other way. Where others blundered from moment to moment, scarcely understanding their own wants, hurts, or hopes, let alone those of others, Kellhus caught each instant—each soul—like a fly. His world, Esmenet had realized, was one without surfaces, one where everything—from word and expression to war and nation—was smoky glass, something to be peered *through* ...

He was the Warrior-Prophet ... Truth. And Truth commanded all things.

She quashed a sudden urge to hug herself in joy and astonishment. She was here—*here!*—at the right hand of the most glorious soul to have walked the world. To kiss Truth. To take Truth between her thighs, to feel him press deep into her womb. It was more than a boon, more than a gift ...

"She smiles," Werjau exclaimed. "How can she smile at a time such as this?"

Esmenet glanced at the burly Galeoth, flushing in embarrassment.

"Because," Kellhus said indulgently, "she sees what you cannot, Werjau."

But Esmenet wasn't so sure ... She simply daydreamed, didn't she? Werjau had simply caught her mooning over Kellhus like an addled juvenile ...

But then, why did the ground thrum so? And the stars ... What *did* she see?

Something ... Something without compare.

Her skin tingled. The Thanes of the Warrior-Prophet watched her, and she looked through their faces, glimpsed their yearning hearts. To think! So many deluded souls, living illusory lives in unreal worlds! So many! It both boggled her and broke her heart.

And at the same time, it was her triumph.

Something absolute.

Her heart fluttered, pinioned by Kellhus's shining gaze. She felt at once smoke and naked flesh—something seen through and something desired.

There's more than me ... More than this—yes!

"Tell us, Esmi," Kellhus hissed through Serwë's mouth. "Tell us what you see!"

There's more than them.

"We must take the knife to them," she said, speaking as she knew her Master would have her speak. "We must show them the demons in their midst."

So much more!

The Warrior-Prophet smiled with her own lips.

"We must kill them," her voice said.

The thing called Sarcellus hurried through the dark streets toward the hill where the Exalt-General and his Columns had quartered. The letter Conphas had sent was simple: *Come quickly. Danger stalks us.* The man had neglected to sign the letter, but then he didn't need to. His meticulous handwriting was unmistakable.

Sarcellus turned down a narrow street that smelled of unwashed Men and animal grease. More derelict Inrithi, he realized. As the Holy War starved, more and more Men of the Tusk had turned to an animal existence, hunting rats, eating things that should not be eaten, and begging ...

The starving wretches came to their feet as he walked between them. They congregated about him, holding out filthy palms, tugging at his sleeves. "*Mercy ...*" they moaned and muttered. "*Merceeee.*" Sarcellus thrust them back, made his way forward. He struck several of the more insistent. Not that he begrudged them, for they'd often proved useful when the hunger grew too great. No one missed beggars.

Besides, they were apt reminders of what Men were in truth.

Pale hands reached from looted silks. Piteous cries seethed through the gloom. Then, in the gravelly voice of a drunkard, a rag-draped man before him said, "Truth shines."

"Excuse me?" Sarcellus snapped, coming to a halt.

He seized the speaker by the shoulders, jerked his head up. Though bitten, the man's face hadn't been battered into submission—far from it. His eyes looked hard as iron. This, Sarcellus realized, was a man who *battered.*

"Truth," the man said, "does not die."

"What's this?" Sarcellus asked, releasing the warrior. "Robbery?"

The iron-eyed man shook his head.

"Ah," Sarcellus said, suddenly understanding. "You belong to him ... What is it you call yourselves?"

"Zaudunyani." The man smiled, and for a moment, it seemed the most terrifying smile Sarcellus had ever witnessed: pale lips pressed into a thin, passionless line.

Then Sarcellus remembered the purpose of his fashioning. How could he forget what he was? His phallus hardened against his breeches ...

"Slaves of the Warrior-Prophet," he said, sneering. "Tell me, do you know *what* I am?"

"Dead," someone said from behind.

Sarcellus laughed, sweeping his gaze over the necks he would break. Oh, rapture! How he would shoot hot across his thigh! He was certain of it!

Yes! With so many! This time ...

But his humour vanished when his look returned to the man with the iron eyes. The face beneath his face twitched into a vestigial frown ... *They're not af—*

Something rained down from above ... Suddenly he found himself drenched. Oil! They'd doused him in oil! He looked from side to side, blowing fluid from his lips, shaking it from his fingertips. His would-be assassins, he saw, had been doused as well.

"Fools!" he exclaimed. "Burn me, and you burn too!"

At the last instant, Sarcellus heard the bowstring twang, the flaming arrow zip through the air. He jerked to the side. The shaft struck the iron-eyed man. Flame leapt up his soiled robes, twined about his cowl.

But rather than fall, the man lunged, his eyes fixed upon Sarcellus, his arms closing in an embrace. The shaft snapped between them. Burning breast met burning breast.

Flame consumed them both. The thing called Sarcellus howled, shrieked with its entire face. It stared in horror at the iron eyes, now wreathed in blazing fire ...

"Truth ..." the man whispered.

Ikurei Conphas. How like a child he looked, his naked form half-twisted in sheets, his face tipped gently back, as though he peered into some distant sky in his dreams. General Martemus stood in the shadows, gazing down at the sleeping form of his Exalt-General, silently rehearsing the command that had brought him here—knife in hand.

"Tonight, Martemus, I will reach out my hand ..."

It was unlike any he'd ever been given.

Martemus had spent most of his life following commands, and though he'd unstintingly tried to execute each and every one, even those that proved disastrous, their origins had always haunted him. No matter how tormented or august the channels, the commands he followed had always come from *somewhere*, from someplace within a beaten and debauched world: peevish officers, spiteful apparati, vainglorious generals ... As a result, he had often thought that thought, so catastrophic for a man who'd been bred to serve: *I am greater than what I obey.*

But the command he followed this night ...

"Tonight, Martemus ..."

It came from nowhere within the circle of this world.

"I will take a life."

To answer such a command, he'd decided, was more than merely akin to worship—it was worship made flesh. All meaningful things, it now seemed to him, were but forms of prayer.

Lessons of the Warrior-Prophet.

Martemus raised the silvery blade to a shaft of moonlight, and for a shining moment it seemed to *fit* Conphas's throat. In his soul's eye, he saw the Imperial Heir dead, beautiful lips perched open in the memory of a final breath, glassy eyes staring far, far into the Outside. He saw blood pooled in folded linen sheets, like water between the petals of a lotus. The General glanced about the luxurious bedchamber, at the dim frescoes prancing along the walls, at the dark carpets swimming across the floor. Would it seem a simpler place, he wondered, when they found his corpse in blooded sheets?

Commands. Through them a voice could become an army, a breath could become blood.

Think of how long you've wanted this!

Dread and exhilaration.

You're a practical man. Strike and be done with it!

Conphas groaned, shifted like a naked virgin beneath the sheets. His eyes fluttered open. Stared at him in dull incomprehension. Flickered to the accusatory knife.

"Martemus?" the young man gasped.

"Truth," the General grated, striking downward.

But there was a flash, and though his arm continued arcing downward, his hand tumbled outward, the knife slipping from nerveless fingers. Dumbstruck, he raised his arm, stared in horror at the stump of his wrist. Blood spilled along the back of his forearm, dribbled like piss from his elbow.

He whirled to the shadows, saw the glistening demon, its skin puckered by hell-fire, its face impossibly extended, clawing the air like a crab ...

"Fucking Dûnyain," it growled.

Something passed through Martemus's neck. Something sharp ...

Martemus's head bounced from the side of the mattress into the shadows, a living expression still flexing across its face. Too horrified to cry out, Conphas scrambled through the tangled sheets, away from the figure that had killed his General. The form backed into the blackness of a far corner, but for an instant Conphas glimpsed something naked and nightmarish— something impossible.

"Who?" he cried.

"Silence!" a familiar voice hissed. "It's *me!*"

"Sarcellus?"

The horror slackened somewhat. But the bewilderment remained ...

Martemus dead?

"This is a nightmare!" Conphas exclaimed. "I still sleep!"

"You don't sleep, I assure you. Though you came close to never awakening ..."

"What happens?" Conphas cried. Despite hollow legs, he strode around the far mahogany post of his bed, stood naked over the crumpled form of his General. The man still wore his field uniform. "Martemus?"

"Belonged to *him*," the voice from the dark corner said.

"Prince Kellhus," Conphas said in dawning recognition. Suddenly he understood all that he needed to know: a battle had just been fought—and won. He grinned in relief—and wondrous admiration. The man had used Martemus! *Martemus!*

And here I thought I'd won the battle for his soul!

"I need a lantern," he snapped, recovering his imperious mien. What was that smell?

"Strike no light!" the disembodied voice cried. "They attacked me tonight as well."

Conphas scowled. Saviour or not, Sarcellus had no business barking commands at his betters.

"As you can see," he said graciously, so as not to imply ingratitude, "my most trusted General is dead. I will have light." He turned to call for his guards ...

"Don't be a fool! We must act fast, otherwise the Holy War is doomed!"

Conphas paused, looked to the corner concealing the Shrial Knight, his head tilted in morbid curiosity. "They burned you, didn't they?" He took two steps toward the shadows. "You smell of pork."

There was a rattle, like that of a bolting beast, and something slick barrelled across the bedchamber, disappeared out the balcony ...

Roaring for his guards, Conphas raced after him, waving past the gossamer sheers. Though he saw nothing in the Caraskand night, he noticed the spray of Martemus's blood across his arms. He heard his guards explode into the room behind him, grinned at their shouts of dismay.

"General Martemus," he called, stepping out of the chill air into their astonished presence, "was a traitor. Bring his body to the engines. See that it's cast to the heathens, where it belongs. Then send for General Sompas."

The truce had ended.

"And the General's head," his towering Captain, Triaxeras, asked in an unsteady voice, "do you wish that cast to the heathens as well?"

"No," Ikurei Conphas said, slipping into a robe held out by one of his haeturi. He laughed at the absurdity of the man's head, which lay like a cabbage near the foot of his bed. It was odd how he could feel so little after all they'd suffered together.

"The General never leaves my side, Triah. You know that."

Fustaras was a zealous soldier. As a Proadjunct in the third maniple of the Selial Column, he was what others in the Imperial Army called a "Threesie," someone who'd signed a third indenture—a third fourteen-year term—rather than taking his Imperial Pension. Though often the bane of junior officers, Threesies like Fustaras were prized by their generals, so much so they were often issued more shares than their titular superiors. Everyone knew Threesies formed the stubborn heart of any Column. They were the men who saw things through.

Which was why, Fustaras supposed, General Sompas had chosen him and several of his fellows for this mission. "When children go astray," the man had said, "they must be beaten."

Dressed, like most Men of the Tusk, in looted Kianene robes, Fustaras and his band prowled the street commonly known as the Galleries—so named, Fustaras supposed, because of the innumerable, tenement-lined alleyways that wound about it. Located in the southeast quarter of the Bowl, it was a notorious gathering place for the Zaudunyani—the cursed heretics. Many would crowd the tenement rooftops and call out prayers to the nearby Heights of the Bull, where that obscene fraud, Prince Kellhus of Atrithau, continued to cower. Others would listen to deranged enthusiasts—they called them Judges—preach from the mouth of various alleyways.

Following his instructions to the letter, Fustaras halted and accosted a Judge where the heretics were most concentrated. "Tell me, friend," he asked in an amiable manner. "What do they say of Truth?"

The emaciated man turned, his pate gleaming pink through a froth of wild, white hair. Without hesitation, he replied, "That it shines."

As though reaching for coppers to toss to beggars, Fustaras clasped the ash club hanging beneath his cloak. "Are you sure?" he asked, his demeanour at once casual and dangerous. He hefted the polished haft. "Perhaps it bleeds."

The man's sparkling gaze darted from Fustaras's eyes to the club, then back. "That too," he said in the rigid manner of someone resolved to master their quailing heart. He pitched his voice so those nearby could hear. "If not, then why the Holy War?"

This particular heretic, Fustaras decided, was too clever by a half. He hoisted the club high, then struck. The man fell to one knee. Blood trickled across his right temple and cheek; he raised two glistening fingers to Fustaras, as though to say, *See* ...

Fustaras struck him again. The Judge fell to the cracked cobble.

Shouts echoed through the street, and Fustaras glimpsed half-starved men running from all directions. Clubs bared, his troop closed in formation about him. Even so, he found himself reconsidering the merits of the General's plan ... There were so many. How could there be so many?

Then he remembered he was a Threesie.

He wiped the flecks of blood from his face with a stained sleeve. "To all those who heed the so-called Warrior-Prophet," he cried. "Know that we, the Orthodox, will doom you as you have doomed—"

Something exploded against his jaw. He pitched backward, clutching his face, stumbled over the inert form of the Judge. He rolled across the hard ground, felt blood pulse over his fingertips. A rock ... Someone had thrown a rock!

His ears ringing, clamour roaring about him, he pressed himself to one knee, then found his feet. Clutching his jaw, he stood, looked around ... and saw his men being cut down. Terror bolted through him.

But the general said—

A wild-eyed Thunyeri with three shrivelled Sranc heads jangling between his thighs reached out and seized him by the throat. For an instant, the man looked scarcely human, he was so tall and so thin.

"*Reära thuning praussa!*" the flaxen-haired barbarian roared, swinging him about. Fustaras glimpsed armed shadows behind, felt his cry gagged into a cough by the thumb crushing his windpipe. "*Fraas kaumrut!*"

There was an instant where he could actually feel the cold of the iron spear tip against the small of his back. A sensation, like sucking deep icy air. Howling faces. The hot rush of blood.

A wheezing, huffing animal ruled its black heart, mewling in pain and fury.

The thing called Sarcellus shuffled through the ruined precincts of some nameless tabernacle. For three days it had skulked through the dark places of the city, unable to close its face for pain. Now, kicking through a clutch of blackened human skulls, it thought of the snow that whistled across the Plains of Agongorea, of white expanses bruised black by pitch. It could remember leaping through the cool cool drifts, soothed rather than bitten by the icy winds. It could remember blood jetting across pristine white, fading into lines of rose.

But the snow was so very far—as far as Holy Golgotterath!—and the fire, it flared as near as his blistered skin. The fire still burned!

Curse-him-curse-him-curse-him-curse-him! Let me gnaw his tongue! Fuck his wounds!

"Do you suffer, Gaörta?"

It jerked like a cat, peered through the cramped digits of its outer face.

As still and glossy black as a statue of diorite, the Synthese regarded him from the summit of several heaped and charred bodies. Its face looked white and wet and inscrutable in the gloom, like something carved from a potato.

The shell of the Old Father ... Aurang, Great General of the World-Breaker, ancient Prince of the Inchoroi.

"It *hurts*, Old Father! *How it hurts!*"

"Savour it, Gaörta, for it's but a taste of what is to come."

The thing called Sarcellus snuffled and blubbered, rolled its inner and outer faces beneath the merciless stars.

"*No,*" it moaned, beating petulant fingers through the debris at its feet. "*Nooo!*"

"Yes," the tiny lips said. "The Holy War is doomed ... You have failed. *You*, Gaörta."

Wild terror lanced through its cringing thoughts: it knew what failure meant, but it couldn't move. There was only obedience before the Architect, the Maker.

"But it wasn't me! It was *them!* The Cishaurim command the Padirajah! It was their—"

"*Fault*, Gaörta?" the Old Father said. "The very poison we would suck from this world?"

The thing called Sarcellus raised its hands in desperate warding. All the monstrous and monumental glory of the Consult seemed to crash down upon him. "I'm sorry, please!"

The tiny eyes closed, but whether in weariness or in contemplation, the thing called Sarcellus could not tell. When they opened, they were as blue as cataracts. "One more task, Gaörta. One more task in the name of *spite*."

It fell to its belly before the Synthese, writhed and grovelled in agony. "Anything!" it gasped. "Anything! I would cut out any heart! Pluck any eye! I would drag the whole world to oblivion!"

"The Holy War is doomed. We must deal with the Cishaurim some other way ..." Again, the eyes clicked shut. "You must ensure this Kellhus dies with the Men of the Tusk. He must not escape."

And the thing called Sarcellus forgot about snow. Vengeance! Vengeance would balm his blasted skin!

"*Now*," the palm-sized expression grated, and Gaörta had the sense of vast power, ancient and hoary, forced through a reed throat. Here and there, small showers of dust trailed down the broken walls.

"Close your face."

Gaörta obeyed as he must, screamed as he must.

Proyas's missive crumpled in his right hand, Cnaiür strode through a carpeted corridor belonging to the humble but strategically located villa where the Conriyan had chosen to sequester his household—or what remained of it. He paused before entering the bright square of the court-yard, stooping beneath the florid double-arched vaults peculiar to Kianene architecture. A dried orange peel, no longer than his thumb, lay curled in the dust encircling the black marble base of the left pilaster. Without thinking, he scooped it into his mouth, winced at the bitterness.

Every day he grew more hungry.

My son! How could he so name my son?

He found Proyas awaiting him near one of three brackish pools at the centre of the courtyard, loitering with two men he didn't recognize: an imperial officer and a Shrial Knight. Mid-morning clouds formed a ponderous procession across the sky, drawing their shadows across the sun-bright confusion of the hills that loomed over the courtyard's shaded porticos, particularly to the south and west.

Caraskand. The city that had become their tomb.

He does this to gall me. To remind me of the object of my hate!

Proyas caught sight of him first. "Cnaiür, good—"

"I don't read," he growled, tossing the crumpled sheaf at the Prince's feet. "If you wish to confer with me, send *word*, not scratches."

Proyas's expression darkened. "But of course," he said tightly. He nodded to the two strangers, as though trying to salvage some rigid semblance of jnanic decorum. "These men have made a claim—of sorts— in a bid to secure my support. I would have you confirm it."

Struck by a sudden horror, Cnaiür stared at the imperial officer, recognizing the insignia stamped into the collar of his cuirass. And of course, there was the blue mantle ...

The man frowned, exchanged a smiling, significant look with his companion.

"He grows lean in wits as well," the officer said in a voice Cnaiür recognized all too well. He suddenly remembered it floating across the corpses of his kinsmen—at the Battle of Kiyuth. Ikurei Conphas ... The Exalt-General stood before him! But how could he fail to recognize him?

But the madness lifts! It lifts!

Cnaiür blinked, saw himself seated upon Conphas's chest, carving off his nose the way a child might draw in the mud. "What does he want?" he barked at Proyas. He glanced at the Shrial Knight, realizing he'd seen the man before as well, though he couldn't recall his name. A small, golden Tusk hung about the Knight-Commander's neck, cupped in the folds of his white surcoat.

Conphas answered in Proyas's stead. "What I want, you barbaric lout, is the *truth*."

"The truth?"

"Lord Sarcellus," Proyas said, "claims to have news of Atrithau."

Cnaiür stared at the man, for the first time noticing the bandages about his hands and the odd network of angry red lines across his sumptuous face. "Atrithau? But how is that possible?"

"Three men have come forward," Sarcellus said, "out of the piety of their hearts. They swear that a man—a veteran of the northern caravans who perished in the desert—told them there was no way Prince Kellhus could be who he claims to be." The Shrial Knight smiled in a peculiar fashion—obviously the burns, or whatever marred his face, were quite painful. "Apparently the scandal of Atrithau," Sarcellus continued inexorably, "is that its King, Aethelarius, has *no live heirs*. The House of Morghund is about to flicker out—forever, they say. And this means that Anasûrimbor Kellhus is a pretender."

The faint throb of Kianene drums filled the silence. Cnaiür turned back to Proyas. "You said they want your support ... For what?"

"Just answer the blasted question!" Conphas exclaimed.

Ignoring the Exalt-General, Cnaiür and Proyas exchanged a look of honesty and admission. Despite their quarrels, such looks had become frighteningly common over the course of the past weeks.

"With my support," Proyas said, "they think they can prosecute Kellhus without inciting war within these cursed walls."

"Prosecute Kellhus?"

"Yes ... As a False Prophet, according to the Law of the Tusk."

Cnaiür scowled. "And why do you need my word?"

"Because I trust you."

Cnaiür swallowed. *Outland dogs!* someone raged. *Kine!*

For some reason a look of alarm flickered across Conphas's face.

"Apparently the illustrious Prince of Conriya," Sarcellus said, "will have no truck with hearsay ..."

"Not," Proyas snapped, "on a matter as ill-omened as this!"

Working his jaw, Cnaiür glared at the Shrial Knight, wondering what could cause such a strange disposition of burns across a man's face. He thought of the Battle of Anwurat, of the relish with which he'd driven his knife into Kellhus's chest—or the thing that had looked like him. He thought of Serwë gasping beneath him, and a pang watered his eyes. Only she knew his heart. Only she understood when he awoke weeping ...

Serwë, first wife of his heart.

I will have her! someone within him wept. *She belongs to me!*

So beautiful ... My proof!

Suddenly everything seemed to slump, as though the world itself had been soaked in numbness and lead. And he realized—without anguish, without heartbreak—that Anasûrimbor Moënghus was beyond him. Despite all his hate, all his tooth-gnashing fury, the blood trail he followed ended here ... In a city.

We're dead. All of us ...

If Caraskand was to be their tomb, he would see certain blood spilled first.

But Moënghus! someone cried. *Moënghus must die!* And yet he could no longer recall the hated face. He saw only a mewling infant ...

"What you say is true," he finally said. He turned to Proyas, held his astonished, brown-eyed gaze. It seemed he could taste the orange peel anew, so bitter were the words.

"The man you call Prince Kellhus is an imposter ... A prince of nothing."

Never, it seemed, had his heart felt so flaccid and cold.

The many-pillared audience hall of the Sapatishah's Palace was as immense as old King Eryeat's dank gallery in Moraör, the ancient Hall of Kings in Oswenta, and yet the glory of the Warrior-Prophet made it seem the hearth room of a hovel. Seated upon Imbeyan's throne of ivory and bone, Saubon watched his approach with trepidation. Cupped in gigantic bowls of iron, the King-Fires crackled in his periphery. Even after all this time they seemed to offend the surrounding magnificence—the imposition of a crude and backward people.

But still, he was King! King of Caraskand.

Draped in white samite, the man who'd once been Prince Kellhus paused beneath him, standing on the round crimson rug the Kianene had used for obeisance. He did not kneel, nor did he seem to blink.

"Why have you summoned me?"

"To warn you ... You must flee. The Council convenes shortly ..."

"But the Padirajah commands the approaches, rules the countryside. Besides, I cannot abandon those who follow me. I cannot abandon you."

"But you must! They will condemn you. Even Proyas!"

"And you, Coithus Saubon? Will you condemn me?"

"No ... Never!"

"But you've already given them your guarantees."

"Who said this? What liar dares—"

"You. You say this."

"But ... But you must understand!"

"I understand. They've ransomed your city. All you need do is pay."

"No! It's not that way. It's not!"

"Then what way is it?"

"It ... It ... It is what it is!"

"For all of your life, Saubon, you've ached for *this*, the trappings of a tyrant—the effects of old Eryeat, your father. Tell me, to whom did you run, Saubon, after your father beat you? Who dabbed your cuts with fleece? Was it to your mother? Or was it to Kussalt, your groom?

"No one beat me! He ... He ..."

"Kussalt, then. Tell me, Saubon, what was more difficult? Losing him on the Plains of Mengedda, or learning of his lifelong hate?"

"Silence!"

"All your long life, no one has known you."

"Silence!"

"All your long life you've suffered, you've questioned—"

"No! No! Silence!"

"—and you've punished those who would love you."

Saubon slapped burly hands about his ears. "Cease! I command it!"

"As you punished Kussalt, as you punish—"

"*Silence-silence-silence!* They told me you would do this! They warned me!"

"Indeed. They warned you against the *truth*. Against wandering into the nets of the Warrior-Prophet."

"How can you know this?" Saubon cried, overcome by incredulous woe. "*How?*"

"Because it's Truth."

"Then fie on it! *Fie on the truth!*"

"And what of your immortal soul?"

"Then let it be damned!" he roared, leaping to his feet. "I embrace it— embrace it all! Damnation in this life! Damnation in *all others*! Torment heaped upon torment! I would bear all to be King for a day! I would see you broken and blooded if that meant I could own this throne! *I would see the God's own eyes plucked out!*"

This last scream pealed through the hollow recesses of the audience hall, returned to him in a haunting shiver: *pluck-plucked-out-out ...*

He fell to his knees before his throne, felt the heat of his King-Fires bite tear-soaked skin. There was shouting, the clank of armour and weaponry. Guards had come rushing ...

But of the Warrior-Prophet there was no sign.

"He-he's not real," Saubon mumbled to the hollows of his court. "He doesn't exist!"

But the gold-ringed fists kept falling. They would never stop.

He'd spent days seated upon the terrace, lost in whatever worlds he searched in his trances. At sunrise and sunset, Esmenet would go to him and leave a bowl of water as he'd directed. She brought him food as well, though he'd asked her not to. She would stare at his broad, motionless back, at his hair waving in the breeze, at the dying sun upon his face, and she would feel like a little girl kneeling before an idol, offering tribute to something monstrous and insatiable: salted fish, dried prunes and figs, unleavened bread—enough to cause a small riot in the lower city.

He touched none of it.

Then one dawn she went out to him, and he wasn't there.

After a desperate rush through the galleries of the palace, she found him in their apartments, unkempt and rakish, joking with Serwë, who had just arisen.

"Esmi-Esmi-Esmi," the swollen-eyed girl pouted. "Could you bring me little Moënghus?"

Too relieved to feel exasperated, Esmenet ducked into the adjoining nursery and plucked the black-haired babe from his cradle. Though his dumbfounded stare made her smile, she found the winter blue of his eyes unnerving.

"I was just saying," Kellhus said as she delivered the child to Serwë, "that the Great Names have summoned me ..." He reached out a haloed hand. "They want to parley."

He mentioned nothing, of course, about his meditation. He never did.

Esmenet took his hand, sat beside him on their bed, only just understanding the implications of what he had said.

"Parley?" she suddenly cried. "Kellhus, they summon you to *condemn you!*"

"Kellhus?" Serwë asked. "What does she mean?"

"That this parley is a *trap*," Esmenet exclaimed. She stared hard at Kellhus. "You know this!"

"What can you mean?" Serwë exclaimed. "Everyone loves Kellhus … Everyone *knows* now."

"No, Serwë. Many hate him—very many. Very many want him dead!"

Serwë laughed in the oblivious way of which only she seemed capable. "Esmenet …" she said, shaking her head as though at a beloved fool. She boosted little Moënghus into the air. "Auntie Esmi forgets," she cooed to the infant. "Yeeesss. She forgets who your father is!"

Esmenet watched dumbstruck. Sometimes she wanted nothing more than to wring the girl's neck. How? How could he love such a simpering fool?

"Esmi …" Kellhus said abruptly. The warning in his voice chilled her heart. She turned to him, shouted *Forgive me!* with her eyes.

But at the same time, she couldn't relent, not now, not after what she had found. "Tell her, Kellhus! Tell her what's about to happen!"

Not again. Not again!

"Listen to me, Esmi. There's no other way. The Zaudunyani and the Orthodox cannot go to war."

"Not even for you?" she cried. "This Holy War, this city, is but a pittance compared to you! Don't you see, Kellhus?" Her desperation swelled into sudden anguish and desolation, and she angrily wiped at her tears. This was too important for selfish grief! *But I've lost so many!*

"Don't you see how precious you are? Think of what Akka said! What if you're the world's only hope?"

He cupped her cheek, brushed her eyebrow with his thumb, which he held warm against her temple.

"Sometimes, Esmi, we must cross death to reach our destination."

She thought of King Shikol in *The Tractate*, the demented Xerashi King who'd commanded the Latter Prophet's execution. She thought of his gilded thighbone, the instrument of judgement, which to this day remained the most potent symbol of evil in Inrithidom. Was this what Inri Sejenus had said to his nameless lover? That loss could somehow secure glory?

But this is madness!

"The Shortest Path," she said, horrified by the teary-eyed contemptuousness of her tone.

But the blond-bearded face smiled.

"Yes," the Warrior-Prophet said. "The Logos."

"Anasûrimbor Kellhus," Gotian intoned in his powerful voice, "I hereby denounce you as a False Prophet, and as a pretender to the warrior-caste. It is the judgement of the Council of Great and Lesser Names that you be scourged in the manner decreed by Scripture."

Serwë heard a wail pierce the thunderous outcry, and only afterward realized that it was her own. Moënghus sobbed in her arms, and she reflexively began rocking him, though she was too frightened to coo re-assurances. The Hundred Pillars had drawn their swords, and now thronged to either side of them, trading fierce glares with the Shrial Knights.

"You judge no one!" someone was bellowing. *"The Warrior-Prophet alone speaks the judgement of the Gods! It is you who've been found wanting! You who shall be punished!"*

"False! False!—"

It seemed a thousand half-starved faces cried a thousand hungry things. Accusations. Curses. Laments. The air was flushed by humid cries. Hundreds had gathered within the ruined shell of the Citadel of the Dog to hear the Warrior-Prophet answer the charges of the Great and Lesser Names. Hot in the sun, the black ruins towered about them: walls unconsummated by vaults, foundations obscured by heaped wreckage, the side of a fallen tower bare and rounded against the debris, like the flanks of a whale breaching the surface of a choppy sea. The Men of the Tusk had congregated across every pitched slope and beneath every monolithic remnant. Fist-waving faces packed every pocket of clear ground.

Instinctively pulling her baby tight to her breast, Serwë glanced around in terror. *Esmi was right ... We shouldn't have come!* She looked up to Kellhus, and wasn't surprised by the divine calm with which he observed the masses. Even here, he seemed the godlike nail which fastened what happened to what *should* happen.

He'll make them see!

But the roar was redoubled, and reverberated through her body. Several men had drawn their knives, as though the sound of fury were grounds enough for murderous riot.

So much hatred.

Even the Great Names, gathered in the clear centre of the fortress's courtyard, looked apprehensive. They gazed blank-faced at the thundering mobs, almost as though they were counting. Already several fights had broken out; she could see the flash of steel and flailing monkey limbs amidst the packed mobs—believers beset by unbelievers.

A starved fanatic with a knife managed to slip past the Hundred Pillars, rushed the Warrior-Prophet ...

... who pinched the knife from his hand as though he were a child, clasped his throat with one hand and lifted him from the ground, like a gasping dog.

The pocked grounds gradually quieted as more and more turned their horrified eyes to the Warrior-Prophet and his thrashing burden—until shortly only the would-be assassin could be heard, gagging. Serwë's skin pimpled in dread. *Why do they do this? Why do they dare his wrath?*

Kellhus tossed the man to the ground, where he lay inert, a heap of slack limbs.

"What is it that you fear?" the Warrior-Prophet asked. His tone was both plaintive and imperious—not the overbearing manner of a King certain of his sanction, but the despotic voice of Truth.

Gotian shouldered his way passed the interceding onlookers. "The wrath of the God," he cried, "who punishes us for harbouring an abomination!"

"No." His flashing eyes found them from among the masses: Saubon, Proyas, Conphas, and the others. "You fear that as my power waxes, yours will wane. You do what you do not in the name of the God, but in the name of avarice. You wouldn't tolerate even the God to possess your Holy War. And yet, in each of your hearts there is an itch, an anguished question that I alone can see: *What if he truly is the Prophet? What doom awaits us then?*"

"*SILENCE!*" Conphas roared, spittle flying from his contorted lips.

"And you, Conphas? What is it that you hide?"

"His words are spears!" Conphas cried to the others. "His very voice is an outrage!"

"But I ask only *your* question: *What if you are wrong?*"

Even Conphas was dumbstruck by the force of these words. It was as though the Warrior-Prophet had made this demand in the God's own voice.

"You turn to fury in the absence of certainty," he continued sadly. "I only ask you this: What moves your soul? What moves you to condemn me? Is it indeed the God? The God strides with certainty, with *glory*, through the hearts of men! Does the God so stride through you? *Does the God so stride through you?*"

Silence. The poignant hush of dread, as though they were a congregation of debauched children suddenly confronted by the rebuke of their godlike father. Serwë felt tears flood her cheeks.

They see! They at last see!

But then a Shrial Knight, the one named Sarcellus, whose face alone remained pious and devoid of hesitation, answered the Warrior-Prophet in a loud, clear voice.

"'All things both sacred and vile,'" the Knight-Commander said, quoting the Tusk, "'speak to the hearts of Men, and they are bewildered, and holding out their hands to darkness, *they name it light.*'"

The Warrior-Prophet stared at him sharply, and quoted in turn: "'Hearken Truth, for it strides fiercely among you, and will not be denied.'"

Possessed of beatific calm, Sarcellus answered: "'Fear him, for he is the deceiver, the Lie made Flesh, come among you to foul the waters of your heart.'"

And the Warrior-Prophet smiled sadly. "Lie made flesh, Sarcellus?" Serwë watched his eyes search the crowds, then settle on the nearby Scylvendi. "Lie made flesh," he repeated, staring into the fiend's embattled face. "The hunt need not end … Remember this when you recall the secret of battle. You still command the ears of the Great."

"False Prophet," Sarcellus continued. "Prince of *nothing*."

As if these words had been a sign, the Shrial Knights rushed the Hundred Pillars, and there was the clash of fierce arms. Someone shrieked, and one of the Knights fell to his knees, grasping in his left hand the gushing stump where his right hand should have been. Another shriek, and then yet another, and then the starving mobs, as though sobered from a drunken stupor by the sight of blood, surged forward.

Serwë screamed, clawed at the Warrior-Prophet's white sleeve, grasped her baby with fierce desperation. *This isn't happening ...*

But it was hopeless. After several moments of howling butchery, the Shrial Knights were upon them. With nightmarish horror she watched the Warrior-Prophet catch a blade in his palms, break it, and then touch the neck of his assailant. The man crumpled. Another he caught by the arm, which suddenly went limp as sackcloth, and then drove his fist through his face, as though the man's head were a melon.

Somewhere impossibly far away, she heard Gotian roar at his men, thunder at them to stop.

She saw a manic-faced Knight rush her, sword raised to the sun, but then he was on the ground, fumbling with a fountain of blood that had bloomed from his side, and then a rough arm was about her, tiger-striped by scars and impossibly strong.

The Scylvendi? The Scylvendi had saved her?

At last bridled by their Grandmaster, the Shrial Knights relented, and stood back. They were lean and wolfish beneath their hauberks. The Tusks they bore on their stained and tattered surcoats looked threadbare and wicked.

It seemed the whole world had erupted in a chorus of howling throats.

Gotian stepped from the sweaty thunder beyond his men, and after glancing a dark moment at Cnaiür, he turned to the Warrior-Prophet. His once aristocratic face looked haggard and bitter, the look of a man who had been harrowed by a hateful world.

"Yield, Anasûrimbor Kellhus," he said hoarsely. "You will be scourged according to Scripture."

Serwë thrashed against the plainsman until he released her. He stared at her with savage horror, and she felt only hate—bone-snapping hate. She stumbled to Kellhus's side, and buried her face and her child against his robes.

"*Yield!*" she sobbed. "My lord and master you must yield! Do not die in this place! You must not die!"

She could feel her Prophet's tender eyes upon her, his divine embrace encompass her. She looked up into his face and saw love in his shining, god-remote eyes. The love of the God for her! For *Serwë*, first wife and lover of the Warrior-Prophet. For the girl who was nothing ...

Glittering tears branched across her cheeks. "I love you!" she cried. "I love you and you cannot die!"

She looked down at the squalling babe between them. "Our son!" she sobbed. *"Our son needs the God!"*

She felt rough hands pull her back, and an ache such as she'd never suffered as they pulled her from his embrace. My *heart! They tear me from my heart!*

"He's the God!" she shrieked. "Can't you see? He's *the God!"*

She struggled against the man who held her, but he was too strong. *"The God!"*

The man who held her spoke: "According to Scripture?" It was Sarcellus.

"According to Scripture," the Grandmaster replied, but there was now pity in his voice.

"But she has a newborn child!" another cried—the Scylvendi ... What did he mean? She looked to him, but he was a dark shadow against the congregation of warlike men, spliced by tears and sunlight.

"It matters not," Gotian replied, his voice hardening with mad resolve.

"My child!" Was there desperation, pain in the Scylvendi's voice?

No ... not your child. Kellhus? What happened?

"Then take it." Curt, as though seeking to snuff further mortification.

Someone pulled her wailing son from her arms. Another heart gone. Another ache.

No ... Moënghus? What's happening?

Serwë shrieked, until it seemed her eyes must shimmer into flame, her face crumble into dust.

The flash of sunlight across a knife. Sarcellus's knife. Sounds. Celebratory and horrified.

Serwë felt her life spill across her breasts. She worked her lips to speak to him, that godlike man so near, to say something final, but there was no sound, no breath. She raised her hands and beads of dark wine fell from her outstretched fingers ...

My Prophet, my love, how could this be?

I know not, sweet Serwë ...

And as sky and the howling faces beneath darkened, she remembered his words, once spoken.

"*You are innocence, sweet Serwë, the one heart I need not teach* …"

Last flare of sunlight, drowsy, as though glimpsed by a child stirring from dreams beneath an airy tree.

Innocence, Serwë.

The limb-vaulted canopy, growing darker, warm-woollen like a shroud. No more sun.

You are the mercy you seek.

But my baby, my—

CHAPTER TWENTY-THREE

CARASKAND

For Men, no circle is ever closed. We walk ever in spirals.

—DRUSAS ACHAMIAN, THE COMPENDIUM OF THE FIRST HOLY WAR

Bring he who has spoken prophecy to the judgement of the priests, and if his prophecy is judged true, acclaim him, for he is clean, and if his prophecy is judged false, bind him to the corpse of his wife, and hang him one cubit above the earth, for he is unclean, an anathema unto the Gods.

—WARRANTS 7:48, THE CHRONICLE OF THE TUSK

Late Winter, 4112 Year-of-the-Tusk, Caraskand

It was as though someone had struck the back of his knees with a staff. Eleäzaras stumbled forward, but was steadied by the strong arms of Lord Chinjosa, Count-Palatine of Antanamera.

No ... No.

"Do you know what this means?" Chinjosa hissed.

Eleäzaras pushed the Palatine away and took two more drunken steps toward Chepheramunni's body. The gloom of his sickroom was alleviated by a cluster of candles at the head of his bed. The bed itself was lavish, set between four marble columns that braced the low vaults of the ceiling. But it reeked of feces, blood, and pestilence.

Chepheramunni's head lay beneath the congregated candles, but his face ...

It was nowhere to be seen.

Where his face *should* have been lay what resembled an overturned spider, its legs clutched in death about its abdomen. What had been Chepheramunni's face lay unspooled across the knuckles and shins of the steepled limbs. Eleäzaras saw familiar fragments: a lone nostril, the haired ridge of an eyebrow. Beneath he glimpsed lidless eyes and the shine of human teeth, bared and lipless.

And just as that fool Skalateas had claimed, nowhere could he sense the bruise of sorcery.

Chepheramunni—a Cishaurim skin-spy.

Impossible.

The Grandmaster of the Scarlet Spires coughed, blinked back uncharacteristic tears. This was too much. The very air seemed nightmarish with mad implication. The ground tipped beneath his feet. Once again, he felt Chinjosa steady him.

"Grandmaster! What does this mean?"

That we're doomed. That I've led my School to its destruction.

A string of catastrophes. The disastrous losses at the battle of Anwurat. General Setpanares killed. Fifteen sorcerers of rank dead between the desert and the plague. And the disaster at Iothiah, which had claimed the lives of two others. The Holy War besieged and starving.

And now this ... To find their hated enemy here, standing with him upon the summit. How much did the Cishaurim know?

"We're doomed," Eleäzaras muttered.

"No, Grandmaster," Chinjosa replied, his own deep voice still tight with horror.

Eleäzaras turned to him. Chinjosa was a large, burly man geared for war in his ring-mail hauberk, over which he wore an open Kianene coat of red silk. The white cosmetics made his strong-featured face stark against his black, square-cut beard. Chinjosa had proven himself indomitable in battle, an able commander, and in Iyokus's absence, a shrewd adviser.

"We *would* be doomed had this abomination led us into battle. Perhaps the Gods have favoured us with their afflictions."

Eleäzaras stared numbly into Chinjosa's face, struck by a further terrifying thought. "You are who you are, Chinjosa?"

The Palatine of Antanamera, the province that had so often proven itself the spine of High Ainon, looked at him sternly. "It *is* me, Grandmaster."

Eleäzaras studied the caste-noble, and it seemed as though the man's simple, warlike strength pulled him back from the brink of despair. Chinjosa was right. This wasn't yet another catastrophe; it was a ... blessing of a sort. But if Chepheramunni could be replaced ... There must be others.

"No one is to know of this, Chinjosa. *No one.*"

The Palatine nodded in the dim light.

If only that Mandate ingrate had broken!

"Remove its head," Eleäzaras said, his voice terse with growing outrage, "then throw the carcass onto the pyre."

Achamian and Xinemus walked the ways of twilight, between light and dark, where only shadows are known. There was no food in this place, no life-giving water, and their bodies, which they carried across their backs the way one might carry a corpse, suffered horribly.

The twilight way. The shadow way. From the port city of Joktha to Caraskand.

When they passed near the camps of the enemy, they could feel the Cishaurim's plucked eyes—brilliant, pure, like a lamplight before a silvered mirror—search for them from beyond the horizon. Many times Achamian felt that otherworldly light throw shadows from their shadows. Many times Achamian thought they were doomed. But always those eyes turned away their inhuman scrutiny, either deceived or ... Achamian could not say why.

Gaining the walls, they revealed themselves beneath a small postern gate. It was night, and torches glittered between the battlements above. With Xinemus slumped against him, Achamian called to the astonished guards: "Open the gates! I am Drusas Achamian, a Mandate Schoolman, and this is Krijates Xinemus, the Marshal of Attrempus ... We have come to share your plight!"

"This city is both doomed and damned," someone shouted down. "Who seeks entry to such a place? Who but madmen or traitors?"

Achamian paused before answering, struck by the bleak conviction of the man's tone. The Men of the Tusk, he realized, had lost all hope.

"Those who would attend their loved ones," he said. "Even unto death."

After a pause, the outer doors burst open and a troop of hollow-cheeked Tydonni seized them. At long last they found themselves inside the horror of Caraskand.

———— ∞ ————

The temple-complex of Csokis, Esmenet had heard some say, was as old as the Great Ziggurat of Xijoser in Shigek. It occupied the heart of the Bowl, and from the limestone-paved reaches of its central campus, the Kalaul, all five of the surrounding heights could be seen. In the centre of the campus rose a great tree, an ancient eucalyptus that Men had called Umiaki since time immemorial. Esmenet wept in its cavernous shadow, staring up at the hanging forms of Kellhus and Serwë. The infant Moënghus dozed in her arms—oblivious.

"Please ... Please wake up, Kellhus, please!"

Before roaring mobs, Incheiri Gotian had stripped Kellhus of his clothing, then whipped him with cedar branches until he'd bled from a hundred places. Afterward, they bound his bleeding body to Serwë's nude corpse, ankle to ankle, wrist to wrist, face to face. Then they lashed the two of them, limbs outstretched, to a great bronze ring, which they hoisted and chained—upside down no less—to the winding girth of Umiaki's lowest and mightiest limb. Esmenet had wailed her voice to nothing.

Now they spun in slow circles, their golden hair mingling in the breeze, their arms and legs sweeping out like those of dancers. Esmenet glimpsed ashen breasts crushed against a shining ribcage, armpit hair twisted into horns, then Serwë's slender back rolled into view, almost mannish because of the deep line of her spine. She glimpsed her sex, bared between outspread legs, pressed against the confusion of Kellhus's genitalia ...

Serwë ... Her face blackening as the blood settled, her limbs and torso carved in grey marble, as perfect in form as any artifice. And Kellhus ...

His face sheened in sweat, his muscular back gleaming white between lines of angry red. His eyes swollen shut.

"But you said!" Esmenet wailed. "You said Truth can't die!"

Serwë dead. Kellhus dying. No matter how long she looked, no matter how deep her reason, no matter how shrill her threats ...

Around and around, the dying and the dead. A mad pendulum.

Holding Moënghus close, Esmenet curled across the waxy mat of leaves. They smelled bitter where her body bruised them.

"Remember when you recall the secret of battle ..."

The Inrithi fell silent as he passed, their eyes following him as they followed kings. Cnaiür knew well the effect his presence worked on other men. Even beneath starred skies, he needed no gold, no herald or banner, to announce the fact of his station. He wore his glory on the skin of his arms. He was Cnaiür urs Skiötha, breaker-of-horses-and-men; others need only look to fear him.

"The hunt need not end ..."

Shut up! Shut up!

The Kalaul, the broad central campus of Csokis, teemed with piteous and despicable humanity. Along the terminus of the campus, Inrithi crowded the monumental steps of temples that looked, to Cnaiür's eyes, as ancient as any he'd seen in Shigek or Nansur. Others skulked beneath the pillared facades of dormitories and half-ruined cloisters. Across the outskirts, Inrithi sat upon mats and muttered to one another. Some even tended small fires, burning aromatic resins and woods—oblations, no doubt, for their Warrior-Prophet. The crowds thickened as he neared the great tree in the Kalaul's heart. He saw men wearing only shirts, their hindquarters smeared with shit. He saw others whose stomachs seemed pinned to their spines. He encountered one bare-chested fool who leapt up and down shaking cupped hands over his head like a rattle. When Cnaiür shouldered the imbecile aside, something like pebbles scattered across the paving stones. He heard the madman wailing about teeth in his wake.

"... the secret of battle ..."

Lies! More lies!

Heedless of the threats and curses that greeted his passage, Cnaiür continued battling forward, pressing through what seemed a malodorous sea of heads, elbows, and shoulders. He paused only when he could clearly view the mighty tree that men called Umiaki. Like an immense, upturned root, it rose black and leafless into the night sky, shrouding its precincts in impenetrable darkness.

"You still command the ears of the Great ..."

No matter how hard Cnaiür peered, he could see nothing of the Dûnyain—or Serwë.

"Does he still breathe?" he cried. "Does his heart still beat?"

The Inrithi massed about him turned to one another, shared looks of anxious bewilderment. No one replied.

Dog-eyed drunks!

He plowed through them in disgust, yanking men aside to move forward. Finally he reached the perimeter of Shrial Knights, one of whom pressed a palm to his chest to hold him back. Cnaiür scowled until the man withdrew his hand, then peered yet again into the darkness beneath Umiaki.

He could see nothing.

For a time, he pondered cutting his way to the tree. Then a procession of Shrial Knights bearing torches passed on the far side of Umiaki, and for a fleeting moment Cnaiür glimpsed his sprawled silhouette—or was it hers?—against the glittering lights.

The forward ranks of Inrithi began shouting, some in rapture, others in derision. Through the uproar, Cnaiür heard a velvety voice, spoken in timbres only his heart could hear.

"It's good that you've come ... Proper."

Cnaiür stared in horror at the figure across the ring. Then the string of torches marched on, and darkness reclaimed the ground beneath Umiaki. The surrounding clamour subsided, fractured into individual shouts.

"All men," the voice said, *"should know their work."*

"I come to watch you suffer!" Cnaiür cried. "I come to watch you die!"

In his periphery, he glimpsed men turning to him in alarm.

"But why? Why would you want such a thing?"

"Because you betrayed me!"

"How? How have I betrayed you?"

"You need only *speak!* You're Dûnyain!"

"You make too much of me ... More even then these Inrithi."

"Because I know! I *alone* know what you are! I alone can destroy you!" He laughed as only a many-blooded Chieftain of the Utemot could, then gestured to the darkness beneath Umiaki. "Witness ..."

"And my father? The hunt need not end—you know this."

Cnaiür stood breathless, as motionless as a horse-laming stone hidden among the Steppe grasses.

"I've made a trade," he said evenly. "I've yielded to the greater hate."

"Have you?"

"Yes! Yes! Look at her! Look at what you've done to her!"

"What I've done, Scylvendi? Or what you've done?"

"She's dead. My Serwë! My Serwë is dead! My prize!"

"Oh, yes ... What will they whisper, now that your proof has passed? How will they measure?"

"They killed her because of you!"

Laughter, full and easy-hearted, like that of a favourite uncle just into his cups.

"Spoken like a true Son of the Steppe!"

"You mock me?"

A heavy hand seized his shoulder. "Enough!" someone was shouting. "Stow your madness! Cease speaking that foul tongue!"

In a single motion, Cnaiür snatched the hand and twisted it about, wrenching tendon and bone. He effortlessly wheeled the fool who'd grabbed him from his place among the others. He struck the cow-faced ingrate to the ground.

"Mock? Who would dare mock a murderer?"

"You!" Cnaiür screamed at the tree. He reached out neck-breaking arms. "You killed her!"

"No, Scylvendi. You did ... When you sold me."

"To save my son!"

And Cnaiür saw her, limp and horrified in Sarcellus's arms, blood spouting across her gown, her eyes drowning in darkness ... The darkness! How many eyes had he watched it consume?

He heard a babe bawling from the black.

"They were supposed to kill the whore!" Cnaiür screamed.

Several Inrithi were shouting at him now. He felt a blow glance his cheek, glimpsed the flash of steel. He grabbed a man about the head, drove his thumbs into his eyes. Something sharp pricked his thigh. Fists pounded against his back. Something—a club or a pommel—cracked against his temple; he released the man, reeling backward. He glimpsed black Umiaki, and heard the Dûnyain laughing, laughing as the Utemot had laughed.

"*Weeper!*"

"You!" he roared, beating down men with stone-fisted blows. "YOU!"

Suddenly the clutching, cutting mob scrambled back from a brawling figure to his right. Several cried out in apology. Cnaiür glanced at the man, who stood almost as tall as he, though not so broad.

"Have you lost your wits, Scylvendi? It's me! Me!"

"*You murdered Serwë.*"

And suddenly, the stranger became Coithus Saubon, dressed in a penitent's shabby robes. What kind of devilry?

"Cnaiür," the Galeoth Prince exclaimed, "who are you speaking to?"

"*You* …" the darkness cackled.

"Scylvendi?"

Cnaiür shook free of the man's firm grip. "This is a fool's vigil," he grated.

He spat, then turned to fight his way free of the stink.

Esmi …

His heart leapt at the thought.

I'm coming, my sweet. I'm so very close!

It seemed he could smell the musky orange of her scent. It seemed he could hear her gasps hot against his cheek, feel her grind against his loins, desperately, as though to smother a perilous fire. It seemed he could see her throwing back her hair—a glimpse of sultry eyes and parted lips.

So very close!

The Tydonni—five Numaineiri knights and a motley of men-at-arms—escorted them through the dark streets. The Tydonni had been courteous enough, given the circumstances of their arrival, but until someone in authority vouched for the two of them, the knights refused to say much of anything. Achamian saw other Men of the Tusk on their route, most of them as wretched as the guards upon the gate. Whether sitting in windows, or leaning with others against the pilasters, they stared, their faces pale and blank, their eyes impossibly bright, as though housing the fires that wasted their frames.

Achamian had seen such looks before. On the Fields of Eleneöt, after the death of Anasûrimbor Celmomas. In great Trysë, watching the fall of the Shinoth Gate. On the Plains of Mengedda, awaiting the approach of dread Tsurumah. The look of horror and fury, of Men who could only exact and never overcome.

The look of Apocalypse.

Whenever Achamian matched their gazes, no threat or challenge was exchanged, only the thoughtless understanding of exhausted brothers. Something—demon or reptile—crawled into the skulls of those who endured the unendurable, and when it looked out their eyes, as it inevitably did, it could recognize itself in others. He belonged, Achamian realized. Not just here in Caraskand with those he loved, but here with the *Holy War*. He belonged with these men—even unto death.

We share the same doom.

Moving slowly for Xinemus's sake, they trudged between two heights whose names Achamian didn't know, and into an area one of the Numaineiri had called the Bowl—where Proyas and his household were supposedly quartered. They passed through a veritable labyrinth of streets and alleyways, and more than once the knights had to ask passersby for directions. Despite everything—the prospect of finding Kellhus and Esmenet, of seeing Proyas after so many bitter months—Achamian found himself pondering the carelessness of his declaration beneath Caraskand's walls: "*I am Drusas Achamian, a Mandate Schoolman ...*"

How long had it been since he'd last spoken those words aloud?

A Mandate Schoolman ...

Was that what he was? And if so, why did he shy from the thought of contacting Atyersus? In all likelihood, they'd learned of his abduction. They were certain to have informants he knew nothing about among the Conriyan contingent at least. He imagined they assumed him dead.

So why not contact them? The threat of the Second Apocalypse hadn't dwindled during his captivity. And the Dreams, they wracked him as they ever did ...

Because I'm no longer one of them.

For all the ferocity with which he'd defended the Gnosis—to the point of sacrificing Xinemus!—he'd forsaken the Mandate. He'd forsaken them, he realized, even before his abduction by the Scarlet Spires. He'd forsaken them for Kellhus ...

I was going to teach him the Gnosis.

Even to think this stole his breath, reminded him that so much more than Esmenet awaited him within these walls. The old mysteries surrounding Maithanet. The threat of the Consult and their skin-spies. The promise and enigma of Anasûrimbor Kellhus. The premonitions of the Second Apocalypse!

But even as his skin pimpled with dread, something balked within him, something old and obdurate, as callous as crocodiles. *Let the mysteries rot!* he found himself thinking. *Let the world crash about us!* For he was Drusas Achamian, a man like any other, and he would have his lover, his wife— his Esmenet. Like so many things in the aftermath of Iothiah, the rest seemed childish, like tropes in an over-read book.

I know you live. I know it!

At long last, their small troop came to a pause before the faceless walls of some compound. Xinemus at his side, Achamian watched while two of the Numaineiri knights fell to arguing with the guards posted before the compound's gate. He turned at the sound of his friend's voice.

"Akka," Xinemus said, scowling in his queer, eyeless fashion. "When we walked as shadows ..."

The Marshal hesitated, and for a moment Achamian feared an onslaught of recriminations. Before Iothiah, the notion of using sorcery to slip past the enemy would have been unthinkable for Xinemus. And yet he'd acquiesced with scarcely a complaint when Achamian had suggested the possibility in Joktha. Did he repent? Or had he, like Achamian, been gouged of his previous cares as well?

"I'm blind," Xinemus continued. "Blind as blind could be, Akka! And yet *I saw them* ... The Cishaurim. I saw them *seeing!*"

Achamian pursed his lips, troubled by the fear-to-hope tone of the Marshal's voice.

"You *did* see," he said carefully, "in a manner ... There's many ways of seeing. And all of us possess eyes that never breach skin. Men are wrong to think nothing lies between blindness and sight."

"And the Cishaurim?" Xinemus pressed. "Is that ... Is that how they—"

"The Cishaurim are masters of this interval. They blind themselves, they say, to better see the World Between. According to some, it's the key to their metaphysics."

"So ..." Xinemus began, unable to contain the passion in his voice.

"Not now, Zin," Achamian said, watching the most senior of the Tydonni knights, a choleric thane called Anmergal, stride toward them from the compound gate. "Some other time ..."

In broken but workable Sheyic, Anmergal stated that Proyas's people had agreed to take them—despite their better judgement. "No one steals *into* Caraskand," he explained. "Only out." Then, heedless of any reply they might make, he barged past them, yelling out to his troops. At the same time, men-at-arms, dressed as Kianene but bearing the Black Eagle of House Nersei on their shields, appeared from the darkness. Within moments, Achamian and Xinemus found themselves ushered into the compound.

They were greeted by an emaciated steward dressed in the threadbare yet lustrous white and black livery of Proyas's House. Soldiers in tow, the man led them down a carpeted hallway. They passed a Kianene woman—a slave, no doubt—kneeling in the doorway of an adjoining chamber, and Achamian found himself shocked, not by her obvious terror, but by the fact that she was the first Kianene he'd seen since entering Caraskand ...

No wonder the city seemed a tomb.

They rounded a corner and found themselves in a tall antechamber. Set between two corpulent pillars—Nilnameshi by the look of them—a door of greening bronze lay partially ajar. The steward ducked his head in. Nodding to someone unseen, he pressed the door open and, after a nervous glance at Xinemus, gestured for them to follow. Achamian cursed the knot in his gut ...

Then found himself staring at Nersei Proyas.

Though more haggard and far thinner—his linen tunic hung from shoulders like sword pommels—the Crown Prince of Conriya still looked much the same. The shock of curly black hair, which his mother had both cursed and adored. The trim beard etching a jaw that, though not as youthful as it once was, remained set in the old way. The nimble brow. And of course the lucid brown eyes, which were deep enough, it seemed, to contain any admixture of passion, no matter how contradictory.

"What is it?" Xinemus asked. "What happens?"

"Proyas ..." Achamian said. He cleared his throat. "It's Proyas, Zin."

The Conriyan Prince stared at Xinemus, his face expressionless. He advanced two steps from a lavishly worked table in what must have been his bedchamber. As though from a stupor, he said, "What happened?"

Achamian said nothing, struck dumb by a rush of unexpected passions. He felt his face grow hot with fury. Xinemus stood beside him, absolutely motionless.

"Speak up," Proyas commanded, his voice ringing with desperation. "What happened?"

"The Scarlet Spires took his eyes," Achamian said evenly. "As a ... As a way to—"

Without warning, the young Prince flew to Xinemus, clutched him in a wild embrace, not cheek to cheek as between men, but as a child might, with his forehead pressed against the Marshal's collar. He shuddered with sobs. Xinemus clutched the back of his head with thick fingers, crushed his beard against his scalp.

A moment of fierce silence passed.

"*Zin,*" Proyas hissed. "Please forgive me! Please, *I beg of you!*"

"Shhh ... It's enough to feel your embrace ... To hear your voice."

"But Zin! Your eyes! Your eyes!"

"Shush, now ... Akka will fix me. You'll see."

Achamian flinched at the words. Hope was never so poison as when it deluded loved ones.

Gasping, Proyas pressed his cheek against the Marshal's shoulder. His glittering look found Achamian, and for a moment they gazed unblinking each at the other.

"You too, Old Teacher," the young man croaked. "Can you find it in your heart to forgive?"

Though Achamian heard the words clearly, they seemed to reach him as though from a great distance, their speaker too distant to truly matter.

No, he realized, he couldn't forgive, not because his heart had hardened, but because it had receded. He saw the boy, Prosha, whom he'd once loved, but he saw a stranger as well, a man who walked questionable and competing paths. A man of faith.

A murderous fanatic.

How could he think these men were his brothers?

With his face as blank as he could manage, Achamian said, "I'm a teacher no longer."

Proyas squeezed shut his eyes. They were hooded in the old way when he opened them. Whatever hardships the Holy War had endured, Proyas the Judge had survived.

"Where are they?" Achamian asked. The circles were so much clearer now. Aside from Xinemus, only Esmenet and Kellhus possessed any claim to his heart. In the whole world, only they mattered.

Proyas visibly stiffened, pressed himself from Xinemus's breast.

"Hasn't anyone told you?"

"No one would tell us anything," Xinemus said. "They feared we were spies."

Achamian couldn't breathe. "Esmenet?" he gasped.

The Prince swallowed, a stricken look upon his face.

"No ... Esmenet is safe." He ran a hand through his cropped hair, both anxious and ominous.

Somewhere, a wick sizzled in a guttering candle.

"And Kellhus?" Xinemus asked. "What about him?"

"You must understand. Much, very much, has happened."

Xinemus pawed the air before him, as though needing to touch those he spoke to. "What are you saying, Proyas?"

"I'm saying Kellhus is dead."

Of all Caraskand, only the great bazaar carried any memory of the Steppe, and even then it was only the bones of such a memory: its flatness purchased by masons, its openness enclosed by dark-windowed facades. No grasses grew between the paving stones.

"*Swazond*," he had said. "The man you have killed is gone from the world, Serwë. He exists only here, a scar upon your arm. It is the mark of his *absence*, of all the ways his soul will not move, and of all the acts he will not commit. A mark of the weight you now bear."

And she had replied, "I don't understand ..."

Such a dear fool, that girl. So innocent.

Cnaiür lay against the ribbed belly of a dead horse, surrounded by ever-widening circles of Kianene dead—victims of the city's glorious sack three weeks before.

"I will bear you," he said to the blackness. And never, it seemed, had he uttered a mightier oath. "You will not want, so long as my back is strong."

Traditional words, uttered by the groom as the memorialist braided his hair in marriage.

He raised the knife to his throat.

Bound to a circle, swinging from the limb of a dark tree.

Bound to Serwë.

Cold and lifeless against him.

Serwë.

Spinning in slow circles.

A fly crawled across her cheek, paused before a breathless nostril. He puffed air across her dead skin, and the fly was gone. *Must keep her clean.*

Her eyes half-open, papyrus-dry.

Serwë! Breathe girl, breathe! I command it!

I come before you. I come before!

Bound skin-to-skin to Serwë.

What have I ... What? What?

A convulsion of some kind.

No ... No! I must focus. I must assess ...

Unblinking eyes, staring down black cheeks, out to the stars.

There's no circumstance beyond ... No circumstance beyond ...

Logos.

I'm one of the Conditioned!

From his shins to his cheek, he could feel her, radiating a cold as deep as her bones.

Breathe! Breathe!

Dry ... And so still! So impossibly still!

Father, please! Please make her breathe!

I ... I can walk no farther.

Face so dark, mottled like something from the sea ... How had she ever smiled?

Focus! What happens?

All is in disarray. And they've killed her. They've murdered my wife.

I gave her to them.

What did you say?

I gave her to them.

Why? Why would you do this?

For you ...

For them.

Something dropped within him, and he tumbled into sleep, cold water rinsing bruised and broken skin.

Dreams followed. Dark tunnels, weary earth.

A ridge, curved like a sleeping woman's hip, against the night sky.

And upon it two silhouettes, black against clouds of stars, impossibly bright.

The figure of a man seated, shoulders crouched like an ape, legs crossed like a priest.

And a tree with branches that swept up and out, forking across the bowl of the night.

And about the Nail of Heaven, the stars revolved, like clouds hurried across winter skies.

And Kellhus stared at the figure, stared at the tree, but he could not move. The firmament cycled, as though night after night passed without day.

Framed by the wheeling heavens, the figure spoke, a million throats in his throat, a million mouths in his mouth ...

WHAT DO YOU SEE?

The silhouette stood, hands clasped like a monk, legs bent like a beast.

TELL ME ...

Whole worlds wailed in terror.

The Warrior-Prophet awoke, his skin tingling against a dead woman's cheek ...

More convulsions.

Father! What happens to me?
Pang upon pang, wresting away his face, beating it into a stranger's.
You weep.

———— ❧ ————

The Zaudunyani on the Heights of the Bull immediately recognized him as a friend of the Warrior-Prophet, and Achamian found himself in a bright reception hall blinking at ivory plaques set in glossy black marble. After several moments, an Ainoni caste-noble called Gayamakri—one of the Nascenti, the others said—arrived and escorted him down dark halls. When Achamian asked him about the white-clad warriors he saw posted throughout the palace, the man yammered on about riots and the evil machinations of the Orthodox. But Achamian only had ears for his leaping heart ...

At long last they paused before two grand doors—cherrywood beneath bronze fretting—and Achamian found himself thinking of jokes he could use to make her laugh ...

"From a sorcerer's tent to a caste-noble's suite ... Hmm."

He could almost hear her laughter, almost see her eyes, wanton with love and devilry.

"So what will it be the next time I die? The Andiamine Heights?"

"She likely sleeps," Gayamakri said apologetically. "Things have been especially hard on her."

Jokes ... What could he be thinking? She would need him, fiercely if what Proyas had said was true. Serwë dead and Kellhus dying. The Holy War starving ... She would need him to hold her. How he would hold her!

Without warning Gayamakri whirled, clutched his hands. "Please!" he hissed. "You must save him! You must!" The man fell to his knees, held him with white-knuckled fervour. "You were his teacher!"

"I-I'll do what I can," Achamian stammered. "On that I give you my word."

Tears branched across the man's cheeks into his beard. He pressed his forehead to Achamian's hands. "Thank you! Thank you!"

At a loss for words, Achamian pulled the Nascenti to his feet. The man fussed with his yellow and white robes, pathetically, as though just remembering a lifetime obsession with jnan.

"You'll remember?" he gasped.

"Of course," Achamian replied. "But first I must confer with Esmenet. Alone ... Do you understand?"

Gayamakri nodded. He backed away three steps, then turned and fled down the hall.

He stood before the tall doors, breathing.

Esmi.

He would hold her while she sobbed. He would speak his every thought, tell her what she'd meant to him through his captivity. He would tell her that he, a Mandate Schoolman, would take her as his wife—his wife! And her eyes would weep wonder ... He almost laughed with joy.

At last!

Rather than knocking, he pressed through the doors the way a husband might. Gloom and the scent of vanilla and balsam greeted him. Only six scattered candles illuminated the suite, which was broad with vaulted ceilings and decked with a luxurious array of carpets, screens, and hangings. Set upon a raised dais, a great pentagonal bed dominated the room's heart, its sheets and blankets knotted as though by passion. To the left, the panelled walls opened onto what looked like a private garden. Outside the sky was bright with stars.

A sorcerer's tent indeed!

He stepped from the lane of light thrown by the doors, peering into the suite's deeper reaches. The bed was empty; he could see that through the gauze. The doors rattled shut behind him, giving him a start.

Where was she?

Then his eyes found her on the far side of the room, curled up on a small couch with her back to the doors—to him. Her hair looked longer, almost purple in the gloom. Her loose gown had fallen, revealing a slender shoulder, both brown and pale. His arousal was immediate, both joyous and desperate.

How many times had he kissed that skin?

Kissing. That was how he would awaken her, crying while kissing her naked shoulder. She would stir, think he was a dream. *"No ... It can't be you. You're dead."* Then he would take her, with slow, fierce tenderness, wrack her with voluptuous rapture. And she would know that at long last her heart had returned.

I've come back for you Esmi ... From death and agony.

He descended the landing before the doors, only to halt when she suddenly bolted upright. She looked about in alarm, then stared at him with swollen and incredulous eyes.

For an instant, she seemed a stranger to him; he saw her with the same youthful and ardent eyes that had discovered her in Sumna so many years ago. Coltish beauty. Freckled cheeks. Full lips and perfect teeth.

There was a breathless moment between them.

"*Esmi ...*" he whispered, unable to say anything else. He'd forgotten how beautiful ...

For a heartbeat she radiated abject horror, as though she looked upon a wraith. But then, miraculously it seemed, she flew to him, her small bare feet winglike with desperation.

Then they were together, recklessly clutching one another. She felt so small, so slender in his arms!

"Oh Akka!" she sobbed, "You were dead! *Dead!*"

"No-no-no, my sweet," he murmured, and let loose a shuddering breath.

"Akka, Akka, oh Akka!"

He ran a shaking hand across the back of her head. Her hair felt like silk against his palm, soothing silk. And her smell—incense soft and woman musky. "Shush, Esmi," he whispered. "Everything will be all right. We're together again!" *Please let me kiss you.*

But she cried louder. "You must save him, Achamian! *You must save him!*"

Small confusions, stirring like vermin.

"Save him? Esmi ... What do you mean?" His arms slackened.

She thrust herself from his embrace, stumbled back in terror, as though remembering some horrible truth.

"Kellhus," she said, her lips trembling.

Achamian beat at the whining fear that flared through him. "What do you mean, Esmi?"

He could feel the blood drop from his face.

"Don't you see! They're *killing him!*"

"Kellhus? Yes ... Of course I'll do everything I can to save him! But please, Esmi! Let me hold you! *I need to hold you!*"

"You must save him Achamian! *You can't let them kill him!*"

Flare of dread, undeniable this time. *No. Must be reasonable. She's suffered as much as I have. She's just not as strong.*

"I won't let anyone do anything to him. I swear it. But just … please …"

Esmi … What have you done?

Her face collapsed about some impossible fact. She sobbed. *"He's … H-he's …"*

Curious sensation—as though submerged in water with lungs emptied of air. "Yes, Esmi … He's the Warrior-Prophet. I too believe! I'll do everything I can to save him."

"No, Achamian …"

Her face was now dead, in the way of those who must carve distances, cut wide what was once close.

Don't say it! Please don't say it!

He looked about the extravagant room, gesturing with his hands. He tried to laugh, then said, "S-some sorcerer's tent, eh?" A sob knifed the back of his throat. "Wha-what will it be the next time I die? The Andi … Th-the Andiamine …" He tried to smile.

"Akka," she whispered. "I carry his child."

Whore after all.

Achamian passed between the congregated Inrithi, between the signal fires of the Shrial Knights, little more than a shadow thrown by an otherworldly sun. He remembered the screams and crashing walls of Iothiah. He remembered blasting hallways through stone and burnt brick. Oh, he knew the might of his song, the thunder of his world-breaking voice!

And he knew the bitter rapture of vengeance.

A great tree soared into the night sky, a hoary old eucalyptus, too ancient not to be named. His first thought was to set it alight, to transform it into a blazing beacon of his wrath—a funeral pyre for the betrayer, the seducer! But he could sense the absences that encircled the man, the three Chorae the Men of the Tusk had bound to his bronze ring. And he could see that he suffered …

Achamian crept beneath the tree, onto the mat of fallen leaves. He clutched his knees and rocked to and fro in the darkness. There she was, an impossible fact made flesh.

Serwë dead.

And there he was, hanging with her, limb to limb, breast to breast …

Kellhus … Naked, slowly rolling as though the ring unravelled the long string of his life.

How could such things come to pass?

Achamian ceased rocking and sat still. He listened to the hemp creak in the breeze. He smelled eucalyptus and death. His body calmed, became the cold vessel of his fury and heartbreak.

Beyond the Shrial Knights encircling the tree, thousands packed the surrounding campus, singing hymns and dirges for their Warrior-Prophet. The cry of a flute pierced the din, wandering, trailing, rising in grief-stricken crescendos, calling out the same godless prayer, the howl, almost animal in its intensity …

Achamian hugged himself in the darkness.

How could such things …

Thumb and forefinger pressed hard against his eyes. Shivering. Cold. Heart like rags bundled about cold stone.

He lifted his face, raised chin and brow to his hate. Tears streamed down his cheeks.

"How? How could you betray me like this? You … *You!* The two people—the only two! You kn-knew how empty my life had been. You knew! I c-can't understand … I try and I try but I can't understand! *How could you do this to me!*"

Images boiled through his thoughts … Esmenet gasping beneath the hot plunge of Kellhus's hips. The brushing of breathless lips. Her startled cry. Her climax. The two of them, naked and entwined beneath blankets, staring at the light of a single candle, and Kellhus asking: *"How did you bear that man? How did you ever bring yourself to lie with a sorcerer?"*

"He fed me. He was a warm plump pillow with gold in his pockets … But he wasn't you, my love. No one is you."

His mouth was wrenched open by a soft inarticulate cry … How. Why. Then savagery.

"I could *break* you, Kellhus. See you *burn! Burn* until your eyes burst! *Dog!* Treacherous dog! I'll see you shriek until you gag on your own heart, until your limbs snap for agony! I can *do it!* I can burn *hosts* with my song! I can pack the anguish of a thousand men into your skin! With tongue and teeth, *I can peel you to nothing! Grind your corpse to chalk!"*

He began weeping. The dark world about him buzzed and burned.

"Damn you ..." he gasped. He couldn't breathe ... Where was the air to breathe?

He rolled his head, like a boy whose anger had been stripped hollow by hurt ... He beat an awkward fist against the dead leaves.

"Damn-you-damn-you-damn-you ..."

He looked around numbly, and wiped at his face with a half-hearted sleeve. Sniffled and tasted the salt of tears in the back of his throat ...

"You've made a whore of her, Kellhus ... You've made a whore of my Esmi ..."

They swayed round in shadowy circles. The sound of laughter carried on the night wind. The dark tree seemed to exhale an endless, ambient breath.

"*Achamian* ..." Kellhus whispered.

The words winded him, struck him dumb with horror.

No ... He's not allowed to speak ...

"*He said you would come.*" Spoken from a dead woman's cheek.

Kellhus stared as though from the surface of a coin, his dark eyes glittering, his face pressed against Serwë's, whose head had drawn back in rigor, gaping mouth filled with dusty teeth. For a moment, it seemed that he lay spread-eagle across a mirror, and that Serwë was no more than his reflection.

Achamian shuddered. *What have they done to you?*

Impossibly, the ring had ceased its ponderous revolutions.

"*I see them, Achamian. They walk among us, hidden in ways you cannot see ...*"

The Consult.

His hackles stirred. Cold sweat set his skin afire.

"*The No-God returns, Akka ... I've seen him! He is as you said. Tsurumah. Mog-Pharau ...*"

"Lies!" Achamian cried. "Lies to spare you my wrath!"

"*My Nascenti ... Tell them to show you what lies in the garden.*"

"What? What lies in the garden?"

But the shining eyes were closed.

A grievous howl echoed across the Kalaul, chilling blood and drawing men with torches to the blackness beneath Umiaki. The ring continued its endless roll.

※

Dawn light streamed over the balcony and through the gauze, etching the bedchamber in radiant surfaces and pockets of black shadow. Stirring in his bed, Proyas scowled at the light, raised an arm against it. For several heartbeats, he lay utterly still, trying to swallow away the pain at the back of his throat—the last residue of the hemoplexy. Then the shame and remorse of the previous evening came flooding back.

Achamian and Xinemus had returned. Akka and Zin ... Both of them irrevocably transformed.

Because of me.

A cold morning breeze tossed through the sheers. Proyas huddled, hoarding whatever warmth his blankets offered. He tried to doze, but found himself fencing with worry and dismay instead. In his boyhood, he'd cherished the luxurious laziness of such mornings. He drifted through legends and fancies, dreaming of all the great things he was destined to accomplish. He studied the shadows thrown by the morning sun and wondered at the way they crept across the walls. On cold mornings like this one, he wrapped his blankets about him, savouring them the way the elderly savoured hot baths. The warmth had never stopped short of his bones as it did now.

Some time passed before Proyas realized someone watched him.

At first he simply blinked, too astonished to move or shout. Both the decor and the design of the compound were Nilnameshi. Aside from extravagantly detailed imagery, the chamber possessed low ceilings propped with fat and fluted columns imported, no doubt, from Invishi or Sappathurai. Almost invisible for the morning glare, a figure reclined against one of the columns flanking the balcony ...

Proyas shot forward from the covers.

"Achamian?"

Several heartbeats passed before his eyes adjusted enough to recognize the man.

"What are you doing, Achamian? What do you want?"

"Esmenet," the sorcerer said. "Kellhus has taken her as his wife ... Did you know that?"

Proyas gaped at the Schoolman, robbed of his outrage by something in his voice: a queer kind of drunkenness, a recklessness, but born of loss instead of drink.

"I knew," he admitted, squinting at Achamian's figure. "But I thought that ..." He trailed and swallowed. "Kellhus will soon be dead."

He immediately felt a fool: it sounded like he offered compensation.

"Esmenet is lost to me," Achamian said. The sorcerer's expression was little more than a shadow against the glare, but somehow Proyas could see its exhausted resolve.

"But how could you say that? You don't—"

"Where's Xinemus?" the Schoolman interrupted.

Proyas raised his eyebrows, gestured with a leftward tilt of his head. "One wall over," he said. "The next room."

Achamian pursed his lips. "Did he tell you?"

"About his eyes?" Proyas looked to the outline of his feet beneath the vermilion covers. "No. I hadn't the courage to ask. I assumed that the Spires ..."

"Because of *me*, Proyas. They blinded him as a way to coerce me."

The message was obvious. *It's not your fault*, he was saying.

Proyas raised a hand as though to pinch more sleep from his eyes. He wiped away tears instead.

Damn you, Akka ... I don't need your protection!

"For the Gnosis?" he asked. "Was that what they wanted?"

Krijates Xinemus, a Marshal of Conriya, blinded for blasphemy's sake.

"In part ... They also thought I had information regarding the Cishaurim."

"Cishaurim?"

Achamian snorted. "The Scarlet Spires are terrified, did you know that? Terrified of what they cannot see."

"It stands to reason: all they do is hide. Eleäzaras still refuses to take the field, even though I'm told they've begun boiling their books out of hunger."

"I doubt they stray far from their latrines," Achamian said, the old twinkle surfacing through the exhaustion of his voice, "the rot they read."

Proyas laughed, and an almost forgotten sense of comfort stole over him. This, he realized, was how they'd once talked, their cares and worries directed outward rather than at each other. But instead of taking heart at the realization, Proyas suffered only more dismay, understanding that what trust and camaraderie had once given them, only dread and exhaustion could now deliver.

A long silence passed between them, fuelled by the sudden collapse of their good humour. Proyas found his gaze wandering to the trains of priapic revellers, brown-skinned and half-nude, that marched across the painted walls, their arms filled with various bounty. With every passing heartbeat it seemed the silence buzzed louder.

Then Achamian said, "Kellhus cannot die."

Proyas pursed his lips. "But of course," he said numbly. "I say he must die, so *you* say he must live." He glanced, not without nervousness, at his nearby work table. The parchment sat in plain view, its raised corners translucent in the sun: Maithanet's letter.

"This has nothing to do with you, Proyas. I am past you."

The tone as much as the words chilled Proyas to the pith.

"Then why are you here?"

"Because of all the Great Names, only you can understand."

"Understand," Proyas repeated, feeling the old impatience rekindle in his heart. "Understand what? No, let me guess ... Only I can understand the significance of the name 'Anasûrimbor.' Only I can understand the peril—"

"Enough!" Achamian shouted. "Can't you see that when you make light of these matters you *make light of me*? When have I ever scoffed at the Tusk? When have I ever mocked the Latter Prophet? When?"

Proyas caught his retort, which had been all the harsher for the truth of what Achamian said.

"Kellhus," he said, "has already been judged."

"Have care, Proyas. Remember King Shikol."

For the Inrithi, the name "Shikol," the Xerashi King who had condemned Inri Sejenus, was synonymous with hatred and tragic presumption. The thought that his own name might someday possess the same poison caused Proyas no small terror.

"Shikol was wrong ... I am right!"

It all came down to Truth.

"I wonder," Achamian said, "what Shikol would say ..."

"What?" Proyas exclaimed. "So the great sceptic thinks a new prophet walks among us? Come, Akka ... It's too absurd!"

These are Conphas's words ... Another unkind thought.

Achamian paused, but whether out of care or hesitation Proyas couldn't tell.

"I'm not sure what he is ... All I know is that he's too important to die."

Sitting rigid in his bed, Proyas peered against the sun, struggling to see his old teacher. Aside from his outline against the blue pillar, the most he could discern were the five lines of white that streaked the black of his beard. Proyas sighed loudly through his nostrils, looked down to his thumbs.

"I thought much the same not so long ago," he admitted. "I worried that what Conphas and the others said was true, that he was the reason the anger of the God burned against us. But I'd shared too many cups with the man not to ... not to realize he's more than simply remarkable ...

"But then ..."

From nowhere, it seemed, a great cloud crawled before the sun, and a dim chill fell across the room. For the first time, Proyas could see his old teacher clearly: the haggard face, the forlorn eyes and meditative brow, the blue smock and woollen travel robes, soiled black about the knees ...

So poor. Why did Achamian always look so poor?

"Then what?" the Schoolman asked, apparently unconcerned with his sudden visibility.

Proyas heaved another sigh, glanced once again at the parchment upon his table. Distant thunder rumbled in on the wind, which whisked through the black cedars below.

"Well," he continued, "first there was the Scylvendi ... His hatred of Kellhus. I thought to myself, 'How could this man, this man who knows Kellhus better than any other, despise him so?'"

"Serwë," Achamian said. "Kellhus once told me the barbarian loved Serwë."

"Cnaiür said much the same when I first asked him ... But there was something, something about his manner, that made me think there was more. He's such a fierce and melancholy man. And complicated—very complicated."

"His skin is too thin," Achamian said. "But I suppose it scars well."

A sour smirk was the most Proyas could afford. "There's more to Cnaiür urs Skiötha than you know, Akka. Mark me. In some ways, he's as extraordinary as Kellhus. Be thankful he's our pet, and not the Padirajah's."

"Your point, Proyas?"

The Conriyan Prince frowned. "The point is that I questioned him about Kellhus again, shortly after we found ourselves besieged ..."

"And?"

"And he told me to go ask Kellhus himself. That was when ..." He hesitated, groping in vain for some delicate way to continue. More thunder piled through the balcony doorways.

"That was when I found Esmenet in his bed."

Achamian closed his eyes for a moment. When he opened them, his gaze was steady.

"And your misgivings became genuine doubts ... I'm touched."

Proyas chose to ignore the sarcasm.

"After that, I no longer dismissed Conphas's arguments out of hand. I mulled things over for a time, at once anguished by all that happened—that happens still!—and terrified that if I sided with Conphas and the others, I would be striking sparks over tinder."

"You feared war between the Orthodox and the Zaudunyani."

"And I fear it still!" Proyas fairly cried. "Though it scarcely seems to matter with the Padirajah waiting with his desert wolves."

How could it all come to this? Such a pass!

"So what decided you?"

"The Scylvendi," Proyas said with a shrug. "Conphas brought forward witnesses who claimed to know a man from the northern caravans, a man who, before he died in the desert, claimed that Atrithau had no princes."

"Hearsay," Achamian said. "Worthless ... You know that. It was probably a ploy on Conphas's part. Dead men have a habit of telling the most convenient tales."

"Which is what I thought, until the Scylvendi confirmed the story."

Achamian leaned forward, his brow knotted in angry shock. "Confirmed? What do you mean?"

"He called Kellhus a prince of nothing."

The Schoolman sat rigid for a time, his eyes lost in the space between them. He knew the penalties for transgressing caste. All men did. The caste-nobles of the Three Seas cherished their ancestor scrolls for more than spiritual or sentimental reasons.

"He could be lying," Achamian mused. "As a way to regain possession of Serwë, maybe?"

"He could be ... Given the way he reacted to her execution—"

"Serwë executed!" the sorcerer exclaimed. "How could such a thing happen? Proyas? How could you *let* such a thing happen? She was just—"

"Ask Gotian!" Proyas blurted. "Trying them according to the Tusk was his idea—his! He thought it would legitimize the affair, make it seem less like ... less—"

"Like what it was?" Achamian cried. "A conspiracy of frightened caste-nobles trying to protect their power and privilege?"

"That depends," Proyas replied stiffly, "on whom you ask ... Either way, we needed to forestall war. And so far—"

"Heaven forfend," Achamian snapped, "that men murder men for faith."

"And heaven forfend that fools perish for their folly. And heaven forfend that mothers miscarry, that children put out their eyes. Heaven forfend that anything horrible happen! I couldn't agree with you more, Akka ..." He smiled sarcastically. To think he'd almost missed the blasphemous old bastard!

"But back to the point. I did not condemn Kellhus out of hand, old tutor. Many things—many!—compelled me to vote with the others. Prophet or not, Anasûrimbor Kellhus is dead."

Achamian had been watching him, his face emptied of expression. "Who said he was a prophet?"

"Enough, Akka, please ... You just said he was too important to die."

"He is, Proyas! *He is!* He's our only hope!"

Proyas rubbed more sleep from the corner of his eyes. He let go a long, exasperated breath.

"So? The Second Apocalypse, is it? Is Kellhus the second coming of Seswatha?" He shook his head. "Please ... Please tell—"

"He's more!" the Schoolman cried with alarming passion. "Far more than Seswatha, as he must be ... The Heron Spear is lost, destroyed when the Scylvendi sacked ancient Cenei. If the Consult were to succeed a second time, if the No-God were to walk again ..." Achamian stared, his eyes rounded in horror.

"Men would have no hope."

Proyas had endured many of these small rants since his childhood. What made them so uncanny, and at the same time so intolerable, was the way Achamian spoke: as though he recounted rather than conjectured. Just then the morning sun flashed anew between a crease in the accumulating clouds. The thunder, however, continued to rumble across wretched Caraskand.

"Akka ..."

The Schoolman silenced him with an outstretched hand. "You once asked me, Proyas, whether I had more than Dreams to warrant my fears. Do you remember?"

All too well. It was the same night Achamian had asked him to write to Maithanet.

"I remember, yes."

Without warning, Achamian stood and stepped out onto the balcony. He vanished into the morning glare only to reappear moments afterward, hoisting something dark in his hands.

By some coincidence, the sun vanished the moment Proyas reached out to shield his eyes.

He stared at the soil- and blood-stained bundle. A pungent odour slowly filled the room.

"Look at it!" Achamian commanded, brandishing it. "Look! Then send your quickest riders out to the Great Names!"

Proyas recoiled, clutched at the covers about his knees. Suddenly he realized what it seemed he'd known all along: Achamian wouldn't relent. And of course not: he was a Mandate Schoolman.

Maithanet ... Most Holy Shriah. Is this what you would have me do? Is it? Certainty in doubt. That was what was holy! That!

"Save your warrant for the others," Proyas muttered. With a flourish he kicked free the sheets and strode naked to the nearby table. The floor was cold enough to ache. Shivers chattered across his skin.

He snatched Maithanet's missive, held it out to the scowling sorcerer.

"Read it," he murmured. Lightning threaded the sky beyond the ruined Citadel of the Dog.

Achamian set down his reeking bundle, grasped the parchment, scanned it. Proyas noticed the black crescents under his fingernails. Instead of looking up in stunned shock as Proyas had expected, the sorcerer frowned and squinted at the sheet. He even held it to what light remained. The room trembled to the crack of thunder.

"Maithanet?" the sorcerer asked, his eyes still rivetted to the Shriah's flawless script. Proyas knew the line he pondered. The impossible always left the deepest marks on the soul.

Assist Drusas Achamian, though he is a blasphemer, for in this wickedness, the Holy shall also follow ...

Achamian set the sheet upon his lap, though he still pinched the corner with his thumb and forefinger. The two men shared a thoughtful gaze ... Confusion and relief warred in his old teacher's eyes.

"Aside from my sword, my harness, and my ancestors," Proyas said, "that letter is the only thing I brought across the desert. The only thing I saved."

"Call them," Achamian said. "Summon the others to Council."

Gone was the golden morning. Rain poured from black skies.

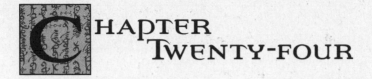

Chapter Twenty-four

CARASKAND

They strike down the weak and call it justice. They ungird their loins and call it reparation. They bark like dogs and call it reason.

—ONTILLAS, *ON THE FOLLY OF MEN*

Late Winter, 4112 Year-of-the-Tusk, Caraskand

Rain fell in windswept skirts of grey. It sizzled across the rooftops and the streets. It gurgled through the gutters, rinsing away flakes of dried blood. It pattered against the still-skinned skulls of the dead. It both kissed the uppermost twigs of ancient Umiaki and plummeted through his darkest hollows. A million beads of water. Converging at the forks between branches, twining into strings, threading the darkness with lines of glittering white. Soon rivulets spiralled down the hemp rope and dropped like marbles along the bronze ring, whence they branched across skin, both living and dead.

Across the Kalaul, thousands ran for cover, shielding themselves with wool cloaks and mantles. Others wailed, held out their hands, beseeching, wondering what the rains omened. The lightning blinded them. The waters bit their cheeks. And the thunder muttered secrets they could not fathom.

They held out their hands, beseeching.

His sleep was fitful, haunted by dreams of Dûnyain words and Dûnyain deeds. *You*, the abomination said, *still command the ears of the Great*. Serwë slumped in Sarcellus's arms, showering blood. *Remember the secret of battle — remember!*

Cnaiür woke to rain and whispers.

The secret of battle ...

The ears of the Great.

Not finding Proyas at his compound, he rode with all due haste to the Sapatishah's Palace on the Kneeling Heights, where the Prince's terrified steward had said he could be found. The rain had started to trail by the time he reached the first echelons of residences about the base of the heights. Momentary sunlight cast fingers of brilliance across the otherwise dark city. As he urged his famished mount upward, Cnaiür cast a look over his shoulder, saw the sun battle through clouds of mountainous black. From height to height, across the confusion of the Bowl all the way to the dark and hazy line of the Triamic Walls, pools of rainwater flashed white, like a thousand coins of silver.

He dismounted in the anarchy of the palace's outer campus. Every heartbeat, it seemed, saw another band of armed riders clack through the gates. With the exception of the Galeoth guardsmen and several near-skeletal Kianene slaves, everyone carried either the mark or the air of caste-nobility. Cnaiür recognized many from previous Councils, though for some reason, none dared to hail him. He followed the Inrithi into the shadows of the Entry Hall, where he fairly collided with a crimson-clad Gaidekki.

The Palatine halted, stared at him agog.

"Sweet Sejenus!" he exclaimed. "Are you well? Was there more fighting on the walls?"

Cnaiür looked down to his chest: red had soaked the white of his tunic almost to his iron-plated girdle.

"Your throat's been cut!" Gaidekki said wondrously.

"Where's Proyas?" Cnaiür snapped.

"With the other dead," the Palatine said darkly, gesturing to the files of men disappearing into the palace's frescoed inner sanctums.

Cnaiür found himself following a band of wild-tempered Thunyeri led by Yalgrota Sranchammer, his flaxen braids adorned with iron nails bent like tusks and the shrunken heads of heathen. At one point, the giant jerked his head about and glared at him. Cnaiür matched his gaze, his soul boiling with thoughts of murder.

"*Ushurrutga!*" the man snorted and turned away, smiling at the guttural laughter of his compatriots.

Cnaiür spat on the walls, then stared wildly about. Wherever he looked, it seemed, he saw men glance away.

All of them! All of them!

Somewhere, he could hear the tribesmen of the Utemot whisper ...

Weeper ...

The vaulted corridor ended in bronze doors, which had been propped open with two busts kicked face down onto the carpets. Old Sapatishahs carved in diorite, Cnaiür imagined, or relics of the Nansur occupation. Through the doors, he found himself in a great chamber, shouldering his way through a crowd of milling caste-nobles. The air hummed with reverberating voices.

Faggot weeper!

The room was circular, and far more ancient in construction than the greater palace—Kyranean or Shigeki, perhaps. A table carved of what looked like white gypsum dominated the central floor, which was covered by a magnificent rug of copper and gold embroidery. Just beyond the rug's outer fringe, a series of concentric tiers rose in the fashion of amphitheatres, providing an unobstructed view of the table below. Constructed of monumental blocks, the encircling wall soared above the back tier, set with sconces and adorned with the distinctive, streamer-like tapestries favoured by the Kianene. A pointed dome of corbelled stone loomed overhead, hanging, it seemed, without the luxury of mortar or vaults. A series of wells about its base provided light, diffuse and white, while high above the central table heathen banners swayed in unseen drafts.

Cnaiür found Proyas standing near the table, his head bent in concentration as he listened to a stocky man in blue and grey. The man's robes were soiled about the knees, and compared with the rakish frames of those about him, he looked almost obscenely fat. Someone shouted from the tiers, and the man turned to the sound, revealing the five white lines that marred his unplaited beard. Cnaiür stared incredulously.

It was the sorcerer. The dead sorcerer ...

What happened here?

"Proyas!" he shouted, for some reason loath to come any closer. "We must speak!"

The Conriyan Prince looked about, and upon locating him, scowled much as Gaidekki had. The sorcerer, however, continued speaking, and Cnaiür found himself waved away with a harried gesture.

"Proyas!" he barked, but the Prince spared him only a furious glance.

Fool! Cnaiür thought. The siege could be broken! He knew what they must do!

The secret of battle. He remembered ...

He found a spot on the tiers with the other Lesser Names and their retinues, and watched the Great Names settle into their usual bickering. The hunger in Caraskand had reached such straits that even the great among the Inrithi had been reduced to eating rats and drinking the blood of their horses. The leaders of the Holy War had grown hollow-cheeked and gaunt, and the hauberks of many, particularly those who'd been fat, hung loosely from their frames, so they resembled juveniles playing in their father's armour. They looked at once foolish and tragic, possessed of the shambling pageantry of dying rulers.

As Caraskand's titular king, Saubon sat in a large black-lacquered seat at the head of the table. He leaned forward, gripping the arms of his chair, as though preparing to exercise a pre-eminence no one else recognized. To his right reclined Conphas, who looked about with the lolling impatience of someone forced to treat lessers as equals. To his left sat Prince Skaiyelt's surviving brother, Hulwarga the Limper, who'd represented Thunyerus ever since Skaiyelt had succumbed to the hemoplexy. Next to Hulwarga sat Gothyelk, the grizzled Earl of Agansanor, his wiry beard as unkempt as usual, his combative look more menacing. To his left sat Proyas, his manner both wary and thoughtful. Though he spoke to the sorcerer, who sat on a smaller seat immediately next to him, his eyes continued to search the faces of those about the table. And lastly, positioned between Proyas and Conphas, sat the decorous Palatine of

Antanamera, Chinjosa, whom according to rumour the Scarlet Spires had installed as interim King-Regent in the wake of Chepheramunni's demise—also to the hemoplexy.

"Where's Gotian?" Proyas demanded of the others.

"Perhaps," Ikurei Conphas said with droll sarcasm, "the Grandmaster learned it was a *sorcerer* you'd summoned us to hear. Shrial Knights, I fear, tend to be rather *Shrial* ..."

Proyas called out to Sarcellus, who sat on the lowest tier, clad ankle to wrist in the white Shrial vestments he typically wore to Council. Bowing low to the Great Names, the Knight-Commander professed ignorance as to his Grandmaster's whereabouts. Cnaiür looked down at his right forearm while he spoke, not so much listening to as memorizing the hateful timbre of the man's voice. He watched the veins and scars ripple as he clenched and unclenched his fist.

When he blinked, he saw the knife gashing Serwë's throat, the shining, spilling red ...

Cnaiür scarcely heard the procedural arguments that followed: something regarding the legalities of continuing without the Holy Shriah's representative. Instead, he watched Sarcellus. Ignoring the Great Names and their debate, the dog was engrossed in counsel with some other Shrial Knight. The spidery network of red lines still marred his sensuous face, though much fainter than when Cnaiür had last seen the man with Proyas and Conphas. His expression appeared calm, but his large brown eyes seemed troubled and distant, as though he pondered matters that rendered this spectacle irrelevant.

What was it the Dûnyain had said?

Lie made flesh.

Cnaiür was hungry, very hungry—he hadn't eaten a true meal for several days now—and the gnawing in his belly lent a curious edge to everything he witnessed, as though his soul no longer had the luxury of fat thoughts and fat impressions. The taste of his horse's blood was fresh upon his lips. For a mad moment, he found himself wondering what Sarcellus's blood would taste like. Would it taste like lies?

Did lies have a taste?

Everything since Serwë's murder seemed unclear, and no matter how hard Cnaiür tried, he could not separate his days from his nights.

Everything overflowed, spilled into everything else. Everything had been fouled—fouled! And the Dûnyain wouldn't shut up!

And then this morning, for no reason whatsoever, he'd simply understood. He'd remembered the secret of battle … *I told him! I showed him the secret!*

And the cryptic words that Kellhus had spoken on the ruined heights of the Citadel became plain as lead.

The hunt need not end!

He understood the Dûnyain's plan—or part of it … If only Proyas would have listened!

Suddenly the shouting about the table trailed, as did the rumbling along the tiers. An astonished hush fell across the ancient chamber, and Cnaiür saw the sorcerer, Achamian, standing at Proyas's side, glaring at the others with the grim fearlessness of an exhausted man.

"Since my presence so offends you," he said in a loud clear voice, "I will not mince words. You have all made a ghastly mistake, a mistake which *must* be undone, for the sake of the Holy War, and for the sake of the World." He paused to appraise their scowling faces. "You must free Anasûrimbor Kellhus."

Cries of outrage and reproach exploded from those about the table and those along the tiers alike. Cnaiür watched, rivetted to his seat, to his martial posture. He did not, it seemed, need to speak to Proyas after all.

"*LISTEN to him!*" the Conriyan Prince screeched over the warring voices. Astonished by the savagery of this outburst, the entire room seemed to catch its breath. But Cnaiür was already breathless.

He seeks to free him!

But did this mean they also knew the Dûnyain's plan?

In the Councils of the Holy War, Proyas had always played the sober foil for the excessive passions of the other Great Names. To hear the man scream in this way was a dismaying thing. The other Great Names fell silent, like children chastised not by their father but by what they'd made their father do.

"This is no travesty," Proyas continued. "This is no joke meant to gall or offend. More, far more, than our lives depend on what decision we make here today. I ask you to decide with me, as does any man with arguments to make. But I demand—*I demand!*—that you listen before making that decision! And this demand, I think, is no real demand at all, since listening without bias, without bigotry, is simply what all wise men do."

Cnaiür glanced across the chamber, noted that Sarcellus watched the drama as intently as any of the others. He even angrily waved at his retinue to fall silent.

Standing before the great Inrithi lords, the sorcerer looked haggard and impoverished in his soiled gear, and he appeared hesitant, as though only now realizing how far he'd strayed from his element. But with his girth and unbroken health, he looked a king in the trappings of a beggar. The Men of the Tusk, on the other hand, looked like wraiths decked in the trappings of kings.

"You've asked," Achamian called out, "why the God punishes the Holy War. What cancer pollutes us? What disease of spirit has stirred the God's wrath against us? But there are many cancers. For the faithful, Schoolmen such as myself are one such cancer. But the Shriah himself has sanctioned our presence among you. So you looked elsewhere, and found the man many call the 'Warrior-Prophet,' and you asked yourself, 'What if this man is false? Would that not be enough for the God's anger to burn against us? A False Prophet?'" He paused, and Cnaiür could see that he swallowed behind pursed lips. "I haven't come to tell you whether Prince Kellhus is truly a Prophet, nor even whether he's a prince of anything at all. I've come, rather, to warn you of a different cancer ... One that you've overlooked, though indeed some of you know of its presence. There are spies among us, my lords ..."—a collective murmur momentarily filled the chamber—"abominations that wear false faces of skin."

The sorcerer bent beneath the table, hoisted a fouled sack of some kind. In a single motion, he unfurled it across the table. Something like silvery eels about a blackened cabbage rolled onto the polished surface, came to rest against an impossible reflection. A severed head?

Lie made flesh ...

A cacophony of exclamations reverberated beneath the chamber's dome.

"—*Deceit! Blasphemous deceit!*—"

"—*is madness! We cannot*—"

"—*but what could it*—"

Surrounded by astonished cries and brandished fists, Cnaiür watched Sarcellus stand, then press his way through the clamour toward the exit. Once again, Cnaiür glimpsed the inflamed lines that marred the Knight-Commander's face ... Suddenly he realized he'd seen the pattern before ... But where? Where?

Anwurat ... Serwë bloodied and screaming. Kellhus naked, his groin smeared red, his face jerking open like fingers about a coal ... A Kellhus who was not Kellhus.

Overcome by a trembling, wolfish hunger, Cnaiür stood and hurried to follow. At last he fathomed everything the Dûnyain had said to him the day he was denounced by the Great Names—the day of Serwë's death. The memory of Kellhus's voice pierced the thunder of the assembled Inrithi ...

Lie made flesh.

A name.

Sarcellus's name.

———— ✦ ————

Sinerses fell to his knees just beyond the raised threshold of the entryway, then pressed his head to the faux-carpet carved into the stone. The Kianene, like most other peoples, considered certain thresholds sacred, but rather than anoint them on the appropriate days as did the Ainoni, they adorned them with elaborately carved renditions of reed-woven rugs. It was, Hanamanu Eleäzaras had decided, a worthy custom. The passage from place to place, he thought, should be marked in stone. Notice needed to be served.

"Grandmaster!" Sinerses gasped, throwing back his head. "I bear word from Lord Chinjosa!"

Eleäzaras had expected the man, but not his agitation. His skin crawling, he looked to his secretaries and ordered them from the room with a vague wave. Like most men of power in Caraskand, Eleäzaras had found himself very interested in the specifics of his dwindling supplies.

Everything it seemed, had conspired against him these past months. Caraskand's slow starvation had reached such a pitch that even sorcerers of rank went hungry—the most desperate had started boiling the leather binding and vellum pages of those texts that had survived the desert. The most glorious School in the Three Seas had been reduced to eating their books! The Scarlet Spires suffered with the rest of the Holy War, so much so that they now discussed meeting with the Great Names and declaring that henceforth the Scarlet Spires would war openly with the Inrithi—something that had been unthinkable mere weeks ago.

Wagers beget wagers, each typically more desperate than the last. In order to preserve his first wager, Eleäzaras now must make a second, one that would expose the Scarlet Spires to the deadly Trinkets of the Padirajah's Thesji Bowmen, who'd so decimated the Imperial Saik, the Emperor's own School, during the Jihads. And this, he knew, could very well weaken the Scarlet Spires beyond any hope of overcoming the Cishaurim.

Chorae! Accursed things. The Tears of the God cared nothing for those who brandished them, Inrithi or Fanim, so long as they weren't sorcerers. Apparently one didn't need to interpret the God correctly to wield Him.

Wager upon wager. Desperation upon desperation. The situation had become so dire, things had been stretched so tight, that any news, Eleäzaras realized, could break the back of his School. The more pinched the note, the more the string could snap.

Even the words of this slave-soldier kneeling at his feet could signal their doom.

Eleäzaras fought for his breath. "What have you learned, Captain?"

"Proyas has brought the Mandate Schoolman to the Council," the man said.

Eleäzaras felt his skin pimple. Ever since hearing of their mission's destruction in Iothiah, he'd found himself dreading the Mandati's return ...

"You mean Drusas Achamian?"

He's come to exact vengeance.

"Yes, Grandmaster. He's—"

"Has he come alone? Are there *any others*?" *Please, please ...* Achamian on his own, they could easily manage. A corps of Mandate sorcerers, however, could prove ruinous. Too many had died already.

No more! We can afford to lose no more!

"No. He seems to be alone, but—"

"Does he bring charges against us? Does he malign our exalted School?"

"He speaks of skin-spies, Grandmaster! *Skin-spies!*"

Eleäzaras stared uncomprehending.

"He says they walk among us," Sinerses continued. "He says they're *everywhere!* He even brought one of their heads in a sack—so hideous, Master! That such a thing—but-but I forget myself! Lord Chinjosa himself sent me ... He seeks instruction. The Mandate sorcerer is demanding the Great Names free the Warrior-Prophet ..."

Prince Kellhus? Eleäzaras blinked, still struggling to make sense of the man's blather ...

Yes! Yes! His friend! They were friends before ... The Mandate fiend was his teacher.

"Free?" Eleäzaras managed to say with some semblance of reserve. "Wh-what are his grounds?"

Sinerses's eyes bulged from his half-starved face. "The *skin-spies* ... He claims this Warrior-Prophet is the only one who can see them."

The Warrior-Prophet. Since marching from the desert, they'd watched the man with growing trepidation—especially when it became apparent how many of their Javreh were secretly taking the Whelming and becoming Zaudunyani. When Ikurei Conphas had come to him promising to destroy the man, Eleäzaras had commanded Chinjosa to support the Exalt-General in all ways. Though he still fretted over the possibility of war between the Orthodox and the Zaudunyani, he'd thought the matter of Anasûrimbor Kellhus's fate, at least, had been sealed.

"What do you mean?"

"He argues that since only this Prophet can see them, he must be released so that the Holy War might be cleansed. Only this way, he claims, will the God turn his anger from us."

As an old master at jnan, Eleäzaras was loath to allow his true passions to surface in the presence of his slaves, but these past days ... had been very hard. The face he showed Sinerses was bewildered—he seemed an old man who'd grown very afraid of the world.

"Muster as many men as you can," he said distantly. "*Immediately!*"

Sinerses fled.

Spies ... Everywhere spies! And if he couldn't find them ... If he couldn't find them ...

The Grandmaster of the Scarlet Spires would speak to this Warrior-Prophet—to this holy man who could see what was hidden in their midst. Throughout his life, Eleäzaras, a sorcerer who could peer into the world's smokiest recesses, had wondered what it was the Holy thought they saw. Now he knew.

Malice.

———————— ⬡ ————————

It hungered, the thing called Sarcellus. For blood. For fucking things living and dead. But more than anything it hungered for consummation. All of it, from its anus to the sham it called its soul, was bent to the ends of its creators. Everything was twisted to the promise of climax, to the jet of hot salt.

But the Architects had been shrewd, so heartlessly astute, when they laid its foundations. So few things—the rarest of circumstances!—could deliver that release. Killing the woman, the Dûnyain's wife, had been such a moment. The mere recollection was enough to make its phallus arch against its breeches, gasp like a fish …

And now that the Mandate sorcerer—accursed Chigra!—had returned seeking to deliver the Dûnyain … The promise! The fury! It had known instantly what it must do. As it strode from the Sapatishah's Palace, the air swam with its yearning, the sun shimmered with its hate.

Although subtle beyond reason, the thing called Sarcellus walked a far simpler world than that walked by men. There was no war of competing passions, no need for discipline or denial. It lusted only to execute the will of its authors. In appeasing its hunger, it appeased the good.

So it had been forged. Such was the cunning of its manufacture.

The Warrior-Prophet must die. There were no interfering passions, no fear, no remorse, no competing lusts. It would kill Anasûrimbor Kellhus before he could be saved, and in so doing …

Find ecstasy.

———————— ⬡ ————————

Cnaiür need only see the route Sarcellus took down the Kneeling Heights to know where the dog was headed. The man rode into the Bowl, which meant he rode to the temple-complex where Gotian and the Shrial

Knights were stationed—and where the Dûnyain and Serwë hung from black-limbed Umiaki.

Cnaiür spat, then hollered for his horse.

By the time he clattered free of the outer campus, he could no longer find the man. He barrelled downward, through the welter of structures that crowded the slopes below the Sapatishah's Palace. Despite his mount's perilous condition, he whipped it to a gallop. They raced past spiked garden walls, along abandoned shop fronts, and beneath looming tenements, turned only where the streets seemed to descend. Csokis, he remembered, lay near the bottom of the Bowl.

The very air seemed to buzz with omens.

Over and over, like a shard of glass in his stomach, images of Kellhus cycled through his thoughts. It seemed he could feel the man's hand clamped about his neck, holding him, impossibly, over the precipice in the Hethanta Mountains. For a panicked moment, he even found it difficult to breathe, to swallow. The sensation passed only when he ran his fingertips along the clotted gash about his throat—his most recent swazond.

How? How can he afflict me so?

But then that was Moënghus's lesson. The Dûnyain made disciples of all men, whether they revered him or no. One need only breathe.

Even my hate! Cnaiür thought. *Even my hate he uses to his advantage!*

Though his heart rankled at this, it rankled far more at the thought of losing Moënghus. Kellhus had spoken true those long months past in the Utemot camp: his heart had only one quarry, and it could not be fed on surrogates. He was bound to the Dûnyain as the Dûnyain was bound to Serwë's corpse—bound by the cutting ropes of an unconquerable hate.

Any shame. Any indignity. He would bear any injury, commit any atrocity, to whet his vengeance. He would see the whole world burn before he would surrender his hate. Hate! That was the obsessive heart of his strength. Not his blade. Not his frame. His neck-breaking, wife-striking, shield-cracking hate! Hatred had secured him the White Yaksh. Hatred had banded his body with the Holy Scars. Hatred had preserved him from the Dûnyain when they crossed the Steppe. Hatred had inured him to the claims these outlanders made on his heart.

Hatred, and hatred alone, had kept him sane.

Of course the Dûnyain had known this.

After Moënghus, Cnaiür had fled to the codes of the People, thinking they could preserve his heart. Having been cheated of them, they'd seemed all the more precious, akin to water in times of great thirst. For years he'd whipped himself down the tracks followed by his tribesmen—whipped himself bloody! To be a man, the memorialists said, was to take and not to be taken, to enslave and not to be enslaved. So he would be first among warriors, the most violent of all men! For this was the most paramount of the Unwritten Laws: a man—a true man!—conquered, and did not suffer himself to be used.

Hence the torment of his pact with Kellhus. All this time Cnaiür had jealously guarded his heart and soul, spitting upon the fiend's every word, never thinking that the man could rule him by manipulating the circumstances *about him*. The Dûnyain had unmanned him no differently than he had these Inrithi fools.

Moënghus! He named him Moënghus! My son!

What better way to gall him? What better way to gull? He had been used. Even now, thinking these very thoughts, the Dûnyain used him!

But it did not matter ...

There were no codes. There was no honour. The world between men was as trackless as the Steppe—as the desert! There were no *men* ... Only beasts, clawing, craving, mewling, braying. Gnawing at the world with their hungers. Beaten like bears into dancing to this absurd custom or that. All these thousands, these Men of the Tusk, killed and died in the name of delusion. Save hunger, nothing commanded the world.

This was the secret of the Dûnyain. This was their monstrosity. This was their fascination.

Ever since Moënghus had abandoned him, Cnaiür had thought *himself* the traitor. Always one thought too many, always one lust, one hunger! But now he knew that the treachery dwelt in the chorus of condemning voices, the recriminations that howled out from nowhere, calling him names, such hateful names!

She was my proof!

Liars! Fools! He would make them see!

Any shame. Any indignity. He would strangle infants in their cribs. He would kneel beneath the fall of hot seed. He would see his hate through!

There was no honour. Only wrath and destruction.

Only hate.

The hunt need not end!

The abandoned tenements fell away, and Cnaiür found himself galloping across one of Caraskand's bazaars. Corpses, little more than sodden bundles of skin, bone, and fabric, flashed beneath. Halfway across the grim expanse, he spied the obelisks of Csokis rising above a low scarp of buildings. After passing through a complex of several mud-brick storehouses, decrepit to the point of collapse, he found an avenue he recognized and whipped his horse along a row of what looked like fire-gutted residences. After a sharp right, his mount was forced by momentum to leap an overturned piss basin, a great stone bowl that must have belonged to a nearby launderer. He felt before he heard his Eumarnan white throw a shoe. The horse screamed, faltered, then limped to a halt—apparently lamed.

Cursing the thing, he leapt to the ground and began sprinting, knowing there was no way for him to overtake the Knight-Commander now. Beyond the first turn, however, the white Kalaul miraculously yawned wide before him, criss-crossed by the water-soaked joints between paving stones and darkened by crowds of starving thousands.

At first, he didn't know whether he should be dismayed or heartened by the sight of so many Inrithi. Most of them, he imagined, would be Zaudunyani, which might prevent Sarcellus from killing the Dûnyain outright—if that was what the man in fact intended to do. Thrusting his way between startled onlookers, Cnaiür gazed across the crowds, searching in vain for the Shrial Knight. He saw the tree, Umiaki, in the distance, dark and hunched against a hazy band of colonnades and temple facades. The sudden certainty that the Dûnyain was dead struck him breathless.

It's over.

It seemed he'd never suffered such a harrowing thought. He frantically peered across the distances. The unobscured sun was boiling steam from the damp masses. He looked to the men crowding about him, and felt a sudden, dizzying relief. Many chanted or sang. Others simply looked to the branches reaching skyward. All seemed anxious with hunger, but nothing more.

He lives still, or there would be a riot …

Cnaiür barged his way forward, was shocked to find the half-starved Inrithi scrambling from his path. He heard voices cry out *"Scylvendi!"* not in salute as they had at Anwurat, but as a curse or a prayer. Soon a great train of men followed him, some jeering, others crying out in exultation. Every face, it seemed, turned to his passage. A broad lane opened before him, reaching nearly all the way to the black tree.

"Scylvendi!" the Men of the Tusk shouted. *"Scylvendi!"*

As before, Shrial Knights guarded the tree, only now arrayed in ranks some three or four men deep—a battle line, in effect. Mounted patrols waded through the near distance. Alone among the Inrithi, the Knights of the Tusk had refused to don Kianene garments, so they looked thread-bare in their tattered gold and white surcoats. Their helms and chainmail, however, still gleamed in the sunlight.

As he approached them, Cnaiür spied Sarcellus standing with Gotian amid a clot of other Shrial officers. The forward Shrial Knights recognized him, and granted him a wide if suspicious berth as he strode toward Sarcellus and the Grandmaster. The two men seemed to be arguing. Umiaki reared behind them, branching dark across sea-blue skies. Glancing across the great mat of leaves, Cnaiür glimpsed the ring hanging beneath Umiaki's chapped bowers. He saw Serwë and the Dûnyain slowly spinning, like two sides of a coin.

How can she be dead?

"Because of you," the Dûnyain whispered. *"Weeper …"*

"But why this moment?" Cnaiür heard the Grandmaster cry over the growing thunder of the masses.

"Because!" Cnaiür boomed in his mightiest battlefield voice. "He bears a grudge no man can fathom!"

Despite the added censers the Great Names had summoned, Achamian found himself gagging at the stench of the thing. He explained how the limbs folded into a sheath, even propping the rotted head to demonstrate the way two limbs fit about a viscous eye socket. Save the odd exclamation of disgust, the assembled caste-nobles watched in mute horror. At some point, a slave had offered him an orange-scented kerchief. When he could tolerate no more, he pressed it to his face, and gestured for the hideous thing's removal.

For several moments, astonished silence ruled the ancient council chamber. The censers hissed and steamed, fogging the nightmarish air. Smeared across the table, the thing's residue, which resembled black mould, continued to reek.

"So this," Conphas finally said, "is the reason we must free the Deceiver?"

Achamian stared at the man, sensing some kind of verbal trap. He'd known from the start that Conphas would be his primary adversary. Proyas had warned him, saying he'd never encountered anyone as formidable in the ways of jnan. Rather than answer, Achamian decided to draw him out, to reveal his role in these weighty matters.

I must discredit him.

"The time for playing your peers for fools is at an end, Ikurei."

The Exalt-General leaned back in his chair. He drew lazy fingertips across the Imperial Suns stamped on the cuirass of his field armour, as though to remind Achamian of the Chorae that lay hidden beneath. It was a gesture as good as any sneer.

"You make it sound," Proyas said, "as though he already knows about these things."

"He does."

"The sorcerer refers to ancient history," Conphas replied. He'd been wearing his blue general's cloak in the traditional Nansur fashion, thrown forward over his left shoulder. He now cast it back with a brisk motion, letting it trail across the copper carpet. "Some time ago, back when the Holy War still camped about Momemn's walls, my uncle discovered that his Prime Counsel was in truth one of these ... things."

"Skeaös?" Proyas exclaimed. "Are you saying *Skeaös* was one of these skin-spies?"

"None other. Since he proved improbably difficult to restrain for someone so aged, my uncle summoned his Imperial Saik. When they insisted no sorcery was involved, I was sent to fetch the good blasphemer, Achamian here, to confirm their assessment. Things became ..." He paused, then actually had the temerity to *wink* at Achamian. "Messy."

"So?" Gothyelk cried in his gruff manner. "Was there any sorcery?"

"No," Achamian replied. "And that's the very thing that makes them so deadly. If they were sorcerous artifacts, they'd be quickly uncovered. As it stands, they're *impossible* to detect ... And this," he said, turning to glare at the Exalt-General, "is precisely what these things have to do with Anasûrimbor Kellhus ...

"Only he can see them."

Several shouts rang beneath the corbelled dome.

"How do you know this?" Hulwarga asked.

Achamian stiffened, once again seeing Kellhus and Serwë swaying beneath the black tree.

"He told me."

"Told you?" Gothyelk growled. "When? When?"

"But what are they?" Chinjosa said.

"He's right," Saubon exclaimed. "This! This is the cancer that pollutes us! It's as I said all along: the Warrior-Prophet has come to *cleanse* us!"

"You move too fast," Conphas snapped. "You gloss over the most important questions!"

"Indeed!" Proyas said. "Such as why, when you knew these things were among us, you said nothing to the Council!"

"*Please,*" the Exalt-General replied, his brows knitted in derision. "What was I to do? For all we know, several of these creatures sit among us this very moment ..." He looked to the rapt faces, mostly bearded, rising around them. "Among you on the tiers," he called with a sweep of his hand. "Or even about this very table ..."

A concerned rumble broke across the room.

"So tell me," Conphas continued, "given the sorcerer's own estimation of these things, whom could I trust? You heard what he said: they're impossible to detect. I did all that I could in fact do ..." He turned his sly eyes to Achamian, though he continued speaking to his fellow Great Names. "I watched, carefully, and when I at last knew who the lead agent was, I *acted.*"

Achamian bolted erect in his chair. He opened his mouth to protest, but it was too late.

"Who?" Chinjosa, Gothyelk, and Hulwarga cried out in near unison.

Conphas shrugged. "Why, the man who calls himself the Warrior-Prophet ... Who else?"

A single jeer pealed through the air, only to be shouted down by a chorus of rebukes.

"Nonsense!" Achamian cried. "This is rank foolishness!"

The Exalt-General's eyebrows popped up, as though amazed that something so obvious could be overlooked. "But you just said that only he could see these abominations, did you not?"

"Yes, but—"

"Then tell us, *how* does he see them?"

Caught unawares, Achamian could only stare at the man. Never, it seemed, had he come to loathe someone so quickly.

"Well, the answer," Conphas said, "seems plain enough to me. He sees them *because he knows who they are.*"

Exclamations rang out.

Flummoxed, Achamian looked up across the raucous tiers, glancing from face to bearded face. Suddenly he realized that what Conphas had said moments earlier was *true.* Even now, skin-spies watched him—he was certain of it! The *Consult* watched him … And laughed.

He found himself clutching the table's edge.

"So how," Saubon was crying, "did he know I would prevail on the Plains of Mengedda? How did he know where to find water in desert sands? How does he know the truth in men's hearts?"

"Because he's the Warrior-Prophet!" someone bellowed from the tiers. "Truth-Bearer! Light-Bringer! The Salvation of—"

"Blasphemy!" Gothyelk roared, beating the table twice with his great fist. "He is False! *False!* There can be no more Prophets! Sejenus is the true voice of God! The only—"

"How can you say that?" Saubon said, as though mourning a wayward brother. "How many times—"

"He's ensorcelled you!" Conphas shouted in the tones of a High Imperial Officer. "Bewitched you all!" When the uproar abated somewhat, he continued, projecting his voice with the same ringing forcefulness. "As I said earlier, we've forgotten the single most important question! *Who?* Who are these abominations that hound us, that skulk unseen in our most secret councils?"

"Just as I said," Chinjosa seconded. "Who?"

Ikurei Conphas looked pointedly at Achamian, daring him to answer …

"Eh, Schoolman?"

He'd been outmatched, Achamian realized. Conphas knew his answer, knew how the others would scoff and dismiss. The Consult was the stuff of children's tales and Mandate madmen. He stared wordlessly at the Exalt-General, struggling to mask his dismay with contempt. Even with proof, they could undo him with mere words. Even with proof, they refused to believe!

The man's eyes mocked him, seemed to say, *You make it too easy ...*

Conphas abruptly turned to the others. "But you've already answered my question, haven't you? When you said these things aren't the issue of sorcery—or at least any sorcery that Schoolmen can see!"

"Cishaurim," Saubon said. "You're saying these things are Cishaurim."

In his periphery, Achamian could see Proyas glaring at him in alarm. *Why don't you speak?*

But an exhaustion had welled through him, a numbing sense of defeat. In his soul's eye, he saw Esmenet beseeching him, her gaze alien with heartbreaking thoughts, treacherous desires ...

How could this happen?

"What else could they be?" Conphas asked, the very voice of sober reason. "You saw it."

"Aye," Chinjosa said, his eyes strangely hesitant. "They belong to the Eyeless Ones. The Snakeheads! There can be no other explanation."

"Indeed," Conphas said, his voice resonating with oratorical gravity. "The man the Zaudunyani call the Warrior-Prophet, the liar who came to us claiming the privileges of a prince, is an agent of the Cishaurim, sent to corrupt us, to sow dissension among us, to destroy the Holy War!"

"And he's *succeeded*," Gothyelk cried out in dismay. "On all points!"

Denials and lamentations shivered through the air. But doom, Achamian knew, had drawn its circle far beyond Caraskand's walls. *I must find some way ...*

"If Kellhus ..." Proyas shouted, commanding the room with rarity of his voice. "If Kellhus is a Cishaurim agent, *then why did he save us in the desert?*"

Achamian turned to his former student, heartened ...

"To save his own skin," the Exalt-General snapped impatiently. "Why else? As much as you distrust my wiles, Proyas, you must believe me on this. Anasûrimbor Kellhus is a Cishaurim spy. We've been watching him ever since Momemn, ever since his wandering eye revealed Skeaös to my uncle."

"What do you mean?" Achamian blurted.

The Exalt-General looked to him contemptuously. "How do you think my uncle, the glorious Emperor of these lands, identified Skeaös as a spy? He saw your Warrior-Prophet exchanging glances far out of proportion to their acquaintance."

"He's not," Achamian found himself shouting, "my Warrior-Prophet!"

He looked about, blinking, as shocked by his outburst as the others around the table.

All this time! He could see them from the very beginning ...

And yet, the man had said nothing. Throughout the march, throughout their endless discussions of the past and the present, Kellhus *had known* about the skin-spies.

Heedless of the caste-nobles' scrutiny, Achamian gasped for breath, clutched his chest. Dread pimpled his skin. Suddenly, so many of Kellhus's questions, especially those regarding the Consult and the No-God, made a different kind of sense ...

He was working me! Using me for my knowledge! Trying to understand what it was he saw!

And he saw Esmenet's soft lips parting about those words, those impossible words ...

"I carry his child."

How? How could she betray him?

He could remember those nights lying side by side in the darkness of his poor tent, feeling her slender back against his chest, and smiling at the press of her toes, which she always pushed between his calves when they were frigid. Ten little toes, each as cold as a raindrop. He could remember the wan yet breathless wonder that would seep through him. How could such a beauty choose him? How could this woman—this world!—feel safe in his wretched arms? The air would be warm with their exhalations, while beyond the stained canvas, across a thousand silent miles, everything would become strange and chill. And he would clutch her, as though they both plummeted ...

And he would curse himself, thinking, *Don't be a fool! She's here! She swore you'd never be alone!*

But he was. He was alone.

He blinked absurd tears from his eyes. Even his mule, Daybreak, was dead ...

He looked to the Great Names, who watched him from about the table. He felt no shame. The Scarlet Spires had carved that from him—or so it seemed. Only desolation, doubt, and hatred.

He did it! He took her!

Achamian remembered Nautzera, in what seemed another lifetime, asking him if the life of Inrau, his student, was worth the Apocalypse. He'd conceded then, had admitted that no man, no love, was worth such a risk. And here, he'd conceded once again. He would save the man who had halved his heart, because his heart was not worth the world, not worth the Second Apocalypse.

Was it?

Was it?

Achamian had slept only a short while the previous night, dozing while Proyas slumbered. And for the first time since becoming a sorcerer of rank within the Mandate, there had been no Dreams of the Old Wars. He had dreamed, rather, of Kellhus and Esmenet gasping and laughing in sweaty sheets.

Sitting speechless before the Great Names, Drusas Achamian realized that he held his Heart in one hand and Apocalypse in the other. And as he hefted them in his soul, it seemed that he couldn't tell which was the heavier.

It was no different for these men.

The Holy War suffered, and someone must die. Even if it meant the World.

They were only one small pocket of confrontation amid a thousand of such pockets scrawling across the Kalaul. But they were, Cnaiür knew, the centre all the same. Dozens of Shrial Knights milled about them, their faces blank and guarded, their eyes wide with looks of worried concentration.

Something was about to happen.

"But he must die, Grandmaster!" Sarcellus cried. "Kill him and save the Holy War!"

Gotian glanced nervously at Cnaiür before looking back to his Knight-Commander. He ran thick fingers through his short, greying hair. Cnaiür had always thought the Shrial Grandmaster a decisive man, but he seemed old and unsure now—even cowed in some strange way by his subordinate's zeal. All the Men of the Tusk had suffered, some more than others, and some in different ways than others. Gotian, it seemed, bore his scars on his spirit.

"I appreciate your concern, Sarcellus, but it has been agreed that—"

"But that's just my point, Grandmaster! This sorcerer offers the Great Names reasons to spare the Deceiver. He gives them incentives. Contrived stories of evil spies that only the Deceiver can see!"

"What do you mean," Cnaiür snapped, "that only *he* can see them?"

Sarcellus turned to him in a manner that smelled wary, though nothing about him appeared troubled.

"This is what the sorcerer argues," he said in a sneering tone.

"Perhaps he does," Cnaiür replied, "but I followed you from the council chamber. The sorcerer had said only that there were spies in our midst, nothing more."

"Are you suggesting," Gotian asked sharply, "that my Knight-Commander is lying?"

"No," Cnaiür replied with a shrug. He felt the deadly calm settle about him. "I merely ask how he knows what he did not hear."

"You're a heathen dog, Scylvendi," Sarcellus declared. "A heathen! By what's right and holy, you should be rotting with the Kianene of Caraskand, not calling the word of a Shrial Knight into question."

With a feral grin, Cnaiür spat between Sarcellus's booted feet. Over the man's shoulder, he saw the great tree, glimpsed Serwë's willowy corpse bound upside down to the Dûnyain—like dead nailed to dead.

Let it be now.

A series of cries erupted from the nearby crowds. Distracted, Gotian commanded both Cnaiür and Sarcellus to lower their hands from their pommels. Neither man complied.

Sarcellus glanced to Gotian, who peered across the crowd, then back to Cnaiür. "You know not what you do, Scylvendi ..." His face *flexed*, twitched like a dying insect. "You know not what you do."

Cnaiür stared in horror, hearing the madness of Anwurat in the surrounding roar.

Lie made flesh …

Shouts added to shouts, until the air fairly hissed with cries and howls. Following Gotian's gaze, Cnaiür turned and glimpsed a cohort of scale-armoured men in blue and scarlet coats through the screen of Shrial Knights: a few at first, clearing away throngs of Inrithi, then hundreds more, forming almost cheek to jowl opposite Gotian's men. So far no blades had been drawn.

Gotian hurried along his ranks, shouting orders, bellowing to the barracks for reinforcements.

Swords were drawn, flourished so they flashed in the sun. More of the strange warriors approached, a deep phalanx of them shoving their way through the crowds of gaunt Inrithi. They were *Javreh,* Cnaiür realized, the slave-soldiers of the Scarlet Spires. What was happening here?

The masses surged about several brawls. Swords rang and clattered— off to the left. Gotian's cries pierced the din. Bewildered, the ranks of Shrial Knights immediately before Cnaiür suddenly broke, rolled back by Javreh with brandished broadswords.

United by shock, both Cnaiür and Sarcellus drew their swords.

But the slave-soldiers halted before them, making way for the sudden appearance of a dozen emaciated slaves bearing a silk- and gauze-draped palanquin with an intricately carved, black-lacquered frame. In one rehearsed motion, the cadaverous men lowered the litter to the ground.

A sudden hush fell over the crowds, so absolute Cnaiür thought he could hear the wind rattle and click through Umiaki behind him. Somewhere in the distance, some wretch shrieked, either wounded or dying.

Dressed in voluminous crimson gowns, an old man stepped from the shrouded litter, looking about with imperious contempt. The breeze wafted through his silky white beard. His eyes glittered dark from beneath painted brows.

"I am Eleäzaras," he declared in a resonant patrician's voice, "Grandmaster of the Scarlet Spires." He glanced over the dumbstruck crowds, then levelled his hawkish eyes on Gotian.

"The one who calls himself the Warrior-Prophet. You will cut him down and deliver him to me."

———— ✇ ————

"Well, it seems the matter is settled," Ikurei Conphas said, his solemn tone belied by the hyena laughing in his gaze.

"Akka?" Proyas whispered. Achamian looked to him, bewildered. For a moment, the Prince had sounded twelve …

It was strange the way memory cared nothing for the form of the past. Perhaps this was why those dying of old age were so often incredulous. Through memory, the past assailed the present, not in queues arranged by calender and chronicle, but as a hungry mob of yesterdays.

Yesterday Esmenet had loved him. Just yesterday she'd begged him not to leave her, not to go to the Sareotic Library. For the rest of his life, he realized, it would always be yesterday.

He looked to the entryway, his attention caught by movement in his periphery. It was Xinemus … One of Proyas's men—Iryssas, he realized—led him across the threshold, then up into the packed tiers. He was dressed in full panoply, wearing the shin-length skirt of a Conriyan knight and a harness of silvered ring-mail beneath a Kianene vest. His beard was oiled and braided, and fell in a fan of ringlets across his upper chest. Compared with the half-wasted Men of the Tusk, he looked robust, majestic, at once exotic and familiar, like an Inrithi prince from faraway Nilnamesh.

The Marshal stumbled twice passing through his fellow caste-nobles, and Achamian could see torment on his blinded face—torment and a curious, almost heartbreaking stubbornness. A determination to resume his place among the mighty.

Achamian swallowed at the knife in his throat.

Zin …

Breathless, he watched the Marshal settle between Gaidekki and Ingiaban, then turn his face to open air, staring out as though the Great Names sat before him rather than below. Achamian remembered the indolent nights he'd spent at Xinemus's coastal villa in Conriya. He remembered drinking anpoi, eating wild hen stuffed with oysters, and their endless talk of things ancient and dead. And suddenly Achamian understood what he had to do …

He had to tell a story.

Esmenet had loved him just yesterday. But then so too had the world ended!

"I've suffered," he called abruptly, and it seemed he heard his voice through Xinemus's ears.

It sounded strong.

"I have suffered," he repeated, pushing himself to his feet. "All of us have suffered. The time for politics and posturing has passed. 'Those who speak truth,' the Latter Prophet tells us, 'have naught to fear, though they should perish for it ...'"

He could feel their eyes: sceptical, curious, and indignant.

"It surprises you, doesn't it, hearing a sorcerer, one of the Unclean, quoting Scripture. I imagine it even offends some of you. Nevertheless, I shall speak the truth."

"So you lied to us before?" Conphas said with the semblance of sombre tact. Always a true son of House Ikurei.

"No more than you," Achamian said, "nor any other man in these chambers. For all of us parse and ration our words, pitch them to the ears of the listener. All of us play jnan—that cursed game! Even though men die, we play it ... And few, Exalt-General, know it better than you!"

Somehow, he'd found that tone or note that stilled tongues and stirred hearts to listen—that voice, he realized, that Kellhus so effortlessly mastered.

"Men think us Mandate Schoolmen drunk on legend, deranged by history. All the Three Seas laugh at us. And why not, when we weep and tug on our beards at the tales you tell your children at night? But this—*this!*—isn't the Three Seas. This is Caraskand, where the Holy War lies trapped and starving, besieged by the fury of the Padirajah. In all likelihood, these are the last days of your life! Think on it! The hunger, the desperation, the terror flailing at your bowel, the horror bolting through your heart!"

"That's enough!" an ashen-faced Gothyelk cried.

"No!" Achamian boomed. "It isn't enough! For what you suffer now, I've suffered my *entire* life—day and night! Doom! Doom lies upon you, darkening your thoughts, weighing your steps. Even now, your heart quickens. Your breath grows tight ...

"But you've still much, much to learn!

"Thousands of years ago, before Men had crossed the Great Kayarsus, before even *The Chronicle of the Tusk* was written, the Nonmen ruled these lands. And like us, they warred amongst themselves, for honour, for riches, and yes, even for faith. But the greatest of their wars they fought, not against themselves, or even against our ancestors—though we would prove to be their ruin. The greatest of their wars they fought against the Inchoroi, a race of monstrosities. A race who exulted in the subtleties of the flesh, forging perversities from life the way we forge swords from iron. Sranc, Bashrag, even Wracu, dragons, are relics of their ancient wars against the Nonmen.

"Led by the great Cû'jara-Cinmoi, the Nonmen Kings battled them across the plains and through the high and deep places of the earth. After ordeal and grievous sacrifice, they beat the Inchoroi back to their first and final stronghold, a place the Nonmen called Min-Uroikas, the 'Pit of Obscenities.' I'll not recount the horrors of that place. Suffice to say the Inchoroi were overthrown, extinguished—or so it was thought. And the Nonmen cast a glamour about Min-Uroikas so that it would remain forever hidden. Then, exhausted and mortally weakened, they retired to the remnants of their ruined world, a triumphant, yet broken, race.

"Centuries later the Men of Eänna descended the Kayarsus, howling multitudes of them, led by their Chieftain-Kings—our fathers of yore. You know their names, for they're enumerated in *The Chronicle of the Tusk*: Shelgal, Mamayma, Nomur, Inshull … They swept the dwindling Nonmen before them, sealing up their great mansions and driving them into the sea. For an age, knowledge of the Inchoroi and Min-Uroikas passed from all souls. Only the Nonmen of Injor-Niyas remembered, and they dared not leave their mountain fastnesses.

"But as the years passed, the enmity between our races waned. Treaties were forged between the remaining Nonmen and the Norsirai of Trysë and Sauglish. Knowledge and goods were exchanged, and Men learned for the first time of the Inchoroi and their wars against the Nonmen. Then under the heirs of Nincaerû-Telesser, a Nonman sorcerer named Cet'ingira—whom you know as Mekeritrig from *The Sagas*—revealed the location of Min-Uroikas to Shaeönanra, the Grandvizier of the ancient Gnostic School of Mangaecca. The glamour about the wicked stronghold was broken, and the Schoolmen of the Mangaecca reclaimed Min-Uroikas—to the woe of us all.

"They called it Anochirwa, 'Hornsreaching,' though to the Men who warred against them, it came to be called Golgotterath ... A name we use to frighten our children still, though it is we who should be frightened."

He paused, searching from face to face.

"I say this because the Nonmen, even though they destroyed the Inchoroi, could not undo Min-Uroikas, for it wasn't—*isn't*—of this world. The Mangaecca ransacked the place, discovering much that the Nonmen had overlooked, including terrible armaments never brought to fruition. And much as a man who dwells in a palace comes to think himself a prince, so the Mangaecca came to think themselves the successors of the Inchoroi. They became enamoured of their inhuman ways, and they fell upon their obscene and degenerate craft, the Tekne, with the curiosity of monkeys. And most importantly—most tragically!—they discovered Mog-Pharau ..."

"The No-God," Proyas said quietly.

Achamian nodded. "Tsurumah, Mursiris, World-Breaker, and a thousand other hated names ... It took them centuries, but just over two thousand years ago, when the High Kings of Kyraneas exacted tribute from these lands, and perhaps raised this very council hall, they finally succeeded in awakening Him ... The No-God ... Near all the world crashed into screams and blood ere his fall."

He smiled and looked at them, blinked tears across his cheeks. "What I've seen in my Dreams," he said softly. "The horrors I have seen ..."

He shook his head, stepped forward as though stumbling clear of some trance.

"Who among you forgets the Plains of Mengedda? Many of you, I know, suffered nightmares, dreams of dying in ancient battles. And all of you saw the bones and bronze arms vomited from that cursed ground. Those things happened, I assure you, for a *reason*. They are the echoes of terrible deeds, the spoor of dread and catastrophe. If any of you doubt the existence or the power of the No-God, then I bid you only recall that ground, which broke for the mere witness of His passing!

"Now everything I've told you is fact, recorded in annals of both Men and Nonmen. But this isn't, as you might think, a story of doom averted—not in the least! For though Mog-Pharau was struck down on the Plains of Mengedda, his accursed attendants recovered his remains.

And this, great lords, is why we Mandate Schoolmen haunt your courts and wander your halls. This is why we bear your taunts and bite our tongues! For two thousand years the Consult has continued its wicked study, for two thousand years they've laboured to resurrect the No-God. Think us mad, call us fools, but it's your wives, your children, we seek to protect. The Three Seas is our charge!

"This is why I come to you now. Heed me, for I know of what I speak!

"These creatures, these skin-spies, that infiltrate your ranks have no relation to the Cishaurim. By calling them such, you simply do what all men do when assailed by the Unknown: you drag it into the circle of what you know. You clothe new enemies in the trappings of old. But these things hail from far outside your circle, from time out of memory! Think of what we saw moments ago! These skin-spies are beyond your craft or ken, beyond that even of the Cishaurim, whom you fear and hate.

"They are agents of the Consult, and their mere existence omens disaster! Only deep mastery of the Tekne could bring such obscenities to life, a mastery that promises the Resurrection of Mog-Pharau is nigh ...

"Need I tell you what that means?

"We Mandate Schoolmen, as you know, dream of the ancient world's end. And of all those dreams, there's one we suffer more than any other: the death of Celmomas, High-King of Kûniüri, on the Fields of Eleneöt." He paused, realized that he panted for breath. "*Anasûrimbor* Celmomas," he said.

There was an anxious rustle through the chamber. He heard someone muttering in Ainoni.

"And in this dream," he continued, pressing his tone nearer to its crescendo, "Celmomas speaks, as the dying sometimes do, a great prophecy. Do not to grieve, he says, for an Anasûrimbor shall return at the end of the world ...

"An *Anasûrimbor*!" he cried, as though that name held the secret of all reason. His voice resounded through the chamber, echoed across the ancient stonework.

"An Anasûrimbor shall return at the end of the world. *And he has* ... He hangs dying even as we speak! Anasûrimbor Kellhus, the man you've condemned, is what we in the Mandate call the Harbinger, the living sign of the end of days. He is our only hope!"

Achamian swept his gaze from the table to the tiers, lowered his opened palms.

"So *you*, the Lords of the Holy War, must ask yourself, what's the wager you would make? *You* who think yourselves doomed, and your wives and children safe ... Are you so certain this man is *merely* what you think? And whence comes this certainty? From wisdom? Or from desperation?

"Are you willing to *risk the very world* to see your bigotries through?"

The silence that closed about his voice was leaden. It was as though a wall of stone faces and glass eyes regarded him. For a long moment no one dared speak, and with startled wonder, Achamian realized he had actually reached them. For once they'd listened with their hearts!

They believe!

Then Ikurei Conphas began stamping his foot and slapping his thigh, calling, *"Hussaa! Hu-hu-hussaaa!"* Another on the tiers, General Sompas, joined him ... *"Hussaa! Hu-hu-hussaaa!"*

A mockery of the traditional Nansur cheer. The laughter was hesitant at first, but within moments, it boomed through the chamber.

The Lords of the Holy War had made their wager.

His crimson gown shimmering in the sunlight, the Grandmaster of the Scarlet Spires took two steps toward them. "You will deliver him," he repeated darkly.

"Sarcellus!" Incheiri Gotian roared, brandishing a Chorae in his left hand. "Kill him! Kill the False Prophet!"

But Cnaiür was already sprinting toward the tree. He whirled, falling into stance several paces before the Knight of the Tusk.

Anything ... Any indignity. Any price!

Sarcellus lowered his sword, opened his arms as though in fellowship. Beyond him, the masses surged and howled across the reaches of the Kalaul. The air hummed with their growing thunder. Smiling, the Knight-Commander stepped closer, pausing at the extreme limit of any sudden lunge.

"We worship the same God, you and I."

The breeze had calmed, and the sun's heat leapt into its wake. It seemed to Cnaiür that he could smell rotting flesh—rotting flesh mingled with the bitter spit of eucalyptus leaves.

Serwë ...

"This," Cnaiür said calmly, "is the sum of my worship."

Rest my sweet, for I shall bear you ...

He clutched his tunic about its blood-clotted collar, tore it to his waist. He raised his broadsword straight before him.

I shall avenge.

Beyond the Knight-Commander, Gotian exchanged shouts with the crimson-gowned Grandmaster. The Javreh, the slave-soldiers of the Scarlet Spires, threw themselves against the ranks of Shrial Knights, who'd linked arms in an effort to hold them—and the surrounding fields of shrieking and bellowing Inrithi—at bay. The surrounding temples and cloisters of Csokis reared in the distance, impassive in the haze. The Five Heights loomed against the surrounding sky.

And Cnaiür grinned as only a Chieftain of the Utemot could grin. The neck of the world, it seemed, lay pressed against the point of his sword.

I shall butcher.

All hungered here. All starved.

Everything, Cnaiür realized, had transpired according to the Dûnyain's mad gambit. What difference did it make whether he perished now, hanging from this tree, or several days hence, when the Padirajah at last overcame the walls? So he'd given himself to his captors, knowing that no man was so innocent as the accused who exposed his accusers.

Knowing that if he survived ...

The secret of battle!

Sarcellus swept his longsword in a series of blinding exercises. His arms snapped out and down, like bolts thrown from siege engines. There was something inhuman to his movements.

Cnaiür neither flinched nor moved. He was a Son of the People, a prodigy born of desolate earth, sent to kill, to reave. He was a savage from dark northern plains, with thunder in his heart and murder in his eyes ... He was Cnaiür urs Skiötha, most violent of all men.

He shrugged his bronzed limbs and planted his feet.

"You will fear," Sarcellus said, "before this is over."

"I cut you once," Cnaiür grated.

He could clearly see the threads of inflamed red branching across his face now. They were creases, he realized. Creases he'd seen open before …

"I know why you loved her," the Shrial Knight snarled. "Such a peach! I think I'll chase the dogs from her corpse—after—and love her again …"

Cnaiür stared, unmoved. Howls rifled the air. Upraised fists hammered the distances—thousands of them.

Just the space of breaths between them now.

Breaths.

Their blades cut open space. Kissed. Circled. Kissed again. Whirling geometries, shocking the air with the staccato ring of steel. Leap. Crouch. Lunge … With bestial grace, the Scylvendi pounded the abomination, pressing him back. But the Shrial Knight's sword was sorcery—it dazzled the air.

Cnaiür fell back, gathered his breath, shook sweat from his mane.

"My flesh," Sarcellus whispered, "has been folded more times than the steel of your sword." He laughed as though utterly unwinded. "Men are dogs and kine … But my kind, we're wolves in the forest, lions on the plain. We're sharks in the sea …"

Emptiness always laughed.

Cnaiür charged the creature, his sword pummelling the space between them. Feint, then a breathtaking sweep. The Shrial Knight leapt, batted away the thunder of his steel.

Iron honed to the absence of surface, sketching circles and points in the air, reaching, probing …

They locked hilts. Leaned against each other. Cnaiür heaved, but the man seemed immovable.

"Such talent!" Sarcellus cried.

Concussion in his face. How? Cnaiür stumbled across leaves and hot stone, rolled to his feet. He glimpsed Umiaki, clutching the sun with a tree's crone fingers. Then Sarcellus's blade was everywhere, cutting, hammering down his guard. A string of desperations saved his life. He leapt clear.

The famished mobs yammered and shrieked. The very ground thrummed beneath his sandals.

Exhaustion and stings, the weight of old wounds.

Their blades scissored, winced apart, brushed sweaty skin, then circled round the sun. Like teeth they clacked and gnashed.

Lathered in sweat. Each breath a knife in his chest.

Pressed to the bowers of Umiaki, he glimpsed Serwë sagging against the Dûnyain, her face black and bent back, her teeth leering from shrunken lips. The surrounding riot thinned. The boundaries between him, the ground, and the black tree crumbled. Something filled him, swept him forward, unleashed his corded arms. And he howled, the very mouth of the Steppe, his sword *raping* the air between …

One. Two. Three … Blows that could have halved bulls.

Sarcellus faltered, stumbled—saved himself with an inhuman leap. Back, pirouetting through the air. Landing in a crouch.

The smile was gone.

His black mane ribboned by sweat, his chest heaving over the hollow of his belly, Cnaiür raised his arms to the tumultuous mobs.

"Who?" he screamed. *"Who will take the knife to my heart?"*

Again he fell upon the Shrial Knight, battered him back from the shadows of Umiaki, from the leaves curled about palmed water. But even as the man's style crumbled beneath his frothing attack, it revealed something beautiful in its precision—as beautiful as it was unconquerable. Suddenly, Sarcellus was swatting his blade as though it were a game. The man's longsword became a glittering wind, scoring his cheek, clipping his shin …

Cnaiür fell back, wailed rabid frustration, bellowed defiance.

A sword tip sheared through his thigh. He skidded in blood, fell forward, bare throat exposed … Stone bruised his bones. Grit gouged his skin.

No …

A powerful voice pierced the roar of the Holy War.

"Sarcellus!"

It was Gotian. He'd broken with Eleäzaras, and was warily approaching his zealous Knight-Commander. The crowds abruptly grew subdued.

"Sarcellus …" The Grandmaster's eyes were slack with disbelief. "Where …"—a hesitant swallow—"where did you learn to fight so?"

The Knight of the Tusk whirled, his face the very mask of reverent subservience.

"My lord, I've—"

Sarcellus suddenly convulsed, coughed blood through gritted teeth. Cnaiür guided his thrashing body to the ground with his sword. Then, within reach of the dumbstruck Grandmaster, he hacked off its head with a single stroke. He gathered the thick maul of black hair in his hand, raised the severed head high. Like bowels from a split belly, its face relaxed, opened like a harem of limbs. Gotian fell to his knees. Eleäzaras stumbled back into his slaves. The mob's thunder—horror, exultation—broke across the Scylvendi. The riot of revelation.

He tossed the hoary thing at the sorcerer's feet.

CHAPTER
TWENTY-FIVE

CARASKAND

What is the meaning of a deluded life?

—AJENCIS, *THE THIRD ANALYTIC OF MEN*

Late Winter, 4112 Year-of-the-Tusk, Caraskand

Crying out to one another in eager terror, the Nascenti cut the Warrior-Prophet from his dead wife. A hush, it seemed, had settled across the whole of Caraskand.

He knew he should be weak unto death, but something inexplicable moved him. He rolled from Serwë, braced his arms against his knees, then waving his frantic disciples away, stood impossibly erect. Hands wrapped him in a shroud of white linen. He stumbled clear of Umiaki's gloom, lifted his face to sun and sky. He could feel awe shiver through the masses—awe of him. He raised his palms to the great hollows of the earth, and it seemed he embraced all the Three Seas.

I think I see, Father ...

Cries of rapture and disbelief rang across the packed reaches of the Kalaul. Several paces away Cnaiür stood dumbstruck, as did Eleäzaras a length behind him. Incheiri Gotian staggered forward, fell to his knees and wept. Kellhus smiled with boundless compassion. Everywhere he looked, he saw men kneeling ...

Yes ... The Thousandfold Thought.

And it seemed there was nothing, no dwarfing frame, that could restrict him to this place, to any place ... He was all things, and all things were his ...

He was one of the Conditioned. Dûnyain.

He was the Warrior-Prophet.

Tears roared down his cheeks. With a haloed hand, he reached beneath his breast, firmly wrested the heart from his ribs. He thrust it high to the thunder of their adulation. Beads of blood seemed to crack the stone at his feet ... He glimpsed Sarcellus's uncoiled face.

I see ...

"They said!" he cried in a booming voice, and the howling chorus trailed into silence.

"They said that I was False, that I caused the anger of the God to burn against us!"

He looked into their wasted faces, answered their fevered eyes. He brandished Serwë's burning heart.

"But I say that we—WE!—are that anger!"

Kascamandri, the indomitable Padirajah of Kian, sent a message to the Men of the Tusk, whom he knew were doomed. The message was an offer—an extremely gracious one, the Padirajah thought. If the Holy War relented, yielded Caraskand and forswore their idolatrous worship of False Gods, they would be spared and given lands. They would be made Grandees of Kian as befitted their rank among the idolatrous nations.

Kascamandri was not so foolish as to think this offer would be accepted outright, but he knew something of desperation, knew that in the competition of hungers, piety often lost in the end. Besides, news that the Holy War had been defeated, not by the swords of the Prophet Fane but by his words, would shake the wicked Thousand Temples to the core.

The reply came in the form of a dozen almost skeletal Inrithi knights, dressed in simple cotton tunics and wearing only knives. After disputing the knives, which the idolaters refused to relinquish, Kascamandri's Ushers received them with all jnanic courtesy and brought them directly to the great Padirajah, his children, and the ornamental Grandees of his court.

There was a moment of astonished silence, for the Kianene could scarce believe the bearded wretches before them could author so much woe. Then, before the first ritual declaration, the twelve men cried out, *"Satephikos kana ta yerishi ankapharas!"* in unison, then drew their knives and cut their own throats.

Horrified, Kascamandri clasped his two youngest daughters tight in his elephantine arms. They sobbed and cried out, while his older children, especially his boys, chirped in excited tones. He turned to his dumbstruck interpreter ...

"Th-they said," the ashen-faced man stammered, "'the Warrior-Prophet shall ... shall *come before you* ...'" He gazed helplessly at his Padirajah's gold-slippered feet.

When he demanded to know just who this Warrior-Prophet was, no one could answer him. Only when little Sirol began crying anew did he cease ranting. Dismissing his slaves, he rushed her to the incense-fogged chambers of his pavilion, promising sweets and other beautiful things.

The following morning the Men of the Tusk filed from the Ivory Gate onto the greening Tertae Plain. War horns pealed from hill to hill. Thousand-throated songs drifted on the breeze. No longer would the Holy War endure hunger and disease. No longer would it suffer itself to be besieged.

It would march.

The tattered columns wound from the gates onto the fields. Stricken with illness, Gothyelk was too weakened to battle, so his middle son, Gonrain, rode in his stead. The Great Names had agreed to give the Tydonni the right flank, so the Earl of Agansanor could watch his son from Caraskand's walls. Then came Ikurei Conphas, flanked by the Sacred Suns of his Imperial Columns. Nersei Proyas followed, at the head of the once magnificent knights of Conriya. And after him came Hulwarga the Limper, whose Thunyeri looked more like savage wraiths than men. Then rode Chinjosa, the Count-Palatine of Antanamera, who'd been appointed King-Regent of High Ainon after Chepheramunni's death. The great army the Scarlet Spires had brought from High Ainon was but a ruined shadow of what it had once been, though those who remained possessed bitter strength. King Saubon was the last to issue from Caraskand's great Ivory Gate, leading trains of wild-eyed Galeoth.

Worried that a precipitous attack would simply drive the idolaters back to the shelter of Caraskand's walls, Kascamandri let the Inrithi form unmolested across the fields. The Men of the Tusk mustered between byres and before abandoned farmsteads, their lines somewhat over a mile in length. The weak stood next to the strong, hauberks rusted, jerkins rotted. Strapless harnesses swung from emaciated frames. The arms of some, it seemed, were no thicker than their swords. Knights wearing Enathpanean vests, cassocks, and khalats milled on horses that looked like starved nags. Even those few noncombatants who'd survived—women and priests for the most part—stood among them. Everyone had come to the Fields of Tertae—all those with strength to bear arms. Everyone had come to conquer or to perish. They formed long, haggard ranks, singing hymns, beating blades against shoulder and shield.

Some one hundred thousand Inrithi had stumbled from the Carathay, and less than fifty thousand now ranged across the plain. Another twenty thousand remained within Caraskand, too weak to do more than cheer. Many had dragged themselves from their sickbeds and now crowded the Triamic Walls, especially about the Ivory Gate. Some cried out encouragement and prayers, while others wept, tormented by the collision of hope and hopelessness.

But on wall and field alike, everyone looked anxiously to the centre of the battle line, hoping for a glimpse of the new banner that graced the threadbare standards of the Holy War. There! through budding grove or across rolling pasture, flaring in the breeze: black on white, a ring bisected by the figure of a man, the Circumfix of the Warrior-Prophet. The glory of it scarcely seemed possible …

War horns sounded the advance, and the grim ranks began marching forward, into distances screened by orchards and copses of ash and sycamore. Kascamandri had ordered his host to draw up more than two miles distant, where rolling plain broadened between the city and the surrounding hills, knowing it would be difficult for the Inrithi to cover the intervening distance without exposing their flanks or opening gaps in their line.

Songs keened over the throbbing of Fanim drums. The deep war chants of the Thunyeri, which had once filled the forests of their homeland with the sound of doom. The keening hymns of the Ainoni, whose cultivated ears savoured the dissonance of human voices. The dirges of the Galeoth and the Tydonni, solemn and foreboding. They sang, the Men of the Tusk, overcome with strange passions: joy that knew no laughter, terror that knew no fear. They sang and they marched, walking with the grace of almost-broken men.

Hundreds collapsed, faint for the lack of food. Their kinsmen hauled them to their feet, dragged them forward through the muck of fallow fields.

First blood was shed to the north, nearest the Triamic Walls. The Tydonni under Thane Unswolka of Numaineiri sighted waves of Fanim cresting the hillocks before them, their black-braided goatees bouncing to the rhythm of their trotting horses. The Numaineiri, their faces painted red to terrify their foes, braced their great kite shields with gaunt shoulders. Their archers loosed thin volleys at the advancing Fanim, only to be answered by dark clouds of arrows fired from horseback. Led by Ansacer, the exiled Sapatishah of Gedea, the dispossessed Grandees of Shigek and Enathpaneah charged with fury into the tall warriors of Ce Tydonn.

Near the centre, opposite the Circumfix, screaming mastodons lumbered forward, their howdahs packed with black-faced Girgashi wearing blue turbans and bearing shields of red-lacquered cowhide. But daring outriders, Anpliean knights under Palatine Gaidekki, had raced forward, setting dead winter grasses and thickets aflame. Oily smoke tumbled skyward, pulled to the southeast by the wind. Several mastodons panicked, causing uproar among King Pilaskanda's Hetmen. But most crashed through the smoke and stamped trumpeting into the Inrithi's midst. Soon little could be seen. Smoke and chaos enveloped the Mark of the Circumfix.

Everywhere along the line Fanim horsemen crested rises, burst from citrus groves, or galloped clear of drifting smoke—magnificent divisions of them. Great Cinganjehoi, leading the proud Grandees of Eumarna and Jurisada, swept into the walking lines of Ainoni: Kishyati and Moserothu under Palatines Soter and Uranyanka. Farther to the south, the Grandees of Chianadyni assembled along the summits of the rising hills, awaiting King Saubon and his marching ranks of Galeoth. Wearing wide-sleeved khalats and Nilnameshi chainmail, they charged down the slopes, riding thoroughbreds raised on the hard frontiers of the Great Salt. Crown

Prince Fanayal and his Coyauri struck Earl Anfirig's blue-tattooed Gesindalmen, then swept into the confused lines of the Agmundrmen under Saubon's personal command.

Along Caraskand's walls the infirm cried and howled to their kinsmen, struggling to see what happened. But through the thundering drums, over the ululating war cries of the heathen, they could hear their brothers sing. Smoke obscured the centre, but nearer the walls they saw the Tydonni stand firm before flurries of Fanim horsemen, fighting with grim and preternatural determination. Suddenly Earl Werijen Greatheart and the knights of Plaideöl broke forward, riding what few nags they possessed, and shattered the astonished Kianene. Then far to the south, someone sighted Athjeäri and the inveterate knights of Gaenri streaming down dark slopes, crashing into the rear of the Chianadyni. Saubon had sent his young nephew to counter any flanking manoeuvres in the hills. After breaking and pursuing the division of cavalry Kascamandri had sent for this very purpose, the brash Earl of Gaenri found himself auspiciously positioned in the heathen's rear.

The Fanim fell back in disarray, while before them, all across the Fields of Tertae, the singing Inrithi resumed their forward march. Many upon the walls limped eastward, toward the Gate of Horns, where they could see the first Men of the Tusk fight clear the smoke of the centre and press onward in the wake of retreating Girgashi horsemen. Then they saw it, the Circumfix, fluttering white and unsullied in the wind …

As though driven by inevitability, the iron men marched forward. When the heathen charged, they grabbed at bridles and were trampled. They punched spears deep into the haunches of Fanim horses. They fended hacking swords, pulled heathen shrieking to the ground, where they knifed them in the armpit, face, or groin. They shrugged off piercing arrows. When the heathen relented, some Men of the Tusk, the madness of battle upon them, hurled their helms at the fleeing horsemen. Time and again the Kianene charged, broke, then withdrew, while the iron men trudged on, through the olive trees, across the fallow fields. They would walk with the God—whether he favoured them or no.

But the Kianene were a proud, warlike people, and the host the Padirajah had assembled was great both in number and in heart. Though dismayed, the pious Warriors of the Solitary God were not undone.

Kascamandri himself took to the field, hoisted by his slaves upon the back of a massive horse. Outdistancing the Inrithi, division after division of Fanim horsemen reformed on the outskirts of the Padirajah's camp. Men cast about for sign of the Cishaurim. Then King Pilaskanda, the Padirajah's tributary and friend, loosed the last of the mastodons upon the black-armoured Thunyeri.

The beasts stormed into the Auglishmen under Earl Goken the Red. Men were gored on great winding tusks, tossed and broken by trunks, split like sacks of fruit beneath colossal stamping feet. From the armoured howdahs strapped to the animals' backs, Girgashi sent arrows into the faces of those shouting below. Then the giant Yalgrota felled one singlehanded, hammering the beast's head with a mighty cudgel. The flint-hearted Auglishmen rallied, hewing the trumpeting beasts with axe and sword. Some mastodons toppled, pulled down by a hundred wounds; others panicked before the fire Prince Hulwarga brought against them and began rampaging through the Girgashi horsemen crowded in their rear.

Across the Tertae Plain, waves of Kianene cavalrymen descended upon the advancing Inrithi. Those watching from the Gate of Horns saw the Padirajah's White Tiger close with the Circumfix. They saw the standards of Gaidekki and Ingiaban falter while those of the Nansur crept forward. The stout-hearted infantrymen of the Selial Column hacked their way into the Padirajah's camp. Then the drums of the heathen went silent, and all the world seemed awash in Inrithi voices raised in triumph and song. Cinganjehoi fled the field. The giant Cojirani, the bloodthirsty Grandee of Mizrai, was slain by Proyas, the Prince of Conriya. Kascamandri, the glorious Padirajah of Kian, fell jawless and dying at the sandalled feet of the Warrior-Prophet. His jowled head was mounted upon the standard of the Circumfix. But his precious children escaped, spirited away by slippery Fanayal, the oldest of his sons.

Pinioned between the advancing Inrithi and the fallen camp, the Grandees of Chianadyni and Girgash charged and charged, but the Galeoth and Ainoni shrugged away their desperation and closed with them. The Men of the Tusk wept as they butchered the despairing heathen, for never had they known such dark glory.

And in the wake of the battle, some climbed the mastodon carcasses, held their swords out to the glare of the sun, and understood things they did not know.

The Holy War had been absolved.

Forgiven.

The surviving Grandees were strung from many-boughed sycamores, and in the evening light they hung, like drowned men floating up from the deep. And though years would pass, none would dare touch them. They would sag from the nails that fixed them, collapse into heaps about the base of their trees. And to anyone who listened, they would whisper a revelation ... The secret of battle.

Indomitable conviction. Unconquerable belief.

Early Spring, 4112, Year-of-the-Tusk, Akssersia

Woollen cloak and furs raised against the rain, Aëngelas rode, part of a long file of horsemen plodding across the Plains of Gâl through never-ending curtains of falling grey. They followed a wide trail of trampled grasses. Now and anon someone would find the untrammelled footprint of a child, small and innocent, dimpling the mud. Men Aëngelas had known his entire life—strong men—wept aloud at the sight.

They called themselves the Werigda, and they searched for their missing wives and children. Two days before they had returned to their camp, warriors flushed with success in the ways of small war, and had found destruction and slaughter instead of their loved ones. Inveterate fighters became panicked husbands and fathers, sprinting through the wreckage crying names. But when they realized their families had been taken and not killed, they became warriors again. And they'd ridden, driven by love and terror.

By mid-morning, colossal stoneworks resolved from the sheets of rain and reared above them: the moss- and lichen-crowded ruins of Myclai, once the capital of Akssersia and the greatest city of the Ancient North save Trysë. Aëngelas knew nothing of the Old Wars, or of ancient and proud Akssersia, but he understood his people were descendants of the Apocalypse. They dwelt among the unearthed bones of greater things.

They followed the track over mounds, beneath headless pillars, and along walls spilling into gravel. The Sranc they followed, Aëngelas knew, were neither Kig'krinaki nor Xoägi'i, the clans that had been their rivals since time immemorial. They followed a different, more wicked clan—one never before encountered. Some of them were even horsed—something unheard of for the Sranc.

They passed through dead Myclai in silence, deaf to her rebuke for the unruined.

By evening the rains had stopped, but deepening cold was added to their horror, and their shivers became shudders. That night they found a firepit, and Aëngelas, poking through the black ash with his knife, retrieved a small pile of little bones. Children's bones. The Werigda gnashed their teeth and howled at the dark heavens.

There could be no sleep that night, so they rode on. The plains seemed a heart-stopping hollow, a great funerary shroud, exposed at all points to abyssal portent, to impossibly cruel designs. What had they done? How had they angered the man-pummelling Gods? Had the Stag-Flame burned too low? Had the sacrificial calves been diseased?

Two more days of wet, shivering fury. Two more days of trembling horror. Aëngelas would see the tracks of barefoot women and children, and he would remember their burnt homes, the bodies of the tribe's adolescents strewn amidst the wreckage, desecrated in unspeakable ways. And he would remember his wife's frightened eyes before he'd left with the others to raid the Xoägi'i. He would remember her words of premonition.

"Do not leave us, Aënga ... The Great Ruiner hunts for us. I've seen him in my dreams!"

Another firepit, more small bones. But this time the ashes were warm. The very ground seemed to whisper with the screams of their loved ones.

They were near. But both they and their horses, Aëngelas told them, were too weary for the grim work of battle. Many were dismayed by these words. Whose child would the Sranc eat, they cried, while they tossed on the hard ground? All of them, Aëngelas said, if the Werigda failed to win the morrow's battle. They must sleep.

That night anguished cries awakened him. Pale, callused hands dragged him from his mat, and he drove his knife through the belly of his assailant. The thunder of hooves crashed around him, and he was struck face first into the turf. He struggled to his knees, crying out to his men, but the gibbering shadows were upon him. His arms were wrenched behind him and cruelly bound. He was stripped of his clothes.

With the other survivors, Aëngelas was driven through the night, pulled by a leather thong cut into his lips. He wept as he ran, knowing all was lost. No more would he make love to Valrissa, his wife. No more would he tease his sons as they sat about the evening fire. Over and over, through the agony of his face, he asked: *What have we done to deserve this? What have we done?*

By the wicked glare of torchlight he saw the Sranc, with their narrow shoulders and dog-deep chests, surfacing from the night as though from the depths of the Sea. Inhumanly beautiful faces, as white as polished bone; armour of lacquered human skin; necklaces of human teeth; and the shrunken faces of men stitched into their round shields. He smelled their sweet stench—like feces and rotted fruit. He heard the nightmarish clacking of their laughter, and from somewhere in the night, the shrieks of the Werigda's horses as they were slaughtered.

And periodically he saw the Nonmen, tall upon their silk-black steeds. What Valrissa had dreamed, he realized, was true: the Great Ruiner hunted them! But why?

They reached the Sranc encampment in the grey light of dawn, a string of naked, brutalized men. A great chorus of wails greeted them— women crying names, children howling *"Da! Daa!"* The Sranc led them into the midst of their huddled loved ones, and in an act of curious mercy, cut them loose. Aëngelas flew to Valrissa and his only remaining son. Wracked by sobs he hugged both of them, clutched at their bent backs. And for an instant he felt hope in the pale warmth of degraded bodies.

"Where's Ileni?" he hissed.

But his wife could only cry "Aënga! Aëngaaa!"

The respite, however, was short-lived. Those men who couldn't find their families, who either knelt alone in the frozen mud or raced scream-ing and searching for faces now dead, were butchered. Then those wives and children without husbands were also hacked to silence, until only those who had been reunited remained.

Under the dark eyes of the Nonmen, the Sranc then began beating the survivors into two rows, until the Werigda were drawn in long threads across snow and dead winter grasses, husbands opposite their wives and children.

Leashed to an iron spike hammered into the ground, Aëngelas cringed from the cold and threw himself over and over against the braided thongs that held him from his wife and son. He spat and raged at the passing Sranc. He tried to summon heartening words, words that might let his family endure, that might grace them with dignity for what was about to come. But he could only weep their names, and curse himself for not strangling them earlier, for not saving them from what was about to happen.

And then, for the first time, he heard the *question*—even though it was not spoken.

An uncanny silence fell across the Werigda, and Aëngelas understood that all of them had heard the impossible voice ... The question had resounded through the souls of all his suffering people.

Then he saw ... *it*. An abomination walking through dawn twilight.

It was half-again taller than a man, with long, folded wings curved like scythes over its powerful frame. Save where it was mottled by black, cancerous spots, its skin was translucent, and sheathed about a great flared skull shaped like an oyster set on edge. And within the gaping jaws of that skull was fused *another*, more manlike, so that an almost human face grinned from its watery features.

The Sranc howled with rapture as it passed, and jerked at their groins as they fell to their knees. The mounted Nonmen lowered their shining scalps. It studied the rows of hapless humans, and then its great black eyes fell upon Aëngelas. Valrissa sobbed, a mere length away.

You ... We sense the old fire in you, manling ...

"I am Werigda!" Aëngelas roared.

Do you know what we are?

"The Great Ruiner," Aëngelas gasped.

Noooo, it cooed, as though his mistake had aroused a delicious shiver. *We are not He ... We are His servant. Save my Brother, we are the last of those who descended from the void ...*

"The Great Ruiner!" Aëngelas cried.

The abomination had walked ever closer throughout this exchange, until it loomed over his wife and child. Valrissa clutched Bengulla to her bosom, held out a tragic warding hand against the hoary figure.

Will you tell us, manling? Tell us what we need to know?

"But I don't know!" Aëngelas cried. "I know nothing of what you ask!"

Effortlessly, the Inchoroi snapped Valrissa's tether, and hoisted her before him, held her as though she were a doll. Bengulla shrieked, "Mama! Mama!"

Once again the question thundered through Aëngelas's soul. He wept, tore at the turf.

"I don't know! I don't know!"

Beneath the monstrosity's claws, Valrissa went very still, like a calf caught in the jaws of a wolf. Her terrified eyes turned from Aëngelas, and rolled upwards beneath their lids, as though trying to peer at the figure behind her.

"Valrissa!" Aëngelas screamed. "*Valrissssaa!*"

Holding her by the throat, the thing languorously picked her clothing away, like the skin of a rotten peach. As her breasts fell free, round-white with soft-pink nipples, a sheet of sunlight flickered across the horizon, and illuminated her lithe curves ... But the hunger that held her from behind remained shadowy—like glistening smoke.

Animal violence overcame Aëngelas, and he strained at his leash, gagged inarticulate fury.

And a husky voice in his soul said: *We are a race of lovers, manling ...*

"Beaaassee!" Aëngelas wept. "I don't knooooowww ..."

The thing's free hand traced a thread of blood between her bosom across the plane of her shuddering belly. Valrissa's eyes returned to Aëngelas, thick with something impossible. She moaned and parted her hanging legs to greet the abomination's hand.

A race of lovers ...

"I *don't know!* I don't! I don't! Beaase stop! *Beaasse!*"

The thing screeched like a thousand falcons as it plunged into her. Glass thunder. Shivering sky. She bent back her head, her face contorted in pain and bliss. She convulsed and groaned, arched to meet the creature's thrusts. And when she climaxed, Aëngelas crumpled, grasped his head between his hands, beat his face against the turf.

The cold felt good against his broken lips.

With an inhuman, dragon gasp, the thing pressed its bruised phallus up across her stomach and washed her sunlit breasts with pungent, black seed. Another thunderous screech, woven by the thin human wail of a woman.

And again it asked the question.

I don't know ...

These things make you weak, it said, tossing her like a sack to cold grasses. With a look, it gave her to the Sranc—to their licentious fury. Once again, it asked the question.

The abomination then gave his weeping son—sweet, innocent Bengulla—to the Sranc, and once again asked the question.

I don't know what you mean ...

And when the Sranc made a womb of Aëngelas himself, it asked—with each raper's thrust, it asked ...

Until the gagging shrieks of his wife and child became the question. Until his own deranged howls became the question ...

His wife and child were dead. Sacks of penetrated flesh with faces that he loved, and still ... they did things.

Always, the same mad, incomprehensible question.

Who are the Dûnyain?

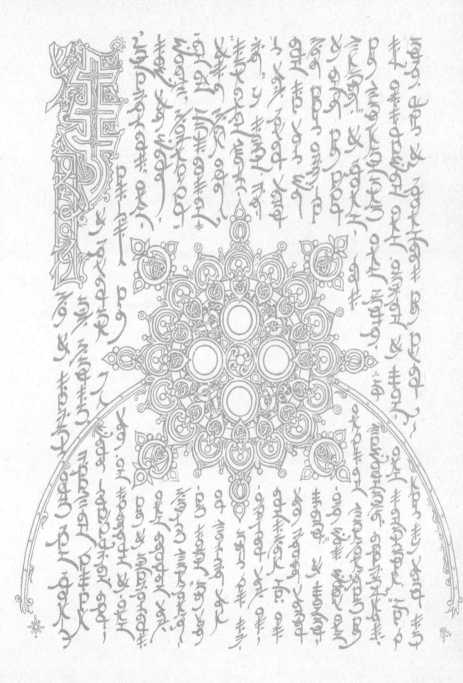

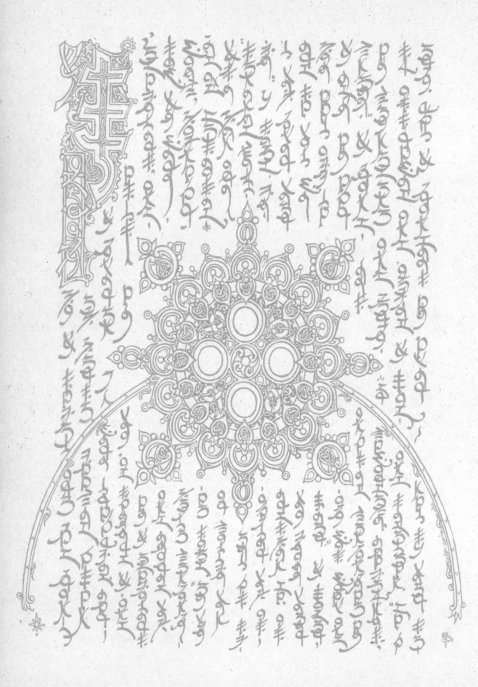

Appendices

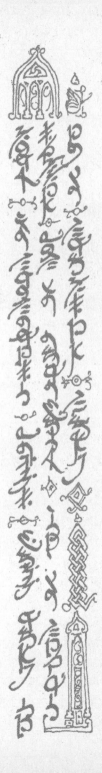

Character and Faction Glossary

Characters

Drusas Achamian, a forty-seven-year-old Mandate sorcerer

Coithus Athjeäri, Saubon's nephew

Bannut, Cnaiür's uncle

Nersei Calmemunis, Proyas's cousin and Conriyan leader of the Vulgar Holy War

Cememketri, Grandmaster of the Imperial Saik

Chepheramunni, King-Regent of High Ainon and leader of the Ainoni contingent

Cnaiür, a forty-four-year-old Scylvendi barbarian, Chieftain of the Utemot

Ikurei Conphas, Exalt-General of Nansur and nephew to the Emperor

Eleäzaras, Grandmaster of the Scarlet Spires

Esmenet, a thirty-one-year-old Sumni prostitute

Geshrunni, slave-soldier and momentary Mandate spy

Hoga Gothyelk, the Earl of Agansanor and leader of the Tydonni contingent

Incheiri Gotian, Grandmaster of the Shrial Knights

Paro Inrau, Shrial Priest and former student of Achamian

Ikurei Istriya, Empress of Nansur and mother of the Emperor

Iyokus, Eleäzaras's Master of Spies

Kascamandri, Padirajah of Kian

Anasûrimbor Kellhus, a thirty-three-year-old Dûnyain monk

Kussalt, Saubon's groom

Maithanet, Shriah of the Thousand Temples

Mallahet, powerful member of the Cishaurim

Martemus, General and Aide-de-Camp to Conphas

Anasûrimbor Moënghus, Kellhus's father

Nautzera, senior member of the Mandate Quorum

Nersei Proyas, Prince of Conriya and former student of Achamian

Cutias Sarcellus, First Knight-Commander of the Shrial Knights

Coithus Saubon, Prince of Galeoth and leader of the Galeoth contingent

Seökti, Heresiarch of the Cishaurim

Serwë, a nineteen-year-old Nymbricani concubine

Seswatha, survivor of the Old Wars and ancient founder of the Mandate

Simas, member of the Quorum and Achamian's former teacher

Skaiyelt, Prince of Thunyerus and leader of the Thunyeri contingent

Skalateas, mercenary sorcerer

Skauras, Kianene Sapatishah-Governor of Shigek

Skeaös, the Emperor's Prime Counsel

Skiötha, Cnaiür's deceased father

Ikurei Xerius III, Emperor of Nansur

Krijates Xinemus, Achamian's friend and Marshal of Attrempus

Xunnurit, Scylvendi King-of-Tribes at the Battle of Kiyuth

Yalgrota, Skaiyelt's giant bondsman

Yursalka, Utemot tribesman

Factions

The Dûnyain: A hidden monastic sect whose members have repudiated history and animal appetite in the hope of finding absolute enlightenment through the control of all desire and circumstance. For two thousand years they have bred their members for both motor reflexes and intellectual acuity.

The Consult: A cabal of magi and generals that survived the death of the No-God in 2155 and has laboured ever since to bring about his return in the so-called Second Apocalypse. Very few in the Three Seas believe the Consult still exists.

The Scylvendi: The ancient nomadic peoples of the Jiünati Steppe. They are both feared and admired for their prowess in war.

Schools

A collective name given to the various academies of sorcerers. The first Schools, both in the Ancient North and in the Three Seas, arose as a response to the Tusk's condemnation of sorcery. The Schools are among the oldest institutions in the Three Seas, and they survive, by and large, because of the terror they inspire and their detachment from the secular and religious powers of the Three Seas.

The Mandate: Gnostic School founded by Seswatha in 2156 to continue the war against the Consult and to protect the Three Seas from the return of the No-God, Mog-Pharau.

The Scarlet Spires: Anagogic School that is the most powerful in the Three Seas and has been de facto ruler of High Ainon since 3818.

The Imperial Saik: Anagogic School indentured to the Emperor of Nansur.

The Mysunsai: Self-proclaimed mercenary School that sells its sorcerous services across the Three Seas.

Inrithi Factions

Synthesizing monotheistic and polytheistic elements, Inrithism, the dominant faith of the Three Seas, is founded on the revelations of Inri Sejenus (c. 2159–2202), the Latter Prophet. The central tenets of Inrithism deal with the immanence of the God in historical events, the unity of the individual deities of the Cults as Aspects of the God as revealed by the Latter Prophet, and the infallibility of the Tusk as scripture.

The Thousand Temples: An institution that provides the ecclesiastical framework of Inrithism. Though based in Sumna, the Thousand Temples is omnipresent throughout the Northwestern and Eastern Three Seas.

The Shrial Knights: A monastic military order under the direct command of the Shriah, created by Ekyannus III, "the Golden," in 2511.

The Conriyans: Conriya is a Ketyai nation of the Eastern Three Seas. Founded after the collapse of the Eastern Ceneian Empire in 3372, it is based around Aöknyssus, the ancient capital of Shir.

The Nansur: The Nansur Empire is a Ketyai nation of the Western Three Seas and the self-proclaimed inheritor of the Ceneian Empire. At the height of its power, the Nansur Empire extended from Galeoth to Nilnamesh, but it has been much reduced by centuries of warfare against the Fanim of Kian.

The Galeoth: Galeoth is a Norsirai nation of the Three Seas, the so-called Middle-North, founded around 3683 by the descendants of refugees from the Old Wars.

The Tydonni: Ce Tydonn is a Norsirai nation of the Eastern Three Seas. It was founded after the collapse of the Ketyai nation of Cengemis in 3742.

The Ainoni: High Ainon is the pre-eminent Ketyai nation of the Eastern Three Seas. It was founded after the collapse of the Eastern Ceneian Empire in 3372 and has been ruled by the Scarlet Spires since the end of the Scholastic Wars in 3818.

The Thunyeri: Thunyerus is a Norsirai nation of the Three Seas. It was founded through the federation of the Thunyeri tribes around 3987, and it only recently converted to Inrithism.

Fanim Factions

Strictly monotheistic, Fanimry is an upstart faith founded on the revelations of the Prophet Fane (3669–3742) and restricted to the Southwestern Three Seas. The central tenets of Fanimry deal with the singularity and transcendence of the God, the falseness of the Gods (who are considered demons by the Fanim), the repudiation of the Tusk as unholy, and the prohibition of all representations of the God.

The Kianene: Kian is the most powerful Ketyai nation of the Three Seas. Extending from the southern frontier of the Nansur Empire to Nilnamesh, it was founded in the wake of the White Jihad, the holy war waged by the first Fanim against the Nansur Empire from 3743 to 3771.

The Cishaurim: Priest-sorcerers of the Fanim, based in Shimeh. Little is known about the metaphysics of Cishaurim sorcery, or the Psûkhe, as the Cishaurim refer to it, beyond the fact that it cannot be perceived by the Few, and that it is in many ways as formidable as the Anagogic sorcery of the Schools.

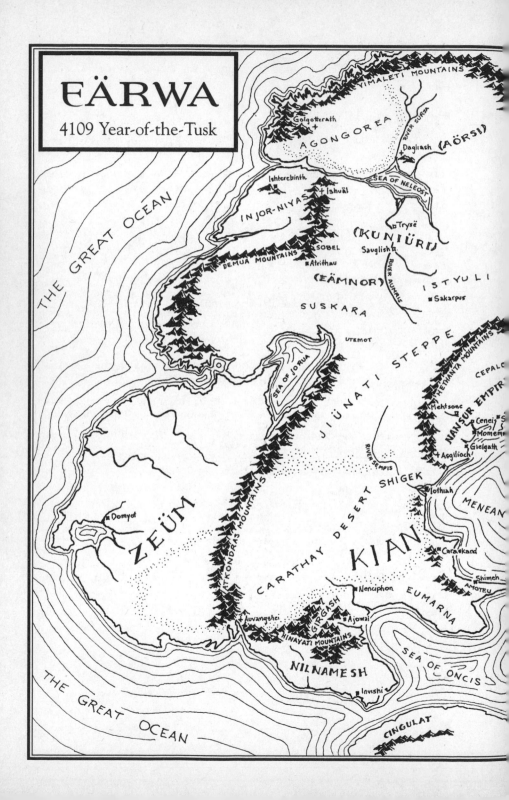

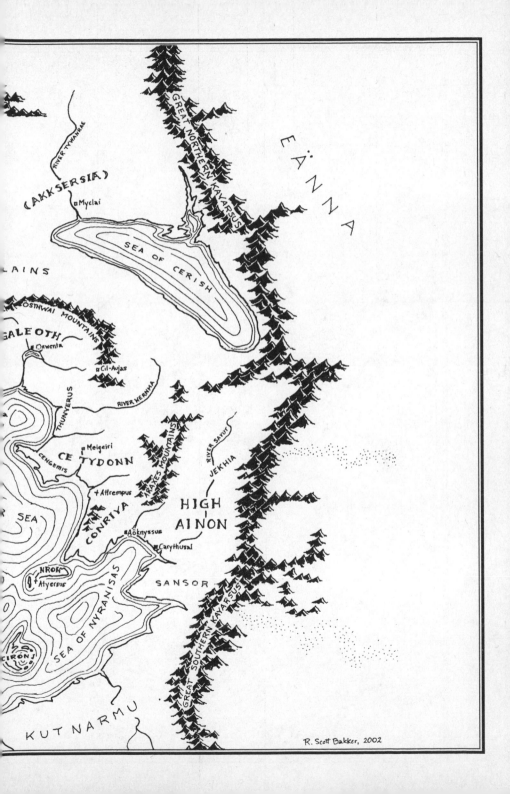

R. Scott Bakker, 2002

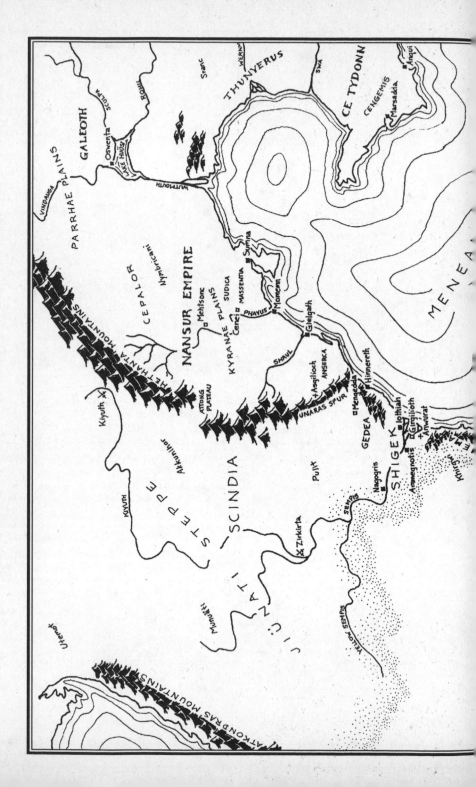

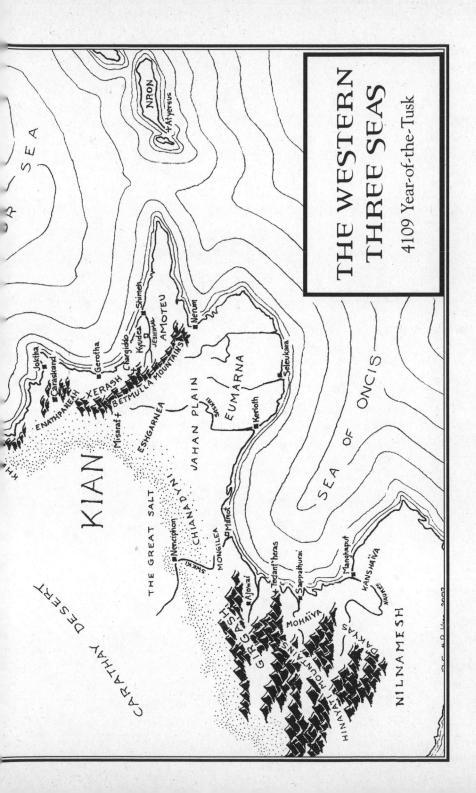

THE WESTERN
THREE SEAS
4109 Year-of-the-Tusk